MEMOIRS

CW01639310

Arthur Golden was born and brought up in Chattanooga, Tennessee. He is a 1978 graduate of Harvard College with a degree in art history, specialising in Japanese art. In 1980 he earned an M.A. in Japanese history from Columbia University where he also learned Mandarin Chinese. After a summer at Beijing University, he went to work at a magazine in Tokyo. In 1988 he received an M.A. in English from Boston University. He has lived and worked in Japan, and since that time has been teaching writing and literature in the Boston area. He now lives in Brookline, Massachusetts, with his wife and children.

Arthur Golden

MEMOIRS OF A GEISHA

VINTAGE BOOKS
London

Published by Vintage 2005

59 60

Copyright © Arthur Golden 1997

The right of Arthur Golden to be identified as the author of this work has been asserted by him in accordance with the Copyright, Designs and Patents Act, 1988

This book is sold subject to the condition that it shall not, by way of trade or otherwise, be lent, resold, hired out, or otherwise circulated without the publisher's prior consent in any form of binding or cover other than that in which it is published and without a similar condition including this condition being imposed on the subsequent purchaser

First published in Great Britain by
Chatto and Windus 1997

First published by Vintage in 1998

Vintage
Random House, 20 Vauxhall Bridge Road,
London SW1V 2SA

www.vintage-books.co.uk

Addresses for companies within The Random House Group Limited can be found at: www.randomhouse.co.uk/offices.htm

The Random House Group Limited Reg. No. 954009

A CIP catalogue record for this book
is available from the British Library

ISBN 9780091887193

Set in 10½/12 Sabon by SX Composing DTP, Rayleigh, Essex

Penguin Random House is committed to a sustainable future for our business, our readers and our planet. This book is made from Forest Stewardship Council® certified paper.

FSC
www.fsc.org
MIX
Paper from
responsible sources
FSC® C018179

Printed and bound in Great Britain by Clays Ltd, Elcograf S.p.A.

TRANSLATOR'S NOTE

ONE EVENING IN the spring of 1936, when I was a boy of fourteen, my father took me to a dance performance in Kyoto. I remember only two things about it. The first is that he and I were the only Westerners in the audience; we had come from our home in the Netherlands only a few weeks earlier, so I had not yet adjusted to the cultural isolation and still felt it acutely. The second is how pleased I was, after months of intensive study of the Japanese language, to find that I could now understand fragments of the conversations I overheard. As for the young Japanese women dancing on the stage before me, I remember nothing of them except a vague impression of brightly colored kimono. I certainly had no way of knowing that in a time and place as far away as New York City nearly fifty years in the future, one among them would become my good friend and would dictate her extraordinary memoirs to me.

As a historian, I have always regarded memoirs as source material. A memoir provides a record not so much of the memoirist as of the memoirist's world. It must differ from biography in that a memoirist can never achieve the perspective that a biographer possesses as a matter of course. Autobiography, if there really is such a thing, is like asking a rabbit to tell us what he looks like hopping through the grasses of the field. How would he know? If we want to hear about the field, on the other hand, no one is in a better circumstance to tell us – so long as we keep in mind that we are missing all those things the rabbit was in no position to observe.

I say this with the certainty of an academician who has based a career on such distinctions. And yet I must confess that the memoirs of my dear friend Nitta Sayuri have impelled me to rethink my views. Yes, she does elucidate for us the very secret world in which she lived – the rabbit's view of the field, if you will. There may well be no better record of the strange life of a geisha than the one Sayuri offers. But she leaves behind as well a record of herself that is far more complete, more accurate, and more compelling than the lengthy chapter examining her life in the book *Glittering Jewels of Japan*, or in the various magazine articles about her that have appeared over the years. It seems that at least in the case of this one unusual subject, no one knew the memoirist as well as the memoirist herself.

That Sayuri should have risen to prominence was largely a matter of chance. Other women have led similar lives. The renowned Kato Yuki – a geisha who captured the heart of George Morgan, nephew of J. Pierpont, and became his bride-in-exile during the first decade of this century – may have lived a life even more unusual in some ways than Sayuri's. But only Sayuri has documented her own saga so completely. For a long while I believed that her choice to do so was a fortuitous accident. If she had remained in Japan, her life would have been too full for her to consider compiling her memoirs. However, in 1956 circumstances in her life led Sayuri to emigrate to the United States. For her remaining forty years, she was a resident of New York City's Waldorf Towers, where she created for herself an elegant Japanese-style suite on the thirty-second floor. Even then her life continued at its frenetic pace. Her suite saw more than its share of Japanese artists, intellectuals, business figures – even cabinet ministers and a gangster or two. I did not meet her until an acquaintance introduced us in 1985. As a scholar of Japan, I had encountered Sayuri's name, though I knew almost nothing about her. Our friendship grew, and she confided in me more and more. One day I asked if she would ever permit her story to be told.

'Well, Jakob-san, I might, if it's you who records it,' she told me.

So it was that we began our task. Sayuri was clear that she wanted to dictate her memoirs rather than write them herself, because, as she explained, she was so accustomed to talking face-to-face that she would hardly know how to proceed with no one in the room to listen. I agreed, and the manuscript was dictated to me over the course of eighteen months. I was never more aware of Sayuri's Kyoto dialect – in which geisha themselves are called *geiko*, and kimono are sometimes known as *obebe* – than when I began to wonder how I would render its nuances in translation. But from the very start I felt myself lost in her world. On all but a few occasions we met in the evening; because of long habit, this was the time when Sayuri's mind was most alive. Usually she preferred to work in her suite at the Waldorf Towers, but from time to time we met in a private room at a Japanese restaurant on Park Avenue, where she was well known. Our sessions generally lasted two or three hours. Although we tape-recorded each session, her secretary was present to transcribe her dictation as well, which she did very faithfully. But Sayuri never spoke to the tape recorder or to the secretary; she spoke always to me. When she had doubts about where to proceed, I was the one who steered her. I regarded myself as the foundation upon which the enterprise was based and felt that her story would never have been told had I not gained her trust. Now I've come to see that the truth may be otherwise. Sayuri chose me as her amanuensis, to be sure, but she may have been waiting all along for the right candidate to present himself.

Which brings us to the central question: Why did Sayuri want her story told? Geisha may not take any formal vow of silence, but their existence is predicated on the singularly Japanese conviction that what goes on during the morning in the office and what goes on during the evening behind closed doors bear no relationship to one another, and must always remain compartmentalized and separate. Geisha simply do not talk for the record about their experiences. Like prostitutes, their lower-class counterparts, geisha are often in the unusual position of knowing whether this or that public figure really does put his pants on one leg at a time like everyone else. Probably it is to their credit that these butterflies of the night regard their roles as a kind of public trust, but in any case, the geisha who violates that trust puts herself in an untenable position. Sayuri's circumstances in telling her story were unusual, in that no one in Japan had power over her any longer. Her ties with her native country had already been severed. This may tell us, at least in part, why she no longer felt constrained to silence, but it does not tell us why she chose to talk. I was afraid to raise the question with her; what if, in examining her own scruples on the subject, she should change her mind? Even when the manuscript was complete, I felt reluctant to ask. Only after she had received her advance from the publisher did I feel it safe to query her: Why had she wanted to document her life?

'What else do I have to do with my time these days?' she replied.

As to whether or not her motives were really as simple as this, I leave the reader to decide.

Though she was eager to have her biography recorded, Sayuri did insist upon several conditions. She wanted the manuscript published only after her death and the deaths of several men who had figured prominently in her life. As it turned out, they all predeceased her. It was a great concern of Sayuri's that no one be embarrassed by her revelations. Whenever possible I have left names unchanged, though Sayuri did hide the identities of certain men even from me through the convention, rather common among geisha, of referring to customers by means of an epithet. When encountering characters such as Mr. Snowshowers – whose moniker suggests itself because of his dandruff – the reader who believes Sayuri is only trying to amuse may have misunderstood her real intent.

When I asked Sayuri's permission to use a tape recorder, I intended it only as a safeguard against any possible errors of transcription on the part of her secretary. Since her death last year, however, I have wondered if I had another motive as well – namely, to preserve her voice, which had a quality of expressiveness I have rarely encountered. Customarily she spoke with a soft tone, as one might expect of a woman who has made a career of entertaining men. But when she wished to bring a scene to life before me, her voice could make me think there were six or eight people in the room. Sometimes still, I play her tapes during the evenings in my study and find it very difficult to believe she is no longer alive.

Jakob Haarhuis
Arnold Rusoff Professor of Japanese History
New York University

I

SUPPOSE THAT YOU and I were sitting in a quiet room overlooking a garden, chatting and sipping at our cups of green tea while we talked about something that had happened a long while ago, and I said to you, 'That afternoon when I met so-and-so . . . was the very best afternoon of my life, and also the very worst afternoon.' I expect you might put down your teacup and say, 'Well, now, which was it? Was it the best or the worst? Because it can't possibly have been both!' Ordinarily I'd have to laugh at myself and agree with you. But the truth is that the afternoon when I met Mr. Tanaka Ichiro really was the best and the worst of my life. He seemed so fascinating to me, even the fish smell on his hands was a kind of perfume. If I had never known him, I'm sure I would not have become a geisha.

I wasn't born and raised to be a Kyoto geisha. I wasn't even born in Kyoto. I'm a fisherman's daughter from a little town called Yoroido on the Sea of Japan. In all my life I've never told more than a handful of people anything at all about Yoroido, or about the house in which I grew up, or about my mother and father, or my older sister – and certainly not about how I became a geisha, or what it was like to be one. Most people would much rather carry on with their fantasies that my mother and grandmother were geisha, and that I began my training in dance when I was weaned from the breast, and so on. As a matter of fact, one day many years ago I was pouring a cup of sake for a man who happened to mention that he had been in Yoroido only the previous week. Well, I felt as a bird must feel when it has flown across the ocean and comes upon a creature that knows its nest. I was so shocked I couldn't stop myself from saying:

'Yoroido! Why, that's where I grew up!'

This poor man! His face went through the most remarkable series of changes. He tried his best to smile, though it didn't come out well because he couldn't get the look of shock off his face.

'Yoroido?' he said. 'You can't mean it.'

I long ago developed a very practiced smile, which I call my 'Noh smile' because it resembles a Noh mask whose features are frozen. Its advantage is that men can interpret it however they want; you can imagine how often I've relied on it. I decided I'd better use it just then, and of course it worked. He let out all his breath and tossed down the cup of sake I'd poured for him before giving an enormous laugh I'm sure was prompted more by relief than anything else.

'The very idea!' he said, with another big laugh. 'You, growing up in a dump like Yoroido. That's like making tea in a bucket!' And when he'd laughed again, he said to me, 'That's why you're so much fun, Sayuri-san. Sometimes you almost make me believe your little jokes are real.'

I don't much like thinking of myself as a cup of tea made in a bucket, but I suppose in a way it must be true. After all, I did grow up in Yoroido, and no one would suggest it's a glamorous spot. Hardly anyone ever visits it. As for the people who live there, they never have occasion to leave. You're probably wondering how I came to leave it myself. That's where my story begins.

In our little fishing village of Yoroido, I lived in what I called a 'tipsy house.' It stood near a cliff where the wind off the ocean was always blowing. As a child it seemed to me as if the ocean had caught a terrible cold, because it was always wheezing and there would be spells when it let out a huge sneeze – which is to say there was a burst of wind with a tremendous spray. I decided our tiny house must have been offended by the ocean sneezing in its face from time to time, and took to leaning back because it wanted to get out of the way. Probably it would have collapsed if my father hadn't cut a timber from a wrecked fishing boat to prop up the eaves, which made the house look like a tipsy old man leaning on his crutch.

Inside this tipsy house I lived something of a lopsided life. Because from my earliest years I was very much like my mother, and hardly at all like my father or older sister. My mother said it was because we were made just the same, she and I – and it was true we both had the same peculiar eyes of a sort you almost never see in Japan. Instead of being dark brown like everyone else's, my mother's eyes were a translucent gray, and mine are just the same. When I was very young, I told my mother I thought someone had poked a hole in her eyes and all the ink had drained out, which she thought very funny. The fortune-tellers said her eyes were so pale because of too much water in her personality, so much that the other four elements were hardly present at all – and this, they explained, was why her features matched so poorly. People in the village often said she ought to have been extremely attractive, because her parents had been. Well, a peach has a lovely taste and so does a mushroom, but you can't put the two together; this was the terrible trick nature had played on her. She had her mother's pouty mouth but her father's angular jaw, which gave the impression of a delicate picture with much too heavy a frame. And her lovely gray eyes were surrounded by thick lashes that must have been striking on her father, but in her case only made her look startled.

My mother always said she'd married my father because she had too much water in her personality and he had too much wood in his. People who knew my father understood right away what she was talking about. Water flows from place to place quickly and always finds a crack to spill through. Wood, on the other hand, holds fast to the earth. In my father's case this was a good thing, for he was a fisherman, and a man with wood in his personality is at ease on the sea. In fact, my father was more at ease on the sea than anywhere else, and never left it far behind him. He smelled like the sea even after he had bathed. When he wasn't fishing, he sat on the floor in our dark front room mending a fishing net. And if a fishing net had been a sleeping creature, he wouldn't even have awakened it, at the speed he worked. He did everything this slowly. Even when he summoned a look of concentration, you could run outside and drain the bath in the time it took him to rearrange his features. His face was very heavily creased, and into each crease he had tucked some worry or other, so that it wasn't really his own face any longer, but more like a tree that had nests of birds in all the branches. He had to struggle constantly to manage it and always looked worn out from the effort.

When I was six or seven, I learned something about my father I'd never known. One day I asked him, 'Daddy, why are you so old?' He hoisted up his eyebrows at this, so that they formed little sagging umbrellas over his eyes. And he let out a long breath, and shook his head and said, 'I don't know.' When I turned to my mother, she gave me a look meaning she would answer the question for me another time. The following day without saying a word, she walked me down the hill toward the village and turned at a path into a graveyard in the woods. She led me to three graves in the corner, with three white marker posts much taller than I was. They had stern-looking black characters written top to bottom on them, but I hadn't attended the school in our little village long enough to know where one ended and the next began. My mother pointed to them and said, 'Natsu, wife of Sakamoto Minoru.' Sakamoto Minoru was the name of my father. 'Died age twenty-four, in the nineteenth year of Meiji.' Then she pointed to the next one: 'Jinichiro, son of Sakamoto Minoru, died age six, in the nineteenth year of Meiji,' and to the next one, which was identical except for the name, Masao, and the age, which was three. It took me a while to understand that my father had been married before, a long time ago, and that his whole family had died. I went back to those graves not long afterward and found as I stood there that sadness was a very heavy thing. My body weighed twice what it had only a moment earlier, as if those graves were pulling me down toward them.

With all this water and all this wood, the two of them ought to have made a good balance and produced children with the proper arrangement of elements. I'm sure it was a surprise to them that they ended up with one of each. For it wasn't just that I resembled my mother and had even inherited her unusual eyes; my sister, Satsu, was as much like my father as anyone could be. Satsu was six years older than me, and of course, being older, she could do things I couldn't do. But Satsu had a remarkable quality of doing everything in a way that seemed like a complete accident. For example, if you asked her to pour a bowl of soup from a pot on the stove, she would get the job done, but in a way that looked like she'd spilled it into the bowl just by luck. One time she even cut herself with a fish, and I don't mean with a knife she was using to clean a fish. She was carrying a fish wrapped in paper up the hill from the village when it slid out and fell against her leg in such a way as to cut her with one of its fins.

Our parents might have had other children besides Satsu and me, particularly since my father hoped for a boy to fish with him. But when I was seven my mother grew terribly ill with what was probably bone cancer, though at the time I had no idea what was wrong. Her only escape from discomfort was to sleep, which she began to do the way a cat does – which is to say, more or less constantly. As the months passed she slept most of the time, and soon began to groan whenever she was awake. I knew something in her was changing quickly, but because of so much water in her personality, this didn't seem worrisome to me. Sometimes she grew thin in a matter of months but grew strong again just as quickly. But by the time I was nine, the bones in her face had begun to protrude, and she never gained weight again afterward. I didn't realize the water was draining out of her because of her illness. Just as seaweed is naturally soggy, you see, but turns brittle as it dries, my mother was giving up more and more of her essence.

Then one afternoon I was sitting on the pitted floor of our dark front room, singing to a cricket I'd found that morning, when a voice called out at the door:

'Oi! Open up! It's Dr. Miura!'

Dr. Miura came to our fishing village once a week, and had made a point of walking up the hill to check on my mother ever since her illness had begun. My father was at home that day because a terrible storm was coming. He sat in his usual spot on the floor, with his two big spiderlike hands tangled up in a fishing net. But he took a moment to point his eyes at me and raise one of his fingers. This meant he wanted me to answer the door.

Dr. Miura was a very important man – or so we believed in our village. He had studied in Tokyo and reportedly knew more Chinese characters than anyone. He was far too proud to notice a creature like me. When I opened the door for him, he slipped out of his shoes and stepped right past me into the house.

'Why, Sakamoto-san,' he said to my father, 'I wish I had your life, out on the sea fishing all day. How glorious! And then on rough days you take a rest. I see your wife is still asleep,' he went on. 'What a pity. I thought I might examine her.'

'Oh?' said my father.

'I won't be around next week, you know. Perhaps you might wake her for me?'

My father took a while to untangle his hands from the net, but at last he stood.

'Chiyo-chan,' he said to me, 'get the doctor a cup of tea.'

My name back then was Chiyo. I wouldn't be known by my geisha name, Sayuri, until years later.

My father and the doctor went into the other room, where my mother lay sleeping. I tried to listen at the door, but I could hear only my mother groaning, and nothing of what they said. I occupied myself with making tea, and soon the doctor came back out rubbing his hands together and looking very stern. My father came to join him, and they sat together at the table in the center of the room.

'The time has come to say something to you, Sakamoto-san,' Dr. Miura began. 'You need to have a talk with one of the women in the village. Mrs. Sugi, perhaps. Ask her to make a nice new robe for your wife.'

'I haven't the money, Doctor,' my father said.

'We've all grown poorer lately. I understand what you're saying. But you owe it to your wife. She shouldn't die in that tattered robe she's wearing.'

'So she's going to die soon?'

'A few more weeks, perhaps. She's in terrible pain. Death will release her.'

After this, I couldn't hear their voices any longer; for in my ears I heard a sound like a bird's wings flapping in panic. Perhaps it was my heart, I don't know. But if you've ever seen a bird trapped inside the great hall of a temple, looking for some way out, well, that was how my mind was reacting. It had never occurred to me that my mother wouldn't simply go on being sick. I won't say I'd never wondered what might happen if she should die; I did wonder about it, in the same way I wondered what might happen if our house were swallowed up in an earthquake. There could hardly be life after such an event.

'I thought I would die first,' my father was saying.

'You're an old man, Sakamoto-san. But your health is good. You might have four or five years. I'll leave you some more of those pills for your wife. You can give them to her two at a time, if you need to.'

They talked about the pills a bit longer, and then Dr. Miura left. My father went on sitting for a long while in silence, with his back to me. He wore no shirt but only his loose-fitting skin; the more I looked at him, the more he began to seem like just a curious collection of shapes and textures. His spine was a path of knobs. His head, with its discolored splotches, might have been a bruised fruit. His arms were sticks wrapped in old leather, dangling from two bumps. If my mother died, how could I go on living in the house with him? I didn't want to be away from him; but whether he was there or not, the house would be just as empty when my mother had left it.

At last my father said my name in a whisper. I went and knelt beside him.

'Something very important,' he said.

His face was so much heavier than usual, with his eyes rolling around almost as though he'd lost control of them. I thought he was struggling to tell me my mother would die soon, but all he said was:

'Go down to the village. Bring back some incense for the altar.'

Our tiny Buddhist altar rested on an old crate beside the entrance to the kitchen; it was the only thing of value in our tipsy house. In front of a rough carving of Amida, the Buddha of the Western Paradise, stood tiny black mortuary tablets bearing the Buddhist names of our dead ancestors.

'But, Father . . . wasn't there anything else?'

I hoped he would reply, but he only made a gesture with his hand that meant for me to leave.

The path from our house followed the edge of the sea cliffs before turning inland toward the village. Walking it on a day like this was difficult, but I remember feeling grateful that the fierce wind drew my mind from the things troubling me. The sea was violent, with waves like stones chipped into blades, sharp enough to cut. It seemed to me the world itself was feeling just as I felt. Was life nothing more than a storm that constantly washed away what had been there only a moment before, and left behind something barren and unrecognizable? I'd never had such a thought before. To escape it, I ran down the path until the village came into view below me. Yoroido was a tiny town, just at the opening of an inlet. Usually the water was spotted with fishermen, but today I could see just a few boats coming back – looking to me, as they always did, like water bugs kicking along the surface. The storm was coming in earnest now; I could hear its roar. The fishermen on the inlet began to soften as they disappeared within the curtain of rain, and then they were gone completely. I could see the storm climbing the slope toward me. The first drops hit me like quail eggs, and in a matter of seconds I was as wet as if I'd fallen into the sea.

Yoroido had only one road, leading right to the front door of the Japan Coastal Seafood Company; it was lined with a number of houses whose front rooms were used for shops. I ran across the street toward the Okada house, where dry goods were sold; but then something happened to me – one of those trivial things with huge consequences, like losing your step and falling in front of a train. The packed dirt road was slippery in the rain, and my feet went out from under me. I fell forward onto one side of my face. I suppose I must have knocked myself into a daze, because I remember only a kind of numbness and a feeling of something in my mouth I wanted to spit out. I heard voices and felt myself turned onto my back; I was lifted and carried. I could tell they were taking me into the Japan Coastal Seafood Company, because I smelled the odor of fish wrapping itself around me. I heard a slapping sound as they slid a catch of fish from one of the wooden tables onto the floor and laid me on its slimy surface. I knew I was wet from the rain, and bloody too, and that I was barefoot and dirty, and wearing peasant clothing. What I didn't know was that this was the moment that would change everything. For it was in this condition I found myself looking up into the face of Mr. Tanaka Ichiro.

I'd seen Mr. Tanaka in our village many times before. He lived in a much larger town nearby but came every day, for his family owned the Japan Coastal Seafood Company. He didn't wear peasant clothing like the fishermen, but rather a man's kimono, with kimono trousers that made him look to me like the illustrations you may have seen of samurai. His skin was smooth and tight as a drum; his cheekbones were shiny hillocks, like the crisp skin of a grilled fish. I'd always found him fascinating. When I was in the street throwing a beanbag with the other children and Mr. Tanaka happened to stroll out of the seafood company, I always stopped what I was doing to watch him.

I lay there on that slimy table while Mr. Tanaka examined my lip, pulling it down with his fingers and tipping my head this way and that. All at once he caught sight of my gray eyes, which were fixed on his face with such fascination, I couldn't pretend I hadn't been staring at him. He didn't give me a sneer, as if to say that I was an impudent girl, and he didn't look away as if it made no difference where I looked or what I thought. We stared at each other for a long moment – so long it gave me a chill even there in the muggy air of the seafood company.

'I know you,' he said at last. 'You're old Sakamoto's little girl.'

Even as a child I could tell that Mr. Tanaka saw the world around him as it really was; he never wore the dazed look of my father. To me, he seemed to see the sap bleeding from the trunks of the pine trees, and the circle of brightness in the sky where the sun was smothered by clouds. He lived in the world that was visible, even if it didn't always please him to be there. I knew he noticed the trees, and the mud, and the children in the street, but I had no reason to believe he'd ever noticed me.

Perhaps this is why when he spoke to me, tears came stinging to my eyes.

Mr. Tanaka raised me into a sitting position. I thought he was going to tell me to leave, but instead he said, 'Don't swallow that blood, little girl. Unless you want to make a stone in your stomach. I'd spit it onto the floor, if I were you.'

'A girl's blood, Mr. Tanaka?' said one of the men. 'Here, where we bring the fish?'

Fishermen are terribly superstitious, you see. They especially don't like women to have anything to do with fishing. One man in our village, Mr. Yamamura, found his daughter playing in his boat one morning. He beat her with a stick and then washed out the boat with sake and lye so strong it bleached streaks of coloring from the wood. Even this wasn't enough; Mr. Yamamura had the Shinto priest come and bless it. All this because his daughter had done nothing more than play where the fish are caught. And here Mr. Tanaka was suggesting I spit blood onto the floor of the room where the fish were cleaned.

'If you're afraid her spit might wash away some of the fish guts,' said Mr. Tanaka, 'take them home with you. I've got plenty more.'

'It isn't the fish guts, sir.'

'I'd say her blood will be the cleanest thing to hit this floor since you or I were born. Go ahead,' Mr. Tanaka said, this time talking to me. 'Spit it out.'

There I sat on that slimy table, uncertain what to do. I thought it would be terrible to disobey Mr. Tanaka, but I'm not sure I would have found the courage to spit if one of the men hadn't leaned to the side and pressed a finger against one nostril to blow his nose onto the floor. After seeing this, I couldn't bear to hold anything in my mouth a moment longer, and spat out the blood just as Mr. Tanaka had told me to do.

All the men walked away in disgust except Mr. Tanaka's assistant, named Sugi. Mr. Tanaka told him to go and fetch Dr. Miura.

'I don't know where to find him,' said Sugi, though what he really meant, I think, was that he wasn't interested in helping.

I told Mr. Tanaka the doctor had been at our house a few minutes earlier.

'Where is your house?' Mr. Tanaka asked me.

'It's the little tipsy house up on the cliffs.'

'What do you mean . . . "tipsy house"?'

'It's the one that leans to the side, like it's had too much to drink.'

Mr. Tanaka didn't seem to know what to make of this. 'Well, Sugi, walk up toward Sakamoto's tipsy house and look for Dr. Miura. You won't have trouble finding him. Just listen for the sound of his patients screaming when he pokes them.'

I imagined Mr. Tanaka would go back to his work after Sugi had left; but instead he stood near the table a long while looking at me. I felt my face beginning to burn. Finally he said something I thought was very clever.

'You've got an eggplant on your face, little daughter of Sakamoto.'

He went to a drawer and took out a small mirror to show it to me. My lip was swollen and blue, just as he'd said.

'But what I really want to know;' he went on, 'is how you came to have such extraordinary eyes, and why you don't look more like your father?'

'The eyes are my mother's,' I said. 'But as for my father, he's so wrinkled I've never known what he really looks like.'

'You'll be wrinkled yourself one day.'

'But some of his wrinkles are the way he's made,' I said. 'The back of his head is as old as the front, but it's as smooth as an egg.'

'That isn't a respectful thing to say about your father,' Mr. Tanaka told me. 'But I suppose it's true.'

Then he said something that made my face blush so red, I'm sure my lips looked pale.

'So how did a wrinkled old man with an egg for a head father a beautiful girl like you?'

In the years since, I've been called beautiful more often than I can remember. Though, of course, geisha are always called beautiful, even those who aren't. But when Mr. Tanaka said it to me, before I'd ever heard of such a thing as a geisha, I could almost believe it was true.

After Dr. Miura tended to my lip, and I bought the incense my father had sent me for, I walked home in a state of such agitation, I don't think there could have been more activity inside me if I'd been an anthill. I would've had an easier time if my emotions had all pulled me in the same direction, but it wasn't so simple. I'd been blown about like a scrap of paper in the wind. Somewhere between the various thoughts about my mother – somewhere past the discomfort in my lip – there nestled a pleasant thought I tried again and again to bring into focus. It was about Mr. Tanaka. I stopped on the cliffs and gazed out to sea, where the waves even after the storm were still like sharpened stones, and the sky had taken on the brown tone of mud. I made sure no one was watching me, and then clutched the incense to my chest and said Mr. Tanaka's name into the whistling wind, over and over, until I felt satisfied I'd heard the music in every syllable. I know it sounds foolish of me – and indeed it was. But I was only a confused little girl.

After we'd finished our dinner and my father had gone to the village to watch the other fishermen play Japanese chess, Satsu and I cleaned the kitchen in silence. I tried to remember how Mr. Tanaka had made me feel, but in the cold quiet of the house it had slipped away from me. Instead I felt a persistent, icy dread at the thought of my mother's illness. I found myself wondering how long it would be until she was buried out in the village graveyard along with my father's other family. What would become of me afterward? With my mother dead, Satsu would act in her place, I supposed. I watched my sister scrub the iron pot that had cooked our soup; but even though it was right before her – even though her eyes were pointed at the thing – I could tell she wasn't seeing it. She went on scrubbing it long after it was clean. Finally I said to her:

'Satsu-san, I don't feel well.'

'Go outside and heat the bath,' she told me, and brushed her unruly hair from her eyes with one of her wet hands.

'I don't want a bath,' I said. 'Satsu, Mommy is going to die –'

'This pot is cracked. Look!'

'It isn't cracked,' I said. 'That line has always been there.'

'But how did the water get out just then?'

'You sloshed it out. I watched you.'

For a moment I could tell that Satsu was feeling something very strongly, which translated itself onto her face as a look of extreme puzzlement, just as so many of her feelings did. But she said nothing further to me. She only took the pot from the stove and walked toward the door to dump it out.

2

THE FOLLOWING MORNING, to take my mind off my troubles, I went swimming in the pond just inland from our house amid a grove of pine trees. The children from the village went there most mornings when the weather was right. Satsu came too sometimes, wearing a scratchy bathing dress she'd made from our father's old fishing clothes. It wasn't a very good bathing dress, because it sagged at her chest whenever she bent over, and one of the boys would scream, 'Look! You can see Mount Fuji!' But she wore it just the same.

Around noontime, I decided to return home for something to eat. Satsu had left much earlier with the Sugi boy, who was the son of Mr. Tanaka's assistant. She acted like a dog around him. When he went somewhere, he looked back over his shoulder to signal that she should follow, and she always did. I didn't expect to see her again until dinnertime, but as I neared the house I caught sight of her on the path ahead of me, leaning against a tree. If you'd seen what was happening, you might have understood it right away; but I was only a little girl. Satsu had her scratchy bathing dress up around her shoulders and the Sugi boy was playing around with her 'Mount Fujis,' as the boys called them.

Ever since our mother first became ill, my sister had grown a bit pudgy. Her breasts were every bit as unruly as her hair. What amazed me most was that their unruliness appeared to be the very thing the Sugi boy found fascinating about them. He jiggled them with his hand, and pushed them to one side to watch them swing back and settle against her chest. I knew I shouldn't be spying, but I couldn't think what else to do with myself while the path ahead of me was blocked. And then suddenly I heard a man's voice behind me say:

'Chiyo-chan, why are you squatting there behind that tree?'

Considering that I was a little girl of nine, coming from a pond where I'd been swimming; and considering that as yet I had no shapes or textures on my body to conceal from anyone . . . well, it's easy to guess what I was wearing.

When I turned – still squatting on the path, and covering my nakedness with my arms as best I could – there stood Mr. Tanaka. I could hardly have been more embarrassed.

'That must be your tipsy house over there,' he said. 'And over there, that looks like the Sugi boy. He certainly looks busy! Who's that girl with him?'

'Well, it might be my sister, Mr. Tanaka. I'm waiting for them to leave.'

Mr. Tanaka cupped his hands around his mouth and shouted, and then I heard the sound of the Sugi boy running away down the path. My sister must have run away too, for Mr. Tanaka told me I could go home and get some clothes now. 'When you see that sister of yours,' he said to me, 'I want you to give her this.'

He handed me a packet wrapped in rice paper, about the size of a fish head. 'It's some Chinese herbs,' he told me. 'Don't listen to Dr. Miura if he tells you they're worthless. Have your sister make tea with them and give the tea to your mother, to ease the pain. They're very precious herbs. Make sure not to waste them.'

'I'd better do it myself in that case, sir. My sister isn't very good at making tea.'

'Dr. Miura told me your mother is sick,' he said. 'Now you tell me your sister can't even be trusted to make tea! With your father so old, what will become of you, Chiyo-chan? Who takes care of you even now?'

'I suppose I take care of myself these days.'

'I know a certain man. He's older now, but when he was a boy about your age, his father died. The very next year his mother died, and then his older brother ran away to Osaka and left him alone. Sounds a bit like you, don't you think?'

Mr. Tanaka gave me a look as if to say that I shouldn't dare to disagree.

'Well, that man's name is Tanaka Ichiro,' he went on. 'Yes, me . . . although back then my name was Morihashi Ichiro. I was taken in by the Tanaka family at the age of twelve. After I got a bit older, I was married to the daughter and adopted. Now I help run the family's seafood company. So things turned out all right for me in the end, you see. Perhaps something like that might happen to you too.'

I looked for a moment at Mr. Tanaka's gray hair and at the creases in his brow like ruts in the bark of a tree. He seemed to me the wisest and most knowledgeable man on earth. I believed he knew things I would never know; and that he had an elegance I would never have; and that his blue kimono was finer than anything I would ever have occasion to wear. I sat before him naked, on my haunches in the dirt, with my hair tangled and my face dirty, with the smell of pond water on my skin.

'I don't think anyone would ever want to adopt me,' I said.

'No? You're a clever girl, aren't you? Naming your house a "tipsy house." Saying your father's head looks like an egg!'

'But it does look like an egg.'

'It wouldn't have been a clever thing to say otherwise. Now run along, Chiyo-chan,' he said. 'You want lunch, don't you? Perhaps if your sister's having soup, you can lie on the floor and drink what she spills.'

From that very moment on, I began to have fantasies that Mr. Tanaka would adopt me. Sometimes I forget how tormented I felt during this period. I suppose I would have grasped at anything that offered me comfort. Often when I felt troubled, I found my mind returning to the same image of my mother, long before she ever began groaning in the mornings from the pains inside her. I was four years old, at the obon festival in our village, the time of year when we welcomed back the spirits of the dead. After a few evenings of ceremonies in the graveyard, and fires outside the entrances of the houses to guide the spirits home, we gathered on the festival's final night at our Shinto shrine, which stood on rocks overlooking the inlet. Just inside the gate of the shrine was a clearing, decorated that evening with colored paper lanterns strung on ropes between the trees. My mother and I danced together for a while with the rest of the villagers, to the music of drums and a flute; but at last I began to feel tired and she cradled me in her lap at the edge of the clearing. Suddenly the wind came up off the cliffs and one of the lanterns caught fire. We watched the flame burn through the cord, and the lantern came floating down, until the wind caught it again and rolled it through the air right toward us with a trail of gold dust streaking into the sky. The ball of fire seemed to settle on the ground, but then my mother and I watched as it rose up on the current of the wind, floating straight for us. I felt my mother release me, and then all at once she threw her arms into the fire to scatter it. For a moment we were both awash in sparks and flames; but then the shreds of fire drifted into the trees and burned out, and no one – not even my mother – was hurt.

A week or so later, when my fantasies of adoption had had plenty of time to ripen, I came home one afternoon to find Mr. Tanaka sitting across from my father at the little table in our house. I knew they were talking about something serious, because they didn't even notice me when I stepped into our entryway. I froze there to listen to them.

'So, Sakamoto, what do you think of my proposal?'

'I don't know, sir,' said my father. 'I can't picture the girls living anywhere else.'

'I understand, but they'd be much better off, and so would you. Just see to it they come down to the village tomorrow afternoon.'

At this, Mr. Tanaka stood to leave. I pretended I was just arriving so we would meet at the door.

'I was talking with your father about you, Chiyo-chan,' he said to me. 'I live across the ridge in the town of Senzuru. It's bigger than Yoroido. I think you'd like it. Why don't you and Satsu-san come there tomorrow? You'll see my house and meet my little daughter. Perhaps you'll stay the night? Just one night, you understand; and then I'll bring you back to your home again. How would that be?'

I said it would be very nice. And I did my best to pretend no one had suggested anything out of the ordinary to me. But in my head it was as though an explosion had occurred. My thoughts were in fragments I could hardly piece together. Certainly it was true that a part of me hoped desperately to be adopted by Mr. Tanaka after my mother died; but another part of me was very much afraid. I felt horribly ashamed for even imagining I might live somewhere besides my tipsy house. After Mr. Tanaka had left, I tried to busy myself in the kitchen, but I felt a bit like Satsu, for I could hardly see the things before me. I don't know how much time passed. At length I heard my father making a sniffling noise, which I took to be crying and which made my face burn with shame. When I finally forced myself to glance his way, I saw him with his hands already tangled up in one of his fishing nets, but standing at the doorway leading into the back room, where my mother lay in the full sun with the sheet stuck to her like skin.

The next day in preparation for meeting Mr. Tanaka in the village, I scrubbed my dirty ankles and soaked for a while in our bath, which had once been the boiler compartment from an old steam engine someone had abandoned in our village; the top had been sawed off and the inside lined with wood. I sat a long while looking out to sea and feeling very independent, for I was about to see something of the world outside our little village for the first time in my life.

When Satsu and I reached the Japan Coastal Seafood Company, we watched the fishermen unloading their catches at the pier. My father was among them, grabbing fish with his bony hands and dropping them into baskets. At one point he looked toward me and Satsu, and then afterward wiped his face on the sleeve of his shirt. Somehow his features looked heavier to me than usual. The men carried the full baskets to Mr. Tanaka's horse-drawn wagon and arranged them in the back. I climbed up on the wheel to watch. Mostly, the fish stared out with glassy eyes, but every so often one would move its mouth, which seemed to me like a little scream. I tried to reassure them by saying:

'You're going to the town of Senzuru, little fishies!

Everything will be okay.'

I didn't see what good it would do to tell them the truth.

At length Mr. Tanaka came out into the street and told Satsu and me to climb onto the bench of the wagon with him. I sat in the middle, close enough to feel the fabric of Mr. Tanaka's kimono against my hand. I couldn't help blushing at this. Satsu was looking right at me, but she didn't seem to notice anything and wore her usual muddled expression.

I passed much of the trip looking back at the fish as they sloshed around in their baskets. When we climbed up over the ridge leaving Yoroido, the wheel passed over a rock and the wagon tipped to one side quite suddenly. One of the sea bass was thrown out and hit the ground so hard it was jolted back to life. To see it flopping and gasping was more than I could bear. I turned back around with tears in my eyes, and though I tried to hide them from Mr. Tanaka, he noticed them anyway. After he had retrieved the fish and we were on our way again, he asked me what was the matter.

'The poor fish!' I said.

'You're like my wife. They're mostly dead when she sees them, but if she has to cook a crab, or anything else still alive, she grows teary-eyed and sings to them.'

Mr. Tanaka taught me a little song – really almost a sort of prayer – that I thought his wife had invented. She sang it for crabs, but we changed the words for the fish:

Suzuki yo suzuki!
Jobutsu shite kure!

Little bass, oh little bass!
Speed yourself to Buddhahood!

Then he taught me another song, a lullaby I'd never heard before. We sang it to a flounder in the back lying in a low basket by itself, with its two button-eyes on the side of its head shifting around.

Nemure yo, ii karei yo!
Niwa ya makiba ni

Tori mo hitsuji mo
Minna nemureba
Hoshi wa mado kara
Gin no hikari o
Sosogu, kono yoru!

Go to sleep, you good flounder!
When all are sleeping –
Even the birds and the sheep
In the gardens and in the fields –
The stars this evening
Will pour their silver light
Through the window.

We topped the ridge a few moments later, and the town of Senzuru came into view below us. The day was drab, everything in shades of gray. It was my first look at the world outside Yoroido, and I didn't think I'd missed much. I could see the thatched roofs of the town around an inlet, amid dull hills, and beyond them the metal-colored sea, broken with shards of white. Inland, the landscape might have been attractive but for the train tracks running across it like a scar.

Senzuru was mainly a dirty, smelly town. Even the ocean had a terrible odor, as if all the fish in it were rotting. Around the legs of the pier, pieces of vegetables bobbed like the jellyfish in our little inlet. The boats were scratched up, some of their timbers cracked; they looked to me as if they'd been fighting with one another.

Satsu and I sat a long while on the pier, until at length Mr. Tanaka called us inside the Japan Coastal Seafood Company's headquarters and led us down a long corridor. The corridor couldn't have smelled more strongly of fish guts if we had actually been inside a fish. But down at the end, to my surprise, was an office, lovely to my nine-year-old eyes. Inside the doorway, Satsu and I stood in our bare feet on a slimy floor of stone. Before us, a step led up to a platform covered with tatami mats. Perhaps this is what impressed me so; the raised flooring made everything look grander. In any case, I considered it the most beautiful room I'd ever seen – though it makes me laugh now to think that the office of a fish wholesaler in a tiny town on the Japan Sea could have made such an impression on anyone.

On the platform sat an old woman on a cushion, who rose when she saw us and came down to the edge to arrange herself on her knees. She was old and cranky-looking, and I don't think you could ever meet anyone who fidgeted more. When she wasn't smoothing her kimono, she was wiping something from the corner of her eye or scratching her nose, all the while sighing as though she felt very sorry there was so much fidgeting to be done.

Mr. Tanaka said to her, 'This is Chiyo-chan and her older sister, Satsu-san.'

I gave a little bow, to which Mrs. Fidget responded with a nod. Then she gave the biggest sigh she'd given yet, and began to pick with one hand at a crusty patch on her neck. I would have liked to look away, but her eyes were fixed on mine.

'Well! You're Satsu-san, are you?' she said. But she was still looking right at me.

'I'm Satsu,' said my sister.

'When were you born?'

Satsu still seemed unsure which of us Mrs. Fidget was addressing, so I answered for her. 'She's the year of the cow,' I said.

The old woman reached out and patted me with her fingers. But she did it in a most peculiar way, by poking me several times in the jaw. I knew she meant it as a pat because she wore a kindly look.

'This one's rather pretty, isn't she? Such unusual eyes! And you can see that she's clever. Just look at her forehead.' Here she turned to my sister again and said, 'Now, then. The year of the cow; fifteen years old; the planet Venus; six, white. Hmm . . . Come a bit closer.'

Satsu did as she was told. Mrs. Fidget began to examine her face, not only with her eyes but with her fingertips. She spent a long while checking Satsu's nose from different angles, and her ears. She pinched the lobes a number of times, then gave a grunt to indicate she was done with Satsu and turned to me.

'You're the year of the monkey. I can tell it just looking at you. What a great deal of water you have! Eight, white; the planet Saturn. And a very attractive girl you are. Come closer.'

Now she proceeded to do the same thing to me, pinching my ears and so on. I kept thinking of how she'd scratched at the crusty patch on her neck with these same fingers. Soon she got to her feet and came down onto the stone floor where we stood. She took a while getting her crooked feet into her zori, but finally turned toward Mr. Tanaka and gave him a look he seemed to understand at once, because he left the room, closing the door behind him.

Mrs. Fidget untied the peasant shirt Satsu was wearing and removed it. She moved Satsu's bosoms around a bit, looked under her arms, and then turned her around and looked at her back. I was in such a state of shock, I could barely bring myself to watch. I'd certainly seen Satsu naked before, but the way Mrs. Fidget handled her body seemed even more indecent to me than when Satsu had held her bathing dress up for the Sugi boy. Then, as if she hadn't done enough already, Mrs. Fidget yanked Satsu's pants to the floor, looked her up and down, and turned her around facing front again.

'Step out of your pants,' she said.

Satsu's face was more confused than I'd seen it in a long while, but she stepped out of her pants and left them on the slimy stone floor. Mrs. Fidget took her by the shoulders and seated her on the platform. Satsu was completely naked; I'm sure she had no more idea why she should be sitting there than I did. But she had no time to wonder about it either, for in an instant Mrs. Fidget had put her hands on Satsu's knees and spread them apart. And without a moment's hesitation she reached her hand between Satsu's legs. After this I could no longer bring myself to watch. I think Satsu must have resisted, for Mrs. Fidget gave a shout, and at the same moment I heard a loud slap, which was Mrs. Fidget smacking Satsu on the leg – as I could tell later from the red mark there. In a moment Mrs. Fidget was done and told Satsu to put her clothes back on. While she was dressing, Satsu gave a big sniff. She may have been crying, but I didn't dare look at her.

Next, Mrs. Fidget came straight at me, and in a moment my

own pants were down around my knees, and my shirt was taken off me just as Satsu's had been. I had no bosoms for the old woman to move around, but she looked under my arms just as she'd done with my sister, and turned me around too, before seating me on the platform and pulling my pants off my legs. I was terribly frightened of what she would do, and when she tried to spread my knees apart, she had to slap me on the leg just as she'd slapped Satsu, which made my throat begin to burn from holding back my tears. She put a finger between my legs and gave what felt to me like a pinch, in such a way that I cried out. When she told me to dress again, I felt as a dam must feel when it's holding back an entire river. But I was afraid if Satsu or I began to sob like little children, we might look bad in Mr. Tanaka's eyes.

'The girls are healthy,' she said to Mr. Tanaka when he came back into the room, 'and very suitable. Both of them are intact. The older one has far too much wood, but the younger one has a good deal of water. Pretty too, don't you think? Her older sister looks like a peasant beside her!'

'I'm sure they're both attractive girls in their way,' he said. 'Why don't we talk about it while I walk you out? The girls will wait here for me.'

When Mr. Tanaka had closed the door behind them, I turned to see Satsu sitting on the edge of the platform, gazing upward toward the ceiling. Because of the shape of her face, tears were pooled along the tops of her nostrils, and I burst into tears myself the moment I saw her upset. I felt myself to blame for what had happened, and wiped her face with the corner of my peasant shirt.

'Who was that horrible woman?' she said to me.

'She must be a fortune-teller. Probably Mr. Tanaka wants to learn as much about us as he can . . .'

'But why should she look at us in that horrible way!'

'Satsu-san, don't you understand?' I said. 'Mr. Tanaka is planning to adopt us.'

When she heard this, Satsu began to blink as if a bug had crawled into her eye. 'What are you talking about?' she said. 'Mr. Tanaka can't adopt us.'

'Father is so old . . . and now that our mother is sick, I think

Mr. Tanaka is worried about our future. There won't be anyone to take care of us.'

Satsu stood, she was so agitated to hear this. In a moment her eyes had begun to squint, and I could see she was hard at work willing herself to believe that nothing was going to take us from our tipsy house. She was squeezing out the things I'd told her in the same way you might squeeze water from a sponge. Slowly her face began to relax again, and she sat down once more on the edge of the platform. In a moment she was gazing around the room as if we'd never had the conversation at all.

Mr. Tanaka's house lay at the end of a lane just outside the town. The glade of pine trees surrounding it smelled as richly as the ocean back on the seacliffs at our house; and when I thought of the ocean and how I would be trading one smell for another, I felt a terrible emptiness I had to pull myself away from, just as you might step back from a cliff after peering over it. The house was grander than anything in Yoroido, with enormous eaves like our village shrine. And when Mr. Tanaka stepped up into his entryway, he left his shoes right where he walked out of them, because a maid came and stowed them on a shelf for him. Satsu and I had no shoes to put away, but just as I was about to walk into the house, I felt something strike me softly on my backside, and a pine cone fell onto the wood floor between my feet. I turned to see a young girl about my age, with very short hair, running to hide behind a tree. She peered out to smile at me with a triangle of empty space between her front teeth and then ran away, looking back over her shoulder so I'd be certain to chase her. It may sound peculiar, but I'd never had the experience of actually meeting another little girl. Of course I knew the girls in my village, but we'd grown up together and had never done anything that might be called 'meeting.' But Kuniko – for that was the name of Mr. Tanaka's little daughter – was so friendly from the first instant I saw her, I thought it might be easy for me to move from one world into another.

Kuniko's clothing was much more refined than mine, and

she wore zori; but being the village girl I was, I chased her out into the woods barefoot until I caught up to her at a sort of playhouse made from the sawed-off branches of a dead tree. She'd laid out rocks and pine cones to make rooms. In one she pretended to serve me tea out of a cracked cup; in another we took turns nursing her baby doll, a little boy named Taro who was really nothing more than a canvas bag stuffed with dirt. Taro loved strangers, said Kuniko, but he was very frightened of earthworms; and by a most peculiar coincidence, so was Kuniko. When we encountered one, Kuniko made sure I carried it outside in my fingers before poor Taro should burst into tears.

I was delighted at the prospect of having Kuniko for a sister. In fact, the majestic trees and the pine smell – even Mr. Tanaka – all began to seem almost insignificant to me in comparison. The difference between life here at the Tanakas' house and life in Yoroido was as great as the difference between the odor of something cooking and a mouthful of delicious food.

As it grew dark, we washed our hands and feet at the well, and went inside to take our seats on the floor around a square table. I was amazed to see steam from the meal we were about to eat rising up into the rafters of a ceiling high above me, with electric lights hanging down over our heads. The brightness of the room was startling; I'd never seen such a thing before. Soon the servants brought our dinner – grilled salted sea bass, pickles, soup, and steamed rice – but the moment we began to eat, the lights went out. Mr. Tanaka laughed; this happened quite often, apparently. The servants went around lighting lanterns that hung on wooden tripods.

No one spoke very much as we ate. I'd expected Mrs. Tanaka to be glamorous, but she looked like an older version of Satsu, except that she smiled a good deal. After dinner she and Satsu began playing a game of go, and Mr. Tanaka stood and called a maid to bring his kimono jacket. In a moment Mr. Tanaka was gone, and after a short delay, Kuniko gestured to me to follow her out the door. She put on straw zori and lent me an extra pair. I asked her where we were going.

'Quietly!' she said. 'We're following my daddy. I do it every time he goes out. It's a secret.'

We headed up the lane and turned on the main street toward the town of Senzuru, following some distance behind Mr. Tanaka. In a few minutes we were walking among the houses of the town, and then Kuniko took my arm and pulled me down a side street. At the end of a stone walkway between two houses, we came to a window covered with paper screens that shone with the light inside. Kuniko put her eye to a hole torn just at eye level in one of the screens. While she peered in, I heard the sounds of laughter and talking, and someone singing to the accompaniment of a shamisen. At length she stepped aside so I could put my own eye to the hole. Half the room inside was blocked from my view by a folding screen, but I could see Mr. Tanaka seated on the mats with a group of three or four men. An old man beside him was telling a story about holding a ladder for a young woman and peering up her robe; everyone was laughing except Mr. Tanaka, who gazed straight ahead toward the part of the room blocked from my view. An older woman in kimono came with a glass for him, which he held while she poured beer. Mr. Tanaka struck me as an island in the midst of the sea, because although everyone else was enjoying the story – even the elderly woman pouring the beer – Mr. Tanaka just went on staring at the other end of the table. I took my eye from the hole to ask Kuniko what sort of place this was.

'It's a teahouse,' she told me, 'where geisha entertain. My daddy comes here almost every night. I don't know why he likes it so. The women pour drinks, and the men tell stories – except when they sing songs. Everybody ends up drunk.'

I put my eye back to the hole in time to see a shadow crossing the wall, and then a woman came into view. Her hair was ornamented with the dangling green bloom of a willow, and she wore a soft pink kimono with white flowers like cutouts all over it. The broad obi tied around her middle was orange and yellow. I'd never seen such elegant clothing. None of the women in Yoroido owned anything more sophisticated than a cotton robe, or perhaps linen, with a simple pattern in indigo. But unlike her clothing, the woman herself wasn't lovely at all. Her teeth protruded so badly that her lips didn't quite cover them, and the narrowness of her head made me wonder if she'd been pressed between two boards as a baby. You may think me cruel to describe her so harshly; but it struck me as odd that even though no one could have called her a beauty, Mr. Tanaka's eyes were fixed on her like a rag on a hook. He went on watching her while everyone else laughed, and when she knelt beside him to pour a few more drops of beer into his glass, she looked up at him in a way that suggested they knew each other very well.

Kuniko took another turn peeking through the hole; and then we went back to her house and sat together in the bath at the edge of the pine forest. The sky was extravagant with stars, except for the half blocked by limbs above me. I could have sat much longer trying to understand all I'd seen that day and the changes confronting me . . . but Kuniko had grown so sleepy in the hot water that the servants soon came to help us out.

Satsu was snoring already when Kuniko and I lay down on our futons beside her, with our bodies pressed together and our arms intertwined. A warm feeling of gladness began to swell inside me, and I whispered to Kuniko, 'Did you know I'm going to come and live with you?' I thought the news would shock her into opening her eyes, or maybe even sitting up. But it didn't rouse her from her slumber. She let out a groan, and then a moment later her breath was warm and moist, with the rattle of sleep in it.

3

BACK AT HOME my mother seemed to have grown sicker in the day I'd been away. Or perhaps it was just that I'd managed to forget how ill she really was. Mr. Tanaka's house had smelled of smoke and pine, but ours smelled of her illness in a way I can't even bear to describe. Satsu was working in the village during the afternoon, so Mrs. Sugi came to help me bathe my mother. When we carried her out of the house, her rib cage was broader than her shoulders, and even the whites of her eyes were cloudy. I could only endure seeing her this way by remembering how I'd once felt stepping out of the bath with her while she was strong and healthy, when the steam had risen from our pale skin as if we were two pieces of boiled radish. I found it hard to imagine that this woman, whose back I'd so often scraped with a stone, and whose flesh had always seemed firmer and smoother to me than Satsu's, might be dead before even the end of summer.

That night while lying on my futon, I tried to picture the whole confusing situation from every angle to persuade myself that things would somehow be all right. To begin with, I wondered, how could we go on living without my mother? Even if we did survive and Mr. Tanaka adopted us, would my own family cease to exist? Finally I decided Mr. Tanaka wouldn't adopt just my sister and me, but my father as well. He couldn't expect my father to live alone, after all. Usually I couldn't fall asleep until I'd managed to convince myself this was true, with the result that I didn't sleep much during those weeks, and mornings were a blur.

On one of these mornings during the heat of the summer, I was on my way back from fetching a packet of tea in the village when I heard a crunching noise behind me. It turned out to be Mr. Sugi – Mr. Tanaka's assistant – running up the path. When he reached me, he took a long while to catch his breath, huffing and holding his side as if he'd just run all the way from Senzuru. He was red and shiny like a snapper, though the day hadn't grown hot yet. Finally he said:

'Mr. Tanaka wants you and your sister . . . to come down to the village . . . as soon as you can.'

I'd thought it odd that my father hadn't gone out fishing that morning. Now I knew why: Today was the day.

'And my father?' I asked. 'Did Mr. Tanaka say anything about him?'

'Just get along, Chiyo-chan,' he told me. 'Go and fetch your sister.'

I didn't like this, but I ran up to the house and found my father sitting at the table, digging grime out of a rut in the wood with one of his fingernails. Satsu was putting slivers of charcoal into the stove. It seemed as though the two of them were waiting for something horrible to happen.

I said, 'Father, Mr. Tanaka wants Satsu-san and me to go down to the village.'

Satsu took off her apron, hung it on a peg, and walked out the door. My father didn't answer, but blinked a few times, staring at the point where Satsu had been. Then he turned his eyes heavily toward the floor and gave a nod. I heard my mother cry out in her sleep from the back room.

Satsu was almost to the village before I caught up with her. I'd imagined this day for weeks already, but I'd never expected to feel as frightened as I did. Satsu didn't seem to realize this trip to the village was any different from one she might have made the day before. She hadn't even bothered to clean the charcoal off her hands; while wiping her hair away she ended up with a smudge on her face. I didn't want her to meet Mr. Tanaka in this condition, so I reached up to rub off the mark as our mother might have done. Satsu knocked my hand away.

Outside the Japan Coastal Seafood Company, I bowed and said good morning to Mr. Tanaka, expecting he would be happy to see us. Instead he was strangely cold. I suppose this should have been my first clue that things weren't going to happen just the way I'd imagined. When he led us to his horse-drawn wagon, I decided he probably wanted to drive us to his house so that his wife and daughter would be in the room when he told us about our adoption.

'Mr. Sugi will be riding in the front with me,' he said, 'so you and Shizu-san had better get into the back.' That's just what he said: 'Shizu-san.' I thought it very rude of him to get my sister's name wrong that way, but she didn't seem to notice. She climbed into the back of the wagon and sat down among the empty fish baskets, putting one of her hands flat onto the slimy planks. And then with that same hand, she wiped a fly from her face, leaving a shiny patch on her cheek. I didn't feel as indifferently about the slime as Satsu did. I couldn't think about anything but the smell, and about how satisfied I would feel to wash my hands and perhaps even my clothes when we reached Mr. Tanaka's house.

During the trip, Satsu and I didn't speak a word, until we topped the hill overlooking Senzuru, when all of a sudden she said:

'A train.'

I looked out to see a train in the distance, making its way toward the town. The smoke rolled downwind in a way that made me think of the skin being shed from a snake. I thought this was clever and tried explaining it to Satsu, but she didn't seem to care. Mr. Tanaka would have appreciated it, I thought, and so would Kuniko. I decided to explain it to both of them when we reached the Tanakas' home.

Then suddenly I realized we weren't headed in the direction of Mr. Tanaka's home at all.

The wagon came to a stop a few minutes later on a patch of dirt beside the train tracks, just outside the town. A crowd of people stood with sacks and crates piled around them. And there, to one side of them, was Mrs. Fidget, standing beside a peculiarly narrow man wearing a stiff kimono. He had soft black hair, like a cat's, and held in one of his hands a cloth bag suspended from a string. He struck me as out of place in Senzuru, particularly there beside the farmers and the fishermen with their crates, and an old hunched woman wearing a rucksack of yams. Mrs. Fidget said something to him, and when he turned and peered at us, I decided at once that I was frightened of him.

Mr. Tanaka introduced us to this man, whose name was Bekku. Mr. Bekku said nothing at all, but only looked closely at me and seemed puzzled by Satsu.

Mr. Tanaka said to him, 'I've brought Sugi with me from Yoroido. Would you like him to accompany you? He knows the girls, and I can spare him for a day or so.'

'No, no,' said Mr. Bekku, waving his hand.

I certainly hadn't expected any of this. I asked where we were going, but no one seemed to hear me, so I came up with an answer for myself. I decided Mr. Tanaka had been displeased by what Mrs. Fidget had told him about us, and that this curiously narrow man, Mr. Bekku, planned to take us somewhere to have our fortunes told more completely. Afterward we would be returned to Mr. Tanaka.

While I tried my best to soothe myself with these thoughts, Mrs. Fidget, wearing a pleasant smile, led Satsu and me some distance down the dirt platform. When we were too far away for the others to hear us, her smile vanished and she said:

'Now listen to me. You're both naughty girls!' She looked around to be sure no one was watching and then hit us on the tops of our heads. She didn't hurt me, but I cried out in surprise. 'If you do something to embarrass me,' she went on, 'I'll make you pay for it! Mr. Bekku is a stern man; you must pay attention to what he says! If he tells you to crawl under the seat of the train, you'll do it. Understand?'

From the expression on Mrs. Fidget's face, I knew I should answer her or she might hurt me. But I was in such shock I couldn't speak. And then just as I'd feared, she reached out and began pinching me so hard on the side of my neck that I couldn't even tell which part of me hurt. I felt as if I'd fallen into a tub of creatures that were biting me everywhere, and I heard myself whimper. The next thing I knew, Mr. Tanaka was standing beside us.

'What's going on here?' he said. 'If you have something more to say to these girls, say it while I'm standing here. There's no cause for you to treat them this way.'

'I'm sure we have a great many more things to talk about. But the train is coming,' Mrs. Fidget said. And it was true: I could see it curling around a turn not far in the distance.

Mr. Tanaka led us back up the platform to where the farmers and old women were gathering up their things. Soon the train came to a stop before us. Mr. Bekku, in his stiff kimono, wedged himself between Satsu and me and led us by our elbows into the train car. I heard Mr. Tanaka say something, but I was too confused and upset to understand it. I couldn't trust what I heard. It might have been:

Mata yo! 'We'll meet again!'

Or this:

Matte yo! 'Wait!'

Or even this:

Ma . . . cleyo! 'Well, let's go!'

When I peered out the window, I saw Mr. Tanaka walking back toward his cart and Mrs. Fidget wiping her hands all over her kimono.

After a moment, my sister said, 'Chiyo-chan!'

I buried my face in my hands; and honestly I would have plunged in anguish through the floor of the train if I could have. Because the way my sister said my name, she hardly needed to say anything more.

'Do you know where we're going?' she said to me.

I think all she wanted was a yes or no answer. Probably it didn't matter to her what our destination was – so long as someone knew what was happening. But, of course, I didn't. I asked the narrow man, Mr. Bekku, but he paid me no attention. He was still staring at Satsu as if he had never seen anything like her before. Finally he squeezed his face into a look of disgust and said:

'Fish! What a stench, the both of you!'

He took a comb from his drawstring bag and began tearing it through her hair. I'm certain he must have hurt her, but I could see that watching the countryside pass by outside the window hurt her even more. In a moment Satsu's lips turned down like a baby's, and she began to cry. Even if she'd hit me and yelled at me, I wouldn't have ached as much as I did watching her whole face tremble. Everything was my fault.

An old peasant woman with her teeth bared like a dog's came over with a carrot for Satsu, and after giving it to her asked where she was going.

'Kyoto,' Mr. Bekku answered.

I felt so sick with worry at hearing this, I couldn't bring myself to look Satsu in the eye any longer. Even the town of Senzuru seemed a remote, faraway place. As for Kyoto, it sounded as foreign to me as Hong Kong, or even New York, which I'd once heard Dr. Miura talk about. For all I knew, they ground up children in Kyoto and fed them to dogs.

We were on that train for many hours, without food to eat. The sight of Mr. Bekku taking a wrapped-up lotus leaf from his bag, and unwrapping it to reveal a rice ball sprinkled with sesame seeds, certainly got my attention. But when he took it in his bony fingers and pressed it into his mean little mouth without so much as looking at me, I felt as if I couldn't take another moment of torment. We got off the train at last in a large town, which I took to be Kyoto; but after a time another train pulled into the station, and we boarded it. This one did take us to Kyoto. It was much more crowded than the first train had been, so that we had to stand. By the time we arrived, as evening was approaching, I felt as sore as a rock must feel when the waterfall has pounded on it all day long.

I could see little of the city as we neared Kyoto Station. But then to my astonishment, I caught a glimpse of rooftops reaching as far as the base of hills in the distance. I could never have imagined a city so huge. Even to this day, the sight of streets and buildings from a train often makes me remember the terrible emptiness and fear I felt on that curious day when I first left my home.

Back then, around 1930, a fair number of rickshaws still operated in Kyoto. In fact, so many were lined up before the station that I imagined no one went anywhere in this big city unless it was in a rickshaw – which couldn't have been further from the truth. Perhaps fifteen or twenty of them sat pitched forward onto their poles, with their drivers squatting nearby, smoking or eating; some of the drivers even lay curled up asleep right there in the filth of the street.

Mr. Bekku led us by our elbows again, as if we were a

couple of buckets he was bringing back from the well. He probably thought I'd have run away if he'd let go of me a moment; but I wouldn't have. Wherever he was taking us, I preferred it to being cast out alone into that great expanse of streets and buildings, as foreign to me as the bottom of the sea.

We climbed into a rickshaw, with Mr Bekku squeezed tightly on the bench between us. He was a good deal bonier under that kimono even than I suspected. We pitched back as the driver raised the poles, and then Mr. Bekku said, 'Tominaga-cho, in Gion.'

The driver said nothing in reply, but gave the rickshaw a tug to get it moving and then set off at a trot. After a block or two I worked up my courage and said to Mr. Bekku, 'Won't you please tell us where we're going?'

He didn't look as if he would reply, but after a moment he said, 'To your new home.'

At this, my eyes filled with tears. I heard Satsu weeping on the other side of Mr. Bekku and was just about to let out a sob of my own when Mr. Bekku suddenly struck her, and she let out a loud gasp. I bit my lip and stopped myself so quickly from crying any further that I think the tears themselves may have come to a halt as they slid down my cheeks.

Soon we turned onto an avenue that seemed as broad as the whole village of Yoroido. I could hardly see the other side for all the people, bicycles, cars, and trucks. I'd never seen a car before. I'd seen photographs, but I remember being surprised at how . . . well, cruel, is the way they looked to me in my frightened state, as though they were designed more to hurt people than to help them. All my senses were assaulted. Trucks rumbled past so close I could smell the scorched rubber odor of their tires. I heard a horrible screech, which turned out to be a streetcar on tracks in the center of the avenue.

I felt terrified as evening settled in around us; but I was never so astonished by anything in my life as by my first glimpse of city lights. I'd never even seen electricity except during part of our dinner at Mr. Tanaka's house. Here, windows were lit along the buildings upstairs and down, and the people on the sidewalks stood under puddles of yellow glow. I could see pinpoints even at the far reaches of the avenue. We turned onto another street, and I saw for the first time the Minamiza Theater standing on the opposite side of a bridge ahead of us. Its tiled roof was so grand, I thought it was a palace.

At length the rickshaw turned down an alleyway of wooden houses. The way they were all packed together, they seemed to share one continuous facade – which once again gave me the terrible feeling of being lost. I watched women in kimono rushing around in a great hurry on the little street. They looked very elegant to me; though, as I later learned, they were mostly maids.

When we came to a halt before a doorway, Mr. Bekku instructed me to get out. He climbed out behind me, and then as if the day hadn't been difficult enough, the worst thing of all happened. For when Satsu tried to get out as well, Mr. Bekku turned and pushed her back with his long arm.

'Stay there,' he said to her. 'You're going elsewhere.'

I looked at Satsu, and Satsu looked at me. It may have been the first time we'd ever completely understood each other's feelings. But it lasted only a moment, for the next thing I knew my eyes had welled up with tears so much I could scarcely see. I felt myself being dragged backward by Mr. Bekku; I heard women's voices and quite a bit of commotion. I was on the point of throwing myself onto the street when suddenly Satsu's mouth fell open at something she saw in the doorway behind me.

I was in a narrow entryway with an ancient-looking well on one side and a few plants on the other. Mr. Bekku had dragged me inside, and now he pulled me up onto my feet. There on the step of the entryway, just slipping her feet into her lacquered zori, stood an exquisitely beautiful woman wearing a kimono lovelier than anything I'd ever imagined. I'd been impressed with the kimono worn by the young bucktoothed geisha in Mr. Tanaka's village of Senzuru; but this one was a water blue, with swirling lines in ivory to mimic the current in a stream. Glistening silver trout tumbled in the current, and the surface of the water was ringed with gold wherever the soft green leaves of a tree touched it. I had no doubt the gown was woven of pure silk, and so was the obi, embroidered in pale greens and yellows. And her clothing wasn't the only extraordinary thing about her; her face was painted a kind of rich white, like the wall of a cloud when lit by the sun. Her hair, fashioned into lobes, gleamed as darkly as lacquer, and was decorated with ornaments carved out of amber, and with a bar from which tiny silver strips dangled, shimmering as she moved.

This was my first glimpse of Hatsumomo. At the time, she was one of the most renowned geisha in the district of Gion; though of course I didn't know any of this then. She was a petite woman; the top of her hairstyle reached no higher than Mr. Bekku's shoulder. I was so startled by her appearance that I forgot my manners – not that I had developed very good manners yet – and stared directly at her face. She was smiling at me, though not in a kindly way. And then she said:

'Mr. Bekku, could you take out the garbage later? I'd like to be on my way.'

There was no garbage in the entryway; she was talking about me. Mr. Bekku said he thought Hatsumomo had enough room to pass.

'*You* may not mind being so close to her,' said Hatsumomo. 'But when I see filth on one side of the street, I cross to the other.'

Suddenly an older woman, tall and knobby, like a bamboo pole, appeared in the doorway behind her.

'I don't know how anyone puts up with you, Hatsumomo-san,' said the woman. But she gestured for Mr. Bekku to pull me onto the street again, which he did. After this she stepped down into the entryway very awkwardly – for one of her hips jutted out and made it difficult for her to walk – and crossed to a tiny cabinet on the wall. She took from it something that looked to me like a piece of flint, along with a rectangular stone like the kind fishermen use to sharpen their knives, and then stood behind Hatsumomo and struck the flint against the stone, causing a little cluster of sparks to jump onto Hatsumomo's back. I didn't understand this at all; but you see, geisha are more superstitious even than fishermen. A geisha will never go out for the evening until someone has sparked a flint on her back for good luck.

After this, Hatsumomo walked away, using such tiny steps that she seemed to glide along with the bottom of her kimono fluttering just a bit. I didn't know that she was a geisha at the time, for she was worlds above the creature I'd seen in Senzuru a few weeks earlier. I decided she must be some sort of stage performer. We all watched her float away, and then Mr. Bekku handed me over to the older woman in the entryway. He climbed back into the rickshaw with my sister, and the driver raised the poles. But I never saw them leave, because I was slumped down in the entryway in tears.

The older woman must have taken pity on me; for a long while I lay there sobbing in my misery without anyone touching me. I even heard her shush up a maid who came from inside the house to speak with her. At length she helped me to my feet and dried my face with a handkerchief she took from one sleeve of her simple gray kimono.

'Now, now, little girl. There's no need to worry so. No one's going to cook you.' She spoke with the same peculiar accent as Mr. Bekku and Hatsumomo. It sounded so different from the Japanese spoken in my village that I had a hard time understanding her. But in any case, hers were the kindest words anyone had said to me all day, so I made up my mind to do what she advised. She told me to call her Auntie. And then she looked down at me, square in the face, and said in a throaty voice:

'Heavens! What startling eyes! You're a lovely girl, aren't you? Mother will be thrilled.'

I thought at once that the mother of this woman, whoever she was, must be very old, because Auntie's hair, knotted tightly at the back of her head, was mostly gray, with only streaks of black remaining.

Auntie led me through the doorway, where I found myself standing on a dirt corridor passing between two closely spaced structures to a courtyard in the back. One of the structures was a little dwelling like my house in Yoroido – two rooms with floors of dirt; it turned out to be the maids' quarters. The other was a small, elegant house sitting up on foundation stones in such a way that a cat might have crawled underneath it. The corridor between them opened onto the dark sky above, which gave me the feeling I was standing in something more like a miniature village than a house – especially since I could see several other small wooden buildings down in the courtyard at the end. I didn't know it at the time, but this was a very typical dwelling for the section of Kyoto in which it stood. The buildings in the courtyard, though they gave the impression of another group of tiny houses, were just a small shed for the toilets and a storehouse of two levels with a ladder on the outside. The entire dwelling fitted into an area smaller than Mr. Tanaka's home in the countryside and housed only eight people. Or rather nine, now that I had arrived.

After I took in the peculiar arrangement of all the little buildings, I noticed the elegance of the main house. In Yoroido, the wood structures were more gray than brown, and rutted by the salty air. But here the wood floors and beams gleamed with the yellow light of electric lamps. Opening off the front hallway were sliding doors with paper screens, as well as a staircase that seemed to climb straight up. One of these doors stood open, so that I was able to see a wood cabinet with a Buddhist altar. These elegant rooms turned out to be for the use of the family – and also Hatsumomo, even though, as I would come to understand, she wasn't a family member at all. When family members wanted to go to the courtyard, they didn't walk down the dirt corridor as the servants did, but had their own ramp of polished wood running along the side of the house. There were even separate toilets – an upper one for family and a lower one for servants.

I had yet to discover most of these things, though I would learn them within a day or two. But I stood there in the corridor a long while, wondering what sort of place this was and feeling very afraid. Auntie had disappeared into the kitchen and was talking in a hoarse voice to somebody. At length the somebody came out. She turned out to be a girl about my age, carrying a wooden bucket so heavy with water that she sloshed half of it onto the dirt floor. Her body was narrow; but her face was plump and almost perfectly round, so that she looked to me like a melon on a stick. She was straining to carry the bucket, and her tongue stuck out of her mouth just the way the stem comes out of the top of a pumpkin. As I soon learned, this was a habit of hers. She stuck her tongue out when she stirred her miso soup, or scooped rice into a bowl, or even tied the knot of her robe. And her face was truly so plump and so soft, with that tongue curling out like a pumpkin stem, that within a few days I'd given her the nickname of 'Pumpkin,' which everyone came to call her – even her customers many years later when she was a geisha in Gion.

When she had put down the bucket near me, Pumpkin retracted her tongue, and then brushed a strand of hair behind her ear while she looked me up and down. I thought she might say something, but she just went on looking, as though she were trying to make up her mind whether or not to take a bite of me. Really, she did seem hungry; and then at last she leaned in and whispered:

'Where on earth did you come from?'

I didn't think it would help to say that I had come from Yoroido; since her accent was as strange to me as everyone else's, I felt sure she wouldn't recognize the name of my village. I said instead that I'd just arrived.

'I thought I would never see another girl my age,' she said to me. 'But what's the matter with your eyes?'

Just then Auntie came out from the kitchen, and after shooing Pumpkin away, picked up the bucket and a scrap of cloth, and led me down to the courtyard. It had a beautiful mossy look, with steppingstones leading to a storehouse in the back; but it smelled horrible because of the toilets in the little shed along one side. Auntie told me to undress. I was afraid she might do to me something like what Mrs. Fidget had done, but instead she only poured water over my shoulders and rubbed me down with the rag. Afterward she gave me a robe, which was nothing more than coarsely woven cotton in the simplest pattern of dark blue, but it was certainly more elegant than anything I'd ever worn before. An old woman who turned out to be the cook came down into the corridor with several elderly maids to peer at me. Auntie told them they would have plenty of time for staring another day and sent them back where they'd come from.

'Now listen, little girl,' Auntie said to me, when we were alone. 'I don't even want to know your name yet. The last girl who came, Mother and Granny didn't like her, and she was here only a month. I'm too old to keep learning new names, until they've decided they're going to keep you.'

'What will happen if they don't want to keep me?' I asked.

'It's better for you if they keep you.'

'May I ask, ma'am . . . what is this place?'

'It's an okiya,' she said. 'It's where geisha live. If you work very hard, you'll grow up to be a geisha yourself. But you won't make it as far as next week unless you listen to me very closely, because Mother and Granny are coming down the stairs in just a moment to look at you. And they'd better like what they see. Your job is to bow as low as you can, and don't look them in the eye. The older one, the one we call Granny, has never liked anyone in her life, so don't worry about what she says. If she asks you a question, don't even answer it, for heaven's sake! I'll answer for you. The one you want to impress is Mother. She's not a bad sort, but she cares about only one thing.'

I didn't have a chance to find out what that one thing was, for I heard a creaking noise from the direction of the front entrance hall, and soon the two women came drifting out onto the walkway. I didn't dare look at them. But what I could see out of the corner of my eye made me think of two lovely bundles of silk floating along a stream. In a moment they were hovering on the walkway in front of me, where they sank down and smoothed their kimono across their knees.

'Umeko-san!' Auntie shouted – for this was the name of the cook. 'Bring tea for Granny.'

'I don't want tea,' I heard an angry voice say.

'Now, Granny,' said a raspier voice, which I took to be Mother's. 'You don't have to drink it. Auntie only wants to be sure you're comfortable.'

'There's no being comfortable with these bones of mine,' the old woman grumbled. I heard her take in a breath to say something more, but Auntie interrupted.

'This is the new girl, Mother,' she said, and gave me a little shove, which I took as a signal to bow. I got onto my knees and bowed so low, I could smell the musty air wafting from beneath the foundation. Then I heard Mother's voice again.

'Get up and come closer. I want to have a look at you.'

I felt certain she was going to say something more to me after I'd approached her, but instead she took from her obi, where she kept it tucked, a pipe with a metal bowl and a long stem made of bamboo. She set it down beside her on the walkway and then brought from the pocket of her sleeve a drawstring bag of silk, from which she removed a big pinch of tobacco. She packed the tobacco with her little finger, stained the burnt orange color of a roasted yam, and then put the pipe into her mouth and lit it with a match from a tiny metal box.

Now she took a close look at me for the first time, puffing on her pipe while the old woman beside her sighed. I didn't feel I could look at Mother directly, but I had the impression of smoke seeping out of her face like steam from a crack in the earth. I was so curious about her that my eyes took on a life of their own and began to dart about. The more I saw of her, the more fascinated I became. Her kimono was yellow, with willowy branches bearing lovely green and orange leaves; it was made of silk gauze as delicate as a spider's web. Her obi was every bit as astonishing to me. It was a lovely gauzy texture too, but heavier-looking, in russet and brown with gold threads woven through. The more I looked at her clothing, the less I was aware of standing there on that dirt corridor, or of wondering what had become of my sister – and my mother and father – and what would become of me. Every detail of this woman's kimono was enough to make me forget myself. And then I came upon a rude shock: for there above the collar of her elegant kimono was a face so mismatched to the clothing that it was as though I'd been patting a cat's body only to discover that it had a bulldog's head. She was a hideous-looking woman, though much younger than Auntie, which I hadn't expected. It turned out that Mother was actually Auntie's younger sister – though they called each other 'Mother' and 'Auntie,' just as everyone else in the okiya did. Actually they weren't really sisters in the way Satsu and I were. They hadn't been born into the same family; but Granny had adopted them both.

I was so dazed as I stood there, with so many thoughts running through my mind, that I ended up doing the very thing Auntie had told me not to do. I looked straight into Mother's eyes. When I did she took the pipe from her mouth, which caused her jaw to fall open like a trapdoor. And even though I knew I should at all costs look down again, her peculiar eyes were so shocking to me in their ugliness that I could do nothing but stand there staring at them. Instead of being white and clear, the whites of her eyes had a hideous yellow cast, and made me think at once of a toilet into which someone had just urinated. They were rimmed with the raw lip of her lids, in which a cloudy moisture was pooled; and all around them the skin was sagging.

I drew my eyes downward as far as her mouth, which still hung open. The colors of her face were all mixed up: the rims of her eyelids were red like meat, and her gums and tongue were gray. And to make things more horrible, each of her lower teeth seemed to be anchored in a little pool of blood at the gums. This was due to some sort of deficiency in Mother's diet over the past years, as I later learned; but I couldn't help feeling, the more I looked at her, that she was like a tree that has begun to lose its leaves. I was so shocked by the whole effect that I think I must have taken a step back, or let out a gasp, or in some way given her some hint of my feelings, for all at once she said to me, in that raspy voice of hers:

'What are you looking at!'

'I'm very sorry, ma'am. I was looking at your kimono,' I told her. 'I don't think I've ever seen anything like it.'

This must have been the right answer – if there was a right answer – because she let out something of a laugh, though it sounded like a cough.

'So you like it, do you?' she said, continuing to cough, or laugh, I couldn't tell which. 'Do you have any idea what it cost?'

'No, ma'am.'

'More than you did, that's for certain.'

Here the maid appeared with tea. While it was served I took

the opportunity to steal a glance at Granny. Whereas Mother was a bit on the plump side, with stubby fingers and a fat neck, Granny was old and shriveled. She was at least as old as my father, but she looked as if she'd spent her years stewing herself into a state of concentrated meanness. Her gray hair made me think of a tangle of silk threads, for I could see right through them to her scalp. And even her scalp looked mean, because of patches where the skin was colored red or brown from old age. She wasn't frowning exactly, but her mouth made the shape of a frown in its natural state anyway.

She took in a great big breath in preparation to speak; and then as she let it out again she mumbled, 'Didn't I say I don't want any tea?' After this, she sighed and shook her head, and then said to me, 'How old are you, little girl?'

'She's the year of the monkey,' Auntie answered for me.

'That fool cook is a monkey,' Granny said.

'Nine years old,' said Mother. 'What do you think of her, Auntie?'

Auntie stepped around in front of me and tipped my head back to look at my face. 'She has a good deal of water.'

'Lovely eyes,' said Mother. 'Did you see them, Granny?'

'She looks like a fool to me,' Granny said. 'We don't need another monkey anyway.'

'Oh, I'm sure you're right,' Auntie said. 'Probably she's just as you say. But she looks to me like a very clever girl, and adaptable; you can see that from the shape of her ears.'

'With so much water in her personality,' Mother said, 'probably she'll be able to smell a fire before it has even begun. Won't that be nice, Granny? You won't have to worry any longer about our storehouse burning with all our kimono in it.'

Granny, as I went on to learn, was more terrified of fire than beer is of a thirsty old man.

'Anyway, she's rather pretty, don't you think?' Mother added.

'There are too many pretty girls in Gion,' said Granny. 'What we need is a smart girl, not a pretty girl. That Hatsumomo is as pretty as they come, and look at what a fool she is!'

After this Granny stood, with Auntie's help, and made her way back up the walkway. Though I must say that to watch Auntie's clumsy gait – because of her one hip jutting out farther than the other – it wasn't at all obvious which of the two women had the easier time walking. Soon I heard the sound of a door in the front entrance hall sliding open and then shut again, and Auntie came back.

'Do you have lice, little girl?' Mother asked me.

'No,' I said.

'You're going to have to learn to speak more politely than that. Auntie, be kind enough to trim her hair, just to be sure.'

Auntie called a servant over and asked for shears.

'Well, little girl,' Mother told me, 'you're in Kyoto now. You'll learn to behave or get a beating. And it's Granny gives the beatings around here, so you'll be sorry. My advice to you is: work very hard, and never leave the okiya without permission. Do as you're told; don't be too much trouble; and you might begin learning the arts of a geisha two or three months from now. I didn't bring you here to be a maid. I'll throw you out, if it comes to that.'

Mother puffed on her pipe and kept her eyes fixed on me. I didn't dare move until she told me to. I found myself wondering if my sister was standing before some other cruel woman, in another house somewhere in this horrible city. And I had a sudden image in my mind of my poor, sick mother propping herself on one elbow upon her futon and looking around to see where we had gone. I didn't want Mother to see me crying, but the tears pooled in my eyes before I could think of how to stop them. With my vision glazed, Mother's yellow kimono turned softer and softer, until it seemed to sparkle. Then she blew out a puff of her smoke, and it disappeared completely.

4

DURING THOSE FIRST few days in that strange place, I don't think I could have felt worse if I'd lost my arms and legs, rather than my family and my home. I had no doubt life would never again be the same. All I could think of was my confusion and misery; and I wondered day after day when I might see Satsu again. I was without my father, without my mother – without even the clothing I'd always worn. Yet somehow the thing that startled me most, after a week or two had passed, was that I had in fact survived. I remember one moment drying rice bowls in the kitchen, when all at once I felt so disoriented I had to stop what I was doing to stare for a long while at my hands; for I could scarcely understand that this person drying the bowls was actually me.

Mother had told me I could begin my training within a few months if I worked hard and behaved myself. As I learned from Pumpkin, beginning my training meant going to a school in another section of Gion to take lessons in things like music, dance, and tea ceremony. All the girls studying to be geisha took classes at this same school. I felt sure I'd find Satsu there when I was finally permitted to go; so by the end of my first week, I'd made up my mind to be as obedient as a cow following along on a rope, in the hopes that Mother would send me to the school right away.

Most of my chores were straightforward. I stowed away the futons in the morning, cleaned the rooms, swept the dirt corridor, and so forth. Sometimes I was sent to the pharmacist to fetch ointment for the cook's scabies, or to a shop on Shijo Avenue to fetch the rice crackers Auntie was so fond of. Happily the worst jobs, such as cleaning the toilets, were the responsibility of one of the elderly maids. But even though I worked as hard as I knew how, I never seemed to make the good impression I hoped to, because my chores every day were more than I could possibly finish; and the problem was made a good deal worse by Granny.

Looking after Granny wasn't really one of my duties – not as Auntie described them to me. But when Granny summoned me I couldn't very well ignore her, for she had more seniority in the okiya than anyone else. One day, for example, I was about to carry tea upstairs to Mother when I heard Granny call out:

'Where's that girl! Send her in here!'

I had to put down Mother's tray and hurry into the room where Granny was eating her lunch.

'Can't you see this room is too hot?' she said to me, after I'd bowed to her on my knees. 'You ought to have come in here and opened the window.'

'I'm sorry, Granny. I didn't know you were hot.'

'Don't I look hot?'

She was eating some rice, and several grains of it were stuck to her lower lip. I thought she looked more mean than hot, but I went directly to the window and opened it. As soon as I did, a fly came in and began buzzing around Granny's food.

'What's the matter with you?' she said, waving at the fly with her chopsticks. 'The other maids don't let in flies when they open the window!'

I apologized and told her I would fetch a swatter.

'And knock the fly into my food? Oh, no, you won't! You'll stand right here while I eat and keep it away from me.'

So I had to stand there while Granny ate her food, and listen to her tell me about the great Kabuki actor Ichimura Uzaemon XIV, who had taken her hand during a moon-viewing party when she was only fourteen. By the time I was finally free to leave, Mother's tea had grown so cold I couldn't even deliver it. Both the cook and Mother were angry with me.

The truth was, Granny didn't like to be alone. Even when she needed to use the toilet, she made Auntie stand just outside the door and hold her hands to help her balance in a squatting position. The odor was so overpowering, poor Auntie nearly broke her neck trying to get her head as far away from it as possible. I didn't have any jobs as bad as this one, but Granny did often call me to massage her while she cleaned her ears with a tiny silver scoop; and the task of massaging her was a good deal worse than you might think. I almost felt sick the first time she unfastened her robe and pulled it down from her shoulders, because the skin there and on her neck was bumpy and yellow like an uncooked chicken's. The problem, as I later learned, was that in her geisha days she'd used a kind of white makeup we call 'China Clay,' made with a base of lead. China Clay turned out to be poisonous, to begin with, which probably accounted in part for Granny's foul disposition. But also as a younger woman Granny had often gone to the hot springs north of Kyoto. This would have been fine except that the lead-based makeup was very hard to remove; traces of it combined with some sort of chemical in the water to make a dye that ruined her skin. Granny wasn't the only one afflicted by this problem. Even during the early years of World War II, you could still see old women on the streets in Gion with sagging yellow necks.

One day after I'd been in the okiya about three weeks, I went upstairs much later than usual to straighten Hatsumomo's room. I was terrified of Hatsumomo, even though I hardly saw her because of the busy life she led. I worried about what might happen if she found me alone, so I always tried to clean her room the moment she left the okiya for her dance lessons. Unfortunately, that morning Granny had kept me busy until almost noon.

Hatsumomo's room was the largest in the okiya, larger in floor space than my entire house in Yoroido. I couldn't think why it should be so much bigger than everyone else's until one of the elderly maids told me that even though Hatsumomo was the only geisha in the okiya now, in the past there'd been as many as three or four, and they'd all slept together in that one room. Hatsumomo may have lived alone, but she certainly made enough mess for four people. When I went up to her room that day, in addition to the usual magazines strewn about, and brushes left on the mats near her tiny makeup stand, I found an apple core and an empty whiskey bottle under the table. The window was open, and the wind must have knocked down the wood frame on which she'd hung her kimono from the night before – or perhaps she'd tipped it over before going to bed drunk and hadn't yet bothered to pick it up. Usually Auntie would have fetched the kimono by now, because it was her responsibility to care for the clothing in the okiya, but for some reason she hadn't. Just as I was standing the frame erect again, the door slid open all at once, and I turned to see Hatsumomo standing there.

'Oh, it's you,' she said. 'I thought I heard a little mousie or something. I see you've been straightening my room! Are you the one who keeps rearranging all my makeup jars? Why do you insist on doing that?'

'I'm very sorry, ma'am,' I said. 'I only move them to dust underneath.'

'But if you touch them,' she said, 'they'll start to smell like you. And then the men will say to me, "Hatsumomo-san, why do you stink like an ignorant girl from a fishing village?" I'm sure you understand that, don't you? But let's have you repeat it back to me just to be sure. Why don't I want you to touch my makeup?'

I could hardly bring myself to say it. But at last I answered her. 'Because it will start to smell like me.'

'That's very good! And what will the men say?'

'They'll say, "Oh, Hatsumomo-san, you smell just like a girl from a fishing village."'

'Hmm . . . there's something about the way you said it that I don't like. But I suppose it will do. I can't see why you girls from fishing villages smell so bad. That ugly sister of yours was here looking for you the other day, and her stench was nearly as bad as yours.'

I'd kept my eyes to the floor until then; but when I heard these words, I looked Hatsumomo right in the face to see whether or not she was telling me the truth.

'You look so surprised!' she said to me. 'Didn't I mention that she came here? She wanted me to give you a message about where she's living. Probably she wants you to go find her, so the two of you can run away together.'

'Hatsumomo-san –'

'You want me to tell you where she is? Well, you're going to have to earn the information. When I think how, I'll tell you. Now get out.'

I didn't dare disobey her, but just before leaving the room I stopped, thinking perhaps I could persuade her.

'Hatsumomo-san, I know you don't like me,' I said. 'If you would be kind enough to tell me what I want to know, I'll promise never to bother you again.'

Hatsumomo looked very pleased when she heard this and came walking toward me with a luminous happiness on her face. Honestly, I've never seen a more astonishing-looking woman. Men in the street sometimes stopped and took their cigarettes from their mouths to stare at her. I thought she was going to come whisper in my ear; but after she'd stood over me smiling for a moment, she drew back her hand and slapped me.

'I told you to get out of my room, didn't I?' she said.

I was too stunned to know how to react. But I must have stumbled out of the room, because the next thing I knew, I was slumped on the wood floor of the hallway, holding my hand to my face. In a moment Mother's door slid open.

'Hatsumomo!' Mother said, and came to help me to my feet. 'What have you done to Chiyo?'

'She was talking about running away, Mother. I decided it would be best if I slapped her for you. I thought you were probably too busy to do it yourself.'

Mother summoned a maid and asked for several slices of fresh ginger, then took me into her room and seated me at the table while she finished a telephone call. The okiya's only telephone for calling outside Gion was mounted on the wall of her room, and no one else was permitted to use it. She'd left the earpiece lying on its side on the shelf, and when she took it up again, she seemed to squeeze it so hard with her stubby fingers that I thought fluid might drip onto the mats.

'Sorry,' she said into the mouthpiece in her raspy voice. 'Hatsumomo is slapping the maids around again.'

During my first few weeks in the okiya I felt an

unreasonable affection for Mother – something like what a fish might feel for the fisherman who pulls the hook from its lip. Probably this was because I saw her no more than a few minutes each day while cleaning her room. She was always to be found there, sitting at the table, usually with an account book from the bookcase open before her and the fingers of one hand flicking the ivory beads of her abacus. She may have been organized about keeping her account books, but in every other respect she was messier even than Hatsumomo. Whenever she put her pipe down onto the table with a click, flecks of ash and tobacco flew out of it, and she left them wherever they lay. She didn't like anyone to touch her futon, even to change the sheets, so the whole room smelled like dirty linen. And the paper screens over the windows were stained terribly on account of her smoking, which gave the room a gloomy cast.

While Mother went on talking on the telephone, one of the elderly maids came in with several strips of freshly cut ginger for me to hold against my face where Hatsumomo had slapped me. The commotion of the door opening and closing woke Mother's little dog, Taku, who was an ill-tempered creature with a smashed face. He seemed to have only three pastimes in life – to bark, to snore, and to bite people who tried to pet him. After the maid had left again, Taku came and laid himself behind me. This was one of his little tricks; he liked to put himself where I would step on him by accident, and then bite me as soon as I did it. I was beginning to feel like a mouse caught in a sliding door, positioned there between Mother and Taku, when at last Mother hung up the telephone and came to sit at the table. She stared at me with her yellow eyes and finally said:

'Now you listen to me, little girl. Perhaps you've heard Hatsumomo lying. Just because she can get away with it doesn't mean you can. I want to know . . . why did she slap you?'

'She wanted me to leave her room, Mother,' I said. 'I'm terribly sorry.'

Mother made me say it all again in a proper Kyoto accent, which I found difficult to do. When I'd finally said it well enough to satisfy her, she went on:

'I don't think you understand your job here in the okiya. We all of us think of only one thing – how we can help Hatsumomo be successful as a geisha. Even Granny. She may seem like a difficult old woman to you, but really she spends her whole day thinking of ways to be helpful to Hatsumomo.'

I didn't have the least idea what Mother was talking about. To tell the truth, I don't think she could have fooled a dirty rag into believing Granny was in any way helpful to anyone.

'If someone as senior as Granny works hard all day to make Hatsumomo's job easier, think how much harder you have to work.'

'Yes, Mother, I'll continue working very hard.'

'I don't want to hear that you've upset Hatsumomo again. The other little girl manages to stay out of her way; you can do it too.'

'Yes, Mother . . . but before I go, may I ask? I've been wondering if anyone might know where my sister is. You see, I'd hoped to send a note to her.'

Mother had a peculiar mouth, which was much too big for her face and hung open much of the time; but now she did something with it I'd never seen her do before, which was to pinch her teeth together as though she wanted me to have a good look at them. This was her way of smiling – though I didn't realize it until she began to make that coughing noise that was her laugh.

'Why on earth should I tell you such a thing?' she said.

After this, she gave her coughing laugh a few more times, before waving her hand at me to say that I should leave the room.

When I went out, Auntie was waiting in the upstairs hall with a chore for me. She gave me a bucket and sent me up a ladder through a trapdoor onto the roof. There on wooden struts stood a tank for collecting rainwater. The rainwater ran down by gravity to flush the little second-floor toilet near Mother's room, for we had no plumbing in those days, even in the kitchen. Lately the weather had been dry, and the toilet had begun to stink. My task was to dump water into the tank so that Auntie could flush the toilet a few times to clear it out.

Those tiles in the noonday sun felt like hot skillets to me; while I emptied the bucket, I couldn't help but think of the cold water of the pond where we used to swim back in our village on the seashore. I'd been in that pond only a few weeks earlier; but it all seemed so far away from me now, there on the roof of the okiya. Auntie called up to me to pick the weeds from between the tiles before I came back down. I looked out at the hazy heat lying on the city and the hills surrounding us like prison walls. Somewhere under one of those rooftops, my sister was probably doing her chores just as I was. I thought of her when I bumped the tank by accident, and water splashed out and flowed toward the street.

About a month after I'd arrived in the okiya, Mother told me the time had come to begin my schooling. I was to accompany Pumpkin the following morning to be introduced to the teachers. Afterward, Hatsumomo would take me to someplace called the 'registry office,' which I'd never heard of, and then late in the afternoon I would observe her putting on her makeup and dressing in kimono. It was a tradition in the okiya for a young girl, on the day she begins her training, to observe the most senior geisha in this way.

When Pumpkin heard she would be taking me to the school the following morning, she grew very nervous.

'You'll have to be ready to leave the moment you wake up,' she told me. 'If we're late, we may as well drown ourselves in the sewer. . . .'

I'd seen Pumpkin scramble out of the okiya every morning so early her eyes were still crusty; and she often seemed on the point of tears when she left. In fact, when she clopped past the kitchen window in her wooden shoes, I sometimes thought I could hear her crying. She hadn't taken to her lessons well – not well at all, as a matter of fact. She'd arrived in the okiya nearly six months before me, but she'd only begun attending the school a week or so after my arrival. Most days when she came back around noon, she hid straightaway in the maids' quarters so no one would see her upset.

The following morning I awoke even earlier than usual and dressed for the first time in the blue and white robe students wore. It was nothing more than unlined cotton decorated with a childlike design of squares; I'm sure I looked no more elegant than a guest at an inn looks wearing a robe on the way to the bath. But I'd never before worn anything nearly so glamorous on my body.

Pumpkin was waiting for me in the entryway with a worried look. I was just about to slip my feet into my shoes when Granny called me to her room.

'No!' Pumpkin said under her breath; and really, her face sagged like wax that had melted. 'I'll be late again. Let's just go and pretend we didn't hear her!'

I'd like to have done what Pumpkin suggested; but already Granny was in her doorway, glowering at me across the formal entrance hall. As it turned out, she didn't keep me more than ten or fifteen minutes; but by then tears were welling in Pumpkin's eyes. When we finally set out, Pumpkin began at once to walk so fast I could hardly keep up with her.

'That old woman is so cruel!' she said. 'Make sure you put your hands in a dish of salt after she makes you rub her neck.'

'Why should I do that?'

'My mother used to say to me, "Evil spreads in the world through touch." And I know it's true too, because my mother brushed up against a demon that passed her on the road one morning, and that's why she died. If you don't purify your hands, you'll turn into a shriveled-up old pickle, just like Granny.'

Considering that Pumpkin and I were the same age and in the same peculiar position in life, I'm sure we would have talked together often, if we could have. But our chores kept us so busy we hardly had time even for meals – which Pumpkin ate before me because she was senior in the okiya. I knew that Pumpkin had come only six months before me, as I've mentioned. But I knew very little else about her. So I asked:

'Pumpkin, are you from Kyoto? Your accent sounds like you are.'

'I was born in Sapporo. But then my mother died when I was five, and my father sent me here to live with an uncle. Last year my uncle lost his business, and here I am.'

'Why don't you run away to Sapporo again?'

'My father had a curse put on him and died last year. I can't run away. I don't have anywhere to go.'

'When I find my sister,' I said, 'you can come with us. We'll run away together.'

Considering what a difficult time Pumpkin was having with her lessons, I expected she would be happy at my offer. But she didn't say anything at all. We had reached Shijo Avenue by now and crossed it in silence. This was the same avenue that had been so crowded the day Mr. Bekku had brought Satsu and me from the station. Now, so early in the morning, I could see only a single streetcar in the distance and a few bicyclists here and there. When we reached the other side, we continued up a narrow street, and then Pumpkin stopped for the first time since we'd left the okiya.

'My uncle was a very nice man,' she said. 'Here's the last thing I heard him say before he sent me away. "Some girls are smart and some girls are stupid," he told me. "You're a nice girl, but you're one of the stupid ones. You won't make it on your own in the world. I'm sending you to a place where people will tell you what to do. Do what they say, and you'll always be taken care of." So if you want to go out on your own, Chiyo-chan, you go. But me, I've found a place to spend my life. I'll work as hard as I have to so they don't send me away. But I'd sooner throw myself off a cliff than spoil my chances to be a geisha like Hatsumomo.'

Here Pumpkin interrupted herself. She was looking at something behind me, on the ground. 'Oh, my goodness, Chiyo-chan,' she said, 'doesn't it make you hungry?'

I turned to find myself looking into the entryway of another okiya. On a shelf inside the door sat a miniature Shinto shrine with an offering of a sweet-rice cake. I wondered if this could be what Pumpkin had seen; but her eyes were pointed toward the ground. A few ferns and some moss lined the stone path leading to the interior door, but I could see nothing else there. And then my eye fell upon it. Outside the entryway, just at the edge of the street, lay a wooden skewer with a single bite of charcoal-roasted squid remaining. The vendors sold them from carts at night. The smell of the sweet basting sauce was a torment to me, for maids like us were fed nothing more than rice and pickles at most meals, with soup once a day, and small portions of dried fish twice a month. Even so, there was nothing about this piece of squid on the ground that I found appetizing. Two flies were walking around in circles on it just as casually as if they'd been out for a stroll in the park.

Pumpkin was a girl who looked as if she could grow fat quickly, given the chance. I'd sometimes heard her stomach making noises from hunger that sounded like an enormous door rolling open. Still, I didn't think she was really planning to eat the squid, until I saw her look up and down the street to be sure no one was coming.

'Pumpkin,' I said, 'if you're hungry, for heaven's sake, take the sweet-rice cake from that shelf. The flies have already claimed the squid.'

'I'm bigger than they are,' she said. 'Besides, it would be sacrilege to eat the sweet-rice cake. It's an offering.'

And after she said this, she bent down to pick up the skewer.

It's true that I grew up in a place where children experimented with eating anything that moved. And I'll admit I did eat a cricket once when I was four or five, but only because someone tricked me. But to see Pumpkin standing there holding that piece of squid on a stick, with grit from the street stuck to it, and the flies walking around . . . She blew on it to try to get rid of them, but they just scampered to keep their balance.

'Pumpkin, you can't eat that,' I said. 'You might as well drag your tongue along on the paving stones!'

'What's so bad about the paving stones?' she said. And with this – I wouldn't have believed it if I hadn't seen it myself – Pumpkin got down on her knees and stuck out her tongue, and gave it a long, careful scrape along the ground. My mouth fell open from shock. When Pumpkin got to her feet again, she looked as though she herself couldn't quite believe what she'd done. But she wiped her tongue with the palm of her hand, spat a few times, and then put that piece of squid between her teeth and slid it off the skewer.

It must have been a tough piece of squid; Pumpkin chewed it the whole way up the gentle hill to the wooden gate of the school complex. I felt a knot in my stomach when I entered, because the garden seemed so grand to me. Evergreen shrubs and twisted pine trees surrounded a decorative pond full of carp. Across the narrowest part of the pond lay a stone slab. Two old women in kimono stood on it, holding lacquered umbrellas to block the early-morning sun. As for the buildings, I didn't understand what I was seeing at the moment, but I now know that only a tiny part of the compound was devoted to the school. The massive building in the back was actually the Kaburenjo Theater – where the geisha of Gion perform *Dances of the Old Capital* every spring.

Pumpkin hurried to the entrance of a long wood building that I thought was servants' quarters, but which turned out to be the school. The moment I stepped into the entryway, I noticed the distinctive smell of roasted tea leaves, which even now can make my stomach tighten as though I'm on my way to lessons once again. I took off my shoes to put them into the cubby nearest at hand, but Pumpkin stopped me; there was an unspoken rule about which cubby to use. Pumpkin was among the most junior of all the girls, and had to climb the other cubbies like a ladder to put her shoes at the top. Since this was my very first morning I had even less seniority; I had to use the cubby above hers.

'Be very careful not to step on the other shoes when you climb,' Pumpkin said to me, even though there were only a few pairs. 'If you step on them and one of the girls sees you do it, you'll get a scolding so bad your ears will blister.'

The interior of the school building seemed to me as old and dusty as an abandoned house. Down at the end of the long hallway stood a group of six or eight girls. I felt a jolt when I set eyes on them, because I thought one might be Satsu; but when they turned to look at us I was disappointed. They all wore the same hairstyle – the *wareshinobu* of a young apprentice geisha – and looked to me as if they knew much more about Gion than either Pumpkin or I would ever know.

Halfway down the hall we went into a spacious classroom in the traditional Japanese style. Along one wall hung a large board with pegs holding many tiny wooden plaques; on each plaque was written a name in fat, black strokes. My reading and writing were still poor; I'd attended school in the mornings in Yoroido, and since coming to Kyoto had spent an hour every afternoon studying with Auntie, but I could read very few of the names. Pumpkin went to the board and took, from a shallow box on the mats, a plaque bearing her own name, which she hung on the first empty hook. The board on the wall, you see, was like a sign-up sheet.

After this, we went to several other classrooms to sign up in just the same way for Pumpkin's other lessons. She was to have four classes that morning – shamisen, dance, tea ceremony, and a form of singing we call *nagauta*. Pumpkin was so troubled about being the last student in all of her classes that she began to wring the sash of her robe as we left the school for breakfast in the okiya. But just as we slipped into our shoes, another young girl our age came rushing across the garden with her hair in disarray. Pumpkin seemed calmer after seeing her.

We ate a bowl of soup and returned to the school as quickly as we could, so that Pumpkin could kneel in the back of the classroom to assemble her shamisen. If you've never seen a shamisen, you might find it a peculiar-looking instrument. Some people call it a Japanese guitar, but actually it's a good deal smaller than a guitar, with a thin wooden neck that has three large tuning pegs at the end. The body is just a little wooden box with cat skin stretched over the top like a drum. The entire instrument can be taken apart and put into a box or a bag, which is how it is carried about. In any case, Pumpkin assembled her shamisen and began to tune it with her tongue poking out, but I'm sorry to say that her ear was very poor, and the notes went up and down like a boat on the waves, without ever settling down where they were supposed to be. Soon the classroom was full of girls with their shamisens, spaced out as neatly as chocolates in a box. I kept an eye on the door in the hopes that Satsu would walk through it, but she didn't.

A moment later the teacher entered. She was a tiny old woman with a shrill voice. Her name was Teacher Mizumi, and this is what we called her to her face. But her surname of Mizumi sounds very close to *nezumi* – 'mouse'; so behind her back we called her Teacher Nezumi – Teacher Mouse.

Teacher Mouse knelt on a cushion facing the class and made no effort at all to look friendly. When the students bowed to her in unison and told her good morning, she just glowered back at them without speaking a word. Finally she looked at the board on the wall and called out the name of the first student.

This first girl seemed to have a very high opinion of herself. After she'd glided to the front of the room, she bowed before the teacher and began to play. In a minute or two Teacher Mouse told the girl to stop and said all sorts of unpleasant things about her playing; then she snapped her fan shut and waved it at the girl to dismiss her. The girl thanked her, bowed again, and returned to her place, and Teacher Mouse called the name of the next student.

This went on for more than an hour, until at length Pumpkin's name was called. I could see that Pumpkin was nervous, and in fact, the moment she began to play, everything seemed to go wrong. First Teacher Mouse stopped her and took the shamisen to retune the strings herself. Then Pumpkin tried again, but all the students began looking at one another, for no one could tell what piece she was trying to play. Teacher Mouse slapped the table very loudly and told them all to face straight ahead; and then she used her folding fan to tap out the rhythm for Pumpkin to follow. This didn't help, so finally Teacher Mouse began to work instead on Pumpkin's manner of holding the plectrum. She nearly sprained every one of Pumpkin's fingers, it seemed to me, trying to make her hold it with the proper grip. At last she gave up even on this and let the plectrum fall to the mats in disgust. Pumpkin picked it up and came back to her place with tears in her eyes.

After this I learned why Pumpkin had been so worried about being the last student. Because now the girl with the disheveled hair, who'd been rushing to the school as we'd left for breakfast, came to the front of the room and bowed.

'Don't waste your time trying to be courteous to me!'

Teacher Mouse squeaked at her. 'If you hadn't slept so late this morning, you might have arrived here in time to learn something.'

The girl apologized and soon began to play, but the teacher paid no attention at all. She just said, 'You sleep too late in the mornings. How do you expect me to teach you, when you can't take the trouble to come to school like the other girls and sign up properly? Just go back to your place. I don't want to be bothered with you.'

The class was dismissed, and Pumpkin led me to the front of the room, where we bowed to Teacher Mouse.

'May I be permitted to introduce Chiyo to you, Teacher,' Pumpkin said, 'and ask your indulgence in instructing her, because she's a girl of very little talent.'

Pumpkin wasn't trying to insult me; this was just the way people spoke back then, when they wanted to be polite. My own mother would have said it the same way.

Teacher Mouse didn't speak for a long while, but just looked me over and then said, 'You're a clever girl. I can see it just from looking at you. Perhaps you can help your older sister with her lessons.'

Of course she was talking about Pumpkin.

'Put your name on the board as early every morning as you can,' she told me. 'Keep quiet in the classroom. I tolerate no talking at all! And your eyes must stay to the front. If you do these things, I'll teach you as best I can.'

And with this, she dismissed us.

In the hallways between classes, I kept my eyes open for Satsu, but I didn't find her. I began to worry that perhaps I would never see her again, and grew so upset that one of the teachers, just before beginning the class, silenced everyone and said to me:

'You, there! What's troubling you?'

'Oh, nothing, ma'am. Only I bit my lip by accident,' I said. And to make good on this – for the sake of the girls around me, who were staring – I gave a sharp bite on my lip and tasted blood.

It was a relief to me that Pumpkin's other classes weren't as painful to watch as the first one had been. In the dance class, for example, the students practiced the moves in unison, with the result that no one stood out. Pumpkin wasn't by any means the worst dancer, and even had a certain awkward grace in the way she moved. The singing class later in the morning was more difficult for her since she had a poor ear; but there again, the students practiced in unison, so Pumpkin was able to hide her mistakes by moving her mouth a great deal while singing only softly.

At the end of each of her classes, she introduced me to the teacher. One of them said to me, 'You live in the same okiya as Pumpkin, do you?'

'Yes, ma' am,' I said, 'the Nitta okiya,' for Nitta was the family name of Granny and Mother, as well as Auntie.

'That means you live with Hatsumomo-san.'

'Yes, ma'am. Hatsumomo is the only geisha in our okiya at present.'

'I'll do my best to teach you about singing,' she said, 'so long as you manage to stay alive!'

After this the teacher laughed as though she'd made a great joke, and sent us on our way.

5

THAT AFTERNOON HATSUMOMO took me to the Gion Registry Office. I was expecting something very grand, but it turned out to be nothing more than several dark tatami rooms on the second floor of the school building, filled with desks and accounting books and smelling terribly of cigarettes. A clerk looked up at us through the haze of smoke and nodded us into the back room. There at a table piled with papers sat the biggest man I'd ever seen in my life. I didn't know it at the time, but he'd once been a sumo wrestler; and really, if he'd gone outside and slammed his weight into the building itself, all those desks would probably have fallen off the tatami platform onto the floor. He hadn't been a good enough sumo wrestler to take a retirement name, as some of them do; but he still liked to be called by the name he'd used in his wrestling days, which was Awajiumi. Some of the geisha shortened this playfully to Awaji, as a nickname.

As soon as we walked in, Hatsumomo turned on her charm. It was the first time I'd ever seen her do it. She said to him, 'Awaji-san!' But the way she spoke, I wouldn't have been surprised if she had run out of breath in the middle, because it sounded like this:

'Awaaa-jii-saaaannnnnnnn!'

It was as if she were scolding him. He put down his pen when he heard her voice, and his two big cheeks shifted up toward his ears, which was his way of smiling.

'Mmm . . . Hatsumomo-san,' he said, 'if you get any prettier, I don't know what I'm going to do!'

It sounded like a loud whisper when he spoke, because

sumo wrestlers often ruin their voice boxes, smashing into one another's throats the way they do.

He may have been the size of a hippopotamus, but Awajiumi was a very elegant dresser. He wore a pin-striped kimono and kimono trousers. His job was to make certain that all the money passing through Gion flowed where it was supposed to; and a trickle from that river of cash flowed directly into his pocket. That isn't to say that he was stealing; it was just the way the system worked. Considering that Awajiumi had such an important job, it was to every geisha's advantage to keep him happy, which was why he had a reputation for spending as much time out of his elegant clothes as in them.

She and Awajiumi talked for a long time, and finally Hatsumomo told him she'd come to register me for lessons at the school. Awajiumi hadn't really looked at me yet, but here he turned his giant head. After a moment he got up to slide open one of the paper screens over the window for more light.

'Why, I thought my eyes had fooled me,' he said. 'You should have told me sooner what a pretty girl you brought with you. Her eyes . . . they're the color of a mirror!'

'A mirror?' Hatsumomo said. 'A mirror has no color, Awaji-san.'

'Of course it does. It's a sparkly gray. When *you* look at a mirror, all you see is yourself, but I know a pretty color when I find it.'

'Do you? Well, it isn't so pretty to me. I once saw a dead man fished out of the river, and his tongue was just the same color as her eyes.'

'Maybe you're just too pretty yourself to be able to see it elsewhere,' Awajiumi said, opening an account book and picking up his pen. 'Anyway, let's register the girl. Now . . . Chiyo, is it? Tell me your full name, Chiyo, and your place of birth.'

The moment I heard these words, I had an image in my mind of Satsu staring up at Awajiumi, full of confusion and fear. She must have been in this same room at some time or other; if I had to register, surely she'd had to register too.

'Sakamoto is my last name,' I said. 'I was born in the town

of Yoroido. You may have heard of it, sir, because of my older sister, Satsu?'

I thought Hatsumomo would be furious with me; but to my surprise she seemed almost pleased about the question I'd asked.

'If she's older than you, she'd have registered already,' Awajiumi said. 'But I haven't come across her. I don't think she's in Gion at all.'

Now Hatsumomo's smile made sense to me; she'd known in advance what Awajiumi would say. If I'd felt any doubts whether she really had spoken to my sister as she claimed, I felt them no longer. There were other geisha districts in Kyoto, though I didn't know much about them. Satsu was somewhere in one of them, and I was determined to find her.

When I returned to the okiya, Auntie was waiting to take me to the bathhouse down the street. I'd been there before, though only with the elderly maids, who usually handed me a small towel and a scrap of soap and then squatted on the tile floor to wash themselves while I did the same. Auntie was much kinder, and knelt over me to scrub my back. I was surprised that she had no modesty whatever, and slung her tube-shaped breasts around as if they were nothing more than bottles. She even whacked me on the shoulder with one several times by accident.

Afterward she took me back to the okiya and dressed me in the first silk kimono I'd ever worn, a brilliant blue with green grasses all around the hem and bright yellow flowers across the sleeves and chest. Then she led me up the stairs to Hatsumomo's room. Before going in, she gave me a stern warning not to distract Hatsumomo in any way, or do anything that might make her angry. I didn't understand it at the time, but now I know perfectly well why she was so concerned. Because, you see, when a geisha wakes up in the morning she is just like any other woman. Her face may be greasy from sleep, and her breath unpleasant. It may be true that she wears a startling hairstyle even as she struggles to open her eyes; but in every other respect she's a woman like any other, and not a geisha at all. Only when she sits before her mirror to apply her makeup with care does she become a geisha. And I don't mean that this is when she begins to look like one. This is when she begins to think like one too.

In the room, I was instructed to sit about an arm's length to the side of Hatsumomo and just behind her, where I could see her face in the tiny dressing mirror on her makeup stand. She was kneeling on a cushion, wearing a cotton robe that clung to her shoulders, and gathering in her hands a half dozen makeup brushes in various shapes. Some of them were broad like fans, while others looked like a chopstick with a dot of soft hair at the end. Finally she turned and showed them to me.

'These are my brushes,' she said. 'And do you remember this?' She took from the drawer of her makeup stand a glass container of stark white makeup and waved it around in the air for me to see. 'This is the makeup I told you never to touch.'

'I haven't touched it,' I said.

She sniffed the closed jar several times and said, 'No, I don't think you have.' Then she put the makeup down and took up three pigment sticks, which she held out for me in the palm of her hand.

'These are for shading. You may look at them.'

I took one of the pigment sticks from her. It was about the size of a baby's finger, but hard and smooth as stone, so that it left no trace of color on my skin. One end was wrapped in delicate silver foil that was flecking away from the pressure of use.

Hatsumomo took the pigment sticks back and held out what looked to me like a twig of wood burned at one end.

'This is a nice dry piece of paulownia wood,' she said, 'for drawing my eyebrows. And this is wax.' She took two half-used bars of wax from their paper wrapping and held them out for me to see.

'Now why do you suppose I've shown you these things?'

'So I'll understand how you put on your makeup,' I said.

'Heavens, no! I've shown them to you so you'll see there isn't any magic involved. What a pity for you! Because it means that makeup alone won't be enough to change poor

Chiyo into something beautiful.'

Hatsumomo turned back to face the mirror and sang quietly to herself as she opened a jar of pale yellow cream. You may not believe me when I tell you that this cream was made from nightingale droppings, but it's true. Many geisha used it as a face cream in those days, because it was believed to be very good for the skin; but it was so expensive that Hatsumomo put only a few dots around her eyes and mouth. Then she tore a small piece of wax from one of the bars and, after softening it in her fingertips, rubbed it into the skin of her face, and afterward of her neck and chest. She took some time to wipe her hands clean on a rag, and then moistened one of her flat makeup brushes in a dish of water and rubbed it in the makeup until she had a chalky white paste. She used this to paint her face and neck, but left her eyes bare, as well as the area around her lips and nose. If you've ever seen a child cut holes in paper to make a mask, this was how Hatsumomo looked, until she dampened some smaller brushes and used them to fill in the cutouts. After this she looked as if she'd fallen face-first into a bin of rice flour, for her whole face was ghastly white. She looked like the demon she was, but even so, I was sick with jealousy and shame. Because I knew that in an hour or so, men would be gazing with astonishment at that face; and I would still be there in the okiya, looking sweaty and plain.

Now she moistened her pigment sticks and used them to rub a reddish blush onto her cheeks. Already during my first month in the okiya, I'd seen Hatsumomo in her finished makeup many times; I stole looks at her whenever I could without seeming rude. I'd noticed she used a variety of tints for her cheeks, depending on the colors of her kimono. There was nothing unusual in this; but what I didn't know until years later was that Hatsumomo always chose a shade much redder than others might have used. I can't say why she did it, unless it was to make people think of blood. But Hatsumomo was no fool; she knew how to bring out the beauty in her features.

When she'd finished applying blush, she still had no eyebrows or lips. But for the moment she left her face like a bizarre white mask and asked Auntie to paint the back of her neck. I must tell you something about necks in Japan, if you don't know it; namely, that Japanese men, as a rule, feel about a woman's neck and throat the same way that men in the West might feel about a woman's legs. This is why geisha wear the collars of their kimono so low in the back that the first few bumps of the spine are visible; I suppose it's like a woman in Paris wearing a short skirt. Auntie painted onto the back of Hatsumomo's neck a design called *sanbon-ashi* – 'three legs.' It makes a very dramatic picture, for you feel as if you're looking at the bare skin of the neck through little tapering points of a white fence. It was years before I understood the erotic effect it has on men; but in a way, it's like a woman peering out from between her fingers. In fact, a geisha leaves a tiny margin of skin bare all around the hairline, causing her makeup to look even more artificial, something like a mask worn in Noh drama. When a man sits beside her and sees her makeup like a mask, he becomes that much more aware of the bare skin beneath.

While Hatsumomo was rinsing out her brushes, she glanced several times at my reflection in the mirror. Finally she said to me:

'I know what you're thinking. You're thinking you'll never be so beautiful. Well, it's perfectly true.'

'I'll have you know,' said Auntie, 'that some people find Chiyo-chan quite a lovely girl.'

'Some people like the smell of rotting fish,' said Hatsumomo. And with that, she ordered us to leave the room so she could change into her underrobe.

Auntie and I stepped out onto the landing, where Mr. Bekku stood waiting near the full-length mirror, looking just as he had on the day he'd taken Satsu and me from our home. As I'd learned during my first week in the okiya, his real occupation wasn't dragging girls from their homes at all; he was a dresser, which is to say that he came to the okiya every day to help Hatsumomo put on her elaborate kimono.

The robe Hatsumomo would wear that evening was hanging on a stand near the mirror. Auntie stood smoothing it until Hatsumomo came out wearing an underrobe in a lovely rust color, with a pattern of deep yellow leaves. What happened next made very little sense to me at the time, because the complicated costume of kimono is confusing to people who aren't accustomed to it. But the way it's worn makes perfect sense if it's explained properly.

To begin with, you must understand that a housewife and a geisha wear kimono very differently. When a housewife dresses in kimono, she uses all sorts of padding to keep the robe from bunching unattractively at the waist, with the result that she ends up looking perfectly cylindrical, like a wood column in a temple hall. But a geisha wears kimono so frequently she hardly needs any padding, and bunching never seems to be a problem. Both a housewife and a geisha will begin by taking off their makeup robes and tucking a silk slip around the bare hips; we call this a *koshimaki* – 'hip wrap.' It's followed by a short-sleeved kimono undershirt, tied shut at the waist, and then the pads, which look like small contoured pillows with strings affixed for tying them into place. In Hatsumomo's case, with her traditional small-hipped, willowy figure, and her experience of wearing kimono for so many years, she didn't use padding at all.

So far, everything the woman has put on will be hidden from the eye when she is fully dressed. But the next item, the underrobe, isn't really an undergarment at all. When a geisha performs a dance, or sometimes even when she walks along the street, she might raise the hem of her kimono in her left hand to keep it out of the way. This has the effect of exposing the underrobe below the knees; so, you see, the pattern and fabric of the underrobe must be coordinated with the kimono. And, in fact, the underrobe's collar shows as well, just like the collar of a man's shirt when he wears a business suit. Part of Auntie's job in the okiya was to sew a silk collar each day onto the underrobe Hatsumomo planned to wear, and then remove it the next morning for cleaning. An apprentice geisha wears a red collar, but of course Hatsumomo wasn't an apprentice; her collar was white.

When Hatsumomo came out of her room, she was wearing all the items I've described – though we could see nothing but her underrobe, held shut with a cord around her waist. Also, she wore white socks we call *tabi*, which button along the side with a snug fit. At this point she was ready for Mr. Bekku to dress her. To see him at work, you'd have understood at once just why his help was necessary. Kimono are the same length no matter who wears them, so except for the very tallest women, the extra fabric must be folded beneath the sash. When Mr. Bekku doubled the kimono fabric at the waist and tied a cord to hold it in place, there was never the slightest buckle. Or if one did appear, he gave a tug here or there, and the whole thing straightened out. When he finished his work, the robe always fit the contours of the body beautifully.

Mr. Bekku's principal job as dresser was to tie the obi, which isn't as simple a job as it might sound. An obi like the one Hatsumomo wore is twice as long as a man is tall, and nearly as wide as a woman's shoulders. Wrapped around the waist, it covers the area from the breastbone all the way to below the navel. Most people who know nothing of kimono seem to think the obi is simply tied in the back as if it were a string; but nothing could be further from the truth. A half dozen cords and clasps are needed to keep it in place, and a certain amount of padding must be used as well to shape the knot. Mr. Bekku took several minutes to tie Hatsumomo's obi. When he was done, hardly a wrinkle could be seen anywhere in the fabric, thick and heavy as it was.

I understood very little of what I saw on the landing that day; but it seemed to me that Mr. Bekku tied strings and tucked fabric at a frantic rate, while Hatsumomo did nothing more than hold her arms out and gaze at her image in the mirror. I felt miserable with envy, watching her. Her kimono was a brocade in shades of brown and gold. Below the waist, deer in their rich brown coloring of autumn nuzzled one another, with golds and rusts behind them in a pattern like fallen leaves on a forest floor. Her obi was plum-colored, interwoven with silver threads. I didn't know it at the time, but the outfit she wore probably cost as much as a policeman or a shopkeeper might make in an entire year. And yet to look at Hatsumomo standing there, when she turned around to glance back at herself in the free-standing mirror, you would have thought that no amount of money on earth could have made a woman look as glamorous as she did.

All that remained were the final touches on her makeup and the ornaments in her hair. Auntie and I followed Hatsumomo back into her room, where she knelt at her dressing table and took out a tiny lacquer box containing rouge for her lips. She used a small brush to paint it on. The fashion at that time was to leave the upper lip unpainted, which made the lower lip look fuller. White makeup causes all sorts of curious illusions; if a geisha were to paint the entire surface of her lips, her mouth would end up looking like two big slices of tuna. So most geisha prefer a poutier shape, more like the bloom of a violet. Unless a geisha has lips of this shape to begin with – and very few do – she nearly always paints on a more circle-shaped mouth than she actually has. But as I've said, the fashion in those days was to paint only the lower lip, and this is what Hatsumomo did.

Now Hatsumomo took the twig of paulownia wood she'd shown me earlier and lit it with a match. After it had burned for a few seconds she blew it out, cooled it with her fingertips, and then went back to the mirror to draw in her eyebrows with the charcoal. It made a lovely shade of soft gray. Next she went to a closet and selected a few ornaments for her hair, including one of tortoiseshell, and an unusual cluster of pearls at the end of a long pin. When she'd slipped them into her hair, she applied a bit of perfume to the bare flesh on the back of her neck, and tucked the flat wooden vial into her obi afterward in case she should need it again. She also put a folding fan into her obi and placed a kerchief in her right sleeve. And with this she turned to look down at me. She wore the same faint smile she had worn earlier, and even Auntie had to sigh, from how extraordinary Hatsumomo looked.

6

WHATEVER ANY OF us may have thought about Hatsumomo, she was like an empress in our okiya since she earned the income by which we all lived. And being an empress she would have been very displeased, upon returning late at night, to find her palace dark and all the servants asleep. That is to say, when she came home too drunk to unbutton her socks, someone had to unbutton them for her; and if she felt hungry, she certainly wasn't going to stroll into the kitchen to prepare something by herself – such as an *umeboshi ochazuke*, which was a favorite snack of hers, made with leftover rice and pickled sour plums, soaked in hot tea. Actually, our okiya wasn't at all unusual in this respect. The job of waiting up to bow and welcome the geisha home almost always fell to the most junior of the 'cocoons' – as the young geisha-in-training were often called. And from the moment I began taking lessons at the school, the most junior cocoon in our okiya was me. Long before midnight, Pumpkin and the two elderly maids were sound asleep on their futons only a meter or so away on the wood floor of the entrance hall; but I had to go on kneeling there, struggling to stay awake until sometimes as late as two o'clock in the morning. Granny's room was nearby, and she slept with her light on and her door opened a crack. The bar of light that fell across my empty futon made me think of a day, not long before Satsu and I were taken away from our village, when I'd peered into the back room of our house to see my mother asleep there. My father had draped fishing nets across the paper screens to darken the room, but it looked so gloomy I decided to open one of the windows; and when I did, a strip of bright sunlight fell across my mother's futon and showed her hand so pale and bony. To see the yellow light streaming from Granny's room onto my futon . . . I had to wonder if my mother was still alive. We were so much alike, I felt sure I would have known if she'd died; but of course, I'd had no sign one way or the other.

One night as the fall was growing cooler, I had just dozed off leaning against a post when I heard the outside door roll open. Hatsumomo would be very angry if she found me sleeping, so I tried my best to look alert. But when the interior door opened, I was surprised to see a man, wearing a traditional, loose-fitting workman's jacket tied shut at the hip and a pair of peasant trousers – though he didn't look at all like a workman or a peasant. His hair was oiled back in a very modern manner, and he wore a closely trimmed beard that gave him the air of an intellectual. He leaned down and took my head in his hands to look me square in the face.

'Why, you're a pretty one,' he said to me in a low voice. 'What's your name?'

I felt certain he must be a workman, though I couldn't think why he'd come so late at night. I was frightened of answering him, but I managed to say my name, and then he moistened a fingertip with his tongue and touched me on the cheek – to take off an eyelash, as it turned out.

'Yoko is still here?' he asked. Yoko was a young woman who spent every day from midafternoon until late evening sitting in our maids' room. Back in those days the okiya and teahouses in Gion were all linked by a private telephone system, and Yoko was kept busier than almost anyone in our okiya, answering that telephone to book Hatsumomo's engagements, sometimes for banquets or parties six months to a year in advance. Usually Hatsumomo's schedule didn't fill up completely until the morning before, and calls continued through the evening from teahouses whose customers wanted her to drop in if she had time. But the telephone hadn't been ringing much tonight, and I thought probably Yoko had fallen asleep just as I had. The man didn't wait for me to answer, but gestured for me to keep quiet, and showed himself down the dirt corridor to the maids' room.

The next thing I heard was Yoko apologizing – for she had indeed fallen asleep – and then she carried on a long conversation with the switchboard operator. She had to be connected with several teahouses before she at least located Hatsumomo and left a message that the Kabuki actor Onoe Shikan had come to town. I didn't know it at the time, but there was no Onoe Shikan; this was just a code.

After this, Yoko left for the night. She didn't seem worried that a man was waiting in the maids' room, so I made up my mind to say nothing to anyone. This turned out to be a good thing, because when Hatsumomo appeared twenty minutes later, she stopped in the entrance hall to say to me:

'I haven't tried to make your life really miserable yet. But if you ever mention that a man came here, or even that I stopped in before the end of the evening, that will change.'

She was standing over me as she said this, and when she reached into her sleeve for something, I could see even in the dim light that her forearms were flushed. She went into the maids' room and rolled the door shut behind her. I heard a short muffled conversation, and then the okiya was silent. Occasionally I thought I heard a soft whimper or a groan, but the sounds were so quiet, I couldn't be sure. I won't say I knew just what they were doing in there, but I did think of my sister holding up her bathing dress for the Sugi boy. And I felt such a combination of disgust and curiosity that even if I'd been free to leave my spot, I don't think I could have.

Once a week or so, Hatsumomo and her boyfriend – who turned out to be a chef in a nearby noodle restaurant – came to the okiya and shut themselves in the maids' room. They met other times in other places as well. I know because Yoko was often asked to deliver messages, and I sometimes overheard. All the maids knew what Hatsumomo was doing; and it's a measure of how much power she had over us that no one spoke a word to Mother or Auntie or Granny. Hatsumomo would certainly have been in trouble for having a boyfriend, much less for bringing him back to the okiya. The time she spent with him earned no revenue, and even took her away from parties at teahouses where she would otherwise have been making money. And besides, any wealthy man who might have been interested in an expensive, long-term relationship would certainly think less of her and even change his mind if he knew she was carrying on with the chef of a noodle restaurant.

One night just as I was coming back from taking a drink of water at the well in the courtyard, I heard the outside door roll open and slam against the door frame with a bang.

'Really, Hatsumomo-san,' said a deep voice, 'you'll wake everyone . . .'

I'd never really understood why Hatsumomo took the risk of bringing her boyfriend back to the okiya – though probably it was the risk itself that excited her. But she'd never before been so careless as to make a lot of noise. I hurried into my position on my knees, and in a moment Hatsumomo was in the formal entrance hall, holding two packages wrapped in linen paper. Soon another geisha stepped in behind her, so tall that she had to stoop to pass through the low doorway. When she stood erect and looked down on me, her lips looked unnaturally big and heavy at the bottom of her long face. No one would have called her pretty.

'This is our foolish lower maid,' said Hatsumomo. 'She has a name, I think, but why don't you just call her "Little Miss Stupid." '

'Well, Little Miss Stupid,' said the other geisha. 'Go and get your big sister and me something to drink, why don't you?' The deep voice I'd heard was hers, and not the voice of Hatsumomo's boyfriend after all.

Usually Hatsumomo liked to drink a special kind of sake called *amakuchi* – which was very light and sweet. But *amakuchi* was brewed only in the winter, and we seemed to have run out. I poured two glasses of beer instead and brought them out. Hatsumomo and her friend had already made their way down to the courtyard, and were standing in wooden shoes in the dirt corridor. I could see they were very drunk, and Hatsumomo's friend had feet much too big for our little wooden shoes, so that she could hardly walk a step without the two of them breaking out in laughter. You may recall that a wooden walkway ran along the outside of the house. Hatsumomo had just set her packages down onto that walkway and was about to open one of them when I delivered the beer.

'I'm not in the mood for beer,' she said, and bent down to empty both glasses underneath the foundation of the house.

'I'm in the mood for it,' said her friend, but it was already too late. 'Why did you pour mine out?'

'Oh, be quiet, Korin!' Hatsumomo said. 'You don't need more to drink anyway. Just look at this, because you're going to die from happiness when you see it!' And here, Hatsumomo untied the strings holding shut the linen paper of one package, and spread out upon the walkway an exquisite kimono in different powdery shades of green, with a vine motif bearing red leaves. Really, it was a glorious silk gauze – though of summer weight, and certainly not appropriate for the fall weather. Hatsumomo's friend, Korin, admired it so much that she drew in a sharp breath and choked on her own saliva – which caused them both to burst out laughing again. I decided the time had come to excuse myself. But Hatsumomo said:

'Don't go away, Little Miss Stupid.' And then she turned to her friend again and told her, 'It's time for some fun, Korin-san. Guess whose kimono this is!'

Korin was still coughing a good deal, but when she was able to speak, she said, 'I wish it belonged to me!'

'Well, it doesn't. It belongs to none other than the geisha we both hate worse than anyone else on earth.'

'Oh, Hatsumomo . . . you're a genius. But how did you get Satoka's kimono?'

'I'm not talking about Satoka! I'm talking about . . . Miss Perfect!'

'Who?'

'Miss "I'm-So-Much-Better-Than-You-Are" . . . that's who!'

There was a long pause, and then Korin said, 'Mameha! Oh, my goodness, it *is* Mameha's kimono. I can't believe I didn't recognize it! How did you manage to get your hands on it?'

'A few days ago I left something at the Kaburenjo Theater during a rehearsal,' Hatsumomo said. 'And when I went back to look for it, I heard what I thought was moaning coming up from the basement stairs. So I thought, "It can't be! This is too much fun!" And when I crept down and turned on the light, guess who I found lying there like two pieces of rice stuck together on the floor?'

'I can't believe it! Mameha?'

'Don't be a fool. She's much too prissy to do such a thing. It was her maid, with the custodian of the theater. I knew she'd do anything to keep me from telling, so I went to her later and told her I wanted this kimono of Mameha's. She started crying when she figured out which one I was describing.'

'And what's this other one?' Korin asked, pointing to the second package that lay on the walkway, its strings still tied.

'This one I made the girl buy with her own money, and now it belongs to me.'

'Her own money?' said Korin. 'What maid has enough money to buy a kimono?'

'Well, if she didn't buy it as she said, I don't want to know where it came from. Anyway, Little Miss Stupid is going to put it away in the storehouse for me.'

'Hatsumomo-san, I'm not allowed in the storehouse,' I said at once.

'If you want to know where your older sister is, don't make me say anything twice tonight. I have plans for you. Afterward you may ask me a single question, and I'll answer it.'

I won't say that I believed her; but of course, Hatsumomo had the power to make my life miserable in any way she wanted. I had no choice but to obey.

She put the kimono – wrapped in its linen paper – into my arms and walked me down to the storehouse in the courtyard. There she opened the door and flipped a light switch with a loud snap. I could see shelves stacked with sheets and pillows, as well as several locked chests and a few folded futons. Hatsumomo grabbed me by the arm and pointed up a ladder along the outside wall.

'The kimono are up there,' she said.

I made my way up and opened a sliding wooden door at the top. The storage loft didn't have shelves like the ground-floor level. Instead the walls were lined with red lacquered cases stacked one on top of the next, nearly as high as the ceiling. A narrow corridor passed between these two walls of cases, with slatted windows at the ends, covered over with screens for ventilation. The space was lit harshly just as below, but much more brightly; so that when I had stepped inside, I could read the black characters carved into the fronts of the cases. They said things like *Kota-Komon*, *Ro* 'Stenciled Designs, Open-Weave Silk Gauze'; and *Kuromontsuki, Awase* – 'Black-Crested Formal Robes with Inner Lining.' To tell the truth, I couldn't understand all the characters at the time, but I did manage to find the case with Hatsumomo's name on it, on a top shelf. I had trouble taking it down, but finally I added the new kimono to the few others, also wrapped in linen paper, and replaced the case where I'd found it. Out of curiosity, I opened another of the cases very quickly and found it stacked to the top with perhaps fifteen kimono, and the others whose lids I lifted were all the same. To see that storehouse crowded with cases, I understood at once why Granny was so terrified of fire. The collection of kimono was probably twice as valuable as the entire villages of Yoroido and Senzuru put together. And as I learned much later, the most expensive ones were in storage somewhere else. They were worn only by apprentice geisha; and since Hatsumomo could no longer wear them, they were kept in a rented vault for safekeeping until they were needed again.

By the time I returned to the courtyard, Hatsumomo had been up to her room to fetch an inkstone and a stick of ink, as well as a brush for calligraphy. I thought perhaps she wanted to write a note and slip it inside the kimono when she refolded it. She had dribbled some water from the well onto her inkstone and was now sitting on the walkway grinding ink. When it was good and black, she dipped a brush in it and smoothed its tip against the stone – so that all the ink was absorbed in the brush and none of it would drip. Then she put it into my hand, and held my hand over the lovely kimono, and said to me:

'Practice your calligraphy, little Chiyo.'

This kimono belonging to the geisha named Mameha –

whom I'd never heard of at the time – was a work of art. Weaving its way from the hem up to the waist was a beautiful vine made of heavily lacquered threads bunched together like a tiny cable and sewn into place. It was a part of the fabric, yet it seemed so much like an actual vine growing there, I had the feeling I could take it in my fingers, if I wished, and tear it away like a weed from the soil. The leaves curling from it seemed to be fading and drying in the autumn weather, and even taking on tints of yellow.

'I can't do it, Hatsumomo-san!' I cried.

'What a shame, little sweetheart,' her friend said to me. 'Because if you make Hatsumomo tell you again, you'll lose the chance to find your sister.'

'Oh, shut up, Korin. Chiyo knows she has to do what I tell her. Write something on the fabric, Miss Stupid. I don't care what it is.'

When the brush first touched the kimono, Korin was so excited she let out a squeal that woke one of the elderly maids, who leaned out into the corridor with a cloth around her head and her sleeping robe sagging all around her. Hatsumomo stamped her foot and made a sort of lunging motion, like a cat, which was enough to make the maid go back to her futon. Korin wasn't happy with the few uncertain strokes I'd made on the powdery green silk, so Hatsumomo instructed me where to mark the fabric and what sorts of marks to make. There wasn't any meaning to them; Hatsumomo was just trying in her own way to be artistic. Afterward she refolded the kimono in its wrapping of linen and tied the strings shut again. She and Korin went back to the front entryway to put their lacquered zori back on their feet. When they rolled open the door to the street, Hatsumomo told me to follow.

'Hatsumomo-san, if I leave the okiya without permission, Mother will be very angry, and –'

'I'm giving you permission,' Hatsumomo interrupted. 'We have to return the kimono, don't we? I hope you're not planning to keep me waiting.'

So I could do nothing but step into my shoes and follow her up the alleyway to a street running beside the narrow Shirakawa Stream. Back in those days, the streets and alleys in Gion were still paved beautifully with stone. We walked along in the moonlight for a block or so, beside the weeping cherry trees that drooped down over the black water, and finally across a wooden bridge arching over into a section of Gion I'd never seen before. The embankment of the stream was stone, most of it covered with patches of moss. Along its top, the backs of the teahouses and okiya connected to form a wall. Reed screens over the windows sliced the yellow light into tiny strips that made me think of what the cook had done to a pickled radish earlier that day. I could hear the laughter of a group of men and geisha. Something very funny must have been happening in one of the teahouses, because each wave of laughter was louder than the one before, until they finally died away and left only the twanging of a shamisen from another party. For the moment, I could imagine that Gion was probably a cheerful place for some people. I couldn't help wondering if Satsu might be at one of those parties, even though Awajiumi, at the Gion Registry Office, had told me she wasn't in Gion at all.

Shortly, Hatsumomo and Korin came to a stop before a wooden door.

'You're going to take this kimono up the stairs and give it to the maid there,' Hatsumomo said to me. 'Or if Miss Perfect herself answers the door, you may give it to her. Don't say anything; just hand it over. We'll be down here watching you.'

With this, she put the wrapped kimono into my arms, and Korin rolled open the door. Polished wooden steps led up into the darkness. I was trembling with fear so much, I could go no farther than halfway up them before I came to a stop. Then I heard Korin say into the stairwell in a loud whisper:

'Go on, little girl! No one's going to eat you unless you come back down with the kimono still in your hands – and then we just might. Right, Hatsumomo-san?'

Hatsumomo let out a sigh at this, but said nothing. Korin was squinting up into the darkness, trying to see me; but Hatsumomo, who stood not much higher than Korin's shoulder, was chewing on one of her fingernails and paying no attention at all. Even then, amid all my fears, I couldn't help noticing how extraordinary Hatsumomo's beauty was. She may have been as cruel as a spider, but she was more lovely chewing on her fingernail than most geisha looked posing for a photograph. And the contrast with her friend Korin was like comparing a rock along the roadside with a jewel. Korin looked uncomfortable in her formal hairstyle with all its lovely ornaments, and her kimono seemed to be always in her way. Whereas Hatsumomo wore her kimono as if it were her skin.

On the landing at the top of the stairs, I knelt in the black darkness and called out:

'Excuse me, please!'

I waited, but nothing happened. 'Louder,' said Korin. 'They aren't expecting you.'

So I called again, 'Excuse me!'

'Just a moment!' I heard a muffled voice say; and soon the door rolled open. The girl kneeling on the other side was no older than Satsu, but thin and nervous as a bird. I handed her the kimono in its wrapping of linen paper. She was very surprised, and took it from me almost desperately.

'Who's there, Asami-san?' called a voice from inside the apartment. I could see a single paper lantern on an antique stand burning beside a freshly made futon. The futon was for the geisha Mameha; I could tell because of the crisp sheets and the elegant silk cover, as well as the *takamakura* – 'tall pillow' – just like the kind Hatsumomo used. It wasn't really a pillow at all, but a wooden stand with a padded cradle for the neck; this was the only way a geisha could sleep without ruining her elaborate hairstyle.

The maid didn't answer, but opened the wrapping around the kimono as quietly as she could, and tipped it this way and that to catch the reflection of the light. When she caught sight of the ink marring it, she gasped and covered her mouth. Tears spilled out almost instantly onto her cheeks, and then a voice called:

'Asami-san! Who's there?'

'Oh, no one, miss!' cried the maid. I felt terribly sorry for her as she dried her eyes quickly against one sleeve. While she was reaching up to slide the door closed, I caught a glimpse of her mistress. I could see at once why Hatsumomo called Mameha 'Miss Perfect.' Her face was a perfect oval, just like a doll's, and as smooth and delicate-looking as a piece of china, even without her makeup. She walked toward the doorway, trying to peer into the stairwell, but I saw no more of her before the maid quickly rolled the door shut.

The next morning after lessons, I came back to the okiya to find that Mother, Granny, and Auntie were closed up together in the formal reception room on the first floor. I felt certain they were talking about the kimono; and sure enough, the moment Hatsumomo came in from the street, one of the maids went to tell Mother, who stepped out into the entrance hall and stopped Hatsumomo on her way up the stairs.

'We had a little visit from Mameha and her maid this morning,' she said.

'Oh, Mother, I know just what you're going to say. I feel terrible about the kimono. I tried to stop Chiyo before she put ink on it, but it was too late. She must have thought it was mine! I don't know why she's hated me so from the moment she came here . . . To think she would ruin such a lovely kimono just in the hopes of hurting me!'

By now, Auntie had limped out into the hall. She cried, '*Matte mashita!*' I understood her words perfectly well; they meant 'We've waited for you!' But I had no idea what she meant by them. Actually, it was quite a clever thing to say because this is what the audience sometimes shouts when a great star makes his entrance in a Kabuki play.

'Auntie, are you suggesting that I had something to do with ruining that kimono?' Hatsumomo said. 'Why would I do such a thing?'

'Everyone knows how you hate Mameha,' Auntie told her. 'You hate anyone more successful than you.'

'Does that suggest I ought to be extremely fond of you, Auntie, since you're such a failure?'

'There'll be none of that,' said Mother. 'Now you listen to me, Hatsumomo. You don't really think anyone is empty-headed enough to believe your little story. I won't have this sort of behavior in the okiya, even from you. I have great respect for Mameha. I don't want to hear of anything like this happening again. As for the kimono, someone has to pay for it. I don't know what happened last night, but there's no dispute about who was holding the brush. The maid saw the girl doing it. The girl will pay,' said Mother, and put her pipe back into her mouth.

Now Granny came out from the reception room and called a maid to fetch the bamboo pole.

'Chiyo has enough debts,' said Auntie. 'I don't see why she should pay Hatsumomo's as well.'

'We've talked about this enough,' Granny said. 'The girl should be beaten and made to repay the cost of the kimono, and that's that. Where's the bamboo pole?'

'I'll beat her myself,' Auntie said. 'I won't have your joints flaring up again, Granny. Come along, Chiyo.'

Auntie waited until the maid brought the pole and then led me down to the courtyard. She was so angry her nostrils were bigger than usual, and her eyes were bunched up like fists. I'd been careful since coming to the okiya not to do anything that would lead to a beating. I felt hot suddenly and the stepping-stones at my feet grew blurry. But instead of beating me, Auntie leaned the pole against the storehouse and then limped over to say quietly to me:

'What have you done to Hatsumomo? She's bent on destroying you. There must be a reason, and I want to know what it is.'

'I promise you, Auntie, she's treated me this way since I arrived. I don't know what I ever did to her.'

'Granny may call Hatsumomo a fool, but believe me, Hatsumomo is no fool. If she wants to ruin your career badly enough, she'll do it. Whatever you've done to make her angry you must stop doing it.'

'I haven't done anything, Auntie, I promise you.'

'You must never trust her, not even if she tries to help you. Already she's burdened you with so much debt you may never work it off.'

'I don't understand . . .' I said, 'about *debt*?'

'Hatsumomo's little trick with that kimono is going to cost you more money than you've ever imagined in your life.

That's what I mean about debt.'

'But . . . how will I pay?'

'When you begin working as a geisha, you'll pay the okiya back for it, along with everything else you'll owe – your meals and lessons; if you get sick, your doctor's fees. You pay all of that yourself. Why do you think Mother spends all her time in her room, writing numbers in those little books? You owe the okiya even for the money it cost to acquire you.'

Throughout my months in Gion, I'd certainly imagined that money must have changed hands before Satsu and I were taken from our home. I often thought of the conversation I'd overheard between Mr. Tanaka and my father, and of what Mrs. Fidget had said about Satsu and me being 'suitable.' I'd wondered with horror whether Mr. Tanaka had made money by helping to sell us, and how much we had cost. But I'd never imagined that I myself would have to repay it.

'You won't pay it back until you've been a geisha a good long time,' she went on. 'And you'll never pay it back if you end up a failed geisha like me. Is that the way you want to spend your future?'

At the moment I didn't much care how I spent my future.

'If you want to ruin your life in Gion, there are a dozen ways to do it,' Auntie said. 'You can try to run away. Once you've done that, Mother will see you as a bad investment; she's not going to put more money into someone who might disappear at any time. That would mean the end of your lessons, and you can't be a geisha without training. Or you can make yourself unpopular with your teachers, so they won't give you the help you need. Or you can grow up to be an ugly woman like me. I wasn't such an unattractive girl when Granny bought me from my parents, but I didn't turn out well, and Granny's always hated me for it. One time she beat me so badly for something I did that she broke one of my hips. That's when I stopped being a geisha. And that's the reason I'm going to do the job of beating you myself, rather than letting Granny get her hands on you.'

She led me to the walkway and made me lie down on my stomach there. I didn't much care whether she beat me or not; it seemed to me that nothing could make my situation worse.

Every time my body jolted under the pole, I wailed as loudly as I dared, and pictured Hatsumomo's lovely face smiling down at me. When the beating was over, Auntie left me crying there. Soon I felt the walkway tremble under someone's footsteps and sat up to find Hatsumomo standing above me.

'Chiyo, I would be ever so grateful if you'd get out of my way.'

'You promised to tell me where I could find my sister, Hatsumomo,' I said to her.

'So I did!' She leaned down so that her face was near mine. I thought she was going to tell me I hadn't done enough yet, that when she thought of more for me to do, she would tell me. But this wasn't at all what happened.

'Your sister is in a *jorou-ya* called Tatsuyo,' she told me, 'in the district of Miyagawa-cho, just south of Gion.'

When she was done speaking, she gave me a little shove with her foot, and I stepped down out of her way.

7

I'D NEVER HEARD the word *jorou-ya* before; so the very next evening, when Auntie dropped a sewing tray onto the floor of the entrance hall and asked my help in cleaning it up, I said to her:

'Auntie, what is a *jorou-ya*?'

Auntie didn't answer, but just went on reeling up a spool of thread.

'Auntie?' I said again.

'It's the sort of place Hatsumomo will end up, if she ever gets what she deserves,' she said.

She didn't seem inclined to say more, so I had no choice but to leave it at that.

My question certainly wasn't answered; but I did form the impression that Satsu might be suffering even more than I was. So I began thinking about how I might sneak to this place called Tatsuyo the very next time I had an opportunity. Unfortunately, part of my punishment for ruining Mameha's kimono was confinement in the okiya for fifty days. I was permitted to attend the school as long as Pumpkin accompanied me; but I was no longer permitted to run errands. I suppose I could have dashed out the door at any time, if I'd wanted to, but I knew better than to do something so foolish. To begin with, I wasn't sure how to find the Tatsuyo. And what was worse, the moment I was discovered missing, Mr. Bekku or someone would be sent to look for me. A young maid had run away from the okiya next door only a few months earlier, and they brought her back the following morning. They beat her so badly over the next few days that her wailing was horrible. Sometimes I had to put my fingers in my ears to shut it out.

I decided I had no choice but to wait until my fifty-day confinement was over. In the meantime, I put my efforts into finding ways to repay Hatsumomo and Granny for their cruelty. Hatsumomo I repaid by scraping up pigeon droppings whenever I was supposed to clean them from the stepping-stones in the courtyard and mixing them in with her face cream. The cream already contained unguent of nightingale droppings, as I've mentioned; so maybe it did her no harm, but it did give me satisfaction. Granny I repaid by wiping the toilet rag around on the inside of her sleeping robe; and I was very pleased to see her sniffing at it in puzzlement, though she never took it off. Soon I discovered that the cook had taken it upon herself to punish me further over the kimono incident – even though no one had asked her to – by cutting back on my twice-monthly portions of dried fish. I couldn't think of how to repay her for this until one day I saw her chasing a mouse down the corridor with a mallet. She hated mice worse than cats did, as it turned out. So I swept mouse droppings from under the foundation of the main house and scattered them here and there in the kitchen. I even took a chopstick one day and gouged a hole in the bottom of a canvas bag of rice, so she'd have to take everything out of all the cabinets and search for signs of rodents.

One evening as I was waiting up for Hatsumomo, I heard the telephone ring, and Yoko came out a moment later and went up the stairs. When she came back down, she was holding Hatsumomo's shamisen, disassembled in its lacquer carrying case.

'You'll have to take this to the Mizuki Teahouse,' she said to me. 'Hatsumomo has lost a bet and has to play a song on a shamisen. I don't know what's gotten into her, but she won't use the one the teahouse has offered. I think she's just stalling, since she hasn't touched a shamisen in years.'

Yoko apparently didn't know I was confined to the okiya, which was no surprise, really. She was rarely permitted to leave the maids' room in case she should miss an important telephone call, and she wasn't involved in the life of the okiya in any way. I took the shamisen from her while she put on her kimono overcoat to leave for the night. And after she had explained to me where to find the Mizuki Teahouse, I slipped into my shoes in the entryway, tingling with nervousness that someone might stop me. The maids and Pumpkin – even the three older women – were all asleep, and Yoko would be gone in a matter of minutes. It seemed to me my chance to find my sister had come at last.

I heard thunder rumble overhead, and the air smelled of rain. So I hurried along the streets, past groups of men and geisha. Some of them gave me peculiar looks, because in those days we still had men and women in Gion who made their living as shamisen porters. They were often elderly; certainly none of them were children. It wouldn't surprise me if some of the people I passed thought I'd stolen that shamisen and was running away with it.

When I reached the Mizuki Teahouse, rain was beginning to fall; but the entrance was so elegant I was afraid to set foot in it. The walls beyond the little curtain that hung in the doorway were a soft orange hue, trimmed in dark wood. A path of polished stone led to a huge vase holding an arrangement of twisted branches from a maple tree with their brilliant red leaves of fall. At length I worked up my courage and brushed past the little curtain. Near the vase, a spacious entryway opened to one side, with a floor of coarsely polished granite. I remember being astounded that all the beauty I'd seen wasn't even the entryway to the teahouse, but only the path leading to the entryway. It was exquisitely lovely – as indeed it should have been; because although I didn't know it, I was seeing for the first time one of the most exclusive teahouses in all of Japan. And a teahouse isn't for tea, you see; it's the place where men go to be entertained by geisha.

The moment I stepped into the entryway, the door before me rolled open. A young maid kneeling on the raised floor inside gazed down at me; she must have heard my wooden shoes on the stone. She was dressed in a beautiful dark blue kimono with a simple pattern in gray. A year earlier I would have taken her to be the young mistress of such an extravagant place, but now after my months in Gion, I recognized at once that her kimono – though more beautiful than anything in Yoroido – was far too simple for a geisha or for the mistress of a teahouse. And of course, her hairstyle was plain as well. Still, she was far more elegant than I was, and looked down at me with contempt.

'Go to the back,' she said.

'Hatsumomo has asked that –'

'Go to the back!' she said again, and rolled the door shut without waiting for me to reply.

The rain was falling more heavily now, so I ran, rather than walked, down a narrow alley alongside the teahouse. The door at the back entrance rolled open as I arrived, and the same maid knelt there waiting for me. She didn't say a word but just took the shamisen case from my arms.

'Miss,' I said, 'may I ask? . . . Can you tell me where the Miyagawa-cho district is?'

'Why do you want to go there?'

'I have to pick up something.'

She gave me a strange look, but then told me to walk along the river until I had passed the Minamiza Theater, and I would find myself in Miyagawa-cho.

I decided to stay under the eaves of the teahouse until the rain stopped. As I stood looking around, I discovered a wing of the building visible between the slats of the fence beside me. I put my eye to the fence and found myself looking across a beautiful garden at a window of glass. Inside a lovely tatami room, bathed in orange light, a party of men and geisha sat around a table scattered with sake cups and glasses of beer. Hatsumomo was there too, and a bleary-eyed old man who seemed to be in the middle of a story. Hatsumomo was amused about something, though evidently not by what the old man was saying. She kept glancing at another geisha with her back to me. I found myself remembering the last time I had peered into a teahouse, with Mr. Tanaka's little daughter, Kuniko, and began to feel that same sense of heaviness I'd felt so long ago at the graves of my father's first family – as if the earth were pulling me down toward it. A certain thought was swelling in my head, growing until I couldn't ignore it any longer. I wanted to turn away from it; but I was as powerless to stop that thought from taking over my mind as the wind is to stop itself from blowing. So I stepped back and sank onto the stone step of the entryway, with the door against my back, and began to cry. I couldn't stop thinking about Mr. Tanaka. He had taken me from my mother and father, sold me into slavery, sold my sister into something even worse. I had taken him for a kind man. I had thought he was so refined, so worldly. What a stupid child I had been! I would never go back to Yoroido, I decided. Or if I did go back, it would only be to tell Mr. Tanaka how much I hated him.

When at last I got to my feet and wiped my eyes on my wet robe, the rain had eased to a mist. The paving stones in the alley sparkled gold from the reflection of the lanterns. I made my way back through the Tominaga-cho section of Gion to the Minamiza Theater, with its enormous tiled roof that had made me think of a palace the day Mr. Bekku brought Satsu and me from the train station. The maid at the Mizuki Teahouse had told me to walk along the river past the Minamiza; but the road running along the river stopped at the theater. So I followed the street behind the Minamiza instead. After a few blocks I found myself in an area without streetlights and nearly empty of people. I didn't know it at the time, but the streets were empty mostly because of the Great Depression; in any other era Miyagawa-cho might have been busier even than Gion. That evening it seemed to me a very sad place – which indeed I think it has always been. The wooden facades looked like Gion, but the place had no trees, no lovely Shirakawa Stream, no beautiful entryways. The only illumination came from lightbulbs in the open doorways, where old women sat on stools, often with two or three women I took to be geisha on the street beside them. They wore kimono and hair ornaments similar to geisha, but their obi were tied in the front rather than the back. I'd never seen this before and didn't understand it, but it's the mark of a prostitute. A woman who must take her sash on and off all night can't be bothered with tying it behind her again and again.

With the help of one of these women, I found the Tatsuyo in a dead-end alley with only three other houses. All were marked with placards near their doors. I can't possibly describe how I felt when I saw the sign lettered 'Tatsuyo,' but I will say that my body seemed to tingle everywhere, so much that I felt I might explode. In the doorway of the Tatsuyo sat an old woman on a stool, carrying on a conversation with a much younger woman on a stool across the alley – though really it was the old woman who did all the talking. She sat leaning back against the door frame with her gray robe sagging partway open and her feet stuck out in a pair of zori. These were zori woven coarsely from straw, of the sort you might have seen in Yoroido, and not at all like the beautifully lacquered zori Hatsumomo wore with her kimono. What was more, this old woman's feet were bare, rather than fitted with the smooth silk tabi. And yet she thrust them out with their uneven nails just as though she were proud of the way they looked and wanted to be sure you noticed them.

'Just another three weeks, you know, and I'm not coming back,' she was saying. 'The mistress thinks I am, but I'm not. My son's wife is going to take good care of me, you know. She's not clever, but she works hard. Didn't you meet her?'

'If I did I don't remember,' the younger woman across the way said. 'There's a little girl waiting to talk with you. Don't you see her?'

At this, the old woman looked at me for the first time. She didn't say anything, but she gave a nod of her head to tell me she was listening.

'Please, ma'am,' I said, 'do you have a girl here named Satsu?'

'We don't have any Satsu,' she said.

I was too shocked to know what to say to this; but in any case, the old woman suddenly looked very alert, because a man was just walking past me toward the entrance. She stood partway and gave him several bows with her hands on her knees and told him, 'Welcome!' When he'd entered, she put herself back down on the stool and stuck her feet out again.

'Why are you still here?' the old woman said to me. 'I told you we don't have any Satsu.'

'Yes, you do,' said the younger woman across the way. 'Your Yukiyo. Her name used to be Satsu, I remember.'

'That's as may be,' replied the old woman. 'But we don't have any Satsu for this girl. I don't get myself into trouble for nothing.'

I didn't know what she meant by this, until the younger woman muttered that I didn't look as if I had even a single sen on me. And she was quite right. A sen – which was worth only one hundredth of a yen – was still commonly used in those days, though a single one wouldn't buy even an empty cup from a vendor. I'd never held a coin of any kind in my hand since coming to Kyoto. When running errands, I asked that the goods be charged to the Nitta okiya.

'If it's money you want,' I said, 'Satsu will pay you.'

'Why should she pay to speak to the likes of you?'

'I'm her little sister.'

She beckoned me with her hand; and when I neared her, she took me by the arms and spun me around.

'Look at this girl,' she said to the woman across the alley. 'Does she look like a little sister to Yukiyo? If our Yukiyo was as pretty as this one, we'd be the busiest house in town! You're a liar, is what you are.' And with this, she gave me a little shove back out into the alley.

I'll admit I was frightened. But I was more determined than frightened, and I'd already come this far; I certainly wasn't going to leave just because this woman didn't believe me. So I turned myself around and gave her a bow, and said to her, 'I apologize if I seem to be a liar, ma'am. But I'm not. Yukiyo is my sister. If you'd be kind enough to tell her Chiyo is here, she'll pay you what you want.'

This must have been the right thing to say, because at last she turned to the younger woman across the alley. 'You go up for me. You're not busy tonight. Besides, my neck is bothering me. I'll stay here and keep an eye on this girl.'

The younger woman stood up from her stool and walked across into the Tatsuyo. I heard her climbing the stairs inside. Finally she came back down and said:

'Yukiyo has a customer. When he's done, someone will tell her to come down.'

The old woman sent me into the shadows on the far side of the door to squat where I couldn't be seen. I don't know how much time passed, but I grew more and more worried that someone in the okiya might discover me gone. I had an excuse for leaving, though Mother would be angry with me just the same; but I didn't have an excuse for staying away. Finally a man came out, picking at his teeth with a toothpick. The old woman stood to bow and thanked him for coming. And then I heard the most pleasing sound I'd heard since coming to Kyoto.

'You wanted me, ma'am?'

It was Satsu's voice.

I sprang to my feet and rushed to where she stood in the doorway. Her skin looked pale, almost gray – though perhaps it was only because she wore a kimono of garish yellows and reds. And her mouth was painted with a bright lipstick like the kind Mother wore. She was just tying her sash in the front, like the women I'd seen on my way there. I felt such relief at seeing her, and such excitement, I could hardly keep from rushing into her arms; and Satsu too let out a cry and covered her hand with her mouth.

'The mistress will be angry with me,' the old woman said.

'I'll come right back,' Satsu told her, and disappeared inside the Tatsuyo again. A moment or so later she was back, and dropped several coins into the woman's hand, who told her to take me into the spare room on the first floor.

'And if you hear me cough,' she added, 'it means the mistress is coming. Now hurry up.'

I followed Satsu into the gloomy entrance hall of the Tatsuyo. Its light was brown more than yellow, and the air smelled like sweat. Beneath the staircase was a sliding door that had come off its track. Satsu tugged it open, and with difficulty managed to shut it behind us. We were standing in a tiny tatami room with only one window covered by a paper screen. The light from outdoors was enough for me to see Satsu's form, but nothing of her features.

'Oh, Chiyo,' she said, and then she reached up to scratch her face. Or at least, I thought she was scratching her face, for I couldn't see well. It took me a moment to understand she was crying. After this I could do nothing to hold back my own tears.

'I'm so sorry, Satsu!' I told her. 'It's all my fault.'

Somehow or other we stumbled toward each other in the dark until we were hugging. I found that all I could think about was how bony she'd grown. She stroked my hair in a way that made me think of my mother, which caused my eyes to well up so much I might as well have been underwater.

'Quiet, Chiyo-chan,' she whispered to me. With her face so close to mine, her breath had a pungent odor when she spoke. 'I'll get a beating if the mistress finds out you were here. Why did it take you so long!'

'Oh, Satsu, I'm so sorry! I know you came to my okiya . . .'

'Months ago.'

'The woman you spoke with there is a monster. She wouldn't give me the message for the longest time.'

'I have to run away, Chiyo. I can't stay here in this place any longer.'

'I'll come with you!'

'I have a train schedule hidden under the tatami mats upstairs. I've been stealing money whenever I can. I have enough to pay off Mrs. Kishino. She gets beaten whenever a girl escapes. She won't let me go unless I pay her first.'

'Mrs. Kishino . . . who is she?'

'The old lady at the front door. She's going away. I don't know who will take her place. I can't wait any longer! This is a horrible spot. Never end up anywhere like this, Chiyo! You'd better go now. The mistress may be here at any moment.'

'But wait. When do we run away?'

'Wait in the corner there, and don't say a word. I have to go upstairs.'

I did as she told me. While she was gone I heard the old woman at the front door greet a man, and then his heavy footsteps ascended the stairs over my head. Soon someone came down again hurriedly, and the door slid open. I felt panicked for a moment, but it was only Satsu, looking very pale.

'Tuesday. We'll run away. Tuesday late at night, five days from now. I have to go upstairs, Chiyo. A man has come for me.'

'But wait, Satsu. Where will we meet? What time?'

'I don't know . . . one in the morning. But I don't know where.'

I suggested we meet near the Minamiza Theater, but Satsu thought it would be too easy for people to find us. We agreed to meet at a spot exactly across the river from it.

'I have to go now,' she said.

'But, Satsu . . . what if I can't get away? Or what if we don't meet up?'

'Just be there, Chiyo! I'll only have one chance. I've waited as long as I can. You have to go now before the mistress comes back. If she catches you here, I may never be able to run away.'

There were so many things I wanted to say to her, but she took me out into the hallway and wrenched the door shut behind us. I would have watched her go up the stairs, but in a moment the old woman from the doorway had taken me by the arm and pulled me out into the darkness of the street.

I ran back from Miyagawa-cho and was relieved to find the okiya as quiet as I'd left it. I crept inside and knelt in the dim light of the entrance hall, dabbing the sweat from my forehead and neck with the sleeve of my robe and trying to catch my breath. I was just beginning to settle down, now that I'd succeeded in not getting caught. But then I looked at the door to the maids' room and saw that it stood open a bit, just wide enough to reach an arm through, and I felt myself go cold. No one ever left it that way. Except in hot weather it was usually closed all the way. Now as I watched it, I felt certain I heard a rustling sound from within. I hoped it was a rat; because if it wasn't a rat, it was Hatsumomo and her boyfriend again. I began to wish I hadn't gone to Miyagawa-cho. I wished it so hard that if such a thing had been possible, I think time itself would have begun to run backward just from the force of all my wishing. I got to my feet and crept down onto the dirt corridor, feeling dizzy from worry and with my throat as dry as a patch of dusty ground. When I reached the door of the maids' room, I brought my eye to the crack to peer inside. I couldn't see well. Because of the damp weather, Yoko had lit charcoal earlier that evening in the brazier set into the floor; only a faint glow remained, and in that dim light, something small and pale was squirming. I almost let out a scream when I saw it, because I was sure it was a rat, with its head bobbing around as it chewed at something. To my horror I could even hear the moist, smacking sounds of its mouth. It seemed to be standing up on top of something, I couldn't tell what. Stretching out toward me were two bundles of what I thought were probably rolled-up fabric, which gave me the impression it had chewed its way up between them, spreading them apart as it went. It was eating something Yoko must have left there in the room. I was just about to shut the door, for I was frightened it might run out into the corridor with me, when I heard a woman's moan. Then suddenly from beyond where the rat was chewing, a head raised up and Hatsumomo was looking straight at me. I jumped back from the door. What I'd thought were bundles of rolled-up fabric were her legs. And the rat wasn't a rat at all. It was her boyfriend's pale hand protruding from his sleeve.

'What is it?' I heard her boyfriend's voice say. 'Is someone there?'

'It's nothing,' Hatsumomo whispered.

'Someone's there.'

'No, it's no one at all,' she said. 'I thought I heard something, but it's no one.'

There was no question in my mind Hatsumomo had seen me. But she apparently didn't want her boyfriend to know. I hurried back to kneel in the hallway, feeling as shaken as if I'd almost been run over by a trolley. I heard groans and noises coming from the maids' room for some time, and then they stopped. When Hatsumomo and her boyfriend finally stepped out into the corridor, her boyfriend looked right at me.

'That girl's in the front hall,' he said. 'She wasn't there when I came in.'

'Oh, don't pay her any attention. She was a bad girl tonight and went out of the okiya when she wasn't supposed to. I'll deal with her later.'

'So there was someone spying on us. Why did you lie to me?'

'Koichi-san,' she said, 'you're in such a bad mood tonight!'

'You aren't the least surprised to see her. You knew she was there all along.'

Hatsumomo's boyfriend came striding up to the front entrance hall and stopped to glower at me before stepping down into the entryway. I kept my eyes to the floor, but I could feel myself blush a brilliant red. Hatsumomo rushed past me to help him with his shoes. I heard her speak to him as I'd never heard her speak to anyone before, in a pleading, almost whining voice.

'Koichi-san, please,' she said, 'calm down. I don't know what's gotten into you tonight! Come again tomorrow . . .'

'I don't want to see you tomorrow.'

'I hate when you make me wait so long. I'll meet you anywhere you say, on the bottom of the riverbed, even.'

'I don't have anywhere to meet you. My wife watches over me too much as it is.'

'Then come back here. We have the maids' room –'

'Yes, if you like sneaking around and being spied on! Just let me go, Hatsumomo. I want to get home.'

'Please don't be angry with me, Koichi-san. I don't know why you get this way! Tell me you'll come back, even if it isn't tomorrow.'

'One day I won't come back,' he said. 'I've told you that all along.'

I heard the outside door roll open, and then it closed again; after a time Hatsumomo came back into the front entrance hall and stood peering down the corridor at nothing. Finally she turned to me and wiped the moisture from her eyes.

'Well, little Chiyo,' she said. 'You went to visit that ugly sister of yours, didn't you?'

'Please, Hatsumomo-san,' I said.

'And then you came back here to spy on me!' Hatsumomo said this so loudly, she woke one of the elderly maids, who propped herself on her elbow to look at us. Hatsumomo shouted at her, 'Go back to sleep, you stupid old woman!' and the maid shook her head and lay back down again.

'Hatsumomo-san, I'll do whatever you want me to do,' I said. 'I don't want to get in trouble with Mother.'

'Of course you'll do whatever I want you to do. That isn't even a subject for discussion! And you're already in trouble.'

'I had to go out to deliver your shamisen.'

'That was more than an hour ago. You went to find your sister, and you made plans to run away with her. Do you think I'm stupid? And then you came back here to spy on me!'

'Please forgive me,' I said. 'I didn't know it was you there! I thought it was –'

I wanted to tell her I'd thought I'd seen a rat, but I didn't think she'd take it kindly.

She peered at me for a time and then went upstairs to her room. When she came back down, she was holding something in her fist.

'You want to run away with your sister, don't you?' she said. 'I think that's a fine idea. The sooner you're out of the okiya, the better for me. Some people think I don't have a heart, but it isn't true. It's touching to imagine you and that fat cow going off to try to make a living someplace, all alone in the world! The sooner you're out of here, the better for me. Stand up.'

I stood, though I was afraid of what she was going to do to me. Whatever she was holding in her fist she wanted to tuck beneath the sash of my robe; but when she stepped toward me, I backed away.

'Look,' she said, and opened her hand. She was holding a number of folded bills – more money than I'd ever seen, though I don't know how much. 'I've brought this from my room for you. You don't need to thank me. Just take it. You'll repay me by getting yourself out of Kyoto so I'll never have to see you again.'

Auntie had told me never to trust Hatsumomo, even if she offered to help me. But when I reminded myself how much Hatsumomo hated me, I understood that she wasn't really helping me at all; she was helping herself to be rid of me. I stood still as she reached into my robe and tucked the bills under my sash. I felt her glassy nails brushing against my skin. She spun me around to retie the sash so the money wouldn't slip, and then she did the strangest thing. She turned me around to face her again, and began to stroke the side of my head with her hand, wearing an almost motherly gaze. The very idea of Hatsumomo behaving kindly toward me was so odd, I felt as if a poisonous snake had come up and begun to rub against me like a cat. Then before I knew what she was doing, she worked her fingers down to my scalp; and all at once she clenched her teeth in fury and took a great handful of my hair, and yanked it to one side so hard I fell to my knees and cried out. I couldn't understand what was happening; but soon Hatsumomo had pulled me to my feet again, and began leading me up the stairs yanking my hair this way and that. She was shouting at me in anger, while I screamed so loudly I wouldn't have been surprised if we'd woken people all up and down the street.

When we reached the top of the stairs, Hatsumomo banged on Mother's door and called out for her. Mother opened it very quickly, tying her sash around her middle and looking angry.

'What is the matter with the two of you!' she said.

'My jewelry!' Hatsumomo said. 'This stupid, stupid girl!' And here she began to beat me. I could do nothing but huddle into a ball on the floor and cry out for her to stop until Mother managed to restrain her somehow. By that time Auntie had come to join her on the landing.

'Oh, Mother,' Hatsumomo said, 'on my way back to the okiya this evening, I thought I saw little Chiyo at the end of the alleyway talking to a man. I didn't think anything of it, because I knew it couldn't be her. She isn't supposed to be out of the okiya at all. But when I went up to my room, I found my jewelry box in disarray, and rushed back down just in time to see Chiyo handing something over to the man. She tried to run away, but I caught her!'

Mother was perfectly silent a long while, looking at me.

'The man got away,' Hatsumomo went on, 'but I think Chiyo may have sold some of my jewelry to raise money. She's planning to run away from the okiya, Mother, that's what I think . . . after we've been so kind to her!'

'All right, Hatsumomo,' Mother said. 'That's quite enough. You and Auntie go into your room and find out what's missing.'

The moment I was alone with Mother, I looked up at her from where I knelt on the floor and whispered, 'Mother, it isn't true . . . Hatsumomo was in the maids' room with her boyfriend. She's angry about something, and she's taking it out on me. I didn't take anything from her!'

Mother didn't speak. I wasn't even sure she'd heard me. Soon Hatsumomo came out and said she was missing a brooch used for decorating the front of an obi.

'My emerald brooch, Mother!' she kept saying, and crying just like a fine actress. 'She's sold my emerald brooch to that horrible man! It was my brooch! Who does she think she is to steal such a thing from me!'

'Search the girl,' Mother said.

Once when I was a little child of six or so, I watched a spider spinning its web in a corner of the house. Before the spider had even finished its job, a mosquito flew right into the web and was trapped there. The spider didn't pay it any attention at first, but went on with what it was doing; only when it was finished did it creep over on its pointy toes and sting that poor mosquito to death. As I sat there on that wooden floor and watched Hatsumomo come reaching for me with her delicate fingers, I knew I was trapped in a web she had spun for me. I could do nothing to explain the cash I was carrying beneath my sash. When she drew it out, Mother took it from her and counted it.

'You're a fool to sell an emerald brooch for so little,' she said to me. 'Particularly since it will cost you a good deal more to replace it.'

She tucked the money into her own sleeping robe, and then said to Hatsumomo:

'You had a boyfriend here in the okiya tonight.'

Hatsumomo was taken aback by this; but she didn't hesitate to reply, 'Whatever gave you such an idea, Mother?'

There was a long pause, and then Mother said to Auntie, 'Hold her arms.'

Auntie took Hatsumomo by the arms and held her from behind, while Mother began to pull open the seams of Hatsumomo's kimono at the thigh. I thought Hatsumomo would resist, but she didn't. She looked at me with cold eyes as Mother gathered up the *koshimaki* and pushed her knees apart. Then Mother reached up between her legs, and when her hand came out again her fingertips were wet. She rubbed her thumb and fingers together for a time, and then smelled them. After this she drew back her hand and slapped Hatsumomo across the face, leaving a streak of moisture.

8

HATSUMOMO WASN'T THE only one angry at me the following day, because Mother ordered that all the maids be denied servings of dried fish for six weeks as punishment for having tolerated Hatsumomo's boyfriend in the okiya. I don't think the maids could have been more upset with me if I'd actually stolen the food from their bowls with my own hands; and as for Pumpkin, she began to cry when she found out what Mother had ordered. But to tell the truth, I didn't feel as uneasy as you might imagine to have everyone glowering at me, and to have the cost of an obi brooch I'd never seen or even touched added to my debts. Anything that made life more difficult for me only strengthened my determination to run away.

I don't think Mother really believed I'd stolen the obi brooch, though she was certainly content to buy a new one at my expense if it would keep Hatsumomo happy. But she had no doubts at all that I'd left the okiya when I shouldn't have, because Yoko confirmed it. I felt almost as though my life itself were slipping away from me when I learned that Mother had ordered the front door locked to prevent me from going out again. How would I escape from the okiya now? Only Auntie had a key, and she kept it around her neck even while she was sleeping. As an extra measure, the job of sitting by the door in the evenings was taken away from me and given to Pumpkin instead, who had to wake Auntie to have the door unlocked when Hatsumomo came home.

Every night I lay on my futon scheming; but as late as Monday, the very day before Satsu and I had arranged to run away, I'd come up with no plan for my escape. I grew so despondent I had no energy at all for my chores, and the maids chided me for dragging my cloth along the woodwork I was supposed to be polishing, and pulling a broom along the corridor I was supposed to be sweeping. I spent a long while Monday afternoon pretending to weed the courtyard while really only squatting on the stones and brooding. Then one of the maids gave me the job of washing the wood floor in the maids' room, where Yoko was seated near the telephone, and something extraordinary happened. I squeezed a rag full of water onto the floor, but instead of snaking along toward the doorway as I would have expected, it ran toward one of the back corners of the room.

'Yoko, look,' I said. 'The water's running uphill.'

Of course it wasn't really uphill. It only looked that way to me. I was so startled by this that I squeezed more water and watched it run into the corner again. And then . . . well, I can't say exactly how it happened; but I pictured myself flowing up the stairs to the second-floor landing, and from there up the ladder, through the trapdoor, and onto the roof beside the gravity-feed tank.

The roof! I was so astonished at the thought, I forgot my surroundings completely; and when the telephone near Yoko rang, I almost cried out in alarm. I wasn't sure what I would do once I reached the roof, but if I could succeed in finding my way down from there, I might meet Satsu after all.

The following evening I made a great show of yawning when I went to bed and threw myself onto my futon as though I were a sack of rice. Anyone watching me would have thought I was asleep within a moment, but actually I could hardly have been more awake. I lay for a long while thinking of my house and wondering what expression would form itself on my father's face when he looked up from the table to see me standing in the doorway. Probably the pockets at his eyes would droop down and he would start to cry, or else his mouth would take on that odd shape that was his way of smiling. I didn't allow myself to picture my mother quite so vividly; just the thought of seeing her again was enough to bring tears to my eyes.

At length the maids settled down onto their futons beside me on the floor, and Pumpkin took up her position waiting for Hatsumomo. I listened to Granny chanting sutras, which she did every night before going to bed. Then I watched her through the partly opened door as she stood beside her futon and changed into her sleeping robe. I was horrified by what I saw when her robe slipped from her shoulders, for I'd never seen her completely naked before. It wasn't just the chicken-like skin of her neck and shoulders; her body made me think of a pile of wrinkled clothing. She looked strangely pitiful to me while she fumbled to unfold the sleeping robe she'd picked up from the table. Everything drooped from her, even her protruding nipples that hung like fingertips. The more I watched her, the more I came to feel that she must be struggling in that cloudy, old lady's mind of hers with thoughts of her own mother and father – who had probably sold her into slavery when she was a little girl – just as I had been struggling with thoughts of my own parents. Perhaps she had lost a sister too. I'd certainly never thought of Granny in this way before. I found myself wondering if she'd started life much as I had. It made no difference that she was a mean old woman and I was just a struggling little girl. Couldn't the wrong sort of living turn anyone mean? I remembered very well that one day back in Yoroido, a boy pushed me into a thorn bush near the pond. By the time I clawed my way out I was mad enough to bite through wood. If a few minutes of suffering could make me so angry; what would years of it do? Even stone can be worn down with enough rain.

If I hadn't already resolved to run away, I'm sure I would have been terrified to think of the suffering that probably lay in wait for me in Gion. Surely it would make me into the sort of old woman Granny had become. But I comforted myself with the thought that by the following day I could begin forgetting even my memories of Gion. I already knew how I would reach the roof; as to how I would climb from there to the street . . . well, I wasn't at all sure. I would have no choice but to take my chances in the dark. Even if I did make it down without hurting myself, reaching the street would be only the beginning of my troubles. However much life in Gion was a struggle, life after running away would surely be more of a struggle. The world was simply too cruel; how could I survive? I lay on my futon in anguish for a while, wondering if I really had the strength to do it . . . but Satsu would be waiting for me. She would know what to do.

Quite some time passed before Granny settled down in her room. By then the maids were snoring loudly. I pretended to turn over on my futon in order to steal a glance at Pumpkin, kneeling on the floor not far away. I couldn't see her face well, but I had the impression she was growing drowsy. Originally I'd planned to wait until she fell asleep, but I had no idea of the time any longer; and besides, Hatsumomo might come home at any moment. I sat up as quietly as I could, thinking that if anyone noticed me I would simply go to the toilet and come back again. But no one paid me any attention. A robe for me to wear on the following morning lay folded on the floor nearby. I took it in my arms and went straight for the stairwell,

Outside Mother's door, I stood listening for a while. She didn't usually snore, so I couldn't judge anything from the silence, except that she wasn't talking on the telephone or making any other sort of noise. Actually, her room wasn't completely silent because her little dog, Taku, was wheezing in his sleep. The longer I listened, the more his wheezing sounded like someone saying my name: 'CHI-yo! CHI-yo!' I wasn't prepared to sneak out of the okiya until I'd satisfied myself Mother was asleep, so I decided to slide the door open and have a look. If she was awake, I would simply say I thought someone had called me. Like Granny Mother slept with the lamp on her table illuminated; so when I opened the door a crack and peered in, I could see the parched bottoms of her feet sticking out of the sheets. Taku lay between her feet with his chest rising and falling, making that wheezy noise that sounded so much like my name.

I shut her door again and changed my clothes in the upstairs hallway. The only thing I lacked now was shoes – and I never considered running away without them, which ought to give you some idea how much I'd changed since the summer. If Pumpkin hadn't been kneeling in the front entrance hall, I would have taken a pair of the wooden shoes used for walking along the dirt corridor. Instead I took the shoes reserved for use in the upstairs toilet. They were of a very poor quality with a single leather thong across the top to hold them in place on the foot. To make matters worse, they were much too big for me; but I had no other option.

After closing the trapdoor silently behind me, I stuffed my sleeping robe under the gravity-feed tank and managed to climb up and straddle my legs over the ridge of the roof. I won't pretend I wasn't frightened; the voices of people on the street certainly seemed a long way below me. But I had no time to waste being afraid, for it seemed to me that at any moment one of the maids, or even Auntie or Mother, might pop up through the trapdoor looking for me. I put the shoes onto my hands to keep from dropping them and began scooting my way along the ridge, which proved to be more difficult than I'd imagined. The roof tiles were so thick they made almost a small step where they overlapped, and they clanked against one another when I shifted my weight unless I moved very slowly Every noise I made echoed off the roofs nearby.

I took several minutes to cross just to the other side of our okiya. The roof of the building next door was a step lower than ours. I climbed down onto it and stopped a moment to look for a path to the street; but despite the moonlight, I could see only a sheet of blackness. The roof was much too high and steep for me to consider sliding down it on a gamble. I wasn't at all sure the next roof would be better; and I began to feel a bit panicky. But I continued along from ridge to ridge until I found myself, near the end of the block, looking down on one side into an open courtyard. If I could make my way to the gutter, I could scoot around it until I came to what I thought was probably a bath shed. From the top of the bath shed, I could climb down into the courtyard easily.

I didn't relish the thought of dropping into the middle of someone else's house. I had no doubt it was an okiya; all the houses along our block were. In all likelihood someone would be waiting at the front door for the geisha to return, and would grab me by the arm as I tried to run out. And what if the front door was locked just as ours was? I wouldn't even have considered this route if I'd had any other choice. But I thought the path down looked safer than anything I'd seen yet.

I sat on the ridge a long while listening for any clues from the courtyard below. All I could hear was laughter and conversation from the street. I had no idea what I would find in the courtyard when I dropped in, but I decided I'd better make my move before someone in my okiya discovered me gone. If I'd had any idea of the damage I was about to do to my future, I would have spun around on that ridge as fast as I could have and scooted right back where I'd come from. But I knew nothing of what was at stake. I was just a child who thought she was embarking on a great adventure.

I swung my leg over, so that in a moment I was dangling along the slope of the roof, just barely clinging to the ridge. I realized with some panic that it was much steeper than I'd thought it would be. I tried to scamper back up, but I couldn't do it. With the toilet shoes on my hands, I couldn't grab onto the ridge of the roof at all, but only hook my wrists over it. I knew I had committed myself, for I would never manage to climb back up again; but it seemed to me that the very moment I let go, I would slide down that roof out of control. My mind was racing with these thoughts, but before I'd made the decision to let go of the ridge, it let go of me. At first I glided down more slowly than I would have expected, which gave me some hope I might stop myself farther down, where the roof curved outward to form the eaves. But then my foot dislodged one of the roof tiles, which slid down with a clattering noise and shattered in the courtyard below. The next thing I knew, I lost my grip on one of the toilet shoes and it slid right past me.

I heard the quiet plop as it landed below, and then a much worse sound – the sound of footsteps coming down a wooden walkway toward the courtyard.

Many times I had seen the way flies stood on a wall or ceiling just as if they were on level ground. Whether they did it by having sticky feet, or by not weighing very much, I had no idea, but when I heard the sound of someone walking below, I decided that whatever I did I would find a way of sticking to that roof just as a fly might do, and I would find it right away. Otherwise I was going to end up sprawled in that courtyard in another few seconds. I tried digging my toes into the roof, and then my elbows and knees. As a final act of desperation I did the most foolish thing of all – I slipped the shoe from my other hand and tried to stop myself by pressing my two palms against the roof tiles. My palms must have been dripping with sweat, because instead of slowing down I began to pick up speed the moment I touched them to the roof. I heard myself skidding with a hissing sound; and then suddenly the roof was no longer there.

For a moment I heard nothing; only a frightening, empty silence. As I fell through the air I had time to form one thought clearly in my mind: I pictured a woman stepping into the courtyard, looking down to see the shattered tile on the ground, and then looking up toward the roof in time to see me fall out of the sky right on top of her; but of course this isn't what happened. I turned as I fell, and landed on my side on the ground. I had the sense to bring an arm up to protect my head; but still I landed so heavily that I knocked myself into a daze. I don't know where the woman was standing, or even if she was in the courtyard at the time I fell out of the sky. But she must have seen me come down off that roof, because as I lay stunned on the ground I heard her say:

'Good heavens! It's raining little girls!'

Well, I would have liked to jump to my feet and run out, but I couldn't do it. One whole side of my body felt dipped in pain. Slowly I became aware of two women kneeling over me. One kept saying something again and again, but I couldn't make it out. They talked between themselves and then picked me up from the moss and sat me on the wooden walkway. I remember only one fragment of their conversation.

'I'm telling you, she came off the roof, ma'am.'

'Why on earth was she carrying toilet slippers with her? Did you go up there to use the toilet, little girl? Can you hear me? What a dangerous thing to do! You're lucky you didn't break into pieces when you fell!'

'She can't hear you, ma'am. Look at her eyes.'

'Of course she can hear me. Say something, little girl!'

But I couldn't say anything. All I could do was think about how Satsu would be waiting for me opposite the Minamiza Theater, and I would never show up.

The maid was sent up the street to knock on doors until she found where I'd come from, while I lay curled up in a ball in a state of shock. I was crying without tears and holding my arm, which hurt terribly when suddenly I felt myself pulled to my feet and slapped across the face.

'Foolish, foolish girl!' said a voice. Auntie was standing before me in a rage, and then she pulled me out of that okiya and behind her up the street. When we reached our okiya, she leaned me up against the wooden door and slapped me again across the face.

'Do you know what you've done?' she said to me, but I couldn't answer. 'What were you thinking! Well, you've ruined everything for yourself . . . of all the stupid things! Foolish, foolish girl!'

I'd never imagined Auntie could be so angry. She dragged me into the courtyard and threw me onto my stomach on the walkway. I began to cry in earnest now, for I knew what was coming. But this time instead of beating me halfheartedly as she had before, Auntie poured a bucket of water over my robe to make the rod sting all the more, and then struck me so hard I couldn't even draw a breath. When she was done beating me, she threw the rod onto the ground and rolled me over onto my back. 'You'll never be a geisha now,' she cried. 'I warned you not to make a mistake like this! And now there's nothing I or anyone else can do to help you.'

I heard nothing more of what she said because of the terrible screams from farther up the walkway. Granny was giving Pumpkin a beating for not having kept a better eye on me.

As it turned out, I'd broken my arm landing as I had in that courtyard. The next morning a doctor came and took me to a clinic nearby. It was late afternoon already by the time I was brought back to the okiya with a plaster cast on my arm. I was still in terrible pain, but Mother called me immediately to her room. For a long while she sat staring at me, patting Taku with one hand and holding her pipe in her mouth with the other.

'Do you know how much I paid for you?' she said to me at last.

'No, ma'am,' I answered. 'But you're going to tell me you paid more than I'm worth.'

I won't say this was a polite way to respond. In fact, I thought Mother might slap me for it, but I was beyond caring. It seemed to me nothing in the world would ever be right again. Mother clenched her teeth together and gave a few coughs in that strange laugh of hers.

'You're right about that!' she said. 'Half a yen might have been more than you're worth. Well, I had the impression you were clever. But you're not clever enough to know what's good for you.'

She went back to puffing at her pipe for a while, and then she said, 'I paid seventy-five yen for you, that's what I paid. Then you went and ruined a kimono, and stole a brooch, and now you've broken your arm, so I'll be adding medical expenses to your debts as well. Plus you have your meals and lessons, and just this morning I heard from the mistress of the Tatsuyo, over in Miyagawa-cho, that your older sister has run away. The mistress there still hasn't paid me what she owes. Now she tells me she's not going to do it! I'll add that to your debt as well, but what difference will it make? You already owe more than you'll ever repay.'

So Satsu had escaped. I'd spent the day wondering, and now I had my answer. I wanted to feel happy for her, but I couldn't.

'I suppose you could repay it after ten or fifteen years as a geisha,' she went on, 'if you happened to be a success. But who would invest another sen in a girl who runs away?'

I wasn't sure how to reply to any of this, so I told Mother I was sorry. She'd been talking to me pleasantly enough until then, but after my apology, she put her pipe on the table and stuck out her jaw so much – from anger, I suppose – that she gave me the impression of an animal about to strike.

'Sorry, are you? I was a fool to invest so much money in you in the first place. You're probably the most expensive maid in all of Gion! If I could sell off your bones to pay back some of your debts, why, I'd rip them right out of your body!'

With this, she ordered me out of the room and put her pipe back into her mouth.

My lip was trembling when I left, but I held my feelings in; for there on the landing stood Hatsumomo. Mr. Bekku was waiting to finish tying her obi while Auntie, with a handkerchief in her hand, stood in front of Hatsumomo, peering into her eyes.

'Well, it's all smeared,' Auntie said. 'There's nothing more I can do. You'll have to finish your little cry and redo your makeup afterward.'

I knew exactly why Hatsumomo was crying. Her boyfriend had stopped seeing her, now that she'd been barred from bringing him to the okiya. I'd learned this the morning before and felt certain Hatsumomo was going to blame her troubles on me. I was eager to get down the stairs before she spotted me, but it was already too late. She snatched the handkerchief from Auntie's hand and made a gesture calling me over. I certainly didn't want to go, but I couldn't refuse.

'You've got no business with Chiyo,' Auntie said to her. 'Just go into your room and finish your makeup.'

Hatsumomo didn't reply, but drew me into her room and shut the door behind us.

'I've spent days trying to decide exactly how I ought to ruin your life,' she said to me. 'But now you've tried to run away, and done it for me! I don't know whether to feel pleased. I was looking forward to doing it myself.'

It was very rude of me, but I bowed to Hatsumomo and slid open the door to let myself out without replying. She might have struck me for it, but she only followed me into the hall and said, 'If you wonder what it will be like as a maid all your life, just have a talk with Auntie! Already you're like two ends of the same piece of string. She has her broken hip; you have your broken arm. Perhaps one day you'll even look like a man, just the way Auntie does!'

'There you go, Hatsumomo,' Auntie said. 'Show us that famous charm of yours.'

*

Back when I was a little girl of five or six, and had never so much as thought about Kyoto once in all my life, I knew a little boy named Noboru in our village. I'm sure he was a nice boy, but he had a very unpleasant smell, and I think that's why he was so unpopular. Whenever he spoke, all the other children paid him no more attention than if a bird had chirped or a frog had croaked, and poor Noboru often sat right down on the ground and cried. In the months after my failed escape, I came to understand just what life must have been like for him; because no one spoke to me at all unless it was to give me an order. Mother had always treated me as though I were only a puff of smoke, for she had more important things on her mind. But now all the maids, and the cook, and Granny did the same.

All that bitter cold winter, I wondered what had become of Satsu, and of my mother and father. Most nights when I lay on my futon I was sick with anxiety, and felt a pit inside myself as big and empty as if the whole world were nothing more than a giant hall empty of people. To comfort myself I closed my eyes and imagined that I was walking along the path beside the sea cliffs in Yoroido. I knew it so well I could picture myself there as vividly as if I really had run away with Satsu and was back at home again. In my mind I rushed toward our tipsy house holding Satsu's hand – though I had never held her hand before – knowing that in another few moments we would be reunited with our mother and father. I never did manage to reach the house in these fantasies; perhaps I was too afraid of what I might find there, and in any case, it was the trip along the path that seemed to comfort me. Then at some point I would hear the cough of one of the maids near me, or the embarrassing sound of Granny passing wind with a groan, and in that instant the smell of the sea air dissolved, the coarse dirt of the path beneath my feet turned into the sheets of my futon once again, and I was left where I'd started with nothing but my own loneliness.

When spring came, the cherry trees blossomed in Maruyama Park, and no one in Kyoto seemed to talk about anything else.

Hatsumomo was busier than usual during the daytime because of all the blossom viewing parties. I envied her the bustling life I saw her prepare for every afternoon. I'd already begun to give up my hopes of awakening one night to find that Satsu had sneaked into our okiya to rescue me, or that in some other way I might hear word of my family in Yoroido. Then one morning as Mother and Auntie were preparing to take Granny on a picnic, I came down the stairs to find a package on the floor of the front entrance hall. It was a box about as long as my arm, wrapped in heavy paper and tied up with frayed twine. I knew it was none of my business; but since no one was around to see me, I went over to read the name and address in heavy characters on the face. It said:

Sakamoto Chiyo
c/o Nitta Kayoko
Gion Tominaga-cho
City of Kyoto, Kyoto Prefecture

I was so astonished that I stood a long while with my hand over my mouth, and I'm sure my eyes were as big around as teacups. The return address, beneath a patch of stamps, was from Mr. Tanaka. I had no idea what could possibly be in the package, but seeing Mr. Tanaka's name there . . . you may find it absurd, but I honestly hoped perhaps he'd recognized his mistake in sending me to this terrible place, and had mailed me something to set me free from the okiya. I can't imagine any package that might free a little girl from slavery; I had trouble imagining it even then. But I truly believed in my heart that somehow when that package was opened, my life would be changed forever.

Before I could figure out what to do next, Auntie came down the stairs and shooed me away from the box, even though it had my name on it. I would have liked to open it myself, but she called for a knife to cut the twine and then took her time unwrapping the coarse paper. Underneath was a layer of canvas sacking stitched up with heavy fishermen's thread. Sewn to the sacking by its corners was an envelope bearing my name. Auntie cut the envelope free and then tore away the sacking to reveal a dark wooden box. I began to get excited about what I might find inside, but when Auntie took off the lid, I felt myself all at once growing heavy. For there, nestled amid folds of white linen, lay the tiny mortuary tablets that had once stood before the altar in our tipsy house. Two of them, which I had never seen before, looked newer than the others and bore unfamiliar Buddhist names, written with characters I couldn't understand. I was afraid even to wonder why Mr. Tanaka had sent them.

For the moment, Auntie left the box there on the floor, with the tablets lined up so neatly inside, and took the letter from the envelope to read it. I stood for what seemed a long while, full of my fears, and not daring even to think. Finally, Auntie sighed heavily and led me by the arm into the reception room. My hands were trembling in my lap as I knelt at the table, probably from the force of trying to keep all my terrible thoughts from rising to the surface of my mind. Perhaps it was really a hopeful sign that Mr. Tanaka had sent me the mortuary tablets. Wasn't it possible that my family would be moving to Kyoto, that we would buy a new altar together and set up the tablets before it? Or perhaps Satsu had asked that they be sent to me because she was on her way back. And then Auntie interrupted my thoughts.

'Chiyo, I'm going to read you something from a man named Tanaka Ichiro,' she said in a voice that was strangely heavy and slow. I don't think I breathed at all while she spread the paper out on the table.

Dear Chiyo:

Two seasons have passed since you left Yoroido, and soon the trees will give birth to a new generation of blossoms. Flowers that grow where old ones have withered serve to remind us that death will one day come to us all.

As one who was once an orphaned child himself, this humble person is sorry to have to inform you of the terrible burden you must bear. Six weeks after you left for your new life in Kyoto, the suffering of your honored mother came to its end, and only a few weeks afterward your honored father departed this world as well. This humble person is deeply sorry for your loss and hopes you will rest assured that the remains of both your honored parents are enshrined in the village cemetery. Services were conducted for them at the Hoko-ji Temple in Senzuru, and in addition the women in Yoroido have chanted sutras. This humble person feels confident that both your honored parents have found their places in paradise.

The training of an apprentice geisha is an arduous path. However, this humble person is filled with admiration for those who are able to recast their suffering and become great artists. Some years ago while visiting Gion, it was my honor to view the spring dances and attend a party afterward at a teahouse, and the experience has left the deepest impression. It gives me some measure of satisfaction to know that a safe place in this world has been found for you, Chiyo, and that you will not be forced to suffer through years of uncertainty. This humble person has been alive long enough to see two generations of children grow up, and knows how rare it is for ordinary birds to give birth to a swan. The swan who goes on living in its parents' tree will die; this is why those who are beautiful and talented bear the burden of finding their own way in the world.

Your sister, Satsu, came through Yoroido late this past fall, but ran away again at once with the son of Mr. Sugi. Mr. Sugi fervently hopes to see his beloved son again in this lifetime, and asks therefore that you please notify him immediately if you receive word from your sister.

Most sincerely yours,

Tanaka Ichiro

Long before Auntie had finished reading this letter, the tears had begun to flow out of me just like water from a pot that boils over. For it would have been bad enough to learn that my mother had died, or that my father had died. But to learn in a single moment that both my mother and my father had died and left me, and that my sister too was lost to me forever . . . at once my mind felt like a broken vase that would not stand. I was lost even within the room around me.

You must think me very naive for having kept alive the hope for so many months that my mother might still be living. But really I had so few things to hope for, I suppose I would have clutched at anything. Auntie was very kind to me while I tried to find my bearings. Again and again she said to me, 'Bear up, Chiyo, bear up. There's nothing more any of us can do in this world.'

When I was finally able to speak, I asked Auntie if she would set up the tablets someplace where I wouldn't see them, and pray on my behalf – for it would give me too much pain to do it. But she refused, and told me I should be ashamed even to consider turning my back on my own ancestors. She helped me set the tablets up on a shelf near the base of the stairwell, where I could pray before them every morning. 'Never forget them, Chiyo-chan,' she said. 'They're all that's left of your childhood.'

9

AROUND THE TIME of my sixty-fifth birthday, a friend sent me an article she'd found somewhere, called 'The Twenty Greatest Geisha of Gion's Past.' Or maybe it was the thirty greatest geisha, I don't remember. But there I was on the list with a little paragraph telling some things about me, including that I'd been born in Kyoto – which of course I wasn't. I can assure you I wasn't one of Gion's twenty greatest geisha either; some people have difficulty telling the difference between something great and something they've simply heard of. In any case, I would have been lucky to end up as nothing more than a bad geisha and an unhappy one, like so many other poor girls, if Mr. Tanaka had never written to tell me that my parents had died and that I would probably never see my sister again.

I'm sure you'll recall my saying that the afternoon when I first met Mr. Tanaka was the very best afternoon of my life, and also the very worst. Probably I don't need to explain why it was the worst; but you may be wondering how I could possibly imagine that anything good ever came of it. It's true that up until this time in my life Mr. Tanaka had brought me nothing but suffering; but he also changed my horizons forever. We lead our lives like water flowing down a hill, going more or less in one direction until we splash into something that forces us to find a new course. If I'd never met Mr. Tanaka, my life would have been a simple stream flowing from our tipsy house to the ocean. Mr. Tanaka changed all that when he sent me out into the world. But being sent out into the world isn't necessarily the same as leaving your home behind you. I'd been in Gion more than six months by the time I received Mr. Tanaka's letter; and yet during that time, I'd never for a moment given up the belief that I would one day find a better life elsewhere, with at least part of the family I'd always known. I was living only half in Gion; the other half of me lived in my dreams of going home. This is why dreams can be such dangerous things: they smolder on like a fire does, and sometimes consume us completely.

During the rest of the spring and all that summer following the letter, I felt like a child lost on a lake in the fog. The days spilled one after another into a muddle. I remember only snippets of things, aside from a constant feeling of misery and fear. One cold evening after winter had come, I sat a long while in the maids' room watching snow falling silently into the okiya's little courtyard. I imagined my father coughing at the lonely table in his lonely house, and my mother so frail upon her futon that her body scarcely sank into the bedding. I stumbled out into the courtyard to try to flee my misery; but of course we can never flee the misery that is within us.

Then in early spring, a full year after the terrible news about my family, something happened. It was the following April, when the cherry trees were in blossom once again; it may even have been a year to the day since Mr. Tanaka's letter. I was almost twelve by then and was beginning to look a bit womanly, even though Pumpkin still looked very much like a little girl. I'd grown nearly as tall as I would ever grow. My body would remain thin and knobby like a twig for a year or two more, but my face had already given up its childish softness and was now sharp around the chin and cheekbones, and had broadened in such a way as to give a true almond shape to my eyes. In the past, men had taken no more notice of me on the streets than if I had been a pigeon; now they were watching me when I passed them. I found it strange to be the object of attention after being ignored for so long.

In any case, very early one morning that April, I awoke from a most peculiar dream about a bearded man. His beard was so heavy that his features were a blur to me, as if someone had censored them from the film. He was standing before me saying something I can't remember, and then all at once he slid open the paper screen over a window beside him with a loud *clack*. I awoke thinking I'd heard a noise in the room. The maids were sighing in their sleep. Pumpkin lay quietly with her round face sagging onto the pillow. Everything looked just as it always did, I'm sure; but my feelings were strangely different. I felt as though I were looking at a world that was somehow changed from the one I'd seen the night before – peering out, almost, through the very window that had opened in my dream.

I couldn't possibly have explained what this meant. But I continued thinking about it while I swept the stepping-stones in the courtyard that morning, until I began to feel the sort of buzzing in my head that comes from a thought circling and circling with nowhere to go, just like a bee in a jar. Soon I put down the broom and went to sit in the dirt corridor, where the cool air from beneath the foundation of the main house drifted soothingly over my back. And then something came to mind that I hadn't thought about since my very first week in Kyoto.

Only a day or two after being separated from my sister, I had been sent to wash some rags one afternoon, when a moth came fluttering down from the sky onto my arm. I flicked it off, expecting that it would fly away, but instead it sailed like a pebble across the courtyard and lay there upon the ground. I didn't know if it had fallen from the sky already dead or if I had killed it, but its little insect death touched me. I admired the lovely pattern on its wings, and then wrapped it in one of the rags I was washing and hid it away beneath the foundation of the house.

I hadn't thought about this moth since then; but the moment it came to mind I got on my knees and looked under the house until I found it. So many things in my life had changed, even the way I looked; but when I unwrapped the moth from its funeral shroud, it was the same startlingly lovely creature as on the day I had entombed it. It seemed to be wearing a robe in subdued grays and browns, like Mother wore when she went to her mah-jongg games at night. Everything about it seemed beautiful and perfect, and so utterly unchanged. If only one thing in my life had been the same as during that first week in Kyoto . . . As I thought of this my mind began to swirl like a hurricane. It struck me that we – that moth and I – were two opposite extremes. My existence was as unstable as a stream, changing in every way; but the moth was like a piece of stone, changing not at all. While thinking this thought, I reached out a finger to feel the moth's velvety surface; but when I brushed it with my fingertip, it turned all at once into a pile of ash without even a sound, without even a moment in which I could see it crumbling. I was so astonished I let out a cry. The swirling in my mind stopped; I felt as if I had stepped into the eye of a storm. I let the tiny shroud and its pile of ashes flutter to the ground; and now I understood the thing that had puzzled me all morning. The stale air had washed away. The past was gone. My mother and father were dead and I could do nothing to change it. But I suppose that for the past year I'd been dead in a way too. And my sister . . . yes, she was gone; but I wasn't gone. I'm not sure this will make sense to you, but I felt as though I'd turned around to look in a different direction, so that I no longer faced backward toward the past, but forward toward the future. And now the question confronting me was this: What would that future be?

The moment this question formed in my mind, I knew with as much certainty as I'd ever known anything that sometime during that day I would receive a sign. This was why the bearded man had opened the window in my dream. He was saying to me, 'Watch for the thing that will show itself to you. Because that thing, when you find it, will be your future.'

I had no time for another thought before Auntie called out to me:

'Chiyo, come here!'

Well, I walked up that dirt corridor as though I were in a trance. It wouldn't have surprised me if Auntie had said, 'You want to know about your future? All right, listen closely . . .' But instead she just held out two hair ornaments on a square of white silk.

'Take these,' she said to me. 'Heaven knows what Hatsumomo was up to last night; she came back to the okiya wearing another girl's ornaments. She must have drunk more than her usual amount of sake. Go find her at the school, ask whose they are, and return them.'

When I took the ornaments, Auntie gave me a piece of paper with a number of other errands written on it as well and told me to come back to the okiya as soon as I had done them all.

Wearing someone else's hair ornaments home at night may not sound so peculiar, but really it's about the same as coming home in someone else's underwear. Geisha don't wash their hair every day, you see, because of their fancy hairstyles. So a hair ornament is a very intimate article. Auntie didn't even want to touch the things, which is why she was holding them on a square of silk. She wrapped them up to give them to me, so that they looked just like the bundled-up moth I'd been holding only a few minutes earlier. Of course, a sign doesn't mean anything unless you know how to interpret it. I stood there staring at the silk bundle in Auntie's hand until she said, 'Take it, for heaven's sake!' Later, on my way to the school, I unfolded it to have another look at the ornaments. One was a black lacquer comb shaped like the setting sun, with a design of flowers in gold around the outside; the other was a stick of blond wood with two pearls at the end holding in place a tiny amber sphere.

I waited outside the school building until I heard the *don* of the bell signaling the end of classes. Soon girls in their blue and white robes came pouring out. Hatsumomo spotted me even before I spotted her, and came toward me with another geisha. You may wonder why she was at the school at all, since she was already an accomplished dancer and certainly knew everything she needed to know about being a geisha. But even the most renowned geisha continued to take advanced lessons in dance throughout their careers, some of them even into their fifties and sixties.

'Why, look,' Hatsumomo said to her friend. 'I think it must be a weed. Look how tall it is!' This was her way of ridiculing me for having grown a finger's-width taller than her.

'Auntie has sent me here, ma'am,' I said, 'to find out whose hair ornaments you stole last night.'

Hatsumomo's smile faded. She snatched the little bundle from my hand and opened it.

'Why, these aren't mine . . .' she said. 'Where did you get them?'

'Oh, Hatsumomo-san!' said the other geisha. 'Don't you remember? You and Kanako took out your hair ornaments while the two of you were playing that foolish game with Judge Uwazumi. Kanako must have gone home with your hair ornaments, and you went home with hers.'

'How disgusting,' said Hatsumomo. 'When do you think Kanako last washed her hair? Anyway, her okiya is right next to yours. Take them for me, would you? Tell her I'll come to fetch mine later, and she'd better not try to keep them.'

The other geisha took the hair ornaments and left.

'Oh, don't go, little Chiyo,' Hatsumomo said to me. 'There's something I want to show you. It's that young girl over there, the one walking through the gate. Her name is Ichikimi.'

I looked at Ichikimi, but Hatsumomo didn't seem to have any more to say about her. 'I don't know her,' I said.

'No, of course not. She's nothing special. A bit stupid, and as awkward as a cripple. But I just thought you'd find it interesting that she's going to be a geisha, and you never will.'

I don't think Hatsumomo could have found anything crueler to say to me. For a year and a half now, I'd been condemned to the drudgery of a maid. I felt my life stretching out before me like a long path leading nowhere. I won't say I wanted to become a geisha; but I certainly didn't want to remain a maid. I stood in the garden of the school a long while, watching the young girls my age chat with one another as they streamed past. They may only have been heading back for lunch, but to me they were going from one important thing to another with lives of purpose, while I on the other hand would go back to nothing more glamorous than scrubbing the stones in the courtyard. When the garden emptied out, I stood worrying that perhaps this was the sign I'd waited for – that other young girls in Gion would move ahead in their lives and leave me behind. This thought gave me such a fright I couldn't stay alone in the garden any longer. I walked down to Shijo Avenue and turned toward the Kamo River. Giant banners on the Minamiza Theater announced the performance of a Kabuki play that afternoon entitled *Shibaraku*, which is one of our most famous plays, though I knew nothing about Kabuki at the time. Crowds streamed up the steps into the theater. Among the men in their dark Western-style suits or kimono, several geisha stood out in brilliant coloring just like autumn leaves on the murky waters of a river. Here again, I saw life in all its noisy excitement passing me by. I hurried away from the avenue, down a side street leading along the Shirakawa Stream, but even there, men and geisha were rushing along in their lives so full of purpose. To shut out the pain of this thought I turned toward the Shirakawa, but cruelly, even its waters glided along with purpose – toward the Kamo River and from there to Osaka Bay and the Inland Sea. It seemed the same message waited for me everywhere. I threw myself onto the little stone wall at the edge of the stream and wept. I was an abandoned island in the midst of the ocean, with no past, to be sure, but no future either. Soon I felt myself coming to a point where I thought no human voice could reach me – until I heard a man's voice say this:

'Why, it's too pretty a day to be so unhappy.'

Ordinarily a man on the streets of Gion wouldn't notice a girl like me, particularly while I was making a fool of myself by crying. If he did notice me, he certainly wouldn't speak to me, unless it was to order me out of his way, or some such thing. Yet not only had this man bothered to speak to me, he'd actually spoken kindly. He'd addressed me in a way that suggested I might be a young woman of standing – the daughter of a good friend, perhaps. For a flicker of a moment I imagined a world completely different from the one I'd always known, a world in which I was treated with fairness, even kindness – a world in which fathers didn't sell their daughters. The noise and hubbub of so many people living their lives of purpose around me seemed to stop; or at least, I ceased to be aware of it. And when I raised myself to look at the man who'd spoken, I had a feeling of leaving my misery behind me there on the stone wall.

I'll be happy to try to describe him for you, but I can think of only one way to do it – by telling you about a certain tree that stood at the edge of the sea cliffs in Yoroido. This tree was as smooth as driftwood because of the wind, and when I was a little girl of four or five I found a man's face on it one day. That is to say, I found a smooth patch as broad as a plate, with two sharp bumps at the outside edge for cheekbones. They cast shadows suggesting eye sockets, and beneath the shadows rose a gentle bump of a nose. The whole face tipped a bit to one side, gazing at me quizzically; it looked to me like a man with as much certainty about his place in this world as a tree has. Something about it was so meditative, I imagined I'd found the face of a Buddha.

The man who'd addressed me there on the street had this same kind of broad, calm face. And what was more, his features were so smooth and serene, I had the feeling he'd go on standing there calmly until I wasn't unhappy any longer. He was probably about forty-five years old, with gray hair combed straight back from his forehead. But I couldn't look at him for long. He seemed so elegant to me that I blushed and looked away.

Two younger men stood to one side of him; a geisha stood to the other. I heard the geisha say to him quietly:

'Why, she's only a maid! Probably she stubbed her toe while running an errand. I'm sure someone will come along to help her soon.'

'I wish I had your faith in people, Izuko-san,' said the man.

'The show will be starting in only a moment. Really, Chairman, I don't think you should waste any more time . . .'

While running errands in Gion, I'd often heard men addressed by titles like 'Department Head' or occasionally 'Vice President.' But only rarely had I heard the title 'Chairman.' Usually the men addressed as Chairman had bald heads and frowns, and swaggered down the street with groups of junior executives scurrying behind. This man before me was so different from the usual chairman that even though I was only a little girl with limited experience of the world, I knew his company couldn't be a terribly important one. A man with an important company wouldn't have stopped to talk to me.

'You're trying to tell me it's a waste of time to stay here and help her,' said the Chairman.

'Oh, no,' the geisha said. 'It's more a matter of having no time to waste. We may be late for the first scene already.'

'Now, Izuko-san, surely at some time you yourself have been in the same state this little girl is in. You can't pretend the life of a geisha is always simple. I should think you of all people –'

'*I've* been in the state *she's* in? Chairman, do you mean . . . making a public spectacle of myself?'

At this, the Chairman turned to the two younger men and asked that they take Izuko ahead to the theater. They bowed and went on their way while the Chairman remained behind. He looked at me a long while, though I didn't dare to look back at him. At length I said:

'Please, sir, what she says is true. I'm only a foolish girl . . . please don't make yourself late on my account.'

'Stand up a moment,' he told me.

I didn't dare disobey him, though I had no idea what he wanted. As it turned out, all he did was take a handkerchief from his pocket to wipe away the grit that had stuck to my face from the top of the stone wall. Standing so close before him, I could smell the odor of talc on his smooth skin, which made me recall the day when the Emperor Taisho's nephew had come to our little fishing village. He'd done nothing more than step out of his car and walk to the inlet and back, nodding to the crowds that knelt before him, wearing a Western-style business suit, the first I'd ever seen – for I peeked at him, even though I wasn't supposed to. I remember too that his mustache was carefully groomed, unlike the hair on the faces of the men in our village, which grew untended like weeds along a path. No one of any importance had ever been in our village before that day. I think we all felt touched by nobility and greatness.

Occasionally in life we come upon things we can't understand because we have never seen anything similar. The Emperor's nephew certainly struck me that way; and so did the Chairman. When he had wiped away the grit and tears from my face, he tipped my head up.

'Here you are . . . a beautiful girl with nothing on earth to be ashamed of,' he said. 'And yet you're afraid to look at me. Someone has been cruel to you . . . or perhaps life has been cruel.'

'I don't know, sir,' I said, though of course I knew perfectly well.

'We none of us find as much kindness in this world as we should,' he told me, and he narrowed his eyes a moment as if to say I should think seriously about what he'd just said.

I wanted more than anything to see the smooth skin of his face once more, with its broad brow, and the eyelids like sheaths of marble over his gentle eyes; but there was such a gulf in social standing between us. I did finally let my eyes flick upward, though I blushed and looked away so quickly that he may never have known I met his gaze. But how can I describe what I saw in that instant? He was looking at me as a musician might look at his instrument just before he begins to play, with understanding and mastery. I felt that he could see into me as though I were a part of him. How I would have loved to be the instrument he played!

In a moment he reached into his pocket and brought something out.

'Do you like sweet plum or cherry?' he said.

'Sir? Do you mean . . . to eat?'

'I passed a vendor a moment ago, selling shaved ice with syrup on it. I never tasted one until I was an adult, but I'd have liked them as a child. Take this coin and buy one. Take my handkerchief too, so you can wipe your face afterward,' he said. And with this, he pressed the coin into the center of the handkerchief, wrapped it into a bundle, and held it out to me.

From the moment the Chairman had first spoken to me, I'd forgotten that I was watching for a sign about my future. But when I saw the bundle he held in his hand, it looked so much like the shrouded moth, I knew I'd come upon the sign at last. I took the bundle and bowed low to thank him, and tried to tell him how grateful I was – though I'm sure my words carried none of the fullness of my feelings. I wasn't thanking him for the coin, or even for the trouble he'd taken in stopping to help me. I was thanking him for . . . well, for something I'm not sure I can explain even now. For showing me that something besides cruelty could be found in the world, I suppose.

I watched him walk away with sickness in my heart – though it was a pleasing kind of sickness, if such a thing exists. I mean to say that if you have experienced an evening more exciting than any in your life, you're sad to see it end; and yet you still feel grateful that it happened. In that brief encounter with the Chairman, I had changed from a lost girl facing a lifetime of emptiness to a girl with purpose in her life. Perhaps it seems odd that a casual meeting on the street could have brought about such change. But sometimes life is like that, isn't it? And I really do think if you'd been there to see what I saw, and feel what I felt, the same might have happened to you.

When the Chairman had disappeared from sight, I rushed up the street to search for the shaved ice vendor. The day wasn't especially hot, and I didn't care for shaved ice; but eating it would make my encounter with the Chairman linger. So I bought a paper cone of shaved ice with cherry syrup on it, and went to sit again on the same stone wall. The taste of the syrup seemed startling and complex, I think only because my senses were so heightened. If I were a geisha like the one named Izuko, I thought, a man like the Chairman might spend time with me. I'd never imagined myself envying a geisha. I'd been brought to Kyoto for the purpose of becoming one, of course; but up until now I'd have run away in an instant if I could have. Now I understood the thing I'd overlooked; the point wasn't to become a geisha, but to *be* one. To become a geisha . . . well, that was hardly a purpose in life. But to be a geisha . . . I could see it now as a stepping-stone to something else. If I was right about the Chairman's age, he was probably no more than forty-five. Plenty of geisha had achieved tremendous success by the age of twenty. The geisha Izuko was probably no more than twenty-five herself. I was still a child, nearly twelve . . . but in another twelve years I'd be in my twenties. And what of the Chairman? He would be no older by that time than Mr. Tanaka was already.

The coin the Chairman had given me was far more than I'd needed for a simple cone of shaved ice. I held in my hand the change from the vendor – three coins of different sizes. At first I'd thought of keeping them forever; but now I realized they could serve a far more important purpose.

I rushed to Shijo Avenue and ran all the way to its end at the eastern edge of Gion, where the Gion Shrine stood. I climbed the steps, but I felt too intimidated to walk beneath the great two-story entrance gate with its gabled roof, and walked around it instead. Across the gravel courtyard and up another flight of steps, I passed through the torii gate to the shrine itself. There I threw the coins into the offertory box – coins that might have been enough to take me away from Gion – and announced my presence to the gods by clapping three times and bowing. With my eyes squeezed tightly shut and my hands together, I prayed that they permit me to become a geisha somehow. I would suffer through any training, bear up under any hardship, for a chance to attract the notice of a man like the Chairman again.

When I opened my eyes, I could still hear the traffic on Higashi-Oji Avenue. The trees hissed in a gust of wind just as they had a moment earlier. Nothing had changed. As to whether the gods had heard me, I had no way of knowing. I could do nothing but tuck the Chairman's handkerchief inside my robe and carry it with me back to the okiya.

10

ONE MORNING QUITE some months later, while we were putting away the *ro* underrobes – the ones made of lightweight silk gauze for hot weather – and bringing out the *hitoe* underrobes instead – the ones with no lining, used in September – I came upon a smell in the entryway so horrible that I dropped the armload of robes I was carrying. The smell was coming from Granny's room. I ran upstairs to fetch Auntie, because I knew at once that something must be terribly wrong. Auntie hobbled down the stairs as quickly as she could and went in to find Granny dead on the floor; and she had died in a most peculiar manner.

Granny had the only electric space heater in our okiya. She used it every single night except during the summer. Now that the month of September had begun and we were putting away the summer-weight underrobes, Granny had begun to use her heater again. That doesn't mean the weather was necessarily cool; we change the weight of our clothing by the calendar, not by the actual temperature outdoors, and Granny used her heater just the same way. She was unreasonably attached to it, probably because she'd spent so many nights of her life suffering miserably from the cold.

Granny's usual routine in the morning was to wrap the cord around the heater before pushing it back against the wall. Over time the hot metal burned all the way through the cord, so that the wire finally came into contact with it, and the whole thing became electrified. The police said that when Granny touched it that morning she must have been immobilized at once, maybe even killed instantly. When she slid down onto the floor, she ended up with her face pressed against the hot metal surface. This was what caused the horrible smell. Happily I didn't see her after she'd died, except for her legs, which were visible from the doorway and looked like slender tree limbs wrapped in wrinkled silk.

For a week or two after Granny died, we were as busy as you can imagine, not only with cleaning the house thoroughly – because in Shinto, death is the most impure of all the things that can happen – but with preparing the house by setting out candles, trays with meal offerings, lanterns at the entrance, tea stands, trays for money that visitors brought, and so on. We were so busy that one evening the cook became ill and a doctor was summoned; it turned out her only problem was that she'd slept no more than two hours the night before, hadn't sat down all day, and had eaten only a single bowl of clear soup. I was surprised too to see Mother spending money almost unrestrainedly, making plans for sutras to be chanted on Granny's behalf at the Chionin Temple, purchasing lotus-bud arrangements from the undertaker – all of it right in the midst of the Great Depression. I wondered at first if her behavior was a testament to how deeply she felt about Granny; but later I realized what it really meant: practically all of Gion would come tramping through our okiya to pay respects to Granny, and would attend the funeral at the temple later in the week; Mother had to put on the proper kind of show.

For a few days all of Gion did indeed come through our okiya, or so it seemed; and we had to feed tea and sweets to all of them. Mother and Auntie received the mistresses of the various teahouses and okiya, as well as a number of maids who were acquainted with Granny; also shopkeepers, wig makers, and hairdressers, most of whom were men; and of course, dozens and dozens of geisha. The older geisha knew Granny from her working days, but the younger ones had never even heard of her; they came out of respect for Mother – or in some cases because they had a relationship of one kind or another with Hatsumomo.

My job during this busy period was to show visitors into the reception room, where Mother and Auntie were waiting for them. It was a distance of only a few steps; but the visitors couldn't very well show themselves in; and besides, I had to keep track of which faces belonged to which shoes, for it was my job to take the shoes to the maids' room to keep the entryway from being too cluttered, and then bring them back again at the proper moment. I had trouble with this at first. I couldn't peer right into the eyes of our visitors without seeming rude, but a simple glimpse of their faces wasn't enough for me to remember them. Very soon I learned to look closely at the kimono they wore.

On about the second or third afternoon the door rolled open, and in came a kimono that at once struck me as the loveliest I'd seen any of our visitors wear. It was somber because of the occasion – a simple black robe bearing a crest – but its pattern of green and gold grasses sweeping around the hem was so rich-looking, I found myself imagining how astounded the wives and daughters of the fishermen back in Yoroido would be to see such a thing. The visitor had a maid with her as well, which made me think perhaps she was the mistress of a teahouse or okiya – because very few geisha could afford such an expense. While she looked at the tiny Shinto shrine in our entryway, I took the opportunity to steal a peek at her face. It was such a perfect oval that I thought at once of a certain scroll in Auntie's room, showing an ink painting of a courtesan from the Heian period a thousand years earlier. She wasn't as striking a woman as Hatsumomo, but her features were so perfectly formed that at once I began to feel even more insignificant than usual. And then suddenly I realized who she was.

Mameha, the geisha whose kimono Hatsumomo had made me ruin.

What had happened to her kimono wasn't really my fault; but still, I would have given up the robe I was wearing not to run into her. I lowered my head to keep my face hidden while I showed her and her maid into the reception room. I didn't think she would recognize me, since I felt certain she hadn't seen my face when I'd returned the kimono; and even if she had, two years had passed since then. The maid who accompanied her now wasn't the same young woman who'd taken the kimono from me that night and whose eyes had filled with tears. Still, I was relieved when the time came for me to bow and leave them in the reception room.

Twenty minutes later, when Mameha and her maid were ready to leave, I fetched their shoes and arranged them on the step in the entryway, still keeping my head down and feeling every bit as nervous as I had earlier. When her maid rolled open the door, I felt that my ordeal was over. But instead of walking out, Mameha just went on standing there. I began to worry; and I'm afraid my eyes and my mind weren't communicating well, because even though I knew I shouldn't do it, I let my eyes flick up. I was horrified to see that Mameha was peering down at me.

'What is your name, little girl?' she said, in what I took to be a very stern tone.

I told her that my name was Chiyo.

'Stand up a moment, Chiyo. I'd like to have a look at you.'

I rose to my feet as she had asked; but if it had been possible to make my face shrivel up and disappear, just like slurping down a noodle, I'm sure I would have done it.

'Come now, I want to have a look at you!' she said. 'Here you are acting like you're counting the toes on your feet.'

I raised my head, though not my eyes, and then Mameha let out a long sigh and ordered me to look up at her.

'What unusual eyes!' she said. 'I thought I might have imagined it. What color would you call them, Tatsumi?'

Her maid came back into the entryway and took a look at me. 'Blue-gray, ma'am,' she replied.

'That's just what I would have said. Now, how many girls in Gion do you think have eyes like that?'

I didn't know if Mameha was speaking to me or Tatsumi, but neither of us answered. She was looking at me with a peculiar expression – concentrating on something, it seemed to me. And then to my great relief, she excused herself and left.

Granny's funeral was held about a week later, on a morning chosen by a fortune-teller. Afterward we began putting the okiya back in order, but with several changes. Auntie moved downstairs into the room that had been Granny's, while Pumpkin – who was to begin her apprenticeship as a geisha before long – took the second-floor room where Auntie had lived. In addition, two new maids arrived the following week, both of them middle-aged and very energetic. It may seem odd that Mother added maids although the family was now fewer in number; but in fact the okiya had always been understaffed because Granny couldn't tolerate crowding.

The final change was that Pumpkin's chores were taken away from her. She was told instead to spend her time practicing the various arts she would depend upon as a geisha. Usually girls weren't given so much opportunity for practice, but poor Pumpkin was a slow learner and needed the extra time if anyone ever did. I had difficulty watching her as she knelt on the wooden walkway every day and practiced her shamisen for hours, with her tongue poking out the side of her mouth like she was trying to lick her cheek clean. She gave me little smiles whenever our eyes met; and really, her disposition was as sweet and kind as could be. But already I was finding it difficult to bear the burden of patience in my life, waiting for some tiny opening that might never come and that would certainly be the only chance I'd ever get. Now I had to watch as the door of opportunity was held wide open for someone else. Some nights when I went to bed, I took the handkerchief the Chairman had given me and lay on my futon smelling its rich talc scent. I cleared my mind of everything but the image of him and the feeling of warm sun on my face and the hard stone wall where I'd sat that day when I met him. He was my bodhisattva with a thousand arms who would help me. I couldn't imagine how his help would come to me, but I prayed that it would.

Toward the end of the first month after Granny's death, one of our new maids came to me one day to say I had a visitor at the door. It was an unseasonably hot October afternoon, and my whole body was damp with perspiration from using our old hand-operated vacuum to clean the tatami mats upstairs in Pumpkin's new room, which had only recently been Auntie's; Pumpkin was in the habit of sneaking rice crackers upstairs, so the tatami needed to be cleaned frequently. I mopped myself with a wet towel as quickly as I could and rushed down, to find a young woman in the entryway, dressed in a kimono like a maid's. I got to my knees and bowed to her. Only when I looked at her a second time did I recognize her as the maid who had accompanied Mameha to our okiya a few weeks earlier. I was very sorry to see her there. I felt certain I was in trouble. But when she gestured for me to step down into the entryway, I slipped my feet into my shoes and followed her out to the street.

'Are you sent on errands from time to time, Chiyo?' she asked me.

So much time had passed since I'd tried to run away that I was no longer confined to the okiya. I had no idea why she was asking; but I told her that I was.

'Good,' she said. 'Arrange for yourself to be sent out tomorrow afternoon at three o'clock, and meet me at the little bridge that arches over the Shirakawa Stream.'

'Yes, ma'am,' I said, 'but may I ask why?'

'You'll find out tomorrow, won't you?' she answered, with a little crinkle of her nose that made me wonder if she was teasing me.

I certainly wasn't pleased that Mameha's maid wanted me to accompany her somewhere – probably to Mameha, I thought, to be scolded for what I'd done. But just the same, the following day I talked Pumpkin into sending me on an errand that didn't really need to be run. She was worried about getting into trouble, until I promised to find a way of repaying her. So at three o'clock, she called to me from the courtyard:

'Chiyo-san, could you please go out and buy me some new shamisen strings and a few Kabuki magazines?' She had been instructed to read Kabuki magazines for the sake of her education. Then I heard her say in an even louder voice, 'Is that all right, Auntie?' But Auntie didn't answer, for she was upstairs taking a nap.

I left the okiya and walked along the Shirakawa Stream to the arched bridge leading into the Motoyoshi-cho section of Gion. With the weather so warm and lovely, quite a number of men and geisha were strolling along, admiring the weeping cherry trees whose tendrils drooped onto the surface of the water. While I waited near the bridge, I watched a group of foreign tourists who had come to see the famous Gion district. They weren't the only foreigners I'd ever seen in Kyoto, but they certainly looked peculiar to me, the big-nosed women with their long dresses and their brightly colored hair, the men so tall and confident, with heels that clicked on the pavement. One of the men pointed at me and said something in a foreign language, and they all turned to have a look. I felt so embarrassed I pretended to find something on the ground so I could crouch down and hide myself.

Finally Mameha's maid came; and just as I'd feared, she led me over the bridge and along the stream to the very same doorway where Hatsumomo and Korin had handed me the kimono and sent me up the stairs. It seemed terribly unfair to me that this same incident was about to cause still more trouble for me – and after so much time had passed. But when the maid rolled open the door for me, I climbed up into the gray light of the stairway. At the top we both stepped out of our shoes and went into the apartment.

'Chiyo is here, ma'am!' she cried.

Then I heard Mameha call from the back room, 'All right, thank you, Tatsumi!'

The young woman led me to a table by an open window, where I knelt on one of the cushions and tried not to look nervous. Very shortly another maid came out with a cup of tea for me – because as it turned out, Mameha had not one maid, but two. I certainly wasn't expecting to be served tea; and in fact, nothing like this had happened to me since dinner at Mr. Tanaka's house years earlier. I bowed to thank her and took a few sips, so as not to seem rude. Afterward I found myself sitting for a long while with nothing to do but listen to the sound of water passing over the knee-high cascade in the Shirakawa Stream outside.

Mameha's apartment wasn't large, but it was extremely elegant, with beautiful tatami mats that were obviously new; for they had a lovely yellow-green sheen and smelled richly of straw. If you've ever looked closely enough at a tatami mat, you'd notice that the border around it is edged in fabric, usually just a strip of dark cotton or linen; but these were edged in a strip of silk with a pattern of green and gold. Not far away in an alcove hung a scroll written in a beautiful hand, which turned out to be a gift to Mameha from the famous calligrapher Matsudaira Koichi. Beneath it, on the wooden base of the alcove, an arrangement of blossoming dogwood branches rose up out of a shallow dish that was irregular in shape with a cracked glaze of the deepest black. I found it very peculiar, but actually it had been presented to Mameha by none other than Yoshida Sakuhei, the great master of the *setoguro* style of ceramics who became a Living National Treasure in the years after World War II.

At last Mameha came out from the back room, dressed exquisitely in a cream kimono with a water design at the hem. I turned and bowed very low on the mats while she drifted over to the table; and when she was there, she arranged herself on her knees opposite me, took a sip of tea the maid served to her, and then said this:

'Now . . . Chiyo, isn't it? Why don't you tell me how you managed to get out of your okiya this afternoon? I'm sure Mrs. Nitta doesn't like it when her maids attend to personal business in the middle of the day.'

I certainly hadn't expected this sort of question. In fact, I couldn't think of anything at all to say, even though I knew it would be rude not to respond. Mameha just sipped at her tea and looked at me with a benign expression on her perfect, oval face. Finally she said:

'You think I'm trying to scold you. But I'm only interested to know if you've gotten yourself into trouble by coming here.'

I was very relieved to hear her say this. 'No, ma'am,' I said. 'I'm supposed to be on an errand fetching Kabuki magazines and shamisen strings.'

'Oh, well, I've got plenty of those,' she said, and then called her maid over and told her to fetch some and put them on the table before me. 'When you go back to your okiya, take them with you, and no one will wonder where you've been. Now, tell me something. When I came to your okiya to pay my respects, I saw another girl your age.'

'That must have been Pumpkin. With a very round face?'

Mameha asked why I called her Pumpkin, and when I explained, she gave a laugh.

'This Pumpkin girl,' Mameha said, 'how do she and Hatsumomo get along?'

'Well, ma'am,' I said, 'I suppose Hatsumomo pays her no more attention than she would a leaf that has fluttered into the courtyard.'

'How very poetic . . . a leaf that has fluttered into the courtyard. Is that the way Hatsumomo treats you as well?'

I opened my mouth to speak, but the truth is, I wasn't sure what to say. I knew very little about Mameha, and it would be improper to speak ill of Hatsumomo to someone outside the okiya. Mameha seemed to sense what I was thinking, for she said to me:

'You needn't answer. I know perfectly well how Hatsumomo treats you: about like a serpent treats its next meal, I should think.'

'If I may ask, ma'am, who has told you?'

'No one has told me,' she said. 'Hatsumomo and I have known each other since I was a girl of six and she was nine. When you've watched a creature misbehaving itself over such a long period, there's no secret in knowing what it will do next.'

'I don't know what I did to make her hate me so,' I said.

'Hatsumomo is no harder to understand than a cat. A cat is happy so long as it's lying in the sun with no other cats around. But if it should think someone else is poking around its meal dish . . . Has anyone told you the story of how Hatsumomo drove young Hatsuoki out of Gion?'

I told her no one had.

'What an attractive girl Hatsuoki was,' Mameha began. 'And a very dear friend of mine. She and your Hatsumomo were sisters. That is to say, they'd both been trained by the same geisha – in this case, the great Tomihatsu, who was already an old woman at the time. Your Hatsumomo never liked young Hatsuoki, and when they both became apprentice geisha, she couldn't bear having her as a rival. So she began to spread a rumor around Gion that Hatsuoki had been caught in a public alleyway one night doing something very improper with a young policeman. Of course there was no truth in it. If Hatsumomo had simply gone around telling the story, no one in Gion would have believed her. People knew how jealous she felt about Hatsuoki. So here's what she did: whenever she came upon someone very drunk – a geisha, or a maid, or even a man visiting Gion, it didn't matter – she whispered the story about Hatsuoki in such a way that the next day the person who'd heard it didn't remember that Hatsumomo had been the source. Soon poor Hatsuoki's reputation was so damaged, it was an easy matter for Hatsumomo to put a few more of her little tricks to use and drive her out.'

I felt a strange relief at hearing that someone besides me had been treated monstrously by Hatsumomo.

'She can't bear to have rivals,' Mameha went on. 'That's the reason she treats you as she does.'

'Surely Hatsumomo doesn't see me as a rival, ma'am,' I said. 'I'm no more a rival to her than a puddle is a rival to the ocean.'

'Not in the teahouses of Gion, perhaps. But within your okiya . . . Don't you find it odd that Mrs. Nitta has never adopted Hatsumomo as her daughter? The Nitta okiya must be the wealthiest in Gion without an heir. By adopting Hatsumomo, not only would Mrs. Nitta solve that problem, but all of Hatsumomo's earnings would then be kept by the okiya, without a single sen of it paid out to Hatsumomo herself. And Hatsumomo is a very successful geisha! You'd think Mrs. Nitta, who's as fond of money as anyone, would have adopted her a long time ago. She must have a very good reason not to do so, don't you think?'

I'd certainly never thought of any of this before, but after listening to Mameha, I felt certain I knew exactly what the reason was.

'Adopting Hatsumomo,' I said, 'would be like releasing the tiger from its cage.'

'It certainly would. I'm sure Mrs. Nitta knows perfectly well what sort of adopted daughter Hatsumomo would turn out to be – the sort that finds a way to drive the Mother out. In any case, Hatsumomo has no more patience than a child. I don't think she could keep even a cricket alive in a wicker cage. After a year or two, she'd probably sell the okiya's collection of kimono and retire. That, young Chiyo, is the reason Hatsumomo hates you so very much. The Pumpkin girl, I don't imagine Hatsumomo feels too worried about Mrs. Nitta adopting her.'

'Mameha-san,' I said, 'I'm sure you recall the kimono of yours that was ruined . . .'

'You're going to tell me you're the girl who put ink on it.'

'Well . . . yes, ma'am. And even though I'm sure you know Hatsumomo was behind it, I do hope that someday I'll be able to show how sorry I am for what happened.'

Mameha gazed at me a long while. I had no notion what she was thinking until she said:

'You may apologize, if you wish.'

I backed away from the table and bowed low to the mats; but before I had a chance to say anything at all, Mameha interrupted me.

'That would be a lovely bow, if only you were a farmer visiting Kyoto for the first time,' she said. 'But since you want to appear cultivated, you must do it like this. Look at me; move farther away from the table. All right, there you are on your knees; now straighten out your arms and put your fingertips onto the mats in front of you. Just the tips of your fingers; not your whole hand. And you mustn't spread your fingers at all; I can still see space between them. Very well, put them on the mats . . . hands together . . . there! Now that looks lovely. Bow as low as you can, but keep your neck perfectly straight, don't let your head drop that way. And for heaven's sake, don't put any weight onto your hands or you'll look like a man! That's fine. Now you may try it again.'

So I bowed to her once more, and told her again how deeply sorry I was for having played a role in ruining her beautiful kimono.

'It was a beautiful kimono, wasn't it?' she said. 'Well, now we'll forget about it. I want to know why you're no longer training to be a geisha. Your teachers at the school tell me you were doing well right up until the moment you stopped taking lessons. You ought to be on your way to a successful career in

Gion. Why would Mrs. Nitta stop your training?'

I told her about my debts, including the kimono and the brooch Hatsumomo had accused me of stealing. Even after I was finished, she went on looking coldly at me. Finally she said:

'There's something more you're not telling me. Considering your debts, I'd expect Mrs. Nitta to feel only more determined to see you succeed as a geisha. You'll certainly never repay her by working as a maid.'

When I heard this, I must have lowered my eyes in shame without realizing it; for in an instant Mameha seemed able to read my very thoughts.

'You tried to run away, didn't you?'

'Yes, ma'am,' I said. 'I had a sister. We'd been separated but we managed to find each other. We were supposed to meet on a certain night to run away together . . . but then I fell off the roof and broke my arm.'

'The roof! You must be joking. Did you go up there to take a last look at Kyoto?'

I explained to her why I'd done it. 'I know it was foolish of me,' I said afterward. 'Now Mother won't invest another sen in my training, since she's afraid I may run away again.'

'There's more to it than that. A girl who runs away makes the mistress of her okiya look bad. That's the way people think here in Gion. "My goodness, she can't even keep her own maids from running away!" That sort of thing. But what will you do with yourself now, Chiyo? You don't look to me like a girl who wants to live her life as a maid.'

'Oh, ma'am . . . I'd give anything to undo my mistakes,' I said. 'It's been more than two years now. I've waited so patiently in the hopes that some opportunity might come along.'

'Waiting patiently doesn't suit you. I can see you have a great deal of water in your personality. Water never waits. It changes shape and flows around things, and finds the secret paths no one else has thought about – the tiny hole through the roof or the bottom of a box. There's no doubt it's the most versatile of the five elements. It can wash away earth; it can put out fire; it can wear a piece of metal down and sweep it away. Even wood, which is its natural complement, can't survive without being nurtured by water. And yet, you haven't drawn on those strengths in living your life, have you?'

'Well, actually, ma'am, water flowing was what gave me the idea of escaping over the roof.'

'I'm sure you're a clever girl, Chiyo, but I don't think that was your cleverest moment. Those of us with water in our personalities don't pick where we'll flow to. All we can do is flow where the landscape of our lives carries us.'

'I suppose I'm like a river that has come up against a dam, and that dam is Hatsumomo.'

'Yes, probably that's true,' she said, looking at me calmly. 'But rivers sometimes wash dams away.'

From the moment of my arrival in her apartment, I'd been wondering why Mameha had summoned me. I'd already decided that it had nothing to do with the kimono; but it wasn't until now that my eyes finally opened to what had been right before me all along. Mameha must have made up her mind to use me in seeking her revenge on Hatsumomo. It was obvious to me they were rivals; why else would Hatsumomo have destroyed Mameha's kimono two years earlier? No doubt Mameha had been waiting for just the right moment, and now, it seemed, she'd found it. She was going to use me in the role of a weed that chokes out other plants in the garden. She wasn't simply looking for revenge; unless I was mistaken, she wanted to be rid of Hatsumomo completely.

'In any case,' Mameha went on, 'nothing will change until Mrs. Nitta lets you resume your training.'

'I don't have much hope,' I said, 'of ever persuading her.'

'Don't worry just now about persuading her. Worry about finding the proper time to do it.'

I'd certainly learned a great many lessons from life already; but I knew nothing at all about patience – not even enough to understand what Mameha meant about finding the proper time. I told her that if she could suggest what I ought to say, I would be eager to speak with Mother tomorrow.

'Now, Chiyo, stumbling along in life is a poor way to

proceed. You must learn how to find the time and place for things. A mouse who wishes to fool the cat doesn't simply scamper out of its hole when it feels the slightest urge. Don't you know how to check your almanac?'

I don't know if you've ever seen an almanac. To open one and flip through the pages, you'd find it crammed with the most complicated charts and obscure characters. Geisha are a very superstitious lot, as I've said. Auntie and Mother, and even the cook and the maids, scarcely made a decision as simple as buying a new pair of shoes without consulting an almanac. But I'd never checked one in my life.

'It's no wonder, all the misfortunes you've experienced,' Mameha told me. 'Do you mean to say that you tried to run away without checking if the day was auspicious?'

I told her my sister had made the decision when we would leave. Mameha wanted to know if I could remember the date, which I managed to do after looking at a calendar with her; it had been the last Tuesday in October 1929, only a few months after Satsu and I were taken from our home.

Mameha told her maid to bring an almanac for that year; and then after asking my sign – the year of the monkey – she spent some time checking and cross-checking various charts, as well as a page that gave my general outlook for the month. Finally she read aloud:

'"A most inauspicious time. Needles, unusual foods, and travel must be avoided at all costs."' Here she stopped to look up at me. 'Do you hear that? Travel. After that it goes on to say that you must avoid the following things . . . let's see . . . "bathing during the hour of the rooster," "acquiring new clothing," "*embarking on new enterprises*," and listen to this one, "*changing residences*."' Here Mameha closed the book and peered at me. 'Were you careful about any of those things?'

Many people have doubts about this sort of fortune-telling; but any doubts you might have would certainly have been swept away if you'd been there to see what happened next. Mameha asked my sister's sign and looked up the same information about her. 'Well,' she said after looking at it for a while, 'it reads, "An auspicious day for small changes."

Perhaps not the best day for something as ambitious as running away, but certainly better than the other days that week or the next.' And then came the surprising thing. 'It goes on to say, "A good day for travel in the direction of the Sheep,"' Mameha read. And when she brought out a map and found Yoroido, it lay to the north northeast of Kyoto, which was indeed the direction corresponding to the zodiac sign of the Sheep. Satsu had checked her almanac. That was probably what she'd done when she left me there in the room under the stairwell at the Tatsuyo for a few minutes. And she'd certainly been right to do it; she had escaped, while I hadn't.

This was the moment when I began to understand how unaware I'd been – not only in planning to run away, but in everything. I'd never understood how closely things are connected to one another. And it isn't just the zodiac I'm talking about. We human beings are only a part of something very much larger. When we walk along, we may crush a beetle or simply cause a change in the air so that a fly ends up where it might never have gone otherwise. And if we think of the same example but with ourselves in the role of the insect, and the larger universe in the role we've just played, it's perfectly clear that we're affected every day by forces over which we have no more control than the poor beetle has over our gigantic foot as it descends upon it. What are we to do? We must use whatever methods we can to understand the movement of the universe around us and time our actions so that we are not fighting the currents, but moving with them.

Mameha took up my almanac again and this time selected several dates over the following weeks that would be auspicious for significant change. I asked whether I should try to speak with Mother on one of the dates, and exactly what I should say.

'It isn't my intention to have you speak with Mrs. Nitta yourself,' she said. 'She'll turn you down in an instant. If I were her, so would I! As far as she knows, there's no one in Gion willing to be your older sister.'

I was very sorry to hear her say this. 'In that case, Mameha-san, what should I do?'

'You should go back to your okiya, Chiyo,' she said, 'and

mention to no one that you've spoken with me.'

After this, she gave me a look that meant I should bow and excuse myself right then, which I did. I was so flustered I left without the Kabuki magazines and shamisen strings Mameha had given me. Her maid had to come running down the street with them.

11

I SHOULD EXPLAIN just what Mameha meant by 'older sister,' even though at the time, I hardly knew much about it myself. By the time a girl is finally ready to make her debut as an apprentice, she needs to have established a relationship with a more experienced geisha. Mameha had mentioned Hatsumomo's older sister, the great Tomihatsu, who was already an old woman when she trained Hatsumomo; but older sisters aren't always so senior to the geisha they train. Any geisha can act as older sister to a younger girl, as long as she has at least one day's seniority.

When two girls are bound together as sisters, they perform a ceremony like a wedding. Afterward they see each other almost as members of the same family, calling each other 'Older Sister' and 'Younger Sister' just as real family members do. Some geisha may not take the role as seriously as they should, but an older sister who does her job properly becomes the most important figure in a young geisha's life. She does a great deal more than just making sure her younger sister learns the proper way of blending embarrassment and laughter when a man tells a naughty joke, or helping her select the right grade of wax to use under her makeup. She must also make sure her younger sister attracts the notice of people she'll need to know. She does this by taking her around Gion and presenting her to the mistresses of all the proper tea-houses, to the man who makes wigs for stage performances, to the chefs at the important restaurants, and so on.

There's certainly plenty of work in all of this. But introducing her younger sister around Gion during the day is only half of what an older sister must do. Because Gion is like a faint star that comes out in its fullest beauty only after the sun has set. At night the older sister must take her younger sister with her to entertain, in order to introduce her to the customers and patrons she's come to know over the years. She says to them, 'Oh, have you met my new younger sister, So-and-so? Please be sure to remember her name, because she's going to be a big star! And please permit her to call on you the next time you visit Gion.' Of course, few men pay high fees to spend the evening chatting with a fourteen-year-old; so this customer probably won't, in fact, summon the young girl on his next visit. But the older sister and the mistress of the teahouse will continue to push her on him until he does. If it turns out he doesn't like her for some reason . . . well, that's another story; but otherwise, he'll probably end up a patron of hers in good time, and very fond of her too – just as he is of her older sister.

Taking on the role of older sister often feels about like carrying a sack of rice back and forth across the city. Because not only is a younger sister as dependent on her older sister as a passenger is on the train she rides; but when the girl behaves badly, it's her older sister who must bear responsibility. The reason a busy and successful geisha goes to all this trouble for a younger girl is because everyone in Gion benefits when an apprentice succeeds. The apprentice herself benefits by paying off her debts over time, of course; and if she's lucky, she'll end up mistress to a wealthy man. The older sister benefits by receiving a portion of her younger sister's fees – as do the mistresses of the various teahouses where the girl entertains. Even the wigmaker, and the shop where hair ornaments are sold, and the sweets shop where the apprentice geisha will buy gifts for her patrons from time to time . . . they may never directly receive a portion of the girl's fees; but certainly they all benefit by the patronage of yet another successful geisha, who can bring customers into Gion to spend money.

It's fair to say that, for a young girl in Gion, nearly everything depends on her older sister. And yet few girls have any say over who their older sisters will be. An established geisha certainly won't jeopardize her reputation by taking on a younger sister she thinks is dull or someone she thinks her patrons won't like. On the other hand, the mistress of an okiya that has invested a great deal of money in training a certain apprentice won't sit quietly and just wait for some dull geisha to come along and offer to train her. So as a result, a successful geisha ends up with far more requests than she can manage. Some she can turn away, and some she can't . . . which brings me to the reason why Mother probably did feel – just as Mameha suggested that not a single geisha in Gion would be willing to act as my older sister.

Back at the time I first came to the okiya, Mother probably had in mind for Hatsumomo to act as my older sister. Hatsumomo may have been the sort of woman who would bite a spider right back, but nearly any apprentice would have been happy to be her younger sister. Hatsumomo had already been older sister to at least two well-known young geisha in Gion. Instead of torturing them as she had me, she'd behaved herself well. It was her choice to take them on, and she did it for the money it would bring her. But in my case, Hatsumomo could no more have been counted on to help me in Gion and then be content with the few extra yen it would bring her than a dog can be counted on to escort a cat down the street without taking a bite out of it in the alley. Mother could certainly have compelled Hatsumomo to be my older sister – not only because Hatsumomo lived in our okiya, but also because she had so few kimono of her own and was dependent on the okiya's collection. But I don't think any force on earth could have compelled Hatsumomo to train me properly. I'm sure that on the day she was asked to take me to the Mizuki Teahouse and introduce me to the mistress there, she would have taken me instead to the banks of the river and said, 'Kamo River, have you met my new younger sister?' and then pushed me right in.

As for the idea of another geisha taking on the task of training me . . . well, it would mean crossing paths with Hatsumomo. Few geisha in Gion were brave enough to do such a thing.

Late one morning a few weeks after my encounter with Mameha, I was serving tea to Mother and a guest in the reception room when Auntie slid open the door.

'I'm sorry to interrupt,' Auntie said, 'but I wonder if you would mind excusing yourself for just a moment, Kayoko-san.' Kayoko was Mother's real name, you see, but we rarely heard it used in our okiya. 'We have a visitor at the door.'

Mother gave one of her coughing laughs when she heard this. 'You must be having a dull day, Auntie,' she said, 'to come announce a visitor yourself. The maids don't work hard enough as it is, and now you're doing their jobs for them.'

'I thought you'd rather hear from me,' Auntie said, 'that our visitor is Mameha.'

I had begun to worry that nothing would come of my meeting with Mameha. But to hear that she had suddenly appeared at our okiya . . . well, the blood rushed to my face so intensely that I felt like a lightbulb just switched on. The room was perfectly quiet for a long moment, and then Mother's guest said, 'Mameha-san . . . well! I'll run along, but only if you promise to tell me tomorrow just what this is all about.'

I took my opportunity to slip out of the room as Mother's guest was leaving. Then in the formal entrance hall, I heard Mother say something to Auntie I'd never imagined her saying. She was tapping her pipe into an ashtray she'd brought from the reception room, and when she handed the ashtray to me, she said, 'Auntie, come here and fix my hair, please.' I'd never before known her to worry in the least about her appearance. It's true she wore elegant clothing. But just as her room was filled with lovely objects and yet was hopelessly gloomy, she herself may have been draped in exquisite fabrics, but her eyes were as oily as a piece of old, smelly fish . . . and really, she seemed to regard her hair the way a train regards its smokestack: it was just the thing that happened to be on top.

While Mother was answering the door, I stood in the maids' room cleaning out the ashtray. And I worked so hard to overhear Mameha and Mother that it wouldn't have surprised me if I had strained all the muscles in my ears.

First Mother said, 'I'm sorry to have kept you waiting, Mameha-san. What an honor to have a visit from you!'

Then Mameha said, 'I hope you'll forgive me for calling so

unexpectedly, Mrs. Nitta.' Or something equally dull. And it went on this way for a while. All my hard work in overhearing it was about as rewarding to me as a man who lugs a chest up the hill only to learn that it's full of rocks.

At last they made their way through the formal entrance hall to the reception room. I was so desperate to overhear their conversation that I grabbed a rag from the maids' room and began polishing the floor of the entrance hall with it. Normally Auntie wouldn't have permitted me to work there while a guest was in the reception room, but she was as preoccupied with eavesdropping as I was. When the maid came out after serving tea, Auntie stood to one side where she wouldn't be seen and made sure the door was left open a crack so she could hear. I listened so closely to their small talk that I must have lost track of everything around me, for suddenly I looked up to see Pumpkin's round face staring right into mine. She was on her knees polishing the floor, even though I was already doing it and she wasn't expected to do chores anymore.

'Who is Mameha?' she whispered to me.

Obviously she had overheard the maids talking among themselves; I could see them huddled together on the dirt corridor just at the edge of the walkway.

'She and Hatsumomo are rivals,' I whispered back. 'She's the one whose kimono Hatsumomo made me put ink on.'

Pumpkin looked like she was about to ask something else, but then we heard Mameha say, 'Mrs. Nitta, I do hope you'll forgive me for disturbing you on such a busy day, but I'd like to talk with you briefly about your maid Chiyo.'

'Oh, no,' Pumpkin said, and looked into my eyes to show how sorry she felt for the trouble I was about to be in.

'Our Chiyo can be a bit of a nuisance,' Mother said. 'I do hope she hasn't been troubling you.'

'No, nothing like that,' Mameha said. 'But I noticed she hasn't been attending the school these past few weeks. I'm so accustomed to running into her from time to time in the hallway . . . Just yesterday I realized she must be terribly ill! I've recently met an extremely capable doctor. I wonder, shall I ask him to stop by?'

'It's very kind of you,' said Mother, 'but you must be thinking of a different girl. You couldn't have run into our Chiyo in the hallway at the school. She hasn't attended lessons there for two years.'

'Are we thinking of the same girl? Quite pretty, with startling blue-gray eyes?'

'She does have unusual eyes. But there must be two such girls in Gion . . . Who would have thought it!'

'I wonder if it's possible that two years have passed since I saw her there,' Mameha said. 'Perhaps she made such a strong impression it still seems very recent. If I may ask, Mrs. Nitta . . . is she quite well?'

'Oh, yes. As healthy as a young sapling, and every bit as unruly if I do say so.'

'Yet she isn't taking lessons any longer? How puzzling.'

'For a young geisha as popular as you, I'm sure Gion must seem an easy place to make a living. But you know, times are very difficult. I can't afford to invest money in just anyone. As soon as I realized how poorly suited Chiyo was –'

'I'm quite sure we're thinking of two different girls,' Mameha said. 'I can't imagine that a businesswoman as astute as you are, Mrs. Nitta, would call Chiyo "poorly suited" . . .'

'Are you certain her name is Chiyo?' Mother asked.

None of us realized it, but as she spoke these words, Mother was rising from the table and crossing the little room. A moment later she slid open the door and found herself staring directly into Auntie's ear. Auntie stepped out of the way just as though nothing had happened; and I suppose Mother was content to pretend the same, for she did nothing more than look toward me and say, 'Chiyo-chan, come in here a moment.'

By the time I slid the door shut behind me and knelt on the tatami mats to bow, Mother had already settled herself at the table again.

'This is our Chiyo,' Mother said.

'The very girl I was thinking of!' said Mameha. 'How do you do, Chiyo-chan? I'm happy that you look so healthy! I was just saying to Mrs. Nitta that I'd begun to worry about you. But you seem quite well.'

'Oh, yes, ma'am, very well,' I answered.

'Thank you, Chiyo,' Mother told me. I bowed to excuse myself, but before I could rise to my feet, Mameha said:

'She's really quite a lovely girl, Mrs. Nitta. I must say, at times I've thought of coming to ask your permission to make her my younger sister. But now that she's no longer in training . . .'

Mother must have been shocked to hear this, because although she'd been on the point of taking a sip of tea, her hand stopped on its way to her mouth and remained motionless there during the time it took me to leave the room. I was nearly back to my place on the floor of the entrance hall when she finally responded.

'A geisha as popular as you, Mameha-san . . . you could have any apprentice in Gion as your younger sister.'

'It's true I'm often asked. But I haven't taken on a new younger sister in more than a year. You'd think that with this terrible Depression, customers would have slowed to a trickle, but really I've never been so busy. I suppose the rich just go right on being rich, even in a time like this.'

'They need their fun more than ever now,' Mother said. 'But you were saying . . . '

'Yes, what was I saying? Well, it makes no difference. I mustn't take any more of your time. I'm pleased that Chiyo is quite healthy after all.'

'Very healthy, yes. But, Mameha-san, wait a moment before you leave, if you don't mind. You were saying you'd almost considered taking on Chiyo as your younger sister?'

'Well, by now she's been out of training so long . . .' Mameha said. 'Anyway, I'm sure you have an excellent reason for the decision you've made, Mrs. Nitta. I wouldn't dare second-guess you.'

'It's heartbreaking, the choices people are forced to make in these times. I just couldn't afford her training any longer! However, if you feel she has potential, Mameha-san, I'm sure any investment you might choose to make in her future would be amply repaid.'

Mother was trying to take advantage of Mameha. No geisha ever paid lesson fees for a younger sister.

'I wish such a thing were possible,' Mameha said, 'but with this terrible Depression . . .'

'Perhaps there's some way I could manage it,' Mother said. 'Though Chiyo is a bit headstrong, and her debts are considerable. I've often thought how shocking it would be if she ever managed to repay them.'

'Such an attractive girl? I'd find it shocking if she couldn't.'

'Anyway, there's more to life than money, isn't there?' Mother said. 'One wants to do one's best for a girl like Chiyo. Perhaps I could see my way to investing a bit more in her . . . just for her lessons, you understand. But where would it all lead?'

'I'm sure Chiyo's debts are very considerable,' Mameha said. 'But even so, I should think she'll repay them by the time she's twenty.'

'Twenty!' said Mother. 'I don't think any girl in Gion has ever done such a thing. And in the midst of this Depression . . .'

'Yes, there is the Depression, it's true.'

'It certainly seems to me our Pumpkin is a safer investment,' Mother said. 'After all, in Chiyo's case, with you as her older sister, her debts will only grow worse before they get better.'

Mother wasn't just talking about my lesson fees; she was talking about fees she would have to pay to Mameha. A geisha of Mameha's standing commonly takes a larger portion of her younger sister's earnings than an ordinary geisha would.

'Mameha-san, if you have a moment longer,' Mother went on, 'I wonder if you would entertain a proposal. If the great Mameha says Chiyo will repay her debts by the age of twenty, how can I doubt it's true? Of course, a girl like Chiyo won't succeed without an older sister such as yourself, and yet our little okiya is stretched to its limits just now. I can't possibly offer you the terms you're accustomed to. The best I could offer from Chiyo's future earnings might be only half what you'd ordinarily expect.'

'Just now I'm entertaining several very generous offers,' Mameha said. 'If I'm going to take on a younger sister, I couldn't possibly afford to do it at a reduced fee.'

'I'm not quite finished, Mameha-san,' Mother replied.

'Here's my proposal. It's true I can afford only half what you might usually expect. But if Chiyo does indeed manage to repay her debts by the age of twenty, as you anticipate, I would turn over to you the remainder of what you ought to have made, plus an additional thirty percent. You would make more money in the long run.'

'And if Chiyo turns twenty without having repaid her debts?' Mameha asked.

'I'm sorry to say that in such a case, the investment would have been a poor one for both of us. The okiya would be unable to pay the fees owed to you.'

There was a silence, and then Mameha sighed.

'I'm very poor with numbers, Mrs. Nitta. But if I understand correctly, you'd like me to take on a task you think may be impossible, for fees that are less than usual. Plenty of promising young girls in Gion would make fine younger sisters to me at no risk whatever. I'm afraid I must decline your proposal.'

'You're quite right,' said Mother. 'Thirty percent is a bit low. I'll offer you double, instead, if you succeed.'

'But nothing if I fail.'

'Please don't think of it as nothing. A portion of Chiyo's fees would have gone to you all along. It's simply that the okiya would be unable to pay you the additional amount you would be owed.'

I felt certain Mameha was going to say no. Instead she said, 'I'd like to find out first how substantial Chiyo's debt really is.'

'I'll fetch the account books for you,' Mother told her.

I heard nothing more of their conversation, for at this point Auntie ran out of patience for my eavesdropping, and sent me out of the okiya with a list of errands. All that afternoon, I felt as agitated as a pile of rocks in an earthquake; because, of course, I had no idea how things would turn out. If Mother and Mameha couldn't come to an agreement, I would remain a maid all my life just as surely as a turtle remains a turtle.

When I returned to the okiya, Pumpkin was kneeling on the walkway near the courtyard, making terrible twanging noises with her shamisen. She looked very pleased when she caught sight of me, and called me over.

'Find some excuse to go into Mother's room,' she said. 'She's been in there all afternoon with her abacus. I'm sure she'll say something to you. Then you have to run back down here and tell me!'

I thought this was a fine idea. One of my errands had been to buy some cream for the cook's scabies, but the pharmacy had been out of it. So I decided to go upstairs and apologize to Mother for having come back to the okiya without it. She wouldn't care, of course; probably she didn't even know I'd been sent to fetch it. But at least it would get me into her room.

As it turned out, Mother was listening to a comedy show on the radio. Normally if I disturbed her at a time like this, she would wave me in and go right on listening to the radio – looking over her account books and puffing at her pipe. But today, to my surprise, she turned off the radio and slapped the account book shut the moment she saw me. I bowed to her and went to kneel at the table.

'While Mameha was here,' she said, 'I noticed you in the formal entrance hall polishing the floor. Were you trying to overhear our conversation?'

'No, ma'am. There was a scratch on the floorboards. Pumpkin and I were doing what we could to buff it out.'

'I only hope you turn out to be a better geisha than you are a liar,' she said, and began to laugh, but without taking her pipe out of her mouth, so that she accidentally blew air into the stem and caused ashes to shoot up out of the little metal bowl. Some of the flecks of tobacco were still burning when they came down onto her kimono. She put the pipe down onto the table and whacked herself with her palm until she was satisfied they'd all been snuffed out.

'Now, Chiyo, you've been here in the okiya more than a year,' she said.

'More than two years, ma'am.'

'In that time I've hardly taken any notice of you. And then today, along comes a geisha like Mameha, to say she wants to be your older sister! How on earth am I to understand this?'

As I saw it, Mameha was actually more interested in harming Hatsumomo than in helping me. But I certainly couldn't say such a thing to Mother. I was about to tell her I had no idea why Mameha had taken an interest in me; but before I could speak, the door to Mother's room slid open, and I heard Hatsumomo's voice say:

'I'm sorry, Mother, I didn't know you were busy scolding the maid!'

'She won't be a maid much longer,' Mother told her. 'We've had a visit today that may interest you.'

'Yes, I gather Mameha has come and plucked our little minnow out of the aquarium,' Hatsumomo said. She drifted over and knelt at the table, so close that I had to scoot away to make room for both of us.

'For some reason,' Mother said, 'Mameha seems to think Chiyo will repay her debts by the age of twenty.'

Hatsumomo's face was turned toward mine. To see her smile, you might have thought she was a mother looking adoringly at a baby. But this is what she said:

'Perhaps, Mother, if you sold her to a whorehouse . . .'

'Stop it, Hatsumomo. I didn't invite you in here to listen to this sort of thing. I want to know what you've done to Mameha lately to provoke her.'

'I may have ruined Miss Prissy's day by strolling past her on the street, perhaps, but other than that I haven't done a thing.'

'She has something in mind. I'd like to know what it is.'

'There's no mystery at all, Mother. She thinks she can get at me by going through Little Miss Stupid.'

Mother didn't respond; she seemed to be considering what Hatsumomo had told her. 'Perhaps,' she said at last, 'she really docs think Chiyo will be a more successful geisha than our Pumpkin and would like to make a bit of money off her. Who can blame her for that?'

'Really, Mother . . . Mameha doesn't need Chiyo in order to make money. Do you think it's an accident she's chosen to waste her time on a girl who happens to live in the same okiya I do? Mameha would probably establish a relationship with your little dog if she thought it would help drive me out of Gion.'

'Come now, Hatsumomo. Why would she want to drive you out of Gion?'

'Because I'm more beautiful. Does she need a better reason? She wants to humiliate me by telling everyone, "Oh, please meet my new younger sister. She lives in the same okiya as Hatsumomo, but she's such a jewel they've entrusted her to *me* for training instead."'

'I can't imagine Mameha behaving that way,' Mother said, almost under her breath.

'If she thinks she can make Chiyo into a more successful geisha than Pumpkin,' Hatsumomo went on, 'she's going to be very surprised. But I'm delighted that Chiyo will be dressed up in a kimono and paraded around. It's a perfect opportunity for Pumpkin. Haven't you ever seen a kitten attacking a ball of string? Pumpkin will be a much better geisha after she's sharpened her teeth on this one.'

Mother seemed to like this, for she raised the edges of her mouth in a sort of smile.

'I had no idea what a fine day this would be,' she said. 'This morning when I woke up, two useless girls were living in the okiya. Now they'll be fighting it out . . . and with a couple of the most prominent geisha in Gion ushering them along!'

12

THE VERY NEXT afternoon Mameha summoned me to her apartment. This time she was seated at the table waiting for me when the maid slid open the door. I was careful to bow properly before coming into the room and then to cross to the table and bow again.

'Mameha-san, I don't know what has led you to this decision . . . ' I began, 'but I can't express how grateful I am –'

'Don't be grateful just yet,' she interrupted. 'Nothing has happened. You'd better tell me what Mrs. Nitta said to you after my visit yesterday.'

'Well,' I said, 'I think Mother was a little confused about why you've taken notice of me . . . and to tell the truth, so am I.' I hoped Mameha would say something, but she didn't. 'As for Hatsumomo –'

'Don't even waste your time thinking about what she says. You already know she'd be thrilled to see you fail, just as Mrs. Nitta would.'

'I don't understand why Mother should want me to fail,' I said, 'considering she'll make more money if I succeed.'

'Except that if you pay back your debts by the age of twenty, she'll owe me a good deal of money. I made a sort of bet with her yesterday,' Mameha said, while a maid served us tea. 'I wouldn't have made the bet unless I felt certain you would succeed. But if I'm going to be your older sister, you may as well know that I have very strict terms.'

I expected her to tell them to me, but she only glowered and said:

'Really, Chiyo, you must stop blowing on your tea that

way. You look like a peasant! Leave it on the table until it's cool enough to drink.'

'I'm sorry,' I said. 'I wasn't aware I was doing it.'

'It's time you were; a geisha must be very careful about the image she presents to the world. Now, as I say, I have very strict terms. To begin with, I expect you to do what I ask without questioning me or doubting me in any way. I know you've disobeyed Hatsumomo and Mrs. Nitta from time to time. You may think that's understandable; but if you ask me, you should have been more obedient in the first place and perhaps none of these unfortunate things would ever have happened to you.'

Mameha was quite right. The world has changed a good deal since; but when I was a child, a girl who disobeyed her elders was soon put in her place.

'Several years ago I took on two new younger sisters,' Mameha continued. 'One worked very hard, but the other slacked off. I brought her here to my apartment one day and explained that I wouldn't tolerate her making a fool of me any longer, but it had no effect. The following month I told her to go and find herself a new older sister.'

'Mameha-san, I promise you, such a thing will never happen with me,' I said. 'Thanks to you, I feel like a ship encountering its first taste of the ocean. I would never forgive myself for disappointing you.'

'Yes, well, that's all fine, but I'm not just talking about how hard you work. You'll have to be careful not to let Hatsumomo trick you. And for heaven's sake, don't do anything to make your debts worse than they are. Don't break even a teacup!'

I promised her I wouldn't; but I must confess that when I thought of Hatsumomo tricking me again . . . well, I wasn't sure how I could defend myself if she tried.

'There's one more thing,' Mameha said. 'Whatever you and I discuss must be kept private. You are never to tell any of it to Hatsumomo. Even if we've only talked about the weather, do you understand? If Hatsumomo asks what I said, you must tell her, "Oh, Hatsumomo-san, Mameha-san never says anything of interest! As soon as I've heard it, it slips right out of my mind. She's the dullest person alive!"'

I told Mameha I understood.

'Hatsumomo is quite clever,' she went on. 'If you give her the slightest hint, you'll be surprised how much she'll figure out on her own.'

Suddenly, Mameha leaned toward me and said in an angry voice, 'What were you two talking about yesterday when I saw you on the street together?'

'Nothing, ma'am!' I said. And though she went on glaring at me, I was so shocked I couldn't say anything further.

'What do you mean, nothing? You'd better answer me, you stupid little girl, or I'll pour ink in your ear tonight while you're sleeping!'

It took me a moment to understand that Mameha was trying to do an imitation of Hatsumomo. I'm afraid it wasn't a very good imitation, but now that I understood what she was doing, I said, 'Honestly, Hatsumomo-san, Mameha-san is always saying the dullest things! I can never remember a single one of them. They just melt away like snowflakes. Are you quite sure you saw us talking yesterday? Because if we talked at all, I can hardly remember it . . . .'

Mameha went on for a time, doing her poor imitation of Hatsumomo, and at the end said I had done an adequate job. I wasn't as confident as she was. Being questioned by Mameha, even when she was trying to act like Hatsumomo, wasn't the same thing as keeping up a facade in front of Hatsumomo herself.

In the two years since Mother had put an end to my lessons, I'd forgotten much of what I'd learned. And I hadn't learned much to begin with, since my mind had been occupied with other things. This is why, when I went back to the school after Mameha agreed to be my older sister, I honestly felt I was beginning my lessons for the very first time.

I was twelve years old by then, and nearly as tall as Mameha. Having grown older may seem like an advantage, but I can assure you it wasn't. Most of the girls at the school had begun their studies much younger, in some cases at the traditional age of three years and three days. Those few who'd started as young as this were mostly the daughters of geisha themselves, and had been raised in such a way that dance and tea ceremony formed as much a part of their daily life as swimming in the pond had for me.

I know I've described something of what it was like to study shamisen with Teacher Mouse. But a geisha must study a great many arts besides shamisen. And in fact, the 'gei' of 'geisha' means 'arts,' so the word 'geisha' really means 'artisan' or 'artist.' My first lesson in the morning was in a kind of small drum we call *tsutsumi*. You may wonder why a geisha should bother learning drums, but the answer is very simple. In a banquet or any sort of informal gathering in Gion, geisha usually dance to nothing more than the accompaniment of a shamisen and perhaps a singer. But for stage performances, such as *Dances of the Old Capital* every spring, six or more shamisen players join together as an ensemble, backed by various types of drums and also a Japanese flute we call *fue*. So you see, a geisha must try her hand at all of these instruments, even though eventually she'll be encouraged to specialize in one or two.

As I say, my early-morning lesson was in the little drum we call *tsutsumi*, which is played in a kneeling position like all the other musical instruments we studied. *Tsutsumi* is different from the other drums because it's held on the shoulder and played with the hand, unlike the larger *okawa*, which rests on the thigh, or the largest drum of all, called *taiko*, which sits edgewise on a stand and is struck with fat drumsticks. I studied them all at one time or other. A drum may seem like an instrument even a child can play, but actually there are various ways of striking each of them, such as – for the big *taiko* – bringing the arm across the body and then swinging the drumstick backhand, you might say, which we call *uchikomi*; or striking with one arm while bringing the other up at the same moment, which we call *sarashi*. There are other methods as well, and each produces a different sound, but only after a great deal of practice. On top of this, the orchestra is always in view of the public, so all these movements must be graceful and attractive, as well as being in unison with the other players. Half the work is in making the right sound; the other half is in doing it the proper way.

Following drums, my next lesson of the morning was in Japanese flute, and after that in shamisen. The method in studying any of these instruments was more or less the same. The teacher began by playing something, and then the students tried to play it back. On occasion we sounded like a band of animals at the zoo, but not often, because the teachers were careful to begin simply. For example, in my first lesson on the flute, the teacher played a single note and we tried one at a time to play it back. Even after only one note, the teacher still found plenty to say.

'So-and-so, you must keep your little finger down, not up in the air. And you, Such-and-such, does your flute smell bad? Well then, why do you wrinkle your nose that way!'

She was very strict, like most of the teachers, and naturally we were afraid of making mistakes. It wasn't uncommon for her to take the flute from some poor girl in order to hit her on the shoulder with it.

After drums, flute, and shamisen, my next lesson was usually in singing. We often sing at parties in Japan; and of course, parties are mostly what men come to Gion for. But even if a girl can't hold a tune and will never be asked to perform in front of others, she must still study singing to help her understand dance. This is because the dances are set to particular pieces of music, often performed by a singer accompanying herself on the shamisen.

There are many different types of songs – oh, far more than I could possibly count – but in our lessons we studied five different kinds. Some were popular ballads; some were long pieces from Kabuki theater telling a story; others were something like a short musical poem. It would be senseless for me to try describing these songs. But let me say that while I find most of them enchanting, foreigners often seem to think they sound more like cats wailing in a temple yard than music. It is true that traditional Japanese singing involves a good deal of warbling and is often sung so far back in the throat that the sound comes out from the nose rather than the mouth. But it's only a matter of what you're accustomed to hearing.

In all of these classes, music and dance were only part of

what we learned. Because a girl who has mastered the various arts will still come off badly at a party if she hasn't learned proper comportment and behavior. This is one reason the teachers always insist upon good manners and bearing in their students, even when a girl is only scurrying down the hall toward the toilet. When you're taking a lesson in shamisen, for example, you'll be corrected for speaking in anything but the most proper language, or for speaking in a regional accent rather than in Kyoto speech, or for slouching, or walking in lumbering steps. In fact, the most severe scolding a girl is likely to receive probably won't be for playing her instrument badly or failing to learn the words to a song, but rather for having dirty fingernails, or being disrespectful, or something of that sort.

Sometimes when I've talked with foreigners about my training, they've asked, 'Well, when did you study flower arranging?' The answer is that I never did. Anyone who sits down in front of a man and begins to arrange flowers by way of entertaining him is likely to look up and find that he has laid his head down on the table to go to sleep. You must remember that a geisha, above all, is an entertainer and a performer. We may pour sake or tea for a man, but we never go and fetch another serving of pickles. And in fact, we geisha are so well pampered by our maids that we scarcely know how to look after ourselves or keep our own rooms orderly, much less adorn a room in a teahouse with flowers.

My last lesson of the morning was in tea ceremony. This is a subject many books are written about, so I won't try to go into much detail. But basically, a tea ceremony is conducted by one or two people who sit before their guests and prepare tea in a very traditional manner, using beautiful cups, and whisks made from bamboo, and so forth. Even the guests are a part of the ceremony because they must hold the cup in a certain manner and drink from it just so. If you think of it as sitting down to have a nice cup of tea . . . well, it's more like a sort of dance, or even a meditation, conducted while kneeling. The tea itself is made from tea leaves ground into a powder and then whisked with boiled water into a frothy green mix we call *matcha*, which is very unpopular with foreigners. I'll admit it does look like green soapy water and has a bitter taste that takes a certain getting used to.

Tea ceremony is a very important part of a geisha's training. It isn't unusual for a party at a private residence to begin with a brief tea ceremony. And the guests who come to see the seasonal dances in Gion are first served tea made by geisha.

My tea ceremony teacher was a young woman of perhaps twenty-five who wasn't a very good geisha, as I later learned; but she was so obsessed with tea ceremony that she taught it as if every movement was absolutely holy. Because of her enthusiasm I quickly learned to respect her teaching, and I must say it was the perfect lesson to have at the end of a long morning. The atmosphere was so serene. Even now, I find tea ceremony as enjoyable as a good night's sleep.

What makes a geisha's training so difficult isn't simply the arts she must learn, but how hectic her life becomes. After spending all morning in lessons, she is still expected to work during the afternoon and evening very much as she always has. And still, she sleeps no more than three to five hours every night. During these years of training, if I'd been two people my life would probably still have been too busy. I would have been grateful if Mother had freed me from my chores as she had Pumpkin; but considering her bet with Mameha, I don't think she ever considered offering me more time for practice. Some of my chores were given to the maids, but most days I was responsible for more than I could manage, while still being expected to practice shamisen for an hour or more during the afternoon. In winter, both Pumpkin and I were made to toughen up our hands by holding them in ice water until we cried from pain, and then practice outside in the frigid air of the courtyard. I know it sounds terribly cruel, but it's the way things were done back then. And in fact, toughening the hands in this way really did help me play better. You see, stage fright drains the feeling from your hands; and when you've already grown accustomed to playing with hands that are numbed and miserable, stage fright presents much less of a problem.

In the beginning Pumpkin and I practiced shamisen

together every afternoon, right after our hour-long lesson in reading and writing with Auntie. We'd studied Japanese with her ever since my arrival, and Auntie always insisted on good behavior. But while practicing shamisen during the afternoon, Pumpkin and I had great fun together. If we laughed out loud Auntie or one of the maids would come scold us; but as long as we made very little noise and plunked away at our shamisens while we talked, we could get away with spending the hour enjoying each other's company. It was the time of day I looked forward to most.

Then one afternoon while Pumpkin was helping me with a technique for slurring notes together, Hatsumomo appeared in the corridor before us. We hadn't even heard her come into the okiya.

'Why, look, it's Mameha's little-sister-to-be!' she said to me. She added the 'to-be' because Mameha and I wouldn't officially be sisters until the time of my debut as an apprentice geisha.

'I might have called you "Little Miss Stupid,"' she went on, 'but after what I've just observed, I think I ought to save that for Pumpkin instead.'

Poor Pumpkin lowered her shamisen into her lap just like a dog putting its tail between its legs. 'Have I done something wrong?' she asked.

I didn't have to look directly at Hatsumomo to see the anger blooming on her face. I was terribly afraid of what would happen next.

'Nothing at all!' Hatsumomo said. 'I just didn't realize what a thoughtful person you are.'

'I'm sorry, Hatsumomo,' Pumpkin said. 'I was trying to help Chiyo by –'

'But Chiyo doesn't want your help. When she wants help with her shamisen, she'll go to her teacher. Is that head of yours just a big, hollow gourd?'

And here Hatsumomo pinched Pumpkin by the lip so hard that the shamisen slid off her lap onto the wooden walkway where she was seated, and fell from there onto the dirt corridor below.

'You and I need to have a little talk,' Hatsumomo said to

her. 'You'll put your shamisen away, and I'll stand here to make sure you don't do anything else stupid.'

When Hatsumomo let go, poor Pumpkin stepped down to pick up her shamisen and begin disassembling it. She gave me a pitiful glance, and I thought she might calm down. But in fact her lip began to quiver; then her whole face trembled like the ground before an earthquake; and suddenly she dropped the pieces of her shamisen onto the walkway and put her hand to her lip – which had already begun to swell – while tears rolled down her cheeks. Hatsumomo's face softened as if the angry sky had broken, and she turned to me with a satisfied smile.

'You'll have to find yourself another little friend,' she said to me. 'After Pumpkin and I have had our talk, she'll know better than to speak a word to you in the future. Won't you, Pumpkin?'

Pumpkin nodded, for she had no choice; but I could see how sorry she felt. We never practiced shamisen together again.

I reported this encounter to Mameha the next time I visited her apartment.

'I hope you took to heart what Hatsumomo said to you,' she told me. 'If Pumpkin isn't to speak a word to you, then you mustn't speak a word to her either. You'll only get her into trouble; and besides, she'll have to tell Hatsumomo what you say. You may have trusted the poor girl in the past, but you mustn't any longer.'

I felt so sad at hearing this, I could hardly speak for a long while. 'Trying to survive in an okiya with Hatsumomo,' I said at last, 'is like a pig trying to survive in a slaughterhouse.'

I was thinking of Pumpkin when I said this, but Mameha must have thought I meant myself. 'You're quite right,' she said. 'Your only defense is to become more successful than Hatsumomo and drive her out.'

'But everyone says she's one of the most popular geisha. I can't imagine how I'll ever become more popular than she is.'

'I didn't say popular,' Mameha replied. 'I said successful. Going to a lot of parties isn't everything. I live in a spacious apartment with two maids of my own, while Hatsumomo – who probably goes to as many parties as I do – continues to live in the Nitta okiya. When I say successful, I mean a geisha who has earned her independence. Until a geisha has assembled her own collection of kimono – or until she's been adopted as the daughter of an okiya, which is just about the same thing – she'll be in someone else's power all her life. You've seen some of my kimono, haven't you? How do you suppose I came by them?'

'I've been thinking that perhaps you were adopted as the daughter of an okiya before you came to live in this apartment.'

'I did live in an okiya until about five years ago. But the mistress there has a natural daughter. She would never adopt another.'

'So if I might ask . . . did you buy your entire collection of kimono yourself?'

'How much do you think a geisha earns, Chiyo! A complete collection of kimono doesn't mean two or three robes for each of the seasons. Some men's lives revolve around Gion. They'll grow bored if they see you in the same thing night after night.'

I must have looked every bit as puzzled as I felt, for Mameha gave a laugh at the expression on my face.

'Cheer up, Chiyo-chan, there's an answer to this riddle. My *danna* is a generous man and bought me most of these robes. That's why I'm more successful than Hatsumomo. I have a wealthy *danna*. She hasn't had one in years.'

I'd already been in Gion long enough to know something of what Mameha meant by a *danna*. It's the term a wife uses for her husband – or rather, it was in my day. But a geisha who refers to her *danna* isn't talking about a husband. Geisha never marry. Or at least those who do no longer continue as geisha.

You see, sometimes after a party with geisha, certain men don't feel satisfied with all the flirting and begin to long for something a bit more. Some of these men are content to make their way to places like Miyagawa-cho, where they'll add the odor of their own sweat to the unpleasant houses I saw on the night I found my sister. Other men work up their courage to lean in bleary-eyed and whisper to the geisha beside them a question about what her 'fees' might be. A lower-class geisha may be perfectly agreeable to such an arrangement; probably she's happy to take whatever income is offered her. A woman like this may call herself a geisha and be listed at the registry office; but I think you should take a look at how she dances, and how well she plays shamisen, and what she knows about tea ceremony before you decide whether or not she really is a proper geisha. A true geisha will never soil her reputation by making herself available to men on a nightly basis.

I won't pretend a geisha never gives in casually to a man she finds attractive. But whether she does or not is her private affair. Geisha have passions like everyone else, and they make the same mistakes. A geisha who takes such a risk can only hope she isn't found out. Her reputation is certainly at stake; but more important, so is her standing with her *danna*, if she has one. What's more, she invites the wrath of the woman who runs her okiya. A geisha determined to follow her passions might take this risk; but she certainly won't do it for spending money she might just as easily earn in some legitimate way.

So you see, a geisha of the first or second tier in Gion can't be bought for a single night, not by anyone. But if the right sort of man is interested in something else – not a night together, but a much longer time – and if he's willing to offer suitable terms, well, in that case a geisha will be happy to accept such an arrangement. Parties and so on are all very nice; but the real money in Gion comes from having a *danna*, and a geisha without one – such as Hatsumomo – is like a stray cat on the street without a master to feed it.

You might expect that in the case of a beautiful woman like Hatsumomo, any number of men would have been eager to propose themselves as her *danna*; and I'm sure there were many who did. She had in fact had a *danna* at one time. But somehow or other she'd so angered the mistress of the Mizuki, which was her principal teahouse, that men who made inquiries forever afterward were told she wasn't available – which they probably took to mean she already had a *danna*, even though it wasn't true. In damaging her relationship with the mistress, Hatsumomo had hurt no one so much as herself. As a very popular geisha, she made enough money to keep Mother happy; but as a geisha without a *danna*, she didn't make enough to gain her independence and move out of the okiya once and for all. Nor could she simply change her registration to another teahouse whose mistress might be more accommodating in helping her find a *danna*; none of the other mistresses would want to damage their relationships with the Mizuki.

Of course, the average geisha isn't trapped in this way. Instead she spends her time charming men in the hopes that one of them will eventually make an inquiry with the mistress of the teahouse about her. Many of these inquiries lead nowhere; the man, when he's investigated, may be found to have too little money; or he may balk when someone suggests he give a gift of an expensive kimono as a gesture of goodwill. But if the weeks of negotiations come to a successful conclusion, the geisha and her new *danna* conduct a ceremony just like when two geisha become sisters. In most cases this bond will probably last six months or so, perhaps longer – because of course, men tire so quickly of the same thing. The terms of the arrangement will probably oblige the *danna* to pay off a portion of the geisha's debts and cover many of her living expenses every month – such as the cost of her makeup and perhaps a portion of her lesson fees, and maybe her medical expenses as well. Things of that sort. Despite all these extravagant expenses, he'll still continue to pay her usual hourly fee whenever he spends time with her, just as her other customers do. But he's also entitled to certain 'privileges.'

These would be the arrangements for an average geisha. But a very top geisha, of which there were probably thirty or forty in Gion, would expect much more. To begin with, she wouldn't even consider tarnishing her reputation with a string of *danna*, but might instead have only one or two in her entire life. Not only will her *danna* cover all of her living expenses, such as her registration fee, her lesson fees, and her meals; what's more, he'll provide her with spending money, sponsor dance recitals for her, and buy her gifts of kimono and jewelry. And when he spends time with her, he won't pay her usual hourly fee; he'll probably pay more, as a gesture of goodwill.

Mameha was certainly one of these top geisha; in fact, as I came to learn, she was probably one of the two or three best-known geisha in all of Japan. You may have heard something about the famous geisha Mametsuki, who had an affair with the prime minister of Japan shortly before World War I and caused something of a scandal. She was Mameha's older sister – which is why they both had 'Mame' in their names. It's common for a young geisha to derive her name from the name of her older sister.

Having an older sister like Mametsuki was already enough to ensure Mameha a successful career. But in the early 1920s, the Japan Travel Bureau began its first international advertising campaign. The posters showed a lovely photograph of the pagoda from the Toji Temple in southeastern Kyoto, with a cherry tree to one side and a lovely young apprentice geisha on the other side looking very shy and graceful, and exquisitely delicate. That apprentice geisha was Mameha.

It would be an understatement to say that Mameha became famous. The poster was displayed in big cities all over the world, with the words 'Come and Visit the Land of the Rising Sun' in all sorts of foreign languages – not only English, but German, French, Russian, and . . . oh, other languages I've never even heard of. Mameha was only sixteen at the time, but suddenly she found herself being summoned to meet every head of state who came to Japan, and every aristocrat from England or Germany, and every millionaire from the United States. She poured sake for the great German writer Thomas Mann, who afterward told her a long, dull story through an interpreter that went on and on for nearly an hour; as well as Charlie Chaplin, and Sun Yat-sen, and later Ernest Hemingway, who got very drunk and said the beautiful red lips on her white face made him think of blood in the snow. In the years since then, Mameha had grown only more famous by putting on a number of widely publicized dance recitals at the Kabukiza Theater in Tokyo, usually attended by the prime minister and a great many other luminaries.

When Mameha had announced her intention of taking me on as her younger sister, I hadn't known any of these things about her, and it's just as well. Probably I would have felt so intimidated, I couldn't have done much more than tremble in her presence.

Mameha was kind enough to sit me down and explain much of this on that day in her apartment. When she was satisfied that I understood her, she said:

'Following your debut, you'll be an apprentice geisha until the age of eighteen. After that you'll need a *danna* if you're to pay back your debts. A very substantial *danna*. My job will be to make sure you're well known in Gion by then, but it's up to you to work hard at becoming an accomplished dancer. If you can't make it at least to the fifth rank by the age of sixteen, nothing I can do will help you, and Mrs. Nitta will be delighted to win her bet with me.'

'But, Mameha-san,' I said, 'I don't understand what dance has to do with it.'

'Dance has everything to do with it,' she told me. 'If you look around at the most successful geisha in Gion, every one of them is a dancer.'

Dance is the most revered of the geisha's arts. Only the most promising and beautiful geisha are encouraged to specialize in it, and nothing except perhaps tea ceremony can compare to the richness of its tradition. The Inoue School of dance, practiced by the geisha of Gion, derives from Noh theater. Because Noh is a very ancient art that has always been patronized by the Imperial court, dancers in Gion consider their art superior to the school of dance practiced in the Pontocho district across the river, which derives from Kabuki. Now, I'm a great admirer of Kabuki, and in fact I've been lucky enough to have as my friends a number of the most famous Kabuki actors of this century. But Kabuki is a relatively young art form; it didn't exist before the 1700s. And it has always been enjoyed by ordinary people rather than patronized by the Imperial court. There is simply no comparing the dance in Pontocho to the Inoue School of Gion.

All apprentice geisha must study dance, but, as I say, only the promising and attractive ones will be encouraged to specialize and go on to become true dancers, rather than shamisen players or singers. Unfortunately, the reason Pumpkin, with her soft, round face, spent so much of her time practicing shamisen was because she hadn't been selected as a dancer. As for me, I wasn't so exquisitely beautiful that I was given no choice but to dance, like Hatsumomo. It seemed to me I would become a dancer only by demonstrating to my teachers that I was willing to work as hard as necessary.

Thanks to Hatsumomo, however, my lessons got off to a very bad start. My instructor was a woman of about fifty, known to us as Teacher Rump, because her skin gathered at her throat in such a way as to make a little rear end there beneath her chin. Teacher Rump hated Hatsumomo as much as anyone in Gion did. Hatsumomo knew this quite well; and so what do you think she did? She went to her – I know this because Teacher Rump told it to me some years later – and said:

'Teacher, may I be permitted to ask you a favor? I have my eye on one of the students in your class, who seems to me a very talented girl. I'd be extremely grateful if you could tell me what you think of her. Her name is Chiyo, and I'm very, very fond of her. I'd be greatly in your debt for any special help you might give her.'

Hatsumomo never needed to say another word after this, because Teacher Rump gave me all the 'special help' Hatsumomo hoped she would. My dancing wasn't bad, really, but Teacher Rump began at once to use me as an example of how things should not be done. For example, I remember one morning when she demonstrated a move to us by drawing her arm across her body just so and then stamping one foot on the mats. We were all expected to copy this move in unison; but because we were beginners, when we finished and stamped our feet, it sounded as if a platter stacked with beanbags had been spilled onto the floor, for not a single foot hit the mats at the same moment as any other. I can assure you I'd done no worse at this than anyone else, but Teacher Rump came and stood before me with that little rear end under her chin quivering, and tapped her folding fan against her thigh a few times before drawing it back and striking me on the side of the head with it.

'We don't stamp at just any old moment,' she said. 'And we don't twitch our chins.'

In dances of the Inoue School, the face must be kept perfectly expressionless in imitation of the masks worn in Noh theater. But for her to complain about my chin twitching at the very moment when her own was trembling in anger . . . well, I was on the edge of tears because she'd struck me, but the other students burst out laughing. Teacher Rump blamed me for the outburst, and sent me out of the classroom in punishment.

I can't say what might have become of me under her care, if Mameha hadn't finally gone to have a talk with her and helped her to figure out what had really happened. However much Teacher Rump might have hated Hatsumomo beforehand, I'm sure she hated her all the more after learning how Hatsumomo had duped her. I'm happy to say she felt so terrible about the way she had treated me that I soon became one of her favorite students.

I won't say I had any natural talent of any kind at all, in dance or in anything else; but I was certainly as determined as anyone to work singlemindedly until I reached my goal. Since meeting the Chairman on the street that day back in the spring, I had longed for nothing so much as the chance to become a geisha and find a place for myself in the world. Now that Mameha had given me that chance, I was intent on making good. But with all my lessons and chores, and with my high expectations, I felt completely overwhelmed in my first six months of training. Then after that, I began to discover little tricks that made everything go more smoothly. For example, I found a way of practicing the shamisen while running errands. I did this by practicing a song in my mind while picturing clearly how my left hand should shift on the neck and how the plectrum should strike the string. In this way, when I put the real instrument into my lap, I could sometimes play a song quite well even though I had tried playing it only once before. Some people thought I'd learned it without practicing, but in fact, I'd practiced it all up and down the alleyways of Gion.

I used a different trick to learn the ballads and other songs we studied at the school. Since childhood I've always been able to hear a piece of music once and remember it fairly well the next day. I don't know why, just something peculiar about my mind, I suppose. So I took to writing the words on a piece of paper before going to sleep. Then when I awoke, while my mind was still soft and impressionable, I read the page before even stirring from my futon. Usually this was enough, but with music that was more difficult, I used a trick of finding images to remind me of the tune. For example, a branch falling from a tree might make me think of the sound of a drum, or a stream flowing over a rock might remind me of bending a string on the shamisen to make the note rise in pitch; and I would picture the song as a kind of stroll through a landscape.

But of course, the greatest challenge of all, and the most important one for me, was dance. For months I tried to make use of the various tricks I'd discovered, but they were of little help to me. Then one day Auntie grew furious when I spilled tea onto a magazine she was reading. The strange thing was that I'd been thinking kind thoughts toward her at the very moment she turned on me. I felt terribly sad afterward and found myself thinking of my sister, who was somewhere in Japan without me; and of my mother, who I hoped was at peace in paradise now; and of my father, who'd been so willing to sell us and live out the end of his life alone. As these thoughts ran through my head, my body began to grow heavy. So I climbed the stairs and went into the room where Pumpkin and I slept – for Mother had moved me there after Mameha's visit to our okiya. Instead of laying myself down on the tatami mats and crying, I moved my arm in a sort of sweeping movement across my chest. I don't know why I did it; it was a move from a dance we'd studied that morning, which seemed to me very sad. At the same time I thought about the Chairman and how my life would be so much better if I could rely on a man like him. As I watched my arm sweep through the air, the smoothness of its movement seemed to express these feelings of sadness and desire. My arm passed through the air with great dignity of movement – not like a leaf fluttering from a tree, but like an ocean liner gliding through the water. I suppose that by 'dignity' I mean a kind of self-confidence, or certainty, such that a little puff of wind or the lap of a wave isn't going to make any difference.

What I discovered that afternoon was that when my body felt heavy, I could move with great dignity. And if I imagined the Chairman observing me, my movements took on such a deep sense of feeling that sometimes each movement of a dance stood for some little interaction with him. Turning around with my head tipped at an angle might represent the question, 'Where shall we spend our day together, Chairman?' Extending my arm and opening my folding fan told how grateful I felt that he'd honored me with his company. And when I snapped my fan shut again later in the dance, this was when I told him that nothing in life mattered more to me than pleasing him.

13

DURING THE SPRING of 1934, after I'd been in training for more than two years, Hatsumomo and Mother decided that the time had come for Pumpkin to make her debut as an apprentice geisha. Of course, no one told me anything about it, since Pumpkin was on orders not to speak with me, and Hatsumomo and Mother wouldn't waste their time even considering such a thing. I found out about it only when Pumpkin left the okiya early one afternoon and came back at the end of the day wearing the hairstyle of a young geisha – the so-called *momoware*, meaning 'split peach.' When I took my first look at her as she stepped up into the entrance hall, I felt sick with disappointment and jealousy. Her eyes never met mine for more than a flicker of an instant; probably she couldn't help thinking of the effect her debut was having on me. With her hair swept back in an orb so beautifully from her temples, rather than tied at the neck as it had always been, she looked very much like a young woman, though still with her same babyish face. For years she and I had envied the older girls who wore their hair so elegantly. Now Pumpkin would be setting out as a geisha while I remained behind, unable even to ask about her new life.

Then came the day Pumpkin dressed as an apprentice geisha for the first time and went with Hatsumomo to the Mizuki Teahouse, for the ceremony to bind them together as sisters. Mother and Auntie went, though I wasn't included. But I did stand among them in the formal entrance hall until Pumpkin came down the stairs assisted by the maids. She wore a magnificent black kimono with the crest of the Nitta okiya and a plum and gold obi; her face was painted white for the very first time. You might expect that with the ornaments in her hair and the brilliant red of her lips, she should have looked proud and lovely; but I thought she looked more worried than anything else. She had great difficulty walking; the regalia of an apprentice geisha is so cumbersome. Mother put a camera into Auntie's hands and told her to go outside and photograph Pumpkin having a flint sparked on her back for good luck the very first time. The rest of us remained crowded inside the entrance hall, out of view. The maids held Pumpkin's arms while she slipped her feet into the tall wooden shoes we call *okobo*, which an apprentice geisha always wears. Then Mother went to stand behind Pumpkin and struck a pose as though she were about to spark a flint, even though, in reality, it was always Auntie or one of the maids who did the job. When at last the photograph was taken, Pumpkin stumbled a few steps from the door and turned to look back. The others were on their way out to join her, but I was the one she looked at, with an expression that seemed to say she was very sorry for the way things had turned out.

By the end of that day, Pumpkin was officially known by her new geisha name of Hatsumiyo. The 'Hatsu' came from Hatsumomo, and even though it ought to have helped Pumpkin to have a name derived from a geisha as well known as Hatsumomo, in the end it didn't work that way. Very few people ever knew her geisha name, you see; they just called her Pumpkin as we always had.

I was very eager to tell Mameha about Pumpkin's debut. But she'd been much busier than usual lately, traveling frequently to Tokyo at the request of her *danna*, with the result that we hadn't set eyes on each other in nearly six months. Another few weeks passed before she finally had time to summon me to her apartment. When I stepped inside, the maid let out a gasp; and then a moment later Mameha came walking out of the back room and let out a gasp as well. I couldn't think what was the matter. And then when I got on my knees to bow to Mameha and tell her how honored I was to see her again, she paid me no attention at all.

'My goodness, has it been so long, Tatsumi?' she said to her maid. 'I hardly recognize her.'

'I'm glad to hear you say it, ma'am,' Tatsumi replied. 'I thought something had gone wrong with my eyes!'

I certainly wondered at the time what they were talking about. But evidently in the six months since I'd last seen them, I'd changed more than I realized. Mameha told me to turn my head this way and that, and kept saying over and over, 'My goodness, she's turned into quite a young woman!' At one point Tatsumi even made me stand and hold my arms out so she could measure my waist and hips with her hands, and then said to me, 'Well, there's no doubt a kimono will fit your body just like a sock fits a foot.' I'm sure she meant this as a compliment, for she had a kindly look on her face when she said it.

Finally Mameha asked Tatsumi to take me into the back room and put me into a proper kimono. I'd arrived in the blue and white cotton robe I'd worn that morning to my lessons at the school, but Tatsumi changed me into a dark blue silk covered with a design of tiny carriage wheels in shades of brilliant yellow and red. It wasn't the most beautiful kimono you would ever see, but when I looked at myself in the full-length mirror as Tatsumi was tying a bright green obi into place around my waist, I found that except for my plain hairstyle, I might have been taken for a young apprentice geisha on her way to a party. I felt quite proud when I walked out of the room, and thought Mameha would gasp again, or something of the sort. But she only rose to her feet, tucked a handkerchief into her sleeve, and went directly to the door, where she slipped her feet into a green pair of lacquered zori and looked back over her shoulder at me.

'Well?' she said. 'Aren't you coming?'

I had no idea where we were going, but I was thrilled at the thought of being seen on the street with Mameha. The maid had put out a pair of lacquered zori for me, in a soft gray. I put them on and followed Mameha down the dark tunnel of the stairwell. As we stepped out onto the street, an elderly woman slowed to bow to Mameha and then, in almost the same movement, turned to bow to me. I scarcely knew what to think of this, for hardly anyone ever took notice of me on the street. The bright sunlight had blinded my eyes so much, I couldn't make out whether or not I knew her. But I bowed back, and in a moment she was gone. I thought probably she was one of my teachers, but then an instant later the same thing happened again – this time with a young geisha I'd often admired, but who had never so much as glanced in my direction before.

We made our way up the street with nearly everyone we passed saying something to Mameha, or at the very least bowing to her, and then afterward giving me a little nod or bow as well. Several times I stopped to bow back, with the result that I fell a step or two behind Mameha. She could see the difficulty I was having, and took me to a quiet alleyway to show me the proper way of walking. My trouble, she explained, was that I hadn't learned to move the upper half of my body independently of the lower half. When I needed to bow to someone, I stopped my feet. 'Slowing the feet is a way of showing respect,' she said. 'The more you slow up, the greater the respect. You might stop altogether to bow to one of your teachers, but for anyone else, don't slow more than you need to, for heaven's sake, or you'll never get anywhere. Go along at a constant pace when you can, taking little steps to keep the bottom of your kimono fluttering. When a woman walks, she should give the impression of waves rippling over a sandbar.'

I practiced walking up and down the alley as Mameha had described, looking straight toward my feet to see if my kimono fluttered as it should. When Mameha was satisfied, we set out again.

Most of our greetings, I found, fell into one of two simple patterns. Young geisha, as we passed them, usually slowed or even stopped completely and gave Mameha a deep bow, to which Mameha responded with a kind word or two and a little nod; then the young geisha would give me something of a puzzled look and an uncertain bow, which I would return much more deeply – for I was junior to every woman we encountered. When we passed a middle-aged or elderly woman, however, Mameha nearly always bowed first; then the woman returned a respectful bow, but not as deep as Mameha's, and afterward looked me up and down before giving me a little nod. I always responded to these nods with the deepest bows I could manage while keeping my feet in motion.

I told Mameha that afternoon about Pumpkin's debut; and for months afterward I hoped she would say the time had come for my apprenticeship to begin as well. Instead, spring passed and summer too, without her saying anything of the sort. In contrast with the exciting life Pumpkin was now leading, I had only my lessons and my chores, as well as the fifteen or twenty minutes Mameha spent with me during the afternoons several times a week. Sometimes I sat in her apartment while she taught me about something I needed to know; but most often she dressed me in one of her kimono and walked me around Gion while running errands or calling on her fortune-teller or wig maker. Even when it rained and she had no errands to run, we walked under lacquered umbrellas, making our way from store to store to check when the new shipment of perfume would arrive from Italy, or whether a certain kimono repair was finished though it wasn't scheduled to be completed for another week.

At first I thought perhaps Mameha took me with her so that she could teach me things like proper posture – for she was constantly rapping me on the back with her closed folding fan to make me stand straighter – and about how to behave toward people. Mameha seemed to know everyone, and always made a point of smiling or saying something kind, even to the most junior maids, because she understood well that she owed her exalted position to the people who thought highly of her. But then one day as we were walking out of a bookstore, I suddenly realized what she was really doing. She had no particular interest in going to the bookstore, or the wig maker, or the stationer. The errands weren't especially important; and besides, she could have sent one of her maids instead of going herself. She ran these errands only so that people in Gion would see us strolling the streets together. She was delaying my debut to give everyone time to take notice of me.

*

One sunny October afternoon we set out from Mameha's apartment and headed downstream along the banks of the Shirakawa, watching the leaves of the cherry trees flutter down onto the water. A great many other people were out strolling for just the same reason, and, as you would expect, all of them greeted Mameha. In nearly every case, at the same time they greeted Mameha, they greeted me.

'You're getting to be rather well known, don't you think?' she said to me.

'I think most people would greet even a sheep, if it were walking alongside Mameha-san.'

'Especially a sheep,' she said. 'That would be so unusual. But really, I hear a great many people asking about the girl with the lovely gray eyes. They haven't learned your name, but it makes no difference. You won't be called Chiyo much longer anyway.'

'Does Mameha-san mean to say –'

'I mean to say that I've been speaking with Waza-san' – this was the name of her fortune-teller – 'and he has suggested the third day in November as a suitable time for your debut.'

Mameha stopped to watch me as I stood there still as a tree and with my eyes the size of rice crackers. I didn't cry out or clap my hands, but I was so delighted I couldn't speak. Finally I bowed to Mameha and thanked her.

'You're going to make a fine geisha,' she said, 'but you'll make an even better one if you put some thought into the sorts of statements you make with your eyes.'

'I've never been aware of making any statement with them at all,' I said.

'They're the most expressive part of a woman's body, especially in your case. Stand here a moment, and I'll show you.'

Mameha walked around the corner, leaving me alone in the quiet alleyway. A moment later she strolled out and walked right past me with her eyes to one side. I had the impression she felt afraid of what might happen if she looked in my direction.

'Now, if you were a man,' she said, 'what would you think?'

'I'd think you were concentrating so hard on avoiding me that you couldn't think about anything else.'

'Isn't it possible I was just looking at the rainspouts along the base of the houses?'

'Even if you were, I thought you were avoiding looking at me.'

'That's just what I'm saying. A girl with a stunning profile will never *accidentally* give a man the wrong message with it. But men are going to notice your eyes and imagine you're giving messages with them even when you aren't. Now watch me once more.'

Mameha went around the corner again, and this time came back with her eyes to the ground, walking in a particularly dreamy manner. Then as she neared me her eyes rose to meet mine for just an instant, and very quickly looked away. I must say, I felt an electric jolt; if I'd been a man, I would have thought she'd given herself over very briefly to strong feelings she was struggling to hide.

'If I can say things like this with ordinary eyes like mine,' she told me, 'think how much more you can say with yours. It wouldn't surprise me if you were able to make a man faint right here on the street.'

'Mameha-san!' I said. 'If I had the power to make a man faint I'm sure I'd be aware of it by now.'

'I'm quite surprised you aren't. Let's agree, then, that you'll be ready to make your debut as soon as you've stopped a man in his tracks just by flicking your eyes at him.'

I was so eager to make my debut that even if Mameha had challenged me to make a tree fall by looking at it, I'm sure I would have tried. I asked her if she would be kind enough to walk with me while I experimented on a few men, and she was happy to do it. My first encounter was with a man so old that, really, he looked like a kimono full of bones. He was making his way slowly up the street with the help of a cane, and his glasses were smeared so badly with grime that it wouldn't have surprised me if he had walked right into the corner of a building. He didn't notice me at all; so we continued toward Shijo Avenue. Soon I saw two businessmen in Western suits, but I had no better luck with them. I think they recognized

Mameha, or perhaps they simply thought she was prettier than I was, for in any case, they never took their eyes off her.

I was about to give up when I saw a delivery boy of perhaps twenty, carrying a tray stacked with lunch boxes. In those days, a number of the restaurants around Gion made deliveries and sent a boy around during the afternoon to pick up the empty boxes. Usually they were stacked in a crate that was either carried by hand or strapped to a bicycle; I don't know why this young man was using a tray. In any case, he was half a block away, walking toward me. I could see that Mameha was looking right at him, and then she said:

'Make him drop the tray.'

Before I could make up my mind whether she was joking, she turned up a side street and was gone.

I don't think it's possible for a girl of fourteen – or for a woman of any age – to make a young man drop something just by looking at him in a certain way; I suppose such things may happen in movies and books. I would have given up without even trying, if I hadn't noticed two things. First, the young man was already eyeing me as a hungry cat might eye a mouse; and second, most of the streets in Gion didn't have curbs, but this one did, and the delivery boy was walking in the street not far from it. If I could crowd him so that he had to step up onto the sidewalk and stumble over the curb, he might drop the tray. I began by keeping my gaze to the ground in front of me, and then tried to do the very thing Mameha had done to me a few minutes earlier. I let my eyes rise until they met the young man's for an instant, and then I quickly looked away. After a few more steps I did the same thing again. By this time he was watching me so intently that probably he'd forgotten about the tray on his arm, much less the curb at his feet. When we were very close, I changed my course ever so slightly to begin crowding him, so that he wouldn't be able to pass me without stepping over the curb onto the sidewalk, and then I looked him right in the eye. He was trying to move out of my way; and just as I had hoped, his feet tangled themselves on the curb, and he fell to one side scattering the lunch boxes on the sidewalk. Well, I couldn't help laughing! And I'm happy to say that the young man began to laugh too. I helped him pick up his boxes, gave him a little smile before he bowed to me more deeply than any man had ever bowed to me before, and then went on his way.

I met up with Mameha a moment later, who had seen it all.

'I think perhaps you're as ready now as you'll ever need to be,' she said. And with that, she led me across the main avenue to the apartment of Waza-san, her fortune-teller, and set him to work finding auspicious dates for all the various events that would lead up to my debut – such as going to the shrine to announce my intentions to the gods, and having my hair done for the first time, and performing the ceremony that would make sisters of Mameha and me.

I didn't sleep at all that night. What I had wanted for so long had finally come to pass, and oh, how my stomach churned! The idea of dressing in the exquisite clothing I admired and presenting myself to a roomful of men was enough to make my palms glisten with sweat. Every time I thought of it, I felt a most delicious nervousness that tingled all the way from my knees into my chest. I imagined myself inside a teahouse, sliding open the door of a tatami room. The men turned their heads to look at me; and of course, I saw the Chairman there among them. Sometimes I imagined him alone in the room, wearing not a Western-style business suit, but the Japanese dress so many men wore in the evenings to relax. In his fingers, as smooth as driftwood, he held a sake cup; more than anything else in the world, I wanted to pour it full for him and feel his eyes upon me as I did.

I may have been no more than fourteen, but it seemed to me I'd lived two lives already. My new life was still beginning, though my old life had come to an end some time ago. Several years had passed since I'd learned the sad news about my family, and it was amazing to me how completely the landscape of my mind had changed. We all know that a winter scene, though it may be covered over one day, with even the trees dressed in shawls of snow, will be unrecognizable the following spring. Yet I had never imagined such a thing could occur within our very selves. When I first learned the news of my family, it was as though I'd been covered over by a blanket of snow. But in time the terrible coldness had melted away to reveal a landscape I'd never seen before or even imagined. I don't know if this will make sense to you, but my mind on the eve of my debut was like a garden in which the flowers have only begun to poke their faces up through the soil, so that it is still impossible to tell how things will look. I was brimming with excitement; and in this garden of my mind stood a statue, precisely in the center. It was an image of the geisha I wanted to become.

14

I'VE HEARD IT said that the week in which a young girl prepares for her debut as an apprentice geisha is like when a caterpillar turns into a butterfly. It's a charming idea; but for the life of me I can't imagine why anyone ever thought up such a thing. A caterpillar has only to spin its cocoon and doze off for a while; whereas in my case, I'm sure I never had a more exhausting week. The first step was to have my hair done in the manner of an apprentice geisha, in the 'split peach' style, which I've mentioned. Gion had quite a number of hairdressers in those days; Mameha's worked in a terribly crowded room above an eel restaurant. I had to spend nearly two hours waiting my turn with six or eight geisha kneeling here and there, even out on the landing of the stairwell. And I'm sorry to say that the smell of dirty hair was overpowering. The elaborate hairstyles geisha wore in those days required so much effort and expense that no one went to the hairdresser more than once a week or so; by the end of that time, even the perfumes they put in their hair weren't of much help.

When at last my turn came, the first thing the hairdresser did was put me over a large sink in a position that made me wonder if he was going to chop off my head. Then he poured a bucket of warm water over my hair and began to scrub it with soap. Actually 'scrub' isn't a strong enough word, because what he did to my scalp using his fingers is more like what a workman does to a field using a hoe. Looking back on it, I understand why. Dandruff is a great problem among geisha, and very few things are more unattractive and make the hair look more unclean. The hairdresser may have had the best motives, but after a while my scalp felt so raw, I was almost in tears from the pain. Finally he said to me, 'Go ahead and cry if you have to. Why do you think I put you over a sink!'

I suppose this was his idea of a clever joke, because after he'd said it he laughed out loud.

When he'd had enough of scraping his fingernails across my scalp, he sat me on the mats to one side and tore a wooden comb through my hair until the muscles of my neck were sore from pulling against him. At length he satisfied himself that the knots were gone, and then combed camellia oil into my hair, which gave it a lovely sheen. I was starting to think the worst was over; but then he took out a bar of wax. And I must tell you that even with camellia oil as a lubricant and a hot iron to keep the wax soft, hair and wax were never meant to go together. It says a great deal about how civilized we human beings are, that a young girl can willingly sit and allow a grown man to comb wax through her hair without doing anything more than whimpering quietly to herself. If you tried such a thing with a dog, it would bite you so much you'd be able to see through your hands.

When my hair was evenly waxed, the hairdresser swept the forelock back and brought the rest up into a large knot like a pincushion on the top of the head. When viewed from the back, this pincushion has a split in it, as if it's cut in two, which gives the hairstyle its name of 'split peach.'

Even though I wore this split-peach hairstyle for a number of years, there's something about it that never occurred to me until quite some time later when a man explained it. The knot – what I've called the 'pincushion' – is formed by wrapping the hair around a piece of fabric. In back where the knot is split, the fabric is left visible; it might be any design or color, but in the case of an apprentice geisha – after a certain point in her life, at least – it's always red silk. One night a man said to me:

'Most of these innocent little girls have no idea how provocative the 'split peach' hairstyle really is! Imagine that you're walking along behind a young geisha, thinking all sorts of naughty thoughts about what you might like to do to her, and then you see on her head this split-peach shape, with a big splash of red inside the cleft . . . And what do you think of?'

Well, I didn't think of anything at all, and I told him so.

'You aren't using your imagination!' he said.

After a moment I understood and turned so red he laughed to see it.

On my way back to the okiya, it didn't matter to me that my poor scalp felt the way clay must feel after the potter has scored it with a sharp stick. Every time I caught a glimpse of myself in the glass of a shop, I felt I was someone to be taken seriously; not a girl anymore, but a young woman. When I reached the okiya, Auntie made me model my hair for her and said all sorts of kind things. Even Pumpkin couldn't resist walking once around me admiringly – though Hatsumomo would have been angry if she'd known. And what do you suppose Mother's reaction was? She stood on her tiptoes to see better – which did her little good, because already I was taller than she was – and then complained that I probably ought to have gone to Hatsumomo's hairdresser rather than Mameha's.

Every young geisha may be proud of her hairstyle at first, but she comes to hate it within three or four days. Because you see, if a girl comes home exhausted from the hairdresser and lays her head down on a pillow for a nap just as she did the night before, her hair will be flattened out of shape. The moment she awakens, she'll have to go right back to the hairdresser again. For this reason, a young apprentice geisha must learn a new way of sleeping after her hair is styled for the first time. She doesn't use an ordinary pillow any longer, but a *takamakura* – which I've mentioned before. It's not so much a pillow as a cradle for the base of the neck. Most are padded with a bag of wheat chaff, but still they're not much better than putting your neck on a stone. You lie there on your futon with your hair suspended in the air, thinking everything is fine until you fall asleep; but when you wake up, you've shifted somehow so that your head has settled back on the mats, and your hairstyle is as flat as if you hadn't bothered to use a tall pillow in the first place. In my case, Auntie helped me to avoid this by putting a tray of rice flour on the mats beneath my hair. Whenever my head drooped back while I slept, my hair sank into the rice flour, which stuck to the wax and ruined my hairstyle. I'd already watched Pumpkin go through this ordeal. Now it was my turn. For a time I woke up every morning with my hair ruined and had to wait in line at the hairdresser for my chance to be tortured.

Every afternoon during the week leading up to my debut, Auntie dressed me in the complete regalia of an apprentice geisha and made me walk up and down the dirt corridor of the okiya to build up my strength. In the beginning I could scarcely walk at all, and worried that I might tip over backward. Young girls dress much more ornately than older women, you see, which means brighter colors and showier fabrics, but also a longer obi. A mature woman will wear the obi tied in back in a manner we call the 'drum knot,' because it makes a tidy little box shape; this doesn't require very much fabric. But a girl younger than around twenty or so wears her obi in a showier fashion. In the case of an apprentice geisha, this means the most dramatic fashion of all, a *darari-obi* – 'dangling obi' – knotted almost as high as the shoulder blades, and with the ends hanging nearly to the ground. No matter how brightly colored a kimono might be, the obi is nearly always brighter. When an apprentice geisha walks down the street in front of you, you notice not her kimono but rather her brilliantly colored, dangling obi – with just a margin of kimono showing at the shoulders and on the sides. To achieve this effect the obi must be so long that it stretches all the way from one end of a room to the other. But it isn't the length of the obi that makes it hard to wear; it's the weight, for it's nearly always made of heavy silk brocade. Just to carry it up the stairs is exhausting, so you can imagine how it feels to wear it – the thick band of it squeezing your middle like one of those awful snakes, and the heavy fabric hanging behind, making you feel as if someone has strapped a traveling trunk to your back.

To make matters worse, the kimono itself is also heavy, with long, swinging sleeves. I don't mean sleeves that drape over the hand onto the ground. You may have noticed that when a woman is wearing kimono and stretches out her arms, the fabric below the sleeve hangs down to form something like a pocket. This baggy pocket, which we call the *furi*, is the part that's so long on the kimono of an apprentice geisha. It can easily drag along the ground if a girl isn't careful; and when she dances, she will certainly trip over her sleeves if she doesn't wrap them many times around the forearm to keep them out of the way,

Years later a famous scientist from Kyoto University when he was very drunk one night, said something about the costume of an apprentice geisha that I've never forgotten. 'The mandrill of central Africa is often considered the showiest of primates,' he said. 'But I believe the apprentice geisha of Gion is perhaps the most brilliantly colored primate of all!'

Finally the day came when Mameha and I were to perform the ceremony binding us as sisters. I bathed early and spent the rest of the morning dressing. Auntie helped me with the finishing touches on my makeup and hair. Because of the wax and makeup covering my skin, I had the strange sensation of having lost all feeling in my face; every time I touched my cheek, I could feel only a vague sense of pressure from my finger. I did it so many times Auntie had to redo my makeup. Afterward as I studied myself in the mirror, a most peculiar thing happened. I knew that the person kneeling before the makeup stand was me, but so was the unfamiliar girl gazing back. I actually reached out to touch her. She wore the magnificent makeup of a geisha. Her lips were flowering red on a stark white face, with her cheeks tinted a soft pink. Her hair was ornamented with silk flowers and sprigs of unhusked rice. She wore a formal kimono of black, with the crest of the Nitta okiya. When at last I could bring myself to stand, I went into the hall and looked in astonishment at myself in the full-length mirror. Beginning at the hem of my gown, an embroidered dragon circled up the bottom of the robe to the middle of my thigh. His mane was woven in threads lacquered with a beautiful reddish tint. His claws and teeth were silver, his eyes gold – real gold. I couldn't stop tears from welling up in my eyes, and had to look straight up at the ceiling to keep them from rolling onto my cheeks. Before leaving the okiya, I took the handkerchief the Chairman had given me and tucked it into my obi for good luck.

Auntie accompanied me to Mameha's apartment, where I expressed my gratitude to Mameha and pledged to honor and respect her. Then the three of us walked to the Gion Shrine, where Mameha and I clapped our hands and announced to the gods that we would soon be bound as sisters. I prayed for their favor in the years ahead, and then closed my eyes and thanked them for having granted me the wish I'd pleaded for three and a half years earlier, that I should become a geisha.

The ceremony was to take place at the Ichiriki Teahouse, which is certainly the best-known teahouse in all of Japan. It has quite a history, partly because of a famous samurai who hid himself there in the early 1700s. If you've ever heard the story of the Forty-seven Ronin – who avenged their master's death and afterward killed themselves by seppuku – well, it was their leader who hid himself in the Ichiriki Teahouse while plotting revenge. Most of the first-class teahouses in Gion are invisible from the street, except for their simple entrances, but the Ichiriki is as obvious as an apple on a tree. It sits at a prominent corner of Shijo Avenue, surrounded by a smooth, apricot-colored wall with its own tiled roof. It seemed like a palace to me.

We were joined there by two of Mameha's younger sisters, as well as by Mother. When we had all assembled in the exterior garden, a maid led us through the entrance hall and down a beautiful meandering corridor to a small tatami room in the back. I'd never been in such elegant surroundings before. Every piece of wood trim gleamed; every plaster wall was perfect in its smoothness. I smelled the sweet, dusty fragrance of *kuroyaki* – 'char-black' – a sort of perfume made by charring wood and grinding it into a soft gray dust. It's very old-fashioned, and even Mameha, who was as traditional a geisha as you would find, preferred something more Western. But all the *kuroyaki* worn by generations of geisha still haunted the Ichiriki. I have some even now which I keep in a wooden vial; and when I smell it, I see myself back there once again.

The ceremony, which was attended by the mistress of the Ichiriki, lasted only about ten minutes. A maid brought a tray with several sake cups, and Mameha and I drank together. I took three sips from a cup, and then passed it to her and she took three sips. We did this with three different cups, and then it was over. From that moment on, I was no longer known as Chiyo. I was the novice geisha Sayuri. During the first month of apprenticeship, a young geisha is known as a 'novice' and cannot perform dances or entertain on her own without her older sister, and in fact does little besides watching and learning. As for my name of Sayuri, Mameha had worked with her fortune-teller a long while to choose it. The sound of a name isn't all that matters, you see; the meaning of the characters is very important as well, and so is the number of strokes used to write them – for there are lucky and unlucky stroke counts. My new name came from 'sa,' meaning 'together,' 'yu,' from the zodiac sign for the Hen – in order to balance other elements in my personality – and 'ri,' meaning 'understanding.' All the combinations involving an element from Mameha's name, unfortunately, had been pronounced inauspicious by the fortune-teller.

I thought Sayuri was a lovely name, but it felt strange not to be known as Chiyo any longer. After the ceremony we went into another room for a lunch of 'red rice,' made of rice mixed with red beans. I picked at it, feeling strangely unsettled and not at all like celebrating. The mistress of the teahouse asked me a question, and when I heard her call me 'Sayuri,' I realized what was bothering me. It was as if the little girl named Chiyo, running barefoot from the pond to her tipsy house, no longer existed. I felt that this new girl, Sayuri, with her gleaming white face and her red lips, had destroyed her.

Mameha planned to spend the early afternoon taking me around Gion to introduce me to the mistresses of the various teahouses and okiya with which she had relationships. But we didn't head out the moment lunch was done. Instead she took me into a room at the Ichiriki and asked me to sit. Of course, a geisha never really 'sits' while wearing kimono; what we call sitting is probably what other people would call kneeling. In any case, after I'd done it, she made a face at me and told me to do it again. The robes were so awkward it took me several tries to manage it properly. Mameha gave me a little ornament in the shape of a gourd and showed me how to wear it dangling on my obi. The gourd, being hollow and light, is thought to offset the heaviness of the body, you see, and many a clumsy young apprentice has relied upon one to help keep her from falling down.

Mameha talked with me a while, and then just when we were ready to leave, asked me to pour her a cup of tea. The pot was empty, but she told me to pretend to pour it anyway She wanted to see how I held my sleeve out of the way when I did it. I thought I knew exactly what she was looking for and tried my best, but Mameha was unhappy with me.

'First of all,' she said, 'whose cup are you filling?'

'Yours!' I said.

'Well, for heaven's sake, you don't need to impress me. Pretend I'm someone else. Am I a man or a woman?'

'A man,' I said.

'All right, then. Pour me a cup again.'

I did so, and Mameha practically broke her neck trying to peer up my sleeve as I held my arm out.

'How do you like that?' she asked me. 'Because that's exactly what's going to happen if you hold your arm so high.'

I tried pouring again with my arm a bit lower. This time, she pretended to yawn and then turned and began a conversation with an imaginary geisha sitting on the other side of her.

'I think you're trying to tell me that I bored you,' I said. 'But how can I bore you just pouring a cup of tea?'

'You may not want me looking up your sleeve, but that doesn't mean you have to act prissy! A man is interested in only one thing. Believe me, you'll understand all too soon what I'm talking about. In the meantime, you can keep him happy by letting him think he's permitted to see parts of your body no one else can see. If an apprentice geisha acts the way you did just then – pouring tea just like a maid would – the poor man will lose all hope. Try it again, but first show me your arm.'

So I drew my sleeve up above my elbow and held my arm out for her to see. She took it and turned it in her hands to look at the top and the bottom.

'You have a lovely arm; and beautiful skin. You should make sure every man who sits near you sees it at least once.'

So I went on, pouring tea again and again, until Mameha felt satisfied that I drew my sleeve out of the way enough to show my arm without being too obvious what I was doing. I looked laughable if I hiked my sleeve up to my elbow; the trick was to act like I was merely pulling it out of the way, while at the same time drawing it a few finger-widths above my wrist to give a view of my forearm. Mameha said the prettiest part of the arm was the underside, so I must always be sure to hold the teapot in such a way that the man saw the bottom of my arm rather than the top.

She asked me to do it again, this time pretending I was pouring tea for the mistress of the Ichiriki. I showed my arm in just the same way, and Mameha made a face at once.

'For heaven's sake, I'm a woman,' she said. 'Why are you showing me your arm that way? Probably you're just trying to make me angry.'

'Angry?'

'What else am I supposed to think? You're showing me how youthful and beautiful you are, while I'm already old and decrepit. Unless you were doing it just to be vulgar . . .'

'How is it vulgar?'

'Why else have you made such a point of letting me see the underside of your arm? You may as well show me the bottom of your foot or the inside of your thigh. If I happen to catch a glimpse of something here or there, well, that's all right. But to make such a point of showing it to me!'

So I poured a few more times, until I'd learned a more demure and suitable method. Whereupon Mameha announced that we were ready to go out into Gion together.

Already by this time, I'd been wearing the complete ensemble of an apprentice geisha for several hours. Now I had to try walking all around Gion in the shoes we call *okobo*. They're quite tall and made of wood, with lovely, lacquered thongs to hold the foot in place. Most people think it very elegant the way they taper down like a wedge, so that the footprint at the bottom is about half the size of the top. But I found it hard to walk delicately in them. I felt as if I had roof tiles strapped to the bottoms of my feet.

Mameha and I made perhaps twenty stops at various okiya and teahouses, though we spent no more than a few minutes at most of them. Usually a maid answered the door, and Mameha asked politely to speak with the mistress; then when the mistress came, Mameha said to her, 'I'd like to introduce my new younger sister, Sayuri,' and then I bowed very low and said, 'I beg your favor, please, Mistress.' The mistress and Mameha would chat for a moment, and then we left. At a few of the places we were asked in for tea and spent perhaps five minutes. But I was very reluctant to drink tea and only wet my lips instead. Using the toilet while wearing kimono is one of the most difficult things to learn, and I wasn't at all sure I'd learned it adequately just yet.

In any case, within an hour I was so exhausted, it was all I could do to keep from groaning as I walked along. But we kept up our pace. In those days, I suppose there were probably thirty or forty first-class teahouses in Gion and another hundred or so of a somewhat lower grade. Of course we couldn't visit them all. We went to the fifteen or sixteen where Mameha was accustomed to entertaining. As for okiya, there must have been hundreds of those, but we went only to the few with which Mameha had some sort of relationship.

Soon after three o'clock we were finished. I would have liked nothing better than to go back to the okiya to fall asleep for a long while. But Mameha had plans for me that very evening. I was to attend my first engagement as a novice geisha.

'Go take a bath,' she said to me. 'You've been perspiring a good deal, and your makeup hasn't held up.'

It was a warm fall day, you see, and I'd been working very hard.

Back at the okiya, Auntie helped me undress and then took pity on me by letting me nap for a half hour. I was back in her good graces again, now that my foolish mistakes were behind me and my future seemed even brighter than Pumpkin's. She woke me after my nap, and I rushed to the bathhouse as quickly as I could. By five, I had finished dressing and applying my makeup. I felt terribly excited, as you can imagine, because for years I'd watched Hatsumomo, and lately Pumpkin, go off in the afternoons and evenings looking beautiful, and now at last my turn had come. The event that evening, the first I would ever attend, was to be a banquet at the Kansai International Hotel. Banquets are stiffly formal affairs, with all the guests arranged shoulder to shoulder in a sort of U-shape around the outside of a big tatami room, and trays of food sitting on little stands in front of them. The geisha, who are there to entertain, move around the center of the room – inside the U-shape made by all the trays, I mean – and spend only a few minutes kneeling before each guest to pour sake and chat. It isn't what you'd call an exciting affair; and as a novice, my role was less exciting even than Mameha's. I stayed to one side of her like a shadow. Whenever she introduced herself, I did the same, bowing very low and saying, 'My name is Sayuri. I'm a novice and beg your indulgence.' After that I said nothing more, and no one said anything to me.

Toward the end of the banquet, the doors at one side of the room were slid open, and Mameha and another geisha performed a dance together, known as *Chi-yo no Tomo* – 'Friends Everlasting.' It's a lovely piece about two devoted women meeting again after a long absence. Most of the men sat picking their teeth through it; they were executives of a large company that made rubber valves, or some such thing, and had gathered in Kyoto for their annual banquet. I don't think a single one of them would have known the difference between dancing and sleepwalking. But for my part, I was entranced. Geisha in Gion always use a folding fan as a prop when dancing, and Mameha in particular was masterful in her movements. At first she closed the fan and, while turning her body in a circle, waved it delicately with her wrist to suggest a stream of water flowing past. Then she opened it, and it became a cup into which her companion poured sake for her to drink. As I say, the dance was lovely, and so was the music, which was played on the shamisen by a terribly thin geisha with small, watery eyes.

A formal banquet generally lasts no more than two hours; so by eight o'clock we were out on the street again. I was just turning to thank Mameha and bid her good night, when she said to me, 'Well, I'd thought of sending you back to bed now, but you seem to be so full of energy. I'm heading to the Komoriya Teahouse. Come along with me and have your first taste of an informal party. We may as well start showing you around as quickly as we can.'

I couldn't very well tell her I felt too tired to go; so I swallowed my real feelings and followed her up the street.

The party, as she explained to me along the way, was to be given by the man who ran the National Theater in Tokyo. He knew all the important geisha in nearly every geisha district in Japan; and although he would probably be very cordial when Mameha introduced me, I shouldn't expect him to say much. My only responsibility was to be sure I always looked pretty and alert. 'Just be sure you don't let anything happen to make you look bad,' she warned.

We entered the teahouse and were shown by a maid to a room on the second floor. I hardly dared to look inside when Mameha knelt and slid open the door, but I could see seven or eight men seated on cushions around a table, with perhaps four geisha. We bowed and went inside, and afterward knelt on the mats to close the door behind us – for this is the way a geisha enters a room. We greeted the other geisha first, as Mameha had told me to do, then the host, at one corner of the table, and afterward the other guests.

'Mameha-san!' said one of the geisha. 'You've come just in time to tell us the story about Konda-san the wig maker.'

'Oh, heavens, I can't remember it at all,' Mameha said, and everyone laughed; I had no idea what the joke was. Mameha led me around the table and knelt beside the host. I followed and positioned myself to one side.

'Mr. Director, please permit me to introduce my new younger sister,' she said to him.

This was my cue to bow and say my name, and beg the director's indulgence, and so on. He was a very nervous man, with bulging eyes and a kind of chicken-bone frailty. He didn't even look at me, but only flicked his cigarette in the nearly full ashtray before him and said:

'What is all the talk about Konda-san the wig maker? All evening the girls keep referring to it, and not a one of them will tell the story.'

'Honestly, I wouldn't know!' Mameha said.

'Which means,' said another geisha, 'that she's too embarrassed to tell it. If she won't, I suppose I'll have to.'

The men seemed to like this idea, but Mameha only sighed.

'In the meantime, I'll give Mameha a cup of sake to calm her nerves,' the director said, and washed out his own sake cup in a bowl of water on the center of the table – which was there for that very reason – before offering it to her.

'Well,' the other geisha began, 'this fellow Konda-san is the best wig maker in Gion, or at least everyone says so. And for years Mameha-san went to him. She always has the best of everything, you know. Just look at her and you can tell.'

Mameha made a mock-angry face.

'She certainly has the best sneer,' said one of the men.

'During a performance,' the geisha went on, 'a wig maker is always backstage to help with changes of costume. Often while a geisha is taking off a certain robe and putting on another one, something will slip here or there, and then suddenly . . . a naked breast! Or . . . a little bit of hair! You know, these things happen. And anyway –'

'All these years I've been working in a bank,' said one of the men. 'I want to be a wig maker!'

'There's more to it than just gawking at naked women. Anyway, Mameha-san always acts very prim and goes behind a screen to change –'

'Let me tell the story,' Mameha interrupted. 'You're going to give me a bad name. I wasn't being prim. Konda-san was always staring at me like he couldn't wait for the next costume change, so I had a screen brought in. It's a wonder Konda-san didn't burn a hole in it with his eyes, trying to see through it the way he did.'

'Why couldn't you just give him a little glimpse now and then,' the director interrupted. 'How can it hurt you to be nice?'

'I've never thought of it that way,' Mameha said. 'You're quite right, Mr. Director. What harm can a little glimpse do? Perhaps you want to give us one right now?'

Everyone in the room burst out laughing at this. Just when things were starting to calm down, the director started it all over by rising to his feet and beginning to untie the sash of his robe.

'I'm only going to do this,' he said to Mameha, 'if you'll give me a glimpse in return . . .'

'I never made such an offer,' Mameha said.

'That isn't very generous of you.'

'Generous people don't become geisha,' Mameha said. 'They become the patrons of geisha.'

'Never mind, then,' the director said, and sat back down. I have to say, I was very relieved he'd given up; because although all the others seemed to be enjoying themselves enormously, I felt embarrassed.

'Where was I?' Mameha said. 'Well, I had the screen brought in one day, and I thought this was enough to keep me safe from Konda-san. But when I hurried back from the toilet at one point, I couldn't find him anywhere. I began to panic, because I needed a wig for my next entrance; but soon we found him sitting on a chest against the wall, looking very weak and sweating. I wondered if there was something wrong with his heart! He had my wig beside him, and when he saw me, he apologized and helped put it on me. Then later that afternoon, he handed me a note he'd written . . .'

Here Mameha's voice trailed off. At last one of the men said, 'Well? What did it say?'

Mameha covered her eyes with her hand. She was too embarrassed to continue, and everyone in the room broke into laughter.

'All right, I'll tell you what he wrote,' said the geisha who'd begun the story. 'It was something like this: "Dearest Mameha. You are the very loveliest geisha in all of Gion," and so forth. "After you have worn a wig, I always cherish it, and keep it in my workshop to put my face into it and smell the scent of your hair many times a day. But today when you rushed to the toilet, you gave me the greatest moment of my life. While you were inside, I hid myself at the door, and the beautiful tinkling sound, more lovely than a waterfall –" '

The men laughed so hard that the geisha had to wait before going on.

' "– and the beautiful tinkling sound, more lovely than a waterfall, made me hard and stiff where I myself tinkle –" '

'He didn't say it that way,' Mameha said. 'He wrote, "the beautiful tinkling sound, more lovely than a waterfall, caused me to swell and bulge at the knowledge that your body was bare . . ." '

'Then he told her,' the other geisha said, 'that he was unable to stand afterward because of the excitement. And he hoped that one day he would experience such a moment again.'

Of course, everyone laughed, and I pretended to laugh too. But the truth is, I was finding it difficult to believe that these men – who had paid so considerably to be there, among women wrapped in beautiful, expensive robes – really wanted to hear the same sorts of stories children back in the pond in Yoroido might have told. I'd imagined feeling out of my depth in a conversation about literature, or Kabuki, or something of that sort. And of course, there were such parties in Gion; it just happened that my first was of the more childish kind.

All through Mameha's story, the man beside me had sat rubbing his splotchy face with his hands and paying little attention. Now he looked at me a long while and then asked, 'What's the matter with your eyes? Or have I just drunk too much?'

He certainly had drunk too much – though I didn't think it would be proper to tell him. But before I could answer, his eyebrows began to twitch, and a moment later he reached up and scratched his head so much that a little cloud of snow spilled onto his shoulders. As it turned out, he was known in Gion as 'Mr. Snowshowers' because of his terrible dandruff. He seemed to have forgotten the question he'd asked me – or maybe he never expected me to answer it – because now he asked my age. I told him I was fourteen.

'You're the oldest fourteen-year-old I've ever seen. Here, take this,' he said, and handed me his empty sake cup.

'Oh, no, thank you, sir,' I replied, 'for I'm only a novice . . .' This was what Mameha had taught me to say, but Mr. Snowshowers didn't listen. He just held the cup in the air until I took it, and then lifted up a vial of sake to pour for me.

I wasn't supposed to drink sake, because an apprentice geisha – particularly one still in her novitiate – should appear childlike. But I couldn't very well disobey him. I held the sake cup out; but he scratched his head again before he poured, and I was horrified to see a few flecks settle into the cup. Mr. Snowshowers filled it with sake and said to me, 'Now drink up. Go on. First of many.'

I gave him a smile and had just begun to raise the cup slowly to my lips – not knowing what else I could do – when, thank heavens, Mameha rescued me.

'It's your first day in Gion, Sayuri. It won't do for you to get drunk,' she said, though she was speaking for the benefit of Mr. Snowshowers. 'Just wet your lips and be done with it.'

So I obeyed her and wet my lips with the sake. And when I say that I wet my lips, I mean I pinched them shut so tightly I nearly sprained my mouth, and then tipped the sake cup until I felt the liquid against my skin. Then I put the cup down on the table hurriedly and said, 'Mmm! Delicious!' while reaching for the handkerchief in my obi. I felt very relieved when I patted my lips with it, and I'm happy to say that Mr. Snowshowers didn't even notice, for he was busy eyeing the cup as it sat there full on the table before him. After a moment he picked it up in two fingers and poured it right down his throat, before standing and excusing himself to use the toilet.

An apprentice geisha is expected to walk a man to the toilet and back, but no one expects a novice to do it. When there isn't an apprentice in the room, a man will usually walk himself to the toilet, or sometimes one of the geisha will accompany him. But Mr. Snowshowers stood there gazing down at me until I realized he was waiting for me to stand.

I didn't know my way around the Komoriya Teahouse, but Mr. Snowshowers certainly did. I followed him down the hall and around a corner. He stepped aside while I rolled open the door to the toilet for him. After I had closed it behind him and was waiting there in the hallway, I heard the sound of someone coming up the stairs, but I thought nothing of it. Soon Mr. Snowshowers was done and we made our way back. When I entered the room, I saw that another geisha had joined the party, along with an apprentice. They had their backs to the door, so that I didn't see their faces until I'd followed Mr. Snowshowers around the table and taken up my place once again. You can imagine how shocked I felt when I saw them; for there, on the other side of the table, was the one woman I would have given anything to avoid. It was Hatsumomo, smiling at me, and beside her sat Pumpkin.

15

HATSUMOMO SMILED WHEN she was happy, like everybody else; and she was never happier than when she was about to make someone suffer. This is why she wore such a beautiful smile on her face when she said:

'Oh, my goodness! What a peculiar coincidence. Why, it's a novice! I really shouldn't tell the rest of this story, because I might embarrass the poor thing.'

I hoped Mameha would excuse herself and take me with her. But she only gave me an anxious glance. She must have felt that leaving Hatsumomo alone with these men would be like running away from a house on fire; we'd be better off to stay and control the damage.

'Really, I don't think there's anything more difficult than being a novice,' Hatsumomo was saying. 'Don't you think so, Pumpkin?'

Pumpkin was a full-fledged apprentice now; she'd been a novice six months earlier. I glanced at her for sympathy, but she just stared at the table with her hands in her lap. Knowing her as I did, I understood that the little wrinkle at the top of her nose meant she felt upset.

'Yes, ma'am,' she said.

'Such a difficult time of life,' Hatsumomo went on. 'I can still remember how hard I found it . . . What is your name, little novice?'

Happily, I didn't have to respond, because Mameha spoke up.

'You're certainly right about it being a difficult time of life for you, Hatsumomo-san. Though of course, you were more awkward than most.'

'I want to hear the rest of the story,' said one of the men.

'And embarrass the poor novice who's just joined us?' Hatsumomo said. 'I'll tell it only if you promise that you won't think about this poor girl as you listen. Be sure to picture some other girl in your mind.'

Hatsumomo could be ingenious in her devilishness. The men might not have pictured the story happening to me earlier, but they certainly would now.

'Let's see, where was I?' Hatsumomo began. 'Oh, yes. Well, this novice I mentioned . . . I can't remember her name, but I ought to give her one to keep you from confusing her with this poor girl. Tell me, little novice . . . what is your name?'

'Sayuri, ma'am,' I said. And my face felt so hot from nervousness that I wouldn't have been surprised if my makeup had simply melted and begun to drip onto my lap.

'Sayuri. How lovely! Somehow it doesn't suit you. Well, let's call this novice in the story "Mayuri." Now then, one day I was walking along Shijo Avenue with Mayuri, on our way to her older sister's okiya. There was a terrible wind, the sort that rattles the windows, and poor Mayuri had so little experience with kimono. She was no heavier than a leaf, and those big sleeves can be just like sails, you know. As we were about to cross the street, she disappeared, and I heard a little sound from behind me, like "Ah . . . ah," but very faint . . . '

Here Hatsumomo turned to look at me.

'My voice isn't high enough,' she said. 'Let me hear you say it. "Ah . . . ah . . ."'

Well, what could I do? I tried my best to make the noise.

'No, no, much higher . . . oh, never mind!' Hatsumomo turned to the man beside her and said under her breath, 'She isn't very bright, is she?' She shook her head for a moment and then went on. 'Anyway, when I turned around, poor Mayuri was being blown backward up the street a full block behind me, with her arms and legs flailing so much she looked like a bug on its back. I nearly tore my obi laughing, but then all of a sudden she stumbled right off the curb into a busy intersection just as a car came zooming along. Thank heavens she was blown onto the hood! Her legs flew up . . . and then if you can picture this, the wind blew right up her kimono, and . . . well, I don't need to tell you what happened.'

'You certainly do!' one of the men said.

'Don't you have any imagination?' she replied. 'The wind blew her kimono right up over her hips. She didn't want everyone to see her naked; so to preserve her modesty, she flipped herself around and ended up with her legs pointing in two different directions, and her private parts pressed against the windshield, right in the driver's face . . .'

Of course, the men were in hysterics by now, including the director, who tapped his sake cup on the tabletop like a machine gun, and said, 'Why doesn't anything like this ever happen to me?'

'Really, Mr. Director,' Hatsumomo said. 'The girl was only a novice! It's not as if the driver got to see anything. I mean, can you imagine looking at the private parts of this girl across the table?' She was talking about me, of course. 'Probably she's no different from a baby!'

'Girls sometimes start getting hair when they're only eleven,' said one of the men.

'How old are you, little Sayuri-san?' Hatsumomo asked me.

'I'm fourteen, ma'am,' I told her, just as politely as I could. 'But I'm an old fourteen.'

Already the men liked this, and Hatsumomo's smile hardened a bit.

'Fourteen?' she said. 'How perfect! And of course, you don't have any hair . . .'

'Oh, but I do. A good deal of it!' And I reached up and patted one hand against the hair on my head.

I guess this must have been a clever thing to do, although it didn't seem particularly clever to me. The men laughed harder than they'd laughed even at Hatsumomo's story. Hatsumomo laughed too, I suppose because she didn't want to seem as if the joke had been on her.

As the laughter died down, Mameha and I left. We hadn't even closed the door behind us before we heard Hatsumomo excusing herself as well. She and Pumpkin followed us down the stairway.

'Why, Mameha-san,' Hatsumomo said, 'this has simply been too much fun! I don't know why we haven't entertained together more often!'

'Yes, it has been fun,' said Mameha. 'I just relish the thought of what the future holds!'

After this, Mameha gave me a very satisfied look. She was relishing the thought of seeing Hatsumomo destroyed.

That night after bathing and removing my makeup, I was standing in the formal entrance hall answering Auntie's questions about my day, when Hatsumomo came in from the street and stood before me. Normally she wasn't back so early, but I knew the moment I saw her face that she'd come back only for the purpose of confronting me. She wasn't even wearing her cruel smile, but had her lips pressed together in a way that looked almost unattractive. She stood before me only a moment, and then drew back her hand and slapped me across the face. The last thing I saw before her hand struck me was a glimpse of her clenched teeth like two strings of pearls.

I was so stunned, I can't recall what happened immediately afterward. But Auntie and Hatsumomo must have begun to argue, because the next thing I heard was Hatsumomo saying, 'If this girl embarrasses me in public again, I'll be happy to slap the other side of her face!'

'How did I embarrass *you*?' I asked her.

'You knew perfectly well what I meant when I wondered if you had hair, but you made me look like a fool. I owe you a favor, little Chiyo. I'll return it soon, I promise.'

Hatsumomo's anger seemed to close itself up, and she walked back out of the okiya, where Pumpkin was waiting on the street to bow to her.

I reported this to Mameha the following afternoon, but she hardly paid any attention.

'What's the problem?' she said. 'Hatsumomo didn't leave a mark on your face, thank heavens. You didn't expect she'd be pleased at your comment, did you?'

'I'm only concerned about what might happen the next time we run into her,' I said.

'I'll tell you what will happen. We'll turn around and leave. The host may be surprised to see us walk out of a party we've just walked into, but it's better than giving Hatsumomo another chance to humiliate you. Anyway, if we run into her, it will be a blessing.'

'Really, Mameha-san, I can't see how it could be a blessing.'

'If Hatsumomo forces us to leave a few teahouses, we'll drop in on more parties, that's all. You'll be known around Gion much faster that way.'

I felt reassured by Mameha's confidence. In fact, when we set out into Gion later, I expected that at the end of the night I would take off my makeup and find my skin glowing with the satisfaction of a long evening. Our first stop was a party for a young film actor, who looked no older than eighteen but had not a single hair on his head, not even eyelashes or eyebrows. He went on to become very famous a few years later, but only because of the manner of his death. He killed himself with a sword after murdering a young waitress in Tokyo. In any case, I thought him very strange until I noticed that he kept glancing at me; I'd lived so much of my life in the isolation of the okiya that I must admit I relished the attention. We stayed more than an hour, and Hatsumomo never showed up. It seemed to me that my fantasies of success might indeed come to pass.

Next we stopped at a party given by the chancellor of Kyoto University. Mameha at once began talking with a man she hadn't seen in some time, and left me on my own. The only space I could find at the table was beside an old man in a stained white shirt, who must have been very thirsty because he was drinking continually from a glass of beer, except when he moved it away from his mouth to burp. I knelt beside him and was about to introduce myself when I heard the door slide open. I expected to see a maid delivering another round of sake, but there in the hallway knelt Hatsumomo and Pumpkin.

'Oh, good heavens!' I heard Mameha say to the man she was entertaining. 'Is your wristwatch accurate?'

'Very accurate,' he said. 'I set it every afternoon by the clock at the train station.'

'I'm afraid Sayuri and I have no choice but to be rude and

excuse ourselves. We were expected elsewhere a half hour ago!'

And with that, we stood and slipped out of the party the very moment after Hatsumomo and Pumpkin entered it.

As we were leaving the teahouse, Mameha pulled me into an empty tatami room. In the hazy darkness I couldn't make out her features, but only the beautiful oval shape of her face with its elaborate crown of hair. If I couldn't see her, then she couldn't see me; I let my jaw sag with frustration and despair, for it seemed I would never escape Hatsumomo.

'What did you say to that horrid woman earlier today?' Mameha said to me.

'Nothing at all, ma'am!'

'Then how did she find us here?'

'I didn't know we would be here myself,' I said. 'I couldn't possibly have told her.'

'My maid knows about my engagements, but I can't imagine . . . Well, we'll go to a party hardly anyone knows about. Naga Teruomi was just appointed the new conductor of the Tokyo Philharmonic last week. He's come into town this afternoon to give everyone a chance to idolize him. I don't much want to go, but . . . at least Hatsumomo won't be there.'

We crossed Shijo Avenue and turned down a narrow alley that smelled of sake and roasted yams. A sprinkle of laughter fell down onto us from the second-story windows brightly lit overhead. Inside the teahouse, a young maid showed us to a room on the second floor, where we found the conductor sitting with his thin hair oiled back and his fingers stroking a sake cup in anger. The other men in the room were in the midst of a drinking game with two geisha, but the conductor refused to join. He talked with Mameha for a while, and soon asked her to put on a dance. I don't think he cared about the dance, really; it was just a way to end the drinking games and encourage his guests to begin paying attention to him again. Just as the maid brought a shamisen to hand to one of the geisha – even before Mameha had taken up her pose – the door slid open and . . . I'm sure you know what I'm going to say. They were like dogs that wouldn't stop following us. It was Hatsumomo and Pumpkin once again.

You should have seen the way Mameha and Hatsumomo smiled at each other. You'd almost have thought they were sharing a private joke – whereas in fact, I'm sure Hatsumomo was relishing her victory in finding us, and as for Mameha . . . well, I think her smile was just a way of hiding her anger. During her dance, I could see her jaw jutting out and her nostrils flared. She didn't even come back to the table afterward, but just said to the conductor:

'Thank you so much for permitting us to drop in! I'm afraid it's so late . . . Sayuri and I must excuse ourselves now . . .'

I can't tell you how pleased Hatsumomo looked as we closed the door behind us.

I followed Mameha down the stairs. On the bottom step she came to a halt and waited. At last a young maid rushed into the formal entrance hall to see us out – the very same maid who'd shown us up the stairs earlier.

'What a difficult life you must have as a maid!' Mameha said to her. 'Probably you want so many things and have so little money to spend. But tell me, what will you do with the funds you've just earned?'

'I haven't earned any funds, ma'am,' she said. But to see her swallowing so nervously, I could tell she was lying.

'How much money did Hatsumomo promise you?'

The maid's gaze fell at once to the floor. It wasn't until this moment that I understood what Mameha was thinking. As we learned some time afterward, Hatsumomo had indeed bribed at least one of the maids in every first-class teahouse in Gion. They were asked to call Yoko – the girl who answered the telephone in our okiya – whenever Mameha and I arrived at a party. Of course, we didn't know about Yoko's involvement at the time; but Mameha was quite right in assuming that the maid in this teahouse had passed a message to Hatsumomo somehow or other.

The maid couldn't bring herself to look at Mameha. Even when Mameha lifted her chin, the girl still pointed her eyes downward just as if they weighed as much as two lead balls. When we left the teahouse, we could hear Hatsumomo's voice coming from the window above – for it was such a narrow alleyway that everything echoed.

'Yes, what *was* her name?' Hatsumomo was saying.

'Sayuko,' said one of the men.

'Not Sayuko. Sayuri,' said another.

'I think that's the one,' Hatsumomo said. 'But really, it's too embarrassing for her. I mustn't tell you! She seems like a nice girl . . .'

'I didn't get much of an impression,' one man said. 'But she's very pretty.'

'Such unusual eyes!' said one of the geisha.

'You know what I heard a man say about her eyes the other day?' Hatsumomo said. 'He told me they were the color of smashed worms.'

'Smashed worms . . . I've certainly never heard a color described that way before.'

'Well, I'll tell you what I was going to say about her,' Hatsumomo went on, 'but you must promise not to repeat it. She has some sort of disease, and her bosoms look just like an old lady's – all droopy and wrinkled – really, it's dreadful! I saw her in a bathhouse once . . .'

Mameha and I had stopped to listen, but when we heard this, she gave me a little push and we walked out of the alley together. Mameha stood for a while looking up and down the street and then said:

'I'm trying to think where we can go, but . . . I can't think of a single place. If that woman has found us here, I suppose she can find us anywhere in Gion. You may as well go back to your okiya, Sayuri, until we come up with a new plan.'

One afternoon during World War II, some years after these events I'm telling you about now, an officer took his pistol out of its holster during a party beneath the boughs of a maple tree and laid it on the straw mat to impress me. I remember being struck by its beauty. The metal had a dull gray sheen; its curves were perfect and smooth. The oiled wood handle was richly grained. But when I thought of its real purpose as I listened to his stories, it ceased to be beautiful at all and became something monstrous instead.

This is exactly what happened to Hatsumomo in my eyes after she brought my debut to a standstill. That isn't to say I'd never considered her monstrous before. But I'd always envied her loveliness, and now I no longer did. While I ought to have been attending banquets every night, and ten or fifteen parties besides, I was forced instead to sit in the okiya practicing dance and shamisen just as though nothing in my life had changed from the year before. When Hatsumomo walked past me down the corridor in her full regalia, with her white makeup glowing above her dark robe just like the moon in a hazy night sky, I'm sure that even a blind man would have found her beautiful. And yet I felt nothing but hatred, and heard my pulse hissing in my ears.

I was summoned to Mameha's apartment several times in the next few days. Each time I hoped she was going to say she'd found a way around Hatsumomo; but she only wanted me to run errands she couldn't entrust to her maid. One afternoon I asked if she had any idea what would become of me.

'I'm afraid you're an exile, Sayuri-san, for the moment,' she replied. 'I hope you feel more determined than ever to destroy that wicked woman! But until I've thought of a plan, it will do you no good to follow me around Gion.'

Of course I was disappointed to hear it, but Mameha was quite right. Hatsumomo's ridicule would do me such harm in the eyes of men, and even in the eyes of women in Gion, that I would be better off staying home.

Happily, Mameha was very resourceful and did manage to find engagements from time to time that were safe for me to attend. Hatsumomo may have closed off Gion from me, but she couldn't close off the entire world beyond it. When Mameha left Gion for an engagement, she often invited me along. I went on a day trip by train to Kobe, where Mameha cut the ribbon for a new factory. On another occasion I joined her to accompany the former president of Nippon Telephone & Telegraph on a tour of Kyoto by limousine. This tour made quite an impression on me, for it was my first time seeing the vast city of Kyoto that lay beyond the bounds of our little Gion, not to mention my first time riding in a car. I'd never really understood how desperately some people lived during these years, until we drove along the river south of the city and saw dirty women nursing their babies under the trees along the railroad tracks, and men squatting in tattered straw sandals among the weeds. I won't pretend poor people never came to Gion, but we rarely saw anyone like these starving peasants too poor even to bathe. I could never have imagined that I – a slave terrorized by Hatsumomo's wickedness – had lived a relatively fortunate life through the Great Depression. But that day I realized it was true.

Late one morning I returned from the school to find a note telling me to bring my makeup and rush to Mameha's apartment. When I arrived, Mr. Itchoda, who was a dresser just like Mr. Bekku, was in the back room tying Mameha's obi before a full-length mirror.

'Hurry up and put on your makeup,' Mameha said to me. 'I've laid a kimono out for you in the other room.'

Mameha's apartment was enormous by the standards of Gion. In addition to her main room, which measured six tatami mats in area, she had two other smaller rooms – a dressing area that doubled as a maids' room, and a room in which she slept. There in her bedroom was a freshly made-up futon, with a complete kimono ensemble on top of it that her maid had laid out for me. I was puzzled by the futon. The sheets certainly weren't the ones Mameha had slept in the night before, for they were as smooth as fresh snow. I wondered about it while changing into the cotton dressing robe I'd brought. When I went to begin applying my makeup, Mameha told me why she had summoned me.

'The Baron is back in town,' she said. 'He'll be coming here for lunch. I want him to meet you.'

I haven't had occasion to mention the Baron, but Mameha was referring to Baron Matsunaga Tsuneyoshi – her *danna*. We don't have barons and counts in Japan any longer, but we did before World War II, and Baron Matsunaga was certainly among the wealthiest. His family controlled one of Japan's large banks and was very influential in finance. Originally his older brother had inherited the title of baron, but he had been assassinated while serving as finance minister in the cabinet of Prime Minister Inukai. Mameha's *danna*, already in his thirties at that time, had not only inherited the title of baron but all of his brother's holdings, including a grand estate in Kyoto not too far from Gion. His business interests kept him in Tokyo much of the time; and something else kept him there as well – for I learned many years later that he had another mistress, in the geisha district of Akasaka in Tokyo. Few men are wealthy enough to afford one geisha mistress, but Baron Matsunaga Tsuneyoshi had two.

Now that I knew Mameha would be spending the afternoon with her *danna*, I had a much better idea why the futon in her bedroom had been made up with fresh sheets.

I changed quickly into the clothing Mameha had set out for me – an underrobe of light green, and a kimono in russet and yellow with a design of pine trees at the hem. By this time one of Mameha's maids was just returning from a nearby restaurant with a big lacquer box holding the Baron's lunch. The foods inside it, on plates and bowls, were ready to be served just as in a restaurant. The largest was a flat lacquer dish with two grilled, salted *ayu* poised on their bellies as though they were swimming down the river together. To one side stood two tiny steamed crabs of the sort that are eaten whole. A trail of streaked salt curved along the black lacquer to suggest the sand they had crossed.

A few minutes later the Baron arrived. I peeked out through a crack at the edge of the sliding door and saw him standing just outside on the landing while Mameha untied his shoes. My first impression was of an almond or some other kind of nut, because he was small and very round, with a certain kind of heaviness, particularly around his eyes. Beards were very fashionable at that time, and the Baron wore a number of long, soft hairs on his face that I'm sure were supposed to resemble a beard, but looked to me more like some sort of garnish, or like the thin strips of seaweed that are sometimes sprinkled onto a bowl of rice.

'Oh, Mameha . . . I'm exhausted,' I heard him say. 'How I hate these long train rides!'

Finally he stepped out of his shoes and crossed the room with brisk little steps. Earlier in the morning, Mameha's dresser had brought an overstuffed chair and a Persian rug from a storage closet across the hall and arranged them near the window. The Baron seated himself there; but as for what happened afterward, I can't say, because Mameha's maid came over to me and bowed in apology before giving the door a gentle push to slide it the rest of the way closed.

I stayed in Mameha's little dressing room for an hour or more while the maid went in and out serving the Baron's lunch. I heard the murmur of Mameha's voice occasionally, but mainly the Baron did the talking. At one point I thought he was angry with Mameha, but finally I overheard enough to understand that he was only complaining about a man he'd met the day before, who'd asked him personal questions that made him angry. At last when the meal was over, the maid carried out cups of tea, and Mameha asked for me. I went out to kneel before the Baron, feeling very nervous – for I'd never met an aristocrat before. I bowed and begged his favor, and thought perhaps he would say something to me. But he seemed to be looking around the apartment, hardly taking notice of me at all.

'Mameha,' he said, 'what happened to that scroll you used to have in the alcove? It was an ink painting of something or other – much better than the thing you have there now.'

'The scroll there now, Baron, is a poem in Matsudaira Koichi's own hand. It has hung in that alcove nearly four years.'

'Four years? Wasn't the ink painting there when I came last month?'

'It wasn't . . . but in any case, the Baron hasn't honored me with a visit in nearly three months.'

'No wonder I'm feeling so exhausted. I'm always saying I ought to spend more time in Kyoto, but . . . well, one thing leads to another. Let's have a look at that scroll I'm talking about. I can't believe it's been four years since I've seen it.'

Mameha summoned her maid and asked her to bring the scroll from the closet. I was given the job of unrolling it. My hands were trembling so much that it slipped from my grasp when I held it up for the Baron to have a look.

'Careful, girl!' he said.

I was so embarrassed that even after I'd bowed and

apologized, I couldn't help glancing at the Baron again and again to see if he seemed angry with me. While I held the scroll up, he seemed to look at me more than at it. But it wasn't a reproachful stare. After a while I realized it was curiosity, which only made me feel more self-conscious.

'This scroll is much more attractive than the one you have in the alcove now, Mameha,' he said. But he still seemed to be looking at me, and made no effort to look away when I glanced at him. 'Calligraphy is so old-fashioned anyway,' he went on. 'You ought to take that thing in the alcove down, and put up this landscape painting again.'

Mameha had no choice but to do as the Baron suggested; she even managed to look as if she thought it was a fine idea. When the maid and I had finished hanging the painting and rolling up the other scroll, Mameha called me over to pour tea for the Baron. To look at us from above, we formed a little triangle – Mameha, the Baron, and me. But of course, Mameha and the Baron did all the talking; as for me, I did nothing more useful than to kneel there, feeling as much out of my element as a pigeon in a nest of falcons. To think I'd ever imagined myself worthy of entertaining the sorts of men Mameha entertained – not only grand aristocrats like the Baron, but the Chairman as well. Even the theater director from several nights earlier . . . he'd hardly so much as glanced at me. I won't say I'd felt worthy of the Baron's company earlier; but now I couldn't help realizing once again that I was nothing more than an ignorant girl from a fishing village. Hatsumomo, if she had her way, would keep me down so low, every man who visited Gion would remain forever out of my reach. For all I knew I might never see Baron Matsunaga again, and never come upon the Chairman. Wasn't it possible Mameha would realize the hopelessness of my cause and leave me to languish in the okiya like a little-worn kimono that had seemed so lovely in the shop? The Baron – who I was beginning to realize was something of a nervous man – leaned over to scratch at a mark on the surface of Mameha's table, and made me think of my father on the last day I'd seen him, digging grime out of ruts in the wood with his fingernails. I wondered what he would think if he could see me kneeling here in Mameha's apartment, wearing a robe more expensive than anything he'd ever laid eyes on, with a baron across from me and one of the most famous geisha in all of Japan at my side. I was hardly worthy of these surroundings. And then I became aware of all the magnificent silk wrapped about my body, and had the feeling I might drown in beauty. At that moment, beauty itself struck me as a kind of painful melancholy.

16

ONE AFTERNOON AS Mameha and I were strolling across the Shijo Avenue Bridge to pick up some new hair ornaments in the Pontocho district – for Mameha never liked the shops selling hair ornaments in Gion – she came to a stop suddenly. An old tugboat was puffing its way beneath the bridge; I thought Mameha was just concerned about the black fumes, but after a moment she turned to me with an expression I couldn't quite understand.

'What is it, Mameha-san?' I asked.

'I may as well tell you, because you'll only hear it from someone else,' she said. 'Your little friend Pumpkin has just won the apprentice's award. It's expected she'll win it a second time as well.'

Mameha was referring to an award for the apprentice who'd earned the most during the previous month. It may seem strange that such an award existed, but there's a very good reason. Encouraging apprentices to earn as much as possible helps shape them into the sort of geisha who will be most appreciated in Gion – that is to say, the ones who will earn a lot not only for themselves but for everyone else too.

Several times Mameha had predicted that Pumpkin would struggle along for a few years and end up the sort of geisha with a few loyal customers – none of them wealthy – and little else. It was a sad picture, and I was pleased to learn that Pumpkin was doing better than that. But at the same time I felt anxiety prickling at my stomach. Pumpkin now seemed to be one of the most popular apprentices in Gion, while I remained one of the most obscure. When I began to wonder what it might mean for my future, the world around me honestly seemed to grow dark.

The most astonishing thing about Pumpkin's success, as I stood there on the bridge thinking about it, was that she'd managed to surpass an exquisite young girl named Raiha, who'd won the award the past several months. Raiha's mother had been a renowned geisha, and her father was a member of one of Japan's most illustrious families, with almost limitless wealth. Whenever Raiha strolled past me, I felt as a simple smelt must feel when a silver salmon glides by. How had Pumpkin managed to outdo her? Hatsumomo had certainly pushed her from the very day of her debut, so much that she'd begun to lose weight lately and hardly looked herself. But regardless of how hard Pumpkin may have worked, could she really have grown more popular than Raiha?

'Oh, now, really,' said Mameha, 'don't look so sad. You ought to be rejoicing!'

'Yes, it's very selfish of me,' I said.

'That isn't what I mean. Hatsumomo and Pumpkin will both pay dearly for this apprentice's award. In five years, no one will remember who Pumpkin is.'

'It seems to me,' I said, 'that everyone will remember her as the girl who surpassed Raiha.'

'No one has surpassed Raiha. Pumpkin may have earned the most money last month, but Raiha is still the most popular apprentice in Gion. Come, I'll explain.'

Mameha led me to a tearoom in the Pontocho district and sat me down.

In Gion, Mameha said, a very popular geisha can always make sure her younger sister earns more than anyone else – if she is willing to risk hurting her own reputation. The reason has to do with the way *ohana*, 'flower fees,' are billed. In the old days, a hundred years or more ago, every time a geisha arrived at a party to entertain, the mistress of the teahouse lit a stick of one-hour incense – called one *ohana*, or 'flower.' The geisha's fees were based on how many sticks of incense had burned by the time she left.

The cost of one *ohana* has always been fixed by the Gion

Registry Office. While I was an apprentice, it was ¥3, which was about the cost of two bottles of liquor, perhaps. It may sound like a lot, but an unpopular geisha earning one *ohana* per hour has a grim life. Probably she spends most evenings sitting around the charcoal brazier waiting for an engagement; even when she's busy, she may earn no more than ¥10 in a night, which won't be enough even to pay back her debts. Considering all the wealth that flows into Gion, she's nothing more than an insect picking at the carcass – compared with Hatsumomo or Mameha, who are magnificent lionesses feasting at the kill, not only because they have engagements all night long every night, but because they charge a good deal more as well. In Hatsumomo's case, she charged one *ohana* every fifteen minutes, rather than one every hour. And in the case of Mameha . . . well, there was no one else in Gion quite like her: she charged one *ohana* every five minutes.

Of course, no geisha keeps all her earnings, not even Mameha. The teahouse where she earned the fees takes a portion; then a much smaller portion goes to the geisha association; and a portion to her dresser; and right on down the line, including a fee she might pay to an okiya in exchange for keeping her account books and tracking her engagements. She probably keeps only a little more than half of what she earns. Still, it's an enormous sum when compared with the livelihood of an unpopular geisha, who every day sinks deeper and deeper into a pit.

Here's how a geisha like Hatsumomo could make her younger sister seem more successful than she really was.

To begin with, a popular geisha in Gion is welcome at nearly any party, and will drop in on many of them for only five minutes. Her customers will be happy to pay the fees, even though she's only saying hello. They know that the next time they visit Gion, she'll probably join them at the table for a while to give them the pleasure of her company. An apprentice, on the other hand, can't possibly get away with such behavior. Her role is to build relationships. Until she becomes a full-fledged geisha at the age of eighteen, she doesn't consider flitting from party to party. Instead she stays for an hour or more, and only then telephones her okiya to ask her older sister's whereabouts, so she can go to another teahouse and be introduced to a new round of guests. While her popular older sister might drop in on as many as twenty parties during an evening, an apprentice probably attends no more than five. But this isn't what Hatsumomo was doing. She was taking Pumpkin with her everywhere she went.

Until the age of sixteen, an apprentice geisha bills one-half *ohana* per hour. If Pumpkin stayed at a party only five minutes, the host was billed the same as if she'd stayed a full hour. On the other hand, no one expected Pumpkin to stay only five minutes. Probably the men didn't mind that Hatsumomo brought her younger sister for only a brief visit one night, or even two. But after a while they must have begun to wonder why she was too busy to stay longer; and why her younger sister didn't remain behind as she was expected to do. Pumpkin's earnings may have been high, you see – perhaps as high as three or four *ohana* every hour. But she was certain to pay for it with her reputation, and so was Hatsumomo.

'Hatsumomo's behavior only shows us how desperate she is,' Mameha concluded. 'She'll do anything to make Pumpkin look good. And you know why, don't you?'

'I'm not sure, Mameha-san.'

'She wants Pumpkin to look good so Mrs. Nitta will adopt her. If Pumpkin is made the daughter of the okiya, her future is assured, and so is Hatsumomo's. After all, Hatsumomo is Pumpkin's sister; Mrs. Nitta certainly wouldn't throw her out. Do you understand what I'm saying? If Pumpkin is adopted, you'll never be free of Hatsumomo . . . unless it's you who is thrown out.'

I felt as the waves of the ocean must feel when clouds have blocked the warmth of the sun.

'I'd hoped to see you as a popular young apprentice before long,' Mameha went on, 'but Hatsumomo certainly has gotten in our way.'

'Yes, she has.'

'Well, at least you're learning how to entertain men properly. You're lucky to have met the Baron. I may not have found a way around Hatsumomo just yet, but to tell the truth –' And here she stopped herself.

'Ma'am?' I said.

'Oh, never mind, Sayuri. I'd be a fool to share my thoughts with you.'

I was hurt to hear this. Mameha must have noticed my feelings at once, for she was quick to say, 'You're living under the same roof as Hatsumomo, aren't you? Anything I say to you could get back to her.'

'I'm very sorry, Mameha-san, for whatever I've done to deserve your low opinion of me,' I told her. 'Can you really imagine I'll run back to the okiya and tell anything to Hatsumomo?'

'I'm not worried about what you'll do. Mice don't get eaten because they run over to where the cat is sleeping and wake it up. You know perfectly well how resourceful Hatsumomo is. You'll just have to trust me, Sayuri.'

'Yes, ma'am,' I replied; for really, there was nothing else I could say.

'I will tell you one thing,' Mameha said, leaning forward a bit, from what I took as excitement. 'You and I will be going to an engagement together in the next two weeks at a place Hatsumomo will never find us.'

'May I ask where?'

'Certainly not. I won't even tell you when. Just be prepared. You'll find out everything you need to know when the proper time comes.'

When I returned to the okiya that afternoon, I hid myself upstairs to look through my almanac. A variety of days in the next two weeks stood out. One was the coming Wednesday, which was a favorable day for traveling westward; I thought perhaps Mameha planned to take me out of the city. Another was the following Monday, which also happened to be *tai-an* – the most auspicious day of the six-day Buddhist week. Finally, the Sunday after had a curious reading: 'A balance of good and bad can open the door to destiny.' This one sounded most intriguing of all.

I heard nothing from Mameha on Wednesday. A few

afternoons later she did summon me to her apartment – on a day my almanac said was unfavorable – but only to discuss a change in my tea ceremony class at the school. After this an entire week passed without a word from her. And then on Sunday around noon, I heard the door of the okiya roll open and put my shamisen down onto the walkway, where I'd been practicing for an hour or so, to rush to the front. I expected to see one of Mameha's maids, but it was only a man from the druggist's making a delivery of Chinese herbs for Auntie's arthritis. After one of our elderly maids took the packet, I was about to return to my shamisen when I noticed the delivery man trying to get my attention. He was holding a piece of paper in one hand so that only I could see it. Our maid was about to roll the door shut, but he said to me, 'I'm sorry to trouble you, miss, but would you mind throwing this away for me?' The maid thought it odd, but I took the paper and pretended to throw it away in the maids' room. It was a note, unsigned, in Mameha's hand.

'Ask Auntie's permission to leave. Tell her I have work for you to do in my apartment and come here no later than one o'clock. Don't let anyone else know where you're going.'

I'm sure Mameha's precautions were very sensible, but in any case, Mother was lunching with a friend, and Hatsumomo and Pumpkin had gone to an afternoon engagement already. No one remained in the okiya but Auntie and the maids. I went straight up to Auntie's room to find her draping a heavy cotton blanket across her futon, preparing for a nap. She stood shivering in her sleeping robe while I spoke to her. The moment she heard that Mameha had summoned me, she didn't even care to know the reason. She just gave a wave of her hand and crawled beneath the blanket to go to sleep.

Mameha was still attending a morning engagement when I arrived at her apartment, but her maid showed me into the dressing room to help me with my makeup, and afterward brought in the kimono ensemble Mameha had set out for me. I'd grown accustomed to wearing Mameha's kimono, but in fact, it's unusual for a geisha to lend out robes from her collection this way. Two friends in Gion might trade kimono for a night or two; but it's rare for an older geisha to show such kindness to a young girl. And in fact, Mameha was going to a great deal of trouble on my behalf; she no longer wore these long-sleeved robes herself and had to retrieve them from storage. I often wondered if she expected to be repaid somehow.

The kimono she'd laid out for me that day was the loveliest yet – an orange silk with a silver waterfall pouring from the knee into a slate-blue ocean. The waterfall was split by brown cliffs, with knotted driftwood at the base embroidered in lacquered threads. I didn't realize it, but the robe was well known in Gion; people who saw it probably thought of Mameha at once. In permitting me to wear it, I think she was rubbing some of her aura off onto me.

After Mr. Itchoda had tied the obi – a russet and brown high-lighted with gold threads – I put the final touches on my makeup and the ornaments in my hair. I tucked the Chairman's handkerchief – which I'd brought from the okiya as I often did – inside my obi, and stood before the mirror gaping at myself. Already it was amazing to me that Mameha had arranged for me to look so beautiful; but to top it off, when she returned to her apartment, she herself changed into a fairly plain kimono. It was a robe the color of a mountain potato, covered with soft gray hatchmarks, and her obi was a simple pattern of black diamonds on a background of deep blue. She had the understated brilliance of a pearl, as she always did; but when we walked down the street together, the women who bowed at Mameha were looking at me.

From the Gion Shrine, we rode north in a rickshaw for a half hour, into a section of Kyoto I'd never seen. Along the way, Mameha told me we would be attending a sumo exhibition as the guests of Iwamura Ken, the founder of Iwamura Electric in Osaka – which, incidentally, was the manufacturer of the heater that had killed Granny. Iwamura's right-hand man, Nobu Toshikazu, who was president of the company, would also be attending. Nobu was quite a fan of sumo and had helped organize the exhibition that afternoon.

'I should tell you,' she said to me, 'that Nobu is . . . a bit peculiar-looking. You'll make a great impression on him by behaving well when you meet him.' After she said this, she gave me a look as if to say she would be terribly disappointed in me if I didn't.

As for Hatsumomo, we wouldn't have to worry about her. Tickets to the exhibition had been sold out weeks before.

At last we climbed out of the rickshaw at the campus of Kyoto University. Mameha led me up a dirt path lined with small pine trees. Western-style buildings closed in on both sides of us, with windows chopped into tiny glass squares by strips of painted wood. I hadn't realized how much Gion seemed like home to me, until I noticed myself feeling out of place at the university. All around us were smooth-skinned young men with their hair parted, some wearing suspenders to keep up their pants. They seemed to find Mameha and me so exotic that they stopped to watch as we strolled past, and even made jokes to one another. Soon we passed through an iron gate with a crowd of older men and a number of women, including quite a few geisha. Kyoto had few places a sumo exhibition could be held indoors, and one was Kyoto University's old Exhibition Hall. The building no longer stands today; but at that time it fit with the Western structures around it about like a shriveled old man in kimono fits with a group of businessmen. It was a big box of a building, with a roof that didn't seem quite substantial enough, but made me think of a lid fitted onto the wrong pot. The huge doors on one side were so badly warped, they bulged against the iron rods fastened across them. Its ruggedness reminded me so much of my tipsy house that I felt sad for a moment.

As I made my way up the stone steps into the building, I spotted two geisha strolling across the gravel courtyard, and bowed to them. They nodded to me in return, and one said something to the other. I thought this very odd – until I looked at them more closely. My heart sank; one of the women was Hatsumomo's friend Korin. I gave her another bow, now that I recognized her, and did my best to smile. The moment they looked away, I whispered to Mameha:

'Mameha-san! I've just seen a friend of Hatsumomo's!'

'I didn't know Hatsumomo had any friends.'

'It's Korin. She's over there . . . or at least, she was a moment ago, with another geisha.'

'I know Korin. Why are you so worried about her? What can she possibly do?'

I didn't have an answer to this question. But if Mameha wasn't concerned, I could think of no reason why I ought to be.

My first impression upon entering the Exhibition Hall was of an enormous empty space reaching up to the roof, beneath which sunlight poured in through screened windows high overhead. The huge expanse was filled with the noise of the crowd, and with smoke from the sweet-rice cakes roasted with miso paste on the grills outside. In the center was a square mound where the wrestlers would compete, dominated by a roof in the style of a Shinto shrine. A priest walked around on it, chanting blessings and shaking his sacred wand adorned with folded paper strips.

Mameha led me down to a tier in the front, where we removed our shoes and began to walk across in our split-toed socks on a little margin of wood. Our hosts were in this row, but I had no idea who they were until I caught sight of a man waving his hand to Mameha; I knew at once that he was Nobu. There was no doubt why Mameha had warned me about his appearance. Even from a distance the skin of his face looked like a melted candle. At some time in his life he had suffered terrible burns; his whole appearance was so tragic-looking, I couldn't imagine the agony he must have endured. Already I was feeling strange from running into Korin; now I began to worry that when I met Nobu, I might make a fool of myself without quite understanding why. As I walked along behind Mameha, I focused my attention not on Nobu but on a very elegant man seated beside him on the same tatami mat, wearing a pinstripe men's kimono. From the moment I set eyes on this man I felt a strange stillness settling over me. He was talking with someone in another box, so that I could see only the back of his head. But he was so familiar to me that for a moment I could make no sense of what I saw. All I knew was that he was out of place there in the Exhibition Hall. Before I could even think why, I saw an image in my mind of him turning toward me on the streets of our litt[le] village.

And then I realized: it was Mr. Tanaka!

He'd changed in some way I couldn't have described. I watched him reach up to smooth his gray hair and was struck by the graceful way he moved his fingers. Why did I find it so peculiarly soothing to look at him? Perhaps I was in a daze at seeing him and hardly knew how I really felt. Well, if I hated anyone in this world, I hated Mr. Tanaka; I had to remind myself of this. I wasn't going to kneel beside him and say, 'Why, Mr. Tanaka, how very honored I am to see you again! What has brought you to Kyoto?' Instead I would find some way of showing him my true feelings, even if it was hardly the proper thing for an apprentice to do. Actually, I'd thought of Mr. Tanaka very little these last few years. But still I owed it to myself not to be kind to him, not to pour his sake into his cup if I could spill it on his leg instead. I would smile at him as I was obliged to smile; but it would be the smile I had so often seen on Hatsumomo's face; and then I would say, 'Oh, Mr. Tanaka, the strong odor of fish . . . it makes me so homesick to sit here beside you!' How shocked he would be! Or perhaps this: 'Why, Mr. Tanaka, you look . . . almost distinguished!' Though in truth, as I looked at him – for by now we'd nearly reached the box in which he sat – he did look distinguished, more distinguished than I could ever have imagined. Mameha was just arriving, lowering herself to her knees to bow. Then he turned his head, and for the first time I saw his broad face and the sharpness of his cheekbones . . . and most of all, his eyelids folded so tightly in the corners and so smooth and flat. And suddenly everything around me seemed to grow quiet, as if he were the wind that blew and I were just a cloud carried upon it.

He was familiar, certainly – more familiar in some ways than my own image in the mirror. But it wasn't Mr. Tanaka at all. It was the Chairman.

17

I HAD SEEN the Chairman during only one brief moment in my life; but I'd spent a great many moments since then imagining him. He was like a song I'd heard once in fragments but had been singing in my mind ever since. Though of course, the notes had changed a bit over time – which is to say that I expected his forehead to be higher and his gray hair not so thick. When I saw him, I had a flicker of uncertainty whether he was really the Chairman; but I felt so soothed, I knew without a doubt I had found him.

While Mameha was greeting the two men, I stood behind awaiting my turn to bow. What if my voice, when I tried to speak, should sound like a rag squeaking on polished wood? Nobu, with his tragic scars, was watching me, but I wasn't sure whether the Chairman had even noticed me there; I was too timid to glance in his direction. When Mameha took her place and began to smooth her kimono over her knees, I saw that the Chairman was looking at me with what I took to be curiosity. My feet actually went cold from all the blood that came rushing into my face.

'Chairman Iwamura . . . President Nobu,' Mameha said, 'this is my new younger sister, Sayuri.'

I'm certain you've heard of the famous Iwamura Ken, founder of Iwamura Electric. And probably you've heard of Nobu Toshikazu as well. Certainly no business partnership in Japan was ever more famous than theirs. They were like a tree and its roots, or like a shrine and the gate that stands before it. Even as a fourteen-year-old girl I'd heard of them. But I'd never imagined for a moment that Iwamura Ken might be the man I'd met on the banks of the Shirakawa Stream. Well, I lowered myself to my knees and bowed to them, saying all the usual things about begging their indulgence and so forth. When I was done, I went to kneel in the space between them. Nobu fell into conversation with a man beside him, while the Chairman, on the other side of me, sat with his hand around an empty teacup on a tray at his knee. Mameha began talking to him; I picked up a small teapot and held my sleeve out of the way to pour. To my astonishment, the Chairman's eyes drifted to my arm. Of course, I was eager to see for myself exactly what he was seeing. Perhaps because of the murky light in the Exhibition Hall, the underside of my arm seemed to shine with the gleaming smoothness of a pearl, and was a beautiful ivory color. No part of my body had ever struck me as lovely in this way before. I was very aware that the Chairman's eyes weren't moving; as long as he kept looking at my arm, I certainly wasn't going to take it away. And then suddenly Mameha fell silent. It seemed to me she'd stopped talking because the Chairman was watching my arm instead of listening to her. Then I realized what was really the matter.

The teapot was empty. What was more, it had been empty even when I'd picked it up.

I'd felt almost glamorous a moment earlier, but now I muttered an apology and put the pot down as quickly as I could. Mameha laughed. 'You can see what a determined girl she is, Chairman,' she said. 'If there'd been a single drop of tea in that pot, Sayuri would have gotten it out.'

'That certainly is a beautiful kimono your younger sister is wearing, Mameha,' the Chairman said. 'Do I recall seeing it on you, back during your days as an apprentice?'

If I felt any lingering doubts about whether this man was really the Chairman, I felt them no longer after hearing the familiar kindness of his voice.

'It's possible, I suppose,' Mameha replied. 'But the Chairman has seen me in so many different kimono over the years, I can't imagine he remembers them all.'

'Well, I'm no different from any other man. Beauty makes quite an impression on me. When it comes to these sumo wrestlers, I can't tell one of them from the next.'

Mameha leaned across in front of the Chairman and

whispered to me, 'What the Chairman is really saying is that he doesn't particularly like sumo.'

'Now, Mameha,' he said, 'if you're trying to get me into trouble with Nobu . . .'

'Chairman Nobu-san has known for years how you feel!'

'Nevertheless. Sayuri, is this your first encounter with sumo?'

I'd been waiting for some excuse to speak with him but before I'd so much as taken a breath we were all startled by a tremendous boom that shook the great building. Our heads turned and the crowd fell silent; but it was nothing more than the closing of one of the giant doors. In a moment we could hear hinges creaking and saw the second door straining its way around in an arc, pushed by two of the wrestlers. Nobu had his head turned away from me; I couldn't resist peering at the terrible burns on the side of his face and his neck, and at his ear, which was misshapen. Then I saw that the sleeve of his jacket was empty. I'd been so preoccupied, I hadn't noticed it earlier; it was folded in two and fastened to this shoulder by a long silver pin.

I may as well tell you, if you don't know it already, that as a young lieutenant in the Japanese marines, Nobu had been severely injured in a bombing outside Seoul in 1910, at the time Korea was being annexed to Japan. I knew nothing about his heroism when I met him – though in fact, the story was familiar all over Japan. If he'd never joined up with the Chairman and eventually become president of Iwamura Electric, probably he would have been forgotten as a war hero. But as it was, his terrible injuries made the story of his success that much more remarkable, so the two were often mentioned together.

I don't know too much about history – for they taught us only arts at the little school – but I think the Japanese government gained control over Korea at the end of the Russo-Japanese War, and a few years afterward made the decision to incorporate Korea into the growing empire. I'm sure the Koreans didn't much like this. Nobu went there as part of a small force to keep things under control. Late one afternoon he accompanied his commanding officer on a visit to a village near Seoul. On the way back to the spot where their horses were tied up, the members of the patrol came under attack. When they heard the horrible shrieking noise of an incoming shell, the commanding officer tried to climb down into a ditch, but he was an old man and moved at about the speed of a barnacle inching its way down a rock. Moments before the shell struck he was still trying to find a foothold. Nobu laid himself over the commanding officer in an effort to save him, but the old man took this badly and tried to climb out. With some effort he raised his head; Nobu tried to push it back down, but the shell struck, killing the commanding officer and injuring Nobu severely. In surgery later that year, Nobu lost his left arm above the elbow.

The first time I saw his pinned sleeve, I couldn't help averting my eyes in alarm. I'd never before seen anyone who'd lost a limb – though when I was a little girl, an assistant of Mr. Tanaka's had lost the tip of his finger one morning while cleaning a fish. In Nobu's case, many people felt his arm to be the least of his problems, because his skin was like an enormous wound. It's hard to describe the way he looked, and probably it would be cruel for me even to try. I'll just repeat what I overheard another geisha say about him once: 'Every time I look at his face, I think of a sweet potato that has blistered in the fire.'

When the huge doors were closed, I turned back to the Chairman to answer his question. As an apprentice I was free to sit as quietly as an arrangement of flowers, if I wanted to; but I was determined not to let this opportunity pass. Even if I made only the slightest impression on him, like a child's foot might make on a dusty floor, at least it would be a start.

'The Chairman asked if this is my first encounter with sumo,' I said. 'It is, and I would be very grateful for anything the Chairman might be kind enough to explain to me.'

'If you want to know what's going on,' said Nobu, 'you'd better talk to me. What is your name, apprentice? I couldn't hear well with the noise of the crowd.'

I turned away from the Chairman with as much difficulty as a hungry child turns away from a plate of food.

'My name is Sayuri, sir,' I said.

'You're Mameha's younger sister; why aren't you 'Mame'

something-or-other?' Nobu went on. 'Isn't that one of your foolish traditions?'

'Yes, sir. But all the names with 'Mame' turned out to be inauspicious for me, according to the fortune-teller.'

'The fortune-teller,' Nobu said with contempt. 'Is he the one who picked your name for you?'

'I'm the one who picked it,' Mameha said. 'The fortune-teller doesn't pick names; he only tells us if they're acceptable.'

'One day, Mameha,' Nobu replied, 'you'll grow up and stop listening to fools.'

'Now, now, Nobu-san,' said the Chairman, 'anyone hearing you talk would think you're the most modern man in the nation. Yet I've never known anyone who believes more strongly in destiny than you do.'

'Every man has his destiny. But who needs to go to a fortune-teller to find it? Do I go to a chef to find out if I'm hungry?' Nobu said. 'Anyway, Sayuri is a very pretty name – though pretty names and pretty girls don't always go together.'

I was beginning to wonder if his next comment would be something like, 'What an ugly younger sister you've taken on, Mameha!' or some such thing. But to my relief, he said:

'Here's a case where the name and the girl go together. I believe she may be even prettier than you, Mameha!'

'Nobu-san! No woman likes to hear that she isn't the prettiest creature around.'

'Especially you, eh? Well, you'd better get used to it. She has especially beautiful eyes. Turn toward me, Sayuri, so I can have another look at them.'

I couldn't very well look down at the mats, since Nobu wanted to see my eyes. Nor could I stare directly back at him without seeming too forward. So after my gaze slipped around a little, like trying to find a footing on ice, I finally let it settle in the region of his chin. If I could have willed my eyes to stop seeing, I would certainly have done it; because Nobu's features looked like poorly sculpted clay. You must remember that I knew nothing as yet about the tragedy that had disfigured him. When I wondered what had happened to him,

I couldn't stop that terrible feeling of heaviness.

'Your eyes certainly do shimmer in a most startling way,' he said.

At that moment a small door opened along the outside of the hall, and a man entered wearing an exceptionally formal kimono with a high black cap on his head, looking as if he'd stepped directly out of a painting of the Imperial court. He made his way down the aisle, leading a procession of wrestlers so huge they had to crouch to pass through the doorway.

'What do you know about sumo, young girl?' Nobu asked me.

'Only that the wrestlers are as big as whales, sir,' I said. 'There's a man working in Gion who was once a sumo wrestler.'

'You must mean Awajiumi. He's sitting just over there, you know.' With his one hand, Nobu pointed toward another tier where Awajiumi sat, laughing about something, with Korin next to him. She must have spotted me, for she gave a little smile and then leaned in to say something to Awajiumi, who looked in our direction.

'He was never much of a wrestler,' Nobu said. 'He liked to slam his opponents with his shoulder. It never worked, stupid man, but it broke his collarbone plenty of times.'

By now the wrestlers had all entered the building and stood around the base of the mound. One by one their names were announced, and they climbed up and arranged themselves in a circle facing the audience. Later, as they made their way out of the hall again so the wrestlers of the opposing side could begin their procession, Nobu said to me:

'That rope in a circle on the ground marks the ring. The first wrestler to be shoved outside it, or to touch the mound with anything but his feet, is the loser. It may sound easy, but how would you like to try pushing one of those giants over that rope?'

'I suppose I could come up behind him with wooden clappers,' I said, 'and hope to scare him so badly he'd jump out.'

'Be serious,' Nobu said.

I won't pretend this was a particularly clever thing for me

to have said, but it was one of my first efforts at joking with a man. I felt so embarrassed, I couldn't think what to say. Then the Chairman leaned toward me.

'Nobu-san doesn't joke about sumo,' he said quietly.

'I don't make jokes about the three things that matter most in life,' Nobu said. 'Sumo, business, and war.'

'My goodness, I think that was a sort of joke,' Mameha said. 'Does that mean you're contradicting yourself?'

'If you were watching a battle,' Nobu said to me, 'or for that matter sitting in the midst of a business meeting, would you understand what was happening?'

I wasn't sure what he meant, but I could tell from his tone that he expected me to say no. 'Oh, not at all,' I answered.

'Exactly. And you can't expect to understand what's going on in sumo, either. So you can laugh at Mameha's little jokes or you can listen to me and learn what it all means.'

'He's tried to teach me about it over the years,' the Chairman said quietly to me, 'but I'm a very poor student.'

'The Chairman is a brilliant man,' Nobu said. 'He's a poor student of sumo because he doesn't care about it. He wouldn't even be here this afternoon, except that he was generous enough to accept my proposal that Iwamura Electric be a sponsor of the exhibition.'

By now both teams had finished their ring-entering ceremonies. Two more special ceremonies followed, one for each of the two *yokozuna*. A *yokozuna* is the very highest rank in sumo – 'just like Mameha's position in Gion,' as Nobu explained it to me. I had no reason to doubt him; but if Mameha ever took half as much time entering a party as these *yokozuna* took entering the ring, she'd certainly never be invited back. The second of the two was short and had a most remarkable face – not at all flabby, but chiseled like stone, and with a jaw that made me think of the squared front end of a fishing boat. The audience cheered him so loudly I covered my ears. His name was Miyagiyama, and if you know sumo at all, you'll understand why they cheered as they did.

'He is the greatest wrestler I have ever seen,' Nobu told me.

Just before the bouts were ready to begin, the announcer listed the winner's prizes. One was a considerable sum of cash offered by Nobu Toshikazu, president of the Iwamura Electric Company. Nobu seemed very annoyed when he heard this and said, 'What a fool! The money isn't from me, it's from Iwamura Electric. I apologize, Chairman. I'll call someone over to have the announcer correct his mistake.'

'There's no mistake, Nobu. Considering the great debt I owe you, it's the least I can do.'

'The Chairman is too generous,' Nobu said. 'I'm very grateful.' And with this, he passed a sake cup to the Chairman and filled it, and the two of them drank together.

When the first wrestlers entered the ring, I expected the bout to begin right away. Instead they spent five minutes or more tossing salt on the mound and squatting in order to tip their bodies to one side and raise a leg high in the air before slamming it down. From time to time they crouched, glowering into each other's eyes, but just when I thought they were going to charge, one would stand and stroll away to scoop up another handful of salt. Finally, when I wasn't expecting it, it happened. They slammed into each other, grabbing at loincloths; but within an instant, one had shoved the other off balance and the match was over. The audience clapped and shouted, but Nobu just shook his head and said, 'Poor technique.'

During the bouts that followed, I often felt that one ear was linked to my mind and the other to my heart; because on one side I listened to what Nobu told me – and much of it was interesting. But the sound of the Chairman's voice on the other side, as he went on talking with Mameha, always distracted me.

An hour or more passed, and then the movement of a brilliant color in Awajiumi's section caught my eye. It was an orange silk flower swaying in a woman's hair as she took her place on her knees. At first I thought it was Korin, and that she had changed her kimono. But then I saw it wasn't Korin at all, it was Hatsumomo.

To see her there when I hadn't expected her . . . I felt a jolt as if I'd stepped on an electric wire. Surely it was only a matter of time before she found a way of humiliating me, even here in this giant hall amid hundreds of people. I didn't mind her making a fool of me in front of a crowd, if it had to happen; but I couldn't bear the thought of looking like a fool in front of the Chairman. I felt such a hotness in my throat, I could hardly even pretend to listen when Nobu began telling me something about the two wrestlers climbing onto the mound. When I looked at Mameha, she flicked her eyes toward Hatsumomo, and then said, 'Chairman, forgive me, I have to excuse myself. It occurs to me Sayuri may want to do the same.'

She waited until Nobu was done with his story, and then I followed her out of the hall.

'Oh, Mameha-san . . . she's like a demon,' I said.

'Korin left more than an hour ago. She must have found Hatsumomo and sent her here. You ought to feel flattered, really, considering that Hatsumomo goes to so much trouble just to torment you.'

'I can't bear to have her make a fool of me here in front of . . . well, in front of all these people.'

'But if you do something she finds laughable, she'll leave you alone, don't you think?'

'Please, Mameha-san . . . don't make me embarrass myself.'

We'd crossed a courtyard and were just about to climb the steps into the building where the toilets were housed; but Mameha led me some distance down a covered passageway instead. When we were out of earshot of anyone, she spoke quietly to me.

'Nobu-san and the Chairman have been great patrons of mine over the years. Heaven knows Nobu can be harsh with people he doesn't like, but he's as loyal to his friends as a retainer is to a feudal lord; and you'll never meet a more trustworthy man. Do you think Hatsumomo understands these qualities? All she sees when she looks at Nobu is . . . "Mr. Lizard." That's what she calls him. "Mameha-san, I saw you with Mr. Lizard last night! Oh, goodness, you look all splotchy. I think he's rubbing off on you." That sort of thing. Now, I don't care what you think of Nobu-san at the moment. In time you'll come to see what a good man he is. But Hatsumomo may very well leave you alone if she thinks you've taken a strong liking to him.'

I couldn't think how to respond to this. I wasn't even sure just yet what Mameha was asking me to do.

'Nobu-san has been talking to you about sumo for much of the afternoon,' she went on. 'For all anyone knows, you adore him. Now put on a show for Hatsumomo's benefit. Let her think you're more charmed by him than you've ever been by anyone. She'll think it's the funniest thing she's ever seen. Probably she'll want you to stay on in Gion just so she can see more of it.'

'But, Mameha-san, how am I going to make Hatsumomo think I'm fascinated by him?'

'If you can't manage such a thing, I haven't trained you properly,' she replied.

When we returned to our box, Nobu had once again fallen into conversation with a man nearby. I couldn't interrupt, so I pretended to be absorbed in watching the wrestlers on the mound prepare for their bout. The audience had grown restless; Nobu wasn't the only one talking. I felt such a longing to turn to the Chairman and ask if he recalled a day several years ago when he'd shown kindness to a young girl . . . but of course, I could never say such a thing. Besides, it would be disastrous for me to focus my attention on him while Hatsumomo was watching.

Soon Nobu turned back to me and said, 'These bouts have been tedious. When Miyagiyama comes out, we'll see some real skill.'

This, it seemed to me, was my chance to dote on him. 'But the wrestling I've seen already has been so impressive!' I said. 'And the things President Nobu has been kind enough to tell me have been so interesting, I can hardly imagine we haven't seen the best already.'

'Don't be ridiculous,' said Nobu. 'Not one of these wrestlers deserves to be in the same ring as Miyagiyama.'

Over Nobu's shoulder, I could see Hatsumomo in a far tier. She was chatting with Awajiumi and didn't appear to be looking at me.

'I know this may seem a very foolish thing to ask,' I said, 'but how can a wrestler as small as Miyagiyama be the greatest?' And if you had seen my face, you might have thought no subject had ever interested me more. I felt ridiculous, pretending to be absorbed by something so trivial; but no one who saw us would have known that we weren't talking about the deepest secrets of our souls. I'm happy to say that at that very moment, I caught a glimpse of Hatsumomo turning her head toward me.

'Miyagiyama only looks small because the others are so much fatter,' Nobu was saying. 'But he's very vain about his size. His height and weight were printed in the newspaper perfectly correctly a few years ago; and yet he was so offended he had a friend hit him on top of the head with a plank, and then gorged himself on sweet potatoes and water, and went down to the newspaper to show them they were wrong.'

Probably I would have laughed at nearly anything Nobu had said – for Hatsumomo's benefit, I mean. But in fact, it really was quite funny to imagine Miyagiyama squinting his eyes shut and waiting for the plank to come banging down. I held that image in my mind and laughed as freely as I dared, and soon Nobu began to laugh with me. We must have looked like the best of friends to Hatsumomo, for I saw her clapping her hands in delight.

Soon I struck upon the idea of pretending that Nobu himself was the Chairman; every time he spoke, I overlooked his gruffness and tried to imagine gentleness instead. Gradually I found myself able to look at his lips and block from my mind the discoloring and the scars, and imagine that they were the Chairman's lips, and that every nuance in his voice was some comment on his feelings about me. At one point I think I convinced myself I wasn't even in the Exhibition Hall, but in a quiet room kneeling beside the Chairman. I hadn't felt such bliss in as long as I could remember. Like a ball tossed in the air that seems to hang motionless before it falls, I felt myself suspended in a state of quiet timelessness. As I glanced around the hall, I saw only the beauty of its giant wooden timbers and smelled the aroma of the sweet-rice cakes. I thought this state might never end; but then at some point I made a comment I don't even remember, and Nobu responded:

'What are you talking about? Only a fool could think such an ignorant thing!'

My smile fell before I could stop it, just as if the strings holding it had been cut. Nobu was looking me square in the eye. Of course, Hatsumomo sat far away, but I felt certain she was watching us. And then it occurred to me that if a geisha or a young apprentice grew teary-eyed in front of a man, wouldn't most anyone take it for infatuation? I might have responded to his harsh comment with an apology; instead I tried to imagine it was the Chairman who had spoken to me so abruptly, and in a moment my lip was trembling. I lowered my head and made a great show of being childish.

To my surprise, Nobu said, 'I've hurt you, haven't I?'

It wasn't difficult for me to sniff theatrically. Nobu went on looking at me for a long moment and then said, 'You're a charming girl.' I'm sure he intended to say something further, but at that moment Miyagiyama came into the hall and the crowd began to roar.

For a long while, Miyagiyama and the other wrestler, whose name was Saiho, swaggered around the mound, scooping up salt and tossing it into the ring, or stamping their feet as sumo wrestlers do. Every time they crouched, facing each other, they made me think of two boulders on the point of tipping over. Miyagiyama always seemed to lean forward a bit more than Saiho, who was taller and much heavier. I thought when they slammed into each other, poor Miyagiyama would certainly be driven back; I couldn't imagine anyone dragging Saiho across that ring. They took up their position eight or nine times without either of the men charging; then Nobu whispered to me:

'*Hataki komi*! He's going to use *hataki komi*. Just watch his eyes.'

I did what Nobu suggested, but all I noticed was that Miyagiyama never looked at Saiho. I don't think Saiho liked being ignored in this way, because he glowered at his opponent as ferociously as an animal. His jowls were so enormous that his head was shaped like a mountain; and from anger his face had begun to turn red. But Miyagiyama continued to act as though he scarcely noticed him.

'It won't last much longer,' Nobu whispered to me.

And in fact, the next time they crouched on their fists, Saiho charged.

To see Miyagiyama leaning forward as he did, you'd have thought he was ready to throw his weight into Saiho. But instead he used the force of Saiho's charge to stand back up on his feet. In an instant he swiveled out of the way like a swinging door, and his hand came down onto the back of Saiho's neck. By now Saiho's weight was so far forward, he looked like someone falling down the stairs. Miyagiyarna gave him a push with all his force, and Saiho brushed right over the rope at his feet. Then to my astonishment, this mountain of a man flew past the lip of the mound and came sprawling right into the first row of the audience. The spectators tried to scamper out of the way; but when it was over, one man stood up gasping for air, because one of Saiho's shoulders had crushed him.

The encounter had scarcely lasted a second. Saiho must have felt humiliated by his defeat, because he gave the most abbreviated bow of all the losers that day and walked out of the hall while the crowd was still in an uproar.

'That,' Nobu said to me, 'is the move called *hataki komi*.'

'Isn't it fascinating,' Mameha said, in something of a daze. She didn't even finish her thought.

'Isn't what fascinating?' the Chairman asked her.

'What Miyagiyama just did. I've never seen anything like it.'

'Yes, you have. Wrestlers do that sort of thing all the time.'

'Well, it certainly has got me thinking . . .' Mameha said.

Later, on our way back to Gion, Mameha turned to me excitedly in the rickshaw. 'That sumo wrestler gave me a most marvelous idea,' she said. 'Hatsumomo doesn't even know it, but she's just been thrown off-balance herself. And she won't even find it out until it's too late.'

'You have a plan? Oh, Mameha-san, please tell it to me!'

'Do you think for a moment I would?' she said. 'I'm not even going to tell it to my own maid. Just be very sure to keep Nobu-san interested in you. Everything depends on him, and on one other man as well.'

'What other man?'

'A man you haven't met yet. Now don't talk about it any

further! I've probably said more than I should already. It's a great thing you met Nobu-san today. He may just prove to be your rescuer.'

I must admit I felt a sickness inside when I heard this. If I was to have a rescuer, I wanted it to be the Chairman and no one else.

18

NOW THAT I knew the identity of the Chairman, I began that very night to read every discarded news magazine I could find in the hopes of learning more about him. Within a week I'd accumulated such a stack of them in my room that Auntie gave me a look as if I'd lost my mind. I did find mention of him in a number of articles, but only in passing, and none told me the sorts of things I really wanted to know. Still, I went on picking up every magazine I found poking out of a trash basket, until one day I came upon a stack of old papers tied in a bundle behind one of the teahouses. Buried in it was a two-year-old issue of a news magazine that happened to feature an article on Iwamura Electric.

It seemed that Iwamura Electric had celebrated its twentieth anniversary in April of 1931. It astonishes me even now to think of it, but this was the same month when I met the Chairman on the banks of the Shirakawa Stream; I would have seen his face in all the magazines, if only I'd looked in them. Now that I knew a date to search for, I managed over the course of time to find many more articles about the anniversary. Most of them came from a collection of junk thrown out after the death of the old granny who lived in an okiya across the alley.

The Chairman had been born in 1890, as I learned, which meant that despite his gray hair he'd been a little over forty when I met him. I'd formed the impression that day he was probably chairman of an unimportant company, but I was quite wrong. Iwamura Electric wasn't as big as Osaka Electric – its chief rival in western Japan, according to all the articles. But the Chairman and Nobu, because of their celebrated partnership, were much better known than the chiefs of much larger companies. In any case, Iwamura Electric was considered more innovative and had a better reputation.

At seventeen the Chairman had gone to work at a small electric company in Osaka. Soon he was supervising the crew that installed wiring for machinery at factories in the area. The demand for electric lighting in households and offices was growing at this time, and during the evenings the Chairman designed a fixture to allow the use of two lightbulbs in a socket built for only one. The director of the company wouldn't build it, however, and so at the age of twenty-two, in 1912, shortly after marrying, the Chairman left to establish his own company.

For a few years things were difficult; then in 1914, the Chairman's new company won the electrical wiring contract for a new building on a military base in Osaka. Nobu was still in the military at this time, since his war wounds made it difficult for him to find a job anywhere else. He was given the task of overseeing the work done by the new Iwamura Electric Company. He and the Chairman quickly became friends, and when the Chairman offered him a job the following year, Nobu took it.

The more I read about their partnership, the more I understood just how well suited they really were to each other. Nearly all the articles showed the same photograph of them, with the Chairman in a stylish three-piece suit of heavy wool, holding in his hand the ceramic two-bulb socket that had been the company's first product. He looked as if someone had just handed it to him and he hadn't yet decided what he was going to do with it. His mouth was slightly open, showing his teeth, and he stared at the camera with an almost menacing look, as though he were about to throw the fixture. By contrast, Nobu stood beside him, half a head shorter and at full attention, with his one hand in a fist at his side. He wore a morning coat and pin-striped trousers. His scarred face was completely without expression, and his eyes looked sleepy. The Chairman – perhaps because of his prematurely gray hair and the difference in their sizes – might almost have been Nobu's father, though he was only two years older. The articles said that while the Chairman was responsible for the company's growth and direction, Nobu was responsible for managing it. He was the less glamorous man with the less glamorous job, but apparently he did it so well that the Chairman often said publicly that the company would never have survived several crises without Nobu's talents. It was Nobu who'd brought in a group of investors and saved the company from ruin in the early 1920s. 'I owe Nobu a debt I can never repay,' the Chairman was quoted more than once as saying.

Several weeks passed, and then one day I received a note to come to Mameha's apartment the following afternoon. By this time I'd grown accustomed to the priceless kimono ensembles that Mameha's maid usually laid out for me; but when I arrived and began changing into an autumn-weight silk of scarlet and yellow, which showed leaves scattered in a field of golden grasses, I was taken aback to find a tear in the back of the gown large enough to put two fingers through. Mameha hadn't yet returned, but I took the robe in my arms and went to speak with her maid.

'Tatsumi-san,' I said, 'the most upsetting thing . . . this kimono is ruined.'

'It isn't ruined, miss. It needs to be repaired is all. Mistress borrowed it this morning from an okiya down the street.'

'She must not have known,' I said. 'And with my reputation for ruining kimono, she'll probably think –'

'Oh, she knows it's torn,' Tatsumi interrupted. 'In fact, the under-robe is torn as well, in just the same place.' I'd already put on the cream-colored underrobe, and when I reached back and felt in the area of my thigh, I saw that Tatsumi was right.

'Last year an apprentice geisha caught it by accident on a nail,' Tatsumi told me. 'But Mistress was very clear that she wanted you to put it on.'

This made very little sense to me; but I did as Tatsumi said. When at last Mameha rushed in, I went to ask her about it while she touched up her makeup.

'I told you that according to my plan,' she said, 'two men will be important to your future. You met Nobu a few weeks ago. The other man has been out of town until now, but with the help of this torn kimono, you're about to meet him. That sumo wrestler gave me such a wonderful idea! I can hardly wait to see how Hatsumomo reacts when you come back from the dead. Do you know what she said to me the other day? She couldn't thank me enough for taking you to the exhibition. It was worth all her trouble getting there, she said, just to see you making big eyes at "Mr. Lizard." I'm sure she'll leave you alone when you entertain him, unless it's to drop by and have a look for herself. In fact, the more you talk about Nobu around her, the better – though you're not to mention a word about the man you'll meet this afternoon.'

I began to feel sick inside when I heard this, even as I tried to seem pleased at what she'd said; because you see, a man will never have an intimate relationship with a geisha who has been the mistress of a close associate. One afternoon in a bathhouse not many months earlier, I'd listened as a young woman tried to console another geisha who'd just learned that her new *danna* would be the business partner of the man she'd dreamed about. It had never occurred to me as I watched her that I might one day be in the same position myself.

'Ma'am,' I said, 'may I ask? Is it part of your plan that Nobu-san will one day become my *danna*?'

Mameha answered me by lowering her makeup brush and staring at me in the mirror with a look that I honestly think would have stopped a train. 'Nobu-san is a fine man. Are you suggesting you'd be ashamed to have him for a *danna*?' she asked.

'No, ma'am, I don't mean it that way. I'm just wondering . . .'

'Very well. Then I have only two things to say to you. First, you're a fourteen-year-old girl with no reputation whatever. You'll be very fortunate ever to become a geisha with sufficient status for a man like Nobu to consider proposing himself as your *danna*. Secondly, Nobu-san has never found a geisha he likes well enough to take as a mistress. If you're the first, I expect you to feel very flattered.'

I blushed with so much heat in my face I might almost have

caught fire. Mameha was quite right; whatever became of me in the years ahead, I would be fortunate even to attract the notice of a man like Nobu. If Nobu was beyond my reach, how much more unreachable the Chairman must be. Since finding him again at the sumo exhibition, I'd begun to think of all the possibilities life presented to me. But now after Mameha's words I felt myself wading through an ocean of sorrow.

I dressed in a hurry and Mameha led me up the street to the okiya where she'd lived until six years earlier, when she'd gained her independence. At the door we were greeted by an elderly maid, who smacked her lips and gave her head a shake.

'We called the hospital earlier,' the maid said. 'The Doctor goes home at four o'clock today. It's nearly three-thirty already, you know.'

'We'll phone him before we go, Kazuko-san,' Mameha replied. 'I'm sure he'll wait for me.'

'I hope so. It would be terrible to leave the poor girl bleeding.'

'Who's bleeding?' I asked in alarm; but the maid only looked at me with a sigh and led us up the stairs to a crowded little hallway on the second floor. In a space about the size of two tatami mats were gathered not only Mameha and me, as well as the maid who'd shown us up, but also three other young women and a tall, thin cook in a crisp apron. They all looked at me warily except for the cook, who draped a towel over her shoulder and began to whet a knife of the sort used to chop the heads off fish. I felt like a slab of tuna the grocer had just delivered, because I could see now that I was the one who was going to do the bleeding.

'Mameha-san . . .' I said

'Now, Sayuri, I know what you're going to say,' she told me – which was interesting, because I had no idea myself what I was going to say. 'Before I became your older sister, didn't you promise to do exactly as I told you?'

'If I'd known it would include having my liver cut out –'

'No one's going to cut out your liver,' said the cook, in a

tone that was supposed to make me feel much better, but didn't.

'Sayuri, we're going to put a little cut in your skin,' Mameha said. 'Just a little one, so you can go to the hospital and meet a certain doctor. You know the man I mentioned to you? He's a doctor.'

'Can't I just pretend to have a stomachache?'

I was perfectly serious when I said this, but everyone seemed to think I'd made a clever joke, for they all laughed, even Mameha.

'Sayuri, we all have your best interests at heart,' Mameha said. 'We only need to make you bleed a little, just enough so the Doctor will be willing to look at you.'

In a moment the cook finished sharpening the knife and came to stand before me as calmly as if she were going to help me with my makeup – except that she was holding a knife, for heaven's sake. Kazuko, the elderly maid who had shown us in, pulled my collar aside with both hands. I felt myself beginning to panic; but fortunately Mameha spoke up.

'We're going to put the cut on her leg,' she said.

'Not the leg,' said Kazuko. 'The neck is so much more erotic.'

'Sayuri, please turn around and show Kazuko the hole in the back of your kimono,' Mameha said to me. When I'd done as she asked, she went on, 'Now, Kazuko-san, how will we explain this tear in the back of her kimono if the cut is on her neck and not her leg?'

'How are the two things related?' Kazuko said. 'She's wearing a torn kimono, and she has a cut on her neck.'

'I don't know what Kazuko keeps gabbing on about,' the cook said. 'Just tell me where you want me to cut her, Mameha-san, and I'll cut her.'

I'm sure I should have been pleased to hear this, but somehow I wasn't.

Mameha sent one of the young maids to fetch a red pigment stick of the sort used for shading the lips, and then put it through the hole in my kimono and swiftly rubbed a mark high up on the back of my thigh.

'You must place the cut exactly there,' Mameha said to the cook.

I opened my mouth, but before I could even speak, Mameha told me, 'Just lie down and be quiet, Sayuri. If you slow us down any further, I'm going to be very angry.'

I'd be lying if I said I wanted to obey her; but of course, I had no choice. So I lay down on a sheet spread out on the wooden floor and closed my eyes while Mameha pulled my robe up until I was exposed almost to the hip.

'Remember that if the cut needs to be deeper, you can always do it again,' Mameha said. 'Start with the shallowest cut you can make.'

I bit my lip the moment I felt the tip of the knife. I'm afraid I may have let out a little squeal as well, though I can't be sure. In any case, I felt some pressure, and then Mameha said:

'Not that shallow. You've scarcely cut through the first layer of skin.'

'It looks like lips,' Kazuko said to the cook. 'You've put a line right in the middle of a red smudge, and it looks like a pair of lips. The Doctor's going to laugh.'

Mameha agreed and wiped off the makeup after the cook assured her she could find the spot. In a moment I felt the pressure of the knife again.

I've never been good at the sight of blood. You may recall how I fainted after cutting my lip the day I met Mr. Tanaka. So you can probably imagine how I felt when I twisted around and saw a rivulet of blood snaking down my leg onto a towel Mameha held against the inside of my thigh. I lapsed into such a state when I saw it that I have no memory at all of what happened next – of being helped into the rickshaw, or of anything at all about the ride, until we neared the hospital and Mameha rocked my head from side to side to get my attention.

'Now listen to me! I'm sure you've heard over and over that your job as an apprentice is to impress other geisha, since they're the ones who will help you in your career, and not to worry about what the men think. Well, forget about all that! It isn't going to work that way in your case. Your future depends on two men, as I've told you, and you're about to meet one of them. You *must* make the right impression. Are you listening to me?'

'Yes, ma'am, every word,' I muttered,

'When you're asked how you cut your jeg the answer is, you were trying to go to the bathroom in kimono, and you fell onto something sharp. You don't even know what it was, because you fainted. Make up all the details you want; just be sure to sound very childish. And act helpless when we go inside. Let me see you do it.'

Well, I laid my head back and let my eyes roll up into my head. I suppose that's how I was really feeling, but Mameha wasn't at all pleased.

'I didn't say act dead I said act *helpless*. Like this . . .'

Mameha put on a dazed look, as if she couldn't make up her mind even where she should point her eyes and kept her hand to her cheek as though she were feeling faint. She made me imitate that look until she was satisfied. I began my performance as the driver helped me to the entrance of the hospital. Mameha walked beside me, tugging my robe this way and that to be sure I still looked attractive.

We entered through the swinging wooden doors and asked for the hospital director; Mameha said he was expecting us. Finally a nurse showed us down a long hallway to a dusty room with a wooden table and a plain folding screen blocking the windows. While we waited, Mameha took off the towel she'd wrapped around my leg and threw it into a wastebasket.

'Remember, Sayuri,' she nearly hissed, 'we want the Doctor to see you looking as innocent and as helpless as possible. Lie back and try to look weak.'

I had no difficulty at all with this. A moment later the door opened and in came Dr. Crab. Of course, his name wasn't really Dr. Crab, but if you'd seen him I'm sure the same name would have occurred to you, because he had his shoulders hunched up and his elbows sticking out so much, he couldn't have done a better imitation of a crab if he'd made a study of it. He even led with one shoulder when he walked, just like a crab moving along sideways. He had a mustache on his face, and was very pleased to see Mameha, though more with an expression of surprise in his eyes than with a smile.

Dr. Crab was a methodical and orderly man. When he closed the door, he turned the handle first so the latch wouldn't make noise, and then gave an extra press on the door to be sure it was shut. After this he took a case from his coat pocket and opened it very cautiously, as though he might spill something if he wasn't careful; but all it contained was another pair of glasses. When he'd exchanged the glasses he wore, he replaced the case in his pocket and then smoothed his coat with his hands. Finally he peered at me and gave a brisk little nod, whereupon Mameha said:

'I'm so sorry to trouble you, Doctor. But Sayuri has such a bright future before her, and now she's had the misfortune of cutting her leg! What with the possibility of scars, and infections and the like, well, I thought you were the only person to treat her.'

'Just so,' said Dr. Crab. 'Now perhaps I might have a look at the injury?'

'I'm afraid Sayuri gets weak at the sight of blood, Doctor,' Mameha said. 'It might be best if she simply turned away and let you examine the wound for yourself. It's on the back of her thigh.'

'I understand perfectly. Perhaps you'd be kind enough to ask that she lie on her stomach on the examination table?'

I couldn't understand why Dr. Crab didn't ask me himself; but to seem obedient, I waited until I'd heard the words from Mameha. Then the Doctor raised my robe almost to my hips, and brought over a cloth and some sort of smelly liquid, which he rubbed on my thigh before saying, 'Sayuri-san, please be kind enough to tell me how the wound was inflicted.'

I took a deep, exaggerated breath, still doing my best to seem as weak as possible. 'Well, I'm rather embarrassed,' I began, 'but the truth is that I was . . . drinking a good deal of tea this afternoon –'

'Sayuri has just begun her apprenticeship,' Mameha said. 'I was introducing her around Gion. Naturally, everyone wanted to invite her in for tea.'

'Yes, I can imagine,' the Doctor said.

'In any case,' I went on, 'I suddenly felt that I had to . . . well, you know . . .'

'Drinking excessive amounts of tea can lead to a strong urge to relieve the bladder,' the Doctor said.

'Oh, thank you. And in fact . . . well, "strong urge" is an understatement, because I was afraid that in another moment everything would begin to look yellow to me, if you know what I mean . . . '

'Just tell the Doctor what happened, Sayuri,' said Mameha.

'I'm sorry,' I said. 'I just mean to say that I had to use the toilet very bad . . . so bad that when I finally reached it . . . well, I was struggling with my kimono, and I must have lost my balance. When I fell, my leg came against something sharp. I don't even know what it was. I think I must have fainted.'

'It's a wonder you didn't void your bladder when you lost consciousness,' said the Doctor.

All this time I'd been lying on my stomach, holding my face up off the examination table for fear of smudging my makeup, and talking while the Doctor looked at the back of my head. But when Dr. Crab made this last comment, I looked over my shoulder at Mameha as best I could. Happily, she was thinking faster than I was, because she said:

'What Sayuri means is that she lost her balance when she tried to stand once again from a squatting position.'

'I see,' the Doctor said. 'The cut was made by a very sharp object. Perhaps you fell on broken glass or a strip of metal.'

'Yes, it certainly felt very sharp,' I said. 'As sharp as a knife!'

Dr. Crab said nothing more, but washed the cut as though he wanted to see how much he could make it hurt, and then afterward used more of the smelly liquid to remove the blood that had dried all down my leg. Finally he told me the cut would need nothing more than cream and a bandage, and gave me instructions on caring for it over the next few days. With this, he rolled my robe down and put away his glasses as though he might break them if he handled them too roughly.

'I'm very sorry you've ruined such a fine kimono,' he said. 'But I'm certainly happy at the chance to have met you. Mameha-san knows I'm always interested in new faces.'

'Oh, no, the pleasure is all mine, Doctor,' I said.

'Perhaps I'll see you one evening quite soon at the Ichiriki Teahouse.'

'To tell the truth, Doctor,' Mameha said, 'Sayuri is a bit of a . . . special property, as I'm sure you can imagine. She already has more admirers than she can handle, so I've been keeping her away from the Ichiriki as much as I can. Perhaps we might visit you at the Shirae Teahouse instead?'

'Yes, I would prefer that myself,' Dr. Crab said. And then he went through the whole ritual of changing his glasses again so that he could look through a little book he took from his pocket. 'I'll be there . . . let me see . . . two evenings from now. I do hope to see you.'

Mameha assured him we would stop by, and then we left.

In the rickshaw on our way back to Gion, Mameha told me I'd done very well.

'But, Mameha-san, I didn't do anything!'

'Oh? Then how do you account for what we saw on the Doctor's forehead?'

'I didn't see anything but the wooden table right in front of my face.'

'Let's just say that while the Doctor was cleaning the blood from your leg, his forehead was beaded with sweat as if we'd been in the heat of summer. But it wasn't even warm in the room, was it?'

'I don't think so.'

'Well, then!' Mameha said.

I really wasn't sure what she was talking about – or exactly what her purpose had been in taking me to meet the Doctor, for that matter. But I couldn't very well ask, because she'd already made it clear she wouldn't tell me her plan. Then just as the rickshaw driver was pulling us across the Shijo Avenue Bridge into Gion once again, Mameha interrupted herself in the middle of a story.

'You know, your eyes really are extraordinarily lovely in that kimono, Sayuri. The scarlets and yellows . . . they make your eyes shine almost silver! Oh, heavens, I can't believe I haven't thought of this idea sooner. Driver!' she called out. 'We've gone too far. Stop here, please.'

'You told me Gion Tominaga-cho, ma'am. I can't drop the poles in the middle of a bridge.'

'You may either let us out here or finish crossing the bridge and then take us back over it again. Frankly, I don't see much point in that.'

The driver set down his poles where we were, and Mameha and I stepped out. A number of bicyclists rang their bells in anger as they passed, but Mameha didn't seem in the least concerned. I suppose she was so certain of her place in the world, she couldn't imagine anyone being troubled by a little matter like her blocking traffic. She took her time, holding up one coin after another from her silk change purse until she'd paid the exact fare, and then led me back across the bridge in the direction we'd come.

'We're going to Uchida Kosaburo's studio,' she announced. 'He's a marvelous artist, and he's going to take a liking to your eyes, I'm sure of it. Sometimes he gets a little . . . distracted, you might say. And his studio is a mess. It may take him a while to notice your eyes, but just keep them pointed where he can see them.'

I followed Mameha through side streets until we came to a little alley. At the end stood a bright red Shinto gate, miniature in size, pressed tightly between two houses. Beyond the gate, we passed between several small pavilions to a flight of stone steps leading up through trees in their brilliant fall coloring. The air wafting from the dank little tunnel of the steps felt as cool as water, so that it seemed to me I was entering a different world altogether. I heard a swishing sound that reminded me of the tide washing the beach, but it turned out to be a man with his back to us, sweeping water from the top step with a broom whose bristles were the color of chocolate.

'Why, Uchida-san!' Mameha said. 'Don't you have a maid to tidy up for you?'

The man at the top stood in full sunlight, so that when he turned to peer down at us, I doubt he saw anything more than a few shapes under the trees. I could see him well, however, and he was quite a peculiar-looking man. In one corner of his mouth was a giant mole like a piece of food, and his eyebrows were so bushy they looked like caterpillars that had crawled down out of his hair and gone to sleep there. Everything about him was in disarray, not only his gray hair, but his kimono, which looked as if he'd slept in it the night before.

'Who is that?' he said.

'Uchida-san! After all these years you still don't recognize my voice?'

'If you're trying to make me angry whoever you are, you're off to a good start. I'm in no mood for interruptions! I'll throw this broom at you, if you don't tell me who you are.'

Uchida-san looked so angry I wouldn't have been surprised if he'd bit off the mole from the corner of his mouth and spat it at us. But Mameha just continued right up the stairs, and I followed her – though I was careful to stay behind so she would be the one struck by the broom.

'Is this how you greet visitors, Uchida-san?' Mameha said as she stepped up into the light.

Uchida squinted at her. 'So it's you. Why can't you just say who you are like everyone else? Here, take this broom and sweep the steps. No one's coming into my house until I've lit incense. Another of my mice has died, and the place smells like a coffin.'

Mameha seemed amused at this and waited until Uchida had left before leaning the broom against a tree.

'Have you ever had a boil?' she whispered to me. 'When Uchida's work goes badly, he gets into this terrible mood. You have to make him blow up, just like lancing a boil, so that he'll settle down again. If you don't give him something to get angry about, he'll start drinking and only get worse.'

'Does he keep pet mice?' I whispered. 'He said another of his mice had died.'

'Heavens, no. He leaves his ink sticks out, and the mice come and eat them and then die from poisoning. I gave him a box to put his inks in, but he won't use it.'

Just then Uchida's door rolled partway open – for he'd given it a shove and gone right back inside. Mameha and I slipped out of our shoes. The interior was a single large room in the style of a farmhouse. I could see incense burning in a far corner, but it hadn't done any good yet, because the smell of dead mouse struck me with as much force as if someone had stuck clay up my nose. The room was even messier than Hatsumomo's at its worst. Everywhere were long brushes, some broken or gnawed, and big wooden boards with half-finished drawings in black-and-white. In the midst of it all was an unmade futon with ink stains on the sheets. I imagined that Uchida would have ink stains all over himself as well, and when I turned to find out, he said to me:

'What are you looking at?'

'Uchida-san, may I present my younger sister, Sayuri,' Mameha said. 'She's come with me all the way from Gion for the honor of meeting you.'

All the way from Gion wasn't really very far; but in any case, I knelt on the mats and went through the ritual of bowing and begging Uchida's favor, although I wasn't convinced he'd heard a word of what Mameha had told him.

'I was having a fine day until lunchtime,' he said, 'and then look what happened!' Uchida crossed the room and held up a board. Fastened onto it with pins was a sketch of a woman from the back, looking to one side and holding an umbrella – except that a cat had evidently stepped in ink and walked across it, leaving perfectly formed paw prints. The cat himself was curled up asleep at the moment in a pile of dirty clothes.

'I brought him in here for the mice and look!' he went on. 'I've a mind to throw him out.'

'Oh, but the paw prints are lovely,' said Mameha. 'I think they improve the picture. What do you think, Sayuri?'

I wasn't inclined to say anything, because Uchida was looking very upset at Mameha's comment. But in a moment I understood that she was trying to 'lance the boil,' as she'd put it. So I put on my most enthusiastic voice and said:

'I'm surprised at how attractive the paw prints are! I think the cat may be something of an artist.'

'I know why you don't like him,' said Mameha. 'You're jealous of his talent.'

'Jealous, am I?' Uchida said. 'That cat's no artist. He's a demon if he's anything!'

'Forgive me, Uchida-san,' Mameha replied. 'It's just as you say. But tell me, are you planning to throw the picture away?

Because if so, I'd be pleased to have it. Wouldn't it look charming in my apartment, Sayuri?'

When Uchida heard this, he tore the picture from the board and said, 'You like it, do you? All right, I'll make you two presents of it!'And then he tore it into two pieces and gave them to her, saying, 'Here's one! And here's the other! Now get out!'

'I so wish you hadn't done that,' Mameha said. 'I think it was the most beautiful thing you've ever produced.'

'Get out!'

'Oh, Uchida-san, I can't possibly! I wouldn't be a friend if I didn't straighten your place a bit before leaving.'

At this, Uchida himself stormed out of the house, leaving the door wide open behind him. We watched him kick the broom Mameha had left leaning against the tree and then nearly slip and fall as he started down the wet steps. We spent the next half hour straightening up the studio, until Uchida came back in a much improved mood, just as Mameha had predicted. He still wasn't what I would call cheerful; and in fact, he had a habit of chewing constantly at the mole in the corner of his mouth, which gave him the look of being worried. I think he felt embarrassed at his earlier behavior, because he never looked directly at either of us. Soon it became apparent that he wasn't going to notice my eyes at all, and so Mameha said to him:

'Don't you think Sayuri is just the prettiest thing? Have you even bothered to look at her?'

It was an act of desperation, I thought, but Uchida only flicked his eyes at me like brushing a crumb from a table. Mameha seemed very disappointed. The afternoon light was already beginning to fade, so we both rose to leave. She gave the most abbreviated bow in saying good-bye. When we stepped outside, I couldn't help stopping a moment to take in the sunset, which painted the sky behind the distant hills in rusts and pinks as striking as the loveliest kimono – even more so, because no matter how magnificent a kimono is, your hands will never glow orange in its light. But in that sunset my hands seemed to have been dipped in some sort of iridescence. I raised them up and gazed at them for a long moment.

'Mameha-san, look,' I said to her, but she thought I was talking about the sunset and turned toward it with indifference. Uchida was standing frozen in the entryway with an expression of concentration on his face, combing one hand through a tuft of his gray hair. But he wasn't looking at the sunset at all. He was looking at me.

If you've ever seen Uchida Kosaburo's famous ink painting of the young woman in a kimono standing in a rapturous state and with her eyes aglow . . . well, from the very beginning he insisted the idea came from what he saw that afternoon. I've never really believed him. I can't imagine such a beautiful painting could really be based on just a girl staring foolishly at her hands in the sunset.

19

THAT STARTLING MONTH in which I first came upon the Chairman again – and met Nobu, and Dr. Crab, and Uchida Kosaburu – made me feel something like a pet cricket that has at last escaped its wicker cage. For the first time in ages I could go to bed at night believing I might not always draw as little notice in Gion as a drop of tea spilled onto the mats. I still had no understanding of Mameha's plan, or of how it would lead me to success as a geisha, or whether success as a geisha would ever lead me to the Chairman. But every night I lay on my futon with his handkerchief pressed against my cheek, reliving again and again my encounter with him. I was like a temple bell that resonates long after it has been struck.

Some weeks passed without word from any of the men, and Mameha and I began to worry. But at last one morning a secretary from Iwamura Electric phoned the Ichiriki Teahouse to request my company for that evening. Mameha was delighted at this news, because she hoped the invitation had come from Nobu. I was delighted too; I hoped it was from the Chairman. Later that day, in Hatsumomo's presence, I told Auntie I would be entertaining Nobu and asked her to help me choose a kimono ensemble. To my astonishment Hatsumomo came along to lend a hand. I'm sure that a stranger seeing us would have imagined we were members of a close family. Hatsumomo never snickered, or made sarcastic comments, and in fact she was helpful. I think Auntie felt as puzzled as I did. We ended up settling on a powdery green kimono with a pattern of leaves in silver and vermilion, and a gray obi with gold threads. Hatsumomo promised to stop by so she could see Nobu and me together.

That evening I knelt in the hallway of the Ichiriki feeling that my whole life had led me to this moment. I listened to the sounds of muffled laughter, wondering if one of the voices was the Chairman's; and when I opened the door and saw him there at the head of the table, and Nobu with his back to me . . . well, I was so captivated by the Chairman's smile – though it was really only the residue of laughter from a moment earlier – that I had to keep myself from smiling back at him. I greeted Mameha first, and then the few other geisha in the room, and finally the six or seven men. When I arose from my knees, I went straight to Nobu, as Mameha expected me to do. I must have knelt closer to him than I realized, however, because he immediately slammed his sake cup onto the table in annoyance and shifted a little distance away from me. I apologized, but he paid me no attention, and Mameha only frowned. I spent the rest of the time feeling out of sorts. Later, as we were leaving together, Mameha said to me:

'Nobu-san is easily annoyed. Be more careful not to irritate him in the future.'

'I'm sorry ma'am. Apparently he isn't as fond of me as you thought . . . '

'Oh, he's fond of you. If he didn't like your company you'd have left the party in tears. Sometimes his temperament seems as gentle as a sack of gravel, but he's a kind man in his way, as you'll discover.'

I was invited to the Ichiriki Teahouse again that week by Iwamura Electric and many times over the weeks that followed – and not always with Mameha. She cautioned me not to stay too long for fear of making myself look unpopular; so after an hour or so I always bowed and excused myself as though I were on my way to another party. Often while I was dressing for these evenings, Hatsumomo hinted she might stop by, but she never did. Then one afternoon when I wasn't expecting it, she informed me she had some free time that evening and would be absolutely certain to come.

I felt a bit nervous, as you can imagine; but things seemed still worse when I reached the Ichiriki and found that Nobu was absent. It was the smallest party I'd attended yet in Gion, with only two other geisha and four men. What if Hatsumomo should arrive and find me entertaining the Chairman without Nobu? I'd made no headway in thinking what to do, when suddenly the door slid open, and with a surge of anxiety I saw Hatsumomo there on her knees in the hallway.

My only recourse, I decided, was to act bored, as though the company of no one but Nobu could possibly interest me. Perhaps this would have been enough to save me that night; but by good fortune Nobu arrived a few minutes afterward in any case. Hatsumomo's lovely smile grew the moment Nobu entered the room, until her lips were as rich and full as drops of blood beading at the edge of a wound. Nobu made himself comfortable at the table, and then at once, Hatsumomo suggested in an almost maternal way that I go and pour him sake. I went to settle myself near him and tried to show all the signs of a girl enchanted. Whenever he laughed, for example, I flicked my eyes toward him as though I couldn't resist. Hatsumomo was delighted and watched us so openly that she didn't even seem aware of all the men's eyes upon her – or more likely, she was simply accustomed to the attention. She was captivatingly beautiful that evening, as she always was; the young man at the end of the table did little more than smoke cigarettes and watch her. Even the Chairman, who sat with his fingers draped gracefully around a sake cup, stole glimpses of her from time to time. I had to wonder if men were so blinded by beauty that they would feel privileged to live their lives with an actual demon, so long as it was a beautiful demon. I had a sudden image in my mind of the Chairman stepping up into the formal entrance hall of our okiya late one night to meet Hatsumomo, holding a fedora in his hand and smiling down at me as he began to unbutton his overcoat. I didn't think he'd ever really be so entranced by her beauty as to overlook the traces of cruelty that would show themselves. But one thing was certain: if Hatsumomo ever understood my feelings for him, she might very well try to seduce him, if for no other reason than to cause me pain.

Suddenly it seemed urgent to me that Hatsumomo leave the party. I knew she was there to observe the 'developing romance,' as she put it; so I made up my mind to show her what she'd come to see. I began by touching my fingertips to my neck or my hairstyle every so often, in order to seem worried about my appearance. When my fingers brushed one of my hair ornaments inadvertently, I came up with an idea. I waited until someone made a joke, and then while laughing and adjusting my hair, I leaned toward Nobu. Adjusting my hair was a strange thing for me to do, I'll admit, since it was waxed into place and hardly needed attention. But my purpose was to dislodge one of my hair ornaments – a cascade of yellow and orange safflowers in silk – and let it fall into Nobu's lap. As it turned out, the wooden spine holding the ornament in my hair was embedded farther than I'd realized; but I managed to slip it out at last, and it bounced against Nobu's chest and fell onto the tatami between his crossed legs. Most everyone noticed, and no one seemed to know what to do. I'd planned to reach into his lap and reclaim it with girlish embarrassment, but I couldn't bring myself to reach between his legs.

Nobu picked it up himself, and turned it slowly by its spine. 'Fetch the young maid who greeted me,' he said. 'Tell her I want the package I brought.'

I did as Nobu asked and returned to the room to find everyone waiting. He was still holding my hair ornament by the spine, so that the flowers dangled down above the table, and made no effort to take the package from me when I offered it to him. 'I was going to give it to you later, on your way out. But it looks as if I'm meant to give it to you now,' he said, and nodded toward the package in a way that suggested I should open it. I felt very embarrassed with everyone watching, but I unfolded the paper wrapping and opened the little wooden box inside to find an exquisite ornamental comb on a bed of satin. The comb, in the shape of a half-circle, was a showy red color adorned with bright flowers.

'It's an antique I found a few days ago,' Nobu said.

The Chairman, who was gazing wistfully at the ornament in its box on the table, moved his lips, but no sound came out at first, until he cleared his throat and then said, with a strange sort of sadness, 'Why, Nobu-san, I had no idea you were so sentimental.'

Hatsumomo rose from the table; I thought I'd succeeded in ridding myself of her, but to my surprise she came around and knelt near me. I wasn't sure what to make of this, until she removed the comb from the box and carefully inserted it into my hair just at the base of the large pincushionlike bun. She held out her hand, and Nobu gave her the ornament of dangling safflowers, which she replaced in my hair as carefully as a mother tending to a baby. I thanked her with a little bow.

'Isn't she just the loveliest creature?' she said, speaking pointedly to Nobu. And then she gave a very theatrical sigh, as though these few moments were as romantic as any she'd experienced, and left the party as I'd hoped she would.

It goes without saying that men can be as distinct from each other as shrubs that bloom in different times of the year. Because although Nobu and the Chairman seemed to take an interest in me within a few weeks of the sumo tournament, several months passed and still we heard nothing from Dr. Crab or Uchida. Mameha was very clear that we ought to wait until we heard from them, rather than finding some pretext for approaching them again, but at length she could bear the suspense no longer and went to check on Uchida one afternoon.

It turned out that shortly after we'd visited him, his cat had been bitten by a badger and within a few days was dead from infection. Uchida had fallen into another drinking spell as a result. For a few days Mameha visited to cheer him up. Finally when his mood seemed to be turning the corner she dressed me in an ice-blue kimono with multicolored ribbons embroidered at the hem – with only a touch of Western-style makeup to 'accentuate the angles,' as she put it – and sent me to him bearing a present of a pearl-white kitten that had cost her I don't know how much money. I thought the kitten was adorable, but Uchida paid it little attention and instead sat squinting his eyes at me, shifting his head this way and that. A few days later, the news came that he wanted me to model in his studio. Mameha cautioned me not to speak a word to him, and sent me off chaperoned by her maid Tatsumi, who spent the afternoon nodding off in a drafty corner while Uchida moved me from spot to spot, frantically mixing his inks and painting a bit on rice paper before moving me again.

If you were to go around Japan and see the various works Uchida produced while I modeled for him during that winter and the years that followed – such as one of his only surviving oil paintings, hanging in the boardroom of the Sumitomo Bank in Osaka – you might imagine it was a glamorous experience to have posed for him. But actually nothing could have been duller. Most of the time I did little more than sit uncomfortably for an hour or more. Mainly I remember being thirsty because Uchida never once offered me anything to drink. Even when I took to bringing my own tea in a sealed jar, he moved it to the other side of the room so it wouldn't distract him. Following Mameha's instructions, I tried never to speak a word, even one bitter afternoon in the middle of February when I probably should have said something and didn't. Uchida had come to sit right before me and stare at my eyes, chewing on the mole in the corner of his mouth. He had a handful of ink sticks and some water that kept icing over, but no matter how many times he ground ink in various combinations of blue and gray, he was never quite satisfied with the color and took it outside to spill it into the snow. Over the course of the afternoon as his eyes bored into me, he became more and more angry and finally sent me away. I didn't hear a word from him for more than two weeks, and later found out he'd fallen into another drinking spell. Mameha blamed me for letting it happen.

As for Dr. Crab, when I first met him he'd as much as promised to see Mameha and me at the Shirae Teahouse; and yet as late as six weeks afterward, we hadn't heard a word from him. Mameha's concern grew as the weeks passed. I still knew nothing of her plan for catching Hatsumomo off-balance, except that it was like a gate swinging on two hinges, one of which was Nobu and the other of which was Dr. Crab. What she was up to with Uchida, I couldn't say, but it struck me as a separate scheme – certainly not in the very center of her plans.

Finally in late February, Mameha ran into Dr. Crab at the Ichiriki Teahouse and learned that he'd been consumed with the opening of a new hospital in Osaka. Now that most of the work was behind him, he hoped to renew my acquaintance at the Shirae Teahouse the following week. You'll recall that Mameha had claimed I would be overwhelmed with invitations if I showed my face at the Ichiriki; this was why Dr. Crab asked that we join him at the Shirae instead. Mameha's real motive was to keep clear of Hatsumomo, of course; and yet as I prepared to meet the Doctor again, I couldn't help feeling uneasy that Hatsumomo might find us anyway. But the moment I set eyes on the Shirae I nearly burst out laughing, for it was certainly a place Hatsumomo would go out of her way to avoid. It made me think of one shriveled little blossom on a tree in full bloom. Gion continued to be a bustling community even during the last years of the Depression, but the Shirae Teahouse, which had never been important to begin with, had only withered further. The only reason a man as wealthy as Dr. Crab patronized such a place is that he hadn't always been so wealthy. During his early years the Shirae was probably the best he could do. Just because the Ichiriki finally welcomed him didn't mean he was free to sever his bond with the Shirae. When a man takes a mistress, he doesn't turn around and divorce his wife.

That evening in the Shirae, I poured sake while Mameha told a story, and all the while Dr. Crab sat with his elbows sticking out so much that he sometimes bumped one of us with them and turned to nod in apology. He was a quiet man, as I discovered; he spent most of his time looking down at the table through his little round glasses, and every so often slipped pieces of sashimi underneath his mustache in a way that made me think of a boy hiding something beneath a floor covering. When we finally left that evening I thought we'd failed and wouldn't see much of him – because normally a man who'd enjoyed himself so little wouldn't bother coming back to Gion. But as it turned out, we heard from Dr. Crab the next week, and nearly every week afterward over the following months.

*

Things went along smoothly with the Doctor, until one afternoon in the middle of March when I did something foolish and very nearly ruined all Mameha's careful planning. I'm sure many a young girl has spoiled her prospects in life by refusing to do something expected of her, or by behaving badly toward an important man, or some such thing; but the mistake I made was so trivial I wasn't even aware I'd done anything.

It happened in the okiya during the course of about a minute, not long after lunch one cold day while I knelt on the wooden walkway with my shamisen. Hatsumomo was strolling past on her way to the toilet. If I'd had shoes I would have stepped down onto the dirt corridor to get out of her way. But as it was, I could do nothing but struggle to get up from my knees, with my legs and arms nearly frozen. If I'd been quicker Hatsumomo probably wouldn't have bothered speaking to me. But during that moment while I rose to my feet, she said:

'The German Ambassador is coming to town, but Pumpkin isn't free to entertain him. Why don't you ask Mameha to arrange for you to take Pumpkin's place?' After this she let out a laugh, as if to say the idea of my doing such a thing was as ridiculous as serving a dish of acorn shells to the Emperor.

The German Ambassador was causing quite a stir in Gion at the time. During this period, in 1935, a new government had recently come to power in Germany; and though I've never understood much about politics, I do know that Japan was moving away from the United States during these years and was eager to make a good impression on the new German Ambassador. Everyone in Gion wondered who would be given the honor of entertaining him during his upcoming visit.

When Hatsumomo spoke to me, I ought to have lowered my head in shame and made a great show of lamenting the misery of my life compared with Pumpkin's. But as it happened, I had just been musing about how much my prospects seemed to have improved and how successfully Mameha and I had kept her plan from Hatsumomo – whatever her plan was. My first instinct when Hatsumomo spoke was to smile, but instead I kept my face like a mask, and felt pleased with myself that I'd given nothing away. Hatsumonio gave me an odd look; I ought to have realized right then that something had passed through her mind. I stepped quickly to one side, and she passed me. That was the end of it, as far as I was concerned.

Then a few days later, Mameha and I went to the Shirae Teahouse to meet Dr. Crab once again. But as we rolled open the door, we found Pumpkin slipping her feet into her shoes to leave. I was so startled to see her, I wondered what on earth could possibly have brought her there. Then Hatsumomo stepped down into the entryway as well, and of course I knew: Hatsumomo had outsmarted us somehow.

'Good evening, Mameha-san,' Hatsumomo said. 'And look who's with you! It's the apprentice the Doctor used to be so fond of.'

I'm sure Mameha felt as shocked as I did, but she didn't show it. 'Why, Hatsumomo-san,' she said, 'I scarcely recognize you . . . but my goodness, you're aging well!'

Hatsumomo wasn't actually old; she was only twenty-eight or twenty-nine. I think Mameha was just looking for something nasty to say.

'I expect you're on your way to see the Doctor,' Hatsumomo said. 'Such an interesting man! I only hope he'll still be happy to see you. Well, good-bye.' Hatsumomo looked cheerful as she walked away, but in the light from the avenue I could see a look of sorrow on Pumpkin's face.

Mameha and I slipped out of our shoes without speaking a word; neither of us knew what to say. The Shirae's gloomy atmosphere seemed as thick as the water in a pond that night. The air smelled of stale makeup; the damp plaster was peeling in the corners of the rooms. I would have given anything to turn around and leave.

When we slid open the door from the hallway, we found the mistress of the teahouse keeping Dr. Crab company. Usually she stayed a few minutes even after we'd arrived, probably to charge the Doctor for her time. But tonight she excused herself the moment we entered and didn't even look up as she passed. Dr. Crab was sitting with his back facing us, so we skipped the formality of bowing and went instead to join him at the table.

'You seem tired, Doctor,' Mameha said. 'How are you this evening?'

Dr. Crab didn't speak. He just twirled his glass of beer on the table to waste time – even though he was an efficient man and never wasted a moment if he could help it.

'Yes, I am rather tired,' he said at last. 'I don't feel much like talking.'

And with that, he drank down the last of his beer and stood to leave. Mameha and I exchanged looks. When Dr. Crab reached the door to the room, he faced us and said, 'I certainly do not appreciate when people I have trusted turn out to have misled me.'

Afterward he left without closing the door.

Mameha and I were too stunned to speak. At length she got up and slid the door shut. Back at the table, she smoothed her kimono and then pinched her eyes closed in anger and said to me, 'All right, Sayuri. What exactly did you say to Hatsumomo?'

'Mameha-san, after all this work? I promise you I would never do anything to ruin my own chances.'

'The Doctor certainly seems to have thrown you aside as though you're no better than an empty sack. I'm sure there's a reason . . . but we won't find it out until we know what Hatsumomo said to him tonight.'

'How can we possibly do that?'

'Pumpkin was here in the room. You must go to her and ask.'

I wasn't at all sure Pumpkin would speak with me, but I said I would try, and Mameha seemed satisfied with this. She stood and prepared to leave, but I stayed where I was until she turned to see what was keeping me.

'Mameha-san, may I ask a question?' I said. 'Now Hatsumomo knows I've been spending time with the Doctor, and probably she understands the reason why. Dr. Crab certainly knows why. You know why. Even Pumpkin may know why! I'm the only one who doesn't. Won't you be kind enough to explain your plan to me?'

Mameha looked as if she felt very sorry I'd asked this

question. For a long moment she looked everywhere but at me, but she finally let out a sigh and knelt at the table again to tell me what I wanted to know.

'You know perfectly well,' she began, 'that Uchida-san looks at you with the eyes of an artist. But the Doctor is interested in something else, and so is Nobu. Do you know what is meant by "the homeless eel"?'

I had no idea what she was talking about, and I said so.

'Men have a kind of . . . well, an "eel" on them,' she said. 'Women don't have it. But men do. It's located –'

'I think I know what you're talking about,' I said, 'but I didn't know it was called an eel.'

'It isn't an eel, really,' Mameha said. 'But pretending it's an eel makes things so much easier to understand. So let's think of it that way. Here's the thing: this eel spends its entire life trying to find a home, and what do you think women have inside them? Caves, where the eels like to live. This cave is where the blood comes from every month when the "clouds pass over the moon," as we sometimes say.'

I was old enough to understand what Mameha meant by the passage of clouds over the moon, because I'd been experiencing it for a few years already. The first time, I couldn't have felt more panicked if I'd sneezed and found pieces of my brain in the handkerchief. I really was afraid I might be dying, until Auntie had found me washing out a bloody rag and explained that bleeding was just part of being a woman.

'You may not know this about eels,' Mameha went on, 'but they're quite territorial. When they find a cave they like, they wriggle around inside it for a while to be sure that . . . well, to be sure it's a nice cave, I suppose. And when they've made up their minds that it's comfortable, they mark the cave as their territory . . . by spitting. Do you understand?'

If Mameha had simply told me what she was trying to say, I'm sure I would have been shocked, but at least I'd have had an easier time sorting it all out. Years later I discovered that things had been explained to Mameha in exactly the same way by her own older sister.

'Here's the part that's going to seem very strange to you,' Mameha went on, as if what she'd already told me didn't. 'Men actually like doing this. In fact, they like it very much. There are even men who do little in their lives besides search for different caves to let their eels live in. A woman's cave is particularly special to a man if no other eel has ever been in it before. Do you understand? We call this "*mizuage*."'

'We call what "*mizuage*"?'

'The first time a woman's cave is explored by a man's eel. That is what we call *mizuage*.'

Now, *mizu* means 'water' and *age* means 'raise up' or 'place on'; so that the term *mizuage* sounds as if it might have something to do with raising up water or placing something on the water. If you get three geisha in a room, all of them will have different ideas about where the term comes from. Now that Mameha had finished her explanation, I felt only more confused, though I tried to pretend it all made a certain amount of sense.

'I suppose you can guess why the Doctor likes to play around in Gion,' Mameha continued. 'He makes a great deal of money from his hospital. Except for what he needs to support his family, he spends it in the pursuit of *mizuage*. It may interest you to know, Sayuri-san, that you are precisely the sort of young girl he likes best. I know this very well, because I was one myself.'

As I later learned, a year or two before I'd first come to Gion, Dr. Crab had paid a record amount for Mameha's *mizuage* – maybe ¥7000 or ¥8000. This may not sound like much, but at that time it was a sum that even someone like Mother – whose every thought was about money and how to get more of it – might see only once or twice in a lifetime. Mameha's *mizuage* had been so costly partly because of her fame; but there was another reason, as she explained to me that afternoon. Two very wealthy men had bid against each other to be her *mizuage* patron. One was Dr. Crab. The other was a businessman named Fujikado. Ordinarily men didn't compete this way in Gion; they all knew each other and preferred to reach agreement on things. But Fujikado lived on the other side of the country and came to Gion only occasionally. He didn't care if he offended Dr. Crab. And Dr. Crab, who claimed to have some aristocratic blood in him, hated self-made men like Fujikadco – even though, in truth, he was a self-made man too, for the most part.

When Mameha noticed at the sumo tournament that Nobu seemed taken with me, she thought at once of how much Nobu resembled Fujikado – self-made and, to a man like Dr. Crab, repulsive. With Hatsumomo chasing me around like a housewife chasing a cockroach, I certainly wasn't going to become famous the way Mameha had and end up with an expensive *mizuage* as a result. But if these two men found me appealing enough, they might start a bidding war, which could put me in the same position to repay my debts as if I'd been a popular apprentice all along. This was what Mameha had meant by 'catching Hatsumomo off-balance.' Hatsumomo was delighted that Nobu found me attractive; what she didn't realize was that my popularity with Nobu would very likely drive up the price of my *mizuage*.

Clearly we had to reclaim Dr. Crab's affections. Without him Nobu could offer what he wanted for my *mizuage* – that is, if he turned out to have any interest in it at all. I wasn't sure he would, but Mameha assured me that a man doesn't cultivate a relationship with a fifteen-year-old apprentice geisha unless he has her *mizuage* in mind.

'You can bet it isn't your conversation he's attracted to,' she told me.

I tried to pretend I didn't feel hurt by this.

20

LOOKING BACK, I can see that this conversation with Mameha marked a shift in my view of the world. Beforehand I'd known nothing about *mizuage*; I was still a naive girl with little understanding. But afterward I could begin to see what a man like Dr. Crab wanted from all the time and money he spent in Gion. Once you know this sort of thing, you can never unknow it. I couldn't think about him again in quite the same way.

Back at the okiya later that night, I waited in my room for Hatsumomo and Pumpkin to come up the stairs. It was an hour or so after midnight when they finally did. I could tell Pumpkin was tired from the way her hands slapped on the steps – because she sometimes came up the steep stairway on all fours like a dog. Before closing the door to their room, Hatsumomo summoned one of the maids and asked for a beer.

'No, wait a minute,' she said. 'Bring two. I want Pumpkin to join me.'

'Please, Hatsumomo-san,' I heard Pumpkin say. 'I'd rather drink spit.'

'You're going to read aloud to me while I drink mine, so you might as well have one. Besides, I hate when people are too sober. It's sickening.'

After this, the maid went down the stairs. When she came up a short time later, I heard glasses clinking on the tray she carried.

For a long while I sat with my ear to the door of my room, listening to Pumpkin's voice as she read an article about a new Kabuki actor. Finally Hatsumomo stumbled out into the hallway and rolled open the door to the upstairs toilet.

'Pumpkin!' I heard her say. 'Don't you feel like a bowl of noodles?'

'No, ma'am.'

'See if you can find the noodle vendor. And get some for yourself so you can keep me company.'

Pumpkin sighed and went right down the stairs, but I had to wait for Hatsumomo to return to her room before creeping down to follow. I might not have caught up with Pumpkin, except that she was so exhausted she couldn't do much more than wander along at about the speed mud oozes down a hill, and with about as much purpose. When I finally found her, she looked alarmed to see me and asked what was the matter.

'Nothing is the matter,' I said, 'except . . . I desperately need your help.'

'Oh, Chiyo-chan,' she said to me – I think she was the only person who still called me that – 'I don't have any time! I'm trying to find noodles for Hatsumomo, and she's going to make me eat some too. I'm afraid I'll throw up all over her.'

'Pumpkin, you poor thing,' I said. 'You look like ice when it has begun to melt.' Her face was drooping with exhaustion, and the weight of all her clothing seemed as if it might pull her right onto the ground. I told her to go and sit down, that I would find the noodles and bring them to her. She was so tired she didn't even protest, but simply handed me the money and sat down on a bench by the Shirakawa Stream.

It took me some time to find a noodle vendor, but at last I returned carrying two bowls of steaming noodles. Pumpkin was sound asleep with her head back and her mouth open as though she were hoping to catch raindrops. It was about two in the morning, and a few people were still strolling around. One group of men seemed to think Pumpkin was the funniest thing they'd seen in weeks – and I admit it was odd to see an apprentice in her full regalia snoring on a bench.

When I'd set the bowls down beside her and awakened her as gently as I knew how, I said, 'Pumpkin, I want so much to ask you a favor, but . . . I'm afraid you won't be happy when you hear what it is.'

'It doesn't matter,' she said. 'Nothing makes me happy anymore.'

'You were in the room earlier this evening when Hatsumomo talked with the Doctor. I'm afraid my whole future may be affected by that conversation. Hatsumomo must have told him something about me that isn't true, because now the Doctor doesn't want to see me any longer.'

As much as I hated Hatsumomo – as much as I wanted to know what she'd done that evening – I felt sorry at once for having raised the subject with Pumpkin. She seemed in such pain that the gentle nudge I gave her proved to be too much. All at once several teardrops came spilling onto her big cheeks as if she'd been filling up with them for years.

'I didn't know, Chiyo-chan!' she said, fumbling in her obi for a handkerchief. 'I had no idea!'

'You mean, what Hatsumomo was going to say? But how could anyone have known?'

'That isn't it. I didn't know anyone could be so evil! I don't understand it . . . She does things for no reason at all except to hurt people. And the worst part is she thinks I admire her and want to be just like her. But I hate her! I've never hated anyone so much before.'

By now poor Pumpkin's yellow handkerchief was smeared with white makeup. If earlier she'd been an ice cube beginning to melt, now she was a puddle.

'Pumpkin, please listen to me,' I said. 'I wouldn't ask this of you if I had any other alternative. But I don't want to go back to being a maid all my life, and that's just what will happen if Hatsumomo has her way. She won't stop until she has me like a cockroach under her foot. I mean, she'll squash me if you don't help me to scurry away!'

Pumpkin thought this was funny, and we both began to laugh. While she was stuck between laughing and crying, I took her handkerchief and tried to smooth the makeup on her face. I felt so touched at seeing the old Pumpkin again, who had once been my friend, that my eyes grew watery as well, and we ended up in an embrace.

'Oh, Pumpkin, your makeup is such a mess,' I said to her afterward.

'It's all right,' she told me. 'I'll just say to Hatsumomo that a drunken man came up to me on the street and wiped a handkerchief all over my face, and I couldn't do anything about it because I was carrying two bowls of noodles.'

I didn't think she would say anything further but finally she sighed heavily.

'I want to help you, Chiyo,' she said, 'but I've been out too long. Hatsumomo will come looking for me if I don't hurry back. If she finds us together . . .'

'I only have to ask a few questions, Pumpkin. Just tell me, how did Hatsumomo find out I've been entertaining the Doctor at the Shirae Teahouse?'

'Oh, that,' said Pumpkin. 'She tried to tease you a few days ago about the German Ambassador, but you didn't seem to care what she said. You looked so calm, she thought you and Mameha must have some scheme going. So she went to Awajiumi at the registry office and asked what teahouses you've been billing at. When she heard the Shirae was one of them, she got this look on her face and we started going there that same night to look for the Doctor. We went twice before we finally found him.'

Very few men of consequence patronized the Shirae. This is why Hatsumomo would have thought of Dr. Crab at once. As I was now coming to understand, he was renowned in Gion as a '*mizuage* specialist.' The moment Hatsumomo thought of him, she probably knew exactly what Mameha was up to.

'What did she say to him tonight? When we called on the Doctor after you left, he wouldn't even speak with us.'

'Well,' Pumpkin said, 'they chatted for a while, and then Hatsumomo pretended that something had reminded her of a story. And she began it, "There's a young apprentice named Sayuri, who lives in my okiya . . ." When the Doctor heard your name . . . I'm telling you, he sat up like a bee had stung him. And he said, "You know her?" So Hatsumomo told him, "Well, of course I know her, Doctor. Doesn't she live in my okiya?" After this she said something else I don't remember, and then, "I shouldn't talk about Sayuri because . . . well, actually, I'm covering up an important secret for her."'

I went cold when I heard this. I was sure Hatsumomo had

thought of something really awful.

'Pumpkin, what was the secret?'

'Well, I'm not sure I know,' Pumpkin said. 'It didn't seem like much. Hatsumomo told him there was a young man who lived near the okiya and that Mother had a strict policy against boyfriends. Hatsumomo said you and this boy were fond of each other and she didn't mind covering up for you because she thought Mother was too strict. She said she even let the two of you spend time together alone in her room when Mother was out. Then she said something like, "Oh, but . . . Doctor, I really shouldn't have told you! What if it gets back to Mother, after all the work I've done to keep Sayuri's secret!" But the Doctor said he was grateful for what Hatsumomo had told him, and he would be certain to keep it to himself.'

I could just imagine how much Hatsumomo must have enjoyed her little scheme. I asked Pumpkin if there was anything more, but she said no.

I thanked her many times for helping me, and told her how sorry I was that she'd had to spend these past few years as a slave to Hatsumomo.

'I guess some good has come of it,' Pumpkin said. 'Just a few days ago, Mother made up her mind to adopt me. So my dream of having someplace to live out my life may come true.'

I felt almost sick when I heard these words, even as I told her how happy I was for her. It's true that I was pleased for Pumpkin; but I also knew that it was an important part of Mameha's plan that Mother adopt me instead.

In her apartment the next day, I told Mameha what I'd learned. The moment she heard about the boyfriend, she began shaking her head in disgust. I understood it already, but she explained to me that Hatsumomo had found a very clever way of putting into Dr. Crab's mind the idea that my 'cave' had already been explored by someone else's 'eel,' so to speak.

Mameha was even more upset to learn about Pumpkin's upcoming adoption.

'My guess,' she said, 'is that we have a few months before the adoption occurs. Which means that the time has come for your *mizuage*, Sayuri, whether you're ready for it or not.'

Mameha went to a confectioner's shop that same week and ordered on my behalf a kind of sweet-rice cake we call *ekubo*, which is the Japanese word for dimple. We call them *ekubo* because they have a dimple in the top with a tiny red circle in the center; some people think they look very suggestive. I've always thought they looked like tiny pillows, softly dented, as if a woman has slept on them, and smudged red in the center from her lipstick, since she was perhaps too tired to take it off before she went to bed. In any case, when an apprentice geisha becomes available for *mizuage*, she presents boxes of these *ekubo* to the men who patronize her. Most apprentices give them out to at least a dozen men, perhaps many more; but for me there would be only Nobu and the Doctor – if we were lucky. I felt sad, in a way, that I wouldn't give them to the Chairman; but on the other hand, the whole thing seemed so distasteful, I wasn't entirely sorry he would be left out of it.

Presenting *ekubo* to Nobu was easy. The mistress of the Ichiriki arranged for him to come a bit early one evening, and Mameha and I met him in a small room overlooking the entrance courtyard. I thanked him for all his thoughtfulness – for he'd been extremely kind to me over the past six months, not only summoning me frequently to entertain at parties even when the Chairman was absent, but giving me a variety of gifts besides the ornamental comb on the night Hatsumomo came. After thanking him, I picked up the box of *ekubo*, wrapped in unbleached paper and tied with coarse twine, then bowed to him and slid it across the table. He accepted it, and Mameha and I thanked him several more times for all his kindness, bowing again and again until I began to feel almost dizzy. The little ceremony was brief, and Nobu carried his box out of the room in his one hand. Later when I entertained at his party he didn't refer to it. Actually, I think the encounter made him a bit uncomfortable.

Dr. Crab, of course, was another matter. Mameha had to begin by going around to the principal teahouses in Gion and asking the mistresses to notify her if the Doctor should show up. We waited a few nights until word came that he'd turned up at a teahouse named Yashino, as the guest of another man. I rushed to Mameha's apartment to change my clothing and then set out for the Yashino with the box of *ekubo* wrapped up in a square of silk.

The Yashino was a fairly new teahouse, built in a completely Western style. The rooms were elegant in their own way, with dark wooden beams and so on, but instead of tatami mats and tables surrounded by cushions, the room into which I was shown that evening had a floor of hardwood, with a dark Persian rug, a coffee table and a few overstuffed chairs. I have to admit it never occurred to me to sit on one of the chairs. Instead I knelt on the rug to wait for Mameha although the floor was terribly hard on my knees. I was still in that position a half hour later when she came in.

'What are you doing?' she said to me. 'This isn't a Japanese-style room. Sit in one of these chairs and try to look as if you belong.'

I did as Mameha said. But when she sat down opposite me, she looked every bit as uncomfortable as I probably did.

The Doctor, it seemed, was attending a party in the next room. Mameha had been entertaining him for some time already. 'I'm pouring him lots of beer so he'll have to go to the toilet,' she told me. 'When he does, I'll catch him in the hallway and ask that he step in here. You must give him the *ekubo* right away. I don't know how he'll react, but it will be our only chance to undo the damage Hatsumomo has done.'

Mameha left, and I waited in my chair a long while. I was hot and nervous, and I worried that my perspiration would cause my white makeup to turn into a crumpled-looking mess as bad as a futon after being slept in. I looked for something to distract myself; but the best I could do was stand from time to time to catch a glimpse of my face in a mirror hanging on the wall.

Finally I heard voices, then a tapping at the door, and Mameha swung it open.

'Just one moment, Doctor, if you please,' she said.

I could see Dr. Crab in the darkness of the hallway, looking as stern as those old portraits you see in the lobbies of banks. He was peering at me through his glasses. I wasn't sure what to do; normally I would have bowed on the mats, so I went ahead and knelt on the rug to bow in the same way, even though I was certain Mameha would be unhappy with me for doing it. I don't think the Doctor even looked at me.

'I prefer to get back to the party,' he said to Mameha. 'Please excuse me.'

'Sayuri has brought something for you, Doctor,' Mameha told him. 'Just for a moment, if you please.'

She gestured for him to come into the room and saw that he was seated comfortably in one of the overstuffed chairs. After this, I think she must have forgotten what she'd told me earlier, because we both knelt on the rug, one of us at each of Dr. Crab's knees. I'm sure the Doctor felt grand to have two such ornately dressed women kneeling at his feet that way.

'I'm sorry that I haven't seen you in several days,' I said to him. 'And already the weather is growing warm. It seems to me as if an entire season has passed!'

The Doctor didn't respond, but just peered back at me.

'Please accept these *ekubo*, Doctor,' I said, and after bowing, placed the package on a side table near his hand. He put his hands in his lap as if to say he wouldn't dream of touching it.

'Why are you giving me this?'

Mameha interrupted. 'I'm so sorry, Doctor. I led Sayuri to believe you might enjoy receiving *ekubo* from her. I hope I'm not mistaken?'

'You are mistaken. Perhaps you don't know this girl as well as you think. I regard you highly, Mameha-san, but it's a poor reflection on you to recommend her to me.'

'I'm sorry, Doctor,' she said. 'I had no idea you felt that way. I've been under the impression you were fond of Sayuri.'

'Very well. Now that everything is clear, I'll go back to the party.'

'But may I ask? Did Sayuri offend you somehow? Things seem to have changed so unexpectedly.'

'She certainly did. As I told you, I'm offended by people who mislead me.'

'Sayuri-san, how shameful of you to mislead the Doctor!' Mameha said to me. 'You must have told him something you knew was untrue. What was it?'

'I don't know!' I said as innocently as I could. 'Unless it was a few weeks ago when I suggested that the weather was getting warmer, and it wasn't really . . .'

Mameha gave me a look when I said this; I don't think she liked it.

'This is between the two of you,' the Doctor said. 'It is no concern of mine. Please excuse me.'

'But, Doctor, before you go,' Mameha said, 'could there be some misunderstanding? Sayuri's an honest girl and would never knowingly mislead anyone. Particularly someone who's been so kind to her.'

'I suggest you ask her about the boy in her neighborhood,' the Doctor said.

I was very relieved he'd brought up the subject at last. He was such a reserved man, I wouldn't have been surprised if he'd refused to mention it at all.

'So that's the problem!' Mameha said to him. 'You must have been talking with Hatsumomo.'

'I don't see why that matters,' he said.

'She's been spreading this story all over Gion. It's completely untrue! Ever since Sayuri was given an important role on the stage in *Dances of the Old Capital*, Hatsumomo has spent all her energy trying to disgrace her.'

Dances of the Old Capital was Gion's biggest annual event. Its opening was only six weeks away, at the beginning of April. All the dance roles had been assigned some months earlier, and I would have felt honored to take one. A teacher of mine had even suggested it, but as far as I knew, my only role would be in the orchestra and not on the stage at all. Mameha had insisted on this to avoid provoking Hatsumomo.

When the Doctor glanced at me, I did my best to look like someone who would be dancing an important role and had known it for some time.

'I'm afraid to say this, Doctor, but Hatsumomo is a known liar,' Mameha went on. 'It's risky to believe anything she says.'

'If Hatsumomo is a liar, this is the first I've heard of it.'

'No one would dream of telling you such a thing,' Mameha said, speaking in a quiet voice as though she really were afraid of being overheard. 'So many geisha are dishonest! No one wants to be the first to make accusations. But either I'm lying to you now or else Hatsumomo was lying when she told you the story. It's a matter of deciding which of us you know better, Doctor, and which of us you trust more.'

'I don't see why Hatsumomo would make up stories just because Sayuri has a role on the stage.'

'Surely you've met Hatsumomo's younger sister, Pumpkin. Hatsumomo hoped Pumpkin would take a certain role, but it seems Sayuri has ended up with it instead. And I was given the role Hatsumomo wanted! But none of this matters, Doctor. If Sayuri's integrity is in doubt, I can well understand that you might prefer not to accept the *ekubo* she has presented to you.'

The Doctor sat a long while looking at me. Finally he said, 'I'll ask one of my doctors from the hospital to examine her.'

'I'd like to be as cooperative as I can,' Mameha replied, 'but I'd have difficulty arranging such a thing, since you haven't yet agreed to be Sayuri's *mizuage* patron. If her integrity is in doubt . . . well, Sayuri will be presenting *ekubo* to a great many men. I'm sure most will be skeptical of stories they hear from Hatsumomo.'

This seemed to have the effect Mameha wanted. Dr. Crab sat in silence a moment. Finally he said, 'I hardly know the proper thing to do. This is the first time I've found myself in such a peculiar position.'

'Please accept the *ekubo*, Doctor and let's put Hatsumomo's foolishness behind us.'

'I've often heard of dishonest girls who arrange *mizuage* for the time of month when a man will be easily deceived. I'm a doctor, you know. I won't be fooled so readily.'

'But no one is trying to fool you!'

He sat just a moment longer and then stood with his shoulders hunched to march, elbow-first, from the room. I was too busy bowing good-bye to see whether he took the *ekubo* with him; but happily, after he and Mameha had left, I looked at the table and saw they were no longer there.

*

When Mameha mentioned my role on the stage, I thought she was making up a story on the spot to explain why Hatsumomo might lie about me. So you can imagine my surprise the next day when I learned she'd been telling the truth. Or if it wasn't exactly the truth, Mameha felt confident that it would be true before the end of the week.

At that time, in the mid-1930s, probably as many as seven or eight hundred geisha worked in Gion; but because no more than sixty were needed each spring for the production of *Dances of the Old Capital*, the competition for roles destroyed more than a few friendships over the years. Mameha hadn't been truthful when she said that she'd taken a role from Hatsumomo; she was one of the very few geisha in Gion guaranteed a solo role every year. But it was quite true that Hatsumomo had been desperate to see Pumpkin on the stage. I don't know where she got the idea such a thing was possible; Pumpkin may have earned the apprentice's award and received other honors besides, but she never excelled at dance. However, a few days before I presented *ekubo* to the Doctor, a seventeen-year-old apprentice with a solo role had fallen down a flight of stairs and hurt her leg. The poor girl was devastated, but every other apprentice in Gion was happy to take advantage of her misfortune by offering to fill the role. It was this role that in the end went to me. I was only fifteen at the time, and had never danced on the stage before – which isn't to say I wasn't ready to. I'd spent so many evenings in the okiya, rather than going from party to party like most apprentices, and Auntie often played the shamisen so that I could practice dance. This was why I'd already been promoted to the eleventh level by the age of fifteen, even though I probably possessed no more talent as a dancer than anyone else. If Mameha hadn't been so determined to keep me hidden from the public eye because of Hatsumomo, I might even have had a role in the seasonal dances the previous year.

This role was given to me in mid-March, so I had only a month or so to rehearse it. Fortunately my dance teacher was very helpful and often worked with me privately during the afternoons. Mother didn't find out what had happened –

Hatsumomo certainly wasn't going to tell her – until several days afterward, when she heard the rumor during a game of mah-jongg. She came back to the okiya and asked if it was true I'd been given the role. After I told her it was, she walked away with the sort of puzzled look she might have worn if her dog Taku had added up the columns in her account books for her.

Of course, Hatsumomo was furious, but Mameha wasn't concerned about it. The time had come, as she put it, for us to toss Hatsumomo from the ring.

21

LATE ONE AFTERNOON a week or so later, Mameha came up to me during a break in rehearsals, very excited about something. It seemed that on the previous day, the Baron had mentioned to her quite casually that he would be giving a party during the coming weekend for a certain kimono maker named Arashino. The Baron owned one of the best-known collections of kimono in all of Japan. Most of his pieces were antiques, but every so often he bought a very fine work by a living artist. His decision to purchase a piece by Arashino had prompted him to have a party.

'I thought I recognized the name Arashino,' Mameha said to me, 'but when the Baron first mentioned it, I couldn't place it. He's one of Nobu's very closest friends! Don't you see the possibilities? I didn't think of it until today, but I'm going to persuade the Baron to invite both Nobu and the Doctor to his little party. The two of them are certain to dislike each other. When the bidding begins for your *mizuage*, you can be sure that neither will sit still, knowing the prize could be taken by the other.'

I was feeling very tired, but for Mameha's sake I clapped my hands in excitement and said how grateful I was to her for coming up with such a clever plan. And I'm sure it was a clever plan; but the real evidence of her cleverness was that she felt certain she'd have no difficulty persuading the Baron to invite these two men to his party. Clearly they would both be willing to come – in Nobu's case because the Baron was an investor in Iwamura Electric, though I didn't know it at the time; and in Dr. Crab's case because . . . well, because the Doctor considered himself something of an aristocrat, even though he probably had only one obscure ancestor with any aristocratic blood, and would regard it as his duty to attend any function the Baron invited him to. But as to why the Baron would agree to invite either of them, I don't know. He didn't approve of Nobu; very few men did. As for Dr. Crab, the Baron had never met him before and might as well have invited someone off the street,

But Mameha had extraordinary powers of persuasion, as I knew. The party was arranged, and she convinced my dance instructor to release me from rehearsals the following Saturday so I could attend it. The event was to begin in the afternoon and run through dinner – though Mameha and I were to arrive after the party was underway. So it was about three o'clock when we finally climbed into a rickshaw and headed out to the Baron's estate, located at the base of the hills in the northeast of the city. It was my first visit to anyplace so luxurious, and I was quite overwhelmed by what I saw; because if you think of the attention to detail brought to bear in making a kimono, well, that same sort of attention had been brought to the design and care of the entire estate where the Baron lived. The main house dated back to the time of his grandfather, but the gardens, which struck me as a giant brocade of textures, had been designed and built by his father. Apparently the house and gardens never quite fit together until the Baron's older brother – the year before his assassination – had moved the location of the pond, and also created a moss garden with stepping-stones leading from the moon-viewing pavilion on one side of the house. Black swans glided across the pond with a bearing so proud they made me feel ashamed to be such an ungainly creature as a human being.

We were to begin by preparing a tea ceremony the men would join when they were ready; so I was very puzzled when we passed through the main gate and made our way not to an ordinary tea pavilion, but straight toward the edge of the pond to board a small boat. The boat was about the size of a narrow room. Most of it was occupied with wooden seats along the edges, but at one end stood a miniature pavilion with its own roof sheltering a tatami platform. It had actual walls with paper screens slid open for air, and in the very center was a square wooden cavity filled with sand, which served as the brazier where Mameha lit cakes of charcoal to heat the water in a graceful iron teakettle. While she was doing this, I tried to make myself useful by arranging the implements for the ceremony. Already I was feeling quite nervous, and then Mameha turned to me after she had put the kettle on the fire and said:

'You're a clever girl, Sayuri. I don't need to tell you what will become of your future if Dr. Crab or Nobu should lose interest in you. You mustn't let either of them think you're paying too much attention to the other. But of course a certain amount of jealousy won't do any harm. I'm certain you can manage it.'

I wasn't so sure, but I would certainly have to try.

A half hour passed before the Baron and his ten guests strolled out from the house, stopping every so often to admire the view of the hillside from different angles. When they'd boarded the boat, the Baron guided us into the middle of the pond with a pole. Mameha made tea, and I delivered the bowls to each of the guests.

Afterward, we took a stroll through the garden with the men, and soon came to a wooden platform suspended above the water, where several maids in identical kimono were arranging cushions for the men to sit on, and leaving vials of warm sake on trays. I made a point of kneeling beside Dr. Crab, and was just trying to think of something to say when, to my surprise, the Doctor turned to me first.

'Has the laceration on your thigh healed satisfactorily?' he asked.

This was during the month of March, you must understand, and I'd cut my leg way back in November. In the months between, I'd seen Dr. Crab more times than I could count; so I have no idea why he waited until that moment to ask me about it, and in front of so many people. Fortunately, I didn't think anyone had heard, so I kept my voice low when I answered.

'Thank you so much, Doctor. With your help it has healed completely.'

'I hope the injury hasn't left too much of a scar,' he said.

'Oh, no, just a tiny bump, really.'

I might have ended the conversation right there by pouring him more sake, perhaps, or changing the subject; but I happened to notice that he was stroking one of his thumbs with the fingers of his other hand. The Doctor was the sort of man who never wasted a single movement. If he was stroking his thumb in this way while thinking about my leg . . . well, I decided it would be foolish for me to change the subject.

'It isn't much of a scar,' I went on. 'Sometimes when I'm in the bath, I rub my finger across it, and . . . it's just a tiny ridge, really. About like this.'

I rubbed one of my knuckles with my index finger and held it out for the Doctor to do the same. He brought his hand up; but then he hesitated. I saw his eyes jump toward mine. In a moment he drew his hand back and felt his own knuckle instead.

'A cut of that sort should have healed smoothly,' he told me.

'Perhaps it isn't as big as I've said. After all, my leg is very . . . well, sensitive, you see. Even just a drop of rain falling onto it is enough to make me shudder!'

I'm not going to pretend any of this made sense. A bump wouldn't seem bigger just because my leg was sensitive; and anyway when was the last time I'd felt a drop of rain on my bare leg? But now that I understood why Dr. Crab was really interested in me, I suppose I was half-disgusted and half-fascinated as I tried to imagine what was going on in his mind. In any case, the Doctor cleared his throat and leaned toward me.

'And . . . have you been practicing?'

'Practicing?'

'You sustained the injury when you lost your balance while you were . . . well, you see what I mean. You don't want that to happen again. So I expect you've been practicing. But how does one practice such a thing?'

After this, he leaned back and closed his eyes. It was clear to me he expected to hear an answer longer than simply a word or two.

'Well, you'll think me very silly, but every night . . .' I

began; and then I had to think for a moment. The silence dragged on, but the Doctor never opened his eyes. He seemed to me like a baby bird just waiting for the mother's beak. 'Every night,' I went on, 'just before I step into the bath, I practice balancing in a variety of positions. Sometimes I have to shiver from the cold air against my bare skin; but I spend five or ten minutes that way.'

The Doctor cleared his throat, which I took as a good sign.

'First I try balancing on one foot, and then the other. But the trouble is . . .'

Up until this point, the Baron, on the opposite side of the platform from me, had been talking with his other guests; but now he ended his story. The next words I spoke were as clear as if I'd stood at a podium and announced them.

'. . . when I don't have any clothing on –'

I clapped a hand over my mouth, but before I could think of what to do, the Baron spoke up. 'My goodness!' he said. 'Whatever you two are talking about over there, it certainly sounds more interesting than what we've been saying!'

The men laughed when they heard this. Afterward the Doctor was kind enough to offer an explanation.

'Sayuri-san came to me late last year with a leg injury,' he said. 'She sustained it when she fell. As a result, I suggested she work at improving her balance.'

'She's been working at it very hard,' Mameha added. 'Those robes are more awkward than they look.'

'Let's have her take them off, then!' said one of the men – though of course, it was only a joke, and everyone laughed.

'Yes, I agree!' the Baron said. 'I never understand why women bother wearing kimono in the first place. Nothing is as beautiful as a woman without an item of clothing on her body.'

'That isn't true when the kimono has been made by my good friend Arashino,' Nobu said.

'Not even Arashino's kimono are as lovely as what they cover up,' the Baron said, and tried to put his sake cup onto the platform, though it ended up spilling. He wasn't drunk, exactly – though he was certainly much further along in his drinking than I'd ever imagined him. 'Don't misunderstand me,' he went on. 'I think Arashino's robes are lovely. Otherwise he wouldn't be sitting here beside me, now would he? But if you ask me whether I'd rather look at a kimono or a naked woman . . . well!'

'No one's asking,' said Nobu. 'I myself am interested to hear what sort of work Arashino has been up to lately.'

But Arashino didn't have a chance to answer; because the Baron, who was taking a last slurp of sake, nearly choked in his hurry to interrupt.

'Mmm . . . just a minute,' he said. 'Isn't it true that every man on this earth likes to see a naked woman? I mean, is that what you're saying, Nobu, that the naked female form doesn't interest you?'

'That isn't what I'm saying,' Nobu said. 'What I'm saying is, I think it's time for us to hear from Arashino exactly what sort of work he's been up to lately.'

'Oh, yes, I'm certainly interested too,' the Baron said. 'But you know, I do find it fascinating that no matter how different we men may seem, underneath it all we're exactly the same. You can't pretend you're above it, Nobu-san. We know the truth, don't we? There isn't a man here who wouldn't pay quite a bit of money just for the chance to watch Sayuri take a bath. Eh? That's a particular fantasy of mine, I'll admit. Now come on! Don't pretend you don't feel the same way I do.'

'Poor Sayuri is only an apprentice,' said Mameha. 'Perhaps we ought to spare her this conversation.'

'Certainly not!' the Baron answered. 'The sooner she sees the world as it really is, the better. Plenty of men act as if they don't chase women just for the chance to get underneath all those robes, but you listen to me, Sayuri; there's only one kind of man! And while we're on this subject, here's something for you to keep in mind. Every man seated here has at some point this afternoon thought of how much he would enjoy seeing you naked. What do you think of that?'

I was sitting with my hands in my lap, gazing down at the wooden platform and trying to seem demure. I had to respond in some way to what the Baron had said, particularly since everyone else was completely silent; but before I could think of what to say Nobu did something very kind. He put his sake cup down onto the platform and stood up to excuse himself.

'I'm sorry Baron, but I don't know the way to the toilet,' he said. Of course, this was my cue to escort him.

I didn't know the way to the toilet any better than Nobu; but I wasn't going to miss the opportunity to remove myself from the gathering. As I rose to my feet, a maid offered to show me the way, and led me around the pond, with Nobu following along behind.

In the house, we walked down a long hallway of blond wood with windows on one side. On the other side, brilliantly lit in the sunshine, stood display cases with glass tops. I was about to lead Nobu down to the end, but he stopped at a case containing a collection of antique swords. He seemed to be looking at the display, but mostly he drummed the fingers of his one hand, on the glass and blew air out his nose again and again, for he was still very angry. I felt troubled by what had happened as well. But I was also grateful to him for rescuing me, and I wasn't sure how to express this. At the next case – a display of tiny netsuke figures carved in ivory – I asked him if he liked antiques.

'Antiques like the Baron, you mean? Certainly not.'

The Baron wasn't a particularly old man – much younger than Nobu, in fact. But I knew what he meant; he thought of the Baron as a relic of the feudal age.

'I'm so sorry,' I said, 'I was thinking of the antiques here in the case.'

'When I look at the swords over there, they make me think of the Baron. When I look at the netsuke here, they make me think of the Baron. He's been a supporter of our company, and I owe him a great debt. But I don't like to waste my time thinking about him when I don't have to. Does that answer your question?'

I bowed to him in reply, and he strode off down the hallway to the toilet, so quickly that I couldn't reach the door first to open it for him.

Later, when we returned to the water's edge, I was pleased to see that the party was beginning to break up. Only a few of the men would remain for dinner. Mameha and I ushered the others up the path to the main gate, where their drivers were waiting for them on the side street. We bowed farewell to the last man, and I turned to find one of the Baron's servants ready to show us into the house.

Mameha and I spent the next hour in the servants' quarters, eating a lovely dinner that included *tai no usugiri* – paper-thin slices of sea bream, fanned out on a leaf-shaped ceramic plate and served with *ponzu* sauce. I would certainly have enjoyed myself if Mameha hadn't been so moody. She ate only a few bites of her sea bream and sat staring out the window at the dusk. Something about her expression made me think she would have liked to go back down to the pond and sit, biting her lip, perhaps, and peering in anger at the darkening sky.

We rejoined the Baron and his guests already partway through their dinner, in what the Baron called the 'small banquet room.' Actually, the small banquet room could have accommodated probably twenty or twenty-five people; and now that the party had shrunk in size, only Mr. Arashino, Nobu, and Dr. Crab remained. When we entered, they were eating in complete silence. The Baron was so drunk his eyes seemed to slosh around in their sockets.

Just as Mameha was beginning a conversation, Dr. Crab stroked a napkin down his mustache twice and then excused himself to use the toilet. I led him to the same hallway Nobu and I had visited earlier. Now that evening had come, I could hardly see the objects because of overhead lights reflected in the glass of the display cases. But Dr. Crab stopped at the case containing the swords and moved his head around until he could see them.

'You certainly know your way around the Baron's house,' he said.

'Oh, no, sir, I'm quite lost in such a grand place. The only reason I can find my way is because I led Nobu-san along this hallway earlier.'

'I'm sure he rushed right through,' the Doctor said. 'A man like Nobu has a poor sensibility for appreciating the items in these cases.'

I didn't know what to say to this, but the Doctor looked at me pointedly.

'You haven't seen much of the world,' he went on, 'but in time you'll learn to be careful of anyone with the arrogance to accept an invitation from a man like the Baron, and then speak to him rudely in his own house, as Nobu did this afternoon.'

I bowed at this, and when it was clear that Dr. Crab had nothing further to say, led him down the hallway to the toilet.

By the time we returned to the small banquet room, the men had fallen into conversation, thanks to the quiet skills of Mameha, who now sat in the background pouring sake. She often said the role of a geisha was sometimes just to stir the soup. If you've ever noticed the way miso settles into a cloud at the bottom of the bowl but mixes quickly with a few whisks of the chopsticks, this is what she meant.

Soon the conversation turned to the subject of kimono, and we all proceeded downstairs to the Baron's underground museum. Along the walls were huge panels that opened to reveal kimono suspended on sliding rods. The Baron sat on a stool in the middle of the room with his elbows on his knees – bleary-eyed still – and didn't speak a word while Mameha guided us through the collection. The most spectacular robe, we all agreed, was one designed to mimic the landscape of the city of Kobe, which is located on the side of a steep hill falling away to the ocean. The design began at the shoulders with blue sky and clouds; the knees represented the hillside; below that, the gown swept back into a long train showing the blue-green of the sea dotted with beautiful gold waves and tiny ships.

'Mameha,' the Baron said, 'I think you ought to wear that one to my blossom-viewing party in Hakone next week. That would be quite something, wouldn't it?'

'I'd certainly like to,' Mameha replied. 'But as I mentioned the other day, I'm afraid I won't be able to attend the party this year.'

I could see that the Baron was displeased, for his eyebrows closed down like two windows being shut. 'What do you mean? Who has booked an engagement with you that you can't break?'

'I'd like nothing more than to be there, Baron. But just this one year, I'm afraid it won't be possible. I have a medical appointment that conflicts with the party.'

'A medical appointment? What on earth does that mean? These doctors can change times around. Change it tomorrow, and be at my party next week just like you always are.'

'I do apologize,' Mameha said, 'but with the Baron's consent, I scheduled a medical appointment some weeks ago and won't be able to change it.'

'I don't recall giving you any consent! Anyway, it's not as if you need to have an abortion, or some such thing . . .'

A long, embarrassed silence followed. Mameha only adjusted her sleeves while the rest of us stood so quietly that the only sound was Mr. Arashino's wheezy breathing. I noticed that Nobu, who'd been paying no attention, turned to observe the Baron's reaction.

'Well,' the Baron said at last. 'I suppose I'd forgotten, now that you mention it . . . We certainly can't have any little barons running around, now can we? But really, Mameha, I don't see why you couldn't have reminded me about this in private . . .'

'I am sorry, Baron.'

'Anyway, if you can't come to Hakone, well, you can't! But what about the rest of you? It's a lovely party, at my estate in Hakone next weekend. You must all come! I do it every year at the height of the cherry blossoms.'

The Doctor and Arashino were both unable to attend. Nobu didn't reply; but when the Baron pressed him, he said, 'Baron, you don't honestly think I'd go all the way to Hakone to look at cherry blossoms.'

'Oh, the blossoms are just an excuse to have a party,' said the Baron. 'Anyway, it doesn't matter. We'll have that Chairman of yours. He comes every year.'

I was surprised to feel flustered at the mention of the Chairman, for I'd been thinking of him on and off throughout the afternoon. I felt for a moment as if my secret had been exposed.

'It troubles me that none of you will come,' the Baron went on. 'We were having such a nice evening until Mameha started talking about things she ought to have kept private. Well, Mameha, I have the proper punishment for you. You're no longer invited to my party this year. What's more, I want you to send Sayuri in your place.'

I thought the Baron was making a joke; but I must confess, I thought at once how lovely it would be to stroll with the Chairman through the grounds of a magnificent estate, without Nobu or Dr. Crab, or even Mameha nearby.

'It's a fine idea, Baron,' said Mameha, 'but sadly, Sayuri is busy with rehearsals.'

'Nonsense,' said the Baron. 'I expect to see her there. Why do you have to defy me every single time I ask something of you?'

He really did look angry; and unfortunately, because he was so drunk, a good deal of saliva came spilling out of his mouth. He tried to wipe it away with the back of his hand, but ended up smearing it into the long black hairs of his beard.

'Isn't there one thing I can ask of you that you won't disregard?' he went on. 'I want to see Sayuri in Hakone. You could just reply, "Yes, Baron," and be done with it.'

'Yes, Baron.'

'Fine,' said the Baron. He leaned back on his stool again, and took a handkerchief from his pocket to wipe his face clean.

I was very sorry for Mameha. But it would be an understatement to say I felt excited at the prospect of attending the Baron's party. Every time I thought of it in the rickshaw back to Gion, I think my ears turned red. I was terribly afraid Mameha would notice, but she just stared out to the side, and never spoke a word until the end of our ride, when she turned to me and said, 'Sayuri, you must be very careful in Hakone.'

'Yes, ma'am, I will,' I replied.

'Keep in mind that an apprentice on the point of having her *mizuage* is like a meal served on the table. No man will wish to eat it, if he hears a suggestion that some other man has taken a bite.'

I couldn't quite look her in the eye after she said this. I knew perfectly well she was talking about the Baron.

22

AT THIS TIME in my life I didn't even know where Hakone was – though I soon learned that it was in eastern Japan, quite some distance from Kyoto. But I had a most agreeable feeling of importance the rest of that week, reminding myself that a man as prominent as the Baron had invited me to travel from Kyoto to attend a party. In fact, I had trouble keeping my excitement from showing when at last I took my seat in a lovely second-class compartment – with Mr. Itchoda, Mameha's dresser, seated on the aisle to discourage anyone from trying to talk with me. I pretended to pass the time by reading a magazine, but in fact I was only turning the pages, for I was occupied instead with watching out of the corner of my eye as people who passed down the aisle slowed to look at me. I found myself enjoying the attention; but when we reached Shizuoka shortly after noon and I stood awaiting the train to Hakone, all at once I could feel something unpleasant welling up inside me. I'd spent the day keeping it veiled from my awareness, but now I saw in my mind much too clearly the image of myself at another time, standing on another platform, taking another train trip – this one with Mr. Bekku – on the day my sister and I were taken from our home. I'm ashamed to admit how hard I'd worked over the years to keep from thinking about Satsu, and my father and mother, and our tipsy house on the sea cliffs. I'd been like a child with my head in a bag. All I'd seen day after day was Gion, so much so that I'd come to think Gion was everything, and that the only thing that mattered in the world was Gion. But now that I was outside Kyoto, I could see that for most people life had nothing to do with Gion at all; and of course, I couldn't stop from thinking of the other life I'd once led. Grief is a most peculiar thing; we're so helpless in the face of it. It's like a window that will simply open of its own accord. The room grows cold, and we can do nothing but shiver. But it opens a little less each time, and a little less; and one day we wonder what has become of it.

Late the following morning I was picked up at the little inn overlooking Mount Fuji, and taken by one of the Baron's motorcars to his summer house amid lovely woods at the edge of a lake. When we pulled into a circular drive and I stepped out wearing the full regalia of an apprentice geisha from Kyoto, many of the Baron's guests turned to stare at me. Among them I spotted a number of women, some in kimono and some in Western-style dresses. Later I came to realize they were mostly Tokyo geisha – for we were only a few hours from Tokyo by train. Then the Baron himself appeared, striding up a path from the woods with several other men.

'Now, *this* is what we've all been waiting for!' he said. 'This lovely thing is Sayuri from Gion, who will probably one day be 'the great Sayuri from Gion.' You'll never see eyes like hers again, I can assure you. And just wait until you see the way she moves . . . I invited you here, Sayuri, so all the men could have a chance to look at you; so you have an important job. You must wander all around – inside the house, down by the lake, all through the woods, everywhere! Now go along and get working!'

I began to wander around the estate as the Baron had asked, past the cherry trees heavy with their blossoms, bowing here and there to the guests and trying not to seem too obvious about looking around for the Chairman. I made little headway, because every few steps some man or other would stop me and say something like, 'My heavens! An apprentice geisha from Kyoto!' And then he would take out his camera and have someone snap a picture of us standing together, or else walk me along the lake to the little moon-viewing pavilion, or wherever, so his friends could have a look at me – just as he might have done with some prehistoric creature he'd captured in a net. Mameha had warned me that everyone would be fascinated with my appearance; because there's nothing quite like an apprentice geisha from Gion. It's true that in the better geisha districts of Tokyo, such as Shimbashi and Akasaka, a girl must master the arts if she expects to make her debut. But many of the Tokyo geisha at that time were very modern in their sensibilities, which is why some were walking around the Baron's estate in Western-style clothing.

The Baron's party seemed to go on and on. By mid-afternoon I'd practically given up any hope of finding the Chairman. I went into the house to look for a place to rest, but the very moment I stepped up into the entrance hall, I felt myself go numb. There he was, emerging from a tatami room in conversation with another man. They said good-bye to each other, and then the Chairman turned to me.

'Sayuri!' he said. 'Now how did the Baron lure you here all the way from Kyoto? I didn't even realize you were acquainted with him.'

I knew I ought to take my eyes off the Chairman, but it was like pulling nails from the wall. When I finally managed to do it, I gave him a bow and said:

'Mameha-san sent me in her place. I'm so pleased to have the honor of seeing the Chairman.'

'Yes, and I'm pleased to see you too; you can give me your opinion about something. Come have a look at the present I've brought for the Baron. I'm tempted to leave without giving it to him.'

I followed him into a tatami room, feeling like a kite pulled by a string. Here I was in Hakone so far from anything I'd ever known, spending a few moments with the man I'd thought about more constantly than anyone, and it amazed me to think of it. While he walked ahead of me I had to admire how he moved so easily within his tailored wool suit. I could make out the swell of his calves, and even the hollow of his back like a cleft where the roots of a tree divide. He took something from the table and held it out for me to see. At first I thought it was an ornamented block of gold, but it turned out to be an antique cosmetics box for the Baron. This one, as the Chairman told me, was by an Edo period artist named Arata Gonroku. It was a pillow-shaped box in gold lacquer, with soft black images of flying cranes and leaping rabbits. When he put it into my hands, it was so dazzling I had to hold my breath as I looked at it.

'Do you think the Baron will be pleased?' he said. 'I found it last week and thought of him at once, but –'

'Chairman, how can you even imagine that the Baron might not feel pleased?'

'Oh, that man has collections of everything. He'll probably see this as third-rate.'

I assured the Chairman that no one could ever think such a thing; and when I gave him back the box, he tied it up in a silk cloth again and nodded toward the door for me to follow. In the entryway I helped him with his shoes. While I guided his foot with my fingertips, I found myself imagining that we'd spent the afternoon together and that a long evening lay ahead of us. This thought transported me into such a state, I don't know how much time passed before I became aware of myself again. The Chairman showed no signs of impatience, but I felt terribly self-conscious as I tried to slip my feet into my *okobo* and ended up taking much longer than I should have.

He led me down a path toward the lake, where we found the Baron sitting on a mat beneath a cherry tree with three Tokyo geisha. They all rose to their feet, though the Baron had a bit of trouble. His face had red splotches all over it from drink, so that it looked as if someone had swatted him again and again with a stick.

'Chairman!' the Baron said. 'I'm so happy you came to my party. I always enjoy having you here, do you know that? That corporation of yours just won't stop growing, will it? Did Sayuri tell you Nobu came to my party in Kyoto last week?'

'I heard all about it from Nobu, who I'm sure was his usual self.'

'He certainly was,' said the Baron. 'A peculiar little man, isn't he?'

I don't know what the Baron was thinking, for he himself was littler than Nobu. The Chairman didn't seem to like this comment, and narrowed his eyes.

'I mean to say,' the Baron began, but the Chairman cut him off.

'I have come to thank you and say good-bye, but first I have something to give you.' And here he handed over the cosmetics box. The Baron was too drunk to untie the silk cloth around it, but he gave it to one of the geisha, who did it for him.

'What a beautiful thing!' the Baron said. 'Doesn't everybody think so? Look at it. Why, it might be even lovelier than the exquisite creature standing beside you, Chairman. Do you know Sayuri? If not, let me introduce you.'

'Oh, we're well acquainted, Sayuri and I,' the Chairman said.

'How well acquainted, Chairman? Enough for me to envy you?' The Baron laughed at his own joke, but no one else did. 'Anyway, this generous gift reminds me that I have something for you, Sayuri. But I can't give it to you until these other geisha have departed, because they'll start wanting one themselves. So you'll have to stay around until everyone has gone home.'

'The Baron is too kind,' I said, 'but really, I don't wish to make a nuisance of myself.'

'I see you've learned a good deal from Mameha about how to say no to everything. Just meet me in the front entrance hall after my guests have left. You'll persuade her for me, Chairman, while she walks you to your car.'

If the Baron hadn't been so drunk, I'm sure it would have occurred to him to walk the Chairman out himself. But the two men said good-bye, and I followed the Chairman back to the house. While his driver held the door for him, I bowed and thanked him for all his kindness. He was about to get into the car, but he stopped.

'Sayuri,' he began, and then seemed uncertain how to proceed. 'What has Mameha told you about the Baron?'

'Not very much, sir. Or at least . . . well, I'm not sure what the Chairman means.'

'Is Mameha a good older sister to you? Does she tell you the things you need to know?'

'Oh, yes, Chairman. Mameha has helped me more than I can say.'

'Well,' he said, 'I'd watch out, if I were you, when a man like the Baron decides he has something to give you.'

I couldn't think of how to respond to this, so I said something about the Baron being kind to have thought of me at all.

'Yes, very kind, I'm sure. Just take care of yourself,' he said, looking at me intently for a moment, and then getting into his car.

I spent the next hour strolling among the few remaining guests, remembering again and again all the things the Chairman had said to me during our encounter. Rather than feeling concerned about the warning he had given me, I felt elated that he had spoken with me for so long. In fact, I had no space in my mind at all to think about my meeting with the Baron, until at last I found myself standing alone in the entrance hall in the fading afternoon light. I took the liberty of going to kneel in a nearby tatami room, where I gazed out at the grounds through a plate-glass window.

Ten or fifteen minutes passed; finally the Baron came striding into the entrance hall. I felt myself go sick with worry the moment I saw him, for he wore nothing but a cotton dressing robe. He had a towel in one hand, which he rubbed against the long black hairs on his face that were supposed to be a beard. Clearly he'd just stepped out of the bath. I stood and bowed to him.

'Sayuri, do you know what a fool I am!' he said to me. 'I've had too much to drink.' That part was certainly true. 'I forgot you were waiting for me! I hope you'll forgive me when you see what I've put aside for you.'

The Baron walked down the hallway toward the interior of the house, expecting me to follow him. But I remained where I was, thinking of what Mameha had said to me, that an apprentice on the point of having her *mizuage* was like a meal served on the table.

The Baron stopped. 'Come along!' he said to me.

'Oh, Baron. I really mustn't. Please permit me to wait here.'

'I have something I'd like to give you. Just come back into my quarters and sit down, and don't be a silly girl.'

'Why, Baron,' I said, 'I can't help but be a silly girl; for that's what I am!'

'Tomorrow you'll be back under the watchful eyes of Mameha, eh? But there's no one watching you here.'

If I'd had the least common sense at that moment, I would have thanked the Baron for inviting me to his lovely party and told him how much I regretted having to impose on him for the use of his motorcar to take me back to the inn. But everything had such a dream-like quality . . . I suppose I'd gone into a state of shock. All I knew for certain was how afraid I felt.

'Come back with me while I dress,' said the Baron. 'Did you drink much sake this afternoon?'

A long moment passed. I was very aware that my face felt as though it had no expression on it at all, but simply hung from my head.

'No, sir,' I managed to say at last.

'I don't suppose you would have. I'll give you as much as you like. Come along.'

'Baron,' I said, 'please, I'm quite sure I'm expected back at the inn.'

'Expected? Who is expecting you?'

I didn't answer this.

'I said, who is expecting you? I don't see why you have to behave this way. I have something to give you. Would you rather I went and fetched it?'

'I'm very sorry,' I said.

The Baron just stared at me. 'Wait here,' he said at last, and walked back into the interior of the house. A short time later he emerged holding something flat, wrapped in linen paper. I didn't have to look closely to know it was a kimono.

'Now then,' he said to me, 'since you insist on being a silly girl, I've gone and fetched your present. Does this make you feel better?'

I told the Baron I was sorry once again.

'I saw how much you admired this robe the other day. I'd like you to have it,' he said.

The Baron set the package down on the table and untied the strings to open it. I thought the kimono would be the one showing a landscape of Kobe; and to tell the truth, I felt as worried as I did hopeful, for I had no idea what I'd do with such a magnificent thing, or how I would explain to Mameha that the Baron had given it to me. But what I saw instead, when the Baron opened the wrapping, was a magnificent dark fabric with lacquered threads and embroidery in silver. He took the robe out and held it up by the shoulders. It was a kimono that belonged in a museum – made in the 1860s, as the Baron told me, for the niece of the very last shogun, Tokugawa Yoshinobu. The design on the robe was of silver birds flying against a night sky, with a mysterious landscape of dark trees and rocks rising up from the hem.

'You must come back with me and try it on,' he said. 'Now don't be a silly girl! I have a great deal of experience tying an obi with my own hands. We'll put you back into your kimono so that no one will ever know.'

I would gladly have exchanged the robe the Baron was offering me for some way out of the situation. But he was a man with so much authority that even Mameha couldn't disobey him. If she had no way of refusing his wishes, how could I? I could sense that he was losing patience; heaven knows he'd certainly been kind in the months since I'd made my debut, permitting me to attend to him while he ate lunch and allowing Mameha to bring me to the party at his Kyoto estate. And here he was being kind once again, offering me a stunning kimono.

I suppose I finally came to the conclusion that I had no choice but to obey him and pay the consequences, whatever they might be. I lowered my eyes to the mats in shame; and in this same dreamlike state I'd been feeling all along, I became aware of the Baron taking my hand and guiding me through the corridors toward the back of his house. A servant stepped into the hallway at one point, but bowed and went back the moment he caught sight of us. The Baron never spoke a word, but led me along until we came to a spacious tatami room, lined along one wall with mirrors. It was his dressing room. Along the opposite wall were closets with all their doors closed.

My hands trembled with fear, but if the Baron noticed he

made no comment. He stood me before the mirrors and raised my hand to his lips; I thought he was going to kiss it, but he only held the back of my hand against the bristles on his face and did something I found peculiar; he drew my sleeve above my wrist and took in the scent of my skin. His beard tickled my arm, but somehow I didn't feel it. I didn't seem to feel anything at all; it was as if I were buried beneath layers of fear, and confusion, and dread . . . And then the Baron woke me from my shock by stepping behind me and reaching around my chest to untie my *obijime*. This was the cord that held my obi in place.

I experienced a moment of panic now that I knew the Baron really intended to undress me. I tried saying something, but my mouth moved so clumsily I couldn't control it; and anyway, the Baron only made noises to shush me. I kept trying to stop him with my hands, but he pushed them away and finally succeeded in removing my *obijime*. After this he stepped back and struggled a long while with the knot of the obi between my shoulderblades. I pleaded with him not to take it off – though my throat was so dry that several times when I tried to speak, nothing came out – but he didn't listen to me and soon began to unwind the broad obi, wrapping and unwrapping his arms around my waist. I saw the Chairman's handkerchief dislodge itself from the fabric and flutter to the ground. In a moment the Baron let the obi fall in a pile to the floor, and then unfastened the *datejime* – the waistband underneath. I felt the sickening sensation of my kimono releasing itself from around my waist. I clutched it shut with my arms, but the Baron pulled them apart. I could no longer bear to watch in the mirror. The last thing I recall as I closed my eyes was the heavy robe being lifted from around my shoulders with a rustle of fabric.

The Baron seemed to have accomplished what he'd set out to do; or at least, he went no further for the moment. I felt his hands at my waist, caressing the fabric of my underrobe. When at last I opened my eyes again, he stood behind me still, taking in the scent of my hair and my neck. His eyes were fixed on the mirror – fixed, it seemed to me, on the waistband that held my underrobe shut. Every time his fingers moved, I tried with the power of my mind to keep them away, but all too soon they began creeping like spiders across my belly and in another moment had tangled themselves in my waistband and begun to pull. I tried to stop him several times, but the Baron pushed my hands away as he'd done earlier. Finally the waistband came undone; the Baron let it slip from his fingers and fall to the floor. My legs were trembling, and the room was nothing more than a blur to me as he took the seams of my underrobe in his hands and started to draw them open. I couldn't stop myself from grabbing at his hands once again.

'Don't be so worried, Sayuri!' the Baron whispered to me. 'For heaven's sake, I'm not going to do anything to you I shouldn't do. I only want to have a look, don't you understand? There's nothing wrong in that. Any man would do the same.'

A shiny bristle from his face tickled against my ear as he said this, so that I had to turn my head to one side. I think he must have interpreted this as a kind of consent, because now his hands began to move with more urgency. He pulled my robe open. I felt his fingers on my ribs, almost tickling me as he struggled to untie the strings holding my kimono undershirt closed. A moment later he'd succeeded. I couldn't bear the thought of what the Baron might see; so even while I kept my face turned away, I strained my eyes to look in the mirror. My kimono undershirt hung open, exposing a long strip of skin down the center of my chest.

By now the Baron's hands had moved to my hips, where they were busy with my *koshimaki.* Earlier that day, when I had wrapped the *koshimaki* several times around me, I'd tucked it more tightly at the waist than I probably needed to. The Baron was having trouble finding the seam, but after several tugs he loosened the fabric, so that with one long pull he was able to draw the entire length of it out from beneath my underrobe. As the silk slid against my skin, I heard a noise coming out of my throat, something like a sob. My hands grabbed for the *koshimaki*, but the Baron pulled it from my reach and dropped it to the floor. Then as slowly as a man might peel the cover from a sleeping child, he drew open my underrobe in a long breathless gesture, as though he were unveiling something magnificent. I felt a burning in my throat that told me I was on the point of crying; but I couldn't bear the thought that the Baron would see my nakedness and also see me cry. I held my tears back somehow, at the very edge of my vision, and watched the mirror so intently that for a long moment I felt as though time had stopped. I'd certainly never seen myself so utterly naked before. It was true that I still wore buttoned socks on my feet; but I felt more exposed now with the seams of my robe held wide apart than I'd ever felt even in a bathhouse while completely unclothed. I watched the Baron's eyes linger here and there on my reflection in the mirror. First he drew the robe still farther open to take in the outline of my waist. Then he lowered his eyes to the darkness that had bloomed on me in the years since I'd come to Kyoto. His eyes remained there a long while; but at length they rose up slowly, passing over my stomach, along my ribs, to the two plum-colored circles – first on one side, and then on the other. Now the Baron took away one of his hands, so that my underrobe settled against me on that side. What he did with his hand I can't say, but I never saw it again. At one point I felt a moment of panic when I saw a naked shoulder protruding from his bathrobe. I don't know what he was doing – and even though I could probably make an accurate guess about it now, I much prefer not to think about it. All I know is that I became very aware of his breath warming my neck. After that, I saw nothing more. The mirror became a blur of silver; I was no longer able to hold back my tears.

At a certain point the Baron's breathing slowed again. My skin was hot and quite damp from fear, so that when he released my robe at last and let it fall, I felt the puff of air against my side almost as a breeze. Soon I was alone in the room; the Baron had walked out without my even realizing it. Now that he was gone, I rushed to dress myself with such desperation that while I knelt on the floor to gather up my undergarments, I kept seeing in my mind an image of a starving child grabbing at scraps of food.

I dressed again as best I could, with my hands trembling. But until I had help, I could go no further than to close my underrobe and secure it with the waistband. I waited in front of the mirror, looking with some concern at the smeared makeup on my face. I was prepared to wait there a full hour if I had to. But only a few minutes passed before the Baron came back with the sash of his bathrobe tight around his plump belly. He helped me into my kimono without a word, and secured it with my *datejime* just as Mr. Itchoda would have done. While he was holding my great, long obi in his arms, measuring it out in loops as he prepared to tie it around me, I began to feel a terrible feeling. I couldn't make sense of it at first; but it seeped its way through me just as a stain seeps across cloth, and soon I understood. It was the feeling that I'd done something terribly wrong. I didn't want to cry in front of the Baron, but I couldn't help it – and anyway, he hadn't looked me in the eye since coming back into the room. I tried to imagine I was simply a house standing in the rain with the water washing down the front of me. But the Baron must have seen, for he left the room and came back a moment later with a handkerchief bearing his monogram. He instructed me to keep it, but after I used it, I left it there on a table.

Soon he led me to the front of the house and went away without speaking a word. In time a servant came, holding the antique kimono wrapped once again in linen paper. He presented it to me with a bow and then escorted me to the Baron's motorcar. I cried quietly in the backseat on the way to the inn, but the driver pretended to take no notice. I was no longer crying about what had happened to me. Something much more frightful was on my mind – namely what would happen when Mr. Itchoda saw my smeared makeup, and then helped me undress and saw the poorly tied knot in my obi, and then opened the package and saw the expensive gift I'd received. Before leaving the car I wiped my face with the Chairman's handkerchief, but it did me little good. Mr. Itchoda took one look at me and then scratched his chin as though he understood everything that had happened. While he was untying my obi in the room upstairs, he said:

'Did the Baron undress you?'

'I'm sorry,' I said.

'He undressed you and looked at you in the mirror. But he

didn't enjoy himself with you. He didn't touch you, or lie on top of you, did he?'

'No, sir.'

'That's fine, then,' Mr. Itchoda said, staring straight ahead. Not another word was spoken between us.

23

I WON'T SAY MY emotions had settled themselves by the time the train pulled into Kyoto Station early the following morning. After all, when a stone is dropped into a pond, the water continues quivering even after the stone has sunk to the bottom. But when I descended the wooden stairs carrying us from the platform, with Mr. Itchoda one step behind me, I came upon such a shock that for a time I forgot everything else.

There in a glass case was the new poster for that season's *Dances of the Old Capital*, and I stopped to have a look at it. Two weeks remained before the event. The poster had been distributed just the previous day, probably while I was strolling around the Baron's estate hoping to meet up with the Chairman. The dance every year has a theme, such as 'Colors of the Four Seasons in Kyoto,' or 'Famous Places from *Tale of the Heike*.' This year the theme was 'The Gleaming Light of the Morning Sun.' The poster, which of course was drawn by Uchida Kosaburo – who'd created nearly every poster since 1919 – showed an apprentice geisha in a lovely green and orange kimono standing on an arched wooden bridge. I was exhausted after my long trip and had slept badly on the train; so I stood for a while before the poster in a sort of daze, taking in the lovely greens and golds of the background, before I turned my attention to the girl in the kimono. She was gazing directly into the bright light of the sunrise, and her eyes were a startling blue-gray. I had to put a hand on the railing to steady myself. I was the girl Uchida had drawn there on that bridge!

On the way back from the train station, Mr. Itchoda

pointed out every poster we passed, and even asked the rickshaw driver to go out of his way so we could see an entire wall of them on the old Daimaru Department Store building. Seeing myself all over the city this way wasn't quite as thrilling as I would have imagined; I kept thinking of the poor girl in the poster standing before a mirror as her obi was untied by an older man. In any case, I expected to hear all sorts of congratulations over the course of the following few days, but I soon learned that an honor like this one never comes without costs. Ever since Mameha had arranged for me to take a role in the seasonal dances, I'd heard any number of unpleasant comments about myself. After the poster, things only grew worse. The next morning, for example, a young apprentice who'd been friendly the week before now looked away when I gave a bow to greet her.

As for Mameha, I went to visit her in her apartment, where she was recovering, and found that she was as proud as if she herself had been the one in the poster. She certainly wasn't pleased that I'd taken the trip to Hakone, but she seemed as devoted to my success as ever – strangely, perhaps even more so. For a while I worried she would view my horrible encounter with the Baron as a betrayal of her. I imagined Mr. Itchoda must have told her about it . . . but if he did, she never raised the subject between us. Neither did I.

Two weeks later the seasonal dances opened. On that first day in the dressing room at the Kaburenjo Theater, I felt myself almost overflowing with excitement, for Mameha had told me the Chairman and Nobu would be in the audience. While putting on my makeup, I tucked the Chairman's handkerchief beneath my dressing robe, against my bare skin. My hair was bound closely to my head with a silk strip, because of the wigs I would be wearing, and when I saw myself in the mirror without the familiar frame of hair surrounding my face, I found angles in my cheeks and around my eyes that I'd never before seen. It may seem odd, but when I realized that the shape of my own face was a surprise to me, I had the sudden insight that nothing in life is ever as simple as we imagine.

An hour later I was standing with the other apprentices in

the wings of the theater, ready for the opening dance. We wore identical kimono of yellow and red, with obis of orange and gold – so that we looked, each of us, like shimmering images of sunlight. When the music began, with that first thump of the drums and the twang of all the shamisens, and we danced out together like a string of beads – our arms outstretched, our folding fans open in our hands – I had never before felt so much a part of something.

After the opening piece, I rushed upstairs to change my kimono. The dance in which I was to appear as a solo performer was called 'The Morning Sun on the Waves,' about a maiden who takes a morning swim in the ocean and falls in love with an enchanted dolphin. My costume was a magnificent pink kimono with a water design in gray, and I held blue silk strips to symbolize the rippling water behind me. The enchanted dolphin prince was played by a geisha named Umiyo; in addition, there were roles for geisha portraying wind, sunlight, and sprays of water – as well as a few apprentices in charcoal and blue kimono at the far reaches of the stage, playing dolphins calling their prince back to them.

My costume change went so quickly that I found myself with a few minutes to peek out at the audience. I followed the sound of occasional drumbeats to a narrow, darkened hallway running behind one of the two orchestra booths at the sides of the theater. A few other apprentices and geisha were already peering out through carved slits in the sliding doors. I joined them and managed to find the Chairman and Nobu sitting together – though it seemed to me the Chairman had given Nobu the better seat. Nobu was peering at the stage intently, but I was surprised to see that the Chairman seemed to be falling asleep. From the music I realized that it was the beginning of Mameha's dance, and went to the end of the hallway where the slits in the doors gave a view of the stage.

I watched Mameha no more than a few minutes; and yet the impression her dance made on me has never been erased. Most dances of the Inoue School tell a story of one kind or another, and the story of this dance – called 'A Courtier Returns to His Wife' – was based on a Chinese poem about a courtier who carries on a long affair with a lady in the

Imperial palace. One night the courtier's wife hides on the outskirts of the palace to find out where her husband has been spending his time. Finally, at dawn, she watches from the bushes as her husband takes leave of his mistress – but by this time she has fallen ill from the terrible cold and dies soon afterward.

For our spring dances, the story was changed to Japan instead of China; but otherwise, the tale was the same. Mameha played the wife who dies of cold and heartbreak, while the geisha Kanako played the role of her husband, the courtier. I watched the dance from the moment the courtier bids good-bye to his mistress. Already the setting was inspiringly beautiful, with the soft light of dawn and the slow rhythm of the shamisen music like a heartbeat in the background. The courtier performed a lovely dance of thanks to his mistress for their night together, and then moved toward the light of rising sun to capture its warmth for her. This was the moment when Mameha began to dance her lament of terrible sadness, hidden to one side of the stage out of view of the husband and mistress. Whether it was the beauty of Mameha's dance or of the story, I cannot say; but I found myself feeling such sorrow as I watched her, I felt as if I myself had been the victim of that terrible betrayal. At the end of the dance, sunlight filled the stage. Mameha crossed to a grove of trees to dance her simple death scene. I cannot tell you what happened after that. I was too overcome to watch any further; and in any case, I had to return backstage to prepare for my own entrance.

While I waited in the wings, I had the peculiar feeling that the weight of the entire building was pressing down on me – because of course, sadness has always seemed to me an oddly heavy thing. A good dancer often wears her white, buttoned socks a size too small, so she can sense the seams in the wooden stage with her feet. But as I stood there trying to find the strength within myself to perform, I had the impression of so much weight upon me that I felt not only the seams in the stage, but even the fibers in the socks themselves. At last I heard the music of the drums and shamisen, and the whisking noise of the clothing as the other dancers moved quickly past me onto the stage; but it's very hard for me to remember anything afterward. I'm sure I raised my arms with my folding fan closed and my knees bent – for this was the position in which I made my entrance. I heard no suggestion afterward that I'd missed my cue, but all I remember clearly is watching my own arms with amazement at the sureness and evenness with which they moved. I'd practiced this dance any number of times; I suppose that must have been enough. Because although my mind had shut down completely, I performed my role without any difficulty or nervousness.

At every performance for the rest of that month, I prepared for my entrance in the same way, by concentrating on 'The Courtier Returns to His Wife,' until I could feel the sadness laying itself over me. We human beings have a remarkable way of growing accustomed to things; but when I pictured Mameha dancing her slow lament, hidden from the eyes of her husband and his mistress, I could no more have stopped myself from feeling that sadness than you could stop yourself from smelling an apple that has been cut open on the table before you.

One day in the final week of performances, Mameha and I stayed late in the dressing room, talking with another geisha. When we left the theater we expected to find no one outside – and indeed the crowd had gone. But as we reached the street, a driver in uniform stepped out of a car and opened the rear door. Mameha and I were on the point of walking right past when Nobu emerged.

'Why, Nobu-san,' Mameha said, 'I was beginning to worry that you no longer cared for Sayuri's company! Every day this past month, we've hoped to hear something from you . . .'

'Who are you to complain about being kept waiting? I've been outside this theater nearly an hour.'

'Have you just come from seeing the dances again?' Mameha said. 'Sayuri is quite a star.'

'I haven't *just* come from anything,' Nobu said. 'I've come from the dances a full hour ago. Enough time has passed for me to make a phone call and send my driver downtown to pick something up for me.'

Nobu banged on the window of the car with his one hand, and startled the poor driver so badly his cap fell off. The driver rolled down the window and gave Nobu a tiny shopping bag in the Western style, made of what looked like silver foil. Nobu turned to me, and I gave him a deep bow and told him how happy I was to see him.

'You're a very talented dancer, Sayuri. I don't give gifts for no reason,' he said, though I don't think this was in any way true. 'Probably that's why Mameha and others in Gion don't like me as much as other men.'

'Nobu-san!' said Mameha. 'Who has ever suggested such a thing?'

'I know perfectly well what you geisha like. So long as a man gives you presents you'll put up with any sort of nonsense.'

Nobu held out the small package in his hand for me to take.

'Why, Nobu-san,' I said, 'what nonsense is it that *you* are asking me to put up with?' I meant this as a joke, of course; but Nobu didn't see it that way.

'Haven't I just said I'm not like other men?' he growled. 'Why don't you geisha ever believe anything told to you? If you want this package, you'd better take it before I change my mind.'

I thanked Nobu and accepted the package, and he banged on the window of the car once again. The driver jumped out to hold the door for him.

We bowed until the car had turned the corner and then Mameha led me back into the garden of the Kaburenjo Theater, where we took a seat on a stone bench overlooking the carp pond and peered into the bag Nobu had given me. It contained only a tiny box, wrapped in gold-colored paper embossed with the name of a famous jewelry store and tied with a red ribbon. I opened it to find a simple jewel, a ruby as big as a peach pit. It was like a giant drop of blood sparkling in the sunlight over the pond. When I turned it in my fingers, the glimmer jumped from one face to another. I could feel each of the jumps in my chest.

'I can see how thrilled you are,' Mameha said, 'and I'm very happy for you. But don't enjoy it too much. You'll have other jewels in your life, Sayuri – plenty of them, I should think. But you'll never have this opportunity again. Take this ruby back to your okiya, and give it to Mother.'

To see this beautiful jewel, and the light that seeped out of it painting my hand pink, and to think of Mother with her sickly yellow eyes and their meat-colored rims . . . well, it seemed to me that giving this jewel to her would be like dressing up a badger in silk. But of course, I had to obey Mameha.

'When you give it to her,' she went on, 'you must be especially sweet and say, 'Mother, I really have no need for a jewel like this and would be honored if you'd accept it. I've caused you so much trouble over the years.' But don't say more, or she'll think you're being sarcastic.'

When I sat in my room later, grinding an ink stick to write a note of thanks to Nobu, my mood grew darker and darker. If Mameha herself had asked me for the ruby, I could have given it to her cheerfully . . . but to give it to Mother! I'd grown fond of Nobu, and was sorry that his expensive gift would go to such a woman. I knew perfectly well that if the ruby had been from the Chairman, I couldn't have given it up at all. In any case, I finished the note and went to Mother's room to speak with her. She was sitting in the dim light, petting her dog and smoking.

'What do you want?' she said to me. 'I'm about to send for a pot of tea.'

'I'm sorry to disturb you, Mother. This afternoon when Mameha and I left the theater, President Nobu Toshikazu was waiting for me –'

'Waiting for Mameha-san, you mean.'

'I don't know, Mother. But he gave me a gift. It's a lovely thing, but I have no use for it.'

I wanted to say that I would be honored if she would take it, but Mother wasn't listening to me. She put her pipe down onto the table and took the box from my hand before I could even offer it to her. I tried again to explain things, but Mother just turned over the box to dump the ruby into her oily fingers.

'What is this?' she asked.

'It's the gift President Nobu gave me. Nobu Toshikazu, of Iwamura Electric, I mean.'

'Don't you think I know who Nobu Toshikazu is?'

She got up from the table to walk over to the window, where she slid back the paper screen and held the ruby into the stream of late-afternoon sunlight. She was doing what I had done on the street, turning the gem around and watching the sparkle move from face to face. Finally she closed the screen again and came back.

'You must have misunderstood. Did he ask you to give it to Mameha?'

'Well, Mameha was with me at the time.'

I could see that Mother's mind was like an intersection with too much traffic in it. She put the ruby onto the table and began to puff on her pipe. I saw every cloud of smoke as a little confused thought released into the air. Finally she said to me, 'So, Nobu Toshikazu has an interest in you, does he?'

'I've been honored by his attention for some time now.'

At this, she put the pipe down onto the table, as if to say that the conversation was about to grow much more serious. 'I haven't watched you as closely as I should have,' she said. 'If you've had any boyfriends, now is the time to tell me.'

'I've never had a single boyfriend, Mother.'

I don't know whether she believed what I'd said or not, but she dismissed me just the same. I hadn't yet offered her the ruby to keep, as Mameha had instructed me to do. I was trying to think of how to raise the subject. But when I glanced at the table where the gem lay on its side, she must have thought I wanted to ask for it back. I had no time to say anything further before she reached out and swallowed it up in her hand.

Finally it happened, one afternoon only a few days later. Mameha came to the okiya and took me into the reception room to tell me that the bidding for my *mizuage* had begun. She'd received a message from the mistress of the Ichiriki that very morning.

'I couldn't be more disappointed at the timing,' Mameha said, 'because I have to leave for Tokyo this afternoon. But you won't need me. You'll know if the bidding goes high, because things will start to happen.'

'I don't understand,' I said. 'What sorts of things?'

'All sorts of things,' she said, and then left without even taking a cup of tea.

She was gone three days. At first my heart raced every time I heard one of the maids approaching. But two days passed without any news. Then on the third day, Auntie came to me in the hallway to say that Mother wanted me upstairs.

I'd just put my foot onto the first step when I heard a door slide open, and all at once Pumpkin came rushing down. She came like water poured from a bucket, so fast her feet scarcely touched the steps, and midway down she twisted her finger on the banister. It must have hurt, because she let out a cry and stopped at the bottom to hold it.

'Where is Hatsumomo?' she said, clearly in pain. 'I have to find her!'

'It looks to me as if you've hurt yourself badly enough,' Auntie said. 'You have to go find Hatsumomo so she can hurt you more?'

Pumpkin looked terribly upset, and not only about her finger; but when I asked her what was the matter, she just rushed to the entryway and left.

Mother was sitting at the table when I entered her room. She began to pack her pipe with tobacco, but soon thought better of it and put it away. On top of the shelves holding the account books stood a beautiful European-style clock in a glass case. Mother looked at it every so often, but a few long minutes passed and still she said nothing to me. Finally I spoke up. 'I'm sorry to disturb you, Mother, but I was told you wanted to see me.'

'The doctor is late,' she said. 'We'll wait for him.'

I imagined she was referring to Dr. Crab, that he was coming to the okiya to talk about arrangements for my *mizuage*. I hadn't expected such a thing and began to feel a tingling in my belly. Mother passed the time by patting Taku, who quickly grew tired of her attentions and made little growling noises.

At length I heard the maids greeting someone in the front

entrance hall below, and Mother went down the stairs. When she came back a few minutes later she wasn't escorting Dr. Crab at all, but a much younger man with smooth silver hair, carrying a leather bag.

'This is the girl,' Mother said to him.

I bowed to the young doctor, who bowed back to me.

'Ma'am,' he said to Mother, 'where shall we . . .?'

Mother told him the room we were in would be fine. The way she closed the door, I knew something unpleasant was about to happen. She began by untying my obi and folding it on the table. Then she slipped the kimono from my shoulders and hung it on a stand in the corner. I stood in my yellow underrobe as calmly as I knew how, but in a moment Mother began to untie the waistband that held my underrobe shut. I couldn't quite stop myself from putting my arms in her way – though she pushed them aside just as the Baron had done, which gave me a sick feeling. After she'd removed the waistband, she reached inside and pulled out my *koshimaki* – once again, just as it had happened in Hakone. I didn't like this a bit, but instead of pulling open my robe as the Baron had, she refolded it around me and told me to lie down on the mats.

The doctor knelt at my feet and, after apologizing, peeled open my underrobe to expose my legs. Mameha had told me a little about *mizuage*, but it seemed to me I was about to learn more. Had the bidding ended, and this young doctor emerged the winner? What about Dr. Crab and Nobu? It even crossed my mind that Mother might be intentionally sabotaging Mameha's plans. The young doctor adjusted my legs and reached between them with his hand, which I had noticed was smooth and graceful like the Chairman's. I felt so humiliated and exposed that I had to cover my face. I wanted to draw my legs together, but I was afraid anything that made his task more difficult would only prolong the encounter. So I lay with my eyes pinched shut, holding my breath. I felt as little Taku must have felt the time he choked on a needle, and Auntie held his jaws open while Mother put her fingers down his throat. At one point I think the doctor had both of his hands between my legs; but at last he took them away, and folded my robe shut. When I opened my eyes, I saw him wiping his hands on a cloth.

'The girl is intact,' he said.

'Well, that's fine news!' Mother replied. 'And will there be much blood?'

'There shouldn't be any blood at all. I only examined her visually.'

'No, I mean during *mizuage*.'

'I couldn't say. The usual amount, I should expect.'

When the young silver-haired doctor had taken his leave, Mother helped me dress and instructed me to sit at the table. Then without any warning, she grabbed my earlobe and pulled it so hard I cried out. She held me like that, with my head close to hers, while she said:

'You're a very expensive commodity, little girl. I underestimated you. I'm lucky nothing has happened. But you may be very sure I'm going to watch you more closely in the future. What a man wants from you, a man will pay dearly to get. Do you follow me?'

'Yes, ma'am!' I said. Of course, I would have said yes to anything, considering how hard she was pulling on my ear.

'If you give a man freely what he ought to pay for, you'll be cheating this okiya. You'll owe money, and I'll take it from you. And I'm not just talking about this!' Here Mother made a gruesome noise with her free hand – rubbing her fingers against her palm to make a squishing sound.

'Men will pay for that,' she went on. 'But they'll pay just to chat with you too. If I find you sneaking off to meet a man, even if it's just for a little talk . . .' And here she finished her thought by giving another sharp tug on my earlobe before letting it go.

I had to work hard to catch my breath. When I felt I could speak again, I said, 'Mother . . . I've done nothing to make you angry!'

'Not yet, you haven't. If you're a sensible girl, you never will.'

I tried to excuse myself, but Mother told me to stay. She tapped out her pipe, even though it was empty; and when she'd filled it and lit it, she said, 'I've come to a decision. Your status here in the okiya is about to change.'

I was alarmed by this and began to say something, but Mother stopped me.

'You and I will perform a ceremony next week. After that, you'll be my daughter just as if you'd been born to me. I've come to the decision to adopt you. One day, the okiya will be yours.'

I couldn't think of what to say, and I don't remember much of what happened next. Mother went on talking, telling me that as the daughter of the okiya I would at some point move into the larger room occupied by Hatsumomo and Pumpkin, who together would share the smaller room where I'd lived up to now. I was listening with only half my mind, until I began slowly to realize that as Mother's daughter, I would no longer have to struggle under Hatsumomo's tyranny. This had been Mameha's plan all along, and yet I'd never really believed it would happen. Mother went on lecturing me. I looked at her drooping lip and her yellowed eyes. She may have been a hateful woman, but as the daughter of this hateful woman, I would be up on a shelf out of Hatsumomo's reach.

In the midst of all of this, the door slid open, and Hatsumomo herself stood there in the hallway.

'What do you want?' Mother said. 'I'm busy.'

'Get out,' she said to me. 'I want to talk with Mother.'

'If you want to talk with me,' Mother said, 'you may ask Sayuri if she'll be kind enough to leave.'

'*Be kind enough to leave, Sayuri*,' Hatsumomo said sarcastically.

And then for the first time in my life, I spoke back to her without the fear that she would punish me for it.

'I'll leave if Mother wants me to,' I told her.

'Mother, would you be kind enough to make Little Miss Stupid leave us alone?' Hatsumomo said.

'Stop making a nuisance of yourself!' Mother told her. 'Come in and tell me what you want.'

Hatsumomo didn't like this, but she came and sat at the table anyway. She was midway between Mother and me, but still so close that I could smell her perfume.

'Poor Pumpkin has just come running to me, very upset,'

she began. 'I promised her I'd speak with you. She told me something very strange. She said, "Oh, Hatsumomo! Mother has changed her mind!" But I told her I doubted it was true.'

'I don't know what she was referring to. I certainly haven't changed my mind about anything recently.'

'That's just what I said to her, that you would never go back on your word. But I'm sure she'd feel better, Mother, if you told her yourself.'

'Told her what?'

'That you haven't changed your mind about adopting her.'

'Whatever gave her that idea? I never had the least intention of adopting her in the first place.'

It gave me a terrible pain to hear this, for I couldn't help thinking of how Pumpkin had rushed down the stairs looking so upset . . . and no wonder, for no one could say anymore what would become of her in life. Hatsumomo had been wearing that smile that made her look like an expensive piece of porcelain, but Mother's words struck her like rocks. She looked at me with hatred.

'So it's true! You're planning to adopt *her*. Don't you remember, Mother, when you said you were going to adopt Pumpkin? You asked me to tell her the news!'

'What you may have said to Pumpkin is none of my concern. Besides, you haven't handled Pumpkin's apprenticeship as well as I expected. She was doing well for a time, but lately . . .'

'You promised, Mother,' Hatsumomo said in a tone that frightened me.

'Don't be ridiculous! You know I've had my eye on Sayuri for years. Why would I turn around and adopt Pumpkin?'

I knew perfectly well Mother was lying. Now she went so far as to turn to me and say this:

'Sayuri-san, when was the first time I raised the subject of adopting you? A year ago, perhaps?'

If you've ever seen a mother cat teaching its young to hunt – the way she takes a helpless mouse and rips it apart – well, I felt as though Mother was offering me the chance to learn how I could be just like her. All I had to do was lie as she lied and say, 'Oh, yes, Mother, you mentioned the subject to me many times!' This would be my first step in becoming a yellow-eyed old woman myself one day, living in a gloomy room with my account books. I could no more take Mother's side than Hatsumomo's. I kept my eyes to the mats so I wouldn't have to see either of them, and said that I didn't remember.

Hatsumomo's face was splotched red from anger. She got up and walked to the door, but Mother stopped her.

'Sayuri will be my daughter in one week,' she said. 'Between now and then, you must learn how to treat her with respect. When you go downstairs, ask one of the maids to bring tea for Sayuri and me.'

Hatsumomo gave a little bow, and then she was gone.

'Mother,' I said, 'I'm very sorry to have been the cause of so much trouble. I'm sure Hatsumomo is quite wrong about any plans you may have made for Pumpkin, but . . . may I ask? Wouldn't it be possible to adopt both Pumpkin and me?'

'Oh, so you know something about business now, do you?' she replied. 'You want to try telling me how to run the okiya?'

A few minutes later, a maid arrived bearing a tray with a pot of tea and a cup – not two cups, but only a single one. Mother didn't seem to care. I poured her cup full and she drank from it, staring at me with her red-rimmed eyes.

24

WHEN MAMEHA RETURNED to town the following day and learned that Mother had decided to adopt me, she didn't seem as pleased as I would have expected. She nodded and looked satisfied, to be sure; but she didn't smile. I asked if things hadn't turned out exactly as she'd hoped.

'Oh, no, the bidding between Dr. Crab and Nobu went just as I'd hoped,' she told me, 'and the final figure was a considerable sum. The moment I found out, I knew Mrs. Nitta would certainly adopt you. I couldn't be more pleased!'

This is what she said. But the truth, as I came to understand in stages over the following years, was something quite different. For one thing, the bidding hadn't been a contest between Dr. Crab and Nobu at all. It had ended up a contest between Dr. Crab and the Baron. I can't imagine how Mameha must have felt about this; but I'm sure it accounts for why she was suddenly so cold to me for a short time, and why she kept to herself the story of what had really happened.

I don't mean to suggest that Nobu was never involved. He did bid quite aggressively for my *mizuage*, but only during the first few days, until the figure passed ¥8000. When he ended up dropping out, it probably wasn't because the bidding had gone too high. Mameha knew from the beginning that Nobu could bid against anyone, if he wanted to. The trouble, which Mameha hadn't anticipated, was that Nobu had no more than a vague interest in my *mizuage*. Only a certain kind of man spends his time and money chasing after *mizuage*, and it turned out that Nobu wasn't one of them. Some months earlier, as you may remember, Mameha had suggested that no man would cultivate a relationship with a fifteen-year-old apprentice unless he was interested in her *mizuage*. This was during the same discussion when she told me, 'You can bet it isn't your conversation he's attracted to.' She may have been right about my conversation, I don't know; but whatever attracted Nobu to me, it wasn't my *mizuage* either.

As for Dr. Crab, he was a man who would probably have chosen suicide the old-fashioned way before allowing someone like Nobu to take a *mizuage* away from him. Of course he wasn't really bidding against Nobu after the first few days, but he didn't know that, and the mistress of the Ichiriki made up her mind not to tell him. She wanted the price to go as high as it could. So when she spoke to him on the telephone she said things like, 'Oh, Doctor, I've just received word from Osaka, and an offer has come in for five thousand yen.' She probably had received word from Osaka – though it might have been from her sister, because the mistress never liked to tell outright lies. But when she mentioned Osaka and an offer in the same breath, naturally Dr. Crab assumed the offer was from Nobu, even though it was actually from the Baron.

As for the Baron, he knew perfectly well his adversary was the Doctor, but he didn't care. He wanted the *mizuage* for himself and pouted like a little boy when he began to think he might not win it. Sometime later a geisha told me about a conversation she'd had with him around this time. 'Do you hear what has been happening?' the Baron said to her. 'I'm trying to arrange a *mizuage*, but a certain annoying doctor keeps getting in my way. Only one man can be the explorer of an undiscovered region, and I want to be that man! But what am I to do? This foolish doctor doesn't seem to understand that the numbers he throws about represent real money!'

As the bidding went higher and higher, the Baron began to talk about dropping out. But the figure had already come so close to a new record that the mistress of the Ichiriki made up her mind to push things still higher by misleading the Baron, just as she'd misled the Doctor. On the telephone she told him that the 'other gentleman' had made a very high bid, and then added, 'However, many people believe he's the sort of gentleman who will go no higher.' I'm sure there may have been people who believed such a thing about the Doctor, but the mistress herself wasn't one of them. She knew that when the Baron made his last bid, whatever it was, the Doctor would top it.

In the end, Dr. Crab agreed to pay ¥11,500 for my *mizuage*. Up to that time, this was the highest ever paid for a *mizuage* in Gion, and possibly in any of the geisha districts in Japan. Keep in mind that in those days, one hour of a geisha's time cost about ¥4, and an extravagant kimono might have sold for ¥1500. So it may not sound like a lot, but it's much more than, say, a laborer might have earned in a year.

I have to confess I don't know much about money. Most geisha pride themselves on never carrying cash with them, and are accustomed to charging things wherever they go. Even now in New York City, I live just the same way. I shop at stores that know me by sight, where the clerks are kind enough to write down the items I want. When the bill comes at the end of the month, I have a charming assistant who pays it for me. So you see, I couldn't possibly tell you how much money I spend, or how much more a bottle of perfume costs than a magazine. So I may be one of the worst people on earth to try explaining anything at all about money. However, I want to pass on to you something a close friend once told me – who I'm sure knows what he's talking about, because he was Japan's Deputy Minister of Finance for a time during the 1960s. Cash, he said, is often worth less one year than it was the year before, and because of this, Mameha's *mizuage* in 1929 actually cost more than mine in 1935, even though mine was ¥11,500 while Mameha's was more like ¥7000 or ¥8000.

Of course, none of this mattered back at the time my *mizuage* was sold. As far as everyone was concerned I had set a new record, and it remained until 1951, when Katsumiyo came along – who in my opinion was one of the greatest geisha of the twentieth century. Still, according to my friend the Deputy Minister of Finance, the real record remained Mameha's until the 1960s. But whether the real record belonged to me, or to Katsumiyo, or to Mameha – or even to Mamemitsu back in the 1890s – you can well imagine that Mother's plump little hands began to itch when she heard about a record amount of cash.

It goes without saying that this is why she adopted me. The fee for my *mizuage* was more than enough to repay all my debts to the okiya. If Mother hadn't adopted me, some of that money would have fallen into my hands – and you can imagine how Mother would have felt about this. When I became the daughter of the okiya, my debts ceased to exist because the okiya absorbed them all. But all of my profits went to the okiya as well, not only then, at the time of my *mizuage*, but forever afterward.

The adoption took place the following week. Already my given name had changed to Sayuri; now my family name changed as well. Back in my tipsy house on the sea cliffs, I'd been Sakamoto Chiyo. Now my name was Nitta Sayuri.

Of all the important moments in the life of a geisha, *mizuage* certainly ranks as high as any. Mine occurred in early July of 1935, when I was fifteen years old. It began in the afternoon when Dr. Crab and I drank sake in a ceremony that bound us together. The reason for this ceremony is that even though the *mizuage* itself would be over with quickly, Dr. Crab would remain my *mizuage* patron until the end of his life – not that it gave him any special privileges, you understand. The ceremony was performed at the Ichiriki Teahouse, in the presence of Mother, Auntie, and Mameha. The mistress of the Ichiriki attended as well, and Mr. Bekku, my dresser – because the dresser is always involved in ceremonies of this sort, representing the interests of the geisha. I was dressed in the most formal costume an apprentice wears, a black, five-crested robe and an underrobe of red, which is the color of new beginnings. Mameha instructed me to behave very sternly, as though I had no sense of humor at all. Considering my nervousness, I found it easy to look stern as I walked down the hallway of the Ichiriki Teahouse, with the train of my kimono pooled around my feet.

After the ceremony we all went to a restaurant known as Kitcho for dinner. This was a solemn event too, and I spoke little and ate even less. Sitting there at dinner, Dr. Crab had probably already begun thinking about the moment that would come later, and yet I've never seen a man who looked more bored. I kept my eyes lowered throughout the meal in the interests of acting innocent, but every time I stole a glance in his direction, I found him peering down through his glasses like a man at a business meeting.

When dinner was over, Mr. Bekku escorted me by rickshaw to a beautiful inn on the grounds of the Nanzen-ji Temple. He'd already visited there earlier in the day to arrange my clothing in an adjoining room. He helped me out of my kimono and changed me into a more casual one, with an obi that required no padding for the knot – since padding would be awkward for the Doctor. He tied the knot in such a way that it would come undone quite easily. After I was fully dressed, I felt so nervous that Mr. Bekku had to help me back into my room and arrange me near the door to await the Doctor's arrival. When he left me there, I felt a horrible sense of dread, as if I'd been about to have an operation to remove my kidneys, or my liver, or some such thing.

Soon Dr. Crab arrived and asked that I order him sake while he bathed in the bath attached to the room. I think he may have expected me to help undress him, because he gave me a strange look. But my hands were so cold and awkward, I don't think I could have done it. He emerged a few minutes later wearing a sleeping robe and slid open the doors to the garden, where we sat on a little wooden balcony, sipping sake and listening to the sound of the crickets and the little stream below us. I spilled sake on my kimono, but the Doctor didn't notice. To tell the truth, he didn't seem to notice much of anything, except a fish that splashed in the pond nearby, which he pointed out to me as if I might never have seen such a thing. While we were there, a maid came and laid out both our futons, side by side.

Finally the Doctor left me on the balcony and went inside. I shifted in such a way as to watch him from the corner of my eye. He unpacked two white towels from his suitcase and set them down on the table, arranging them this way and that until they were just so. He did the same with the pillows on one of the futons, and then came and stood at the door until I rose from my knees and followed him.

While I was still standing, he removed my obi and told me

to make myself comfortable on one of the futons. Everything seemed so strange and frightening to me, I couldn't have been comfortable no matter what I'd done. But I lay down on my back and used a pillow stuffed with beans to prop up my neck. The Doctor opened my robe and took a long while to loosen each of the garments beneath it step by step, rubbing his hands over my legs, which I think was supposed to help me relax. This went on for a long time, but at last he fetched the two white towels he'd unpacked earlier. He told me to raise my hips and then spread them out beneath me.

'These will absorb the blood,' he told me.

Of course, a *mizuage* often involves a certain amount of blood, but no one had explained to me exactly why. I'm sure I should have kept quiet or even thanked the Doctor for being so considerate as to put down towels, but instead I blurted out, 'What blood?' My voice squeaked a little as I said it, because my throat was so dry. Dr. Crab began explaining how the 'hymen' – though I didn't know what that could possibly be – frequently bled when torn . . . and this, that, and the other . . . I think I became so anxious hearing it all that I rose up a little from the futon, because the Doctor put his hand on my shoulder and gently pushed me back down.

I'm sure this sort of talk would be enough to quash some men's appetite for what they were about to do; but the Doctor wasn't that sort of man. When he'd finished his explanation, he said to me, 'This is the second time I will have the opportunity of collecting a specimen of your blood. May I show you?'

I'd noticed that he'd arrived with not only his leather overnight bag, but also a small wooden case. The Doctor fetched a key ring from the pocket of his trousers in the closet and unlocked the case. He brought it over and swung it open down the middle to make a kind of freestanding display. On both sides were shelves with tiny glass vials, all plugged with corks and held in place by straps. Along the bottom shelf were a few instruments, such as scissors and tweezers; but the rest of the case was crowded with these glass vials, perhaps as many as forty or fifty of them. Except for a few empty ones on the top shelf, they all held something inside, but I had no idea what. Only when the Doctor brought the lamp from the table was I able to see white labels along the tops of each vial, marked with the names of various geisha. I saw Mameha's name there, as well as the great Mamekichi's. I saw quite a number of other familiar names as well, including Hatsumomo's friend Korin.

'This one,' the Doctor said as he removed one of the vials, 'belongs to you.'

He'd written my name wrong, with a different character for the 'ri' of Sayuri. But inside the vial was a shriveled-looking thing I thought resembled a pickled plum, though it was brownish rather than purple. The Doctor removed the cork and used tweezers to take it out.

'This is a cotton swab that was drenched in your blood,' he said, 'from the time you cut your leg, you'll recall. I don't normally save the blood of my patients, but I was . . . very taken with you. After collecting this sample, I made up my mind that I would be your *mizuage* patron. I think you'll agree it will make an unusual specimen, to possess not just a sample of your blood collected at *mizuage*, but also a sample taken from a laceration on your leg quite a number of months earlier.'

I hid my disgust while the Doctor went on to show me several other vials, including Mameha's. Hers contained not a cotton swab, but a small wadding of white fabric that was stained the color of rust and had grown quite stiff. Dr. Crab seemed to find all these samples fascinating, but for my part . . . well, I pointed my face in their direction in order to be polite, but when the Doctor wasn't watching, I looked elsewhere.

Finally he closed his case and set it aside before taking off his glasses, folding them and putting them on the table nearby. I was afraid the moment had come, and indeed, Dr. Crab moved my legs apart and arranged himself on his knees between them. I think my heart was beating at about the same speed as a mouse's. When the Doctor untied the sash of his sleeping robe, I closed my eyes and brought a hand up to cover my mouth, but I thought better of it at the last moment in case I should make a bad impression, and let my hand settle near my head instead.

The Doctor's hands burrowed around for a while, making me very uncomfortable in much the same way as the young silver-haired doctor had a few weeks earlier. Then he lowered himself until his body was poised just above mine. I put all the force of my mind to work in making a sort of mental barrier between the Doctor and me, but it wasn't enough to keep me from feeling the Doctor's 'eel,' as Mameha might have called it, bump against the inside of my thigh. The lamp was still lit, and I searched the shadows on the ceiling for something to distract me, because now I felt the Doctor pushing so hard that my head shifted on the pillow. I couldn't think what to do with my hands, so I grabbed the pillow with them and squeezed my eyes tighter. Soon there was a great deal of activity going on above me, and I could feel all sorts of movement inside me as well. There must have been a very great deal of blood, because the air had an unpleasant metallic smell. I kept reminding myself how much the Doctor had paid for this privilege; and I remember hoping at one point that he was enjoying himself more than I was. I felt no more pleasure there than if someone had rubbed a file over and over against the inside of my thigh until I bled.

Finally the homeless eel marked its territory, I suppose, and the Doctor lay heavily upon me, moist with sweat. I didn't at all like being so close to him, so I pretended to have trouble breathing in the hopes he would take his weight off me. For a long while he didn't move, but then all at once he got to his knees and was very businesslike again. I didn't watch him, but from the corner of my eye I couldn't help seeing that he wiped himself off using one of the towels beneath me. He tied the sash of his robe, and then put on his glasses, not noticing a little smear of blood at the edge of one lens, and began to wipe between my legs using towels and cotton swabs and the like, just as though we were back in one of the treatment rooms at the hospital. The worst of my discomfort had passed by this time, and I have to admit I was almost fascinated lying there, even with my legs spread apart so revealingly, as I watched him open the wooden case and take out the scissors. He cut away a piece of the bloody towel beneath me and stuffed it, along with a cotton ball he'd used, into the glass vial with my misspelled name on it. Then he gave a formal bow and said, 'Thank you very much.' I couldn't very well bow back while lying down, but it made no difference, because the Doctor stood at once and went off to the bath again.

I hadn't realized it, but I'd been breathing very quickly from nervousness. Now that it was over and I was able to catch my breath, I probably looked as though I were in the middle of being operated upon, but I felt such relief I broke into a smile. Something about the whole experience seemed so utterly ridiculous to me; the more I thought about it, the funnier it seemed, and in a moment I was laughing. I had to keep quiet because the Doctor was in the next room. But to think that the course of my entire future had been altered by this? I imagined the mistress of the Ichiriki making telephone calls to Nobu and the Baron while the bidding was under way, all the money that had been spent, and all the trouble. How strange it would have been with Nobu, since I was beginning to think of him as a friend. I didn't even want to wonder what it might have been like with the Baron.

While the Doctor was still in the bath, I tapped on the door to Mr. Bekku's room. A maid rushed in to change the bedsheets, and Mr. Bekku came to help me put on a sleeping robe. Later, after the Doctor had fallen asleep, I got up again and bathed quietly. Mameha had instructed me to stay awake all night, in case the Doctor should awaken and need something. But even though I tried not to sleep, I couldn't help drifting off. I did manage to awaken in the morning in time to make myself presentable before the Doctor saw me.

After breakfast, I saw Dr. Crab to the front door of the inn and helped him into his shoes. Just before he walked away, he thanked me for the evening and gave me a small package. I couldn't make up my mind whether it might be a jewel like Nobu had given me or a few cuttings from the bloody towel of the night before! But when I worked up my courage to open it back in the room, it turned out to be a package of Chinese herbs. I didn't know what to make of them until I asked Mr. Bekku, who said I should make tea once a day with the herbs to discourage pregnancy. 'Be cautious with them, because they're very costly,' he said. 'But don't be too cautious. They're still cheaper than an abortion.'

It's strange and very hard to explain, but the world looked different to me after *mizuage*. Pumpkin, who hadn't yet had hers, now seemed inexperienced and childlike to me somehow, even though she was older. Mother and Auntie, as well as Hatsumomo and Mameha had all been through it, of course, and I was probably much more aware than they were of having this peculiar thing in common with them. After *mizuage* an apprentice wears her hair in a new style, and with a red silk band at the base of the pincushion bun, rather than a patterned one. For a time I was so aware of which apprentices had red hair bands and which had patterned ones that I scarcely seemed to notice anything else while walking along the street, or in the hallways of the little school. I had a new respect for the ones who had been through *mizuage*, and felt much more worldly than the ones who hadn't.

I'm sure all apprentices feel changed by the experience of *mizuage* in much the same way I did. But for me it wasn't just a matter of seeing the world differently. My day-to-day life changed as well, because of Mother's new view of me. She was the sort of person, I'm sure you realize, who noticed things only if they had price tags on them. When she walked down the street, her mind was probably working like an abacus: 'Oh, there's little Yukiyo, whose stupidity cost her poor older sister nearly a hundred yen last year! And here comes Ichimitsu, who must be very pleased at the payments her new *danna* is making.' If Mother were to walk alongside the Shirakawa Stream on a lovely spring day when you could almost see beauty itself dripping into the water from the tendrils of the cherry trees, she probably wouldn't even notice any of it – unless . . . I don't know . . . she had a plan to make money from selling the trees, or some such thing.

Before my *mizuage*, I don't think it made any difference to Mother that Hatsumomo was causing trouble for me in Gion. But now that I had a high price tag on me, she put a stop to Hatsumomo's troublemaking without my even having to ask it of her. I don't know how she did it. Probably she just said, 'Hatsumomo, if your behavior causes problems for Sayuri and costs this okiya money, you'll be the one to pay it!' Ever since my mother had grown ill, my life had certainly been difficult; but now for a time, things became remarkably uncomplicated. I won't say I never felt tired or disappointed; in fact, I felt tired much of the time. Life in Gion is hardly relaxing for the women who make a living there. But it was certainly a great relief to be freed from the threat of Hatsumomo. Inside the okiya too, life was almost pleasurable. As the adopted daughter, I ate when I wanted. I chose my kimono first instead of waiting for Pumpkin to choose hers – and the moment I'd made my choice, Auntie set to work sewing the seams to the proper width, and basting the collar onto my underrobe, before she'd touched even Hatsumomo's. I didn't mind when Hatsumomo looked at me with resentment and hatred because of the special treatment I now received. But when Pumpkin passed me in the okiya with a worried look, and kept her eyes averted from mine even when we were face-to-face, it caused me terrible pain. I'd always had the feeling our friendship would have grown if only circumstances hadn't come between us. I didn't have that feeling any longer.

With my *mizuage* behind me, Dr. Crab disappeared from my life almost completely. I say 'almost' because even though Mameha and I no longer went to the Shirae Teahouse to entertain him, I did run into him occasionally at parties in Gion. The Baron, on the other hand, I never saw again. I didn't yet know about the role he'd played in driving up the price of my *mizuage*, but as I look back I can understand why Mameha may have wanted to keep us apart. Probably I would have felt every bit as uncomfortable around the Baron as Mameha would have felt having me there. In any case, I can't pretend I missed either of these men.

But there was one man I was very eager to see again, and I'm sure I don't need to tell you I'm talking about the Chairman. He hadn't played any role in Mameha's plan, so I didn't expect my relationship with him to change or come to an end just because my *mizuage* was over. Still, I have to admit I felt very relieved a few weeks afterward to learn that Iwamura Electric had called to request my company once again. When I arrived that evening, both the Chairman and Nobu were present. In the past I would certainly have gone to sit beside Nobu; but now that Mother had adopted me, I wasn't obliged to think of him as my savior any longer. As it happened, a space beside the Chairman was vacant, and so with a feeling of excitement I went to take it. The Chairman was very cordial when I poured him sake, and thanked me by raising his cup in the air before drinking it; but all evening long he never looked at me. Whereas Nobu, whenever I glanced in his direction, glared back at me as though I were the only person in the room he was aware of. I certainly knew what it was like to long for someone, so before the evening was over I made a point of going to spend a bit of time with him. I was careful never to ignore him again after this.

A month or so passed, and then one evening during a party I happened to mention to Nobu that Mameha had arranged for me to appear in a festival in Hiroshima. I wasn't sure he was listening when I told him, but the very next day when I returned to the okiya after my lessons, I found in my room a new wooden travel trunk he'd sent me as a gift. The trunk was much finer even than the one I'd borrowed from Auntie for the Baron's party in Hakone. I felt terribly ashamed of myself for having thought I could simply discard Nobu now that he was no longer central to any plans Mameha might have had. I wrote him a note of thanks, and told him I looked forward to expressing my gratitude in person when I saw him the following week, at a large party Iwamura Electric had planned some months in advance.

But then a peculiar thing happened. Shortly before the party I received a message that my company wouldn't be needed after all. Yoko, who worked at the telephone in our okiya, was under the impression the party had been canceled. As it happened, I had to go to the Ichiriki that night anyway for another party. Just as I was kneeling in the hallway to enter, I saw the door to a large banquet room down at the end slide open, and a young geisha named Katsue came out. Before she closed the door, I heard what I felt certain was the sound of the Chairman's laughter coming from inside the room. I was very puzzled by this, so I rose from my knees and went to catch Katsue before she left the teahouse.

'I'm very sorry to trouble you,' I said, 'but have you just come from the party given by Iwamura Electric?'

'Yes, it's quite lively. There must be twenty-five geisha and nearly fifty men . . .'

'And . . . Chairman Iwamura and Nobu-san are both there?' I asked her.

'Not Nobu. Apparently he went home sick this morning. He'll be very sorry to have missed it. But the Chairman is there; why do you ask?'

I muttered something – I don't remember what it was – and she left.

Up until this moment I'd somehow imagined that the Chairman valued my company as much as Nobu did. Now I had to wonder whether it had all been an illusion, and Nobu was the only one who cared.

25

MAMEHA MAY ALREADY have won her bet with Mother, but she still had quite a stake in my future. So during the next few years she worked to make my face familiar to all her best customers, and to the other geisha in Gion as well. We were still emerging from the Depression at this time; formal banquets weren't as common as Mameha would have liked. But she took me to plenty of informal gatherings, not only parties in the teahouses, but swimming excursions, sight-seeing tours, Kabuki plays, and so on. During the heat of summer when everyone felt most relaxed, these casual gatherings were often quite a lot of fun, even for those of us supposedly hard at work entertaining. For example, a group of men sometimes decided to go floating in a canal boat along the Kamo River, to sip sake and dangle their feet in the water. I was too young to join in the carousing, and often ended up with the job of shaving ice to make snow cones, but it was a pleasant change nevertheless.

Some nights, wealthy businessmen or aristocrats threw geisha parties just for themselves. They spent the evening dancing and singing, and drinking with the geisha, often until well after midnight. I remember on one of these occasions, the wife of our host stood at the door to hand out envelopes containing a generous tip as we left. She gave Mameha two of them, and asked her the favor of delivering the second to the geisha Tomizuru, who had 'gone home earlier with a headache,' as she put it. Actually she knew as well as we did that Tomizuru was her husband's mistress, and had gone with him to another wing of the house to keep him company for the night.

Many of the glamorous parties in Gion were attended by famous artists, and writers, and Kabuki actors, and sometimes they were very exciting events. But I'm sorry to tell you that the average geisha party was something much more mundane. The host was likely to be the division head of a small company, and the guest of honor one of his suppliers, or perhaps one of his employees he'd just promoted, or something along those lines. Every so often, some well-meaning geisha admonished me that as an apprentice, my responsibility – besides trying to look pretty – was to sit quietly and listen to conversations in the hopes of one day becoming a clever conversationalist myself. Well, most of the conversations I heard at these parties didn't strike me as very clever at all. A man might turn to the geisha beside him and say, 'The weather certainly is unusually warm, don't you think?' And the geisha would reply with something like, 'Oh, yes, very warm!' Then she'd begin playing a drinking game with him, or try to get all the men singing, and soon the man who'd spoken with her was too drunk to remember he wasn't having as good a time as he'd hoped. For my part, I always considered this a terrible waste. If a man has come to Gion just for the purpose of having a relaxing time, and ends up involved in some childish game such as paper-scissors-stone . . . well, in my view he'd have been better off staying at home and playing with his own children or grandchildren – who, after all, are probably more clever than this poor, dull geisha he was so unfortunate as to sit beside.

Every so often, though, I was privileged to overhear a geisha who really was clever, and Mameha was certainly one of these. I learned a great deal from her conversations. For example, if a man said to her, 'Warm weather, don't you think?' she had a dozen replies ready. If he was old and lecherous, she might say to him, 'Warm? Perhaps it's just the effect on you of being around so many lovely women!' Or if he was an arrogant young businessman who didn't seem to know his place, she might take him off his guard by saying, 'Here you are sitting with a half-dozen of the best geisha in Gion, and all you can think to talk about is the weather.' One time when I happened to be watching her, Mameha knelt beside a very young man who couldn't have been more than nineteen or twenty; he probably wouldn't have been at a geisha party at all if his father hadn't been the host. Of course, he didn't know what to say or how to behave around geisha, and I'm sure he felt nervous; but he turned to Mameha very bravely and said to her, 'Warm, isn't it?' She lowered her voice and answered him like this:

'Why, you're certainly right about it being warm. You should have seen me when I stepped out of the bath this morning! Usually when I'm completely naked, I feel so cool and relaxed. But this morning, there were little beads of sweat covering my skin all the way up my body – along my thighs, and on my stomach, and . . . well, other places too.'

When that poor boy set his sake cup down on the table, his fingers were trembling. I'm sure he never forgot that geisha party for the rest of his life.

If you ask me why most of these parties were so dull, I think probably there are two reasons. First, just because a young girl has been sold by her family and raised from an early age to be a geisha doesn't mean she'll turn out to be clever, or have anything interesting to say. And second, the same thing goes for the men. Just because a man has made enough money to come to Gion and waste it however he chooses doesn't mean he's fun to be around. In fact, many of the men are accustomed to being treated with a great deal of respect. Sitting back with their hands on their knees and big frowns on their faces is about as much work as they plan to do in the way of being entertaining. One time I listened to Mameha spend an entire hour telling stories to a man who never even looked in her direction, but just watched the others in the room while she talked. Oddly enough, this was just what he wanted, and he always asked for Mameha when he came to town.

After two more years of parties and outings – all the while continuing with my studies and participating in dance performances whenever I could – I made the shift from being an apprentice to being a geisha. This was in the summer of 1938, when I was eighteen years old. We call this change 'turning the collar,' because an apprentice wears a red collar while a geisha wears a white one. Though if you were to see an apprentice and a geisha side by side, their collars would be the last thing you'd notice. The apprentice, with her elaborate, long-sleeved kimono and dangling obi, would probably make you think of a Japanese doll, whereas the geisha would look simpler, perhaps, but also more womanly.

The day I turned my collar was one of the happiest days of Mother's life; or at least, she acted more pleased than I'd ever seen her. I didn't understand it at the time, but it's perfectly clear to me now what she was thinking. You see, a geisha, unlike an apprentice, is available to a man for more than just pouring his tea, provided the terms are suitable. Because of my connection with Mameha and my popularity in Gion, my standing was such that Mother had plenty of cause for excitement – excitement being, in Mother's case, just another word for money.

Since moving to New York I've learned what the word 'geisha' really means to most Westerners. From time to time at elegant parties, I've been introduced to some young woman or other in a splendid dress and jewelry. When she learns I was once a geisha in Kyoto, she forms her mouth into a sort of smile, although the corners don't turn up quite as they should. She has no idea what to say! And then the burden of conversation falls to the man or woman who has introduced us – because I've never really learned much English, even after all these years. Of course, by this time there's little point even in trying, because this woman is thinking, 'My goodness . . . I'm talking with a prostitute . . .' A moment later she's rescued by her escort, a wealthy man a good thirty or forty years older than she is. Well, I often find myself wondering why she can't sense how much we really have in common. She is a kept woman, you see, and in my day, so was I.

I'm sure there are a great many things I don't know about these young women in their splendid dresses, but I often have the feeling that without their wealthy husbands or boyfriends, many of them would be struggling to get by and might not have the same proud opinions of themselves. And of course the same thing is true for a first-class geisha. It is all very well for a geisha to go from party to party and be popular with a great many men; but a geisha who wishes to become a star is completely dependent on having a *danna*. Even Mameha, who became famous on her own because of an advertising campaign, would soon have lost her standing and been just another geisha if the Baron hadn't covered the expenses to advance her career.

No more than three weeks after I turned my collar, Mother came to me one day while I was eating a quick lunch in the reception room, and sat across the table a long while puffing on her pipe. I'd been reading a magazine, but I stopped out of politeness – even though Mother didn't seem at first to have much to say to me. After a time she put down her pipe and said, 'You shouldn't eat those yellow pickles. They'll rot your teeth. Look at what they did to mine.'

It had never occurred to me that Mother believed her stained teeth had anything to do with eating pickles. When she'd finished giving me a good view of her mouth, she picked up her pipe again and took in a puff of smoke.

'Auntie loves yellow pickles, ma'am,' I said, 'and her teeth are fine.'

'Who cares if Auntie's teeth are fine? She doesn't make money from having a pretty little mouth. Tell the cook not to give them to you. Anyway, I didn't come here to talk with you about pickles. I came to tell you that this time next month you'll have a *danna*.'

'A *danna*? But, Mother, I'm only eighteen . . .'

'Hatsumomo didn't have a danna until she was twenty. And of course, that didn't last . . . You ought to be very pleased.'

'Oh, I am very pleased. But won't it require a lot of my time to keep a *danna* happy? Mameha thinks I should establish my reputation first, just for a few years.'

'Mameha! What does she know about business? The next time I want to know when to giggle at a party, I'll go and ask her.'

Nowadays young girls, even in Japan, are accustomed to jumping up from the table and shouting at their mothers, but in my day we bowed and said, 'Yes, ma'am,' and apologized for having been troublesome; and that's exactly how I responded.

'Leave the business decisions to me,' Mother went on. 'Only a fool would pass up an offer like the one Nobu Toshikazu has made.'

My heart nearly stopped when I heard this. I suppose it was obvious that Nobu would one day propose himself as my *danna*. After all, he'd made an offer for my *mizuage* several years earlier, and since then had certainly asked for my company more frequently than any other man. I can't pretend I hadn't thought of this possibility; but that isn't to say I'd ever believed it was the course my life would really take. On the day I first met Nobu at the sumo tournament, my almanac reading had been, 'A balance of good and bad can open the door to destiny.' Nearly every day since, I'd thought of it in one way or another. Good and bad . . . well, it was Mameha and Hatsumomo; it was my adoption by Mother and the *mizuage* that had brought it about; and of course it was the Chairman and Nobu. I don't mean to suggest I disliked Nobu. Quite the opposite. But to become his mistress would have closed off my life from the Chairman forever.

Mother must have noticed something of the shock I felt at hearing her words – or in any case, she wasn't pleased at my reaction. But before she could respond we heard a noise in the hallway outside like someone suppressing a cough, and in a moment Hatsumomo stepped into the open doorway. She was holding a bowl of rice, which was very rude of her – she never should have walked away from the table with it. When she'd swallowed, she let out a laugh.

'Mother!' she said. 'Are you trying to make me choke?' Apparently she'd been listening to our conversation while she ate her lunch. 'So the famous Sayuri is going to have Nobu Toshikazu for her *danna*,' she went on. 'Isn't that sweet!'

'If you've come here to say something useful, then say it,' Mother told her.

'Yes, I have,' Hatsumomo said gravely, and she came and knelt at the table. 'Sayuri-san, you may not realize it, but one of the things that goes on between a geisha and her *danna* can cause the geisha to become pregnant, do you understand?

And a man will become very upset if his mistress gives birth to another man's child. In your case, you must be especially careful, because Nobu will know at once, if the child should happen to have two arms like the rest of us, that it can't possibly be his!'

Hatsumomo thought her little joke was very funny.

'Perhaps you should cut off one of your arms, Hatsumomo,' said Mother, 'if it will make you as successful as Nobu Toshikazu has been.'

'And probably it would help, too, if my face looked like this!' she said, smiling, and picked up her rice bowl so we could see what was in it. She was eating rice mixed with red adzuki beans and, in a sickening way, it did look like blistered skin.

As the afternoon progressed I began to feel dizzy; with a strange buzzing in my head, and soon made my way to Mameha's apartment to talk with her. I sat at her table sipping at my chilled barley tea – for we were in the heat of summer – and trying not to let her see how I felt. Reaching the Chairman was the one hope that had motivated me all through my training. If my life would be nothing more than Nobu, and dance recitals, and evening after evening in Gion, I couldn't think why I had struggled so.

Already Mameha had waited a long while to hear why I'd come, but when I set my glass of tea down on the table, I was afraid my voice would crack if I tried to speak. I took a few more moments to compose myself, and then finally swallowed and managed to say, 'Mother tells me that within a month it's likely I'll have a *danna*.'

'Yes, I know. And the *danna* will be Nobu Toshikazu.'

By this time I was concentrating so hard on holding myself back from crying, I could no longer speak at all.

'Nobu-san is a good man,' she said, 'and very fond of you.'

'Yes, but, Mameha-san . . . I don't know how to say it . . . this was never what I imagined!'

'What do you mean? Nobu-san has always treated you kindly.'

'But, Mameha-san, I don't want kindness!'

'Don't you? I thought we all wanted kindness. Perhaps what you mean is that you want something more than kindness. And that is something you're in no position to ask.'

Of course, Mameha was quite right. When I heard these words, my tears simply broke through the fragile wall that had held them, and with a terrible feeling of shame, I laid my head upon the table and let them drain out of me. Only when I'd composed myself afterward did Mameha speak.

'What did you expect, Sayuri?' she asked

'Something besides this!'

'I understand you may find Nobu difficult to look at, perhaps. But –'

'Mameha-san, it isn't that. Nobu-san is a good man, as you say. It's just that –'

'It's just that you want your destiny to be like Shizue's. Is that it?'

Shizue, though she wasn't an especially popular geisha, was considered by everyone in Gion to be the most fortunate of women. For thirty years she'd been the mistress of a pharmacist. He wasn't a wealthy man, and she wasn't a beauty; but you could have looked all over Kyoto and not found two people who enjoyed each other's company as they did. As usual, Mameha had come closer to the truth than I wanted to admit.

'You're eighteen years old, Sayuri,' she went on. 'Neither you nor I can know your destiny. You may never know it! Destiny isn't always like a party at the end of the evening. Sometimes it's nothing more than struggling through life from day to day.'

'But, Mameha-san, how cruel!'

'Yes, it is cruel,' she said. 'But none of us can escape destiny.'

'Please, it isn't a matter of escaping my destiny, or anything of that sort. Nobu-san is a good man, just as you say. I know I should feel nothing but gratitude for his interest, but . . . there are so many things I've dreamed about.'

'And you're afraid that once Nobu has touched you, after that they can never be? Really, Sayuri, what did you think life as a geisha would be like? We don't become geisha so our lives will be satisfying. We become geisha because we have no other choice.'

'Oh, Mameha-san . . . please . . . have I really been so foolish to keep my hopes alive that perhaps one day –'

'Young girls hope all sorts of foolish things, Sayuri. Hopes are like hair ornaments. Girls want to wear too many of them. When they become old women they look silly wearing even one.'

I was determined not to lose control of my feelings again. I managed to hold in all my tears except the few that squeezed out of me like sap from a tree.

'Mameha-san,' I said, 'do you have. . . strong feelings for the Baron?'

'The Baron has been a good *danna* to me.'

'Yes, of course that's true, but do you have feelings for him as a man? I mean, some geisha do have feelings for their *danna*, don't they?'

'The Baron's relationship with me is convenient for him, and very beneficial to me. If our dealings were tinged with passion . . . well, passion can quickly slip over into jealousy, or even hatred. I certainly can't afford to have a powerful man upset with me. I've struggled for years to carve out a place for myself in Gion, but if a powerful man makes up his mind to destroy me, well, he'll do it! If you want to be successful, Sayuri, you must be sure that men's feelings remain always under your control. The Baron may be hard to take at times, but he has plenty of money, and he's not afraid to spend it. And he doesn't want children, thank heavens. Nobu will certainly be a challenge for you. He knows his own mind much too well. I won't be surprised if he expects more of you than the Baron has expected of me.'

'But, Mameha-san, what about your own feelings? I mean, hasn't there ever been a man . . .'

I wanted to ask if there had ever been a man who brought out feelings of passion in her. But I could see that her irritation with me, if it had been only a bud until then, had burst into full bloom now. She drew herself up with her hands in her lap; I think she was on the point of rebuking me, but I apologized for my rudeness at once, and she settled back again.

'You and Nobu have an *en*, Sayuri, and you can't escape it,' she said.

I knew even then that she was right. An *en* is a karmic bond lasting a lifetime. Nowadays many people seem to believe their lives are entirely a matter of choice; but in my day we viewed ourselves as pieces of clay that forever show the fingerprints of everyone who has touched them. Nobu's touch had made a deeper impression on me than most. No one could tell me whether he would be my ultimate destiny, but I had always sensed the *en* between us. Somewhere in the landscape of my life Nobu would always be present. But could it really be that of all the lessons I'd learned, the hardest one lay just ahead of me? Would I really have to take each of my hopes and put them away where no one would ever see them again, where not even I would ever see them?

'Go back to the okiya, Sayuri,' Mameha told me. 'Prepare for the evening ahead of you. There's nothing like work for getting over a disappointment.'

I looked up at her with the idea of making one last plea, but when I saw the expression on her face, I thought better of it. I can't say what she was thinking; but she seemed to be peering into nothingness with her perfect oval face creased in the corners of her eyes and mouth from strain. And then she let out a heavy breath, and gazed down into her teacup with what I took as a look of bitterness.

A woman living in a grand house may pride herself on all her lovely things; but the moment she hears the crackle of fire she decides very quickly which are the few she values most. In the days after Mameha and I had spoken, I certainly came to feel that my life was burning down around me; and yet when I struggled to find even a single thing that would still matter to me after Nobu had become my *danna*, I'm sorry to say that I failed. One evening while I was kneeling at a table in the Ichiriki Teahouse, trying not to think too much about my feelings of misery, I had a sudden thought of a child lost in the snowy woods; and when I looked up at the white-haired men I was entertaining, they looked so much like snowcapped trees all around me that I felt for one horrifying moment I might be the sole living human in all the world.

The only parties at which I managed to convince myself that my life might still have some purpose, however small, were the ones attended by military men. Already in 1938, we'd all grown accustomed to daily reports about the war in Manchuria; and we were reminded every day of our troops overseas by things like the so-called Rising Sun Lunch Box – which was a pickled plum in the center of a box of rice, looking like the Japanese flag. For several generations, army and navy officers had come to Gion to relax. But now they began to tell us, with watery eyes after their seventh or eighth cup of sake, that nothing kept their spirits up so much as their visits to Gion. Probably this was the sort of thing military officers say to the women they talk with. But the idea that I – who was nothing more than a young girl from the seashore – might truly be contributing something important to the nation . . . I won't pretend these parties did anything to lessen my suffering; but they did help remind me just how selfish my suffering really was.

A few weeks passed, and then one evening in a hallway at the Ichiriki, Mameha suggested the time had come to collect on her bet with Mother. I'm sure you'll recall that the two of them had wagered about whether my debts would be repaid before I was twenty. As it turned out, of course, they'd been repaid already though I was only eighteen. 'Now that you've turned your collar,' Mameha said to me, 'I can't see any reason to wait longer.'

This is what she said, but I think the truth was more complicated. Mameha knew that Mother hated settling debts, and would hate settling them still more when the stakes went higher. My earnings would go up considerably after I took a *danna*; Mother was certain to grow only more protective of the income. I'm sure Mameha thought it best to collect what she was owed as soon as possible, and worry about future earnings in the future.

Several days afterward, I was summoned downstairs to the reception room of our okiya to find Mameha and Mother across the table from each other, chatting about the summer weather. Beside Mameha was a gray-haired woman named Mrs. Okada, whom I'd met a number of times. She was mistress of the okiya where Mameha had once lived, and she still took care of Mameha's accounting in exchange for a portion of the income. I'd never seen her look more serious, peering down at the table with no interest in the conversation at all.

'There you are!' Mother said to me. 'Your older sister has kindly come to visit, and has brought Mrs. Okada with her. You certainly owe them the courtesy of joining us.'

Mrs. Okada spoke up, with her eyes still on the tabletop. 'Mrs. Nitta, as Mameha may have mentioned on the telephone, this is more a business call than a social call. There's no need for Sayuri to join us. I'm sure she has other things to do.'

'I won't have her showing disrespect to the two of you,' Mother replied. 'She'll join us at the table for the few minutes you're here.'

So I arranged myself beside Mother, and the maid came in to serve tea. Afterward Mameha said, 'You must be very proud, Mrs. Nitta, of how well your daughter is doing. Her fortunes have surpassed expectations! Wouldn't you agree?'

'Well now, what do I know about your expectations, Mameha-san?' said Mother. After this she clenched her teeth and gave one of her peculiar laughs, looking from one of us to the other to be sure we appreciated her cleverness. No one laughed with her, and Mrs. Okada just adjusted her glasses and cleared her throat. Finally Mother added, 'As for my own expectations, I certainly wouldn't say Sayuri has surpassed them.'

'When we first discussed her prospects a number of years ago,' Mameha said, 'I had the impression you didn't think much of her. You were reluctant even to have me take on her training.'

'I wasn't sure it was wise to put Sayuri's future in the hands of someone outside the okiya, if you'll forgive me,' said Mother. 'We do have our Hatsumomo, you know.'

'Oh, come now, Mrs. Nitta!' Mameha said with a laugh.

'Hatsumomo would have strangled the poor girl before she'd have trained her!'

'I admit Hatsumomo can be difficult. But when you spot a girl like Sayuri with something a little different, you have to be sure to make the right decisions at the right times – such as the arrangement you and I made, Mameha-san. I expect you've come here today to settle our account?'

'Mrs. Okada has been kind enough to write up the figures,' Mameha replied. 'I'd be grateful if you would have a look at them.'

Mrs. Okada straightened her glasses and took an accounting book from a bag at her knee. Mameha and I sat in silence while she opened it on the table and explained her columns of figures to Mother.

'These figures for Sayuri's earnings over the past year,' Mother interrupted. 'My goodness, I only wish we'd been so fortunate as you seem to think! They're higher even than the total earnings for our okiya.'

'Yes, the numbers are most impressive,' Mrs. Okada said, 'but I do believe they are accurate. I've kept careful track through the records of the Gion Registry Office.'

Mother clenched her teeth and laughed at this, I suppose because she was embarrassed at having been caught in her lie. 'Perhaps I haven't watched the accounts as carefully as I should have,' she said.

After ten or fifteen minutes the two women agreed on a figure representing how much I'd earned since my debut. Mrs. Okada took a small abacus from her bag and made a few calculations, writing down numbers on a blank page of the account book. At last she wrote down a final figure and underscored it. 'Here, then, is the amount Mameha-san is entitled to receive.'

'Considering how helpful she has been to our Sayuri,' Mother said, 'I'm sure Mameha-san deserves even more. Unfortunately, according to our arrangements, Mameha agreed to take half of what a geisha in her position might usually take, until after Sayuri had repaid her debts. Now that the debts are repaid, Mameha is of course entitled to the other half, so that she will have earned the full amount.'

'My understanding is that Mameha did agree to take half wages,' Mrs Okada said, 'but was ultimately to be paid double. This is why she agreed to take a risk. If Sayuri had failed to repay her debts, Mameha would have received nothing more than half wages. But Sayuri has succeeded, and Mameha is entitled to double.'

'Really, Mrs. Okada, can you imagine me agreeing to such terms?' Mother said. 'Everyone in Gion knows how careful I am with money. It's certainly true that Mameha has been helpful to our Sayuri. I can't possibly pay double, but I'd like to propose offering an additional ten percent. If I may say so, it seems generous, considering that our okiya is hardly in a position to throw money around carelessly.'

The word of a woman in Mother's position should have been assurance enough – and with any woman but Mother, it certainly would have been. But now that she'd made up her mind to lie . . . well, we all sat in silence a long moment. Finally Mrs. Okada said, 'Mrs. Nitta, I do find myself in a difficult position. I remember quite clearly what Mameha told me.'

'Of course you do,' Mother said. 'Mameha has her memory of the conversation, and I have mine. What we need is a third party and happily, we have one here with us. Sayuri may only have been a girl at the time, but she has quite a head for numbers.'

'I'm sure her memory is excellent,' Mrs. Okada remarked. 'But one can hardly say she has no personal interest. After all, she is the daughter of the okiya.'

'Yes, she is,' said Mameha; and this was the first time she'd spoken up in quite a while. 'But she's also an honest girl. I'm prepared to accept her answer, provided that Mrs. Nitta will accept it too.'

'Of course I will,' Mother said, and put down her pipe. 'Now then, Sayuri, which is it?'

If I'd been given a choice between sliding off the roof to break my arm again just the way I did as a child, or sitting in that room until I came up with an answer to the question they were asking me, I certainly would have marched right up the stairs and climbed the ladder onto the roof. Of all the women in Gion, Mameha and Mother were the two most influential in my life, and it was clear to me I was going to make one of them angry. I had no doubt in my mind of the truth; but on the other hand, I had to go on living in the okiya with Mother. Of course, Mameha had done more for me than anyone in Gion. I could hardly take Mother's side against her.

'Well?' Mother said to me.

'As I recall, Mameha did accept half wages. But you agreed to pay her double earnings in the end, Mother. I'm sorry, but this is the way I remember it.'

There was a pause, and then Mother said, 'Well, I'm not as young as I used to be. It isn't the first time my memory has misled me.'

'We all have these sorts of problems from time to time,' Mrs. Okada replied. 'Now, Mrs. Nitta, what was this about offering Mameha an additional ten percent? I assume you meant ten percent over the double you originally agreed to pay her.'

'If only I were in a position to do such a thing,' Mother said.

'But you offered it only a moment ago. Surely you haven't changed your mind so quickly?'

Mrs. Okada wasn't gazing at the tabletop any longer, but was staring directly at Mother. After a long moment she said, 'I suppose we'll let it be. In any case, we've done enough for one day. Why don't we meet another time to work out the final figure?'

Mother wore a stern expression on her face, but she gave a little bow of assent and thanked the two of them for coming.

'I'm sure you must be very pleased,' Mrs. Okada said, while putting away her abacus and her accounting book, 'that Sayuri will soon be taking a *danna*. And at only eighteen years of age! How young to take such a big step.'

'Mameha would have done well to take a *danna* at that age herself,' Mother replied.

'Eighteen is a bit young for most girls,' Mameha said, 'but I'm certain Mrs. Nitta has made the right decision in Sayuri's case.'

Mother puffed on her pipe a moment, peering at Mameha across the table. 'My advice to you, Mameha-san,' she said, 'is that you stick to teaching Sayuri about that pretty way of rolling her eyes. When it comes to business decisions, you may leave them to me.'

'I would never presume to discuss business with you, Mrs. Nitta. I'm convinced your decision is for the best . . . But may I ask? Is it true the most generous offer has come from Nobu Toshikazu?'

'His has been the only offer. I suppose that makes it the most generous.'

'The only offer? What a pity . . . The arrangements are so much more favorable when several men compete. Don't you find it so?'

'As I say, Mameha-san, you can leave the business decisions to me. I have in mind a very simple plan for arranging favorable terms with Nobu Toshikazu.'

'If you don't mind,' Mameha said, 'I'd be very eager to hear it.'

Mother put her pipe down on the table. I thought she was going to reprimand Mameha, but in fact she said, 'Yes, I'd like to tell it to you, now that you mention it. You may be able to help me. I've been thinking that Nobu Toshikazu will be more generous if he finds out an Iwamura Electric heater killed our Granny. Don't you think so?'

'Oh, I know very little about business, Mrs. Nitta.'

'Perhaps you or Sayuri should let it slip in conversation the next time you see him. Let him know what a terrible blow it was. I think he'll want to make it up to us.'

'Yes, I'm sure that's a good idea,' Mameha said. 'Still, it's disappointing . . . I had the impression another man had expressed interest in Sayuri.'

'A hundred yen is a hundred yen, whether it comes from this man or that one.'

'That would be true in most cases,' Mameha said. 'But the man I'm thinking of is General Tottori Junnosuke . . .'

At this point in the conversation, I lost track of what the two of them were saying; for I'd begun to realize that Mameha was making an effort to rescue me from Nobu. I certainly hadn't expected such a thing. I had no idea whether she'd changed her mind about helping me, or whether she was thanking me for taking her side against Mother . . . Of course, it was possible she wasn't really trying to help me at all, but had some other purpose. My mind went on racing with these thoughts, until I felt Mother tapping my arm with the stem of her pipe.

'Well?' she said.

'Ma'am?'

'I asked if you know the General.'

'I've met him a few times, Mother,' I said. 'He comes to Gion often.'

I don't know why I gave this response. The truth is, I'd met the General more than a few times. He came to parties in Gion every week, though always as the guest of someone else. He was a bit on the small side – shorter than I was, in fact. But he wasn't the sort of person you could overlook, any more than you could overlook a machine gun. He moved very briskly and was always puffing on one cigarette after another, so that wisps of smoke drifted in the air around him like the clouds around a train idling on the tracks. One evening while slightly drunk, the General had talked to me for the longest time about all the various ranks in the army and found it very funny that I kept mixing them up. General Tottori's own rank was *sho-jo*, which meant 'little general' – that is to say, the lowest of the generals – and foolish girl that I was, I had the impression this wasn't very high. He may have played down the importance of his rank from modesty; and I didn't know any better than to believe him.

By now Mameha was telling Mother that the General had just taken a new position. He'd been put in charge of something called 'military procurement' – though as Mameha went on to explain it, the job sounded like nothing more than a housewife going to the market. If the army had a shortage of ink pads, for example, the General's job was to make sure it got the ink pads it needed, and at a very favorable price.

'With his new job,' said Mameha, 'the General is now in a position to take a mistress for the first time. And I'm quite sure he has expressed an interest in Sayuri.'

'Why should it matter to me if he's expressed an interest in Sayuri?' Mother said. 'These military men never take care of a geisha the way a businessman or an aristocrat does.'

'That may be true, Mrs. Nitta. But I think you'll find that General Tottori's new position could be of great help to the okiya.'

'Nonsense! I don't need help taking care of the okiya. All I need is steady, generous income, and that's the one thing a military man can't give me.'

'Those of us in Gion have been fortunate so far,' Mameha said. 'But shortages will affect us, if the war continues.'

'I'm sure they would, if the war continued,' Mother said. 'This war will be over in six months.'

'And when it is, the military will be in a stronger position than ever before. Mrs. Nitta, please don't forget that General Tottori is the man who oversees all the resources of the military. No one in Japan is in a better position to provide you with everything you could want, whether the war continues or not. He approves every item passing through all the ports in Japan.'

As I later learned, what Mameha had said about General Tottori wasn't quite true. He was in charge of only one of five large administrative areas. But he was senior to the men who oversaw the other districts, so he may as well have been in charge. In any case, you should have seen how Mother behaved after Mameha had said this. You could almost see her mind at work as she thought about having the help of a man in General Tottori's position. She glanced at the teapot, and I could just imagine her thinking, 'Well, I haven't had any trouble getting tea; not yet . . . though the price has gone up . . .' And then probably without even realizing what she was doing, she put one hand inside her obi and squeezed her silk bag of tobacco as if to see how much remained.

Mother spent the next week going around Gion and making one phone call after another to learn as much as she could about General Tottori. She was so immersed in this task that sometimes when I spoke to her; she didn't seem to hear me. I think she was so busy with her thoughts, her mind was like a train pulling too many cars.

During this period I continued seeing Nobu whenever he

came to Gion, and did my best to act as though nothing had changed. Probably he'd expected I would be his mistress by the middle of July. Certainly I'd expected it; but even when the month came to a close, his negotiations seemed to have led nowhere. Several times during the following weeks I noticed him looking at me with puzzlement. And then one night he greeted the mistress of the Ichiriki Teahouse in the curtest manner I'd ever seen, by strolling past without so much as a nod. The mistress had always valued Nobu as a customer and gave me a look that seemed surprised and worried all at once. When I joined the party Nobu was giving, I couldn't help noticing signs of anger – a rippling muscle in his jaw, and a certain briskness with which he tossed sake into his mouth. I can't say I blamed him for feeling as he did. I thought he must consider me heartless, to have repaid his many kindnesses with neglect. I fell into a gloomy spell thinking these thoughts, until the sound of a sake cup set down with a *tick* startled me out of it. When I looked up, Nobu was watching me. Guests all around him were laughing and enjoying themselves, and there he sat with his eyes fixed on me, as lost in his thoughts as I had been in mine. We were like two wet spots in the midst of burning charcoal.

26

DURING SEPTEMBER OF that year, while I was still eighteen years old, General Tottori and I drank sake together in a ceremony at the Ichiriki Teahouse. This was the same ceremony I'd first performed with Mameha when she became my older sister; and later with Dr. Crab just before my *miziuage*. In the weeks afterward, everyone congratulated Mother for having made such a favorable alliance.

On that very first night after the ceremony, I went on the General's instructions to a small inn in the northwest of Kyoto called Suruya, with only three rooms. I was so accustomed by this time to lavish surroundings that the shabbiness of the Suruya surprised me. The room smelled of mildew, and the tatami were so bloated and sodden that they seemed to make a sighing noise when I stepped on them. Plaster had crumbled near the floor in one corner. I could hear an old man reading a magazine article aloud in an adjacent room. The longer I knelt there, the more out of sorts I felt, so that I was positively relieved when the General finally arrived – even though he did nothing more, after I had greeted him, than turn on the radio and sit drinking a beer.

After a time he went downstairs to take a bath. When he returned to the room, he took off his robe at once and walked around completely naked toweling his hair; with his little round belly protruding below his chest and a great patch of hair beneath it. I had never seen a man naked before, and I found the General's sagging bottom almost comical. But when he faced me I must admit my eyes went straight to where . . . well, to where his 'eel' ought to have been. Something was flapping around there, but only when the

General lay on his back and told me to take off my clothes did it begin to surface. He was such a strange little nugget of a man, but completely unabashed about telling me what to do. I'd been afraid I'd have to find some way of pleasing him, but as it turned out, all I had to do was follow orders. In the three years since my *mizuage*, I'd forgotten the sheer terror I'd felt when the Doctor finally lowered himself onto me. I remembered it now, but the strange thing was that I didn't feel terror so much as a kind of vague queasiness. The General left the radio on – and the lights as well, as if he wanted to be sure I saw the drabness of the room clearly, right down to the water stain on the ceiling.

As the months passed, this queasiness went away, and my encounters with the General became nothing more than an unpleasant twice-weekly routine. Sometimes I wondered what it might be like with the Chairman; and to tell the truth, I was a bit afraid it might be distasteful, just as with the Doctor and the General. Then something happened to make me see things differently. Around this time a man named Yasuda Akira, who'd been in all the magazines because of the success of a new kind of bicycle light he'd designed, began coming to Gion regularly. He wasn't welcome at the Ichiriki yet and probably couldn't have afforded it in any case, but he spent three or four evenings a week at a little teahouse called Tatematsu, in the Tominagacho section of Gion, not far from our okiya. I first met him at a banquet one night during the spring of 1939, when I was nineteen years old. He was so much younger than the men around him – probably no more than thirty – that I noticed him the moment I came into the room. He had the same sort of dignity as the Chairman. I found him very attractive sitting there with his shirtsleeves rolled up and his jacket behind him on the mats. For a moment I watched an old man nearby, who raised up his chopsticks with a little piece of braised tofu and his mouth already as wide as it would go; this gave me the impression of a door being slid open so that a turtle could march slowly through. By contrast it made me almost weak to see the way Yasuda-san, with his graceful, sculpted arm, put a bite of braised beef into his mouth with his lips parted sensuously.

I made my way around the circle of men, and when I came to him and introduced myself, he said, 'I hope you'll forgive me.'

'Forgive you? Why, what have you done?' I asked him.

'I've been very rude,' he replied. 'I haven't been able to take my eyes off you all evening.'

On impulse I reached into my obi for the brocade card holder I kept there, and discreetly removed one card, which I passed to him. Geisha always carry name cards with them just as businessmen carry business cards. Mine was very small, half the size of an ordinary calling card, printed on heavy rice paper with only the words 'Gion' and 'Sayuri' written on it in calligraphy. It was spring, so I was carrying cards decorated with a colorful spray of plum blossoms in the background. Yasuda admired it for a moment before putting it into his shirt pocket. I had the feeling no words we spoke could be as eloquent as this simple interaction, so I bowed to him and went on to the next man.

From that day, Yasuda-san began asking me to the Tatematsu Teahouse every week to entertain him. I was never able to go as often as he wanted me. But about three months after we first met, he brought me a kimono one afternoon as a gift. I felt very flattered, even though in truth it wasn't a sophisticated robe – woven with a poor quality silk in somewhat garish colors, and with a commonplace design of flowers and butterflies. He wanted me to wear it for him one evening soon, and I promised him I would. But when I returned to the okiya with it that night, Mother saw me carrying the package up the stairs and took it away from me to have a look. She sneered when she saw the robe, and said she wouldn't have me seen in anything so unattractive. The very next day, she sold it.

When I found out what she'd done, I said to her as boldly as I dared that the robe had been given to me as a gift, not to the okiya, and that it wasn't right for her to have sold it.

'Certainly it was your robe,' she said. 'But you are the daughter of the okiya. What belongs to the okiya belongs to you, and the other way around as well.'

I was so angry at Mother after this that I couldn't even

bring myself to look at her. As for Yasuda-san, who'd wanted to see the robe on me, I told him that because of its colors and its butterfly motif, I could wear it only very early in the spring, and since it was now already summer; nearly a year would have to pass before he could see me in it. He didn't seem too upset to hear this.

'What is a year?' he said, looking at me with penetrating eyes. 'I'd wait a good deal longer; depending on what I was waiting for.'

We were alone in the room, and Yasuda-san put his beer glass down on the table in a way that made me blush. He reached out for my hand, and I gave it to him expecting that he wanted to hold it a long moment in both of his before letting it go again. But to my surprise he brought it quickly to his lips and began kissing the inside of my wrist quite passionately, in a way I could feel as far down as my knees. I think of myself as an obedient woman; up until this time I'd generally done the things told to me by Mother; or Mameha, or even Hatsumomo when I'd had no other choice; but I felt such a combination of anger at Mother and longing for Yasuda-san that I made up my mind right then to do the very thing Mother had ordered me most explicitly not to do. I asked him to meet me in that very teahouse at midnight, and I left him there alone.

Just before midnight I came back and spoke to a young maid. I promised her an indecent sum of money if she would see to it that no one disturbed Yasuda-san and me in one of the upstairs rooms for half an hour. I was already there, waiting in the dark, when the maid slid open the door and Yasuda-san stepped inside. He dropped his fedora onto the mats and pulled me to my feet even before the door was closed. To press my body against his felt so satisfying, like a meal after a long spell of hunger. No matter how hard he pressed himself against me, I pressed back harder. Somehow I wasn't shocked to see how expertly his hands slipped through the seams in my clothing to find my skin. I won't pretend I experienced none of the clumsy moments I was accustomed to with the General, but I certainly didn't notice them in the same way. My encounters with the General reminded me of a time as a child when I'd struggled to climb a tree and pluck away a certain leaf at the top. It was all a matter of careful movements, bearing the discomfort until I finally reached my goal. But with Yasuda-san I felt like a child running freely down a hill. Sometime later when we lay exhausted upon the mats together, I moved his shirttail aside and put my hand on his stomach to feel his breathing. I had never in my life been so close to another human being before, though we hadn't spoken a word.

It was only then that I understood: it was one thing to lie still on the futon for the Doctor or the General. It would be something quite different with the Chairman.

Many a geisha's day-to-day life has changed dramatically after taking a *danna*; but in my case, I could hardly see any change at all. I still made the rounds of Gion at night just as I had over the past few years. From time to time during the afternoons I went on excursions, including some very peculiar ones, such as accompanying a man on a visit to his brother in the hospital. But as for the changes I'd expected – the prominent dance recitals paid for by my *danna*, lavish gifts provided by him, even a day or two of paid leisure time – well, none of these things happened. It was just as Mother had said. Military men didn't take care of a geisha the way a businessman or an aristocrat did.

The General may have brought about very little change in my life, but it was certainly true that his alliance with the okiya was invaluable, at least from Mother's point of view. He covered many of my expenses just as a *danna* usually does – including the cost of my lessons, my annual registration fee, my medical expenses, and . . . oh, I don't even know what else – my socks, probably. But more important, his new position as director of military procurement was everything Mameha had suggested, so that he was able to do things for us no other *danna* could have done. For example, Auntie grew ill during March of 1939. We were terribly worried about her; and the doctors were of no help; but after a telephone call to the General, an important doctor from the military hospital in the Kamigyo Ward called on us and provided Auntie with a packet of medicine that cured her. So although the General may not have sent me to Tokyo for dance recitals, or presented me with precious gems, no one could suggest our okiya didn't do well by him. He sent regular deliveries of tea and sugar; as well as chocolates, which were becoming scarce even in Gion. And of course, Mother had been quite wrong about the war ending within six months. We couldn't have believed it at the time, but we'd scarcely seen the beginning of the dark years just yet.

During that fall when the General became my *danna*, Nobu ceased inviting me to parties where I'd so often entertained him. Soon I realized he'd stopped coming to the Ichiriki altogether. I couldn't think of any reason he should do this, unless it was to avoid me. With a sigh, the mistress of the Ichiriki agreed that I was probably right. At the New Year I wrote Nobu a card, as I did with all of my patrons, but he didn't respond. It's easy for me to look back now and tell you casually how many months passed; but at the time I lived in anguish. I felt I'd wronged a man who had treated me kindly – a man I'd come to think of as a friend. What was more, without Nobu's patronage, I was no longer invited to Iwamura Electric's parties, which meant I hardly stood any chance at all of seeing the Chairman.

Of course, the Chairman still came regularly to the Ichiriki even though Nobu didn't. I saw him quietly upbraiding a junior associate in the hallway one evening, gesturing with a fountain pen for emphasis, and I didn't dare disturb him to say hello. Another night, a worried-looking young apprentice named Naotsu, with a terrible underbite, was walking him to the toilet when he caught sight of me. He left Naotsu standing there to come and speak with me. We exchanged the usual pleasantries. I thought I saw in his faint smile, the kind of subdued pride men often seem to feel when gazing on their own children. Before he continued on his way, I said to him, 'Chairman, if there's ever an evening when the presence of another geisha or two might be helpful . . .'

This was very forward of me, but to my relief the Chairman didn't take offense.

'That's a fine idea, Sayuri,' he said. 'I'll ask for you.'

But the weeks passed, and he didn't.

One evening late in March I dropped in on a very lively party given by the Governor of Kyoto Prefecture at a teahouse called Shunju. The Chairman was there, on the losing end of a drinking game, looking exhausted in shirtsleeves and with his tie loosened. Actually the Governor had lost most of the rounds, as I learned, but held his sake better than the Chairman.

'I'm so glad you're here, Sayuri,' he said to me. 'You've got to help me. I'm in trouble.'

To see the smooth skin of his face splotched red, and his arms protruding from rolled-up shirtsleeves, I thought at once of Yasuda-san on that night at the Tatematsu Teahouse. For the briefest moment I had a feeling that everything in the room had vanished but the Chairman and me, and that in his slightly drunken state I might lean in toward him until his arms went around me, and put my lips on his. I even had a flicker of embarrassment that I'd been so obvious in my thoughts that the Chairman must have understood them . . . but if so, he seemed to regard me just the same. To help him, all I could do was conspire with another geisha to slow the pace of the game. The Chairman seemed grateful for this, and when it was all over, he sat and talked with me a long while, drinking glasses of water to sober up. Finally he took a handkerchief from his pocket, identical to the one tucked inside my obi, and wiped his forehead with it, and then smoothed his coarse hair back along his head before saying to me:

'When was the last time you spoke with your old friend Nobu?'

'Not in quite some time, Chairman,' I said. 'To tell the truth, I have the impression Nobu-san may be angry with me.'

The Chairman was looking down into his handkerchief as he refolded it. 'Friendship is a precious thing, Sayuri,' he said. 'One mustn't throw it away.'

I thought about this conversation often over the weeks that followed. Then one day late in April, I was putting on my makeup for a performance of *Dances of the Old Capital*, when a young apprentice I hardly knew came to speak with me. I put down my makeup brush, expecting her to ask a favor – because our okiya was still well supplied with things others in Gion had learned to do without. But instead she said:

'I'm terribly sorry to trouble you, Sayuri-san, but my name is Takazuru. I wondered if you would mind helping me. I know you were once very good friends with Nobu-san . . .'

After months and months of wondering about him, and feeling terribly ashamed for what I'd done, just to hear Nobu's name when I didn't expect it was like opening storm shutters and feeling the first draft of air.

'We must all help each other whenever we can, Takazuru,' I said. 'And if it's a problem with Nobu-san, I'm especially interested. I hope he's well.'

'Yes, he is well, ma'am, or at least I think so. He comes to the Awazumi Teahouse, in East Gion. Do you know it?'

'Oh, yes, I know it,' I said. 'But I had no idea Nobu-san visited there.'

'Yes, ma'am, quite often,' Takazuru told me. 'But . . . may I ask, Sayuri-san? You've known him a long while, and . . . well, Nobu-san is a kind man, isn't he?'

'Takazuru-san, why do you ask me? If you've been spending time with him, surely you know whether or not he is kind!'

'I'm sure I must sound foolish. But I'm so confused! He asks for me every time he comes to Gion, and my older sister tells me he's as good a patron as any girl could hope for. But now she's angry with me because I've cried in front of him several times. I know I shouldn't do it, but I can't even promise I won't do it again!'

'He is being cruel to you, is he?'

By way of answering, poor Takazuru clenched her trembling lips together, and in a moment tears began to pool at the edges of her lids, so much that her little round eyes seemed to gaze up at me from two puddles.

'Sometimes Nobu-san doesn't know how harsh he sounds,' I told her. 'But he must like you, Takazuru-san. Otherwise, why would he ask for you?'

'I think he asks for me only because I'm someone to be mean to,' she said. 'One time he did say my hair smelled clean, but then he told me what a nice change that was.'

'It's strange that you see him so often,' I said. 'I've been hoping for months to run into him.'

'Oh, please don't, Sayuri-san! He already says how nothing about me is as good as you. If he sees you again, he'll only think the worse of me. I know I shouldn't bother you with my problems, ma'am, but . . . I thought you might know something I could do to please him. He likes stimulating conversation, but I never know what to say. Everyone tells me I'm not a very bright girl.'

People in Kyoto are trained to say things like this; but it struck me that this poor girl might be telling the truth. It wouldn't have surprised me if Nobu regarded her as nothing more than the tree where the tiger might sharpen its claws. I couldn't think of anything helpful, so in the end I suggested she read a book about some historical event Nobu might find interesting, and tell the story to him bit by bit when they met. I myself had done this sort of thing from time to time – for there were men who liked nothing more than to sit back with their eyes watery and half-closed, and listen to the sound of a woman's voice. I wasn't sure it would work with Nobu, but Takazuru seemed very grateful for the idea.

Now that I knew where to find Nobu, I was determined to go and see him. I felt terribly sorry I'd made him angry with me; and of course, I might never see the Chairman again without him. I certainly didn't want to cause Nobu pain, but I thought perhaps by meeting with him I could find some way of resuming our friendship. The trouble was, I couldn't drop in uninvited at the Awazumi, for I had no formal relationship with the teahouse. So in the end I made up my mind to stroll past during the evening whenever I could, in the hopes of bumping into Nobu on his way there. I knew his habits well enough to make a fair guess about the time he might arrive.

For eight or nine weeks I kept up this plan. Then at last one evening I spotted him emerging from the back of a limousine in the dark alleyway ahead of me. I knew it was him, because the empty sleeve of his jacket, pinned at the shoulder, gave him an unmistakable silhouette. The driver was handing him his briefcase as I neared. I stopped in the light of a lantern there in the alley, and let out a little gasp that would sound like delight. Nobu looked in my direction just as I'd hoped.

'Well, well,' he said. 'One forgets how lovely a geisha can look.' He spoke in such a casual tone, I had to wonder whether he knew it was me.

'Why, sir, you sound like my old friend Nobu-san,' I said. 'But you can't be him, for I have the impression he has disappeared completely from Gion!'

The driver closed the door, and we stood in silence until the car pulled away.

'I'm so relieved,' I said, 'to see Nobu-san again at last! And what luck for me that he should be standing in the shadows rather than in the light.'

'Sometimes I don't have the least idea what you're talking about, Sayuri. You must have learned this from Mameha. Or maybe they teach it to all geisha.'

'With Nobu-san standing in the shadows, I'm unable to see the angry expression on his face.'

'I see,' he said. 'So you think I'm angry with you?'

'What else am I to think, when an old friend disappears for so many months? I suppose you're going to tell me that you've been too busy to come to the Ichiriki.'

'Why do you say it as if it couldn't possibly be true?'

'Because I happen to know that you've been coming to Gion often. But don't bother to ask me how I know. I won't tell you unless you agree to come on a stroll with me.'

'All right,' said Nobu. 'Since it's a pleasant evening –'

'Oh, Nobu-san, don't say that. I'd much rather you said, "Since I've bumped into an old friend I haven't seen in so long, I can't think of anything I'd rather do than go on a stroll with her."'

'I'll take a walk with you,' he said. 'You may think whatever you like about my reasons for doing it.'

I gave a little bow of assent to this, and we set off together down the alley in the direction of Maruyama Park. 'If Nobu-san wants me to believe he isn't angry,' I said, 'he should act friendlier, instead of like a panther who hasn't been fed for months. No wonder poor Takazuru is so terrified of you . . .'

'So she's spoken to you, has she?' said Nobu. 'Well, if she weren't such an infuriating girl –'

'If you don't like her, why do you ask for her every time you come to Gion?'

'I've never asked for her, not even once! It's her older sister who keeps pushing her at me. It's bad enough you've reminded me of her. Now you're going to take advantage of bumping into me tonight to try to shame me into liking her!'

'Actually, Nobu-san, I didn't "bump" into you at all. I've been strolling down that alley for weeks just for the purpose of finding you.'

This seemed to give Nobu something to think about, for we walked along in silence a few moments. Finally he said, 'I shouldn't be surprised. You're as conniving a person as I know.'

'Nobu-san! What else was I to do?' I said. 'I thought you had disappeared completely. I might never have known where to find you, if Takazuru hadn't come to me in tears to say how badly you've been treating her.'

'Well, I have been hard on her, I suppose. But she isn't as clever as you – or as pretty, for that matter. If you've been thinking I'm angry with you, you're quite right.'

'May I ask what I have done to make an old friend so angry?'

Here Nobu stopped and turned to me with a terribly sad look in his eyes. I felt a fondness welling up in me that I've known for very few men in my life. I was thinking how much I had missed him, and how deeply I had wronged him. But though I'm ashamed to admit it, my feelings of fondness were tinged with pity.

'After a considerable amount of effort,' he said, 'I have discovered the identity of your *danna*.'

'If Nobu-san had asked me, I would have been glad to tell him.'

'I don't believe you. You geisha are the most close-mouthed group of people. I asked around Gion about your *danna*, and one after another they all pretended not to know. I never would have found out, if I hadn't asked Michizono to come entertain me one night, just the two of us.'

Michizono, who was about fifty at the time, was a sort of legend in Gion. She wasn't a beautiful woman, but she could sometimes put even Nobu in a good mood just from the way she crinkled her nose at him when she bowed hello.

'I made her play drinking games with me,' he went on, 'and I won and won until poor Michizono was quite drunk. I could have asked her anything at all and she would have told me.'

'What a lot of work!' I said.

'Nonsense. She was very enjoyable company. There was nothing like work about it. But shall I tell you something? I have lost respect for you, now that I know your *danna* is a little man in uniform whom no one admires.'

'Nobu-san speaks as if I have any choice over who my *danna* is. The only choice I can ever make is what kimono I'll wear. And even then –'

'Do you know why that man has a desk job? It's because no one trusts him with anything that matters. I understand the army very well, Sayuri. Even his own superiors have no use for him. You may as well have made an alliance with a beggar! Really, I was once very fond of you, but –'

'Once? Is Nobu-san not fond of me any longer?'

'I have no fondness for fools.'

'What a cold thing to say! Are you only trying to make me cry? Oh, Nobu-san! Am I a fool because my *danna* is a man you can't admire?'

'You geisha! There was never a more irritating group of people. You go around consulting your almanacs, saying, "Oh, I can't walk toward the east today, because my horoscope says it's unlucky!" But then when it's a matter of something affecting your entire lives, you simply look the other way.'

'It's less a matter of looking the other way than of closing our eyes to what we can't stop from happening.'

'Is that so? Well, I learned a few things from my talk with Michizono that night when I got her drunk. You are the daughter of the okiya, Sayuri. You can't pretend you have no influence at all. It's your duty to use what influence you have, unless you want to drift through life like a fish belly-up on the stream.'

'I wish I could believe life really is something more than a stream that carries us along, belly-up.'

'All right, if it's a stream, you're still free to be in this part of it or that part, aren't you? The water will divide again and again. If you bump, and tussle, and fight, and make use of whatever advantages you might have –'

'Oh, that's fine, I'm sure, when we have advantages.'

'You'd find them everywhere, if you ever bothered to look! In my case, even when I have nothing more than – I don't know – a chewed-up peach pit, or something of the sort, I won't let it go to waste. When it's time to throw it out, I'll make good and certain to throw it at somebody I don't like!'

'Nobu-san, are you counseling me to throw peach pits?'

'Don't joke about it; you know perfectly well what I'm saying. We're very much alike, Sayuri. I know they call me "Mr. Lizard" and all of that, and here you are, the loveliest creature in Gion. But that very first time I saw you at the sumo tournament years ago – what were you, fourteen? – I could see what a resourceful girl you were even then.'

'I've always believed that Nobu-san thinks me more worthy than I really am.'

'Perhaps you're right. I thought you had something more to you, Sayuri. But it turns out you don't even understand where your destiny lies. To tie your fortunes to a man like the General! I would have taken proper care of you, you know. It makes me so furious to think about it! When this General is gone from your life, he'll leave nothing for you to remember him by. Is this how you intend to waste your youth? A woman who acts like a fool is a fool, wouldn't you say?'

If we rub a fabric too often, it will quickly grow threadbare; and Nobu's words had rasped against me so much, I could no longer maintain that finely lacquered surface Mameha had always counseled me to hide behind. I felt lucky to be standing in shadow, for I was certain Nobu would think still less of me if he saw the pain I was feeling. But I suppose my silence must have betrayed me; for with his one hand he took my shoulder and turned me just a fraction, until the light fell on my face. And when he looked me in the eyes, he let out a long sigh that sounded at first like disappointment.

'Why do you seem so much older to me, Sayuri?' he said after a moment. 'Sometimes I forget you're still a girl. Now you're going to tell me I've been too harsh with you.'

'I cannot expect that Nobu-san should act like anyone but Nobu-san,' I said.

'I react very badly to disappointment, Sayuri. You ought to know that. Whether you failed me because you're too young or because you aren't the woman I thought . . . either way you failed me, didn't you?'

'Please, Nobu-san, it frightens me to hear you say these things. I don't know if I can ever live my life by the standards you use for judging me . . .'

'What standards are those, really? I expect you to go through life with your eyes open! If you keep your destiny in mind, every moment in life becomes an opportunity for moving closer to it. I wouldn't expect this sort of awareness from a foolish girl like Takazuru, but –'

'Hasn't Nobu-san been calling me foolish all evening?'

'You know better than to listen to me when I'm angry.'

'So Nobu-san isn't angry any longer. Then will he come to see me at the Ichiriki Teahouse? Or invite me to come and see him? In fact, I'm in no particular hurry this evening. I could come in even now, if Nobu-san asked me to.'

By now we had walked around the block, and were standing at the entrance to the teahouse. 'I won't ask you,' he said, and rolled open the door.

I couldn't help but let out a great sigh when I heard this; and I call it a great sigh because it contained many smaller sighs within it – one sigh of disappointment, one of frustration, one of sadness . . . and I don't know what else.

'Oh, Nobu-san,' I said, 'sometimes you're so difficult for me to understand.'

'I'm a very easy man to understand, Sayuri,' he said. 'I don't like things held up before me that I cannot have.'

Before I had a chance to reply, he stepped into the teahouse and rolled the door shut behind him.

27

DURING THE SUMMER of that year, 1939, I was so busy with engagements, occasional meetings with the General, dance performances, and the like, that in the morning when I tried to get up from my futon, I often felt like a bucket filled with nails. Usually by midafternoon I managed to forget my fatigue, but I often wondered how much I was earning through all my efforts. I never really expected to find out, however, so I was quite taken aback when Mother called me into her room one afternoon and told me I'd earned more in the past six months than both Hatsumomo and Pumpkin combined.

'Which means,' she said, 'that it's time for you to exchange rooms with them.'

I wasn't as pleased to hear this as you might imagine. Hatsumomo and I had managed to live side by side these past few years by keeping away from each other. But I regarded her as a sleeping tiger, not a defeated one. Hatsumomo certainly wasn't going to think of Mother's plan as 'exchanging rooms'; she was going to feel that her room had been taken away from her.

When I saw Mameha that evening, I told her what Mother had said to me, and mentioned my fears that the fire inside Hatsumomo might flare up again.

'Oh, well, that's fine,' said Mameha. 'That woman won't be beaten once and for all until we see blood. And we haven't seen it yet. Let's give her a bit of a chance and see what sort of a mess she makes for herself this time.'

Early the next morning, Auntie came upstairs in the okiya to lay down the rules for moving our belongings. She began by taking me into Hatsumomo's room and announcing that a certain corner now belonged to me; I could put anything I wanted there, and no one else could touch it. Then she brought Hatsumomo and Pumpkin into my smaller room and set up a similar space for the two of them. After we'd swapped all our belongings, the move would be complete.

I set to work that very afternoon carrying my things through the hall. I wish I could say I'd accumulated a collection of beautiful objects as Mameha probably had by my age; but the mood of the nation had changed greatly. Cosmetics and permanents had recently been banned as luxuries by the military government – though of course those of us in Gion, as playthings of the men in power, still did more or less as we pleased. Lavish gifts, however, were almost unheard of, so I'd accumulated nothing more over the years than a few scrolls, inkstones, and bowls, as well as a collection of stereoscopic photos of famous views, with a lovely viewer made of sterling silver, which the Kabuki actor Onoe Yoegoro XVII had given to me. In any case, I carried these things across the hall – along with my makeup, undergarments, books, and magazines – and piled them in the corner of the room. But as late as the following evening, Hatsumomo and Pumpkin still hadn't begun moving their things out. On the way back from my lessons at noon on the third day, I made up my mind that if Hatsumomo's bottles and ointments were still crowded together on the makeup stand, I would go ask Auntie to help me.

When I reached the top of the stairs, I was surprised to see both Hatsumomo's door and mine standing open. A jar of white ointment lay broken on the hallway floor. Something seemed to be amiss, and when I stepped into my room, I saw what it was. Hatsumomo was sitting at my little table, sipping at what looked like a small glass of water – and reading a notebook that belonged to me!

Geisha are expected to be discreet about the men they know; so you may be puzzled to hear that several years earlier while still an apprentice, I'd gone into a paper store one afternoon and bought a beautiful book of blank pages to begin keeping a diary about my life. I wasn't foolish enough to write down the sorts of things a geisha is never expected to reveal. I wrote only about my thoughts and feelings. When I had something to say about a particular man, I gave him a code name. So for example, I referred to Nobu as 'Mr. Tsu,' because he sometimes made a little scornful noise with his mouth that sounded like 'Tsu!' And I referred to the Chairman as 'Mr. Haa,' because on one occasion he'd taken in a deep breath and let it out slowly in a way that sounded like 'Haa,' and I'd imagined him waking up beside me as he said it – so of course, it made a strong impression on me. But I'd never thought for a moment that anyone would see the things I'd written.

'Why, Sayuri, I'm so pleased to see you!' Hatsumomo said 'I've been waiting to tell vou how much I'm enjoying your diary. Some of the entries are *most* interesting . . . and really, your writing style is charming! I'm not much impressed with your calligraphy, but –'

'Did you happen to notice the interesting thing I wrote on the front page?'

'I don't think I did. Let's see . . . "Private." Well, now here's an example of what I'm talking about with your calligraphy.'

'Hatsumomo, please put the book down on the table and leave my room.'

'Really! I'm shocked at you, Sayuri. I'm only trying to be helpful! Just listen for a moment, and you'll see. For example: Why did you choose to give Nobu Toshikazu the name "Mr. Tsu"? It doesn't suit him at all. I think you should have called him "Mr. Blister" or maybe "Mr. One-Arm." Don't you agree? You can change it if you want and you don't even have to give me any credit.'

'I don't know what you're talking about, Hatsumomo. I haven't written anything about Nobu at all.'

Hatsumomo sighed, as if to tell me what an inept liar I was, and then began paging through my journal. 'If it isn't Nobu you were writing about, I want you to tell me the name of the man you're referring to here. Let's see . . . ah, here it is: "Sometimes I see Mr. Tsu's face blooming with anger when a geisha has been staring at him. But for my part, I can look at him as long as I want, and he seems to be pleased by it. I think his fondness for me grows from his feeling that I don't find the look of his skin and his missing arm as strange and frightening as so many girls do." I guess what you're telling me is that you know someone else who looks *just like* Nobu. I think you should introduce them! Think how much they'll have in common.'

By this time I was feeling sick at heart – I can't think of any better way of describing it. For it's one thing to find your secrets suddenly exposed, but when your own foolishness has exposed them . . . well, if I was prepared to curse anyone, it was myself for keeping the journal in the first place and stowing it where Hatsumomo could find it. A shopkeeper who leaves his window open can hardly be angry at the rainstorm for ruining his wares.

I went to the table to take the journal from Hatsumomo, but she clutched it to her chest and stood. In her other hand she picked up the glass of what I'd thought was water. Now that I stood close to her I could smell the odor of sake. It wasn't water at all. She was drunk.

'Sayuri, *of course* you want your journal back, and *of course* I'm going to give it to you,' she said. But she was walking toward the door as she said it. 'The trouble is, I haven't finished reading it. So I'll take it back to my room . . . unless you'd rather I took it to Mother. I'm sure she'll be pleased to see the passages you've written about her.'

I mentioned earlier that a broken bottle of ointment lay on the floor of the hallway. This was how Hatsumomo did things, making a mess and not even bothering to tell the maids. But now as she left my room, she got what she deserved. Probably she'd forgotten about the bottle because she was drunk; in any case she stepped right into the broken glass and let out a little shriek. I saw her look at her foot a moment and make a gasping noise, but then she kept on going.

I felt myself panicking as she stepped into her room. I thought of trying to wrestle the book from her hands . . . but then I remembered Mameha's realization at the sumo tournament. To rush after Hatsumomo was the obvious thing. I'd be better off to wait until she began to relax, thinking she'd won, and then take the journal from her when she wasn't expecting it. This seemed to me a fine idea . . . until a moment later when I had an image of her hiding it in a place I might never find.

By now she'd closed the door. I went to stand outside it and called out quietly, 'Hatsumomo-san, I'm sorry if I seemed angry. May I come in?'

'No, you may not,' she said.

I slid the door open anyway. The room was in terrible disarray, because Hatsumomo had put things everywhere in her efforts at moving. The journal was sitting on the table while Hatsumomo held a towel against her foot. I had no idea how I would distract her, but I certainly didn't intend to leave the room without the journal.

She may have had the personality of a water rat, but Hatsumomo was no fool. If she'd been sober, I wouldn't even have tried to outsmart her right then. But considering her state at the moment . . . I looked around the floor at the piles of underclothing, bottles of perfume, and all the other things she'd scattered in disarray. The closet door was open, and the tiny safe where she kept her jewelry stood ajar; pieces were spilling out onto the mats as though she'd sat there earlier in the morning drinking and trying them on. And then one object caught my eye as clearly as a single star burning in a black sky.

It was an emerald obi brooch, the very one Hatsumomo had accused me of stealing years earlier; on the night I'd found her and her boyfriend in the maids' room. I'd never expected to see it again. I walked directly to the closet and reached down to pluck it from among the jewelry lying there.

'What a wonderful idea!' Hatsumomo said. 'Go ahead and steal a piece of my jewelry. Truthfully, I'd rather have the cash you'll have to pay me.'

'I'm so pleased you don't mind!' I told her. 'But how much cash will I have to pay for this?'

As I said these words, I walked over and held the brooch up before her. The radiant smile she'd worn now faded, just as the darkness fades from a valley when the sun rises on it. In that moment, while Hatsumomo sat stunned, I simply reached down to the table with my other hand and took the journal away.

I had no notion how Hatsumomo would react, but I walked out the door and closed it behind me. I thought of going straight to Mother to show her what I'd found, but of course, I couldn't very well go there with the journal in my hand. As quickly as I could, I slid open the door to the closet where in-season kimono were kept and stashed the journal on a shelf between two robes wrapped in tissue paper. It took no more than a few seconds; but all the while my back tingled from the sensation that at any moment Hatsumomo might open her door and spot me. After I'd shut the closet door again, I rushed into my room and began opening and closing the drawers to my makeup stand to give Hatsumomo the impression I'd hid the journal there.

When I came out into the hallway, she was watching me from the doorway of her room, wearing a little smile as though she found the whole situation amusing. I tried to look worried – which wasn't too difficult – and carried the brooch with me into Mother's room to lay it on the table before her. She put aside the magazine she was reading and held it up to admire it.

'This is a lovely piece,' she said, 'but it won't go far on the black market these days. No one pays much for jewels like this one.'

'I'm sure Hatsumomo will pay very dearly for it, Mother,' I said. 'Do you remember the brooch I'm supposed to have stolen from her years ago, the one that was added to my debts? This is it. I've just found it on the floor near her jewelry box.'

'Do you know,' said Hatsumomo, who had come into the room and now stood behind me. 'I believe Sayuri is right. That is the brooch I lost! Or at least, it looks like it. I never thought I'd see it again!'

'Yes, it's very difficult to find things when you're drunk all the time,' I said. 'If only you'd looked in your jewelry box more closely.'

Mother put the brooch down on the table and went on glowering at Hatsumomo.

'I found it in her room,' Hatsumomo said. 'She'd hidden it in her makeup stand.'

'Why were you looking through her makeup stand?' Mother said.

'I didn't want to have to tell you this, Mother, but Sayuri left something on her table and I was trying to hide it for her. I know I should have brought it to you at once, but . . . she's been keeping a journal, you see. She showed it to me last year. She's written some very incriminating things about certain men, and . . . truthfully, there are some passages about you too, Mother.'

I thought of insisting it wasn't true; but none of it mattered in any case. Hatsumomo was in trouble, and nothing she was going to say would change the situation. Ten years earlier when she had been the okiya's principal earner, she probably could have accused me of anything she'd wanted. She could have claimed I'd eaten the tatami mats in her room, and Mother would have charged me the cost of new ones. But now at last the season had changed; Hatsumomo's brilliant career was dying on the branch, while mine had begun to blossom. I was the daughter of the okiya and its prime geisha. I don't think Mother even cared where the truth lay.

'There is no journal, Mother,' I said. 'Hatsumomo is making it up.'

'Am I?' said Hatsumomo. 'I'll just go find it, then, and while Mother reads through it, you can tell her how I made it up.'

Hatsumomo went to my room, with Mother following. The hallway floor was a terrible mess. Not only had Hatsumomo broken a bottle and then stepped on it, she'd tracked ointment and blood all around the upstairs hall – and much worse, onto the tatami mats in her own room, Mother's room, and now mine as well. She was kneeling at my dressing table when I looked in, closing the drawers very slowly and looking a bit defeated.

'What journal is Hatsumomo talking about?' Mother asked me.

'If there's a journal, I'm certain Hatsumomo will find it,' I said.

At this, Hatsumomo put her hands into her lap and gave a

little laugh as though the whole thing had been some sort of game, and she'd been cleverly outwitted.

'Hatsumomo,' Mother said to her, 'you'll repay Sayuri for the brooch you accused her of stealing. What's more, I won't have the tatami in this okiya defiled with blood. They'll be replaced, and at your expense. This has been a very costly day for you, and it's hardly past noon. Shall I hold off calculating the total, just in case you're not quite finished?'

I don't know if Hatsumomo heard what Mother said. She was too busy glaring at me, and with a look on her face I wasn't accustomed to seeing.

If you'd asked me, while I was still a young woman, to tell you the turning point in my relationship with Hatsumomo, I would have said it was my *mizuage*. But even though it's quite true that my *mizuage* lifted me onto a high shelf where Hatsumomo could no longer reach me, she and I might well have gone on living side by side until we were old women, if nothing else had happened between us. This is why the real turning point, as I've since come to see it, occurred the day when Hatsumomo read my journal, and I discovered the obi brooch she'd accused me of stealing.

By way of explaining why this is so, let me tell you something Admiral Yamamoto Isoroku once said during an evening at the Ichiriki Teahouse. I can't pretend I was well acquainted with Admiral Yamamoto – who's usually described as the father of the Japanese Imperial Navy – but I was privileged to attend parties with him on a number of occasions. He was a small man; but keep in mind that a stick of dynamite is small too. Parties always grew noisier after the Admiral arrived. That night, he and another man were in the final round of a drinking game, and had agreed that the loser would go buy a condom at the nearest pharmacy – just for the embarrassment of it, you understand; not for any other purpose. Of course, the Admiral ended up winning, and the whole crowd broke into cheers and applause.

'It's a good thing you didn't lose, Admiral,' said one of his aides. 'Think of the poor pharmacist looking up to find Admiral Yamamoto Isoroku on the other side of the counter!'

Everyone thought this was very funny, but the Admiral replied that he'd never had any doubt about winning.

'Oh, come now!' said one of the geisha. 'Everyone loses from time to time! Even you, Admiral!'

'I suppose it's true that everyone loses at some time,' he said. 'But never me.'

Some in the room may have considered this an arrogant thing to say, but I wasn't one of them. The Admiral seemed to me the sort of man who really was accustomed to winning. Finally someone asked him the secret of his success.

'I never seek to defeat the man I am fighting,' he explained. 'I seek to defeat his confidence. A mind troubled by doubt cannot focus on the course to victory. Two men are equals – *true* equals – only when they both have equal confidence.'

I don't think I realized it at the time, but after Hatsumomo and I quarreled over my journal, her mind – as the Admiral would have put it – began to be troubled by doubt. She knew that under no circumstances would Mother take her side against me any longer; and because of that, she was like a fabric taken from its warm closet and hung out of doors where the harsh weather will gradually consume it.

If Mameha were to hear me explaining things in this way, she would certainly speak up and say how much she disagreed. Her view of Hatsumomo was quite different from mine. She believed Hatsumomo was a woman bent on self-destruction, and that all we needed to do was to coax her along a path she was certain to follow in any case. Perhaps Mameha was right; I don't know. It's true that in the years since my *mizuage*, Hatsumomo had gradually been afflicted by some sort of disease of the character – if such a thing exists. She'd lost all control over her drinking, for example, and of her bouts of cruelty too. Until her life began to fray, she'd always used her cruelty for a purpose, just as a samurai draws his sword – not for slashing at random, but for slashing at enemies. But by this time in her life, Hatsumomo seemed to have lost sight of who her enemies were, and sometimes struck out even at Pumpkin. From time to time during parties, she even made insulting comments to the men she was entertaining. And another thing: she was no longer as beautiful as she'd once been. Her skin was waxy-looking, and her features puffy. Or perhaps I was only seeing her that way. A tree may look as beautiful as ever; but when you notice the insects infesting it, and the tips of the branches that are brown from disease, even the trunk seems to lose some of its magnificence.

Everyone knows that a wounded tiger is a dangerous beast; and for this reason, Mameha insisted that we follow Hatsumomo around Gion during the evenings over the next few weeks. Partly, Mameha wanted to keep an eye on her, because neither of us would have been surprised if she'd sought out Nobu to tell him about the contents of my journal, and about all my secret feelings for 'Mr. Haa,' whom Nobu might have recognized as the Chairman. But more important, Mameha wanted to make Hatsumomo's life difficult for her to bear.

'When you want to break a board,' Mameha said, 'cracking it in the middle is only the first step. Success comes when you bounce up and down with all your weight until the board snaps in half.'

So every evening, except when she had an engagement she couldn't miss, Mameha came to our okiya around dusk and waited to walk out the door behind Hatsumomo. Mameha and I weren't always able to stay together, but usually at least one of us managed to follow her from engagement to engagement for a portion of the evening. On the first night we did this, Hatsumomo pretended to find it amusing. But by the end of the fourth night she was looking at us through squinted, angry eyes, and had difficulty acting cheerful around the men she tried to entertain. Then early the following week, she suddenly wheeled around in an alleyway and came toward us.

'Let me see now,' she said. 'Dogs follow their owners. And the two of you are following me around, sniffing and sniffing. So I guess you want to be treated like dogs! Shall I show you what I do with dogs I don't like?'

And with this, she drew back her hand to strike Mameha on the side of the head. I screamed, which must have made Hatsumomo stop to think about what she was doing. She stared at me a moment with eyes burning before the fire went out of them and she walked away. Everyone in the alley had noticed what was happening, and a few came over to see if Mameha was all right. She assured them she was fine and then said sadly:

'Poor Hatsumomo! It must be just as the doctor said. She really does seem to be losing her mind.'

There was no doctor, of course, but Mameha's words had the effect she'd hoped for. Soon a rumor had spread all over Gion that a doctor had declared Hatsumomo mentally unstable.

For years Hatsumomo had been very close to the famous Kabuki actor Bando Shojiro VI. Shojiro was what we call an *onna-gata*, which means that he always played women's roles. Once, in a magazine interview, he said that Hatsumomo was the most beautiful woman he'd ever seen, and that on the stage he often imitated her gestures to make himself seem more alluring. So you can well imagine that whenever Shojiro was in town, Hatsumomo visited him.

One afternoon I learned that Shojiro would attend a party later that evening at a teahouse in the geisha district of Pontocho, on the other side of the river from Gion. I heard this bit of news while preparing a tea ceremony for a group of naval officers on leave. Afterward I rushed back to the okiya, but Hatsumomo had already dressed and snuck out. She was doing what I'd once done, leaving early so that no one would follow her. I was very eager to explain to Mameha what I'd learned, so I went straight to her apartment. Unfortunately, her maid told me she'd left a half hour earlier 'to worship.' I knew exactly what this meant: Mameha had gone to a little temple just at the eastern edge of Gion to pray before the three tiny *jizo* statues she'd paid to have erected there. A *jizo*, you see, honors the soul of a departed child; in Mameha's case, they were for the three children she'd aborted at the Baron's request. Under other circumstances I might have gone searching for her, but I couldn't possibly disturb her in such a private moment; and besides, she might not have wanted me to know even that she'd gone there. Instead I sat in her apartment and permitted Tatsumi to serve me tea while I waited. At last, with something of a weary look about her; Mameha came home. I didn't want to raise the subject at first, and so for a time we chatted about the upcoming Festival of the Ages, in which Mameha was scheduled to portray Lady Murasaki Shikibu, author of *The Tale of Genji.* Finally Mameha looked up with a smile from her cup of brown tea – Tatsumi had been roasting the leaves when I arrived – and I told her what I'd discovered during the course of the afternoon.

'How perfect!' she said. 'Hatsumomo's going to relax and think she's free of us. With all the attention Shojiro is certain to give her at the party, she may feel renewed. Then you and I will come drifting in like some sort of horrid smell from the alleyway, and ruin her evening completely.'

Considering how cruelly Hatsumomo had treated me over the years, and how very much I hated her, I'm sure I ought to have been elated at this plan. But somehow conspiring to make Hatsumomo suffer wasn't the pleasure I might have imagined. I couldn't help remembering one morning as a child, when I was swimming in the pond near our tipsy house and suddenly felt a terrible burning in my shoulder. A wasp had stung me and was struggling to free itself from my skin. I was too busy screaming to think of what to do, but one of the boys pulled the wasp off and held it by the wings upon a rock, where we all gathered to decide exactly how to murder it. I was in great pain because of the wasp, and certainly felt no kindness toward it. But it gave me a terrible sensation of weakness in my chest to know that this tiny struggling creature could do nothing to save itself from the death that was only moments away. I felt the same sort of pity toward Hatsumomo.

During evenings when we trailed her around Gion until she returned to the okiya just to get away from us, I felt almost as though we were torturing her.

In any case, around nine o'clock that night, we crossed the river to the Pontocho district. Unlike Gion, which sprawls over many blocks, Pontocho is just a single long alleyway stretched out along one bank of the river. People call it an 'eel's bed' because of its shape. The autumn air was a bit chilly that night, but Shojiro's party was outdoors anyway, on a wooden verandah standing on stilts above the water. No one paid us much attention when we stepped out through the glass doors. The verandah was beautifully lit with paper lanterns, and the river shimmered gold from the lights of a restaurant on the opposite bank. Everyone was listening to Shojiro, who was in the middle of telling a story in his singsong voice; but you should have seen the way Hatsumomo's expression soured when she caught sight of us. I couldn't help remembering a damaged pear I'd held in my hand the day before, because amid the cheerful faces, Hatsumomo's expression was like a terrible bruise.

Mameha went to kneel on a mat right beside Hatsumomo, which I considered very bold of her. I knelt toward the other end of the verandah, beside a gentle-looking old man who turned out to be the koto player Tachibana Zensaku, whose scratchy old records I still own. Tachibana was blind, I discovered that night. Regardless of my purpose in coming, I would have been content to spend the evening just chatting with him, for he was such a fascinating, endearing man. But we'd hardly begun to talk when suddenly everyone burst out laughing.

Shojiro was quite a remarkable mimic. He was slender like the branch of a willow, with elegant, slow-moving fingers, and a very long face he could move about in extraordinary ways; he could have fooled a group of monkeys into thinking he was one of them. At that moment he was imitating the geisha beside him, a woman in her fifties. With his effeminate gestures – his pursed lips, his rolls of the eyes – he managed to look so much like her that I didn't know whether to laugh or just sit with my hand over my mouth in astonishment. I'd seen Shojiro on the stage, but this was something much better.

Tachibana leaned in toward me and whispered, 'What's he doing?'

'He's imitating an older geisha beside him.'

'Ah,' said Tachibana. 'That would be Ichiwari.' And then he tapped me with the back of his hand to make sure he had my attention. 'The director of the Minamiza Theater,' he said, and held out his little finger below the table where no one else could see it. In Japan, you see, holding up the little finger means 'boyfriend' or 'girlfriend.' Tachibana was telling me that the older geisha, the one named Ichiwari, was the theater director's mistress. And in fact the director was there too, laughing louder than anyone.

A moment later, still in the midst of his mimicry, Shojiro stuck one of his fingers up his nose. At this, everyone let out a laugh so loud you could feel the verandah trembling. I didn't know it at the time, but picking her nose was one of Ichiwari's well-known habits. She turned bright red when she saw this, and held a sleeve of her kimono over her face, and Shojiro, who had drunk a good bit of sake, imitated her even then. People laughed politely, but only Hatsumomo seemed to find it really funny; for at this point Shojiro was beginning to cross the line into cruelty. Finally the theater director said, 'Now, now, Shojiro-san, save some energy for your show tomorrow! Anyway, don't you know you're sitting near one of Gion's greatest dancers? I propose that we ask for a performance.'

Of course, the director was talking about Mameha.

'Heavens, no. I don't want to see any dancing just now,' Shojiro said. As I came to understand over the years, he preferred to be the center of attention himself. 'Besides, I'm having fun.'

'Shojiro-san, we mustn't pass up an opportunity to see the famous Mameha,' the director said, speaking this time without a trace of humor. A few geisha spoke up as well, and finally Shojiro was persuaded to ask her if she would perform, which he did as sulkily as a little boy. Already I could see Hatsumomo looking displeased. She poured more sake for Shojiro, and he poured more for her. They exchanged a long look as if to say their party had been spoiled.

A few minutes passed while a maid was sent to fetch a shamisen and one of the geisha tuned it and prepared to play. Then Mameha took her place against the backdrop of the teahouse and performed a few very short pieces. Nearly anyone would have agreed that Mameha was a lovely woman, but very few people would have found her more beautiful than Hatsumomo; so I can't say exactly what caught Shojiro's eye. It may have been the sake he'd drunk, and it may have been Mameha's extraordinary dancing – for Shojiro was a dancer himself. Whatever it was, by the time Mameha came back to join us at the table, Shojiro seemed quite taken with her and asked that she sit beside him. When she did, he poured her a cup of sake, and turned his back on Hatsumomo as if she were just another adoring apprentice.

Well, Hatsumomo's mouth hardened, and her eyes shrank to about half their size. As for Mameha, I never saw her flirt with anyone more deliberately than she did with Shojiro. Her voice grew high and soft, and her eyes swished from his chest to his face and back again. From time to time she drew the fingertips of her hand across the base of her throat as though she felt self-conscious about the splotchy blush that had appeared there. There wasn't really any blush, but she acted it so convincingly, you wouldn't have known it without looking closely. Then one of the geisha asked Shojiro if he'd heard from Bajiru-san.

'Bajiru-san,' said Shojiro, in his most dramatic manner, 'has abandoned me!'

I had no idea who Shojiro was talking about, but Tachibana, the old koto player, was kind enough to explain in a whisper that 'Bajiru-san' was the English actor Basil Rathbone – though I'd never heard of him at the time. Shojiro had taken a trip to London a few years earlier and staged a Kabuki performance there. The actor Basil Rathbone had admired it so much that with the help of an interpreter the two of them had developed something of a friendship. Shojiro may have lavished attention on women like Hatsumomo or Mameha, but the fact remained that he was homosexual; and since his trip to England, he'd made it a running joke that his heart was destined to be broken because Bajiru-san had no interest in men.

'It makes me sad,' said one of the geisha quietly, 'to witness the death of a romance.'

Everyone laughed except for Hatsumomo, who went on glowering at Shojiro.

'The difference between me and Bajiru-san is this. I'll show you,' Shojiro said; and with this he stood and asked Mameha to join him. He led her off to one side of the room, where they had a bit of space.

'When I do my work, I look like this,' he said. And he sashayed from one side of the room to the other, waving his folding fan with a most fluid wrist, and letting his head roll back and forth like a ball on a seesaw. 'Whereas when Bajiru-san does his work, he looks like this.' Here he grabbed Mameha, and you should have seen the astonished expression on her face when he dipped her toward the floor in what looked like a passionate embrace, and planted kisses all over her face. Everyone in the room cheered and clapped. Everyone except Hatsumomo, that is.

'What is he doing?' Tachibana asked me quietly. I didn't think anyone else had heard, but before I could reply, Hatsumomo cried out:

'He's making a fool of himself! That's what he's doing.'

'Oh, Hatsumomo-san,' said Shojiro, 'you're jealous, aren't you!'

'Of course she is!' said Mameha. 'Now you must show us how the two of you make up. Go on, Shojiro-san. Don't be shy! You must give her the very same kisses you gave to me! It's only fair. And in the same way.'

Shojiro didn't have an easy time of it, but soon he succeeded in getting Hatsumomo to her feet. Then with the crowd behind him, he took her in his arms and bent her back. But after only an instant, he jerked upright again with a shout, and grabbed his lip. Hatsumomo had bitten him; not enough to make him bleed, but certainly enough to give him a shock. She was standing with her eyes squinted in anger and her teeth exposed; and then she drew back her hand and slapped him. I think her aim must have been bad from all the sake she'd drunk, because she hit the side of his head rather than his face.

'What happened?' Tachibana asked me. His words were as clear in the quiet of the room as if someone had rung a bell. I didn't answer, but when he heard Shojiro's whimper and the heavy breathing of Hatsumomo, I'm sure he understood.

'Hatsumomo-san, please,' said Mameha, speaking in a voice so calm it sounded completely out of place, 'as a favor to me . . . *do* try to calm down.'

I don't know if Mameha's words had the precise effect she was hoping for, or whether Hatsumomo's mind had already shattered. But Hatsumomo threw herself at Shojiro and began hitting him everywhere. I do think that in a way she went crazy. It wasn't just that her mind seemed to have fractured; the moment itself seemed disconnected from everything else. The theater director got up from the table and rushed over to restrain her. Somehow in the middle of all this, Mameha slipped out and returned a moment later with the mistress of the teahouse. By that time the theater director was holding Hatsumomo from behind. I thought the crisis was over, but then Shojiro shouted at Hatsumomo so loudly, we heard it echo off the buildings across the river in Gion.

'You monster!' he screamed. 'You've bitten me!'

I don't know what any of us would have done without the calm thinking of the mistress. She spoke to Shojiro in a soothing voice, while at the same time giving the theater director a signal to take Hatsumomo away. As I later learned, he didn't just take her inside the teahouse; he took her downstairs to the front and shoved her out onto the street.

Hatsumomo didn't return to the okiya at all that night. When she did come back the following day, she smelled as if she had been sick to her stomach, and her hair was in disarray. She was summoned at once to Mother's room and spent a long while there.

A few days afterward, Hatsumomo left the okiya, wearing a simple cotton robe Mother had given her, and with her hair as I'd never seen it, hanging in a mass around her shoulders. She carried a bag containing her belongings and jewelry, and didn't say good-bye to any of us, but just walked out to the street. She didn't leave voluntarily; Mother had thrown her out. And in fact, Mameha believed Mother had probably been trying to get rid of Hatsumomo for years. Whether or not this is true, I'm sure Mother was pleased at having fewer mouths to feed, since Hatsumomo was no longer earning what she once had, and food had never been more difficult to come by.

If Hatsumomo hadn't been renowned for her wickedness, some other okiya might have wanted her even after what she'd done to Shojiro. But she was like a teakettle that even on a good day might still scald the hand of anyone who used it.

Everyone in Gion understood this about her.

I don't know for sure what ever became of Hatsumomo. A few years after the war, I heard she was making a living as a prostitute in the Miyagawa-cho district. She couldn't have been there long, because on the night I heard it, a man at the same party swore that if Hatsumomo was a prostitute, he would find her and give her some business of his own. He did go looking for her, but she was nowhere to be found. Over the years, she probably succeeded in drinking herself to death. She certainly wouldn't have been the first geisha to do it.

In just the way that a man can grow accustomed to a bad leg, we'd all grown accustomed to having Hatsumomo in our okiya. I don't think we quite understood all the ways her presence had afflicted us until long after she'd left, when things that we hadn't realized were ailing slowly began to heal. Even when Hatsumomo had been doing nothing more than sleeping in her room, the maids had known she was there, and that during the course of the day she would abuse them. They'd lived with the kind of tension you feel if you walk across a frozen pond whose ice might break at any moment. And as for Pumpkin, I think she'd grown to be dependent on her older sister and felt strangely lost without her.

I'd already become the okiya's principal asset, but even I took some time to weed out all the peculiar habits that had taken root because of Hatsumomo. Every time a man looked at me strangely, I found myself wondering if he'd heard something unkind about me from her; even long after she was gone. Whenever I climbed the stairs to the second floor of the okiya, I still kept my eyes lowered for fear that Hatsumomo would be waiting there on the landing, eager for someone to abuse. I can't tell you how many times I reached that last step and looked up suddenly with the realization that there was no Hatsumomo, and there never would be again. I knew she was gone, and yet the very emptiness of the hall seemed to suggest something of her presence. Even now, as an older woman, I sometimes lift the brocade cover on the mirror of my makeup stand, and have the briefest flicker of a thought that I may find her there in the glass, smirking at me.

28

IN JAPAN WE refer to the years from the Depression through World War II as *kuraitani* – the valley of darkness, when so many people lived like children whose heads had slipped beneath the waves. As is often the case, those of us in Gion didn't suffer quite as badly as others. While most Japanese lived in the dark valley all through the 1930s, for example, in Gion we were still warmed by a bit of sun. And I'm sure I don't need to tell you why; women who are mistresses of cabinet ministers and naval commanders are the recipients of enormous good fortune, and they pass that good fortune along to others. You might say Gion was like a pond high up on a mountaintop, fed by streams of rich springwater. More water poured in at some spots than others, but it raised the pond as a whole.

Because of General Tottori, our okiya was one of the spots where the rich springwater came pouring in. Things grew worse and worse around us during the course of several years; and yet long after the rationing of goods had begun, we continued to receive regular supplies of foodstuffs, tea, linens, and even some luxuries like cosmetics and chocolate. We might have kept these things to ourselves and lived behind closed doors, but Gion isn't that sort of place. Mother passed much of it along and considered it well spent, not because she was a generous woman, of course, but because we were all like spiders crowded together on the same web. From time to time people came asking for help, and we were pleased to give it when we could. At some point in the fall of 1941 for example, the military police found a maid with a box containing probably ten times more ration coupons than her okiya was supposed to have. Her mistress sent her to us for safekeeping until arrangements could be made to take her to the countryside, because of course, every okiya in Gion hoarded coupons; the better the okiya, the more it usually had. The maid was sent to us rather than to someone else because General Tottori had instructed the military police to leave us alone. So you see, even within that mountaintop pond that was Gion, we were the fish swimming in the very warmest water of all.

As the darkness continued to settle over Japan, there did finally come a time when even the pinpoint of light in which we'd managed to keep ourselves suddenly went out. It happened at a single moment, early one afternoon just a few weeks before New Year's Day, in December 1942. I was eating my breakfast – or at least, my first meal of the day, for I'd been busy helping to clean the okiya in preparation for the New Year – when a man's voice called out at our entrance. I thought he was probably just making a delivery, so I went on with my meal, but a moment later the maid interrupted me to say a military policeman had come looking for Mother.

'A military policeman?' I said. 'Tell him Mother is out.'

'Yes, I did, ma'am. He'd like to speak with you instead.'

When I reached the front hall, I found the policeman removing his boots in the entryway. Probably most people would have felt relieved just to note that his pistol was still snapped inside its leather case, but as I say, our okiya had lived differently right up until that moment. Ordinarily a policeman would have been more apologetic even than most visitors, since his presence would alarm us. But to see him tugging at his boots . . . well, this was his way of saying he planned to come in whether we invited him or not.

I bowed and greeted him, but he did nothing more than glance at me as though he would deal with me later. Finally he pulled up his socks and pulled down his cap, and then stepped up into the front entrance hall and said he wanted to see our vegetable garden. Just like that, with no word of apology for troubling us. You see, by this time nearly everyone in Kyoto, and probably the rest of the country, had converted their decorative gardens into vegetable gardens – everyone but people like us, that is. General Tottori provided us with enough food that we didn't need to plow up our garden, and were instead able to go on enjoying the hair moss and spearflowers, and the tiny maple in the corner. Since it was winter, I hoped the policeman would look only at the spots of frozen ground where the vegetation had died back, and imagine that we'd planted squash and sweet potatoes amid the decorative plants. So after I'd led him down to the courtyard, I didn't say a word; I just watched as he knelt down and touched the dirt with his fingers. I suppose he wanted to feel whether or not the ground had been dug up for planting.

I was so desperate for something to say that I blurted out the first thing that came to mind. 'Doesn't the dusting of snow on the ground make you think of foam on the ocean?' He didn't answer me, but just stood up to his full height and asked what vegetables we had planted.

'Officer,' I said, 'I'm terribly sorry, but the truth is, we haven't had an opportunity to plant any vegetables at all. And now that the ground is so hard and cold . . .'

'Your neighborhood association was quite right about you!' he said, taking off his cap. He brought out from his pocket a slip of paper and began to read a long list of misdeeds our okiya had committed. I don't even remember them all – hoarding cotton materials, failing to turn in metal and rubber goods needed for the war effort, improper use of ration tickets, all sorts of things like that. It's true we had done these things, just as every other okiya in Gion had. Our crime, I suppose, was that we'd enjoyed more good fortune than most, and had survived longer and in better shape than all but a very few.

Luckily for me, Mother returned just then. She didn't seem at all surprised to find a military policeman there; and in fact, she behaved more politely toward him than I'd ever seen her behave toward anyone. She led him into our reception room and served him some of our ill-gotten tea. The door was closed, but I could hear them talking for a long while. At one point when she came out to fetch something, she pulled me aside and told me this:

'General Tottori was taken into custody this morning. You'd better hurry and hide our best things, or they'll be gone tomorrow.'

Back in Yoroido I used to swim on chilly spring days, and afterward lie on the rocks beside the pond to soak up the heat of the sun. If the sunlight vanished suddenly behind a cloud, as it often did, the cold air seemed to close about my skin like a sheet of metal. The moment I heard of the General's misfortune, standing there in the front entrance hall, I had that same feeling. It was as though the sun had vanished, possibly for good, and I was now condemned to stand wet and naked in the icy air. Within a week of the policeman's visit, our okiya had been stripped of the things other families had lost long ago, such as stores of food, undergarments, and so forth. We'd always been Mameha's source for packets of tea; I think she'd been using them to purchase favors. But now her supplies were better than ours, and she became our source instead. Toward the end of the month, the neighborhood association began confiscating many of our ceramics and scrolls to sell them on what we called the 'gray market,' which was different from the black market. The black market was for things like fuel oil, foods, metals, and so on – mostly items that were rationed or illegal to trade. The gray market was more innocent; it was mainly housewives selling off their precious things to raise cash. In our case, though, our things were sold to punish us as much as for any other reason, and so the cash went to benefit others. The head of the neighborhood association, who was mistress of a nearby okiya, felt deeply sorry whenever she came to take our things away But the military police had given orders; no one could do anything but obey.

If the early years of the war had been like an exciting voyage out to sea, you might say that by about the middle of 1943 we all realized the waves were simply too big for our craft. We thought we would drown, all of us; and many did. It wasn't just that day-to-day life had grown increasingly miserable; no one dared admit it, but I think we'd all begun worrying about the outcome of the war. No one had fun any longer; many people seemed to feel it was unpatriotic even to have a good time. The closest thing to a joke I heard during this period was something the geisha Raiha said one night. For months we'd heard rumors that the military government planned to shut down all the geisha districts in Japan; lately we'd begun to realize that it really was going to happen. We were all wondering what would become of us, when suddenly Raiha spoke up.

'We can't waste our time thinking about such things,' she said. 'Nothing is bleaker than the future, except perhaps the past.'

It may not sound funny to you; but that night we laughed until tears beaded in the corners of our eyes. One day soon the geisha districts would indeed close. When they did, we were certain to end up working in the factories. To give you some idea of what life in the factories was like, let me tell you about Hatsumomo's friend Korin.

During the previous winter, the catastrophe that every geisha in Gion feared most had actually happened to Korin. A maid tending the bath in her okiya had tried to burn newspapers to heat the water, but had lost control of the flames. The entire okiya was destroyed, along with its collection of kimono. Korin ended up working in a factory south of the city fitting lenses into the equipment used for dropping bombs from airplanes. She came back to visit Gion from time to time as the months passed, and we were horrified at how much she'd changed. It wasn't just that she seemed more and more unhappy; we'd all experienced unhappiness, and were prepared for it in any case. But she had a cough that was as much a part of her as a song is part of a bird; and her skin was stained as though she'd soaked it in ink – since the coal the factories used was of a very low grade and covered everything in soot as it burned. Poor Korin was forced to work double shifts while being fed no more than a bowl of weak broth with a few noodles once a day, or watery rice gruel flavored with potato skin.

So you can imagine how terrified we were of the factories. Every day that we awakened to find Gion still open, we felt grateful.

Then one morning in January of the following year, I was standing in line at the rice store in the falling snow, holding my ration coupons, when the shopkeeper next door put out his head and called into the cold:

'It's happened!'

We all of us looked at one another. I was too numbed with cold to care what he was talking about, for I wore only a heavy shawl around my peasant's clothing; no one wore kimono during the day any longer. Finally the geisha in front of me brushed the snow from her eyebrows and asked him what he was talking about. 'The war hasn't come to an end, has it?' she asked.

'The government has announced the closing of the geisha districts,' he said. 'All of you are to report to the registry office tomorrow morning.'

For a long moment we listened to the sound of a radio inside his shop. Then the door rumbled closed again, and there was nothing but the soft hiss of the falling snow. I looked at the despair on the faces of the other geisha around me and knew in an instant that we were all thinking the same thing: Which of the men we knew would save us from life in the factories?

Even though General Tottori had been my *danna* until the previous year, I certainly wasn't the only geisha acquainted with him. I had to reach him before anyone else did. I wasn't properly dressed for the weather, but I put my ration coupons back into the pocket of my peasant pants and set out at once for the northwest of the city. The General was rumored to be living in the Suruya Inn, the same one where we'd met during the evenings twice a week for so many years.

I arrived there an hour or so later, burning with the cold and dusted all over with snow. But when I greeted the mistress, she took a long look at me before bowing in apology and saying she had no idea who I was.

'It's me, mistress . . . Sayuri! I've come to speak with the General.'

'Sayuri-san . . . my heavens! I never thought to see you looking like the wife of a peasant.'

She led me inside at once, but wouldn't present me to the

General until she'd first taken me upstairs and dressed me in one of her kimono. She even put on me a bit of makeup she'd stashed away, so the General would know me when he saw me.

When I entered his room, General Tottori was sitting at the table listening to a drama on the radio. His cotton robe hung open, exposing his bony chest and the thin gray hairs. I could see that his hardships of the past year had been far worse than mine. After all, he'd been accused of awful crimes – negligence, incompetence, abuse of power, and so forth; some people considered him lucky to have escaped prison. An article in a magazine had even blamed him for the Imperial Navy's defeats in the South Pacific, saying that he'd failed to oversee the shipment of supplies. Still, some men bear hardships better than others; and with one look at the General I could see that the weight of this past year had pressed down upon him until his bones had grown brittle, and even his face had come to look a bit misshapen. In the past he'd smelled of sour pickles all the time. Now as I bowed low on the mats near him, he had a different sort of sour smell.

'You're looking very well, General,' I said, though of course this was a lie. 'What a pleasure it is to see you again!'

The General switched off the radio. 'You're not the first to come to me,' he said. 'There's nothing I can do to help you, Sayuri.'

'But I rushed here so quickly! I can't imagine how anyone reached you before I did!'

'Since last week nearly every geisha I know has been to see me, but I don't have friends in power any longer. I don't know why a geisha of your standing should come to me anyway. You're liked by so many men with influence.'

'To be liked and to have true friends willing to help are two very different things,' I said.

'Yes, so they are. What sort of help have you come to me for anyway?'

'Any help at all, General. We talk about nothing these days in Gion but how miserable life in a factory will be.'

'Life will be miserable for the lucky ones. The rest won't even live to see the end of the war.'

'I don't understand.'

'The bombs will fall soon,' the General said. 'You can be certain the factories will take more than their share. If you want to be alive when this war is over, you'd better find someone who can tuck you away in a safe place. I'm sorry I'm not that man. I've already exhausted what influence I had.'

The General asked after Mother's health, and Auntie's, and soon bid me good-bye. I learned only much later what he meant about exhausting his influence. The proprietress of the Suruya had a young daughter; the General had arranged to send her to a town in northern Japan.

On the way back to the okiya, I knew the time had come for me to act; but I couldn't think what to do. Even the simple task of holding my panic at arm's length seemed more than I could manage. I went by the apartment where Mameha was now living – for her relationship with the Baron had ended several months earlier and she'd moved into a much smaller space. I thought she might know what course I should take, but in fact, she was in nearly as much of a panic as I was.

'The Baron will do nothing to help me,' she said, her face pale with worry. 'I've been unable to reach the other men I have in mind. You had better think of someone, Sayuri, and go to him as quickly as you can.'

I'd been out of touch with Nobu for more than four years by that time; I knew at once I couldn't approach him. As for the Chairman . . . well, I would have grabbed at any excuse just to speak with him, but I could never have asked him for a favor. However warmly he may have treated me in the hallways, I wasn't invited to his parties, even when lesser geisha were. I felt hurt by this, but what could I do? In any case, even if the Chairman had wanted to help me, his quarrels with the military government had been in the newspapers lately. He had too many troubles of his own.

So I spent the rest of that afternoon going from teahouse to teahouse in the biting cold, asking about a number of men I hadn't seen in weeks or even months. None of the mistresses knew where to find them.

That evening, the Ichiriki was busy with farewell parties. It was fascinating to see how differently all the geisha reacted to the news. Some looked as though their spirits had been murdered within them; others were like statues of the Buddha – calm and lovely, but painted over with a layer of sadness. I can't say how I myself looked, but my mind was like an abacus. I was so busy with scheming and plotting – thinking which man I would approach, and how I would do it – that I scarcely heard the maid who told me I was wanted in another room. I imagined a group of men had requested my company; but she led me up the stairs to the second floor and along a corridor to the very back of the teahouse. She opened the door of a small tatami room I'd never entered before. And there at the table, alone with a glass of beer, sat Nobu.

Before I could even bow to him or speak a word, he said, 'Sayuri-san, you've disappointed me!'

'My goodness! I haven't had the honor of your company for four years, Nobu-san, and already in an instant I've disappointed you. What could I have done wrong so quickly?'

'I had a little bet with myself that your mouth would fall open at the sight of me.'

'The truth is, I'm too startled even to move!'

'Come inside and let the maid close the door. But first, tell her to bring another glass and another beer. There's something you and I must drink to.'

I did as Nobu told me, and then knelt at the end of the table with a corner between us. I could feel Nobu's eyes upon my face almost as though he were touching me. I blushed as one might blush under the warmth of the sun, for I'd forgotten how flattering it felt to be admired.

'I see angles in your face I've never seen before,' he said to me. 'Don't tell me you're going hungry like everyone else. I'd never expected such a thing of you.'

'Nobu-san looks a bit thin himself.'

'I have food enough to eat, just no time for eating it.'

'I'm glad at least that you are keeping busy.'

'That's the most peculiar thing I've ever heard. When you see a man who has kept himself alive by dodging bullets, do you feel glad for him that he has something to occupy his time?'

'I hope Nobu-san doesn't mean to say that he is truly in fear for his life . . .'

'There's no one out to murder me, if that's what you mean. But if Iwamura Electric is my life, then yes, I'm certainly in fear for it. Now tell me this: What has become of that *danna* of yours?'

'The General is doing as well as any of us, I suppose. How kind of you to ask.'

'Oh, I don't mean it kindly at all.'

'Very few people wish him well these days. But to change the subject, Nobu-san, am I to suppose that you have been coming here to the Ichiriki night after night, but keeping yourself hidden from me by using this peculiar upstairs room?'

'It is a peculiar room, isn't it? I think it's the only one in the teahouse without a garden view. It looks out on the street, if you open those paper screens.'

'Nobu-san knows the room well.'

'Not really. It's the first time I've used it.'

I made a face at him when he said this, to show I didn't believe him.

'You may think what you want, Sayuri, but it's true I've never been in this room before. I think it's a bedroom for overnight guests, when the mistress has any. She was kind enough to let me use it tonight when I explained to her why I'd come.'

'How mysterious . . . So you had a purpose in coming. Will I find out what it is?'

'I hear the maid returning with our beer,' Nobu said. 'You'll find out when she's gone.'

The door slid open, and the maid placed the beer on the table. Beer was a rare commodity during this period, so it was quite something to watch the gold liquid rising in the glass. When the maid had left, we raised our glasses, and Nobu said:

'I have come here to toast your *danna*!'

I put down my beer when I heard this. 'I must say, Nobu-san, there are few things any of us can find to be cheerful about. But it would take me weeks even to begin imagining why you should wish to drink in honor of my *danna*.'

'I should have been more specific. Here's to the foolishness of your *danna*! Four years ago I told you he was an unworthy man, and he has proved me right. Wouldn't you say?'

'The truth is . . . he isn't my *danna* any longer.'

'Just my point! And even if he were, he couldn't do a thing for you, could he? I know Gion is going to close, and everyone's in a panic about it. I received a telephone call at my office today from a certain geisha . . . I won't name her . . . but can you imagine? She asked if I could find her a job at Iwamura Electric.'

'If you don't mind my asking, what did you tell her?'

'I don't have a job for anyone, hardly even myself. Even the Chairman may be out of a job soon, and end up in prison if he doesn't start doing as the government orders. He's persuaded them we don't have the means to manufacture bayonets and bullet casings, but now they want us to design and build fighter airplanes! I mean, honestly, fighter airplanes? We manufacture appliances! Sometimes I wonder what these people are thinking.'

'Nobo-san should speak more quietly.'

'Who's going to hear me? That General of yours?'

'Speaking of the General,' I said, 'I did go to see him today, to ask for his help.'

'You're lucky he was still alive to see you.'

'Has he been ill?'

'Not ill. But he'll get around to killing himself one of these days, if he has the courage.'

'Please, Nobu-san.'

'He didn't help you, did he?'

'No, he said he'd already used up whatever influence he had.'

'That wouldn't have taken him long. Why didn't he save what little influence he had for you?'

'I haven't seen him in more than a year.'

'You haven't seen me in more than four years. And I have saved my best influence for you. Why didn't you come to me before now?'

'But I've imagined you angry with me all this time. Just look at you, Nobu-san! How could I have come to you?'

'How could you not? I can save you from the factories. I have access to the perfect haven. And believe me, it is perfect, just like a nest for a bird. You're the only one I'll give it to, Sayuri. And I won't give it even to you, until you've bowed on the floor right here in front of me and admitted how wrong you were for what happened four years ago. You're certainly right I'm angry with you! We may both be dead before we see each other again. I may have lost the one chance I had. And it isn't enough that you brushed me aside: you wasted the very ripest years of your life on a fool, a man who won't pay even the debt he owes to his country, much less to you. He goes on living as if he's done nothing wrong!'

You can imagine how I was feeling by this time; for Nobu was a man who could hurl his words like stones. It wasn't just the words themselves or their meaning, but the way he said them. At first I'd been determined not to cry, regardless of what he said; but soon it occurred to me that crying might be the very thing Nobu wanted of me. And it felt so easy, like letting a piece of paper slip from my fingers. Every tear that slid down my cheeks I cried for a different reason. There seemed so much to mourn! I cried for Nobu, and for myself; I cried at wondering what would become of us all. I even cried for General Tottori, and for Korin, who had grown so gray and hollow from life in the factory. And then I did what Nobu demanded of me. I moved away from the table to make room, and I bowed low to the floor.

'Forgive me for my foolishness,' I said.

'Oh, get up off the mats. I'm satisfied if you tell me you won't make the same mistake again.'

'I will not.'

'Every moment you spent with that man was wasted! That's just what I told you would happen, isn't it? Perhaps you've learned enough by now to follow your destiny in the future.'

'I will follow my destiny, Nobu-san. There's nothing more I want from life.'

'I'm pleased to hear that. And where does your destiny lead you?'

'To the man who runs Iwamura Electric,' I said. Of course, I was thinking of the Chairman.

'So it does,' Nobu said. 'Now let us drink our beers together.'

I wet my lips – for I was far too confused and upset to be thirsty. Afterward Nobu told me about the nest he'd set aside. It was the home of his good friend Arashino Isamu, the kimono maker. I don't know if you remember him, but he was the guest of honor at the party on the Baron's estate years earlier at which Nobu and Dr. Crab were present. Mr. Arashino's home, which was also his workshop, was on the banks of the Kamo River shallows, about five kilometers upstream from Gion. Until a few years earlier, he and his wife and daughter had made kimono in the lovely Yuzen style for which he was famous. Lately, however, all the kimono makers had been put to work sewing parachutes – for they were accustomed to working with silk, after all. It was a job I could learn quickly, said Nobu, and the Arashino family was very willing to have me. Nobu himself would make the necessary arrangements with the authorities. He wrote the address of Mr. Arashino's home on a piece of paper and gave it to me.

I told Nobu a number of times how grateful I was. Each time I told him, he looked more pleased with himself. Just as I was about to suggest that we take a walk together in the newly fallen snow, he glanced at his watch and drained the last sip of his beer.

'Sayuri,' he said to me, 'I don't know when we will see each other again or what the world will be like when we do. We may both have seen many horrible things. But I will think of you every time I need to be reminded that there is beauty and goodness in the world.'

'Nobu-san! Perhaps you ought to have been a poet!'

'You know perfectly well there's nothing poetic about me.'

'Do your enchanting words mean you're about to leave? I was hoping we might take a stroll together.'

'It's much too cold. But you may see me to the door, and we'll say good-bye there.'

I followed Nobu down the stairs and crouched in the entryway of the teahouse to help him into his shoes. Afterward I slipped my feet into the tall wooden *geta* I was wearing because of the snow, and walked Nobu out to the street. Years earlier a car would have been waiting for him, but only government officials had cars these days, for almost no one could find the gasoline to run them. I suggested walking him to the trolley.

'I don't want your company just now,' Nobu said. 'I'm on my way to a meeting with our Kyoto distributor. I have too many things on my mind as it is.'

'I must say, Nobu-san, I much preferred your parting words in the room upstairs.'

'In that case, stay there next time.'

I bowed and told Nobu good-bye. Most men would probably have turned to look over their shoulders at some point; but Nobu just plodded through the snow as far as the corner, and then turned up Shijo Avenue and was gone. In my hand I held the piece of paper he'd given me, with Mr. Arashino's address written on it. I realized I was squeezing it so hard in my fingers that if it were possible to crush it, I'm sure I would have. I couldn't think why I felt so nervous and afraid. But after gazing a moment at the snow still falling all around me, I looked at Nobu's deep footprints leading to the corner and had the feeling I knew just what was troubling me. When would I ever see Nobu again? Or the Chairman? Or for that matter, Gion itself? Once before, as a child, I'd been torn from my home. I suppose it was the memory of those horrible years that made me feel so alone.

29

YOU MAY THINK that because I was a successful young geisha with a great many admirers, someone else might have stepped forward to rescue me even if Nobu hadn't. But a geisha in need is hardly like a jewel dropped on the street, which anyone might be happy to pick up. Every one of the hundreds of geisha in Gion was struggling to find a nest from the war in those final weeks, and only a few were lucky enough to find one. So you see, every day I lived with the Arashino family, I felt myself more and more in Nobu's debt.

I discovered how fortunate I really was during the spring of the following year, when I learned that the geisha Raiha had been killed in the firebombing of Tokyo. It was Raiha who'd made us laugh by saying that nothing was as bleak as the future except the past. She and her mother had been prominent geisha, and her father was a member of a famous merchant family; to those of us in Gion, no one had seemed more likely to survive the war than Raiha. At the time of her death she was apparently reading a book to one of her young nephews on her father's estate in the Denenchofu section of Tokyo, and I'm sure she probably felt as safe there as she had in Kyoto. Strangely, the same air raid that killed Raiha also killed the great sumo wrestler Miyagiyama. Both had been living in relative comfort. And yet Pumpkin, who had seemed so lost to me, managed to survive the war, though the lens factory where she was working on the outskirts of Osaka was bombed five or six times. I learned that year that nothing is so unpredictable as who will survive a war and who won't. Mameha survived, working in a small hospital in Fukui Prefecture as a nurse's assistant; but her maid Tatsumi was killed by the terrible bomb that fell on Nagasaki, and her dresser, Mr. Itchoda, died of a heart attack during an air raid drill. Mr. Bekku, on the other hand, worked on a naval base in Osaka and yet survived somehow. So did General Tottori, who lived in the Suruya Inn until his death in the mid-1950s, and the Baron too – though I'm sorry to say that in the early years of the Allied Occupation, the Baron drowned himself in his splendid pond after his title and many of his holdings were taken away. I don't think he could face a world in which he was no longer free to act on his every whim.

As for Mother, there was never a moment's doubt in my mind that she would survive. With her highly developed ability to benefit from other people's suffering, she fell so naturally into work in the gray market that it was as if she'd done it all along; she spent the war growing richer instead of poorer by buying and selling other people's heirlooms. Whenever Mr. Arashino sold a kimono from his collection in order to raise cash, he asked me to contact Mother so she could recover it for him. Many of the kimono sold in Kyoto passed through her hands, you see. Mr. Arashino probably hoped Mother would forgo her profit and hold his kimono a few years until he could buy them back again; but she never seemed able to find them – or at least, that was what she said.

The Arashinos treated me with great kindness during the years I lived in their home. In the daytime, I worked with them sewing parachutes. At night I slept alongside their daughter and grandson on futons spread out on the floor of the workshop. We had so little charcoal, we burned compressed leaves for warmth – or newspapers and magazines; anything we could find. Of course food had grown still more scarce; you can't imagine some of the things we learned to eat, such as soybean dregs, usually given to livestock, and a hideous thing called *nukapan*, made by frying rice bran in wheat flour. It looked like old, dried leather though I'm sure leather would probably have tasted better. Very occasionally we had small quantities of potatoes, or sweet potatoes; dried whale meat; sausage made from seals; and sometimes sardines, which we Japanese had never regarded as anything more than fertilizer.

I grew so thin during these years that no one would have recognized me on the streets of Gion. Some days the Arashinos' little grandson, Juntaro, cried from hunger – which is when Mr. Arashino usually decided to sell a kimono from his collection. This was what we Japanese called the 'onion life' – peeling away a layer at a time and crying all the while.

One night in the spring of 1944, after I'd been living with the Arashino family no more than three or four months, we witnessed our first air raid. The stars were so clear, we could see the silhouettes of the bombers as they droned overhead, and also the shooting stars – as they seemed to us – that flew up from the earth and exploded near them. We were afraid we would hear the horrible whistling noise and watch Kyoto burst into flames all around us; and if it had, our lives would have ended right then, whether we had died or not – because Kyoto is as delicate as a moth's wing; if it had been crushed, it could never have recovered as Osaka and Tokyo, and so many other cities, were able to do. But the bombers passed us over, not only that night but every night. Many evenings we watched the moon turn red from the fires in Osaka, and sometimes we saw ashes floating through the air like falling leaves – even there in Kyoto, fifty kilometers away. You can well imagine that I worried desperately about the Chairman and Nobu, whose company was based in Osaka, and who both had homes there as well as in Kyoto. I wondered too what would become of my sister, Satsu, wherever she was. I don't think I'd ever been consciously aware of it, but since the very week she'd run away, I'd carried a belief shrouded somewhere in the back of my mind that the courses of our lives would one day bring us together again. I thought perhaps she might send a letter to me in care of the Nitta okiya, or else come back to Kyoto looking for me. Then one afternoon while I was taking little Juntaro for a walk along the river, picking out stones from the edge of the water and throwing them back in, it occurred to me that Satsu never would come back to Kyoto to find me. Now that I was living an impoverished life myself, I could see that traveling to some far-off city for any reason at all was out of the question. And in any case, Satsu and I probably wouldn't recognize each other on the street even if she did come. As for my fantasy that she might write me a letter . . . well, I felt like a foolish girl again; had it really taken me all these years to understand that Satsu had no way of knowing the name of the Nitta okiya? She couldn't write me if she wanted to – unless she contacted Mr. Tanaka, and she would never do such a thing. While little Juntaro went on throwing stones into the river, I squatted beside him and trickled water onto my face with one hand, smiling at him all the while and pretending I'd done it to cool myself. My little ruse must have worked, because Juntaro seemed to have no idea that anything was the matter.

Adversity is like a strong wind. I don't mean just that it holds us back from places we might otherwise go. It also tears away from us all but the things that cannot be torn, so that afterward we see ourselves as we really are, and not merely as we might like to be. Mr. Arashino's daughter, for example, suffered the death of her husband during the war, and afterward poured herself into two things: caring for her little boy and sewing parachutes for the soldiers. She seemed to live for nothing else. When she grew thinner and thinner, you knew where every gram of her was going. By the war's end, she clutched at that child as though he were the cliff's edge that kept her from falling to the rocks below.

Because I'd lived through adversity once before, what I learned about myself was like a reminder of something I'd once known but had nearly forgotten – namely, that beneath the elegant clothing, and the accomplished dancing, and the clever conversation, my life had no complexity at all, but was as simple as a stone falling toward the ground. My whole purpose in everything during the past ten years had been to win the affections of the Chairman. Day after day I watched the swift water of the Kamo River shallows rushing below the workshop; sometimes I threw a petal into it, or a piece of straw, knowing that it would be carried all the way to Osaka before washing out into the sea. I wondered if perhaps the Chairman, sitting at his desk, might look out his window one afternoon and see that petal or that straw and perhaps think of me. But soon I began to have a troubling thought. The

Chairman might see it, perhaps, though I doubted he would; but even if he did, and he leaned back in his chair to think of the hundred things the petal might bring to mind, I might not be one of them. He had often been kind to me, it was true; but he was a kind man. He'd never shown the least sign of recognizing that I had once been the girl he'd comforted, or that I cared for him, or thought of him.

One day I came to a realization, more painful in some ways even than my sudden understanding that Satsu and I were unlikely to be reunited. I'd spent the previous night nursing a troubling thought, wondering for the first time what might happen if I reached the end of my life and still the Chairman had never taken any special notice of me. That next morning I looked carefully at my almanac in the hopes of finding some sign that my life wouldn't be lived without purpose. I was feeling so dejected that even Mr. Arashino seemed to recognize it, and sent me on an errand to purchase sewing needles at the dry goods store thirty minutes away. On my walk back, strolling along the roadside as the sun was setting, I was nearly run down by an army truck. It's the closest I've ever come to being killed. Only the next morning did I notice that my almanac had warned against travel in the direction of the Rat, precisely the direction in which the dry goods store lay; I'd been looking only for a sign about the Chairman, and hadn't noticed. From this experience I understood the danger of focusing only on what isn't there. What if I came to the end of my life and realized that I'd spent every day watching for a man who would never come to me? What an unbearable sorrow it would be, to realize I'd never really tasted the things I'd eaten, or seen the places I'd been, because I'd thought of nothing but the Chairman even while my life was drifting away from me. And yet if I drew my thoughts back from him, what life would I have? I would be like a dancer who had practiced since childhood for a performance she would never give.

The war ended for us in August of 1945. Most anyone who lived in Japan during this time will tell you that it was the very bleakest moment in a long night of darkness. Our country wasn't simply defeated, it was destroyed – and I don't mean by all the bombs, as horrible as those were. When your country has lost a war and an invading army pours in, you feel as though you yourself have been led to the execution ground to kneel, hands bound, and wait for the sword to fall. During a period of a year or more, I never once heard the sound of laughter – unless it was little Juntaro, who didn't know any better. And when Juntaro laughed, his grandfather waved a hand to shush him. I've often observed that men and women who were young children during these years have a certain seriousness about them; there was too little laughter in their childhoods.

By the spring of 1946, we'd all come to recognize that we would live through the ordeal of defeat. There were even those who believed Japan would one day be renewed. All the stories about invading American soldiers raping and killing us had turned out to be wrong; and in fact, we gradually came to realize that the Americans on the whole were remarkably kind. One day an entourage of them came riding through the area in their trucks. I stood watching them with the other women from the neighborhood. I'd learned during my years in Gion to regard myself as the inhabitant of a special world that separated me from other women; and in fact, I'd felt so separated all these years that I'd only rarely wondered how other women lived – even the wives of the men I'd entertained. Yet there I stood in a pair of torn work pants, with my stringy hair hanging along my back. I hadn't bathed in several days, for we had no fuel to heat the water more than a few times each week. To the eyes of the American soldiers who drove past, I looked no different from the women around me; and as I thought of it, who could say I was any different? If you no longer have leaves, or bark, or roots, can you go on calling yourself a tree? 'I am a peasant,' I said to myself, 'and not a geisha at all any longer.' It was a frightening feeling to look at my hands and see their roughness. To draw my mind away from my fears, I turned my attention again to the truckloads of soldiers driving past. Weren't these the very American soldiers we'd been taught to hate, who had bombed our cities with such horrifying weapons? Now they rode through our neighborhood, throwing pieces of candy to the children.

Within a year after the surrender, Mr. Arashino had been encouraged to begin making kimono once again. I knew nothing about kimono except how to wear them, so I was given the task of spending my days in the basement of the workshop annex, tending to the vats of dye as they boiled. This was a horrid job, partly because we couldn't afford any fuel but *tadon*, which is a kind of coal dust held together by tar; you cannot imagine the stench when it burns. Over time Mr. Arashino's wife taught me how to gather the proper leaves, stems, and bark to make the dyes myself, which may sound like something of a promotion. And it might have been, except that one of the materials – I never found out which – had the strange effect of pickling my skin. My delicate dancer's hands, which I'd once nurtured with the finest creams, now began to peel like the papery outside of an onion, and were stained all over the color of a bruise. During this time – impelled probably by my own loneliness – I became involved in a brief romance with a young tatami maker named Inoue. I thought he looked quite handsome, with his soft eyebrows like smudges on his delicate skin and a perfect smoothness to his lips. Every few nights during the course of several weeks, I sneaked into the annex to let him in. I didn't realize quite how gruesome my hands looked until one night when the fire under the vats was burning so brightly we could see each other. After Inoue caught a glimpse of my hands, he wouldn't let me touch him with them!

To allow my skin some relief, Mr. Arashino gave me the task of gathering spiderworts during the summertime. The spiderwort is a flower whose juice is used for painting the silks before they're masked with starch and then dyed. They tend to grow around the edges of ponds and lakes during the rainy season. I thought gathering them sounded like a pleasant job, so one morning in July, I set out with my rucksack, ready to enjoy the cool, dry day; but soon I discovered that spiderworts are devilishly clever flowers. As far as I could tell, they'd enlisted every insect in western Japan as an ally. Whenever I tore off a handful of flowers, I was attacked by divisions of ticks and mosquitoes; and to make matters worse, one time I stepped on a hideous little frog. Then after I'd spent a miserable week gathering the flowers, I took on what I thought would be a much easier task, of squeezing them in a press to extract their juices. But if you've never smelled the juice of a spiderwort . . . well, I was very glad at the end of the week to go back to boiling dyes once again.

I worked very hard during those years. But every night when I went to bed, I thought of Gion. All the geisha districts in Japan had reopened within a few months of the surrender; but I wasn't free to go back until Mother summoned me. She was making quite a good living selling kimono, artwork, and Japanese swords to American soldiers. So for the time being, she and Auntie remained on the little farm west of Kyoto where they had set up shop, while I continued to live and work with the Arashino family.

Considering that Gion was only a few kilometers away, you may think I visited there often. And yet in the nearly five years I lived away, I went only once. It was one afternoon during the spring, about a year after the end of the war, while I was on my way back from picking up medicine for little Juntaro at the Kamigyo Prefectural Hospital. I took a walk along Kawaramachi Avenue as far as Shijo and crossed the bridge from there into Gion. I was shocked to see whole families crowded together in poverty along the river's edge.

In Gion I recognized a number of geisha, though of course they didn't recognize me; and I didn't speak a word to them, hoping for once to view the place as an outsider might. In truth, though, I could scarcely see Gion at all as I strolled through it; I saw instead only my ghostly memories. When I walked along the banks of the Shirakawa Stream, I thought of the many afternoons Mameha and I had spent walking there. Nearby was the bench where Pumpkin and I had sat with two bowls of noodles on the night I asked for her help. Not far away was the alleyway where Nobu had chastened me for taking the General as my *danna*. From there I walked half a block to the corner of Shijo Avenue where I'd made the young delivery man drop the lunch boxes he was carrying. In all of these spots, I felt I was standing on a stage many hours after the dance had ended, when the silence lay as heavily upon the empty theater as a blanket of snow. I went to our okiya and stared with longing at the heavy iron padlock on the door. When I was locked in, I wanted to be out. Now life had changed so much that, finding myself locked out, I wanted to be inside again. And yet I was a grown woman – free, if I wished, to stroll out of Gion at that very moment and never come back.

One bitter cold afternoon in November, three years after the end of the war, I was warming my hands over the dye vats in the annex when Mrs. Arashino came down to say that someone wished to see me. I could tell from her expression that the visitor wasn't just another of the women from the neighborhood. But you can imagine my surprise when I reached the top of the stairs and saw Nobu. He was sitting in the workshop with Mr. Arashino, holding an empty teacup as though he'd been there chatting for some time already. Mr. Arashino stood when he saw me.

'I have some work in the next room, Nobu-san,' he said. 'You two can stay here and talk. I'm delighted you've come to see us.'

'Don't fool yourself, Arashino,' Nobu replied. 'Sayuri is the person I've come to see.'

I thought this an unkind thing for Nobu to have said, and not at all funny; but Mr. Arashino laughed when he heard it and rolled the door of the workshop closed behind him.

'I thought the whole world had changed,' I said. 'But it can't be so, for Nobu-san has stayed exactly the same.'

'I never change,' he said. 'But I haven't come here to chat. I want to know what's the matter with you.'

'Nothing is the matter. Hasn't Nobu-san been receiving my letters?'

'Your letters all read like poems! You never talk about anything but "the beautiful, trickling water" or some such nonsense.'

'Why, Nobu-san, I'll never waste another letter on you!'

'I'd rather you didn't, if that's how they sound. Why can't you just tell me the things I want to know, such as when you're coming back to Gion? Every month I telephone the Ichiriki to ask about you, and the mistress gives some excuse or other. I thought I might find you ill with some horrible disease. You're skinnier than you were, I suppose, but you look healthy enough to me. What's keeping you?'

'I certainly think of Gion every day.'

'Your friend Mameha came back a year or more ago. Even Michizono, as old as she is, showed up the day it reopened. But no one has been able to tell me why Sayuri won't come back.'

'To tell the truth, the decision isn't mine. I've been waiting for Mother to reopen the okiya. I'm as eager to get back to Gion as Nobu-san is to have me there.'

'Then call that mother of yours and tell her the time has come. I've been patient the past six months. Didn't you understand what I was telling you in my letters?'

'When you said you wanted me back in Gion, I thought you meant that you hoped to see me there soon.'

'If I say I want to see you back in Gion, what I mean is, I want you to pack your bags and go back to Gion. I don't see why you need to wait for that mother of yours anyway! If she hasn't had the sense to go back by now, she's a fool.'

'Few people have anything good to say about her, but I can assure you she's no fool. Nobu-san might even admire her, if he came to know her. She's making a fine living selling souvenirs to American soldiers.'

'The soldiers won't be here forever. You tell her your good friend Nobu wants you back in Gion.' At this, he took a little package with his one hand and tossed it onto the mats next to me. He didn't say a word afterward, but only sipped at his tea and looked at me.

'What is Nobu-san throwing at me?' I said.

'It's a gift I've brought. Open it.'

'If Nobu-san is giving me a gift, first I must bring my gift for him.'

I went to the corner of the room, where I kept my trunk of belongings, and found a folding fan I'd long ago decided to give to Nobu. A fan may seem a simple gift for the man who'd saved me from life in the factories. But to a geisha, the fans we use in dance are like sacred objects – and this wasn't just an ordinary dancer's fan, but the very one my teacher had given me when I reached the level of *shisho* in the Inoue School of dance. I'd never before heard of a geisha parting with such a thing – which was the very reason I'd decided to give it to him.

I wrapped the fan in a square of cotton and went back to present it to him. He was puzzled when he opened it, as I knew he would be. I did my best to explain why I wanted him to have it.

'It's kind of you,' he said, 'but I'm unworthy of this gift. Offer it to someone who appreciates dance more than I do.'

'There's no one else I would give it to. It's a part of me, and I have given it to Nobu-san.'

'In that case, I'm very grateful and I'll cherish it. Now open the package I've brought you.'

Wrapped inside paper and string, and padded with layers of newspaper, was a rock about the size of a fist. I'm sure I was at least as puzzled to receive a rock as Nobu must have been by the fan I'd given him. When I looked at it more closely, I saw it wasn't a rock at all, but a piece of concrete.

'You have in your hand some rubble from our factory in Osaka,' Nobu told me. 'Two of our four factories were destroyed. There's a danger our whole company may not survive the next few years. So you see, if you've given me a piece of yourself with that fan, I suppose I've just given you a piece of myself as well.'

'If it's a piece of Nobu-san, then I will cherish it.'

'I didn't give it to you to cherish. It's a piece of concrete! I want you to help me turn it into a lovely jewel for you to keep.'

'If Nobu-san knows how to do such a thing, please tell me, and we'll all be rich!'

'I have a task for you to do in Gion. If it works out as I hope, our company will be back on its feet in a year or so. When I ask you for that piece of concrete back and replace it with a jewel instead, the time will have come at last for me to become your *danna*.'

My skin felt as cold as glass when I heard this; but I showed no sign of it. 'How mysterious, Nobu-san. A task *I* could undertake, which would be helpful to Iwamura Electric?'

'It's an awful task. I won't lie to you. During the final two years before Gion closed, there was a man named Sato who used to go to parties as a guest of the Prefectural Governor. I want you to come back so you can entertain him.'

I had to laugh when I heard this. 'How horrible a task can that be? However much Nobu-san dislikes him, I'm sure I've entertained worse.'

'If you remember him, you'll know exactly how horrible it is. He's irritating, and he acts like a pig. He tells me he always sat across the table so he could stare at you. You're the only thing he ever talks about – when he talks, that is; because mostly he just sits. Maybe you saw him mentioned in the news magazines last month; he was just appointed to be a Deputy Minister of Finance.'

'My goodness!' I said. 'He must be very capable.'

'Oh, there are fifteen or more men who hold that title. I know he's capable of pouring sake into his mouth; that's the only thing I've ever seen him do. It's a tragedy that the future of a great company like ours should be affected by a man like him! It's a terrible time to be alive, Sayuri.'

'Nobu-san! You mustn't say a thing like that.'

'Why on earth not? No one's going to hear me.'

'It isn't a matter of who hears you. It's your attitude! You shouldn't think that way.'

'Why shouldn't I? The company has never been in worse condition. All through the war, the Chairman resisted what the government told him to do. By the time he finally agreed to cooperate, the war was almost over, and nothing we ever made for them – not one thing – was taken into battle. But has that stopped the Americans from classifying Iwamura Electric as a *zaibatsu* just like Mitsubishi? It's ridiculous. Compared to Mitsubishi, we were like a sparrow watching a lion. And there's something worse: if we can't convince them of our case, Iwamura Electric will be seized, and its assets sold to pay war reparations! Two weeks ago I'd have said that was bad enough, but now they've appointed this fellow Sato to make a recommendation about our case. Those Americans think they were clever to appoint a Japanese. Well, I'd rather have seen a dog take the job than this man.' Suddenly Nobu interrupted himself. 'What on earth is the matter with your hands?'

Since coming up from the annex, I'd kept my hands hidden as best I could. Obviously Nobu had caught sight of them somehow. 'Mr. Arashino was kind enough to give me the job of making dyes.'

'Let's hope he knows how to remove those stains,' said Nobu. 'You can't go back to Gion looking like that.'

'Nobu-san, my hands are the least of my problems. I'm not sure I can go back to Gion at all. I'll do my best to persuade Mother, but truthfully, it isn't my decision. Anyway, I'm sure there are other geisha who'll be helpful –'

'There aren't other geisha! Listen to me, I took Deputy Minister Sato to a teahouse the other day with half a dozen people. He didn't speak a word for an hour, and then finally he cleared his throat and said, "This isn't the Ichiriki." So I told him, "No, it's not. You certainly got that right!" He grunted like a pig, and then said, "Sayuri entertains at the Ichiriki." So I told him, "No, Minister, if she were in Gion at all, she would come right here and entertain us. But I told you – she isn't in Gion!" So then he took his sake cup –'

'I hope you were more polite with him than that,' I said.

'I certainly wasn't! I can tolerate his company for about half an hour. After that I'm not responsible for the things I say. That's exactly the reason I want you there! And don't tell me again it isn't your decision. You owe this to me, and you know it perfectly well. Anyway, the truth is . . . I'd like the chance to spend some time with you myself . . .'

'And I would like to spend time with Nobu-san.'

'Just don't bring any illusions with you when you come.'

'After the past few years, I'm sure I don't have any left. But is Nobu-san thinking of something in particular?'

'Don't expect me to become your *danna* in a month, that's what I'm saying. Until Iwamura Electric has recovered, I'm in no position to make such an offer. I've been very worried about the company's prospects. But to tell the truth, Sayuri, I feel better about the future after seeing you again.'

'Nobu-san! How kind!'

'Don't be ridiculous, I'm not trying to flatter you. Your destiny and mine are intertwined. But I'll never be your *danna* if Iwamura Electric doesn't recover. Perhaps the recovery, just like my meeting you in the first place, is simply meant to be.'

During the final years of the war, I'd learned to stop wondering what was meant to be and what wasn't. I'd often said to the women in the neighborhood that I wasn't sure if I'd ever go back to Gion – but the truth is, I'd always known I would. My destiny, whatever it was, awaited me there. In these years away, I'd learned to suspend all the water in my personality by turning it to ice, you might say. Only by stopping the natural flow of my thoughts in this way could I bear the waiting. Now to hear Nobu refer to my destiny . . . well, I felt he'd shattered the ice inside me and awakened my desires once again.

'Nobu-san,' I said, 'if it's important to make a good impression on Deputy Minister Sato, perhaps you should ask the Chairman to be there when you entertain him.'

'The Chairman is a busy man.'

'But surely if the Minister is important to the future of the company –'

'You worry about getting yourself there. I'll worry about what's best for the company. I'll be very disappointed if you're not back in Gion by the end of the month.'

Nobu rose to leave, for he had to be back in Osaka before nightfall. I walked him to the entryway to help him into his coat and shoes, and put his fedora on his head for him. When I was done, he stood looking at me a long while. I thought he was about to say he found me beautiful – for this was the sort of comment he sometimes made after gazing at me for no reason.

'My goodness, Sayuri, you do look like a peasant!' he said. He had a scowl on his face as he turned away.

30

THAT VERY NIGHT while the Arashinos slept, I wrote to Mother by the light of the *tadon* burning under the dye vats in the annex. Whether my letter had the proper effect or whether Mother was already prepared to reopen the okiya, I don't know; but a week later an old woman's voice called out at the Arashinos' door, and I rolled it open to find Auntie there. Her cheeks had sunken where she'd lost teeth, and the sickly gray of her skin made me think of a piece of sashimi left on the plate overnight. But I could see that she was still a strong woman; she was carrying a bag of coal in one hand and foodstuffs in the other, to thank the Arashinos for their kindness toward me.

The next day I said a tearful farewell and went back to Gion, where Mother, Auntie, and I set about the task of putting things back in order. When I'd had a look around the okiya, the thought crossed my mind that the house itself was punishing us for our years of neglect. We had to spend four or five days on only the worst of the problems: wiping down the dust that lay as heavily as gauze over the woodwork; fishing the remains of dead rodents from the well; cleaning Mother's room upstairs, where birds had torn up the tatami mats and used the straw to make nests in the alcove. To my surprise, Mother worked as hard as any of us, partly because we could afford only a cook and one adult maid, though we did also have a young girl named Etsuko. She was the daughter of the man on whose farm Mother and Auntie had been living. As if to remind me of how many years had passed since I first came to Kyoto as a nine-year-old girl, Etsuko herself was nine. She seemed to regard me with the same fear I'd once felt toward

Hatsumomo, even though I smiled at her whenever I could. She stood as tall and thin as a broom, with long hair that trailed behind her as she scurried about. And her face was narrow like a grain of rice, so that I couldn't help thinking that one day she too would be thrown into the pot just as I had been, and would fluff up white and delicious, to be consumed.

When the okiya was livable again, I set out to pay my respects around Gion. I began by calling on Mameha, who was now in a one-room apartment above a pharmacy near the Gion Shrine; since her return a year earlier, she'd had no *danna* to pay for anything more spacious. She was startled when she first saw me – because of the way my cheekbones protruded, she said. The truth was, I felt just as startled to see her. The beautiful oval of her face was unchanged, but her neck looked sinewy and much too old for her. The strangest thing was that she sometimes held her mouth puckered like an old woman's, because her teeth, though I could see no difference in them, had been quite loose at one time during the war and still caused her pain.

We talked for a long while, and then I asked if she thought *Dances of the Old Capital* would resume the following spring. The performances hadn't been seen in a number of years.

'Oh, why not?' she said. 'The theme can be the "Dance in the Stream"!'

If you've ever visited a hot springs resort or some such place, and been entertained by women masquerading as geisha who are really prostitutes, you'll understand Mameha's little joke. A woman who performs the 'Dance in the Stream' is really doing a kind of striptease. She pretends to wade into deeper and deeper water, all the while raising her kimono to keep the hem dry, until the men finally see what they've been waiting for, and begin to cheer and toast one another with sake.

'With all the American soldiers in Gion these days,' she went on, 'English will get you further than dance. Anyway, the Kaburenjo Theater has been turned into a *kyabarei*.'

I'd never heard this word before, which came from the

English 'cabaret,' but I learned soon enough what it meant. Even while living with the Arashino family, I'd heard stories about American soldiers and their noisy parties. Still I was shocked when I stepped into the entryway of a teahouse later that afternoon and found – instead of the usual row of men's shoes at the base of the step – a confusion of army boots, each of which looked as big to me as Mother's little dog Taku had been. Inside the front entrance hall, the first thing I saw was an American man in his underwear squeezing himself beneath the shelf of an alcove while two geisha, both laughing, tried to pull him out. When I looked at the dark hair on his arms and chest, and even on his back, I had the feeling I'd never seen anything quite so beastly. He'd apparently lost his clothing in a drinking game and was trying to hide, but soon he let the women draw him out by the arms and lead him back down the hall and through a door. I heard whistling and cheering when he entered.

About a week after my return, I was finally ready to make my first appearance as a geisha again. I spent a day rushing from the hairdresser's to the fortune-teller's; soaking my hands to remove the last of the stains; and searching all over Gion to find the makeup I needed. Now that I was nearing thirty, I would no longer be expected to wear white makeup except on special occasions. But I did spend a half hour at my makeup stand that day, trying to use different shades of Western-style face powder to hide how thin I'd grown. When Mr. Bekku came to dress me, young Etsuko stood and watched just as I had once watched Hatsumomo; and it was the astonishment in her eyes, more than anything I saw while looking in the mirror, that convinced me I truly looked like a geisha once again.

When at last I set out that evening, all of Gion was blanketed in a beautiful snow so powdery the slightest wind blew the roofs clean. I wore a kimono shawl and carried a lacquered umbrella, so I'm sure I was as unrecognizable as the day I'd visited Gion looking like a peasant. I recognized only about half the geisha I passed. It was easy to tell those who'd lived in Gion before the war, because they gave a little bow of courtesy as they passed, even when they didn't seem to recognize me. The others didn't bother with more than a nod.

Seeing soldiers here and there on the streets, I dreaded what I might find when I reached the Ichiriki. But in fact, the entryway was lined with the shiny black shoes worn by officers; and strangely enough, the teahouse seemed quieter than in my days as an apprentice. Nobu hadn't yet arrived – or at least, I didn't see any sign of him – but I was shown directly into one of the large rooms on the ground floor and told he would join me there shortly Ordinarily I would have waited in the maids' quarters up the hallway, where I could warm my hands and sip a cup of tea; no geisha likes a man to find her idle. But I didn't mind waiting for Nobu – and besides, I considered it a privilege to spend a few minutes by myself in such a room. I'd been starved for beauty over the past five years, and this was a room that would have astonished you with its loveliness. The walls were covered with a pale yellow silk whose texture gave a kind of presence, and made me feel held by them just as an egg is held by its shell.

I'd expected Nobu to arrive by himself, but when I finally heard him in the hallway, it was clear he'd brought Deputy Minister Sato with him. I didn't mind if Nobu found me waiting, as I've mentioned; but I thought it would be disastrous to give the Minister reason to think I might be unpopular. So I slipped quickly through the adjoining doors into an unused room. As it turned out, this gave me a chance to listen to Nobu struggle to be pleasant.

'Isn't this quite a room, Minister?' he said. I heard a little grunt in reply. 'I requested it especially for you. That painting in the Zen style is really something, don't you think?' Then after a long silence, Nobu added, 'Yes, it's a beautiful night. Oh, did I already ask if you've tasted the Ichiriki Teahouse's own special brand of sake?'

Things continued in this way, with Nobu probably feeling about as comfortable as an elephant trying to act like a butterfly. When at length I went into the hallway and slid open the door, Nobu seemed very relieved to see me.

I got my first good look at the Minister only after introducing myself and going to kneel at the table. He didn't look at all familiar, though he'd claimed to have spent hours staring at me. I don't know how I managed to forget him, because he had a very distinctive appearance; I've never seen anyone who had more trouble just lugging his face around. He kept his chin tucked against his breastbone as though he couldn't quite hold up his head, and he had a peculiar lower jaw that protruded so that his breath seemed to blow right up his nose. After he gave me a little nod and said his name, it was a long while before I heard any sound from him other than grunts, for a grunt seemed to be his way of responding to almost anything.

I did my best to make conversation until the maid rescued us by arriving with a tray of sake. I filled the Minister's cup and was astonished to watch him pour the sake directly into his lower jaw in the same way he might have poured it into a drain. He shut his mouth for a moment and then opened it again, and the sake was gone, without any of the usual signs people make when they swallow. I wasn't really sure he'd swallowed at all until he held out his empty cup.

Things went on like this for fifteen minutes or more while I tried to put the Minister at his ease by telling him stories and jokes, and asking him a few questions. But soon I began to think perhaps there was no such thing as 'the Minister at his ease.' He never gave me an answer of more than a single word. I suggested we play a drinking game; I even asked if he liked to sing. The longest exchange we had in our first half hour was when the Minister asked if I was a dancer.

'Why yes, I am. Would the Minister like me to perform a short piece?'

'No,' he said. And that was the end of it.

The Minister may not have liked making eye contact with people, but he certainly liked to study his food, as I discovered after a maid arrived with dinner for the two men. Before putting anything in his mouth, he held it up with his chopsticks and peered at it, turning it this way and that. And if he didn't recognize it, he asked me what it was. 'It's a piece of yam boiled in soy sauce and sugar,' I told him when he held up something orange. Actually I didn't have the least idea whether it was yam, or a slice of whale liver; or anything else, but I didn't think the Minister wanted to hear that. Later, when he held up a piece of marinated beef and asked me about it, I decided to tease him a bit.

'Oh, that's a strip of marinated leather,' I said. 'It's a specialty of the house here! It's made from the skin of elephants. So I guess I should have said "elephant leather."'

'Elephant leather?'

'Now Minister, you know I'm teasing you! It's a piece of beef. Why do you look at your food so closely? Did you think you would come here and eat dog or something?'

'I've eaten dog, you know,' he said to me.

'That's very interesting. But we don't have any dog here tonight. So don't look at your chopsticks anymore.'

Very soon we began playing a drinking game. Nobu hated drinking games, but he kept quiet after I made a face at him. We may have let the Minister lose a bit more often than we should have, because later, as we were trying to explain the rules to a drinking game he'd never played, his eyes became as unsteady as corks floating in the surf. All at once he stood up and headed off toward one corner of the room.

'Now, Minister,' Nobu said to him, 'exactly where are you planning on going?'

The Minister's answer was to let out a burp, which I considered a very well-spoken reply because it was apparent he was about to throw up. Nobu and I rushed over to help him, but he'd already clamped his hand over his mouth. If he'd been a volcano, he would have been smoking by this time, so we had no choice but to roll open the glass doors to the garden to let him vomit onto the snow there. You may be appalled at the thought of a man throwing up into one of these exquisite decorative gardens, but the Minister certainly wasn't the first. We geisha try to help a man down the hallway to the toilet, but sometimes we can't manage it. If we say to one of the maids that a man has just visited the garden, they all know exactly what we mean and come at once with their cleaning supplies.

Nobu and I did our best to keep the Minister kneeling in the doorway with his head suspended over the snow. But despite our efforts he soon tumbled out headfirst. I did my best to shove him to one side, so he would at least end up in snow that hadn't yet been vomited upon. But the Minister was as bulky as a thick piece of meat. All I really did was turn him onto his side as he fell.

Nobu and I could do nothing but look at each other in dismay at the sight of the Minister lying perfectly still in the deep snow, like a branch that had fallen from a tree.

'Why, Nobu-san,' I said, 'I didn't know how much fun your guest was going to be.'

'I believe we've killed him. And if you ask me, he deserved it. What an irritating man!'

'Is this how you act toward your honored guests? You must take him out onto the street and walk him around a bit to wake him up. The cold will do him good.'

'He's lying in the snow. Isn't that cold enough?'

'Nobu-san!' I said. And I suppose this was enough of a reprimand, for Nobu let out a sigh and stepped down into the garden in his stocking feet to begin the task of bringing the Minister back to consciousness. While he was busy with this, I went to find a maid who could help, because I couldn't see how Nobu would get the Minister back up into the teahouse with only one arm. Afterward I fetched some dry socks for the two men and alerted a maid to tidy the garden after we'd left.

When I returned to the room, Nobu and the Minister were at the table again. You can imagine how the Minister looked – and smelled. I had to peel his wet socks off his feet with my own hands, but I kept my distance from him while doing it. As soon as I was done, he slumped back onto the mats and was unconscious again a moment later.

'Do you think he can hear us?' I whispered to Nobu.

'I don't think he hears us even when he's conscious,' Nobu said. 'Did you ever meet a bigger fool in your life?'

'Nobu-san, quietly!' I whispered. 'Do you think he actually enjoyed himself tonight? I mean, is this the sort of evening you had in mind?'

'It isn't a matter of what I had in mind. It's what he had in mind.'

'I hope that doesn't mean we'll be doing the same thing again next week.'

'If the Minister is pleased with the evening, I'm pleased with the evening.'

'Nobu-san, really! You certainly weren't pleased. You looked as miserable as I've ever seen you. Considering the Minister's condition, I think we can assume he isn't having the best night of his life either . . .'

'You can't assume anything, when it comes to the Minister.'

'I'm sure he'll have a better time if we can make the atmosphere more . . . festive somehow. Wouldn't you agree?'

'Bring a few more geisha next time, if you think it will help,' Nobu said. 'We'll come back next weekend. Invite that older sister of yours.'

'Mameha's certainly clever, but the Minister is so exhausting to entertain. We need a geisha who's going to, I don't know, make a lot of noise! Distract everyone. You know, now that I think of it . . . it seems to me we need another guest as well, not just another geisha.'

'I can't see any reason for that.'

'If the Minister is busy drinking and sneaking looks at me, and you're busy growing increasingly fed up with him, we're not going to have a very festive evening,' I said. 'To tell the truth, Nobu-san, perhaps you should bring the Chairman with you next time.'

You may wonder if I'd been plotting all along to bring the evening to this moment. It's certainly true that in coming back to Gion, I'd hoped more than anything else to find a way of spending time with the Chairman. It wasn't so much that I craved the chance to sit in the same room with him again, to lean in and whisper some comment and take in the scent of his skin. If those sorts of moments would be the only pleasure life offered me, I'd be better off shutting out that one brilliant source of light to let my eyes begin to adjust to the darkness. Perhaps it was true, as it now seemed, that my life was falling toward Nobu. I wasn't so foolish as to imagine I could change the course of my destiny. But neither could I give up the last traces of hope.

'I've considered bringing the Chairman,' Nobu replied. 'The Minister is very impressed with him. But I don't know,

Sayuri. I told you once already. He's a busy man.'

The Minister jerked on the mats as if someone had poked him, and then managed to pull himself up until he was sitting at the table. Nobu was so disgusted at the sight of his clothing that he sent me out to bring back a maid with a damp towel. After the maid had cleaned the Minister's jacket and left us alone again, Nobu said:

'Well, Minister, this certainly has been a wonderful evening! Next time we'll have even more fun, because instead of throwing up on just me, you might be able to throw up on the Chairman, and perhaps another geisha or two as well!'

I was very pleased to hear Nobu mention the Chairman, but I didn't dare react.

'I like this geisha,' said the Minister. 'I don't want another one.'

'Her name is Sayuri, and you'd better call her that, or she won't agree to come. Now stand up, Minister. It's time for us to get you home.'

I walked them as far as the entryway, where I helped them into their coats and shoes and watched the two of them set out in the snow. The Minister was having such a hard time, he would have trudged right into the gate if Nobu hadn't taken him by the elbow to steer him.

Later the same night, I dropped in with Mameha on a party full of American officers. By the time we arrived, their translator was of no use to anyone because they'd made him drink so much; but the officers all recognized Mameha. I was a bit surprised when they began humming and waving their arms, signaling to her that they wanted her to put on a dance. I expected we would sit quietly and watch her, but the moment she began, several of the officers went up and started prancing around alongside. If you'd told me it would happen, I might have felt a little uncertain beforehand; but to see it . . . well, I burst out laughing and enjoyed myself more than I had in a long while. We ended up playing a game in which Mameha and I took turns on the shamisen while the American officers danced around the table. Whenever we stopped the music, they had to rush back to their places. The last to sit drank a penalty glass of sake.

In the middle of the party I commented to Mameha how peculiar it was to see everyone having so much fun without speaking the same language – considering that I'd been at a party with Nobu and another Japanese man earlier that evening, and we'd had an awful time. She asked me a bit about the party.

'Three people can certainly be too few,' she said after I'd told her about it, 'particularly if one of them is Nobu in a foul mood.'

'I suggested he bring the Chairman next time. And we need another geisha as well, don't you think? Someone loud and funny'

'Yes,' said Mameha, 'perhaps I'll stop by . . .'

I was puzzled at first to hear her say this. Because really, no one on earth would have described Mameha as 'loud and funny.' I was about to tell her again what I meant, when all at once she seemed to recognize our misunderstanding and said, 'Yes, I'm interested to stop by . . . but I suppose if you want someone loud and funny, you ought to speak to your old friend Pumpkin.'

Since returning to Gion, I'd encountered memories of Pumpkin everywhere. In fact, the very moment I'd stepped into the okiya for the first time, I'd remembered her there in the formal entrance hall on the day Gion had closed, when she'd given me a stiff farewell bow of the sort she was obliged to offer the adopted daughter. I'd gone on thinking of her again and again all during that week as we cleaned. At one point, while helping the maid wipe the dust from the woodwork, I pictured Pumpkin on the walkway right before me, practicing her shamisen. The empty space there seemed to hold a terrible sadness within it. Had it really been so many years since we were girls together? I suppose I might easily have put it all out of my mind, but I'd never quite learned to accept the disappointment of our friendship running dry. I blamed the terrible rivalry that Hatsumomo had forced upon us. My adoption was the final blow of course, but still I couldn't help holding myself partly accountable. Pumpkin had shown me only kindness. I might have found some way to thank her for that.

Strangely, I hadn't thought of approaching Pumpkin until Mameha suggested it. I had no doubt our first encounter would be awkward, but I mulled it over the rest of that night and decided that maybe Pumpkin would appreciate being introduced into a more elegant circle, as a change from the soldiers' parties. Of course, I had another motive as well. Now that so many years had passed, perhaps we might begin to mend our friendship.

I knew almost nothing about Pumpkin's circumstances, except that she was back in Gion, so I went to speak with Auntie, who had received a letter from her several years earlier. It turned out that in the letter, Pumpkin had pleaded to be taken back into the okiya when it reopened, saying she would never find a place for herself otherwise. Auntie might have been willing to do it, but Mother had refused on the grounds that Pumpkin was a poor investment.

'She's living in a sad little okiya over in the Hanami-cho section,' Auntie told me. 'But don't take pity on her and bring her back here for a visit. Mother won't want to see her. I think it's foolish for you to speak with her anyway.'

'I have to admit,' I said, 'I've never felt right about what happened between Pumpkin and me . . .'

'Nothing happened between you. Pumpkin fell short and you succeeded. Anyway, she's doing very well these days. I hear the Americans can't get enough of her. She's crude, you know, in just the right sort of way for them.'

That very afternoon I crossed Shijo Avenue to the Hanami-cho section of Gion, and found the sad little okiya Auntie had told me about. If you remember Hatsumomo's friend Korin, and how her okiya had burned during the darkest years of the war . . . well, that fire had damaged the okiya next door as well, and this was where Pumpkin was now living. Its exterior walls were charred all along one side, and a part of the tiled roof that had burned away was crudely patched with wooden boards. I suppose in sections of Tokyo or Osaka, it might have been the most intact building in the neighborhood; but it stood out in the middle of Kyoto.

A young maid showed me into a reception room that smelled of wet ash, and came back later to serve me a cup of weak tea. I waited a long while before Pumpkin at last came and slid open the door. I could scarcely see her in the dark hallway outside, but just knowing she was there made me feel such warmth, I rose from the table to go and embrace her. She took a few steps into the room and then knelt and gave a bow as formal as if I'd been Mother. I was startled by this, and stopped where I stood.

'Really, Pumpkin . . . it's only me!' I said.

She wouldn't even look at me, but kept her eyes to the mats like a maid awaiting orders. I felt very disappointed and went back to my place at the table.

When we'd last seen each other in the final years of the war, Pumpkin's face had still been round and full just as in childhood, but with a more sorrowful look. She had changed a great deal in the years since. I didn't know it at the time, but after the closing of the lens factory where she'd worked, Pumpkin spent more than two years in Osaka as a prostitute. Her mouth seemed to have shrunken in size – perhaps because she held it taut, I don't know. And though she had the same broad face, her heavy cheeks had thinned, leaving her with a gaunt elegance that was astonishing to me. I don't mean to suggest Pumpkin had become a beauty to rival Hatsumomo or anything of the sort, but her face had a certain womanliness that had never been there before.

'I'm sure the years have been difficult, Pumpkin,' I said to her, 'but you look quite lovely.'

Pumpkin didn't reply to this. She just inclined her head faintly to indicate she'd heard me. I congratulated her on her popularity and tried asking about her life since the war; but she remained so expressionless that I began to feel sorry I'd come.

Finally after an awkward silence, she spoke.

'Have you come here just to chat, Sayuri? Because I don't have anything to say that will interest you.'

'The truth is,' I said, 'I saw Nobu Toshikazu recently and . . . actually, Pumpkin, he'll be bringing a certain man to Gion from time to time. I thought perhaps you'd be kind enough to help us entertain him.'

'But of course, you've changed your mind now that you've seen me.'

'Why, no,' I said. 'I don't know why you say that. Nobu Toshikazu and the Chairman – Iwamura Ken, I mean . . . Chairman Iwamura – would appreciate your company greatly. It's as simple as that.'

For a moment Pumpkin just knelt in silence, peering down at the mats. 'I've stopped believing that anything in life is "as simple as that," she said at last. 'I know you think I'm stupid –'

'Pumpkin!'

'– but I think you probably have some other reason you're not going to tell me about.'

Pumpkin gave a little bow, which I thought very enigmatic. Either it was an apology for what she'd just said, or perhaps she was about to excuse herself.

'I suppose I do have another reason,' I said. 'To tell the truth, I'd hoped that after all these years, perhaps you and I might be friends, as we once were. We've survived so many things together . . . including Hatsumomo! It seems only natural to me that we should see each other again.'

Pumpkin said nothing.

'Chairman Iwamura and Nobu will be entertaining the Minister again next Saturday at the Ichiriki Teahouse,' I told her. 'If you'll join us, I'd be very pleased to see you there.'

I'd brought her a packet of tea as a gift, and now I untied it from its silk cloth and placed it on the table. As I rose to my feet, I tried to think of something kind to tell her before leaving, but she looked so puzzled, I thought it best just to go.

31

IN THE FIVE or so years since I'd last seen the Chairman, I'd read from time to time in the newspapers about the difficulties he'd suffered – not only his disagreements with the military government in the final years of the war, but his struggle since then to keep the Occupation authorities from seizing his company. It wouldn't have surprised me if all these hardships had aged him a good deal. One photograph of him in the Yomiuri newspaper showed a strained look around his eyes from worry, like the neighbor of Mr. Arashino's who used to squint up at the sky so often, watching for bombers. In any case, as the weekend neared I had to remind myself that Nobu hadn't quite made up his mind that he would bring the Chairman. I could do nothing but hope.

On Saturday morning I awakened early and slid back the paper screen over my window to find a cold rain falling against the glass. In the little alleyway below, a young maid was just climbing to her feet again after slipping on the icy cobblestones. It was a drab, miserable day, and I was afraid even to read my almanac. By noon the temperature had dropped still further; and I could see my breath as I ate lunch in the reception room, with the sound of icy rain tapping against the window. Any number of parties that evening were canceled because the streets were too hazardous, and at nightfall Auntie telephoned the Ichiriki to be sure Iwamura Electric's party was still on. The mistress told us the telephone lines to Osaka were down, and she couldn't be sure. So I bathed and dressed, and walked over to the Ichiriki on the arm of Mr. Bekku, who wore a pair of rubber overshoes he'd borrowed from his younger brother, a dresser in the Pontocho district.

The Ichiriki was in chaos when I arrived. A water pipe had burst in the servants' quarters, and the maids were so busy, I couldn't get the attention of a single one. I showed myself down the hallway to the room where I'd entertained Nobu and the Minister the week before. I didn't really expect anyone to be there, considering that both Nobu and the Chairman would probably be traveling all the way from Osaka – and even Mameha had been out of town and might very well have had trouble returning. Before sliding open the door, I knelt a moment with my eyes closed and one hand on my stomach to calm my nerves. All at once it occurred to me that the hallway was much too quiet. I couldn't hear even a murmur from within the room. With a terrible feeling of disappointment I realized the room must be empty. I was about to stand and leave when I decided to slide open the door just in case; and when I did, there at the table, holding a magazine with both hands, sat the Chairman, looking at me over the top of his reading glasses. I was so startled to see him, I couldn't even speak. Finally I managed to say:

'My goodness, Chairman! Who has left you here all by yourself? The mistress will be very upset.'

'She's the one who left me,' he said, and slapped the magazine shut. 'I've been wondering what happened to her.'

'You don't even have a thing to drink. Let me bring you some sake.'

'That's just what the mistress said. At this rate you'll never come back, and I'll have to go on reading this magazine all night. I'd much rather have your company.' And here he removed his reading glasses, and while stowing them in his pocket, took a long look at me through narrowed eyes.

The spacious room with its pale yellow walls of silk began to seem very small to me as I rose to join the Chairman, for I don't think any room would have been enough to contain all that I was feeling. To see him again after so long awakened something desperate inside me. I was surprised to find myself feeling sad, rather than joyful, as I would have imagined. At times I'd worried that the Chairman might have fallen headlong into old age during the war just as Auntie had done. Even from across the room, I'd noticed that the corners of his eyes were creased more sharply than I remembered them. The skin around his mouth, too, had begun to sag, though it seemed to me to give his strong jaw a kind of dignity. I stole a glimpse of him as I knelt at the table, and found that he was still watching me without expression. I was about to start a conversation, but the Chairman spoke first.

'You are still a lovely woman, Sayuri.'

'Why, Chairman,' I said, 'I'll never believe another word you say. I had to spend a half hour at my makeup stand this evening to hide the sunken look of my cheeks.'

'I'm sure you've suffered worse hardships during the past several years than losing a bit of weight. I know I certainly have.'

'Chairman, if you don't mind my saying it . . . I've heard a little bit from Nobu-san about the difficulties your company is facing –'

'Yes, well, we needn't talk about that. Sometimes we get through adversity only by imagining what the world might be like if our dreams should ever come true.'

He gave me a sad smile that I found so beautiful, I lost myself staring at the perfect crescent of his lips.

'Here's a chance for you to use your charm and change the subject,' he said.

I hadn't even begun to reply before the door slid open and Mameha entered, with Pumpkin right behind her. I was surprised to see Pumpkin; I hadn't expected she would come. As for Mameha, she'd evidently just returned from Nagoya and had rushed to the Ichiriki thinking she was terribly late. The first thing she asked – after greeting the Chairman and thanking him for something he'd done for her the week before – was why Nobu and the Minister weren't present. The Chairman admitted he'd been wondering the same thing.

'What a peculiar day this has been,' Mameha said, talking almost to herself, it seemed. 'The train sat just outside Kyoto Station for an hour, and we couldn't get off. Two young men finally jumped out through the window. I think one of them may have hurt himself. And then when I finally reached the Ichiriki a moment ago, there didn't seem to be anyone here. Poor Pumpkin was wandering the hallways lost! You've met

Pumpkin, haven't you, Chairman?'

I hadn't really looked closely at Pumpkin until now, but she was wearing an extraordinary ash-gray kimono, which was spotted below the waist with brilliant gold dots that turned out to be embroidered fireflies, set against an image of mountains and water in the light of the moon. Neither mine nor Mameha's could compare with it. The Chairman seemed to find the robe as startling as I did, because he asked her to stand and model it for him. She stood very modestly and turned around once.

'I figured I couldn't set foot in a place like the Ichiriki in the sort of kimono I usually wear,' she said. 'Most of the ones at my okiya aren't very glamorous, though the Americans can't seem to tell the difference.'

'If you hadn't been so frank with us, Pumpkin,' Mameha said, 'we might have thought this was your usual attire.'

'Are you kidding me? I've never worn a robe this beautiful in my life. I borrowed it from an okiya down the street. You won't believe what they expect me to pay them, but I'll never have the money, so it doesn't make any difference, now does it?'

I could see that the Chairman was amused – because a geisha never spoke in front of a man about anything as crass as the cost of a kimono. Mameha turned to say something to him, but Pumpkin interrupted.

'I thought some big shot was going to be here tonight.'

'Maybe you were thinking of the Chairman,' Mameha said. 'Don't you think he's a "big shot"?'

'He knows whether he's a big shot. He doesn't need me to tell him.'

The Chairman looked at Mameha and raised his eyebrows in mock surprise. 'Anyway, Sayuri told me about some other guy,' Pumpkin went on.

'Sato Noritaka, Pumpkin,' the Chairman said. 'He's a new Deputy Minister of Finance.'

'Oh, I know that Sato guy. He looks just like a big pig.'

We all laughed at this. 'Really, Pumpkin,' Mameha said, 'the things that come out of your mouth!'

Just then the door slid open and Nobu and the Minister

entered, both glowing red from the cold. Behind them was a maid carrying a tray with sake and snacks. Nobu stood hugging himself with his one arm and stamping his feet, but the Minister just clumped right past him to the table. He grunted at Pumpkin and jerked his head to one side, telling her to move so he could squeeze in beside me. Introductions were made, and then Pumpkin said: 'Hey, Minister, I'll bet you don't remember me, but I know a lot about you.'

The Minister tossed into his mouth the cupful of sake I'd just poured for him, and looked at Pumpkin with what I took to be a scowl.

'What do you know?' said Mameha. 'Tell us something.'

'I know the Minister has a younger sister who's married to the mayor of Tokyo,' Pumpkin said. 'And I know he used to study karate, and broke his hand once.'

The Minister looked a bit surprised, which told me that these things must be true.

'Also, Minister, I know a girl you used to know,' Pumpkin went on. 'Nao Itsuko. We worked in a factory outside Osaka together. You know what she told me? She said the two of you did "you-know-what" together a couple of times.'

I was afraid the Minister would be angry, but instead his expression softened until I began to see what I felt certain was a glimmer of pride.

'She was a pretty girl, she was, that Itsuko,' he said, looking at Nobu with a subdued smile.

'Why, Minister,' Nobu replied, 'I'd never have guessed you had such a way with the ladies.' His words sounded very sincere, but I could see the barely concealed look of disgust on his face. The Chairman's eyes passed over mine; he seemed to find the whole encounter amusing.

A moment later the door slid open and three maids came into the room carrying dinner for the men. I was a bit hungry and had to avert my eyes from the sight of the yellow custard with gingko nuts, served in beautiful celadon cups. Later the maids came back with dishes of grilled tropical fish laid out on beds of pine needles. Nobu must have noticed how hungry I looked, for he insisted I taste it. Afterward the Chairman offered a bite to Mameha, and also to Pumpkin, who refused.

'I wouldn't touch that fish for anything,' Pumpkin said. 'I don't even want to look at it.'

'What's wrong with it?' Mameha asked.

'If I tell you, you'll only laugh at me.'

'Tell us, Pumpkin,' Nobu said.

'Why should I tell you? It's a big, long story, and anyway nobody's going to believe it.'

'Big liar!' I said.

I wasn't actually calling Pumpkin a liar. Back before the closing of Gion, we used to play a game we called 'big liar,' in which everyone had to tell two stories, only one of which was true. Afterward the other players tried to guess which was which; the ones who guessed wrong drank a penalty glass of sake.

'I'm not playing,' said Pumpkin.

'Just tell the fish story then,' said Mameha, 'and you don't have to tell another.'

Pumpkin didn't look pleased at this; but after Mameha and I had glowered at her for a while, she began.

'Oh, all right. It's like this. I was born in Sapporo, and there was an old fisherman there who caught a weird-looking fish one day that was able to speak.'

Mameha and I looked at each other and burst out laughing.

'Laugh if you want to,' Pumpkin said, 'but it's perfectly true.'

'Now, go on, Pumpkin. We're listening,' said the Chairman.

'Well, what happened was, this fisherman laid the fish out to clean it, and it began making noises that sounded just like a person talking, except the fisherman couldn't understand it. He called a bunch of other fishermen over, and they all listened for a while. Pretty soon the fish was nearly dead from being out of the water too long, so they decided to go ahead and kill it. But just then an old man made his way through the crowd and said he could understand every single word the fish was saying, because it was speaking in Russian.'

We all burst out laughing, and even the Minister made a few grunting noises. When we'd calmed down Pumpkin said, 'I knew you wouldn't believe it, but it's perfectly true!'

'I want to know what the fish was saying,' said the Chairman.

'It was nearly dead, so it was kind of . . . whispering. And when the old man leaned down and put his ear to the fish's lips –'

'Fish don't have lips!' I said.

'All right, to the fish's . . . whatever you call those things,' Pumpkin went on. 'To the edges of its mouth. And the fish said, "Tell them to go ahead and clean me. I have nothing to live for any longer. The fish over there who died a moment ago was my wife." '

'So fish get married!' said Mameha. 'They have husbands and wives!'

'That was before the war,' I said. 'Since the war, they can't afford to marry. They just swim around looking for work.'

'This happened way before the war,' said Pumpkin. 'Way, way before the war. Even before my mother was born.'

'Then how do you know it's true?' said Nobu. 'The fish certainly didn't tell it to you.'

'The fish died then and there! How could it tell me if I wasn't born yet? Besides, I don't speak Russian.'

'All right, Pumpkin,' I said, 'so you believe the Chairman's fish is a talking fish too.'

'I didn't say that. But it looks *exactly* like that talking fish did. I wouldn't eat it if I was starving to death.'

'If you hadn't been born yet,' said the Chairman, 'and even your mother hadn't been born, how do you know what the fish looked like?'

'You know what the Prime Minister looks like, don't you?' she said. 'But have you ever met him? Actually, you probably have. Let me pick a better example. You know what the Emperor looks like, but you've never had the honor of meeting him!'

'The Chairman has had the honor, Pumpkin,' Nobu said.

'You know what I mean. Everybody knows what the Emperor looks like. That's what I'm trying to say.'

'There are pictures of the Emperor,' said Nobu. 'You can't have seen a picture of the fish.'

'The fish is famous where I grew up. My mother told me all

about it, and I'm telling you, it looks like that thing right there on the table!'

'Thank heavens for people like you, Pumpkin,' said the Chairman. 'You make the rest of us seem positively dull.'

'Well, that's my story. I'm not telling another one. If the rest of you want to play "big liar," somebody else can start.'

'I'll start,' said Mameha. 'Here's my first story. When I was about six years old I went out one morning to draw water from the well in our okiya, and I heard the sound of a man clearing his throat and coughing. It was coming from inside the well. I woke up the mistress, and she came out to listen to it. When we held a lantern over the well, we couldn't find anyone there at all, but we continued to hear him until after the sun had come up. Then the sounds stopped and we never heard them again.'

'The other story is the true one,' said Nobu, 'and I haven't even heard it.'

'You have to listen to them both,' Mameha went on. 'Here's my second. One time I went with several geisha to Osaka to entertain at the home of Akita Masaichi.' He was a famous businessman who'd made a fortune before the war. 'After we sang and drank for hours, Akita-san fell asleep on the mats, and one of the other geisha snuck us into the next room and opened a big chest full of all kinds of pornography. There were pornographic woodblock prints, including some by Hiroshige –'

'Hiroshige never made pornographic prints,' said Pumpkin.

'Yes, he did, Pumpkin,' the Chairman said. 'I've seen some of them.'

'And also,' Mameha went on, 'he had pictures of all sorts of fat European women and men, and some reels of movies.'

'I knew Akita Masaichi well,' said the Chairman. 'He wouldn't have had a collection of pornography. The other one is true.'

'Now, really, Chairman,' Nobu said. 'You believe a story about a man's voice coming out of a well?'

'I don't have to believe it. All that matters is whether Mameha thinks it's true.'

Pumpkin and the Chairman voted for the man in the well.

The Minister and Nobu voted for the pornography. As for me, I'd heard both of these before and knew that the man in the well was the true one. The Minister drank his penalty glass without complaining; but Nobu grumbled all the while, so we made him go next.

'I'm not going to play this game,' he said.

'You're going to play it, or you're going to drink a penalty glass of sake every round,' Mameha told him.

'All right, you want two stories, I'll tell you two stories,' he said. 'Here's the first one. I've got a little white dog, named Kubo. One night I came home, and Kubo's fur was completely blue.'

'I believe it,' said Pumpkin. 'It had probably been kidnapped by some sort of demon.'

Nobu looked as if he couldn't quite imagine that Pumpkin was serious. 'The next day it happened again,' he went on tentatively, 'only this time Kubo's fur was bright red.'

'Definitely demons,' said Pumpkin. 'Demons love red. It's the color of blood.'

Nobu began to look positively angry when he heard this. 'Here's my second story. Last week I went to the office so early in the morning that my secretary hadn't yet arrived. All right, which is the true one?'

Of course, we all chose the secretary except for Pumpkin, who was made to drink a penalty glass of sake. And I don't mean a cup; I mean a glass. The Minister poured it for her, adding drop by drop after the glass was full, until it was bulging over the rim. Pumpkin had to sip it before she could pick the glass up. I felt worried just watching her, for she had a very low tolerance for alcohol.

'I can't believe the story about the dog isn't true,' she said after she'd finished the glass. Already I thought I could hear her words slurring a bit. 'How could you make something like that up?'

'How could I make it up? The question is, how could you believe it? Dogs don't turn blue. Or red. And there aren't demons.'

It was my turn to go next. 'My first story is this. One night some years ago, the Kabuki actor Yoegoro got very drunk and told me he'd always found me beautiful.'

'This one isn't true,' Pumpkin said. 'I know Yoegoro.'

'I'm sure you do. But nevertheless, he told me he found me beautiful, and ever since that night, he's sent me letters from time to time. In the corner of every letter, he glues one little curly black hair.'

The Chairman laughed at this, but Nobu sat up, looking angry; and said, 'Really, these Kabuki actors. What irritating people!'

'I don't get it. What do you mean a *curly* black hair?' Pumpkin said; but you could see from her expression that she figured out the answer right away.

Everyone fell silent, waiting for my second story. It had been on my mind since we'd started playing the game, though I was nervous about telling it, and not at all certain it was the right thing to do.

'Once when I was a child,' I began, 'I was very upset one day, and I went to the banks of the Shirakawa Stream and began to cry . . .'

As I began this story, I felt almost as though I were reaching across the table to touch the Chairman on the hand. Because it seemed to me that no one else in the room would see anything unusual in what I was saying, whereas the Chairman would understand this very private story – or at least, I hoped he would. I felt I was having a conversation with him more intimate than any we'd ever had; and I could feel myself growing warm as I spoke. Just before continuing, I glanced up, expecting to find the Chairman looking at me quizzically. Instead, he didn't seem even to be paying attention. All at once I felt so vain, like a girl posturing for the crowds as she walks along, only to discover the street is empty.

I'm sure everyone in the room had grown tired of waiting for me by this time, because Mameha said, 'Well? Go on.' Pumpkin mumbled something too, but I couldn't understand her.

'I'm going to tell another story,' I said. 'Do you remember the geisha Okaichi? She died in an accident during the war. Many years before, she and I were talking one day, and she told me she'd always been afraid a heavy wooden box would fall right onto her head and kill her. And that's exactly how she died. A crate full of scrap metal fell from a shelf.'

I'd been so preoccupied, I didn't realize until this moment that neither of my stories was true. Both were partially true; but it didn't concern me very much in any case, because most people cheated while playing this game. So I waited until the Chairman had chosen a story – which was the one about Yoegoro and the curly hair – and declared him right. Pumpkin and the Minister had to drink penalty glasses of sake.

After this it was the Chairman's turn.

'I'm not very good at this sort of game,' he said. 'Not like you geisha, who are so adept at lying.'

'Chairman!' said Mameha, but of course she was only teasing.

'I'm concerned about Pumpkin, so I'm going to make this simple. If she has to drink another glass of sake, I don't think she'll make it.'

It was true that Pumpkin was having trouble focusing her eyes. I don't even think she was listening to the Chairman until he said her name.

'Just listen closely, Pumpkin. Here's my first story. This evening I came to attend a party at the Ichiriki Teahouse. And here's my second. Several days ago, a fish came walking into my office – no, forget that. You might even believe in a walking fish. How about this one. Several days ago, I opened my desk drawer; and a little man jumped out wearing a uniform and began to sing and dance. All right, now which one is true?'

'You don't expect me to believe a man jumped out of your drawer,' Pumpkin said.

'Just pick one of the stories. Which is true?'

'The other one. I don't remember what it was.'

'We ought to make you drink a penalty glass for that, Chairman,' said Mameha.

When Pumpkin heard the words 'penalty glass,' she must have assumed she'd done something wrong, because the next thing we knew, she'd drunk half a glassful of sake, and she wasn't looking well. The Chairman was the first to notice, and took the glass right out of her hand.

'You're not a drain spout, Pumpkin.' the Chairman said. She stared at him so blankly, he asked if she could hear him.

'She might be able to hear you,' Nobu said, 'but she certainly can't see you.'

'Come on, Pumpkin,' the Chairman said. 'I'm going to walk you to your home. Or drag you, if I have to.'

Mameha offered to help, and the two of them led Pumpkin out together, leaving Nobu and the Minister sitting at the table with me.

'Well, Minister,' Nobu said at last, 'how was your evening?'

I think the Minister was every bit as drunk as Pumpkin had been; but he muttered that the evening had been very enjoyable. 'Very enjoyable, indeed,' he added, nodding a couple of times. After this, he held out his sake cup for me to fill, but Nobu plucked it from his hand.

32

ALL THROUGH THAT winter and the following spring, Nobu went on bringing the Minister to Gion once or even twice every week. Considering how much time the two of them spent together during these months, you'd think the Minister would eventually have realized that Nobu felt toward him just as an ice pick feels toward a block of ice; but if he did, he never showed the least sign. To tell the truth, the Minister never seemed to notice much of anything, except whether I was kneeling beside him and whether his cup was full of sake. This devotion made my life difficult at times; when I paid too much attention to the Minister, Nobu grew short-tempered, and the side of his face with less scarring turned a brilliant red from anger. This was why the presence of the Chairman, Mameha, and Pumpkin was so valuable to me. They played the same role straw plays in a packing crate.

Of course I valued the Chairman's presence for another reason as well. I saw more of him during these months than I'd ever seen of him before, and over time I came to realize that the image of him in my mind, whenever I lay on my futon at night, wasn't really how he looked, not exactly. For example, I'd always pictured his eyelids smooth with almost no lashes at all; but in fact they were edged with dense, soft hair like little brushes. And his mouth was far more expressive than I'd ever realized – so expressive, in fact, that he often hid his feelings only very poorly. When he was amused by something but didn't want to show it, I could nevertheless spot his mouth quivering in the corners. Or when he was lost in thought – mulling over some problem he'd encountered during the day, perhaps – he sometimes turned a sake cup around and around in his hand and put his mouth into a deep frown that made creases all the way down the sides of his chin. Whenever he was carried away in this state I considered myself free to stare at him unabashedly. Something about his frown, and its deep furrows, I came to find inexpressibly handsome. It seemed to show how thoroughly he thought about things, and how seriously he was taken in the world. One evening while Mameha was telling a long story, I gave myself over so completely to staring at the Chairman that when I finally came to myself again, I realized that anyone watching me would have wondered what I was doing. Luckily the Minister was too dazed with drink to have noticed; as for Nobu, he was chewing a bite of something and poking around on the plate with his chopsticks, paying no attention either to Mameha or to me. Pumpkin, though, seemed to have been watching me all along. When I looked at her, she wore a smile I wasn't sure how to interpret.

One evening toward the end of February, Pumpkin came down with the flu and was unable to join us at the Ichiriki. The Chairman was late that night as well, so Mameha and I spent an hour entertaining Nobu and the Minister by ourselves. We finally decided to put on a dance, more for our own benefit than for theirs. Nobu wasn't much of a devotee, and the Minister had no interest at all. It wasn't our first choice as a way to pass the time, but we couldn't think of anything better.

First Mameha performed a few brief pieces while I accompanied her on the shamisen. Afterward we exchanged places. Just as I was taking up the starting pose for my first dance – my torso bent so that my folding fan reached toward the ground and my other arm stretched out to one side – the door slid open and the Chairman entered. We greeted him and waited while he took a seat at the table. I was delighted he'd arrived, because although I knew he'd seen me on the stage, he'd certainly never watched me dance in a setting as intimate as this one. At first I'd intended to perform a short piece called 'Shimmering Autumn Leaves,' but now I changed my mind and asked Mameha to play 'Cruel Rain' instead. The story behind 'Cruel Rain' is of a young woman who feels deeply moved when her lover takes off his kimono jacket to cover her during a rainstorm, because she knows him to be an enchanted spirit whose body will melt away if he becomes wet. My teachers had often complimented me on the way I expressed the woman's feelings of sorrow; during the section when I had to sink slowly to my knees, I rarely allowed my legs to tremble as most dancers did. Probably I've mentioned this already, but in dances of the Inoue School the facial expression is as important as the movement of the arms or legs. So although I'd like to have stolen glances at the Chairman as I was dancing, I had to keep my eyes positioned properly at all times, and was never able to do it. Instead, to help give feeling to my dance, I focused my mind on the saddest thing I could think of, which was to imagine that my *danna* was there in the room with me – not the Chairman, but rather Nobu. The moment I formulated this thought, everything around me seemed to droop heavily toward the earth. Outside in the garden, the eaves of the roof dripped rain like beads of weighted glass. Even the mats themselves seemed to press down upon the floor. I remember thinking that I was dancing to express not the pain of a young woman who has lost her supernatural lover, but the pain I myself would feel when my life was finally robbed of the one thing I cared most deeply about. I found myself thinking, too, of Satsu; I danced the bitterness of our eternal separation. By the end I felt almost overcome with grief; but I certainly wasn't prepared for what I saw when I turned to look at the Chairman.

He was sitting at the near corner of the table so that, as it happened, no one but me could see him. I thought he wore an expression of astonishment at first, because his eyes were so wide. But just as his mouth sometimes twitched when he tried not to smile, now I could see it twitching under the strain of a different emotion. I couldn't be sure, but I had the impression his eyes were heavy with tears. He looked toward the door, pretending to scratch the side of his nose so he could wipe a finger in the corner of his eye; and he smoothed his eyebrows as though they were the source of his trouble. I was so shocked to see the Chairman in pain that I felt almost disoriented for a moment. I made my way back to the table, and Mameha and Nobu began to talk. After a moment the Chairman interrupted.

'Where is Pumpkin this evening?'

'Oh, she's ill, Chairman,' said Mameha.

'What do you mean? Won't she be here at all?'

'No, not at all,' Mameha said. 'And it's a good thing, considering she has the stomach flu.'

Mameha went back to talking. I saw the Chairman glance at his wristwatch and then, with his voice still unsteady, he said:

'Mameha, you'll have to excuse me. I'm not feeling very well myself this evening.'

Nobu said something funny just as the Chairman was sliding the door shut, and everyone laughed. But I was thinking a thought that frightened me. In my dance, I'd tried to express the pain of absence. Certainly I had upset myself doing it, but I'd upset the Chairman too; and was it possible he'd been thinking of Pumpkin – who, after all, was absent? I couldn't imagine him on the brink of tears over Pumpkin's illness, or any such thing, but perhaps I'd stirred up some darker, more complicated feelings. All I knew was that when my dance ended, the Chairman asked about Pumpkin; and he left when he learned she was ill. I could hardly bring myself to believe it. If I'd made the discovery that the Chairman had developed feelings for Mameha, I wouldn't have been surprised. But Pumpkin? How could the Chairman long for someone so . . . well, so lacking in refinement?

You might think that any woman with common sense ought to have given up her hopes at this point. And I did for a time go to the fortune-teller every day, and read my almanac more carefully even than usual, searching for some sign whether I should submit to what seemed my inevitable destiny. Of course, we Japanese were living in a decade of crushed hopes. I wouldn't have found it surprising if mine had died off just like so many other people's. But on the other hand, many believed the country itself would one day rise again; and we all knew such a thing could never happen if we resigned ourselves to living forever in the rubble. Every time I happened to read an account in the newspaper of some little shop that had made, say, bicycle parts before the war, and was now back in business almost as though the war had never happened, I had to tell myself that if our entire nation could emerge from its own dark valley, there was certainly hope that I could emerge from mine.

Beginning that March and running all through the spring, Mameha and I were busy with *Dances of the Old Capital*, which was being staged again for the first time since Gion had closed in the final years of the war. As it happened, the Chairman and Nobu grew busy as well during these months, and brought the Minister to Gion only twice. Then one day during the first week of June, I heard that my presence at the Ichiriki Teahouse had been requested early that evening by Iwamura Electric. I had an engagement booked weeks before that I couldn't easily miss; so by the time I finally slid open the door to join the party, I was half an hour late. To my surprise, instead of the usual group around the table, I found only Nobu and the Minister.

I could see at once that Nobu was angry. Of course, I imagined he was angry at me for making him spend so much time alone with the Minister – though to tell the truth, the two of them weren't 'spending time together' any more than a squirrel is spending time with the insects that live in the same tree. Nobu was drumming his fingers on the tabletop, wearing a very cross expression, while the Minister stood at the window gazing out at the garden.

'All right, Minister!' Nobu said, when I'd settled myself at the table. 'That's enough of watching the bushes grow. Are we supposed to sit here and wait for you all night?'

The Minister was startled, and gave a little bow of apology before coming to take his place on a cushion I'd set out for him. Usually I had difficulty thinking of anything to say to him, but tonight my task was easier since I hadn't seen him in so long.

'Minister,' I said, 'you don't like me anymore!'

'Eh?' said the Minister, who managed to rearrange his features so they showed a look of surprise.

'You haven't been to see me in more than a month! Is it because Nobu-san has been unkind, and hasn't brought you to Gion as often as he should have?'

'Nobu-san isn't unkind,' said the Minister. He blew several breaths up his nose before adding, 'I've asked too much of him already.'

'Keeping you away for a month? He certainly is unkind. We have so much to catch up on.'

'Yes,' Nobu interrupted, 'mostly a lot of drinking.'

'My goodness, but Nobu-san is grouchy tonight. Has he been this way all evening? And where are the Chairman, and Mameha and Pumpkin? Won't they be joining us?'

'The Chairman isn't available this evening,' Nobu said. 'I don't know where the others are. They're your problem, not mine.'

In a moment, the door slid back, and two maids entered carrying dinner trays for the men. I did my best to keep them company while they ate – which is to say, I tried for a while to get Nobu to talk; but he wasn't in a talking mood; and then I tried to get the Minister to talk, but of course, it would have been easier to get a word or two out of the grilled minnow on his plate. So at length I gave up and just chattered away about whatever I wanted, until I began to feel like an old lady talking to her two dogs. All this while I poured sake as liberally as I could for both men. Nobu didn't drink much, but the Minister held his cup out gratefully every time. Just as the Minister was beginning to take on that glassy-eyed look, Nobu, like a man who has just woken up, suddenly put his own cup firmly on the table, wiped his mouth with his napkin, and said:

'All right, Minister, that's enough for one evening. It's time for you to be heading home.'

'Nobu-san!' I said. 'I have the impression your guest is just beginning to enjoy himself.'

'He's enjoyed himself plenty. We're sending him home early for once, thank heavens. Come on, then, Minister! Your wife will be grateful.'

'I'm not married,' said the Minister. But already he was pulling up his socks and getting ready to stand.

I led Nobu and the Minister up the hallway to the entrance, and helped the Minister into his shoes. Taxis were still uncommon because of gasoline rationing, but the maid summoned a rickshaw and I helped the Minister into it. Already I'd noticed that he was acting a bit strangely, but this evening he pointed his eyes at his knees and wouldn't even say good-bye. Nobu remained in the entryway, glowering out into the night as if he were watching clouds gather, though in fact it was a clear evening. When the Minister had left, I said to him, 'Nobu-san, what in heaven's name is the matter with the two of you?'

He gave me a look of disgust and walked back into the teahouse. I found him in the room, tapping his empty sake cup on the table with his one hand. I thought he wanted sake, but he ignored me when I asked – and the vial turned out to be empty, in any case. I waited a long moment, thinking he had something to say to me, but finally I spoke up.

'Look at you, Nobu-san. You have a wrinkle between your eyes as deep as a rut in the road.'

He let the muscles around his eyes relax a bit, so that the wrinkle seemed to dissolve. 'I'm not as young as I once was, you know,' he told me.

'What is that supposed to mean?'

'It means there are some wrinkles that have become permanent features, and they aren't going to go away just because you say they should.'

'There are good wrinkles and bad wrinkles, Nobu-san. Never forget it.'

'You aren't as young as you once were yourself, you know.'

'Now you've stooped to insulting me! You're in a worse mood even than I'd feared. Why isn't there any alcohol here? You need a drink.'

'I'm not insulting you. I'm stating a fact.'

'There are good wrinkles and bad wrinkles, and there are good facts and bad facts,' I said. 'The bad facts are best avoided.'

I found a maid and asked that she bring a tray with scotch and water, as well as some dried squid as a snack – for it had struck me that Nobu hadn't eaten much of his dinner. When the tray arrived, I poured scotch into a glass, filled it with water; and put it before him.

'There,' I said, 'now pretend that's medicine, and drink it.' He took a sip; but only a very small one. 'All of it,' I said.

'I'll drink it at my own pace.'

'When a doctor orders a patient to take medicine, the patient takes the medicine. Now drink up!'

Nobu drained the glass, but he wouldn't look at me as he did it. Afterward I poured more and ordered him to drink again.

'You're not a doctor!' he said to me. 'I'll drink at my own pace.'

'Now, now, Nobu-san. Every time you open your mouth, you get into worse trouble. The sicker the patient, the more the medication.'

'I won't do it. I hate drinking alone.'

'All right, I'll join you,' I said. I put some ice cubes in a glass and held it up for Nobu to fill. He wore a little smile when he took the glass from me – certainly the first smile I'd seen on him all evening – and very carefully poured twice as much scotch as I'd poured into his, topped by a splash of water. I took his glass from him, dumped its contents into a bowl in the center of the table, and then refilled it with the same amount of scotch he'd put into mine, plus an extra little shot as punishment.

While we drained our glasses, I couldn't help making a face; I find drinking scotch about as pleasurable as slurping up rainwater off the roadside. I suppose making these faces was all for the best, because afterward Nobu looked much less grumpy. When I'd caught my breath again, I said, 'I don't know what has gotten into you this evening. Or the Minister for that matter.'

'Don't mention that man! I was beginning to forget about him, and now you've reminded me. Do you know what he said to me earlier?'

'Nobu-san,' I said, 'it is my responsibility to cheer you up, whether you want more scotch or not. You've watched the Minister get drunk night after night. Now it's time you got drunk yourself.'

Nobu gave me another disagreeable look, but he took up his glass like a man beginning his walk to the execution ground, and looked at it for a long moment before drinking it all down. He put it on the table and afterward rubbed his eyes with the back of his hand as if he were trying to clear them.

'Sayuri,' he said, 'I must tell you something. You're going to hear about it sooner or later. Last week the Minister and I had a talk with the proprietress of the Ichiriki. We made an inquiry about the possibility of the Minister becoming your *danna*.'

'The Minister?' I said. 'Nobu-san, I don't understand. Is that what you wish to see happen?'

'Certainly not. But the Minister has helped us immeasurably, and I had no choice. The Occupation authorities were prepared to make their final judgment *against* Iwamura Electric, you know. The company would have been seized. I suppose the Chairman and I would have learned to pour concrete or something, for we would never have been permitted to work in business again. However, the Minister made them reopen our case, and managed to persuade them we were being dealt with much too harshly. Which is the truth, you know.'

'Yet Nobu-san keeps calling the Minister all sorts of names,' I said. 'It seems to me –'

'He deserves to be called any name I can think of! I don't like the man, Sayuri. It doesn't make me like him any better to know I'm in his debt.'

'I see,' I said. 'So I was to be given to the Minister because –'

'No one was trying to give you to the Minister. He could never have afforded to be your *danna* anyway. I led him to believe Iwamura Electric would be willing to pay – which of course we wouldn't have been. I knew the answer beforehand or I wouldn't have asked the question. The Minister was terribly disappointed, you know. For an instant I felt almost sorry for him.'

There was nothing funny in what Nobu had said. And yet I couldn't help but laugh, because I had a sudden image in my mind of the Minister as my *danna*, leaning in closer and closer to me, with his lower jaw sticking out, until suddenly his breath blew up my nose.

'Oh, so you find it funny, do you?' Nobu said to me.

'Really, Nobu-san . . . I'm sorry but to picture the Minister –'

'I don't want to picture the Minister! It's bad enough to have sat there beside him, talking with the mistress of the Ichiriki.'

I made another scotch and water for Nobu, and he made one for me. It was the last thing I wanted; already the room seemed cloudy. But Nobu raised his glass, and I had no choice but to drink with him. Afterward he wiped his mouth with his napkin and said, 'It's a terrible time to be alive, Sayuri.'

'Nobu-san, I thought we were drinking to cheer ourselves up.'

'We've certainly known each other a long time, Sayuri. Maybe . . . fifteen years! Is that right?' he said. 'No, don't answer. I want to tell you something, and you're going to sit right there and listen to it. I've wanted to tell you this a long while, and now the time has come. I hope you're listening, because I'm only going to say it once. Here's the thing: I don't much like geisha; probably you know that already. But I've always felt that you, Sayuri, aren't exactly like all the others.'

I waited a moment for Nobu to continue, but he didn't.

'Is that what Nobu-san wanted to tell me?' I asked.

'Well, doesn't that suggest that I ought to have done all kinds of things for you? For example . . . ha! For example, I ought to have bought you jewelry.'

'You have bought me jewelry. In fact, you've always been much too kind. To me, that is; you certainly aren't kind to everybody.'

'Well, I ought to have bought you more of it. Anyway, that isn't what I'm talking about. I'm having trouble explaining myself. What I'm trying to say is, I've come to understand what a fool I am. You laughed earlier at the idea of having the Minister for a *danna*. But just look at me: a one-armed man with skin like – what do they call me, the lizard?'

'Oh, Nobu-san, you must never talk about yourself that way . . .'

'The moment has finally come. I've been waiting years. I

had to wait all through your nonsense with that General. Every time I imagined him with you . . . well, I don't even want to think about that. And the very idea of this foolish Minister! Did I tell you what he said to me this evening? This is the worst thing of all. After he found out he wasn't going to be your *danna*, he sat there a long while like a pile of dirt, and then finally said, "I thought you told me I could be Sayuri's *danna*." Well, I hadn't said any such thing! "We did the best we could, Minister, and it didn't work out," I told him. So then he said, "Could you arrange it just once?" I said, "Arrange what once? For you to be Sayuri's *danna* just once? You mean, one evening?" And then he nodded! Well, I said, "You listen to me, Minister! It was bad enough going to the mistress of the teahouse to propose a man like you as *danna* to a woman like Sayuri. I only did it because I knew it wouldn't happen. But if you think –"'

'You didn't say that!'

'I certainly did. I said, "But if you think I would arrange for you to have even a quarter of a second alone with her . . . Why should you have her? And anyway, she isn't mine to give, is she? To think that I would go to her and ask such a thing!"'

'Nobu-san, I hope the Minister didn't take this too badly, considering all he's done for Iwamura Electric.'

'Now wait just a moment. I won't have you thinking I'm ungrateful. The Minister helped us because it was his job to help us. I've treated him well these past months, and I won't stop now. But that doesn't mean I have to give up what I've waited more than ten years for, and let him have it instead! What if I'd come to you as he wanted me to? Would you have said, "All right, Nobu-san, I'll do it for you"?'

'Please . . . How can I answer such a question?'

'Easily. Just tell me you would never have done such a thing.'

'But Nobu-san, I owe such a debt to you . . . If you asked a favor of me, I could never turn it down lightly.'

'Well, this is new! Have you changed, Sayuri, or has there always been a part of you I didn't know?'

'I've often thought Nobu-san has much too high an opinion of me . . .'

'I don't misjudge people. If you aren't the woman I think you are, then this isn't the world I thought it was. Do you mean to say you could consider giving yourself to a man like the Minister? Don't you feel there's right and wrong in this world, and good and bad? Or have you spent too much of your life in Gion?'

'My goodness, Nobu-san . . . it's been years since I've seen you so enraged . . .'

This must have been exactly the wrong thing to say because all at once Nobu's face flared in anger. He grabbed his glass in his one hand and slammed it down so hard it cracked, spilling ice cubes onto the tabletop. Nobu turned his hand to see a line of blood across his palm.

'Oh, Nobu-san!'

'Answer me!'

'I can't even think of the question right now . . . please, I have to go fetch something for your hand –'

'Would you give yourself to the Minister, no matter who asked it of you? If you're a woman who would do such a thing, I want you to leave this room right now and never speak to me again!'

I couldn't understand how the evening had taken this dangerous turn; but it was perfectly clear to me I could give only one answer. I was desperate to fetch a cloth for Nobu's hand – his blood had trickled onto the table already – but he was looking at me with such intensity I didn't dare to move.

'I would never do such a thing,' I said.

I thought this would calm him, but for a long, frightening moment he continued to glower at me. Finally he let out his breath.

'Next time, speak up before I have to cut myself for an answer.'

I rushed out of the room to fetch the mistress. She came with several maids and a bowl of water and towels. Nobu wouldn't let her call a doctor; and to tell the truth, the cut wasn't as bad as I'd feared. After the mistress left, Nobu was strangely silent. I tried to begin a conversation, but he showed no interest.

'First I can't calm you down,' I said at last, 'and now I can't get you to speak. I don't know whether to make you drink more, or if the liquor itself is the problem.'

'We've had enough liquor, Sayuri. It's time you went and brought back that rock.'

'What rock?'

'The one I gave you last fall. The piece of concrete from the factory. Go and bring it.'

I felt my skin turn to ice when I heard this – because I knew perfectly well what he was saying. The time had come for Nobu to propose himself as my *danna*.

'Oh, honestly, I've had so much to drink, I don't know whether I can walk at all!' I said. 'Perhaps Nobu-san will let me bring it the next time we see each other?'

'You'll get it tonight. Why do you think I stayed on after the Minister left? Go get it while I wait here for you.'

I thought of sending a maid to retrieve the rock for me; but I knew I could never tell her where to find it. So with some difficulty I made my way down the hall, slid my feet into my shoes, and sloshed my way – as it felt to me, in my drunken state – through the streets of Gion.

When I reached the okiya, I went to my room and found the piece of concrete, wrapped in a square of silk and stowed on a shelf of my closet. I unwrapped it and left the silk on the floor; though I don't know exactly why. As I left, Auntie – who must have heard me stumbling and come up to see what was the matter – met me in the upstairs hallway and asked why I was carrying a rock in my hand.

'I'm taking it to Nobu-san, Auntie,' I said. 'Please, stop me!'

'You're drunk, Sayuri. What's gotten into you this evening?'

'I have to give it back to him. And . . . oh, it will be the end of my life if I do. Please stop me.'

'Drunk, and sobbing. You're worse than Hatsumomo! You can't go back out like this.'

'Then please call the Ichiriki. And have them tell Nobu-san I won't be there. Will you?'

'Why is Nobu-san waiting for you to bring him a rock?'

'I can't explain. I can't . . .'

'It makes no difference. If he's waiting for you, you'll have to go,' she said to me, and led me by the arm back into my room, where she dried my face with a cloth and touched up my makeup by the light of an electric lantern. I was limp while she did it; she had to support my chin in her hand to keep my head from rolling. She grew so impatient that she finally grabbed my head with both hands and made it clear she wanted me to keep it still.

'I hope I never see you acting this way again, Sayuri. Heaven knows what's come over you.'

'I'm a fool, Auntie.'

'You've certainly been a fool this evening,' she said. 'Mother will be very angry if you've done something to spoil Nobu-san's affection for you.'

'I haven't yet,' I said. 'But if you can think of anything that will . . . '

'That's no way to talk,' Auntie said to me. And she didn't speak another word until she was finished with my makeup.

I made my way back to the Ichiriki Teahouse, holding that heavy rock in both my hands. I don't know whether it was really heavy, or whether my arms were simply heavy from too much to drink. But by the time I joined Nobu in the room again, I felt I'd used up all the energy I had. If he spoke to me about becoming his mistress, I wasn't at all sure I would be able to dam up my feelings.

I set the rock on the table. Nobu picked it up with his fingers and held it in the towel wrapped around his hand.

'I hope I didn't promise you a jewel this big,' he said. 'I don't have that much money. But things are possible now that weren't possible before.'

I bowed and tried not to look upset. Nobu didn't need to tell me what he meant.

33

THAT VERY NIGHT while I lay on my futon with the room swaying around I me, I made up my mind to be like the fisherman who hour after hour scoops out fish with his net. Whenever thoughts of the Chairman drifted up from within me, I would scoop them out, and scoop them out again, and again, until none of them were left. It would have been a clever system, I'm sure, if I could have made it work. But when I had even a single thought of him, I could never catch it before it sped away and carried me to the very place from which I'd banished my thoughts. Many times I stopped myself and said: Don't think of the Chairman, think of Nobu instead. And very deliberately, I pictured myself meeting Nobu somewhere in Kyoto. But then something always went wrong. The spot I pictured might be where I'd often imagined myself encountering the Chairman, for example . . . and then in an instant I was lost in thoughts of the Chairman once again.

I went on this way for weeks, trying to remake myself. Sometimes when I was free for a while from thinking about the Chairman, I began to feel as if a pit had opened up within me. I had no appetite even when little Etsuko came late at night carrying me a bowl of clear broth. The few times I did manage to focus my mind clearly on Nobu, I grew so numbed I seemed to feel nothing at all. While putting on my makeup, my face hung like a kimono from a rod. Auntie told me I looked like a ghost. I went to parties and banquets as usual, but I knelt in silence with my hands in my lap.

I knew Nobu was on the point of proposing himself as my *danna*, and so I waited every day for the news to reach me.

But the weeks dragged on without any word. Then one hot afternoon at the end of June, nearly a month after I'd given back the rock, Mother brought in a newspaper while I was eating lunch, and opened it to show me an article entitled 'Iwamura Electric Secures Financing from Mitsubishi Bank.' I expected to find all sorts of references to Nobu and the Minister, and certainly to the Chairman; but mostly the article gave a lot of information I can't even remember. It told that Iwamura Electric's designation had been changed by the Allied Occupation authorities from . . . I don't remember – a Class Something to a Class Something-Else. Which meant, as the article went on to explain, that the company was no longer restricted from entering into contracts, applying for loans, and so forth. Several paragraphs followed, all about rates of interest and lines of credit; and then finally about a very large loan secured the day before from the Mitsubishi Bank. It was a difficult article to read, full of numbers and business terms. When I finished, I looked up at Mother, kneeling on the other side of the table.

'Iwamura Electric's fortunes have turned around completely,' she said. 'Why didn't you tell me about this?'

'Mother, I hardly even understand what I've just read.'

'It's no wonder we've heard so much from Nobu Toshikazu these past few days. You must know he's proposed himself as your *danna*. I was thinking of turning him down. Who wants a man with an uncertain future? Now I can see why you've seemed so distracted these past few weeks! Well, you can relax now. It's finally happening. We all know how fond you've been of Nobu these many years.'

I went on gazing down at the table just like a proper daughter. But I'm sure I wore a pained expression on my face; because in a moment Mother went on:

'You mustn't be listless this way when Nobu wants you in his bed. Perhaps your health isn't what it should be. I'll send you to a doctor the moment you return from Amami.'

The only Amami I'd ever heard of was a little island not far from Okinawa; I couldn't imagine this was the place she meant. But in fact, as Mother went on to tell me, the mistress of the Ichiriki had received a telephone call that very morning from Iwamura Electric concerning a trip to the island of Amami the following weekend. I'd been asked to go, along with Mameha and Pumpkin, and also another geisha whose name Mother couldn't remember. We would leave the following Friday afternoon.

'But Mother . . . it makes no sense at all,' I said. 'A weekend trip as far as Amami? The boat ride alone will take all day.'

'Nothing of the sort. Iwamura Electric has arranged for all of you to travel there in an airplane.'

In an instant I forgot my worries about Nobu, and sat upright as quickly as if someone had poked me with a pin. 'Mother!' I said. 'I can't possibly fly on an airplane.'

'If you're sitting in one and the thing takes off, you won't be able to help it!' she replied. She must have thought her little joke was very funny because she gave one of her huffing laughs.

With gasoline so scarce, there couldn't possibly be an airplane, I decided, so I made up my mind not to worry – and this worked well for me until the following day, when I spoke with the mistress of the Ichiriki. It seemed that several American officers on the island of Okinawa traveled by air to Osaka several weekends a month. Normally the airplane flew home empty and returned a few days later to pick them up. Iwamura Electric had arranged for our group to ride on the return trips. We were going to Amami only because the empty airplane was available; otherwise we'd probably have been on our way to a hot-springs resort, and not fearing for our lives at all. The last thing the mistress said to me was, 'I'm just grateful it's you and not me flying in the thing.'

When Friday morning came, we set out for Osaka by train. In addition to Mr. Bekku, who came to help us with our trunks as far as the airport, the little group consisted of Mameha, Pumpkin, and me, as well as an elderly geisha named Shizue. Shizue was from the Pontocho district rather than Gion, and had unattractive glasses and silver hair that made her look even older than she really was. What was worse, her chin had a big cleft in the middle, like two breasts. Shizue seemed to view the rest of us as a cedar views the weeds growing beneath it. Mostly she stared out the window of the train; but every so often she opened the clasp of her orange and red handbag to take out a piece of candy, and looked at us as if she couldn't see why we had to trouble her with our presence.

From Osaka Station we traveled to the airport in a little bus not much larger than a car, which ran on coal and was very dirty. At last after an hour or so, we climbed down beside a silver airplane with two great big propellers on the wings. I wasn't at all reassured to see the tiny wheel on which the tail rested; and when we went inside, the aisle sloped downward so dramatically I felt sure the airplane was broken.

The men were onboard already, sitting in seats at the rear and talking business. In addition to the Chairman and Nobu, the Minister was there, as well as an elderly man who, as I later learned, was regional director of the Mitsubishi Bank. Seated beside him was a man in his thirties with a chin just like Shizue's, and glasses as thick as hers too. As it turned out, Shizue was the longtime mistress of the bank director, and this man was their son.

We sat toward the front of the airplane and left the men to their dull conversation. Soon I heard a coughing noise and the airplane trembled . . . and when I looked out the window, the giant propeller outside had begun to turn. In a matter of moments it was whirling its swordlike blades inches from my face, making the most desperate humming noise. I felt sure it would come tearing through the side of the airplane and slice me in half. Mameha had put me in a window seat thinking the view might calm me once we were airborne, but now that she saw what the propeller was doing, she refused to switch seats with me. The noise of the engines grew worse and the airplane began to bump along, turning here and there. Finally the noise reached its most terrifying volume yet, and the aisle tipped level. After another few moments we heard a thump and began to rise up into the air. Only when the ground was far below us did someone finally tell me the trip was seven hundred kilometers and would take nearly four hours. When I heard this, I'm afraid my eyes glazed over with tears, and everyone began to laugh at me.

I pulled the curtains over the window and tried to calm myself by reading a magazine. Quite some time later, after Mameha had fallen asleep in the seat beside me, I looked up to find Nobu standing in the aisle.

'Sayuri, are you well?' he said, speaking quietly so as not to wake Mameha.

'I don't think Nobu-san has ever asked me such a thing before,' I said. 'He must be in a very cheerful mood.'

'The future has never looked more promising!'

Mameha stirred at the sound of our talking, so Nobu said nothing further, and instead continued up the aisle to the toilet. Just before opening the door, he glanced back toward where the other men were seated. For an instant I saw him from an angle I'd rarely seen, which gave him a look of fierce concentration. When his glance flicked in my direction, I thought he might pick up some hint that I felt as worried about my future as he felt reassured about his. How strange it seemed, when I thought about it, that Nobu understood me so little. Of course, a geisha who expects understanding from her *danna* is like a mouse expecting sympathy from the snake. And in any case, how could Nobu possibly understand anything about me, when he'd seen me solely as a geisha keeping my true self carefully concealed? The Chairman was the only man I'd ever entertained as Sayuri the geisha who had also known me as Chiyo – though it was strange to think of it this way, for I'd never realized it before. What would Nobu have done if he had been the one to find me that day at the Shirakawa Stream? Surely he would have walked right past . . . and how much easier it might have been for me if he had. I wouldn't spend my nights yearning for the Chairman. I wouldn't stop in cosmetics shops from time to time, to smell the scent of talc in the air and remind myself of his skin. I wouldn't strain to picture his presence beside me in some imaginary place. If you'd asked me why I wanted these things, I would have answered, Why does a ripe persimmon taste delicious? Why does wood smell smoky when it burns?

But here I was again, like a girl trying to catch mice with her hands. Why couldn't I stop thinking about the Chairman?

I'm sure my anguish must have shown clearly on my face

when the door to the toilet opened a moment later, and the light snapped off. I couldn't bear for Nobu to see me this way, so I laid my head against the window, pretending to be asleep. After he passed by, I opened my eyes again. I found that the position of my head had caused the curtains to pull open, so that I was looking outside the airplane for the first time since shortly after we'd lifted off the runway. Spread out below was a broad vista of aqua blue ocean, mottled with the same jade green as a certain hair ornament Mameha sometimes wore. I'd never imagined the ocean with patches of green. From the sea cliffs in Yoroido, it had always looked the color of slate. Here the sea stretched all the way out to a single line pulled across like a wool thread where the sky began. This view wasn't frightening at all, but inexpressibly lovely. Even the hazy disk of the propeller was beautiful in its own way, and the silver wing had a kind of magnificence, and was decorated with those symbols that American warplanes have on them. How peculiar it was to see them there, considering the world only five years earlier. We had fought a brutal war as enemies; and now what? We had given up our past; this was something I understood fully, for I had done it myself once. If only I could find a way of giving up my future . . .

And then a frightening image came to mind: I saw myself cutting the bond of fate that held me to Nobu, and watching him fall all the long way into the ocean below.

I don't mean this was just an idea or some sort of daydream. I mean that all at once I understood exactly how to do it. Of course I wasn't really going to throw Nobu into the ocean, but I did have an understanding, just as clearly as if a window had been thrown open in my mind, of the one thing I could do to end my relationship with him forever. I didn't want to lose his friendship; but in my efforts to reach the Chairman, Nobu was an obstacle I'd found no way around. And yet I could cause him to be consumed by the flames of his own anger; Nobu himself had told me how to do it, just a moment after cutting his hand that night at the Ichiriki Teahouse only a few weeks earlier. If I was the sort of woman who would give myself to the Minister, he'd said, he wanted me to leave the room right then and would never speak to me again.

The feeling that came over me as I thought of this . . . it was like a fever breaking. I felt damp everywhere on my body. I was grateful Mameha remained asleep beside me; I'm sure she would have wondered what was the matter, to see me short of breath, wiping my forehead with my fingertips. This idea that had come to me, could I really do such a thing? I don't mean the act of seducing the Minister; I knew perfectly well I could do that. It would be like going to the doctor for a shot. I'd look the other way for a time, and it would be over. But could I do such a thing to Nobu? What a horrible way to repay his kindness. Compared with the sorts of men so many geisha had suffered through the years, Nobu was probably a very desirable *danna*. But could I bear to live a life in which my hopes had been extinguished forever? For weeks I'd been working to convince myself I could live it; but could I really? I thought perhaps I understood how Hatsumomo had come by her bitter cruelty, and Granny her meanness. Even Pumpkin, who was scarcely thirty, had worn a look of disappointment for many years. The only thing that had kept me from it was hope; and now to sustain my hopes, would I commit an abhorrent act? I'm not talking about seducing the Minister; I'm talking about betraying Nobu's trust.

During the rest of the flight, I struggled with these thoughts. I could never have imagined myself scheming in this way, but in time I began to imagine the steps involved just like in a board game: I would draw the Minister aside at the inn – no, not at the inn, at some other place – and I would trick Nobu into stumbling upon us . . . or perhaps it would be enough for him to hear it from someone else? You can imagine how exhausted I felt by the end of the trip. Even as we left the airplane, I must still have looked very worried, because Mameha kept reassuring me that the flight was over and I was safe at last.

We arrived at our inn about an hour before sunset. The others admired the room in which we would all be staying, but I felt so agitated I could only pretend to admire it. It was as spacious as the largest room at the Ichiriki Teahouse, and furnished beautifully in the Japanese style, with tatami mats and gleaming wood. One long wall was made entirely of glass doors, beyond which lay extraordinary tropical plants – some with leaves nearly as big as a man. A covered walkway led down through the leaves to the banks of a stream.

When the luggage was in order, we were all of us quite ready for a bath. The inn had provided folding screens, which we opened in the middle of the room for privacy. We changed into our cotton gowns and made our way along a succession of covered walkways, leading through the dense foliage to a luxurious hot-springs pool at the other end of the inn. The men's and women's entrances were shielded by partitions, and had separate tiled areas for washing. But once we were immersed in the dark water of the springs and moved out beyond the partition's edge, the men and women were together in the water. The bank director kept making jokes about Mameha and me, saying he wanted one of us to fetch a certain pebble, or twig, or something of the sort, from the woods at the edge of the springs – the joke being, of course, that he wanted to see us naked. All this while, his son was engrossed in conversation with Pumpkin; and it didn't take us long to understand why Pumpkin's bosoms, which were fairly large, kept floating up and exposing themselves on the surface while she jabbered away as always without noticing.

Perhaps it seems odd to you that we all bathed together, men and women, and that we planned to sleep in the same room later that night. But actually, geisha do this sort of thing all the time with their best customers – or at least they did in my day. A single geisha who values her reputation will certainly never be caught alone with a man who isn't her *danna*. But to bathe innocently in a group like this, with the murky water cloaking us . . . that's quite another matter. And as for sleeping in a group, we even have a word for it in Japanese – *zakone*, 'fish sleeping.' If you picture a bunch of mackerel thrown together into a basket, I suppose that's what it means.

Bathing in a group like this was innocent, as I say. But that doesn't mean a hand never strayed where it shouldn't, and this thought was very much on my mind as I soaked there in the hot springs. If Nobu had been the sort of man to tease, he might have drifted over toward me; and then after we'd chatted for a time he might suddenly have grabbed me by the hip, or . . . well, almost anywhere, to tell the truth. The proper next step would be for me to scream and Nobu to laugh, and that would be the end of it. But Nobu wasn't the sort of man to tease. He'd been immersed in the bath for a time, in conversation with the Chairman, but now he was sitting on a rock with only his legs in the water, and a small, wet towel draped across his hips; he wasn't paying attention to the rest of us, but rubbing at the stump of his arm absentmindedly and peering into the water. The sun had set by now, and the light faded almost to evening but Nobu sat in the brightness of a paper lantern. I'd never before seen him so exposed. The scarring that I thought was at its worst on one side of his face was every bit as bad on his damaged shoulder though his other shoulder was beautifully smooth like an egg. And now to think that I was considering betraying him . . . He would think I had done it for only one reason, and would never understand the truth. I couldn't bear the thought of hurting Nobu or of destroying his regard for me. I wasn't at all sure I could go through with it.

After breakfast the following morning, we all took a walk through the tropical forest to the sea cliffs nearby where the stream from our inn poured over a picturesque little waterfall into the ocean. We stood a long while admiring the view; even when we were all ready to leave, the Chairman could hardly tear himself away. On the return trip I walked beside Nobu, who was still as cheerful as I'd ever seen him. Afterward we toured the island in the back of a military truck fitted with benches, and saw bananas and pineapples growing on the trees, and beautiful birds. From the mountaintops, the ocean looked like a crumpled blanket in turquoise, with stains of dark blue.

That afternoon we wandered the dirt streets of the little village, and soon came upon an old wood building that looked like a warehouse, with a sloped roof of thatch. We ended up walking around to the back, where Nobu climbed stone steps to open a door at the corner of the building, and the sunlight fell across a dusty stage built out of planking.

Evidently it had at one time been a warehouse but was now the town's theater. When I first stepped inside I didn't think very much about it. But after the door banged shut and we'd made our way to the street again, I began to feel that same feeling of a fever breaking because in my mind I had an image of myself lying there on the rutted flooring with the Minister as the door creaked open and sunlight fell across us. We would have no place to hide; Nobu couldn't possibly fail to see us. In many ways I'm sure it was the very spot I'd half-hoped to find. But I wasn't thinking of these things; I wasn't really thinking at all, so much as struggling to put my thoughts into some kind of order. They felt to me like rice pouring from a torn sack.

As we walked back up the hill toward our inn, I had to fall back from the group to take my handkerchief from my sleeve. It was certainly very warm there on that road, with the afternoon sun shining full onto our faces. I wasn't the only one perspiring. But Nobu came walking back to ask if I was all right. When I couldn't manage to answer him right away, I hoped he would think it was the strain of walking up the hill.

'You haven't looked well all weekend, Sayuri. Perhaps you ought to have stayed in Kyoto.'

'But when would I have seen this beautiful island?'

'I'm sure this is the farthest you've ever been from your home. We're as far from Kyoto now as Hokkaido is.'

The others had walked around the bend ahead. Over Nobu's shoulder I could see the eaves of the inn protruding above the foliage. I wanted to reply to him, but I found myself consumed with the same thoughts that had troubled me on the airplane, that Nobu didn't understand me at all. Kyoto wasn't my home; not in the sense Nobu seemed to mean it, of a place where I'd been raised, a place I'd never strayed from. And in that instant, while I peered at him in the hot sun, I made up my mind that I would do this thing I had feared. I would betray Nobu, even though he stood there looking at me with kindness. I tucked away my handkerchief with trembling hands, and we continued up the hill, not speaking a word.

By the time I reached the room, the Chairman and Mameha had already taken seats at the table to begin a game of go against the bank director, with Shizue and her son looking on. The glass doors along the far wall stood open; the Minister was propped on one elbow staring out, peeling the covering off a short stalk of cane he'd brought back with him. I was desperately afraid Nobu would engage me in a conversation I'd be unable to escape, but in fact, he went directly over to the table and began talking with Mameha. I had no idea as yet how I would lure the Minister to the theater with me, and even less idea how I would arrange for Nobu to find us there. Perhaps Pumpkin would take Nobu for a walk if I asked her to? I didn't feel I could ask such a thing of Mameha, but Pumpkin and I had been girls together; and though I won't call her crude, as Auntie had called her, Pumpkin did have a certain coarseness in her personality and would be less aghast at what I was planning. I would need to direct her explicitly to bring Nobu to the old theater; they wouldn't come upon us there purely by accident.

For a time I knelt gazing out at the sunlit leaves and wishing I could appreciate the beautiful tropical afternoon. I kept asking myself whether I was fully sane to be considering this plan; but whatever misgivings I may have felt, they weren't enough to stop me from going ahead with it. Clearly nothing would happen until I succeeded in drawing the Minister aside, and I couldn't afford to call attention to myself when I did it. Earlier he'd asked a maid to bring him a snack, and now he was sitting with his legs around a tray, pouring beer into his mouth and dropping in globs of salted squid guts with his chopsticks. This may seem like a nauseating idea for a dish, but I can assure you that you'll find salted squid guts in bars and restaurants here and there in Japan. It was a favorite of my father's, but I've never been able to stomach it. I couldn't even watch the Minister as he ate.

'Minister,' I said to him quietly, 'would you like me to find you something more appetizing?'

'No,' he said, 'I'm not hungry.' I must admit this raised in my mind the question of why he was eating in the first place. By now Mameha and Nobu had wandered out the back door in conversation, and the others, including Pumpkin, were gathered around the go board on the table. Apparently the

Chairman had just made a blunder, and they were laughing. It seemed to me my chance had come.

'If you're eating out of boredom, Minister,' I said, 'why don't you and I explore the inn? I've been eager to see it, and we haven't had the time.'

I didn't wait for him to reply but stood and walked from the room. I was relieved when he stepped out into the hallway a moment later to join me. We walked in silence down the corridor, until we came to a bend where I could see that no one was coming from either direction. I stopped.

'Minister, excuse me,' I said, 'but . . . shall we take a walk back down to the village together?'

He looked very confused by this.

'We have an hour or so left in the afternoon,' I went on, 'and I remember something I'd very much like to see again.'

After a long pause, the Minister said, 'I'll need to use the toilet first.'

'Yes, that's fine,' I told him. 'You go and use the toilet; and when you're finished, wait right here for me and we'll take a walk together. Don't go anywhere until I come and fetch you.'

The Minister seemed agreeable to this and continued up the corridor. I went back toward the room. And I felt so dazed – now that I was actually going through with my plan – that when I put my hand on the door to slide it open, I could scarcely feel my fingers touching anything at all.

Pumpkin was no longer at the table. She was looking through her travel trunk for something. At first when I tried to speak, nothing came out. I had to clear my throat and try again.

'Excuse me, Pumpkin,' I said. 'Just one moment of your time . . .'

She didn't look eager to stop what she was doing, but she left her trunk in disarray and came out into the hallway with me. I led her some distance down the corridor, and then turned to her and said:

'Pumpkin, I need to ask a favor.'

I waited for her to tell me she was happy to help, but she just stood with her eyes on me.

'I hope you won't mind my asking –'

'Ask,' she said.

'The Minister and I are about to go for a walk. I'm going to take him to the old theater, and –'

'Why?'

'So that he and I can be alone.'

'The Minister?' Pumpkin said incredulously.

'I'll explain some other time, but here's what I want you to do. I want you to bring Nobu there and . . . Pumpkin, this will sound very strange. I want you to discover us.'

'What do you mean, "discover" you?'

'I want you to find some way of bringing Nobu there and opening the back door we saw earlier, so that . . . he'll see us.'

While I was explaining this, Pumpkin had noticed the Minister waiting in another covered walkway through the foliage. Now she looked back at me.

'What are you up to, Sayuri?' she said.

'I don't have time to explain it now. But it's terribly important, Pumpkin. Truthfully, my entire future is in your hands. Just make sure it's no one but you and Nobu – not the Chairman, for heaven's sake, or anyone else. I'll repay you in any way you'd like.'

She looked at me for a long moment. 'So it's time for a favor from Pumpkin again, is it?' she said. I didn't feel certain what she meant by this, but rather than explaining it to me, she left.

I wasn't sure whether or not Pumpkin had agreed to help. But all I could do at this point was go to the doctor for my shot, so to speak, and hope that she and Nobu would appear. I joined the Minister in the corridor and we set out down the hill.

As we walked around the bend in the road and left the inn behind us, I couldn't help remembering the day Mameha had cut me on the leg and taken me to meet Dr. Crab. On that afternoon I'd felt myself in some sort of danger I couldn't fully understand, and I felt much the same way now. My face was as hot in the afternoon sun as if I'd sat too close to the hibachi; and when I looked at the Minister, sweat was running down his temple onto his neck. If all went well he would soon be pressing that neck against me . . . and at this thought I took my folding fan from my obi, and waved it until my arm was tired, trying to cool both myself and him. All the while, I kept up a flow of conversation, until a few minutes later, when we came to a stop before the old theater with its thatched roof. The Minister seemed puzzled. He cleared his throat and looked up at the sky.

'Will you come inside with me for a moment, Minister?' I said.

He didn't seem to know what to make of this, but when I walked down the path beside the building, he plodded along behind me. I climbed the stone steps and opened the door for him. He hesitated only a moment before walking inside. If he had frequented Gion all his life, he'd certainly have understood what I had in mind – because a geisha who lures a man to an isolated spot has certainly put her reputation at stake, and a first-class geisha will never do such a thing casually. But the Minister just stood inside the theater, in the patch of sunlight, like a man waiting for a bus. My hands were trembling so much as I folded my fan and tucked it into my obi again, I wasn't at all certain I could see my plan through to the end. The simple act of closing the door took all my strength; and then we were standing in the murky light filtering under the eaves. Still, the Minister stood inert, with his face pointed toward a stack of straw mats in the corner of the stage.

'Minister . . .' I said.

My voice echoed so much in the little hall, I spoke more quietly afterward.

'I understand you had a talk with the mistress of the Ichiriki about me. Isn't that so?'

He took in a deep breath, but ended up saying nothing.

'Minister, if I may,' I said, 'I'd like to tell you a story about a geisha named Kazuyo. She isn't in Gion any longer, but I knew her well at one time. A very important man – much like you, Minister – met Kazuyo one evening and enjoyed her company so much that he came back to Gion every night to see her. After a few months of this, he asked to be Kazuyo's *danna*, but the mistress of the teahouse apologized and said it wouldn't be possible. The man was very disappointed; but then one afternoon Kazuyo took him to a quiet spot where they could be alone. Someplace very much like this empty theater. And she explained to him that . . . even though he couldn't be her *danna* –'

The moment I said these last words, the Minister's face changed like a valley when the clouds move away and sunlight rushes across it. He took a clumsy step toward me. At once my heart began to pound like drums in my ears. I couldn't help looking away from him and closing my eyes. When I opened them again, the Minister had come so close, we were nearly touching, and then I felt the damp fleshiness of his face against my cheek. Slowly he brought his body toward mine until we were pressed together. He took my arms, probably to pull me down onto the planking, but I stopped him.

'The stage is too dusty,' I said. 'You must bring over a mat from that stack.'

'We'll go over there,' the Minister replied.

If we had lain down upon the mats in the corner, Nobu wouldn't have seen us in the sunlight when he opened the door.

'No, we mustn't,' I said. 'Please bring a mat here.'

The Minister did as I asked, and then stood with his hands by his side, watching me. Until this moment I'd half-imagined something would stop us; but now I could see that nothing would. Time seemed to slow. My feet looked to me like someone else's when they stepped out of my lacquered zori and onto the mat.

Almost at once, the Minister kicked off his shoes and was against me, with his arms around me tugging at the knot in my obi. I didn't know what he was thinking, because I certainly wasn't prepared to take off my kimono. I reached back to stop him. When I'd dressed that morning, I still hadn't quite made up my mind; but in order to be prepared, I'd very deliberately put on a gray underrobe I didn't much like – thinking it might be stained before the end of the day – and a lavender and blue kimono of silk gauze, as well as a durable silver obi. As for my undergarments, I'd shortened my *koshimaki* – my 'hip wrap' – by rolling it at the waist, so that if I decided after all to seduce the Minister, he'd have no trouble finding his way inside it. Now, when I withdrew his hands from around me, he gave me a puzzled look. I think he believed I was stopping him, and he looked very relieved as I lay down on the mat. It wasn't a tatami, but a simple sheet of woven straw; I could feel the hard flooring beneath. With one hand I folded back my kimono and underrobe on one side so that my leg was exposed to the knee. The Minister was still fully dressed, but he lay down upon me at once, pressing the knot of my obi into my back so much, I had to raise one hip to make myself more comfortable. My head was turned to the side as well, because I was wearing my hair in a style known as *tsubushi shimada*, with a dramatic chignon looped in the back, which would have been ruined if I'd put any weight on it. It was certainly an uncomfortable arrangement, but my discomfort was nothing compared with the uneasiness and anxiety I felt. Suddenly I wondered if I'd been thinking at all clearly when I'd put myself in this predicament. The Minister raised himself on one arm and began fumbling inside the seam of my kimono with his hand, scratching my thighs with his fingernails. Without thinking about what I was doing, I brought my hands up to his shoulders to push him away . . . but then I imagined Nobu as my *danna*, and the life I would live without hope; and I took my hands away and settled them onto the mat again. The Minister's fingers were squirming higher and higher along the inside of my thigh; it was impossible not to feel them. I tried to distract myself by focusing on the door. Perhaps it would open even now, before the Minister had gone any further; but at that moment I heard the jingling of his belt, and then the zip of his pants and a moment later he was forcing himself inside me. Somehow I felt like a fifteen-year-old girl again, because the feeling was so strangely reminiscent of Dr. Crab. I even heard myself whimper. The Minister was holding himself up on his elbows with his face above mine I could see him out of only one corner of my eye. When viewed up close like this with his jaw protruding toward me he looked more like an animal than a human. And even this wasn't the worst part, for with his jaw jutted forward, the Minister's lower lip became like a cup in which his saliva began to pool. I don't know if it was the squid guts he'd eaten, but his saliva had a kind of gray thickness to it, which made me think of the residue left on the cutting board after fish have been cleaned.

When I'd dressed that morning, I'd tucked several sheets of a very absorbent rice paper into the back of my obi. I hadn't expected to need them until afterward, when the Minister would want them for wiping himself off – if I decided to go through with it, that is. Now it seemed I would need a sheet much sooner, to wipe my face when his saliva spilled onto me. With so much of his weight on my hips, however, I couldn't get my hand into the back of my obi. I let out several little gasps as I tried, and I'm afraid the Minister mistook them for excitement – for in any case, he suddenly grew even more energetic, and now the pool of saliva in his lip was being jostled with such violent shock waves I could hardly believe it held together rather than spilling out in a stream. All I could do was pinch my eyes shut and wait. I felt as sick as if I had been lying in the bottom of a little boat, tossed about on the waves, and with my head banging again and again against the side. Then all at once the Minister made a groaning noise, and held very still for a bit, and at the same time I felt his saliva spill onto my cheek.

I tried again to reach the rice paper in my obi, but now the Minister was lying collapsed upon me, breathing as heavily as if he'd just run a race. I was about to push him off when I heard a scraping sound outside. My feelings of disgust had been so loud within me, they'd nearly drowned out everything else. But now that I remembered Nobu, I could feel my heart pounding once again. I heard another scrape; it was the sound of someone on the stone steps. The Minister seemed to have no idea what was about to happen to him. He raised his head and pointed it toward the door with only the mildest interest, as if he expected to see a bird there. And then the door creaked open and the sunlight flooded over us. I had to squint, but I could make out two figures. There was

Pumpkin; she had come to the theater just as I'd hoped she would. But the man peering down from beside her wasn't Nobu at all. I had no notion of why she had done it, but Pumpkin had brought the Chairman instead.

34

I CAN SCARCELY REMEMBER anything after that door opened – for I think the blood may have drained out of me, I went so cold and numb. I know the Minister climbed off me, or perhaps I pushed him off. I do remember weeping and asking if he'd seen the same thing I had, whether it really had been the Chairman standing there in the doorway. I hadn't been able to make out anything of the Chairman's expression, with the late-afternoon sun behind him; and yet when the door closed again, I couldn't help imagining I'd seen on his face some of the shock I myself was feeling. I didn't know if the shock was really there – and I doubted it was. But when we feel pain, even the blossoming trees seem weighted with suffering to us; and in just the same way, after seeing the Chairman there . . . well, I would have found my own pain reflected on anything I'd looked at.

If you consider that I'd taken the Minister to that empty theater for the very purpose of putting myself in danger – so that the knife would come slamming down onto the chopping block, so to speak – I'm sure you'll understand that amid the worry, and fear, and disgust that almost overwhelmed me, I'd also been feeling a certain excitement. In the instant before that door opened, I could almost sense my life expanding just like a river whose waters have begun to swell; for I had never before taken such a drastic step to change the course of my own future. I was like a child tiptoeing along a precipice overlooking the sea. And yet somehow I hadn't imagined a great wave might come and strike me there, and wash everything away.

When the chaos of feelings receded, and I slowly became

aware of myself again, Mameha was kneeling above me. I was puzzled to find that I wasn't in the old theater at all any longer, but rather looking up from the tatami floor of a dark little room at the inn. I don't recall anything about leaving the theater, but I must have done it somehow. Later Mameha told me I'd gone to the proprietor to ask for a quiet place to rest; he'd recognized that I wasn't feeling well, and had gone to find Mameha soon afterward.

Fortunately Mameha seemed willing to believe I was truly ill, and left me there. Later, as I wandered back toward the room in a daze and with a terrible feeling of dread, I saw Pumpkin step out into the covered walkway ahead of me. She stopped when she caught sight of me; but rather than hurrying over to apologize as I half-expected she might, she turned her focus slowly toward me like a snake that had spotted a mouse.

'Pumpkin,' I said, 'I asked you to bring Nobu, not the Chairman. I don't understand –'

'Yes, it must be hard for you to understand, Sayuri, when life doesn't work out perfectly!'

'Perfectly? Nothing worse could have happened . . . did you misunderstand what I was asking you?'

'You really do think I'm stupid!' she said.

I was bewildered, and stood a long moment in silence. 'I thought you were my friend,' I said at last.

'I thought you were my friend too, once. But that was a long time ago.'

'You talk as if I've done something to harm you, Pumpkin, but –'

'No, you'd never do anything like that, would you? Not the perfect Miss Nitta Sayuri! I suppose it doesn't matter that you took my place as the daughter of the okiya? Do you remember that, Sayuri? After I'd gone out of my way to help you with that Doctor – whatever his name was. After I'd risked making Hatsumomo furious at me for helping you! Then you turned it all around and stole what was mine. I've been wondering all these months just why you brought me into this little gathering with the Minister. I'm sorry it wasn't so easy for you to take advantage of me this time –'

'But Pumpkin,' I interrupted, 'couldn't you just have refused to help me? Why did you have to bring the Chairman?'

She stood up to her full height. 'I know perfectly well how you feel about him,' she said. 'Whenever there's nobody looking, your eyes hang all over him like fur on a dog.'

She was so angry, she had bitten her lip; I could see a smudge of lipstick on her teeth. She'd set out to hurt me, I now realized, in the worst way she could.

'You took something from me a long time ago, Sayuri. How does it feel now?' she said. Her nostrils were flared, her face consumed with anger like a burning twig. It was as though the spirit of Hatsumomo had been living trapped inside her all these years, and had finally broken free.

During the rest of that evening, I remember nothing but a blur of events, and how much I dreaded every moment ahead of me. While the others sat around drinking and laughing, it was all I could do to pretend to laugh. I must have spent the entire night flushed red, because from time to time Mameha touched my neck to see if I was feverish. I'd seated myself as far away from the Chairman as I could, so that our eyes would never have to meet; and I did manage to make it through the evening without confronting him. But later, as we were all preparing for bed, I stepped into the hallway as he was coming back into the room. I ought to have moved out of his way, but I felt so ashamed, I gave a brief bow and hurried past him instead, making no effort to hide my unhappiness.

It was an evening of torment, and I remember only one other thing about it. At some point after everyone else was asleep, I wandered away from the inn in a daze and ended up on the sea cliffs, staring out into the darkness with the sound of the roaring water below me. The thundering of the ocean was like a bitter lament. I seemed to see beneath everything a layering of cruelty I'd never known was there – as though the trees and the wind, and even the rocks where I stood, were all in alliance with my old girlhood enemy Hatsumomo. The howling of the wind and the shaking of the trees seemed to mock me. Could it really be that the stream of my life had divided forever? I removed the Chairman's handkerchief from my sleeve, for I'd taken it to bed that evening to comfort myself one last time. I dried my face with it, and held it up into the wind. I was about to let it dance away into the darkness, when I thought of the tiny mortuary tablets that Mr. Tanaka had sent me so many years earlier. We must always keep something to remember those who have left us. The mortuary tablets back in the okiya were all that remained of my childhood. The Chairman's handkerchief would be what remained of the rest of my life.

Back in Kyoto, I was carried along in a current of activity over the next few days. I had no choice but to put on my makeup as usual, and attend engagements at the teahouses just as though nothing had changed in the world. I kept reminding myself what Mameha had once told me, that there was nothing like work for getting over a disappointment; but my work didn't seem to help me in any way. Every time I went into the Ichiriki Teahouse, I was reminded that one day soon Nobu would summon me there to tell me the arrangements had been settled at last. Considering how busy he'd been over the past few months, I didn't expect to hear from him for some time – a week or two, perhaps. But on Wednesday morning, three days after our return from Amami, I received word that Iwamura Electric had telephoned the Ichiriki Teahouse to request my presence that evening.

I dressed late in the afternoon in a yellow kimono of silk gauze with a green underrobe and a deep blue obi interwoven with gold threads. Auntie assured me I looked lovely but when I saw myself in the mirror, I seemed like a woman defeated. I'd certainly experienced moments in the past when I felt displeased with the way I looked before setting out from the okiya; but most often I managed to find at least one feature I could make use of during the course of the evening. A certain persimmon-colored underrobe, for example, always brought out the blue in my eyes, rather than the gray no matter how exhausted I felt. But this evening my face seemed utterly hollow beneath my cheekbones – although I'd put on Western-style makeup just as I usually did – and even my hairstyle seemed lopsided to me. I couldn't think of any way to improve my appearance, other than asking Mr. Bekku to retie my obi just a finger's-width higher, to take away some of my downcast look.

My first engagement was a banquet given by an American colonel to honor the new governor of Kyoto Prefecture. It was held at the former estate of the Sumitomo family, which was now the headquarters of the American army's seventh division. I was amazed to see that so many of the beautiful stones in the garden were painted white, and signs in English – which of course I couldn't read – were tacked to the trees here and there. After the party was over, I made my way to the Ichiriki and was shown upstairs by a maid, to the same peculiar little room where Nobu had met with me on the night Gion was closing. This was the very spot where I'd learned about the haven he'd found to keep me safe from the war; it seemed entirely appropriate that we should meet in this same room to celebrate his becoming my *danna* – though it would be anything but a celebration for me. I knelt at one end of the table, so that Nobu would sit facing the alcove. I was careful to position myself so he could pour sake using his one arm, without the table in his way; he would certainly want to pour a cup for me after telling me the arrangements had been finalized. It would be a fine night for Nobu. I would do my best not to spoil it.

With the dim lighting and the reddish cast from the tea-colored walls, the atmosphere was really quite pleasant. I'd forgotten the very particular scent of the room – a combination of dust and the oil used for polishing wood – but now that I smelled it again, I found myself remembering details about that evening with Nobu years earlier that I couldn't possibly have called to mind otherwise. He'd had holes in both of his socks, I remembered; through one a slender big toe had protruded, with the nail neatly groomed. Could it really be that only five and a half years had passed since that evening? It seemed an entire generation had come and gone; so many of the people I'd once known were dead. Was this the life I'd come back to Gion to lead? It was just as Mameha had once told me: we don't become geisha because we want our lives to be happy; we become geisha because we have no choice. If my mother had lived, I might be a wife and mother at the seashore myself, thinking of Kyoto as a faraway place where the fish were shipped – and would my life really be any worse? Nobu had once said to me, 'I'm a very easy man to understand, Sayuri. I don't like things held up before me that I cannot have.' Perhaps I was just the same; all my life in Gion, I'd imagined the Chairman before me, and now I could not have him.

After ten or fifteen minutes of waiting for Nobu, I began to wonder if he was really coming. I knew I shouldn't do it, but I laid my head down on the table to rest, for I'd slept poorly these past nights. I didn't fall asleep, but I did drift for a time in my general sense of misery. And then I seemed to have a most peculiar dream. I thought I heard the tapping sound of drums in the distance, and a hiss like water from a faucet, and then I felt the Chairman's hand touching my shoulder. I knew it was the Chairman's hand because when I lifted my head from the table to see who had touched me, he was there. The tapping had been his footsteps; the hissing was the door in its track. And now he stood above me with a maid waiting behind him. I bowed and apologized for falling asleep. I felt so confused that for a moment I wondered if I was really awake; but it wasn't a dream. The Chairman was seating himself on the very cushion where I'd expected Nobu to sit, and yet Nobu was nowhere to be seen. While the maid placed sake on the table, an awful thought began to take hold in my mind. Had the Chairman come to tell me Nohu had been in an accident, or that some other horrible thing had happened to him? Otherwise, why hadn't Nobu himself come? I was about to ask the Chairman, when the mistress of the teahouse peered into the room.

'Why, Chairman,' she said, 'we haven't seen you in weeks!'

The mistress was always pleasant in front of guests, but I could tell from the strain in her voice that she had something else on her mind. Probably she was wondering about Nobu, just as I was. While I poured sake for the Chairman, the mistress came and knelt at the table. She stopped his hand before he took a sip from his cup, and leaned toward him to breathe in the scent of the vapors.

'Really, Chairman, I'll never understand why you prefer this sake to others,' she said. 'We opened some this afternoon, the best we've had in years. I'm sure Nobu-san will appreciate it when he arrives.'

'I'm sure he would,' the Chairman said. 'Nobu appreciates fine things. But he won't be coming tonight.'

I was alarmed to hear this; but I kept my eyes to the table. I could see that the mistress was surprised too, because of how quickly she changed the subject.

'Oh, well,' she said, 'anyway, don't you think our Sayuri looks charming this evening!'

'Now, Mistress, when has Sayuri not looked charming?' said the Chairman. 'Which reminds me . . . let me show you something I've brought.'

The Chairman put onto the table a little bundle wrapped in blue silk; I hadn't noticed it in his hand when he'd entered the room. He untied it and took out a short, fat scroll, which he began to unroll. It was cracked with age and showed – in miniature – brilliantly colored scenes of the Imperial court. If you've ever seen this sort of scroll, you'll know that you can unroll it all the way across a room and survey the entire grounds of the Imperial compound, from the gates at one end to the palace at the other. The Chairman sat with it before him, unrolling it from one spindle to the other – past scenes of drinking parties, and aristocrats playing kickball with their kimonos cinched up between their legs – until he came to a young woman in her lovely twelve-layered robes, kneeling on the wood floor outside the Emperor's chambers.

'Now what do you think of that!' he said.

'It's quite a scroll,' the mistress said. 'Where did the Chairman find it?'

'Oh, I bought it years ago. But look at this woman right here. She's the reason I bought it. Don't you notice anything about her?'

The mistress peered at it; afterward the Chairman turned it for me to see. The image of the young woman, though no bigger than a large coin, was painted in exquisite detail. I didn't notice it at first, but her eyes were pale . . . and when I looked more closely I saw they were blue-gray. They made me think at once of the works Uchida had painted using me as a model. I blushed and muttered something about how beautiful the scroll was. The mistress admired it too for a moment, and then said:

'Well, I'll leave the two of you. I'm going to send up some of that fresh, chilled sake I mentioned. Unless you think I should save it for the next time Nobu-san comes?'

'Don't bother,' he said. 'We'll make do with the sake we have.'

'Nobu-san is . . . quite all right, isn't he?'

'Oh, yes,' said the Chairman. 'Quite all right.'

I was relieved to hear this; but at the same time I felt myself growing sick with shame. If the Chairman hadn't come to give me news about Nobu, he'd come for some other reason – probably to berate me for what I'd done. In the few days since returning to Kyoto, I'd tried not to imagine what he must have seen: the Minister with his pants undone, me with my bare legs protruding from my disordered kimono . . .

When the mistress left the room, the sound of the door closing behind her was like a sword being drawn from its sheath.

'May I please say, Chairman,' I began as steadily as I could, 'that my behavior on Amami –'

'I know what you're thinking, Sayuri. But I haven't come here to ask for your apology. Sit quietly a moment. I want to tell you about something that happened quite a number of years ago.'

'Chairman, I feel so confused,' I managed to say. 'Please forgive me, but –'

'Just listen. You'll understand soon enough why I'm telling it to you. Do you recall a restaurant named Tsumiyo? It closed toward the end of the Depression, but . . . well, never mind; you were very young at the time. In any case, one day quite some years ago – eighteen years ago, to be exact – I went there for lunch with several of my associates. We were accompanied by a certain geisha named Izuko, from the Pontocho district.'

I recognized Izuko's name at once.

'She was everybody's favorite back in those days,' the

Chairman went on. 'We happened to finish up our lunch a bit early, so I suggested we take a stroll by the Shirakawa Stream on our way to the theater.'

By this time I'd removed the Chairman's handkerchief from my obi; and now, silently, I spread it onto the table and smoothed it so that his monogram was clearly visible. Over the years the handkerchief had taken on a stain in one corner, and the linen had yellowed; but the Chairman seemed to recognize it at once. His words trailed off, and he picked it up.

'Where did you get this?'

'Chairman,' I said, 'all these years I've wondered if you knew I was the little girl you'd spoken to. You gave me your handkerchief that very afternoon, on your way to see the play Shibaraku. You also gave me a coin –'

'Do you mean to say . . . even when you were an apprentice, you knew that I was the man who'd spoken to you?'

'I recognized the Chairman the moment I saw him again, at the sumo tournament. To tell the truth, I'm amazed the Chairman remembered me.'

'Well, perhaps you ought to look at yourself in the mirror sometime, Sayuri. Particularly when your eyes are wet from crying, because they become . . . I can't explain it. I felt I was seeing right through them. You know, I spend so much of my time seated across from men who are never quite telling me the truth; and here was a girl who'd never laid eyes on me before, and yet was willing to let me see straight into her.'

And then the Chairman interrupted himself.

'Didn't you ever wonder why Mameha became your older sister?' he asked me.

'Mameha?' I said. 'I don't understand. What does Mameha have to do with it?'

'You really don't know, do you?'

'Know what, Chairman?'

'Sayuri, I am the one who asked Mameha to take you under her care. I told her about a beautiful young girl I'd met, with startling gray eyes, and asked that she help you if she ever came upon you in Gion. I said I would cover her expenses if necessary. And she did come upon you, only a few months later. From what she's told me over the years, you would certainly never have hecome a geisha without her help.'

It's almost impossible to describe the effect the Chairman's words had on me. I'd always taken it for granted that Mameha's mission had been personal – to rid herself and Gion of Hatsumomo. Now that I understood her real motive, that I'd come under her tutelage because of the Chairman . . . well, I felt I would have to look back at all the comments she'd ever made to me and wonder about the real meaning behind them. And it wasn't just Mameha who'd suddenly been transformed in my eyes; even I seemed to myself to be a different woman. When my gaze fell upon my hands in my lap, I saw them as hands the Chairman had made. I felt exhilarated, and frightened, and grateful all at once. I moved away from the table to bow and express my gratitude to him; but before I could even do it, I had to say:

'Chairman, forgive me, but I so wish that at some time years ago, you could have told me about . . . all of this. I can't say how much it would have meant to me.'

'There's a reason why I never could, Sayuri, and why I had to insist that Mameha not tell you either. It has to do with Nobu.'

To hear mention of Nobu's name, all the feeling drained out of me – for I had the sudden notion that I understood where the Chairman had been leading all along.

'Chairman,' I said, 'I know I've been unworthy of your kindness. This past weekend, when I –'

'I confess, Sayuri,' he interrupted, 'that what happened on Amami has been very much on my mind.'

I could feel the Chairman looking at me; I couldn't possibly have looked back at him.

'There's something I want to discuss with you,' he went on. 'I've been wondering all day how to go about it. I keep thinking of something that happened many years ago. I'm sure there must be a better way to explain myself, but . . . I do hope you'll understand what I'm trying to say.'

Here he paused to take off his jacket and fold it on the mats beside him. I could smell the starch in his shirt, which made me think of visiting the General at the Suruya Inn and his room that often smelled of ironing.

'Back when Iwamura Electric was still a young company,' the Chairman began, 'I came to know a man named Ikeda, who worked for one of our suppliers on the other side of town. He was a genius at solving wiring problems. Sometimes when we had difficulty with an installation, we asked to borrow him for a day, and he straightened everything out for us. Then one afternoon when I was rushing home from work, I happened to run into him at the pharmacist. He told me he was feeling very relaxed, because he'd quit his job. When I asked him why he'd done it, he said, 'The time came to quit. So I quit!' Well, I hired him right there on the spot. Then a few weeks later I asked him again, 'Ikeda-san, why did you quit your job across town?' He said to me, 'Mr. Iwamura, for years I wanted to come and work for your company. But you never asked me. You always called on me when you had a problem, but you never asked me to work for you. Then one day I realized that you never *would* ask me, because you didn't want to hire me away from one of your suppliers and jeopardize your business relationship. Only if I quit my job first, would you then have the opportunity to hire me. So I quit.'

I knew the Chairman was waiting for me to respond, but I didn't dare speak.

'Now, I've been thinking,' he went on, 'that perhaps your encounter with the Minister was like Ikeda quitting his job. And I'll tell you why this thought has been on my mind. It's something Pumpkin said after she took me down to the theater. I was extremely angry with her, and I demanded she tell me why she'd done it. For the longest time she wouldn't even speak. Then she told me something that made no sense at first. She said you'd asked her to bring Nobu.'

'Chairman, please,' I began unsteadily, 'I made such a terrible mistake. . .'

'Before you say anything further, I only want to know why you did this thing. Perhaps you felt you were doing Iwamura Electric some sort of . . . favor. I don't know. Or maybe you owed the Minister something I'm unaware of.'

I must have given my head a little shake, because the Chairman stopped speaking at once.

'I'm deeply ashamed, Chairman,' I managed to say at last, 'but . . . my motives were purely personal.'

After a long moment he sighed and held out his sake cup. I poured for him, with the feeling that my hands were someone else's, and then he tossed the sake into his mouth and held it there before swallowing. Seeing him with his mouth momentarily full made me think of myself as an empty vessel swelled up with shame.

'All right, Sayuri,' he said, 'I'll tell you exactly why I'm asking. It will be impossible for you to grasp why I've come here tonight, or why I've treated you as I have over the years, if you don't understand the nature of my relationship with Nobu. Believe me, I'm more aware than anyone of how difficult he can sometimes be. But he is a genius; I value him more than an entire team of men combined.'

I couldn't think of what to do or say, so with trembling hands I picked up the vial to pour more sake for the Chairman. I took it as a very bad sign that he didn't lift his cup.

'One day when I'd known you only a short time,' he went on, 'Nobu brought you a gift of a comb, and gave it to you in front of everyone at the party. I hadn't realized how much affection he felt for you until that very moment. I'm sure there were other signs before, but somehow I must have overlooked them. And when I realized how he felt, the way he looked at you that evening . . . well, I knew in a moment that I couldn't possibly take away from him the thing he so clearly wanted. It never diminished my concern for your welfare. In fact, as the years have gone by, it has become increasingly difficult for me to listen dispassionately while Nobu talks about you.'

Here the Chairman paused and said, 'Sayuri, are you listening to me?'

'Yes, Chairman, of course.'

'There's no reason you would know this, but I owe Nobu a great debt. It's true I'm the founder of the company and his boss. But when Iwamura Electric was still quite young, we had a terrible problem with cash flow and very nearly went out of business. I wasn't willing to give up control of the company and I wouldn't listen to Nobu when he insisted on bringing in investors. He won in the end, even though it caused a rift between us for a time; he offered to resign, and I almost let him. But of course, he was completely right, and I was wrong. I'd have lost the company without him. How do you repay a man for something like that? Do you know why I'm called 'Chairman' and not 'President'? It's because I resigned the title so Nobu would take it – though he tried to refuse. This is why I made up my mind, the moment I became aware of his affection for you, that I would keep my interest in you hidden so that Nobu could have you. Life has been cruel to him, Sayuri. He's had too little kindness.'

In all my years as a geisha, I'd never been able to convince myself even for a moment that the Chairman felt any special regard for me. And now to know that he'd intended me for . . .

'I never meant to pay you so little attention,' he went on. 'But surely you realize that if he'd ever picked up the slightest hint of my feelings, he would have given you up in an instant.'

Since my girlhood, I'd dreamed that one day the Chairman would tell me he cared for me; and yet I'd never quite believed it would really happen. I certainly hadn't imagined he might tell me what I hoped to hear, and also that Nobu was my destiny. Perhaps the goal I'd sought in life would elude me, but at least during this one moment, it was within my power to sit in the room with the Chairman and tell him how deeply I felt.

'Please forgive me for what I am about to say,' I finally managed to begin.

I tried to continue, but somehow my throat made up its mind to swallow – though I can't think what I was swallowing, unless it was a little knot of emotion I pushed back down because there was no room in my face for any more.

'I have great affection for Nobu, but what I did on Amami . . .' Here I had to hold a burning in my throat a long moment before I could speak again. 'What I did on Amami, I did because of my feelings for you, Chairman. Every step I have taken in my life since I was a child in Gion, I have taken in the hope of bringing myself closer to you.'

When I said these words, all the heat in my body seemed to

rise to my face. I felt I might float up into the air, just like a piece of ash from a fire, unless I could focus on something in the room. I tried to find a smudge on the tabletop, but already the table itself was glazing over and disappearing in my vision.

'Look at me, Sayuri.'

I wanted to do as the Chairman asked, but I couldn't.

'How strange,' he went on quietly almost to himself, 'that the same woman who looked me so frankly in the eye as a girl, many years ago, can't bring herself to do it now.'

Perhaps it ought to have been a simple task to raise my eyes and look at the Chairman; and yet somehow I couldn't have felt more nervous if I'd stood alone on a stage with all of Kyoto watching. We were sitting at a corner of the table, so close that when at length I wiped my eyes and raised them to meet his, I could see the dark rings around his irises. I wondered if perhaps I should look away and make a little bow and then offer to pour him a cup of sake . . . but no gesture would have been enough to break the tension. As I was thinking these thoughts, the Chairman moved the vial of sake and the cup aside, and then reached out his hand and took the collar of my robe to draw me toward him. In a moment our faces were so close, I could feel the warmth of his skin. I was still struggling to understand what was happening to me – and what I ought to do or say. And then the Chairman pulled me closer, and he kissed me.

It may surprise you to hear that this was the first time in my life anyone had ever really kissed me. General Tottori had sometimes pressed his lips against mine when he was my *danna*; but it had been utterly passionless. I'd wondered at the time if he simply needed somewhere to rest his face. Even Yasuda Akira – the man who'd bought me a kimono, and whom I'd seduced one night at the Tatematsu Teahouse – must have kissed me dozens of times on my neck and face, but he never really touched my lips with his. And so you can imagine that this kiss, the first real one of my life, seemed to me more intimate than anything I'd ever experienced. I had the feeling I was taking something from the Chairman, and that he was giving something to me, something more private than anyone had ever given me before. There was a certain very startling taste, as distinctive as any fruit or sweet, and when I tasted it, my shoulders sagged and my stomach swelled up; because for some reason it called to mind a dozen different scenes I couldn't think why I should remember. I thought of the head of steam when the cook lifted the lid from the rice cooker in the kitchen of our okiya. I saw a picture in my mind of the little alleyway that was the main thoroughfare of Pontocho, as I'd seen it one evening crowded with well-wishers after Kichisaburo's last performance, the day he'd retired from the Kabuki theater. I'm sure I might have thought of a hundred other things, for it was as if all the boundaries in my mind had broken down and my memories were running free. But then the Chairman leaned back away from me again, with one of his hands upon my neck. He was so close, I could see the moisture glistening on his lip, and still smell the kiss we'd just ended.

'Chairman,' I said, 'why?'

'Why what?'

'Why . . . everything? Why have you kissed me? You've just been speaking of me as a gift to Nobu-san.'

'Nobu gave you up, Sayuri. I've taken nothing away from him.'

In my confusion of feelings, I couldn't quite understand what he meant.

'When I saw you there with the Minister, you had a look in your eyes just like the one I saw so many years ago at the Shirakawa Stream,' he told me. 'You seemed so desperate, like you might drown if someone didn't save you. After Pumpkin told me you'd intended that encounter for Nobu's eyes, I made up my mind to tell him what I'd seen. And when he reacted so angrily. . . well, if he couldn't forgive you for what you'd done, it was clear to me he was never truly your destiny.'

One afternoon back when I was a child in Yoroido, a little boy named Gisuke climbed a tree to jump into the pond. He climbed much higher than he should have; the water wasn't deep enough. But when we told him not to jump, he was afraid to climb back down because of rocks under the tree. I ran to the village to find his father, Mr. Yamashita, who came walking so calmly up the hill, I wondered if he realized what danger his son was in. He stepped underneath the tree just as the boy – unaware of his father's presence – lost his grip and fell. Mr. Yamashita caught him as easily as if someone had dropped a sack into his arms, and set him upright. We all of us cried out in delight, and skipped around at the edge of the pond while Gisuke stood blinking his eyes very quickly, little tears of astonishment gathering on his lashes.

Now I knew exactly what Gisuke must have felt. I had been plummeting toward the rocks, and the Chairman had stepped out to catch me. I was so overcome with relief, I couldn't even wipe away the tears that spilled from the corners of my eyes. His shape was a blur before me, but I could see him moving closer, and in a moment he'd gathered me up in his arms just as if I were a blanket. His lips went straight for the little triangle of flesh where the edges of my kimono came together at my throat. And when I felt his breath on my neck, and the sense of urgency with which he almost consumed me, I couldn't help thinking of a moment years earlier, when I'd stepped into the kitchen of the okiya and found one of the maids leaning over the sink, trying to cover up the ripe pear she held to her mouth, its juices running down onto her neck. She'd had such a craving for it, she'd said and begged me not to tell Mother.

35

NOW, NEARLY FORTY years later, I sit here looking back on that evening with the Chairman as the moment when all the grieving voices within me fell silent. Since the day I'd left Yoroido, I'd done nothing but worry that every turn of life's wheel would bring yet another obstacle into my path; and of course, it was the worrying and the struggle that had always made life so vividly real to me. When we fight upstream against a rocky undercurrent, every foothold takes on a kind of urgency.

But life softened into something much more pleasant after the Chairman became my *danna*. I began to feel like a tree whose roots had at last broken into the rich, wet soil deep beneath the surface. I'd never before had occasion to think of myself as more fortunate than others, and yet now I was. Though I must say, I lived in that contented state a long while before I was finally able to look back and admit how desolate my life had once been. I'm sure I could never have told my story otherwise; I don't think any of us can speak frankly about pain until we are no longer enduring it.

On the afternoon when the Chairman and I drank sake together in a ceremony at the Ichiriki Teahouse, something peculiar happened. I don't know why, but when I sipped from the smallest of the three cups we used, I let the sake wash over my tongue, and a single drop of it spilled from the corner of my mouth. I was wearing a five-crested kimono of black, with a dragon woven in gold and red encircling the hem up to my thighs. I recall watching the drop fall beneath my arm and roll down the black silk on my thigh, until it came to a stop at the heavy silver threads of the dragon's teeth. I'm sure most geisha would call it a bad omen that I'd spilled sake; but to me, that droplet of moisture that had slipped from me like a tear seemed almost to tell the story of my life. It fell through empty space, with no control whatsoever over its destiny; rolled along a path of silk; and somehow came to rest there on the teeth of that dragon. I thought of the petals I'd thrown into the Kamo River shallows outside Mr. Arashino's workshop, imagining they might find their way to the Chairman. It seemed to me that, somehow, perhaps they had.

In the foolish hopes that had been so dear to me since girlhood, I'd always imagined my life would be perfect if I ever became the Chairman's mistress. It's a childish thought, and yet I'd carried it with me even as an adult. I ought to have known better: How many times already had I encountered the painful lesson that although we may wish for the barb to be pulled from our flesh, it leaves behind a welt that doesn't heal? In banishing Nobu from my life forever, it wasn't just that I lost his friendship; I also ended up banishing myself from Gion.

The reason is so simple, I ought to have known beforehand it would happen. A man who has won a prize coveted by his friend faces a difficult choice: he must either hide his prize away where the friend will never see it – if he can – or suffer damage to the friendship. This was the very problem that had arisen between Pumpkin and me: our friendship had never recovered after my adoption. So although the Chairman's negotiations with Mother to become my *danna* dragged out over several months, in the end it was agreed that I would no longer work as a geisha. I certainly wasn't the first geisha to leave Gion; besides those who ran away, some married and left as wives, others withdrew to set up teahouses or okiya of their own. In my case, however, I was trapped in a peculiar middle ground. The Chairman wanted me out of Gion to keep me out of sight of Nobu, but he certainly wasn't going to marry me, he was already married. Probably the perfect solution, and the one that the Chairman proposed, would have been to set me up with my own teahouse or inn – one that Nobu would never have visited. But Mother was unwilling to have me leave the okiya; she would have earned no revenues from my relationship with the Chairman if I had ceased to be a member of the Nitta family, you see. This is why in the end, the Chairman agreed to pay the okiya a very considerable sum each month on the condition that Mother permit me to end my career. I continued to live in the okiya, just as I had for so many years; but I no longer went to the little school in the mornings, or made the rounds of Gion to pay my respects on special occasions; and of course, I no longer entertained during the evenings.

Because I'd set my sights on becoming a geisha only to win the affections of the Chairman, probably I ought to have felt no sense of loss in withdrawing from Gion. And yet over the years I'd developed many rich friendships, not only with other geisha but with many of the men I'd come to know. I wasn't banished from the company of other women just because I'd ceased entertaining; but those who make a living in Gion have little time for socializing. I often felt jealous when I saw two geisha hurrying to their next engagement, laughing together over what had happened at the last one. I didn't envy them the uncertainty of their existence; but I did envy that sense of promise I could well remember, that the evening ahead might yet hold some mischievous pleasure.

I did see Mameha frequently. We had tea together at least several times a week. Considering all that she had done for me since childhood – and the special role she'd played in my life on the Chairman's behalf – you can imagine how much I felt myself in her debt. One day in a shop I came upon a silk painting from the eighteenth century showing a woman teaching a young girl calligraphy. The teacher had an exquisite oval face and watched over her pupil with such benevolence, it made me think of Mameha at once, and I bought it for her as a gift. On the rainy afternoon when she hung it on the wall of her dreary apartment, I found myself listening to the traffic that hissed by on Higashi-oji Avenue. I couldn't help remembering, with a terrible feeling of loss, her elegant apartment from years earlier, and the enchanting sound out those windows of water rushing over the knee-high cascade in the Shirakawa Stream. Gion itself had seemed to me like an exquisite piece of antique fabric back then; but so much had changed. Now Mameha's simple one-room apartment had mats the color of stale tea and smelled of herbal potions from the Chinese pharmacy below – so much so that her kimono themselves sometimes gave off a faint medicinal odor.

After she'd hung the ink painting on the wall and admired it for a while, she came back to the table. She sat with her hands around her steaming teacup, peering into it as though she expected to find the words she was looking for. I was surprised to see the tendons in her hands beginning to show themselves from age. At last, with a trace of sadness, she said:

'How curious it is, what the future brings us. You must take care, Sayuri, never to expect too much.'

I'm quite sure she was right. I'd have had an easier time over the following years if I hadn't gone on believing that Nobu would one day forgive me. In the end I had to give up questioning Mameha whether he'd asked about me; it pained me terribly to see her sigh and give me a long, sad look, as if to say she was sorry I hadn't known better than to hope for such a thing.

In the spring of the year after I became his mistress, the Chairman purchased a luxurious house in the northeast of Kyoto and named it *Eishin-an* – 'Prosperous Truth Retreat.' It was intended for guests of the company, but in fact the Chairman made more use of it than anyone. This was where he and I met to spend the evenings together three or four nights a week, sometimes even more. On his busiest days he arrived so late he wanted only to soak in a hot bath while I talked with him, and then afterward fall asleep. But most evenings he arrived around sunset, or soon after, and ate his dinner while we chatted and watched the servants light the lanterns in the garden.

Usually when he first came, the Chairman talked for a time about his workday. He might tell me about troubles with a new product, or about a traffic accident involving a truckload of pans, or some such thing. Of course I was happy to sit and listen, but I understood perfectly well that the Chairman wasn't telling these things to me because he wanted me to know them. He was clearing them from his mind, just like draining water from a bucket. So I listened closely not to his words, but to the tone of his voice, because in the same way that sound rises as a bucket is emptied, I could hear the Chairman's voice softening as he spoke. When the moment was right, I changed the subject, and soon we were talking about nothing so serious as business, but about everything else instead, such as what had happened to him that morning on the way to work, or something about the film we may have watched a few nights earlier there at the *Eishin-an*, or perhaps I told him a funny story I might have heard from Mameha, who on some evenings came to join us there. In any case, this simple process of first draining the Chairman's mind and then relaxing him with playful conversation had the same effect water has on a towel that has dried stiffly in the sun. When he first arrived and I washed his hands with a hot cloth, his fingers felt rigid, like heavy twigs. After we had talked for a time, they bent as gracefully as if he were sleeping.

I expected that this would be my life, entertaining the Chairman in the evenings and occupying myself during the daylight hours in any way I could. But in the fall of 1952, I accompanied the Chairman on his second trip to the United States. He'd traveled there the winter before, and no experience of his life had ever made such an impression on him; he said he felt he understood for the first time the true meaning of prosperity. Most Japanese at this time had electricity only during certain hours, for example, but the lights in American cities burned around the clock. And while we in Kyoto were proud that the floor of our new train station was constructed of concrete rather than old-fashioned wood, the floors of American train stations were made of solid marble. Even in small American towns, the movie theaters were as grand as our National Theater, said the Chairman, and the public bathrooms everywhere were spotlessly clean. What amazed him most of all was that every family in the United States owned a refrigerator, which could be purchased with the wages earned by an average worker in only a month's time. In Japan, a worker needed fifteen months' wages to buy such a thing; few families could afford it.

In any case, as I say, the Chairman permitted me to accompany him on his second trip to America. I traveled alone by rail to Tokyo, and from there we flew together on an airplane bound for Hawaii, where we spent a few remarkable days. The Chairman bought me a bathing suit – the first I'd ever owned – and I sat wearing it on the beach with my hair hanging neatly at my shoulders just like other women around me. Hawaii reminded me strangely of Amami; I worried that the same thought might occur to the Chairman, but if it did, he said nothing about it. From Hawaii, we continued to Los Angeles and finally to New York. I knew nothing about the United States except what I'd seen in movies; I don't think I quite believed that the great buildings of New York City really existed. And when I settled at last into my room at the Waldorf-Astoria Hotel, and looked out the window at the mountainous buildings around me and the smooth, clean streets below, I had the feeling I was seeing a world in which anything was possible. I confess I'd expected to feel like a baby who has been taken away from its mother; for I had never before left Japan, and couldn't imagine that a setting as alien as New York City would make me anything but fearful. Perhaps it was the Chairman's enthusiasm that helped me to approach my visit there with such goodwill. He'd taken a separate room, which he used mostly for business; but every night he came to stay with me in the suite he'd arranged. Often I awoke in that strange bed and turned to see him there in the dark, sitting in a chair by the window holding the sheer curtain open, staring at Park Avenue below. One time after two o'clock in the morning, he took me by the hand and pulled me to the window to see a young couple dressed as if they'd come from a ball, kissing under the street lamp on the corner.

Over the next three years I traveled with the Chairman twice more to the United States. While he attended to business during the day, my maid and I took in the museums and restaurants – and even a ballet, which I found breathtaking. Strangely, one of the few Japanese restaurants we were able to find in New York was now under the management of a chef

I'd known well in Gion before the war. During lunch one afternoon, I found myself in his private room in the back, entertaining a number of men I hadn't seen in years – the vice president of Nippon Telephone & Telegraph; the new Japanese Consul-General, who had formerly been mayor of Kobe; a professor of political science from Kyoto University. It was almost like being back in Gion once again.

In the summer of 1956, the Chairman – who had two daughters by his wife, but no son – arranged for his eldest daughter to marry a man named Nishioka Minoru. The Chairman's intention was that Mr. Nishioka take the family name of Iwamura and become his heir; but at the last moment, Mr. Nishioka had a change of heart, and informed the Chairman that he did not intend to go through with the wedding. He was a very temperamental young man, but in the Chairman's estimation, quite brilliant. For a week or more the Chairman was upset, and snapped at his servants and me without the least provocation. I'd never seen him so disturbed by anything.

No one ever told me why Nishioka Minoru changed his mind, but no one had to. During the previous summer, the founder of one of Japan's largest insurance companies had dismissed his son as president, and turned his company over instead to a much younger man – his illegitimate son by a Tokyo geisha. It caused quite a scandal at the time. Things of this sort had happened before in Japan, but usually on a much smaller scale, in family-owned kimono stores or sweets shops – businesses of that sort. The insurance company director described his firstborn in the newspapers as 'an earnest young man whose talents unfortunately can't be compared with' and here he named his illegitimate son, without ever giving any hint of their relationship. But it made no difference whether he gave a hint of it or not, everyone knew the truth soon enough.

Now, if you were to imagine that Nishioka Minoru, after already having agreed to become the Chairman's heir, had discovered some new bit of information – such as that the Chairman had recently fathered an illegitimate son . . . well,

I'm sure that in this case, his reluctance to go through with the marriage would probably seem quite understandable. It was widely known that the Chairman lamented having no son, and was deeply attached to his two daughters. Was there any reason to think he wouldn't become equally attached to an illegitimate son – enough, perhaps, to change his mind before death and turn over to him the company he'd built? As to the question of whether or not I really had given birth to a son of the Chairman's . . . if I had, I'd certainly be reluctant to talk too much about him, for fear that his identity might become publicly known. It would be in no one's best interest for such a thing to happen. The best course, I feel, is for me to say nothing at all; I'm sure you will understand.

A week or so after Nishioka Minoru's change of heart, I decided to raise a very delicate subject with the Chairman. We were at the *Eishin-an*, sitting outdoors after dinner on the veranda overlooking the moss garden. The Chairman was brooding, and hadn't spoken a word since before dinner was served.

'Have I mentioned to Danna-sama,' I began, 'that I've had the strangest feeling lately?'

I glanced at him, but I could see no sign that he was even listening.

'I keep thinking of the Ichiriki Teahouse,' I went on, 'and truthfully, I'm beginning to recognize how much I miss entertaining.'

The Chairman just took a bite of his ice cream, and then set his spoon down on the dish again.

'Of course, I can never go back to work in Gion; I know that perfectly well. And yet I wonder, Danna-sama . . . isn't there a place for a small teahouse in New York City?'

'I don't know what you're talking about,' he said. 'There's no reason why you should want to leave Japan.'

'Japanese businessmen and politicians are showing up in New York these days as commonly as turtles plopping into a pond,' I said. 'Most of them are men I've known already for years. It's true that leaving Japan would be an abrupt change. But considering that Danna-sama will be spending more and more of his time in the United States . . .' I knew this was true, because he'd already told me about his plan to open a branch of his company there.

'I'm in no mood for this, Sayuri,' he began. I think he intended to say something further, but I went on as though I hadn't heard him.

'They say that a child raised between two cultures often has a very difficult time,' I said. 'So naturally, a mother who moves with her child to a place like the United States would probably be wise to make it her permanent home.'

'Sayuri –'

'Which is to say,' I went on, 'that a woman who made such a choice would probably never bring her child back to Japan at all.'

By this time the Chairman must have understood what I was suggesting – that I remove from Japan the only obstacle in the way of Nishioka Minoru's adoption as his heir. He wore a startled look for an instant. And then, probably as the image formed in his mind of my leaving him, his peevish humor seemed to crack open like an egg, and out of the corner of his eye came a single tear, which he blinked away just as swiftly as swatting a fly.

In August of that same year, I moved to New York City to set up my own very small teahouse for Japanese businessmen and politicians traveling through the United States. Of course, Mother tried to ensure that any business I started in New York City would be an extension of the Nitta okiya, but the Chairman refused to consider any such arrangement. Mother had power over me as long as I remained in Gion; but I broke my ties with her by leaving. The Chairman sent in two of his accountants to ensure that Mother gave me every last yen to which I was entitled.

I can't pretend I didn't feel afraid so many years ago, when the door of my apartment here at the Waldorf Towers closed behind me for the first time. But New York is an exciting city. Before long it came to feel at least as much a home to me as Gion ever did. In fact, as I look back, the memories of many long weeks I've spent here with the Chairman have made my life in the United States even richer in some ways than it was in Japan. My little teahouse, on the second floor of an old club off Fifth Avenue, was modestly successful from the very beginning; a number of geisha have come from Gion to work with me there, and even Mameha sometimes visits. Nowadays I go there myself only when close friends or old acquaintances have come to town. I spend my time in a variety of other ways instead. In the mornings I often join a group of Japanese writers and artists from the area to study subjects that interest us – such as poetry or music or, during one month-long session, the history of New York City. I lunch with a friend most days. And in the afternoons I kneel before my makeup stand to prepare for one party or another – sometimes here in my very own apartment. When I lift the brocade cover on my mirror, I can't help but remember the milky odor of the white makeup I so often wore in Gion. I dearly wish I could go back there to visit; but on the other hand, I think I would be disturbed to see all the changes. When friends bring photographs from their trips to Kyoto, I often think that Gion has thinned out like a poorly kept garden, increasingly overrun with weeds. After Mother's death a number of years ago, for example, the Nitta okiya was torn down and replaced with a tiny concrete building housing a bookshop on the ground floor and two apartments overhead.

Eight hundred geisha worked in Gion when I first arrived there. Now the number is less than sixty, with only a handful of apprentices, and it dwindles further every day – because of course the pace of change never slows, even when we've convinced ourselves it will. On his last visit to New York City, the Chairman and I took a walk through Central Park. We happened to be talking about the past; and when we came to a path through pine trees, the Chairman stopped suddenly He'd often told me of the pines bordering the street outside Osaka on which he'd grown up; I knew as I watched him that he was remembering them. He stood with his two frail hands on his cane and his eyes closed, and breathed in deeply the scent of the past.

'Sometimes,' he sighed, 'I think the things I remember are more real than the things I see.'

As a younger woman I believed that passion must surely fade with age, just as a cup left standing in a room will gradually give up its contents to the air. But when the Chairman and I returned to my apartment, we drank each other up with so much yearning and need that afterward I felt myself drained of all the things the Chairman had taken from me, and yet filled with all that I had taken from him. I fell into a sound sleep and dreamed that I was at a banquet back in Gion, talking with an elderly man who was explaining to me that his wife, whom he'd cared for deeply, wasn't really dead because the pleasure of their time together lived on inside him. While he spoke these words, I drank from a bowl of the most extraordinary soup I'd ever tasted; every briny sip was a kind of ecstasy. I began to feel that all the people I'd ever known who had died or left me had not in fact gone away, but continued to live on inside me just as this man's wife lived on inside him. I felt as though I were drinking them all in – my sister, Satsu, who had run away and left me so young; my father and mother; Mr. Tanaka, with his perverse view of kindness; Nobu, who could never forgive me; even the Chairman. The soup was filled with all that I'd ever cared for in my life; and while I drank it, this man spoke his words right into my heart. I awoke with tears streaming down my temples, and I took the Chairman's hand, fearing that I would never be able to live without him when he died and left me. For he was so frail by then, even there in his sleep, that I couldn't help thinking of my mother back in Yoroido. And yet when his death happened only a few months later, I understood that he left me at the end of his long life just as naturally as the leaves fall from the trees.

I cannot tell you what it is that guides us in this life; but for me, I fell toward the Chairman just as a stone must fall toward the earth. When I cut my lip and met Mr. Tanaka, when my mother died and I was cruelly sold, it was all like a stream that falls over rocky cliffs before it can reach the ocean. Even now that he is gone I have him still, in the richness of my memories. I've lived my life again just telling it to you.

It's true that sometimes when I cross Park Avenue, I'm

struck with the peculiar sense of how exotic my surroundings are. The yellow taxicabs that go sweeping past, honking their horns; the women with their briefcases, who look so perplexed to see a little old Japanese woman standing on the street corner in kimono. But really, would Yoroido seem any less exotic if I went back there again? As a young girl I believed my life would never have been a struggle if Mr. Tanaka hadn't torn me away from my tipsy house. But now I know that our world is no more permanent than a wave rising on the ocean. Whatever our struggles and triumphs, however we may suffer them, all too soon they bleed into a wash, just like watery ink on paper.

ACKNOWLEDGMENTS

ALTHOUGH THE CHARACTER of Sayuri and her story are completely invented, the historical facts of a geisha's day-to-day life in the 1930s and 1940s are not. In the course of my extensive research I am indebted to one individual above all others. Mineko Iwasaki, one of Gion's top geisha in the 1960s and 1970s, opened her Kyoto home to me during May 1992, and corrected my every misconception about the life of a geisha – even though everyone I knew who had lived in Kyoto, or who lived there still, told me never to expect such candor. While brushing up my Japanese on the airplane, I worried that Mineko, whom I had not yet met, might talk with me for an hour about the weather and call it an interview. Instead she took me on an insider's tour of Gion, and together with her husband, Jin, and her sisters, Yaetchiyo and the late Kuniko, patiently answered all my questions about the ritual of a geisha's life in intimate detail. She became, and remains, a good friend. I have the fondest memories of her family's trip to visit us in Boston, and the otherworldly sense my wife and I felt while watching tennis on television in our living room with our new friend, a Japanese woman in her forties who also happened to be one of the last geisha trained in the old tradition.

To Mineko, thank you for everything.

I was introduced to Mineko by Mrs. Reiko Nagura, a long-time friend and a fiercely intelligent woman of my mother's generation, who speaks Japanese, English, and German with equal fluency. She won a prize for a short story she wrote in English while an undergraduate at Barnard, only a few years after first coming to the United States to study, and soon became a lifelong friend of my grandmother's. The affection between her family and mine is now in its fourth generation. Her home has been a regular haven on my visits to Tokyo; I owe her a greater debt than I can express. Along with every other kindness she has done for me, she read over my manuscript at various stages and offered a great many invaluable suggestions.

During the years I have worked on this novel, my wife, Trudy, has provided more help and support than I had any right to expect. Beyond her endless patience, her willingness to drop everything and read when I needed her eye, and her frankness and extreme thoughtfulness, she has given me that greatest of gifts: constancy and understanding.

Robin Desser of Knopf is the kind of editor every writer dreams about: passionate, insightful, committed, always helpful – and a load of fun besides.

For her warmth, her directness, her professionalism, and her charm, there's no one quite like Leigh Feldman. I am extremely lucky to have her for an agent.

Helen Bartlett, you know all you did to help me from early on. Thanks to you, and to Denise Stewart.

I'm very grateful to my good friend Sara Laschever, for her careful reading of the manuscript, her generous involvement, and her many thoughtful suggestions and ideas.

Teruko Craig was kind enough to spend hours talking with me about her life as a schoolgirl in Kyoto during the war. I am grateful also to Liza Dalby, the only American woman ever to become a geisha, and to her excellent book, *Geisha*, an anthropological study of geisha culture, which also recounts her experiences in the Pontocho district; she generously lent me a number of useful Japanese and English books from her personal collection.

Thanks also to Kiharu Nakamura, who has written about her experiences as a geisha in the Shimbashi district of Tokyo, and kindly spent an evening talking with me during the course of my research.

I am grateful, too, for the thoughtful insights and empathetic concern of my brother, Stephen.

Robert Singer, curator of Japanese art at the Los Angeles

County Museum of Art, went to considerable trouble while I was in Kyoto to show me firsthand how aristocrats there once lived.

Bowen Dees, whom I met on an airplane, permitted me to read his unpublished manuscript about his experiences in Japan during the Allied Occupation.

I'm thankful also to Allan Palmer for giving me the benefit of his extensive knowledge of tea ceremony and Japanese superstitions.

John Rosenfield taught me Japanese art history as no one else can, and made a university as gigantic as Harvard feel like a small college. I'm grateful to him for helpful advice all along the way.

I'm profoundly in Barry Minsky's debt, for the valuable role he played as I worked to bring this novel into being.

In addition, for their kindnesses too numerous to recount, thanks to David Kuhn, Merry White, Kazumi Aoki, Yasu Ikuma, Megumi Nakatani, David Sand, Yoshio Imakita, Mameve Medwed, the late Celia Millward, Camilla Trinchieri, Barbara Shapiro, Steve Weisman, Yoshikata Tsukamoto, Carol Janeway of Knopf, Lynn Pleshette, Denise Rusoff, David Schwab, Alison Tolman, Lidia Yagoda, Len Rosen and Diane Fader.

For my wife, Trudy,
and my children, Hays and Tess

A Note About the Author

Arthur Golden was born and brought up in Chattanooga, Tennessee. He is a 1978 graduate of Harvard College with a degree in art history, specializing in Japanese art. In 1980 he earned an M.A. in Japanese history from Columbia University where he also learned Mandarin Chinese. After a summer at Beijing University, he went to work at a magazine in Tokyo. In 1988 he received an M.A. in English from Boston University. He has lived and worked in Japan, and since that time has been teaching writing and literature in the Boston area. He now lives in Brookline, Massachusetts, with his wife and children.

www.vintage-books.co.uk